IN A CITY ON TH
THEY HAD T

JASON BECK: Captain .... .pper *Sarah B. Watson*, he sailed into San Francisco bearing a cargo of Carolina rice, making landfall in a city about to explode. When a cowardly act by unknown thugs threatens his livelihood, he turns to the Committee of Vigilance for justice. But ultimately it will be another Sarah—this one a flesh-and-blood woman—who will determine his destiny.

SARAH ROCKWELL: The owner of a respectable boardinghouse, she is appalled by the Committee and its threat of tyranny. A woman of beauty and substance, she vows to take a stand against it . . . and to draw her new boarder, Captain Beck, to the cause.

THOMAS TRELAYNE: A young theatrical manager who came to San Francisco to find freedom for his ideas finds his life changed by two leading ladies. One will break his heart and lead him to mad, reckless behavior; the other will inspire him to take a public political stand—and in a city that's become a powder keg, there's no telling which act could be more deadly.

MOLLY GRAY: Another of Sarah's boarders, she's a talented actress prepared to play any part for any man, but in San Francisco the cost of desire—and deceit—can be high.

ABEL CALVERT: A rich banker and a high-ranking member of the Committee, he is also a man of hidden allegiances and haunting secrets. Even as he seeks to expand his power, there is one woman capable of moving him to a dangerous passion that could destroy everything he's worked for.

WILLIAM TECUMSEH SHERMAN: A retired army officer who first came to California during the war with Mexico, he now manages a bank and has accepted the ceremonial appointment as general of California militia. But when the Committee of Vigilance marches its legions through the streets of San Francisco, only Sherman steps forward to stand in their way.

DICKIE HOWELL: An orphan and a wharf rat, he moves with ease through the seamy black alleys of the city. Despite Sarah Rockwell's attempts to educate him, he dreams of a life at sea. But his journey to manhood will begin on land, as he plays a crucial role in the fight for San Francisco's future.

The Committee of Vigilance

A NOVEL OF GOLD RUSH SAN FRANCISCO

John Byrne Cooke

BANTAM BOOKS
New York Toronto London Sydney Auckland

THE COMMITTEE OF VIGILANCE

A Bantam Book/October 1994

ISBN 0-553-56869-8

Published simultaneously in the United States and Canada

Bantam Books are published by Bantam Books, a division of Bantam Doubleday
Dell Publishing Group, Inc. Its trademark, consisting of the words "Bantam Books"
and the portrayal of a rooster, is Registered in U.S. Patent and Trademark Office
and in other countries. Marca Registrada. Bantam Books, 1540 Broadway, New
York, New York 10036.

PRINTED IN THE UNITED STATES OF AMERICA

OPM 0 9 8 7 6 5 4 3 2 1

For my mother, who passed on to me
her love of sailing and the sea

FIAT JUSTITIA RUAT CŒLUM

COMMITTEE
OF
VIGILANCE

SAN FRANCISCO

NO CREED, NO PARTY, NO SECTIONAL ISSUES

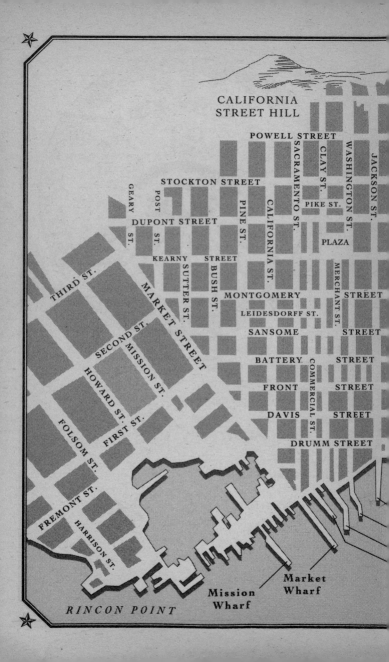

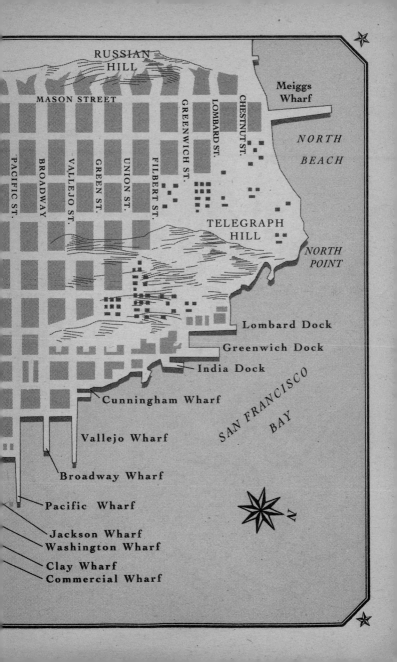

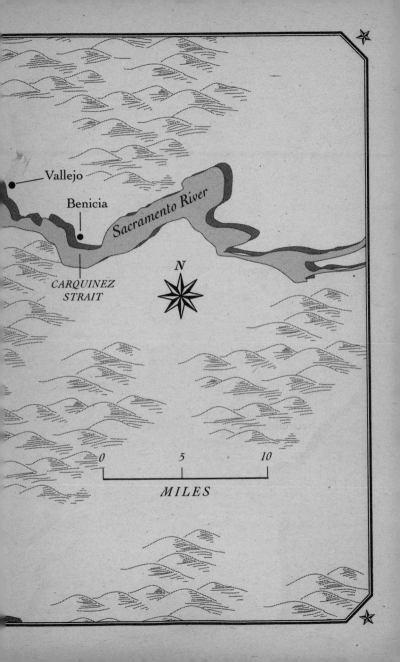

Prologue

illy Bemis moved along the street like an otter, which was a creature he had never seen. He was a small man, and light of foot. He treated the ladies and the dark-suited gentlemen in their Sunday best, the rough miners in their calico shirts, the Chinamen and the even more flamboyant Spaniards and—brightest of all, like jungle birds—the tarts in their stylish finery, as motionless objects. He imagined that he was invisible, gliding among them unnoticed. Make no waves and you can come and go as you please, his dad had told him, emphasizing the lesson with a painful tug on Billy's ear.

The wind was brisk from the west, the city cool beneath the low clouds that stretched across the peninsula and halfway to the Contra Costa shore, where sunlight brightened the wooded hills. As always, the wind carried a fine dust from the sand dunes west of the city. It was a breeze you could get your teeth into, the city's wags liked to say. Some of the men and even a few of the ladies on the street wore white handkerchiefs tied over their noses and mouths, which gave them the appearance of genteel highwaymen.

A carriage rattled past Billy, raising a trail of dust that blew across the street like the skewed wake of a ship.

On the corner of Jackson, a man was selling handkerchiefs from a small table. Billy picked a silver coin from his pocket purse and received a folded square of linen in return. He shook it out, refolded it into a large triangle, and tied it over the lower portion of his face. Beneath the mask he smiled. Who's to cry "thief" when the gentry look like highwaymen?

Bells rang from a Methodist church two streets away. Billy turned down Pacific Street and increased his pace. Mustn't be late. He made it his practice to be on time and to do a job of work well. That was the way to assure repeat business, his father had taught him.

Telegraph Hill loomed to Billy's left, its sparse mantle of stunted brush and parched grass waving in the wind. It wasn't natural to have hills in a city. A sensible city was built on a flat place beside a river, like London or Sydney. But those towns had become inhospitable to Billy Bemis.

He pulled his woolen coat about him. Nearly July and a body was glad for such a coat, even now as the sun peered briefly through the fast-moving clouds before being shut out again. The day would become pleasantly warm if the sun shone, but the wind off the water would keep it from growing hot. Just let the wind keep blowing, and everything would go according to plan.

Nearing the wharves, Billy turned into an alley. He was surprised to find it neatly cobbled. The stones were new and rough, not smooth and rounded like good British cobblestones that had been polished by generations of shoes and boots and hooves.

The narrow passage reeked of urine—equine, feline and human. Smells worse than a tart's crack, Billy thought. He moved lightly over the rough stones. If God should suddenly pluck out his eyes he would know this was not London by the smell of the place. In London there would have been dog shit, but there were few dogs in San Francisco. Too expensive to ship them 'round the Horn. Cats now, that was different. Cats were worth their weight in gold, to keep the mice and rats in check. The salt air was familiar enough, but the brimstone scent of soft coal burnt in a million hearths was missing too, replaced here by the sharp fragrance of fresh-sawn wood, like a spice overlaying the more familiar, less pleasant smells. In this town, everything was new and made of wood.

Mingled with the smell of fresh sawdust was another, older but still sharp—the dry stench of smoke. It was not the friendly char of wood burnt in a kitchen stove or warming some merchant's hearth. This scent carried hints of paint and furniture and clothing. It spoke of destruction.

Billy left the alley and came on a block of burned storehouses that were partly razed, victims of the fire that had consumed the city seven weeks before, on the fourth of May. The remaining skeletons stood aslant, ready to fall. Tomorrow the carpenters would be back, tearing down the old and sawing new wood to build again.

Smoke and sawdust. Death and rebirth. In two short years the city by the bay had risen from its own ashes not once but five times, and no worse charge could be made against a man than to brand him an incendiary.

The image of Johnny Jenkins' dying dance came suddenly fresh and vivid to Billy's mind. The stranglers hanged poor Johnny, and he was only a thief. But then Johnny was slow of wit, and none too careful. Imagine rowing off in an open boat with the sodding merchant's safe!

Out on the bay a bell buoy gonged. In answer, the city's clocks struck half after nine. It was a ragged chorus. Billy felt a sudden longing for the peal of English church bells and the taste of bitter ale, and cobbled streets where the footpads and fencing culls had their place and the toffs had theirs, like two kingdoms separated by an invisible wall. Here, the lines were drawn less certainly. One class of criminals ruled the roost and hired others to do its bidding, but if a man kept his wits about him, he could fill his pockets with gold.

Gold was the magic word on this coast. It was the only currency that mattered. There was precious little silver, and no copper at all, in Billy's purse. Gold had brought a quarter of a million men to California in less than two years and it had built San Francisco from a cluster of adobe huts to a city of forty thousand souls. From Hamburg and Whampoa and Liverpool and New York and Capetown and Callao and Valparaiso and a hundred other ports the vessels came. They came, but they did not leave. Scarcely had they dropped anchor in the bay before the crews were ashore and gone, heading pell-mell for the mines. Billy could see the masts at the foot of Pacific Street and along the waterfront to the south, spilling over into Mission Bay. Like jackstraws on end or the trunks of some ancient forest denuded by a long-forgotten fire, the masts marked the final anchorages of the ghost fleet. Six hundred ships, they said, rotting in the bay, all abandoned for the love of gold. Many had been beached and built over as part of the fill that had already extended the city's waterfront a hundred yards across the mudflats.

"Forty-niners" the first arrivals called themselves now, to let it be known that they were not common riffraff like the later immigrants. Billy sniffed. He had come 'round the Horn in '41, when the gold lay undiscovered in a thousand California streams. But he was not for California then. Billy Bemis was for Australia in '41, much against his will, transported by order of the Crown.

He hesitated as he turned the corner by the Noggin of Ale. From inside came the laughter of men who cared not a whit that the gentry were off to church all solemn and pious, the head stranglers and their wives up in the front pews for all to see. The thought of a tankard of beer made Billy lick his lips, but he clamped his mouth shut and kept on toward the wharves. He had no wish to be recognized in this neighborhood today.

Along the waterfront the buildings were warehouses, block upon block of them, thrown up in a hurry to contain the merchants' goods. Some said they were full to the rafters with flour and other necessities, held in reserve to drive up the price. On any other day, the streets would be crowded with stevedores and draymen and warehousemen. Today they were empty.

In Front Street Billy moved slowly, seeking shelter, but not too near the appointed meeting place. He heard a footfall and melted into a doorway, his hand finding the haft of the dirk beneath his coat. Two figures emerged from the nearest cross street. That would be them. In good time, too. But not good enough to catch Billy Bemis unawares.

"Top o' the mornin' to ye, Tom," Billy said when the two drew abreast of his hiding place.

"Lord strike me!" Tom Leary put his good hand to his chest and drew back from the masked man in the doorway. "Is that you, Billy? You give me a start."

Billy pulled the handkerchief off his face and stuffed it in his coat pocket. "I see you're wearin' your Sunday finery, Tom."

Tom held up his left hand, which was made of leather. "You'd be surprised how few notice it. A hook, now, that they remember." His real hand, smashed by a rock wielded by an English warder in an Irish prison, had been cut off at the wrist by a kindly doctor and fed to the pigs along with the other offal.

"You're a sneaky sod, Billy," said the second of the pair, whose hair was tied in a sailor's pigtail. He slipped into the doorway. "We're daft," he muttered. "Poor Johnny ten days in his grave and we're courting the hangman."

Tom Leary seized the front of the man's coat. "There's three ways you can leave this town, Michael Dunn. Scragged by the stranglers and straight to hell, like poor stupid Johnny, put aboard a ship with a pistol at your back, or strolling the deck of a steamboat like a proper gentleman with gold in your pocket. Which is your preference?"

"You know I've a fondness for gold, Tom." Michael wore steel-rimmed spectacles. One lens was clear, the other black, to cover the socket that no longer contained an eye.

The rhythms of Sydney town in Michael's voice aroused in Billy a brief longing to see the Southern Cross in the night sky. They had come together from Sydney three months before, Billy Bemis and Michael Dunn, placed forcibly aboard ship and warned never to return. On the merchantman they fell in with Tom Leary, an impressed seaman who jumped ship in San Francisco to follow his newfound friends in seeking his fortune. Here in the gold port they were called "Sydney ducks," despite the fact that of the three only Michael Dunn was born in Australia. That mattered not a smidgen to the disdainful gentlemen of California, who reserved the worst of their arrogance for recent arrivals from Australia. They were Sydney ducks one and all. "A bunch of thieving convicts" declared the *Alta California*, the city's leading newspaper, despite the common knowledge that only one man in six had first crossed the equator on a convict transport.

Tom Leary turned loose of Michael's coat and pushed him away. "Aye, you're fond of gold, but you'd plug yer brother's bum for a farthing."

"Not for no farthing, it weren't." Michael giggled.

Tom raised his leather hand and Michael clung to Billy for protection. "Back when we was kiddies, me brother Jimmy got half a crown from an officer for sucking him off. I plugged Jimmy's bum and stole the coin when he were asleep."

"Get off me!" Billy shoved Michael away. "Come on now. He'll be here afore long." He led them to a nearby alley that was choked with empty barrels and crates marked in a dozen languages, none intelligible to any of the three.

"Hide yourselves," Billy said. "Keep still until I call you."

Footsteps approached the alley. Tom Leary grabbed Michael's arm and pulled him behind a packing crate.

A large, elegantly dressed man came into view. "You're on time," he said to Billy.

"A man of me word, guv."

The man looked up and down Front Street, then stepped into the alley and unbuttoned his fly to urinate against the brick wall of a warehouse. He was a portly man, cloaked in a cape, his face shadowed by a silk top hat. He carried an ebony cane with a gold head, although Billy knew that he walked perfectly well without it.

"You have found trustworthy assistants?"

"Two of the best. You got the gold?"

The man rebuttoned his fly before drawing a pouch of gold dust from an inside pocket of his frock coat. The motion revealed a small revolver tucked in his waistband. Billy recognized it as a Colt's pocket model, .31 caliber. He had one much like it in his own coat, but not so new and shiny.

"No one is to know who I am."

"Nor I, guv. That's the thing, isn't it?"

"If you are caught, you are on your own."

"Well, now, there's the rub. If I was brought before you and your strangler friends for judgment, am I to hang without a peep?"

"I cannot raise a hand to save you without endangering myself."

"Ah, well. But you could speak for mercy, guv. For banishment, say, or time in jail. That way I wouldn't have to say who give me the gold and told me what to do."

The man placed the tip of his cane against Billy's chest. "It would be your word against the word of a gentleman."

Billy had suspected this would be his employer's attitude. In a proper court of law he might have a chance to name the man who hired him and get a fair hearing, but the stranglers held their trials in secret.

"It won't be just my word, guv." He raised his voice. "Here now, boys."

Tom Leary stepped into view, followed by Michael Dunn.

"You were to come alone!" The portly man stepped back to the mouth of the alley, pointing the cane like a weapon. There was a black hole in the tip. Billy judged it to be .31 caliber, perhaps .32.

"There's no cause to worry, now, guv." Billy held up his hands in a placating gesture. "We wouldn't betray a trust, none of us. Not unless we felt the touch of hemp to our necks. It's only me knows your name and I'll never breathe it to a living soul so long as I'm safe and well."

The man lowered the cane, still scowling. He tossed over the pouch, which disappeared into Billy's coat in a trice. The town clocks struck a quarter to ten.

"Remain here for five minutes." The man fixed them each with his gaze and took his leave.

Billy portioned out the gold dust into the two smaller pouches he had brought, keeping for himself a somewhat larger share. He passed the pouches to Tom Leary and Michael Dunn. "When the clocks sound a quarter past, and then a few minutes more, not a moment sooner."

"Right you are, Billy." Michael Dunn pocketed his pouch and shifted from foot to foot, eager to be off. "We're grateful for this, Tom and me. We'll stand you a beer tonight. If there's a beer to be found."

Billy stepped into the street. The portly man was gone. "All right, then, off you go. Have a care, Tom."

When they were out of sight, Billy moved off briskly in the opposite direction, but he slowed once he was a street or two removed from the meeting place. He turned up Sacramento and walked like a man out for a Sunday stroll. At Powell, where the streets gave way to the sand hills, Billy turned right, admiring the new homes. On his left, brush-covered hills blocked the view to the Golden Gate. Nearby, a steam paddy stood idle in a partially excavated lot, awaiting the resumption of work on Monday morning.

At Pacific Street, Billy sat on the steps of a half-finished house, as if resting himself on a pleasant Sunday morning. Here the smell of fresh-sawn wood was strong. There were fine homes already lining both sides of Broadway, a block farther north. Broadway was to be a thoroughfare to the west, they said, when they made a cut in the hill. Billy shook his head at the wasted effort. When the gold ran out, the city would sink back into the sandy peninsula. The skeletons of the ships would disintegrate. In ten or twenty years, this place would be as it was before, a lonely outpost on a desolate coast.

He took from his coat pocket a pouch of tobacco and the new pipe he had purchased just over a week before. It was a fine Missouri corncob, seasoning well, but his pleasure in the feel of it diminished as he remembered Johnny Jenkins.

Poor Johnny rose before his eyes, dancing in the night to music only Johnny could hear. The music of angels, maybe. More than likely Johnny skipped to the devil's tune now, although a preacher had prayed over him before the stranglers brought him out, they said. When the preacher took too long about it, the head strangler had told him to get it over quick.

To give him his due, Johnny was a cool one, smoking his cigar when they marched him out, looking more like a spectator at the festive occasion instead of the star attraction. The Plaza had been full to overflowing, everyone cheering and laughing and drinking like a circus was in town, but when the stranglers threw a rope over the beam of the Custom House the throng fell quiet, if only for a moment. Then every man who could get a hand on it grabbed the rope and hauled away, and Johnny Jenkins' eyes bugged out and he shit his breeches and the crowd cheered.

Billy Bemis had seen it all, standing beside Tom Leary and Michael Dunn. He had puffed on his old pipe as he watched Johnny dance in the air until the movement stopped. He had lost the pipe later that night and bought the new one the following day.

The clocks sounded a quarter past ten. Billy tamped the Virginia tobacco with his thumb, trying to shut the image from his mind. The wind was at his back, blowing steadily from the west. It was a good wind, picking up as the sky cleared. Gritty dust settled on Billy's clothes. A buggy rolled down Pacific, but there was no one afoot within his view.

He waited five minutes, then dropped the unlit pipe into the outer pocket of his jacket and rose. He tied the new handkerchief once more about his face and went to the back of the house. He had made his preparations before dawn. The jug of turpentine was where he had left it, concealed beneath the back porch, amidst the sawdust and scraps of lumber that were swept out of the house at the end of each day's work. There was no shortage of handy fuel in this town. No, indeed.

Crouched down by the steps, Billy was concealed from the nearby houses. Moving quickly now, he uncorked the jug and poured a thin stream of turpentine along a trail of sawdust that was an inch deep, three fingers wide, and three yards long. The makeshift fuse ran next to the foundation, sheltered from the wind. When it was soaked along its length, Billy emptied the rest of the turpentine on the scraps and shavings beneath the porch and tossed the jug aside. He struck a lucifer, shielded it with his hands, and touched it to the sawdust trail.

The flame flared and burned, almost invisible in the bright sunlight. Billy had tested just such a fuse the day before, down by the docks. It would take the flame a few minutes to burn the three yards to the steps, and a few minutes was all he needed to get clear.

"Right, then," he said. Keeping the house between himself and the occupied dwellings along Pacific Street, he moved up the slope and north on Powell to Broadway, where he passed three children playing in the sandy soil of a newly fenced yard. Turning right again and left at the next street, he zigzagged over to Vallejo and then to Green Street as the town clocks struck half past ten.

Church bells that had been awaiting the signal drowned out the municipal timekeepers, those of a Catholic church at Powell and Filbert dominating the competition as they pealed out a doleful Gregorian melody. Somewhere behind Billy, another bell joined the chorus, monotonous and insistent, but its alarm was lost in the general clamor of piety.

There were a few people on the streets here, walking idly of a Sunday. None looked Billy's way. His risk was greatest now, as the first alarms struggled to make themselves heard above the church bells, but who could point to one man and say "That's him"? If by bad luck he were stopped by the stranglers he would become a Sunday drunk like his dad, almost incoherent, stumbling toward his rooming house, a threat to no one.

Damn their souls anyway! Who were they to make a man fear for his life? "Regulators," they had styled themselves when they first organized two weeks ago to aid the city police in patrolling the streets at night. Now, in the blink of an eye, they were "The San Francisco Committee of Vigilance," a power unto themselves. They called themselves by numbers instead of names and they held their meetings in secret. They broke into homes in the night and hauled off whomever they pleased. Those they took were "notorious scoundrels," they said, and "known to be bad characters." Some they put aboard outbound steamers without the formality of a judge's ruling and some they held for trial. But they scragged Johnny Jenkins for stealing a safe so every footpad in San Francisco would know they were as likely to hang you as transport you, and if one thing was certain it was that no incendiary would be given safe passage to warmer climes.

Halfway up the slope of Telegraph Hill, Billy shucked off his coat and paused to catch his breath. The city was bright with sunshine and the wind was strong from the west. The church bells had concluded their Sunday chorus and the fire alarms rang clearly now, carrying across the town. As Billy watched, the doors of a church flew open and the congregation hastened forth, looking about fearfully. But it was too late. The church bells had done their job, drowning out the early warnings and allowing the fires to take hold.

From his vantage point, Billy could see all three conflagrations. At Pacific and Powell streets, the half-built house was in flames. Pushed by the westerly wind, the fire reached out to the row of houses along Pacific. It would jump to Broadway soon and then it would threaten the whole city. The second fire, in the shantytown north of Broadway and east of Montgomery, was Michael's work. The third cloud rose from the warehouses at the waterfront, where Tom Leary had done his job. The waterfront had escaped the fire of May 4, but it would not escape this time. The fire companies would see the Powell Street blaze as the greatest threat, coming from windward. They would race to make a line if they could, and down by the water the warehouses, full of goods going begging for buyers, would burn unchecked, as Billy's employer intended.

Another few minutes' climb brought Billy to the top of Telegraph Hill. He dropped to the ground beside the signal house where a watchman kept lookout for ships entering the Golden Gate. The house was empty now, the watchman at church or taking his Sunday at home. Soon enough, he'd be passing buckets.

In the city below, people were fleeing from the homes and buildings nearest the fires. A fire engine came in sight on Dupont Street, the men straining at the rope. They might save a few lives, but there would be no stopping the flames. In time, the fires would join. The city's churchgoing folk would spend their Sunday morning fighting to save their homes and their churches and their places of business. Prayer would come later.

Billy took from his pocket the Missouri corncob pipe and a box of lucifers. He put a match to the bowl and savored the taste, which was marred only slightly by the rawness of the pipe.

"Well done," he said to no one but himself. He would enjoy his pipe, taking in the spectacle, but he would not linger long. Michael Dunn and Tom Leary would look for him tonight in the Noggin of Ale, if it survived the fire, but they would look in vain. In a short time he would buy a ticket like a regular toff and take the steamer to Sacramento. On arrival he would treat himself to a ten-dollar dinner. The gold remaining in his pouch after these indulgences would be enough to last the summer. Enough to pay for warm arms to hold him when he fancied. Enough for two hot meals a day and all the ale he liked. The miners said there was no fog to chill a summer's night in Sacramento. Hot as the Australian outback, they said. And there were no stranglers there.

Other figures were climbing the slopes of the hill now, men and women stopping often to look back at the fires, children racing toward the summit.

Look back and you'll turn to salt, Billy thought.

An explosion rocked the town. At Dupont and Jackson streets, in the path of the flames, splintered timbers spinning through the air marked where firemen were blasting a firebreak.

Billy Bemis smoked his pipe and watched the city burn.

Book One

Chapter 1

The clipper appeared between the headlands of the Golden Gate like a ghost ship. She was barely an outline at first, a wraith in the mists of a light rain squall, taking on form as she cleared the throat of the narrow passage and moved forth upon the great bay, unexpected and unwelcomed. Seagulls wheeled overhead. Closer to the water, brown pelicans glided past the vessel on still wings.

The tillerman of a fishing smack saw her first. "Ship to port, Captain," he said. His face was wet with rain and salt spray. The little boat was beating out to sea against a fresh breeze and a strong tide.

The captain, a stout Gloucester man, turned from overseeing the preparation of the nets. His eyes widened with surprise when he saw the ship. He had not expected to meet any vessels coming through the Gate on such a day. He looked to the clipper's bows, praying she was not the *Flying Dutchman*, breathing more easily when he made out her prosaic name—*Sarah B. Watson*. She had the raked bow and the narrow hull of a true clipper.

"I'd like to meet the man who will approach this bay when he can see no further than a dozen lengths of his own vessel," the captain said. The bones of a score of ships already adorned the rocky coast beyond the Gate, testifying to the dangers of seeking the narrow channel in bad weather. Seamen said finding the Golden Gate when it was fog-shrouded or girdled in rain clouds was more difficult than gaining entrance to a reluctant virgin's passage.

"Let's have a look at her," the captain said.

The man at the tiller called "Ready about," and then, "Helm's alee!" Fishermen laid hold of the sheets as the boat came into the wind, sails flapping, and fell off on the opposite tack.

It was midafternoon. On either side of the turbulent channel, the vaulting headlands glowered darkly, cloaked in their coats of brown. The rain that was spawned as the sea air struck the coast fell almost entirely on the waters of the bay, where it gave no relief to the parched countryside. The winter had been dry.

"She's shipshape in Bristol fashion, that one," the tillerman ventured.

"She is that." The fisher captain noted the sleek lines of the China clipper and the fresh paint that adorned her down to the waterline. The yards were shiny black, braced square before the wind. The topmasts were white, the bulwarks green, the anchors and ironwork blacked, the chains and fastenings free of rust. Even the gilt scrollwork that adorned the bowsprit and stern was newly touched up. The *Sarah B. Watson*'s master had taken advantage of a calm day or two recently to put her in order before entering port. She was fully laden and rode low in the water, as did all ships inbound to San Francisco Bay. The fisher captain judged her to be about twelve hundred tons capacity and two hundred feet overall.

The smack passed across the clipper's bows and was well clear of the ship when she cut the fishing boat's wake sixty yards astern. The captain could hear the hiss of the curling foam under the *Sarah B. Watson*'s prow. Sailors scampered in her rigging like monkeys, shaking out sails. They moved as if they enjoyed the task, more like a crew at the start of a voyage around Cape Horn than at the end of one.

The captain cupped his hands to his mouth and shouted, "Ahoy the *Sarah B. Watson*! Where are you from?"

After a moment an enormous man raised a speaking trumpet at the aft rail and sent the words of his proud reply booming across the water like cannon shot. "We are one hundred nine days out of Boston, by way of Charleston!"

"That's a fair passage," the fisher captain remarked. In '49 or '50, it would have been a record passage. In '51, the *Flying Cloud* had dropped her anchor in San Francisco Bay eighty-nine days and twenty-one hours after hoisting it in New York, and now passages of over a hundred days were scarcely noticed.

"What's your cargo?" the fisherman asked of the clipper.

"Carolina rice," came the answer, less proud this time, it seemed.

As the ship fell astern of the smack she ran up a house flag. The fisher captain raised a spyglass and trained it on the scrap of cloth. It was the pennant of Farnum & Kent, a smaller line than some, but well respected. He lowered the glass and studied the ship's wake as the distance between the two vessels lengthened. A following wind was a helmsman's greatest challenge, but the clipper's wake was straight as a die.

Aboard the *Sarah B. Watson*, the helmsman surveyed the sails that dotted the bay. Fishing boats were the most numerous—offshore Gloucestermen and lateen-rigged Italian feluccas and sailing dories and everything in between. Among them moved larger vessels—smacks and packets, coasters and cutters and schooners of all sizes, even a few pleasure yachts of varied designs—tacking this way and that in the steady westerly breeze that raised whitecaps on the water. Unbound by the rules of the wind, sidewheel steam tugs and two large ferries ploughed through the water, their purposeful movements oblivious to the forces of nature.

Two ships, a medium clipper and a bluff-bowed merchantman, were under way for the Gate, there being little danger in departing the bay while weather shrouded the coast. The *Sarah B. Watson* passed between them, serene in the false calm of a vessel running before the wind, leaving the clipper to port and the squat cargo carrier to starboard.

Ahead, in a crescent stretching from Alcatraz Island to Blossom Rock and on toward Goat Island, ships and barks and brigs lay at anchor, awaiting their turns at the wharves or awaiting a cargo, or awaiting the devil himself, for all the helmsman knew. Lighters and ships' boats plied among them. Beyond the ships and Goat Island lay the wooded hills of Contra Costa, the bay's eastern shore.

The huge man who had returned the fishing smack's hail emerged from the chart house, where he had stowed the speaking trumpet. In a gale he might use it to call orders to the crew. In a sheltered bay, however vast, his own voice was sufficient.

His name was Melchior. Just that and no more. A mane of grizzled curls covered his head and more adorned his face and chin. Blue eyes peered from beneath thick brows that were still solid black.

"A good passage, Jason."

"Aye," the helmsman agreed.

Melchior addressed the helmsman by his Christian name only when no one else was about. They were alone on the poop deck except for the ship's cat, a calico named Veronica after a comely Maori maiden who had stolen a forgotten seaman's heart. The cat ventured on deck only when the ship was on an even keel. She sat now by Jason's feet, cleaning her tail.

"We be signalling for a pilot now." The broad inflections of Cornwall sounded in Melchior's speech.

"Aye." Jason wished he could remain at the helm through this watch and the next and yield it only to go to his bunk for a few hours' rest. Arrival in port spelled the end of the ship's joyous motion as it moved across deep waters. Both Jason Beck and the *Sarah B. Watson* were most content when they were far from the sight of land. But the signal must be given. The ship had slipped through the coastal squalls without seeing the offshore pilot boat.

"I've rigged out the small gun," Melchior said.

The *Sarah B. Watson* carried four brass cannon of varying sizes. When she tiptoed through the pirate-ridden waters of the China Sea, all four were on deck, primed and manned day and night.

Melchior raised a hand and a sharp report boomed from the foredeck, but there was no need for the signal.

The ship's appearance in the Golden Gate had been observed by sharp eyes atop Telegraph Hill and announced by semaphore to the city below and a pilot vessel on the bay. Even now, the boat was standing out from North Point.

The ship hove to as the boat came alongside and delivered the pilot, then fell off as it sheared away. The clipper was nearing Alcatraz. From the rocks of the island a thousand seabirds rose as one, taking unaccountable alarm at the close passage of the vessel. A sentry raised a hand in greeting from the walls of the fort atop the island. The helmsman waved in reply, then turned his attention to the pilot as he climbed to the poop.

"Unseasonal weather, Pilot," Melchior said. At the appearance of the stranger, the cat Veronica got to her feet and trotted into the chart house.

"Can't say as to that, Captain," the pilot allowed. "Ain't been here long enough to say what's seasonal and what ain't."

" 'Tis not me's the skipper here," Melchior informed him. "I be Melchior, first mate. Cap'n Beck be the master." He nodded toward the man at the helm, then walked to the forward rail of the poop and signalled to Brad Keith, a seaman on the weather deck below, to come up.

"Will Clum, Captain Beck," the pilot introduced himself, doing his best to contain his surprise. The *Sarah B. Watson*'s master was barefoot like a common sailor and he was dressed as a sailor dressed, although his trousers and coat were of finer fabric and cut, now that Clum saw them close up. He was bearded and long-haired, like many at the end of a passage 'round the Horn. The brown hair was tied at the nape of his neck with a bit of ribbon. He sported a small golden ring in one ear like a Barbary pirate. It was unusually flamboyant trapping for the master of a Yankee clipper, as Jason Beck was well aware.

"Didn't expect to find myself needed today," Clum said. "Didn't expect to find the master at the wheel, neither. You have made port here before?"

"Twice before, Mr. Clum," Jason said. "In thirty-six and forty-nine."

"I would have liked to see this bay in thirty-six, before all the fuss and bother."

"It was the end of the earth then. A few Spaniards and Indians, and a handful of Yankees trading in hides and tallow."

The pilot looked aloft, appraising the set of the sails and finding no way to improve it. The ship's rigging was freshly tarred. He noted that like most of the larger clippers the *Sarah B. Watson* had converted to split topsails for ease of handling. Amidship, the second mate stood on the weather deck with a speaking trumpet in his hand, ready to relay orders to sailors in the rigging.

Clum said, "There's few who'll brave the Gate on such a day, even masters who have made this port a dozen times."

"With my hand on the wheel, Pilot, the *Sarah B.* will never find a rock in a wave. She knows I love her better than any woman." Jason yielded the wheel to Brad Keith. The young seaman had a steady hand. "She's your ship now, Mr. Clum."

Jason Beck was forty years old and he had been at sea since he was ten. His eyes, which appeared at first glance to be black, were actually a brown so dark that the pupils in their centers were almost indistinguishable, giving them an appearance of bottomlessness. At the corners, the skin was wrinkled from a lifetime of squinting against sun and wind. Of medium height, compact, he was no taller than Will Clum, but the pilot felt small and plain beside him. It was a matter of bearing more than height or dress. Beck's stance bespoke a self-assured authority so natural that Clum wondered how he could ever have mistaken the enormous mate for the master. The *Sarah B. Watson* was Clum's to command for a time, but she was Jason Beck's ship.

"What is your cargo, Captain?"

"Rice, Mr. Clum. She's full to the scuppers with rice."

"Bags or bunkers?"

"Every grain of it in bags. I'll not have loose grain aboard my ship."

Loose grain was a notoriously hazardous cargo, given to shifting unpredictably in heavy weather. And whether loose or in bags it was an invitation to vermin, but with a cat aboard the mice and rats would be kept in check.

"You won't need the grain docks, then," Clum said.

"Any dock will do, Mr. Clum. When I have seen my owner, we'll know where the cargo is bound."

"We'll trim up and steer for the little extreme clipper there at anchor, if you please, Captain Beck." They were in sight of the city now.

At a nod from Jason, Seaman Keith spun the wheel while Melchior and the second mate called out orders to the sailors on deck and in the rigging. By custom, a ship's master never spoke directly to the crew. He spoke to the mates, and the mates conveyed his orders. At sea Jason honored the custom mainly in the breach. In port he observed it as a formality expected by pilots and customs officers and other officials that might otherwise be led to misjudge a ship's master who sported a golden earring.

"Not much wire rigging aboard your ship, Captain," Clum observed. Many of the better ships were converting to wire, for its durability.

"Better rope than wire aboard ship, Mr. Clum. Better rope than wire, better wind than fire."

Rope and beams and planks were made from living things that grew on land and found new life at sea. It was in their nature to float. It was in the nature of steel wire and iron plates to sink. It was in the nature of fire to consume whatever it touched and then to look for more fuel. Jason Beck knew that the days of the wooden-hulled sailing ships were numbered, but he would retire to the land before he sailed a vessel made of iron and steel or accepted a master's berth aboard a steamship with fire in her belly. Better rope than wire. Better wind than fire.

Under the pilot's orders the clipper trimmed her sails further and headed on a reach that would bring her to the harbor. As she came under the lee of the peninsula the sea breeze diminished, blowing west-sou'westerly here, and her pace slowed. At a word from Melchior, sailors swarmed into the rigging, where they clewed up the royals, topgallants and courses, hauled down the upper topsail yards, and set about furling the sails.

By the mainmast, four seamen performed the hated job of pumping ship, but they heaved on the pump handles with a will, making the plungers clank and the ornate iron flywheels spin with a soft hum, while glancing now and then at the city that overflowed the sand hills on the east shore of the peninsula.

Well off the wharves, a steam tug stood by for the clipper's hail and the pilot's directions to her berth or anchorage. Beside the tug, six dockside crimps in a longboat waved and shouted to get the sailors' attention, promising to satiate whichever of their vices most needed attention at the end of a Cape Horn passage.

"Steady, lads," cautioned the second mate. He licked his lips at the thought of the taste of whiskey. Aboard the *Sarah B. Watson*, as aboard most American merchant vessels, spirits were banned at sea in the interest of obtaining insurance at the lowest possible rates.

Jason glanced at the tug and the crimps. "What's the sounding off the end of that wharf there, Mr. Clum?" He pointed to a prominent wharf in the midst of the rest.

"Pacific Wharf is dredged to four fathoms at mean low water, Captain Beck. She's on the ebb now, about half-gone."

"Water to spare. Shall we have a bit of fun?"

"Fun, Captain Beck?"

Jason didn't reply. He regarded the pilot calmly, his dark eyes bright. He had issued a challenge and he was waiting to see if Will Clum was man enough to accept it.

"All right, Captain. And just what might be your idea of a little fun?"

"Melchior." Jason turned to the mate.

"Just like Singapore, Cap'n?" There was a glint of humor in the eyes that watched Jason from beneath the black brows.

"Just like Singapore."

Melchior hove his considerable bulk across the poop with an agility that surprised Will Clum. "Mr. Rooney!" he called to the second mate. "Have your lads look sharp!"

To the seaman at the wheel, he said, "Do like I tell you, young Brad, and be quick when I speak."

On the Pacific Wharf, sailors and landsmen alike

stopped what they were doing and turned to look, then to stare, as the clipper passed by the puffing tug and bore down on the wharf. In her wake, the crimps squawked in anger at being ignored, then argued among themselves over who was to row in pursuit.

Driven by her lower topsails, the spanker, and a single jib, the *Sarah B. Watson* glided among the ships at anchor, her pace stately but inexorable. The afternoon steamer to Sacramento veered out of her way, paddles churning, and let loose a blast of warning from her whistle. Ships under sail had right of way over steam-powered vessels, but the steamer's master felt the right had been abused. The passengers flocked to the aft rail while the onlookers at the outer end of the wharf began to edge nervously toward the land.

"What're they up to?" an old salt wondered aloud. He was seated on the wharf with his back to a piling, stoking his pipe with a three-fingered hand. He got to his feet. Aboard the oncoming ship the sailors went about their tasks without alarm. At the main topgallant yard, a sailor's voice carried over the water. "Who's going to pay for Paddy Doyle's boots?" he demanded to know. At the word *boots*, the men on the footropes heaved up the furled sail, bringing it atop the yard, where they would lash it in place with rope gaskets to finish off the harbor stow. Intent on their work, they didn't even look ahead.

When it seemed that the ship would surely smash into the end of the wharf, the helmsman spun the wheel hard over. As the two-hundred-foot vessel hove into the wind, sailors hauled down the jib and spanker while others heaved on the braces, squaring the lower topsails to the breeze. The sails were taken aback, the light wind filling them from forward now, pushing against the ship's momentum. The *Sarah B. Watson* slowed until she was dead in the water, her port rail not ten yards from where the old salt was dancing with glee.

"Clew up!" cried a voice, and the last sails were gathered to their yards.

"Toss over your line!" the old salt called out. "I'll make her fast."

A sailor heaved a coil of slender rope attached to the loop of a thick hawser. The old man caught the coil and turned to the gawkers, who were moving forward now that the imagined danger was past. "Lend a hand here!" he shouted. With the help of two fishmongers he hauled the mooring line to the wharf and wrestled the loop over a piling.

The crowd surged forward, Custom House officers and dockhands vying for position with idlers and draymen and boardinghouse runners and Sandwich Islanders and Chinamen who had chanced to witness the clipper's unorthodox arrival. Carts and wagons clattered between the vegetable and fish stands and slop shops that were built along the sides of the wharf.

"There you are, Pilot," Jason Beck said to Will Clum. "No sense clambering down to a pitching longboat when we can deliver you to the dock."

Clum permitted himself a smile. "Thank you kindly, Captain Beck."

"By God, Jason Beck! I should have known it was you!"

Jason found himself facing the old salt who had taken such delight in the ship's arrival. The Nordic tones in the man's voice summoned up a memory. Jason looked to the man's right hand. "Finn Warren? From the *Essex*?"

"The same! And you the skipper now!" Finn Warren waggled his three-fingered hand in Jason's face. "I never forget you, see? But you was just a boy then, and I remember you kindly."

Jason flushed with embarrassment. Because of his youthful inexperience, Finn Warren's hand had been caught between an anchor chain and a capstan. Seamen's lore held that the natives of Finland were unlucky to have in a ship's crew, but no harm had come to anyone on the *Essex* while Finn Warren served aboard her, save through the carelessness of Jason Beck.

"I am still sorry for that, Finn. And sorry to find you on the beach."

"Oh, I'm beached for good this time, lad. I came ashore in fifty-two and made my pile. Just a small pile it is, but sufficient to an old seaman's needs. I been luckier than most."

"I never thought to see you a landsman, Finn."

"It's pleasant here, Jason. Not too cold in winter, not

too hot in summer. The women are saucy, and you can always smell the sea."

"You there!" A voice cut through the babel on deck. A young man, tall and thin and neatly dressed, forced his way toward Jason. "Where might I find your captain in this hullabaloo?"

"I am Captain Beck."

The young man reddened, unaware that he was the second person in less than an hour to mistake the ship's master for a seaman. "Forgive me, Captain. By your reputation I had formed an image of—an older man. I am Ned Rollick, first secretary to Mr. Kent."

"I was expecting Mr. Kent himself."

Rollick's Adam's apple was prominent in his thin neck. It bobbed up and down as he swallowed nervously. "Commercial affairs have kept him at the firm's offices, I'm afraid. If you aren't too busy to come with me . . ." With a glance at Finn Warren, he left the suggestion hanging.

"You've much to do, Jason," the old seaman said. "Tomorrow we'll have a brandy together and talk of old times."

"With luck we'll be outward bound on tomorrow's tide, Finn. Come aboard this evening and we'll share a glass."

"You never been one for the pleasures of the land, Jason Beck. You reckon you'll get them to make sail again in less than a day?" He glanced about the deck and Jason followed his gaze.

The crew were coiling down the hauling ends—clews and bunts and downhauls and braces and halyards— making them fast to belaying pins at the pinrails, but they were hampered in their work by the crowd. Jason saw a crimp offer a flask to a seaman named Grimes. Grimes took a long draught and wiped his mouth on his sleeve while the crimp spoke urgently about the other pleasures to be found in the gold port.

Jason would soothe the crew with a promise of more shore leave in the Sandwich Isles. He would tell them anything to make them accept the fastest possible turnabout in San Francisco. They would have leave tonight and come back aboard blind drunk in the morning, and by the turn of the tide they would be fit enough.

"Are there stevedores available to handle the rice?" he asked of Ned Rollick.

Rollick seemed ill at ease. "You will have to discuss this with Mr. Kent, Captain. There is a problem—"

"What kind of problem?"

Rollick's Adam's apple bobbed. "I'm afraid we cannot unload the cargo today. Mr. Kent will—"

"Not unload today? Why not?"

"Mr. Kent would prefer to explain the circumstances to you himself, Captain. I'm to take you to him straight-away, if you will just come with me."

Nothing Jason could do or say would pry anything further from the increasingly embarrassed Ned Rollick. He saw that the clerk was only an errand boy with no authority to explain matters more fully, so he left the ship in Melchior's charge and accompanied Rollick away from the wharves, into the teeming streets of the town.

Chapter 2

rom the low ridge between California Street Hill and Russian Hill, which rose above the western edge of the city, a young woman watched the unorthodox arrival of the China clipper at the Pacific Wharf.

Her name was Sarah Rockwell. She wore a violet day dress beneath a cape of gray silk, and a violet bonnet fringed in black. The colors and the black fringe showed her to be in the final stages of a widow's mourning. Nearly three years had passed since her husband's death, but Sarah Rockwell still grieved, and so long as she grieved she felt it proper to dress in mourning.

She was twenty-four years old.

The sight of a full-rigged ship rounding North Point had caught her eye as she arrived atop the ridge, only a little out of breath from the climb, and she followed the vessel's progress with interest. When the ship neared the Pacific Wharf and turned at the last into the wind, she clapped her hands in delight.

To her surprise, another pair of hands added their applause to her own. She turned to discover a young woman about her own age, standing not far away. The young woman was taller than Sarah. She was elegantly dressed in silk and taffeta the color of a yellow rose, and she shaded her face with a matching parasol. Her hair was blond and her jaunty hat was beyond the bounds of conservative fashion.

"That was an audacious maneuver," Sarah said. The young woman nodded slightly and turned away, walking north along the ridge toward the outstretched arm of Russian Hill. Sarah raised her voice. "I am Sarah Rockwell. We might as well introduce ourselves, since there is no one here to do it for us."

The young woman looked back. "That would not be proper, because you are a lady and I am not."

Sarah felt her face redden as the blond woman walked away, glad that no one had seen her mistake a prostitute for a lady. San Francisco had made her careless of social distinctions, but that very informality was one of the qualities she valued most in her adopted home. Here, a sailor's daughter who had married well was accepted as a lady, even though she kept a boardinghouse.

Sarah looked over the city, her pleasure in the day and the sight of the clipper ship spoiled. San Francisco had welcomed her in a time of trouble. It had given her shelter and healed her. And now she must leave it behind.

Half an hour's walk brought her down off the brush-covered hill to the planked streets of the commercial district. At a lively pace, she had often covered the same distance in half the time. Today she let her fancy divert her from the most direct course to her destination. She chose her favorite streets and lingered before a few of the shops where she had done business, beginning the process of taking her leave.

The city was much changed since she first saw it. The rush of building and immigration that had created a metropolis overnight at the start of the gold rush had slowed, but it continued nevertheless. Sarah's boardinghouse, once an outpost beyond the western fringe of the city, favored in '53 for its quiet and the splendid view of the bay, was now one among many homes along Mason and Jackson and the surrounding streets, its view cut off by the newer houses, except from the third floor windows.

As she walked, the clouds broke and scattered, revealing the sun as Sarah arrived at Montgomery Street. The bright warmth and the bustle of the street revived her spirits. For four blocks, from California to Jackson, Montgomery was paved with square blocks of granite and it looked as solid and respectable as any street in Boston. It seemed to Sarah that optimism was in the very air here. Workingmen and frock-coated gentlemen alike strode along with purpose. The men looked at Sarah, but they did not pause to turn and watch as she passed them by, in part because of her widow's weeds and in part because of their haste to get on about their business.

The protection Sarah gained from her display of mourning was a lesser reason for her maintaining it so long. As a widow, she was somewhat shielded from crude advances. Even the riffraff and the drunkards accorded her a modicum of respect. First in her black dresses and later in the less severe colors of second mourning and ordinary mourning, she had grown accustomed to the freedom of making her way alone, unmolested. When she left San Francisco she would leave her mourning behind, and the protection it provided.

She crossed Sacramento Street and entered the office of the San Francisco *Herald*. A clean-shaven man of about thirty looked up from a desk behind the mahogany counter, where he was writing rapidly on a lined tablet. He rose when he saw that his visitor was a lady. In the rear of the one-room shop, a printer was setting type for the next morning's edition.

"Good afternoon, madam." The man's voice betrayed a trace of an Irish brogue.

"I wish to place an advertisement to sell my boardinghouse." The words cost Sarah a good deal of effort, but they sounded ordinary enough, she judged.

The man took a form and filled in the particulars Sarah gave him. Two-story frame house in good repair, located at Mason and Jackson Streets. Finished attic with two rooms. Seven bedrooms in all. Yard and drying ground. Fenced property. Apply to owner, Mrs. Sarah Rockwell.

"I have heard tell of your house, Mrs. Rockwell. You are well spoken of. What price are you asking?"

"Three thousand five hundred dollars."

The man's surprise was plain. "I take it you are in no great hurry to sell."

"Why do you say so?"

"Real estate is very slow just now, Mrs. Rockwell. Lots that sold a few years past for three hundred dollars are going begging at thirty. Houses are more difficult to move. And a frame house, now that everyone is going to brick, well, I realize that commercial affairs are not a woman's concern, but as owner of the house, you must—"

"I am well aware of the state of business, sir. I read the *Herald* daily."

The man regarded Sarah with new interest. "Do you, now? And what do you think of it?"

"I think it is by far the best newspaper in the city. Mr. Nugent's editorials would put most eastern papers to shame."

The man smiled, obviously pleased. He bowed slightly. "Modesty compels me to stop you before you embarrass me further, Mrs. Rockwell. I am John Nugent, publisher and editor of the *Herald*. Forgive me for not introducing myself sooner."

Nugent's good humor revealed itself in the thickening of his brogue. He had come from Galway as a boy, but the lilt of his childish tongue had long ago been tamed by years spent among men of many different accents in his adopted land.

Sarah was delighted. "I had imagined an older man. Someone more like God."

Nugent laughed. "Is that how I sound in print?"

"You write forcefully, with authority and good sense."

"That should tell you I'm not God. After all, if he had good sense, he never would have created man. I mean, we're a quarrelsome species, you'll have to admit. You have only to look at San Francisco politics to see that."

"I look at our politics through your eyes, Mr. Nugent, and I see everything clearly."

"Ah! Now that reveals a wisdom as divine as your beauty, Mrs. Rockwell. But forgive me, you're in mourning."

Sarah was enjoying the banter, most of all because the publisher treated her as an equal. For the first time, she wished she had packed her mourning clothes away.

Nugent looked over the notes he had made, all business now. "This will be one dollar a day or four dollars per week. How long do you want to continue the ad?"

"Until further notice."

"Shall I lower the price if you don't sell within a certain time?"

Sarah hesitated. She knew the figure was high, but it was no more than the boardinghouse was worth. She had made improvements since buying it in '53. It seemed unfair that the present business conditions threatened her with a loss.

"I will let you know if I'm prepared to lower the price." She paid him for the first week, and she said, "I hope you won't become involved in the quarrel between Mr. King and the *Times*. It has brought out the worst in the other papers."

"They're outdoing themselves today," Nugent said. "Have you seen the *Bulletin*?"

"I read only the *Herald*."

"I appreciate your loyalty, Mrs. Rockwell, but you are missing some grand entertainment." Nugent took the day's *Evening Bulletin* from his desk and set it on the counter before her. He opened it to the second page and pointed to an item. "This came out on the streets an hour ago. They say Casey has already demanded a retraction."

Sarah read the article quickly. In it, James King of William, editor of the *Bulletin*, employed his customary fulminating style to attack James Casey, a city councilman and publisher of the *Sunday Times*. For several months, the two had been exchanging insults in the press. What Sarah knew of the quarrel she had learned in the pages of Nugent's *Herald* and from the conversations of her boarders. King, a failed banker, had added his father's Christian name to his surname in the District of Columbia, where he was born, to distinguish himself from other James Kings there. In San Francisco he kept it as a badge of distinction, one his enemies thought pretentious. He had bought the *Bulletin* in October and since then had attacked Catholics and Democrats indiscriminately, as well as any who supported them. His diatribes had made him many enemies, James Casey's *Times* foremost among them.

Sarah thought the article merely scurrilous until she

read the final paragraph: *The fact that Casey has been an inmate of Sing Sing prison in New York is no offense against the laws of this state, nor is the fact of his having stuffed himself through the ballot box as elected to the Board of Supervisors from a district where it was said he was not a candidate—*

"This is slanderous!" Sarah exclaimed. "Mr. King must know Casey was appointed to fill a vacancy in his district."

"Bravo, Mrs. Rockwell. You are uncommonly well informed, for a lady. As always, King of William overlooks the evidence that would blunt his attack. It's his style. That last bit is more serious, to my way of seeing it. He's inciting to riot there. He's practically called for a mob to lynch Casey."

Sarah read the rest: *—stuffed himself through the ballot box as elected to the Board of Supervisors from a district where it was said he was not a candidate, any justification for Mr. Bagley to shoot Casey, however richly the latter may deserve to have his neck stretched for such fraud on the people.*

"What does he mean about Mr. Bagley shooting Casey?"

"There was a street fight last fall," Nugent said. "Bagley and some Democratic thugs waylaid Casey. He was unarmed, but he got the better of them and chased them off with their own revolvers. He's got spunk, there's no denying that."

"But Mr. Casey supports the Democrats."

"Rival factions. As I've written many times, King is wasting his time attacking the Democrats. Leave them alone and they'll destroy themselves."

"We have enough real problems in this city without men like Mr. King making things worse," Sarah said. She gathered herself to leave. "I hope you will keep yourself and your paper above the fray, Mr. Nugent. Good afternoon."

"The *Herald* will maintain its standards, Mrs. Rockwell. I thank you for your trade."

A clock struck five as Sarah stepped into the street. It was time to be getting home. She moved north along Montgomery Street, scolding herself for taking the city's troubles too much to heart. Even something as remote from her own life as a newspaper quarrel upset her unreasonably. Politics were at the root of the fight between the *Times* and the *Bulletin*. San Francisco's politics, like those in every American city, were rough-and-tumble. The Democrats, as always, claimed the allegiance of the disaffected and the dispossessed, but now the Democrats were split between northern and southern wings, arguing over slavery and free soil. Unable to exploit the schism, the Whigs, tired and aimless, fell into disarray. The Republican Party, formed three years before to support free soil and oppose slavery, showed signs of displacing the Whigs as the party of power and property, while the Know-Nothings contented themselves by whipping up fear of foreigners and Catholics.

It annoyed Sarah that such distant arguments should affect San Francisco. Here of all places, she believed, politics should be argued reasonably, in good fellowship. But politics was a man's world, and good fellowship was not the way of men in the modern age. If they found themselves returned to the Garden of Eden, Sarah felt certain that men would choose up sides between Eve and the serpent, form political parties, and hold an election to determine the outcome.

At Washington Street a crowd blocked the way. The street was strangely quiet. Sarah heard a shout from beyond the gathering, but she couldn't make out the words. She pushed through the throng. As she was about to break free of it a sailor grabbed her roughly and pulled her back. Sarah struggled to free her arm from the seaman's grip, but he held her tightly. A gold ring glinted in his left ear. His dark eyes met hers for a moment and he nodded toward the street, where two men stood alone on the planks, separated by forty feet. "There's trouble here, miss."

As he spoke, the smaller of the two men in the street cried out, "Defend yourself!" He shrugged off his short cloak and held out one arm toward the taller man. A woman screamed.

It took Sarah a moment to realize that the object the smaller man held in his outstretched hand was a revolver.

Chapter 3

t was seven years since Jason Beck had seen San Francisco and the changes in the port city astonished him. In 1849 the gold rush was just beginning. Then, the town of Yerba Buena, lately renamed San Francisco, had been an encampment of plank hovels and tents and a few old Spanish adobes. Most of the men walking the streets were miners, full of haste to reach the gold diggings, a hundred miles inland. Now the miners were fewer and the town was transformed. The rough tents were gone, replaced by orderly blocks of three- and four-story buildings, many of them faced with brick and stone. The streets were planked with three-inch lumber and many of the gentlemen who trod the planks were as fashionably attired as any Boston banker. There were fashionably dressed ladies about as well, some walking unescorted, to Jason's surprise, but the character of the place was set by the workingmen. Outnumbering the gentlemen merchants by twenty to one, they were a ragtag assortment of Chinamen, *chilenos*, Negroes, East Indians, Yankees and Turks, draymen, laborers, sailors and miners, speaking a cacophony of foreign tongues as well as several rough varieties of English. Here, as in all port cities, there were many Kanakas because the Sandwich Islanders were first-class sailors.

The polyglot nature of the inhabitants was no novelty

to the master of a China clipper. Jason's own crew boasted men from a dozen lands.

"There were three thousand souls in this port in forty-nine," he said. "Most of those were hell-bent for the gold country."

"They say there are fifty thousand now, Captain," Ned Rollick replied. "There may be somewhat fewer at present. It is very difficult to obtain precise figures. The miners leave the mountains in the fall when the rains drive them out of the river bottoms. They go back in spring." The lack of an accurate census appeared to trouble the clerk, but Jason was troubled by a memory.

In '49 he had entered San Francisco Bay on a breezy day when the moisture off the sea and the dust off the land combined to form a haze that turned golden in the afternoon sun, as if the ether itself were permeated with the ore being traded with such abandon in the streets of the burgeoning city. Mesmerized by the siren song of El Dorado, Jason's entire crew had deserted within hours of dropping anchor. It had taken him three weeks to cajole and coerce a handful of men into signing on as a makeshift crew to man his ship on the return voyage to Boston. That adventure had cost him his profit from nine months at sea and he had vowed he would not dock again at San Francisco until the gold madness was done. Now Wentworth Farnum and Stephen Kent believed they could increase their profits by carrying Carolina rice to San Francisco on their ships' westbound voyage to the Orient, but Jason had been skeptical from the outset. Five minutes after Ned Rollick ushered him into Stephen Kent's second-story office in a brick building on Sansome Street, his skepticism was replaced by anger.

"A storeship! Never!" Jason rose to his feet so suddenly that the chair on which he had been sitting tipped over and fell to the pine floor with a clatter.

Kent didn't blink. He was older than Jason, barrel-chested, with a ruddy countenance. He had been a ship's captain himself and was not intimidated by the outburst. He now presided over an enormous teak desk whose surface was hidden under sheaves of paper collected in haphazard piles. The fittings of his office included a ba-

rometer on the wall and a brass cleat as large as a pistol
on the desk, which he used as a paperweight.

"Just until the market improves, Captain Beck. If we
sell the rice now, if we are able to sell it at all, we will
take a loss."

"I never wanted the damned stuff in the first place,
Mr. Kent!" Jason fought to control himself. "As for
beating up this coast instead of making straight for
China—I could have the *Sarah B.* full of silk and ivory
by now." He heard again the steady song of the southeast trades as he passed Callao on the coast of Peru. If
he had allowed them to carry him westward he might
have been in Whampoa—Canton's port—for a week
now, ready to weigh anchor and set course for the Straits
of Sunda with a drunken crew.

"Listen here. You get that rice off my ship and you
can store it until it's worth its weight in gold."

Kent heaved himself upright and pushed a heap of paper aside to sit on the corner of his desk. He had thick
white hair and a weather-beaten face that was clean
shaven but for curling whiskers down to his jawline.
"Can't afford the storage, Captain. Every penny we add
to the price of that rice will make us less competitive."

"Hang and be damned! Pay the storage and I will
earn more than enough to cover it by bringing a cargo
from China to Boston in record time. Take the storage
from my profits if you like!" Jason was part owner of
the *Sarah B. Watson.* He received a commensurate share
of the profits from every voyage.

Kent shook his head. "Can't do it, Captain. I've auctioneers and jobbers to deal with. By holding your cargo
offshore we have an advantage over the competition. It is
our best chance to sell it soon."

"The *Sarah B.* is not a storeship!"

"Many a vessel has served in that capacity here."

"Aye, and many of those will never sail again. They
are beached and built over! They have become part of
the land, but I'll not see that happen to my ship!"

"Nor I, Captain Beck. The *Sarah B.* is the flagship of
this house. We have no intention of beaching her, or you.
In a few weeks the price will rise, I assure you. You will
be running before the trades by the middle of June."

In spite of Kent's obstinacy, Jason found that he liked the man. Until today he had known only the firm's senior partner, Wentworth Farnum. In '49, Jason's ship had brought Farnum to San Francisco to establish a California office. Farnum had returned to Boston in '50 after making Stephen Kent, one of his most experienced captains, his partner, and giving him charge of business in the gold port. Like Jason Beck, Kent was a self-made man. He was bluff and direct, qualities Jason admired. Still, the prospect of staying indefinitely in San Francisco was abhorrent to him. "In two weeks I won't have a crew."

"Then we will hire another. This is not forty-nine, Captain. I am well aware of what happened to you here. Your disinclination to visit this port is legend in the firm. But you must understand that the bloom is off the rose so far as the gold rush is concerned. The easy pickings are gone. For every seaman who deserts to the diggings there are two more coming out of the hills flat bust, as the miners say, looking for a vessel."

Kent gave Jason a moment to consider what he had said, then steered the conversation toward a safer channel. "You made a fine passage, Captain. How was the Horn?"

"We came around under reefed topsails. Sleet and rain and snow, and water in the lee scuppers to a man's waist. For all that, we got 'round in six days."

Kent remembered himself as an able seaman clinging for dear life to an ice-coated topgallant yard on his first passage around the Horn. Like the other sailors, he had beaten his hands against the sail to keep them from freezing.

"I can't say I miss it." He peered intently at Jason. "But you, Captain, you would miss it, or I judge you wrongly. Would you prefer a desk, like me?"

"Nay. You'll not warp me to a desk, Mr. Kent. Not so long as I'm fit to stand a weather deck."

Kent nodded. He knew other men like Jason Beck. The sea was like a drug to them, or perhaps more like a necessary elixir. Keep them ashore for too long and something withered in their souls.

The clock on the wall struck twice in clear, delicate

tones, although its hands stood at five o'clock. Jason smiled inwardly. Stephen Kent might claim to prefer the land, but his clock kept time by ship's bells.

"Come, Captain." Kent got to his feet. "We'll close up shop here and we'll quench our thirst together at the Bank Exchange. You will find that a few weeks ashore are not the end of the world."

"I must get my ship to anchor."

"Is your mate a capable man?"

"Capable? Aye. He'll make a master when you need him."

"I will send Ned Rollick to give him word."

Jason made no objection. Melchior would choose a safe anchorage. As they passed through the clerk's office, Jason instructed Rollick to tell Melchior to keep the crew aboard for the night.

In the street, the winds had dropped. Brilliant yellow light from the westering sun illuminated the city. Jason was glad to be out of doors, but his uneasiness returned when he noticed, not for the first time, how the land seemed to roll beneath him. At sea he gave no more thought to keeping his balance than a gull gave to flight. Here he walked a weaving course, but so long as he had his sea legs he did not belong to the land.

Three weeks, Kent said. If he were kept three weeks ashore his sea legs would abandon him and the land would be solid and unmoving. He would sooner dump the damned rice overboard than stay marooned in this port where his luck seemed to fail him.

"What's the ballast here now? Still sand?" Once the rice was sold, the *Sarah B. Watson* would need tons of ballast to keep her steady for the passage to China.

"Sand and rock." Kent led the way around a corner. "We are still chewing away at the hills and there is always grading going on as we extend the streets."

"There were hills closer to the shore in forty-nine."

"Aye. They cut down the hills and extended the waterfront. Sold lots to their friends, filled in beyond them, and sold more waterfront lots to the next group of friends. They speculate in everything, these merchants. Flour, rice and land most of all. Lately even real estate has come on hard times."

As they threaded their way among pedestrians and drays, hackneys and horsemen, Jason found the smells of the city almost overwhelming. At sea he lived with wood and canvas, salt and tar. The wind carried away a man's stink and kept him clean, except in the fo'c'sle when the ship lay becalmed. But Jason Beck had not slept before the mast in many years, and a ship's master did not venture into the fo'c'sle.

"We set about planking the streets in fifty-three," Kent was saying. "At least we have sewers now, thank God. You never saw old Montgomery Street in winter. We used to throw packing crates or brush into the mud, or anything else that was handy. It was once paved with crates of Virginia tobacco. A dozen merchants imported tobacco at the same time and they couldn't give it away. This business of glut and famine is nothing new."

Kent saw that Jason was listening with only half an ear. "I am sorry your cargo has come at a bad time, Captain. But it is not your fault or mine. No one could have foreseen the present conditions."

"Which are?"

"Last year there was a financial panic. Some of the city's leading institutions failed. Since then, things have been very unsettled. The community is nervous, and nervous men try to hedge their bets. There is too much speculation, and little trust in business here."

"Landsman's troubles are no concern of mine."

"They are when they affect your cargo."

"Aye." The concession was grudging.

"I know you don't give a tinker's damn about these things, Captain. You would prefer to leave them to me. But I will tell you the nature of my worries, just so you know the burdens a shipowner carries. In February of this year, some of the commission merchants formed a monopoly to control the price of flour. In fifty-three they drove flour to fifty dollars a barrel before they were broken by new shipments from the east. But things are different now. We're beginning to produce our own wheat, and there's flour from Oregon. This new cartel got the price up to fifteen dollars, but there is plenty of flour and the word got out. Now the bubble has burst and flour is falling, which makes things bad for rice. This port buys the cheapest grain. Has from the start. When the surplus stocks of flour are gone, rice will return to normal, if there is such a thing in this place."

"I saw the scheming of these men once before," Jason said. "I swore I would have no more to do with them. Now they hold me hostage."

"But not for long. They haven't the grip on things they did back then."

Jason prayed the shipowner was right. He had become acquainted with the methods of San Francisco's merchants in '49. So dependent was the gold-rush port on supplies from the eastern States, any man with a few dollars in capital could set himself up as an importer. The "commission merchants" ordered goods from eastern shippers for just ten percent down. They charged outrageous prices and many prospered. But in their greed they often overstocked vital commodities. When prices fell because of a glut, some went bankrupt. In consequence, the commercial community was unstable, rife with fear and greed and ambition.

As they reached Montgomery Street, Kent was nearly knocked off his feet by a smaller man who careened into him and strode on without pausing.

"Now see here!" Kent protested, but the man's attention was fixed on another man coming out of an office across the street and partway down the block.

"Come on! Come on now!" the smaller man cried.

The other man, taller and powerfully built, saw the speaker approaching and stopped where he was. On the street, a space opened around the smaller man as the passersby fell back.

"Come on, then!" the man shouted again.

"That's Casey," Kent said. "Good God! He's after King of William."

The open space on the street widened like a ship's wake. It reached the taller man and passed him by, leaving him alone to face the small man's challenge.

"Are you armed?" the one called Casey demanded of the tall man. He wore a short cloak that concealed his hands.

The tall man said something that was lost in the noise of the street. Apparently he had tried to make a joke, but his smile was halfhearted. His arms were folded, his left hand inside the right breast of his coat.

Casey strode forward until he had closed half the distance between himself and his quarry. "Prepare to defend yourself!" he said.

Oblivious to the scene in the street, a young woman in a gray cape pushed through the crowd that had gathered around Jason and Kent. Jason took her arm as she tried to force her way past him. Her face was smooth and unlined and her eyes bright with resentment when they met his. She tried to pull free but he kept his grip. "There's trouble here, miss," he warned her, and nodded toward the street. They were the first words he had spoken to a woman since the Chilean port of Antofagasta. The woman there had been a soft-spoken *chilena* who was fluent in the silent language of passion but understood no English.

At that moment, Casey let his short cloak fall to the ground and Jason saw that he held a revolver.

"Defend yourself!" Casey cried. Across the street, the tall man dropped his free arm and brought the other out from under his coat. Wide-eyed, Casey raised his pistol. Shouts came from the crowd and a woman screamed.

The onlookers surged back as Casey fired.

"Oh, Lord!" the tall man staggered. "Oh, Lord!" He clutched his shoulder. "Oh, my arm!"

Casey braced his pistol against one knee and used both hands to cock it while three men rushed to assist the wounded man. They supported him on either side and led him through the doorway of the Pacific Express Company.

With his pistol cocked, Casey looked up, found his quarry missing, and became aware for the first time that a hundred pairs of eyes were upon him. The onlookers began to move, giving him a wide berth. Casey bent to retrieve his cloak. He threw it over the hand holding the gun and moved off up Washington Street.

Jason was aware of every sight and sound as the thoroughfare came back to life. Forty years' experience in street and saloon brawls had trained him to summon all his resources on short notice, but since he had been a ship's captain his own participation in such affrays was less frequent.

"He will get away!" The cry came from a man across the street, one of a pair of well-dressed merchants who had witnessed the shooting.

"Don't let the police have him!" called the second merchant.

"Why don't they want the police to have him?" Jason said.

Stephen Kent found his voice. "Because the police are Democrats, like Casey."

From the other side of Washington Street a man moved to intercept Casey. He took hold of his arm when he reached him. Casey tried to shrug off the grip in a halfhearted manner, then seemed to change his mind and allowed the man to lead him away.

Jason became aware that he was holding the young woman's arm. She had made no further attempt to free herself since the shooting. He released her and nodded in apology. "I meant no offense, miss. Just to keep you from harm."

"I thank you, sir." Her voice was almost inaudible. She looked back once as she started off, then vanished among the onlookers, who were talking among themselves, raising a hubbub in the street and moving every which way like a school of fish that had lost their bearings, it seemed to Jason.

"The fat is in the fire now," Kent said.

"What is it all about?"

Kent snorted. "Come along. The best saloon in the city is just here. You will need a drink to understand San Francisco politics. They are a witch's brew."

Kent led the way to the Bank Exchange, which proved to be a drinking house favored by the city's merchants and bankers. The familiar smells of spirits and tobacco smoke evoked memories in Jason of saloons in other ports, but this was no seamen's grogshop. It was surprisingly light, despite the mahogany wainscoting and the figured wallpaper, which was the color of claret wine. Ornate mirrors and chandeliers reflected the numerous gaslights, making the saloon nearly as bright as day.

Kent noted Jason's surprise. "Oh yes. We've gas lighting now. In the street too. Next thing they'll be putting it aboard ship."

"Not on my vessel."

Heads turned as Kent ushered Jason through the crowded room toward the bar. To a man, the saloon's clientele wore top hats and dark coats. They were not accustomed to finding seamen in their midst. Once upon a time such scrutiny had made Jason Beck self-conscious, but no more. He knew the prevailing sentiment among the watchers was not scorn, but envy.

"Stephen!" An impeccably dressed man hailed Kent and motioned the two of them to his table. "Lively doin's just now," he said as they sat. "Jim Casey threw down on King of William and plugged him where he stood. Story is, King didn't defend himself." He saw the glances between Kent and Beck. "Could be you've already heard tell of it."

"We saw it," Kent said.

"Did you, now? I'd have given a day's dust to be there. But I'm forgetting my city manners. Who is this jack tar?"

"He is Captain Jason Beck of our ship *Sarah B. Watson*. Captain, Abel Calvert. Mr. Calvert is the better half of Calvert and Winston, bankers. Or perhaps he is somewhat more than one half?" Kent raised his eyebrows.

"I am the bank, Winston's the banker." Calvert regarded Jason Beck with unconcealed good humor. "Well, Captain, are you traveling in disguise?" Calvert was a few inches shorter than Jason and some years older. His weathered face might have belonged to a sailor. When they shook hands Calvert's grip was hard as any seaman's.

"I have come straight from my ship, Mr. Calvert. We only made port this afternoon." Jason didn't add that even with more time to prepare himself for going ashore he would have come clad as he was now, without putting on a captain's airs.

"Welcome, then. Is it true that you have nothing to drink while you are at sea?"

"Water and tea, Mr. Calvert." The prohibition against spirits aboard ship did not strictly apply to the master, but Jason observed it to the letter because he knew from his own years before the mast that sailors were loath to give allegiance to a master who retreated to his cabin to indulge pleasures that were forbidden them.

"You must have what we called in the mountains a powerful dry. You there, missy!" Calvert hailed a white-aproned waiter girl, clad like the rest of the female staff in a starched white blouse and full black skirts. "Brandy punches twice around! Now, Stephen, tell me about Casey and King."

While Kent related what he and Jason had witnessed, Calvert carefully clipped the end from a Havana cigar with a small silver tool. "First blood to Casey," he said when Kent was done, "but not the last, I'll bet money. Smoke, Captain?"

Jason accepted the cigar and lit it as the waiter girl arrived with six brandy punches. Calvert paid with a gold coin, motioning Stephen Kent's money away.

"Do you take an interest in politics, Captain?" the banker asked.

"I leave politics to landsmen, Mr. Calvert. Except where they concern my ship or my cargo."

"We have a cargo of rice to sell," Kent explained.

"You have my sympathy." To Jason, Calvert said, "This shooting shouldn't concern you. Casey and King of William are newspaper editors on opposite sides of the political fence. King's a Know-Nothing of sorts. An old Whig, or a new Republican, if you like. Doesn't mince words in his paper. Trumpets like a bull elk in heat. He's just found out there's a limit to what some men will take."

"Since King of William began his paper last October, he has accomplished what no other force could have done," Kent said. "He has united the Northern and Southern Democrats, at least in their hatred of him and his paper. Behind all the bombast there are the usual sordid motives—political jobs and patronage, and local enmities that have nothing to do with politics."

"The town is nervous," Calvert said. "Business is bad. That's at the bottom of it. Everyone's looking for a scapegoat. King of William blames the Democrats and the Catholics and whoever else strikes his fancy. Truth is, we're in a stew of our own making. Too much credit, too much risk. The first flush of gold brought high times, but high times don't last forever. Times are tight now. Folks don't like it."

Wreathed in pungent smoke, Jason listened and learned as the warmth of the brandy spread through his body. There was no better place to learn the affairs of any port city than in the saloons, where spirits loosened even a cautious man's tongue. Here in the Bank Exchange he learned more than he wished to know about the tangled skein of politics and commerce that kept the citizens of San Francisco at each other's throats, but although he listened with great care, he found no hint of how he might rid the *Sarah B. Watson* of her troublesome cargo and put out to sea once more. When a newcomer loomed over the table, he welcomed the interruption.

"Rum business, this Casey thing," the man said without preliminaries. He was tall and solid, heavy without being fat.

Calvert's gaze held no welcome. Neither he nor Kent made any move to introduce the large man to Jason.

"What news of King's wound?" Calvert said.

"Shot through the left shoulder," the man said.

"Will he live?" Kent asked.

"There are a dozen physicians with him now. They say he will live." The man swayed on his feet and steadied himself with a walking stick. His flushed face and heavy-lidded eyes showed the effects of drink, but when he leaned over the table his words were precisely spoken and his tone was conspiratorial.

"Casey's given himself up to the police. The Committee of Thirteen meets tonight. Pioneer Hall. Eight o'clock." He withdrew his free hand from a coat pocket and opened it to reveal a large coin stamped from some base metal. He exposed the coin for only a moment before dropping it back in the pocket and turning away. Jason had an impression that the coin bore an emblem of a large eye.

"Jonathan Frye," Stephen Kent said to Jason. "One of the wealthiest merchants in this city."

"He should learn to keep his trap shut when he's liquored up." Calvert's face was expressionless as he watched Frye's large form move across the saloon, stopping here and there to speak in another man's ear.

Jason had been appraising Calvert since Kent had introduced them. In his dark brown coat, velvet waistcoat, spotless boiled shirt and black satin cravat, the banker was as fashionably dressed as any man in the saloon. Yet his hat was beaver, in the D'Orsay style, the crown wider at the top than where it joined the brim. It was of top quality and apparently quite new, but years out of style. And for all of the banker's elegant clothes, Jason thought he detected a bit of playacting in the way Calvert disported himself in his finery. "Where do you stand in all this, Mr. Calvert, if you don't mind my asking?"

"I don't mind at all, Captain Beck. But if you are truly interested in how I see the local politics, you will have to know my background." Calvert puffed on his cigar and regarded Jason thoughtfully. "I got here the long way 'round, you might say. Left home in twenty-seven for the Stoney Mountains to trap beaver with the American Fur Company. Something like running off to sea, I suppose, but I headed inland instead. Turned free trapper and kept at it until the fur trade played out, and those were the best years of my life. After that I went to the Oregon country, along with some of my pards. Summer of forty-eight, we heard talk of gold at Sutter's Fort, so I come down for a look-see. Got here early and struck it rich, to put it plain and simple."

"Abel is the only man I know who dug his fortune out of the ground," Kent said. "The rest got rich by supplying what the miners needed and by finding other ways to profit from the great migration to this coast."

Calvert kept his eyes on Jason. "I've known hard times and I've fought other men to stay alive, Captain. As a consequence, my outlook is not the same as some who came by their money the easy way. I've got no patience for this political squabbling. I support the Citizens Reform ticket. We stay out of national and state politics. Our concern is what's best for the city."

Jason was pleased to learn that his ability to take the measure of landsmen was not dulled by the long voyage. Beneath the banker's clothing he had sensed a man who had lived his life out of doors. A man more like himself and Stephen Kent than the others in this room.

Kent got to his feet. "Mrs. Kent will be worrying about me if she has heard of the shooting," he said by way of taking his leave. Jason rose to join him. "Thanks for the drinks, Abel," Kent said to Calvert. "And let me know if you run across anyone who might buy a few hundred tons of rice."

"I ain't in the grain business, but I will keep an ear to the wind for you, Stephen." He looked to Jason. "It's from Carolina?"

"The best quality."

"I will do what I can. Here's hoping you will soon be in deep water again." With a glance at Stephen Kent he added, "And here's hoping the rest of us will not. To you, Captain, I will offer an old trapper's advice. Hang on to your topknot and keep your powder dry."

Chapter 4

Outside the Bank Exchange, Jason turned to Kent. "Mr. Kent," he began, but Kent raised a hand in friendly protest.

"Stephen to you, Jason. We're both old sea dogs. I'm the older, but we'll overlook that."

"All right then, Stephen. Mightn't this shooting take the merchants' minds off scheming over the cost of rice and flour?"

"It might."

"Who else could help us sell the rice now, besides Mr. Calvert?"

"I know some commission merchants who might help."

"We must give them incentive. That's something merchants understand."

"All right," Kent agreed. "What sort of incentive?"

"We forgo a profit. We price the cargo at our cost. The merchant who sells it to keep the profit. No man to represent the cargo exclusively unless he puts up fifteen percent of the price. It's a method I learned from the Chinese, to sell in a hurry."

"It goes against the grain of a Yankee trader to forgo a profit."

"I'll make it up from Canton to Boston. Tomorrow we'll see your merchant friends together."

"All right. Faced with a loss, I'll regard breaking even as a bargain," Kent said. They shook hands and parted.

At the Pacific Wharf, Jason found the ship's gig waiting for him, manned by the *Sarah B. Watson*'s coxswain, a plump Kanaka named Jolly Jim, and Seaman Grimes. Jason noted that Grimes was sober. A little distance down the wharf a clutch of dockside crimps lurked like rats, but they kept their distance from the sailors.

Jolly Jim saw the direction of Jason's glance. "They got a song to sing, Cap'n. Tell all about pretty *wahine* they got just for me. Tell Grimes what a handsome boy he is. Got *wahine* for him too. Good rum for free, almost, they say."

Jason felt his cares lighten. "And what did you tell them, Jim?" He kept his countenance sober.

"I tell these California man I break his hand if he put it on my arm. I tell him I break his arm if he give Grimes more to drink. California man they go away."

Jason took pleasure at being back on the water. The winds had dropped to a light breeze that scarcely rocked the gig as a surly Grimes propelled it with practiced strokes of the oars. To the west the clouds were breaking and turning orange and crimson as the sun dropped toward the hills of Marin, north of the Golden Gate.

Melchior had chosen to anchor the *Sarah B.* at the southerly end of the anchorage, close to Goat Island. He was awaiting Jason when he climbed the Jacob's ladder to the deck.

Jason noticed that the men on deck and in the rigging paused in their tasks to watch him and Melchior. They would be glad to hear that the cargo was not sold, for that would promise them shore leave over the coming days. But learning that the ship might be kept at San Francisco for weeks would only encourage those who felt the lure of the gold country.

"Come," Jason said, and Melchior accompanied him aft. In the privacy of his cabin he told the mate what he had learned, and how he and Stephen Kent hoped to rid themselves of the rice.

"Give the port watch leave tomorrow morning at eight bells. Twenty-four hours. Starboard watch the next day. We'll continue like that while we're in port, but say nothing to them about how long we may be here. Let them think we will depart any day. The watch aboard to be kept busy. I want her ready to sail."

"Aye, Cap'n."

For a few days the crew would return to the ship out of habit. And then? Would they heed the siren song that had stolen his other crew, seven years ago? Or had the song lost its power?

"By God, I want her ready," Jason said again, although there was no need to give an order to Melchior twice.

"We'll lose some of 'em if we be kept here long, Jason," Melchior ventured.

"It can't be helped. God willing, we'll sail within the week."

Jason took his supper alone. There was singing from the foredeck, and the sound of a Spanish guitar. The crew had learned they were to go ashore. Their throats were dry and their peckers hard in anticipation, and they sang to keep from jumping overboard to swim for land. After nearly four months on sea watches—four hours on, four hours off—they would sleep a restless harbor sleep tonight, preparing themselves for one furious debauch ashore, in case that was all they were allowed.

When Stephen Kent and Captain Beck left him in the Bank Exchange, Abel Calvert rose from his table and moved through the saloon, stopping to greet men with whom he did business. In every gathering the talk was of the shooting. Reports on King of William's condition varied from concerns that he would die before the night was out to assurances that he would be up and about the next day. Rumor said that Casey had surrendered himself to the police and was taken to the County Jail on Broadway for safekeeping. Whether to keep him safe for trial or to preserve him from his enemies was a subject of much debate, with a majority coming down in favor of the latter opinion. More than once Calvert heard references to the Vigilance Committee of 1851, and the chance that it would be revived.

He took a hasty supper at a French café on California Street, then walked to the Plaza, which had been the village square of old Yerba Buena, still surrounded by

Spanish adobes when Calvert first came down from Oregon to follow the rumors of gold. It lay a block west of Montgomery Street, between Clay and Washington, sloping upward to the west. The Americans had renamed it Portsmouth Square, but most forty-niners and many later arrivals called it the Plaza still. It was used for public meetings and was the city's natural gathering place in times of unrest. As such, it served as a barometer of the public mood.

The sun had set while Calvert ate, and dusk lay thick over the city, but even before he reached the open square he could see the fringes of a large crowd. A burst of applause and shouting rose from the gathering as he crossed Clay Street and moved along Kearny, behind the assembly. From the high ground at the southwest corner of the square, a man on a packing crate harangued the assembly.

"The police are Casey's friends!" he shouted. "Do you think the likes of Scannell and Billy Mulligan will let him come to trial?"

The crowd roared its certainty that such a thing would never come to pass.

"Abel!" A call from close at hand turned Calvert's attention to the figure of Stephen Kent, waving at him from the steps of the City Hall, which faced the Plaza from Kearny Street.

Calvert climbed the steps to the shipowner's side. "How long has this been going on?"

"Over an hour, they say. I've just arrived myself. Mrs. Kent wanted me to stay at home, but I thought it best to take the measure of the town."

"So did I. It seems this shooting has set the badger loose."

"Much more of this and they will storm the jail."

"Then it's true Casey is there?"

"Yes. There's a crowd there too. The mayor begged them to go home an hour ago, they say, but it did no good."

"Let's have a look."

From the Plaza to the County Jail was three blocks along Kearny. The jail was midway between Kearny and Dupont on the north side of Broadway. Several hundred men were in the street before the jail, but they lacked the animation of the gathering at the Plaza.

"They are still a crowd, not yet a mob," Kent observed.

A column of volunteer militia armed with muskets entered Broadway from Dupont, bringing a tentative cheer from the men in the street. The column crossed Broadway and turned right on a course that would put them between the jail and the crowd. The crowd fell silent. The militia marched the length of the block, to Kearny, and turned about, the column doubling back on itself. When it reached Dupont again, it turned once more.

Seeing that the volunteers intended to protect the jail rather than put themselves at the disposal of the gathering, the onlookers muttered their dissatisfaction and a few taunted the militia.

A tattoo of hoofbeats sounded above the grumblings. Ten horsemen came up Broadway from the bay side, riding two by two. The leader paused to confer with the officer of militia, then dispersed his men to the perimeter of the crowd. A man stepped from the gathering and spoke to the militia commander. The two men walked off behind the crowd, still talking. They stopped not far from Kent and Calvert.

"That's Captain Ashe," Kent said. "He'll have a sense of things." He led the way to the two men.

"Captain. Stephen Kent, of Farnum and Kent. Do you know Mr. Calvert?"

"I bank with Calvert and Winston, but I have not had the pleasure." Ashe was a solid man with an air of authority. "This is Captain Farren. You may know him as Volney Howard's law partner."

"I'm afraid not," Kent said.

There was handshaking all around, and Calvert said to Ashe, "I take it these are your militia."

"Not exactly, Mr. Calvert. Captain Farren and I are with the Blues. These are California Guards. They would just as soon let the crowd hoist Casey from a roof beam, but for now they will obey my orders. It helps that the Lancers came along." Ashe indicated the horsemen.

"I wish we had our own men," Farren said. "If the vigilants come out in force, the Guards will go over."

Farren was much younger than Ashe, almost a boy, Calvert thought. But San Francisco was a young man's town and boys became men quickly here, as they had in the Rocky Mountains.

"Tomorrow we'll muster the Blues," Ashe said. "Tonight we must make do with what we have."

Calvert knew the militia captain by reputation and he was impressed now by the man in person. Richard Ashe had served as a Texas Ranger in the Mexican War and had been sheriff of San Joaquin County for three years after coming to California. He left that post when he was appointed United States naval agent for the port of San Francisco three years ago. As a Southerner, he belonged to the "Chivalry" wing of the Democratic Party, like many in the Blues.

A nearby clock struck eight times. Calvert took out his watch and confirmed the hour. "I am pleased that you have matters in hand. And pleased to know you, sir." He tipped his hat to Ashe.

Kent followed him as he started off. "You're going to Pioneer Hall?"

"Yes. And you?"

"I'm not on the committee."

"There will be a meeting later on, at Post and Company's warehouse. Ten o'clock, I believe. That's where we'll enlist the men, if it comes to that."

"I pray God it does not," Kent said.

"So do I. But you come along to Post's just in case. The town is up for blood and we will need some level-headed men to keep this from getting out of hand."

Ten minutes' walk brought Calvert to the hall that was the meeting place for the Society of California Pioneers. The door to the hall was flanked by two guards armed with Colt's Navy revolvers. Calvert opened his palm to reveal a coin like the one Jonathan Frye had revealed at the Bank Exchange. It bore the image of an eye and the legend of the Vigilance Committee. He was admitted at once. Another guard ushered him to a room where ten men sat around a large oaken table, Frye among them.

"What news of King?" Calvert asked without ceremony.

"His condition is grave, but the doctors are hopeful."

The speaker was William Tell Coleman. Calvert was not surprised to see the young merchant at the head of the table. Coleman, like Calvert, had been a founder of the Vigilance Committee in 1851. When the organization disbanded, both were among the Committee of Thirteen who kept the association alive against the chance that it might be needed again. Coleman had gone back to the eastern States in '52 but had returned earlier this year. Calvert considered him a stuck-up prig, but he had a gift for bringing men of different views together in common purpose, despite his youth. He was twenty-seven years old.

"Dr. Cole has examined King," said Jonathan Frye. "He judges the wound not to be fatal."

"He should know," another man said, provoking a few chuckles around the table. Dr. Beverly Cole was a noted physician who had accidentally shot himself two years before when his revolver dropped from his coat. The ball had passed through his stomach and for a time the wound was thought to be mortal, but he had recovered. He got about now with the aid of crutches, and it was said that the entry wound was not yet fully healed, but he had survived an injury that might have killed a lesser man.

"We're waiting for Truett and Smiley," Coleman informed Calvert. "While we wait, we are discussing what to do about James Casey and Charles Cora."

"What's Cora got to do with it?"

Frye snorted. "You might as well ask what the devil has to do with sin."

Calvert took a seat at the foot of the table. The addition of Charles Cora's name to the deliberations raised the chances of mischief twentyfold. Six months before, Cora, a gambler and whoremonger, had shot and killed the U.S. marshal for San Francisco, a man named Richardson. Richardson was a drunken lout by most accounts. He had insulted Cora's common-law wife, a notorious trollop who called herself Belle Cora. Later Richardson threatened Cora's life in the Metropolitan Saloon. Calvert had witnessed the threat and never doubted its seriousness. Soon after, Cora had shot Richardson in an alley. There were no witnesses to the shooting and Cora had pleaded self-defense at his trial. A revolver had been found in Richardson's coat. The jury was unable to reach a unanimous verdict and Cora had languished in jail since then, awaiting a second trial. In the interim, it came out that Belle Cora had made flagrant attempts to bribe the jurors.

"Cora and Casey are as like as two peas in a pod," said a small man who sat beside Frye. Calvert recognized him as James Dows, a commission merchant who had not been on the original Committee of Thirteen. He looked like a schoolboy sitting in a chair too large for his diminutive stature, but there was nothing boyish in his cocksure manner. "Neither one will get the justice they deserve in this city. The police and the courts—"

"The police and the courts aren't to blame for a hung jury," Calvert cut him off. Not a man in this room had sat on Cora's jury, nor had anyone of their social standing. The city's merchants routinely evaded jury duty, considering it beneath them. Calvert himself had begged off three times in as many years, citing the demands of his business. If the jury lists were packed with Democrats and riffraff by the police, who were mostly Irish and mostly Democrats, the merchants who sat on the Committee of Thirteen had themselves partly to blame.

The door to the room opened and two men entered. One had to stoop slightly to clear the doorframe.

"We apologize for our tardiness," the tall man said in a deep voice that was surprisingly soft. His name was Miers Truett. The other was Thomas Smiley. He was rotund, of average height, with a quick intelligence that worked most fiercely for his own benefit. He appeared to grow larger as he moved away from Truett and took a seat beside Coleman. Truett, even seated, loomed over the rest.

"We are gathered to decide if we shall reassemble the Committee of Vigilance," Coleman said for their benefit. "It has been suggested that we place a notice in tomorrow's papers, calling for volunteers. It has also been suggested that one of our aims should be to assure a new trial for Charles Cora before such a committee, if we vote to take public action."

While Coleman and the others filled in Truett and

Smiley on the deliberations, Calvert watched the men around the table and measured their mood. There was an eagerness here, one he recognized from his years in the mountains. It was the impatience of a wolf or a panther once it had the scent of blood, or of a young Indian buck who had tasted battle but never felt its wounds. Yet in a city where it seemed half the men were veterans of the Mexican War and brandished military ranks as badges of honor, not a man present had smelled powder burned in anger.

Abel Calvert had fought for his life more than once, and lived to tell about it. But not to men like these. His stories had been related around mountain campfires to others like himself, men who had shared the trapper's life. He would not see their like again, and it was a bitter draught to swallow. When he went down to Oregon in '43 he had believed at first that the beaver trade would revive in time, but he soon saw that pipe dream for what it was. The truth was, the beaver streams were trapped out, and even if the beaver came back the beaver hats that had fueled the trade would not.

Men like these had seen to that. They had milked the fur trade for all it was worth and then moved on without a backward look or a moment's concern over what would happen to the trappers' life. They saw new fortunes to be made in the trade with China. They replaced beaver hats with top hats made of silk, and nourished a market for all things Chinese.

For five years, Abel Calvert had longed for revenge on the top-hatted merchants for their ruination of the mountain life, never dreaming he'd have a chance to take it for real. And then, in '48, he had seen his chance, when rumors raced north from California, telling of gold found on the American River. Calvert took the plunge, and he made his pile. He got out of the diggings when his fortune was secure, but unlike most of the miners he neither drank nor gambled it away. He set himself up first in business, as a commission merchant, then in banking when the commissions trebled his pile. He invested cautiously, conservatively, and for the most part he had insulated himself against the wild swings in the fortunes of the city.

He chuckled under his breath, which caused a few of the men to look in his direction, but Calvert gave no indication of his thoughts. He was remembering his pards the Putnam brothers, Jed and Bat, cursing all silk-hatted merchants up, down and sideways, swearing vengeance. Bat had gone Injun and Jed was running some kind of a road ranch in the Big Horns. Only Abel Calvert had come down from the mountains to battle the enemy on his own ground, and my, look at him now. Yes, Mr. Calvert. No, Mr. Calvert. Whatever you please, Mr. Calvert. Everyone had good manners for a respectable man of property. But to this day he had never worn a silk hat. He had whipped the merchants and the bankers at their own game and he wore his beaver hat proud on his head while he did it.

The talk had turned to the city's militia, and how many companies might come over to the Vigilance Committee if it gave the call.

"Who is captain of the City Guards now?" Coleman asked.

"Walton," someone said. "He'll bring them 'round."

"We can count on the Sarsfield Guards and National Lancers," Miers Truett intoned.

Like the city's volunteer fire companies, the companies of militia were formed by men with similar backgrounds and beliefs. For the most part, each company would choose its course as a whole.

Thomas Smiley leaned forward, enthusiasm for the venture plainly written on his round, florid face. "I have spoken with Frederick Macondray. The California Guards are ours."

The eagerness of the men around him reminded Calvert of a group of boys who wanted to play at grown men's games, and he sensed that there would be no stopping them until they had their fun.

"Enough talk," Jonathan Frye said sharply. "We all know what we're about here. I move the question as amended."

William Tell Coleman rapped the table with his knuckles. "All in favor of commencing enlistments for a new Committee of Vigilance this evening at Post and

Company and placing a notice in tomorrow's papers, sig-
nify by saying aye."

"Aye," said twelve of the thirteen men present.

"The vote is unanimous," Coleman intoned.

"*No!*" Calvert struck the table with the flat of his hand.
The sound echoed about the walls like a pistol shot. He
got to his feet. "For the record, *gentlemen*, the vote is not
unanimous. Ten James Caseys and Charles Coras are
not worth putting our commerce and our honor at risk,
and that's what you are doing. I bow to the majority.
And I will support you. But for the record, I oppose this
motion as a bunch of damn foolishness."

Now go on and have your fun, he thought, but he did
not put the thought into words. There were some insults
even a silk-hatted merchant wouldn't swallow.

Chapter 5

'm going ashore," Jason told Melchior the next morning. They were standing together on the poop deck. The day was breezy and clear, growing warm as the sun rose higher over the Contra Costa hills. On the weather deck, the men of the port watch made ready to lower a longboat. They were cleaned up and dressed in their best, and their eyes went often to the city.

"I will have the boat stand by at the dock for ee, Cap'n, once the watch is ashore."

"I won't need the boat. I will get a room in the town while we're in port."

Melchior turned his broad face fully toward Jason, the black brows arched in surprise. "Bunkin' ashore, are ee, Cap'n?"

"We're trapped here so long as this damned rice is aboard. I'm going to find a way to get rid of it."

When he arrived on the wharf, Jason was besieged by half a dozen boardinghouse runners, young boys who assured him, every one, that the house they solicited for was an accommodation without parallel, although most were squalid seaman's doss houses.

"Captain Beck! Captain Beck! Please, sir!" they cried. They knew the names of the captains and mates of every new ship in port within minutes, it seemed, as if the gulls carried word to them before the anchors touched the water.

" 'Scuse me, Captain," came an older voice to Jason's ear. He found Finn Warren standing beside him. In the midst of the previous day's reverses, he had forgotten his promise to share a glass with his old shipmate.

Finn beckoned to one of the boys. "Dickie! You come here. The rest of you, clear off!" The smallest of the pack scampered forward, while the rest ran to catch up with the sailors. Finn took the boy by the arm. "Dickie, this be Captain Beck of the *Sarah B. Watson*."

"I know, Captain Warren. She's a China clipper, and none better!"

"Captain Warren, Finn?"

"They try to swell my head with flattery, Jason. This be Dickie Howell."

Jason appraised the boy. He was dirty and he smelled, but he was no dirtier and smelled no worse than the others, and he lacked a certain slyness that Jason recognized in the older boys. He had seen that same look in the companions of his youth and he knew it betrayed a hardening of the spirit in the face of an inhospitable world. Dickie Howell still had the gleam of hope in his eyes.

"He's a good lad," Finn was saying, "and he serves a house better than most. It ain't grand, now. You've not grown high-and-mighty?"

"I've no need of grand accommodations, Finn."

"Well, then. The landlady of Dickie's house be a state-of-Mainer and a fine cook."

"I am obliged to you, Finn. We will have that drink this afternoon. At four bells of the dog watches, if that suits you."

Finn gave a nod, very pleased. "Have Dickie bring you to the Noggin of Ale."

Jason hoisted his valise. "Lead the way, boy."

"The Noggin ain't the most grand, neither!" Finn called after them, but Jason knew the sort of grogshop favored by Finn Warren. As a cabin boy he had been introduced to the demon rum by Finn and three of his shipmates. They had laughed to see Jason fall on his face in the street and laughed again when he vomited in his own bunk back aboard ship. But that night's misery had become a bond of friendship later, one that stood him in good stead when he grew to be a seaman.

"Mind where you step, Captain Beck."

Lost in his memories, Jason had nearly trod in a pile of horse dung. Dickie's warning saved him having to scrape off his best shoes, which the ship's boy had polished that morning.

"Well, now, boy. It's Richard, is it?"

"Yes, Captain Beck! Richard Howell at your service." Jason could not know it, but he had just leapfrogged a host of other men in Dickie Howell's estimation, by the simple act of being the first grown-up person to call him Richard.

"The landlady of your house, would that be your mother?"

"No, Captain. My mother's dead."

"And your father?"

"I never knowed him, Captain. 'That bugger were long gone afore you seed the light of day,' my mother said. Alls I got from the two of them was the life of a wharf rat."

Jason looked at Dickie Howell more closely. The boy was about ten years of age, with no physical deformities. He wore shoes that were dirty and cracked, torn canvas pants too short for him by half a foot, and a rough woolen shirt. His coat was cut of finer cloth, out of keeping with the rest of his clothing. He was unafraid, and uncommonly well-spoken for a wharf rat, despite the ease with which he repeated his dead mother's profanity.

"Do you know this city well, Richard Howell?"

"Every street and alley, Captain. I come here with me mum in forty-nine."

"Do you know the banking houses and importers? The auctioneers too?"

"Yes, Captain. When I'm not on the docks for the new ships in port, I carry messages for the merchant houses."

"Then if you've no other business today, young Richard, I will hire you to show me about. This morning I will be an hour or two with my shipowner. When we're done with that, you will show me the lay of the land and then take me to the Noggin of Ale, and I will give you a dollar."

"Excuse me, Captain, but I can make a dollar in an hour, running messages for the banks."

"Gold ports be damned. All right then, I will pay you three dollars, and I promise you won't have to run a step. Is that sufficient?"

"Yes, Captain." Dickie disguised his delight. The truth was, he was lucky to make a dollar in a whole morning carrying messages for the merchants and bankers.

They had left the wharf and were making their way along Washington Street. It seemed to Jason that the streets were unusually quiet for a working day, although it was nearing eight o'clock. At Sansome, he was surprised to see a dozen men, several carrying muskets, marching down the middle of the street.

"Is there some sort of parade today?"

"They're militia, Captain, going to join the Vigilance Committee."

"What vigilance committee?"

"It's in all the newspapers, Captain. Yesterday, Mr. Casey shot Mr. King, right in Montgomery Street."

"I know about that. I saw it."

"You did?" Dickie was wide-eyed.

"What's it got to do with a vigilance committee?"

"The police have got Mr. Casey and the Vigilance Committee's going to hang him. They're enlisting volunteers just over there."

Two blocks away, where Sansome crossed Sacramento, Jason saw that the cross street was blocked by a crowd. "Come," he said. They followed along after the squad of marching men until they reached the edge of the throng, which cheered and parted to let the armed volunteers through, then closed again behind them.

Sacramento Street from Sansome to Montgomery was a solid mass of men. By standing on the sidewalk and looking over the heads of the crowd, Jason could see a score of muskets held high by as many hands, all moving through the mob toward a building halfway along the block. There was a palpable tension in the air, although the mood of the crowd was almost festive.

"Hang and be damned," he muttered under his breath. It seemed that Casey's shooting of King of William had set off an uproar that might last for several days. In Jason's experience, civil unrest brought normal commerce to a standstill. Still, if he acted now, before the merchant community got caught up in the excitement . . .

"How far are we from your boardinghouse, Dickie?"

"Not far, Captain. Ten minutes' walk, if we go quickly."

"Then let us go quickly. First to the boardinghouse, then to my shipowner. You know the offices of Farnum and Kent?"

"Just down here, Sansome Street near Jackson. I know them all, Captain."

The boy led Jason back along Sansome to Clay Street. There they turned left and walked up the gently rising slope until they reached Powell. "Do you fancy doxies, Captain?" Dickie asked, taking Jason off guard.

"Doxies? I thought you were taking me to an honest boardinghouse, young Richard."

"I am, Captain. Alls I wanted to say is, that's the best parlor house in town. That one there. Ask for Mrs. Wickliff and say Dickie Howell sent you."

They were in a neighborhood of respectable frame homes. The boy pointed to a rambling two-story house that stood at the southwest corner of Powell and Clay. There were lace curtains in the windows. A Chinese girl was sweeping the long porch that faced east toward the bay.

"The girls are pretty, and they're clean too," Dickie said. "It's a parlor house. No common seamen allowed in there. Be sure and tell them you're a ship's captain."

"Now see here, young Richard. There are some things a man prefers to discuss with another man. A grown man."

"I'm sorry, Captain. I didn't mean to offend." Dickie put on a suitably wounded expression.

"All right, now," Jason said as they set off northward on Powell. "Tell me the truth. Do young wharf rats still hide under the ships' gangways and try to look up the ladies' skirts?"

Dickie's mouth fell open. "How did you know!"

"I know because I was a wharf rat myself. I knew every seaman's grogshop and every pushing academy in Boston. Once a ship dropped anchor, I knew where the crew drank and whored, just as you know these things in San Francisco."

Dickie's face was a picture of astonishment. "You was a wharf rat?"

"And an orphan, young Richard," Jason said. "At your age I was plying the Boston wharves much as you ply those of San Francisco now." May fortune smile on you as she has smiled on me, he thought. "When the opportunity came I put that life behind me, and you can do the same. You needn't spend your life on the wharves."

"That's what Mrs. Rockwell says. She's teaching me to read and write. Sometimes I eat my supper there and she gives me a lesson. I must have the lesson if I want supper. She gave me my coat too."

Jason admired Mrs. Rockwell's ingenuity and he was pleased to learn that Dickie had not stolen his coat, as he had first supposed.

"Excuse me, Captain, but is a pushing academy a whorehouse?"

"I thought a pushing academy was a whorehouse the world over."

"My mates and I, we call them pumping houses, on account of you go there to get pumped."

"No need to explain lad." In his own youth Jason had shocked more than one sea captain with his premature knowledge of grown-up pleasures, but he was embarrassed in his turn all the same.

"How much farther, Richard?"

"We're here. It's that house. The white one."

They were on Mason Street nearing Jackson, at the western limit of the city. The land sloped gently upward to the west. A few hundred yards west of Mason Street, the slope became steeper, rising to the ridge that extended from Russian Hill to California Street Hill, which hid the Golden Gate from sight.

The house Dickie was pointing to stood on a corner lot. With its white clapboards and green shutters, it would not have been out of place in New Bedford or Marblehead. Atop the peak of the gable, a weather vane in the shape of a ship under full sail pointed nor'west by west. Dormers in the roof suggested a furnished attic. Bedsheets were hung to dry in the garden behind the house and wisteria grew on a trellis by the steps that led to front door and the veranda. A simple sign offered ROOMS TO LET—DAY, WEEK OR MONTH.

At the back door, a young woman was negotiating the purchase of vegetables with a Chinaman while a gray cat rubbed against her skirts. When she turned to wave at Dickie, Jason saw that she was remarkably pretty, and better dressed than any household servant in Boston.

"Listen here, Richard," he said. "Once I'm settled in my room, I want you to introduce me to the scullery maid."

"The scullery maid only comes in the afternoon, Captain, to help with the cleaning and to serve supper."

"Who's that, then?"

"That's Mrs. Rockwell."

Based on what Dickie Howell had said about Mrs. Rockwell, Jason had imagined himself welcomed by a strapping Yankee harridan, or an Irishwoman of the sort he had often encountered astride the quarterdeck of a sailor's doss house. He was obliged to abandon his prejudice in haste.

The Chinaman bowed and took his leave, trotting between the shafts of his vegetable cart. Mrs. Rockwell went into the kitchen and Jason followed Dickie toward the front door, which opened as they climbed the steps to the veranda. A man in a military uniform stepped out, all gold braid and piping, with a revolver strapped to his side. He held the door for a young woman who stood scarcely more than five feet tall. Her hair was black, her skin so fair it was almost translucent, like the surface of a pearl. Her eyes met Jason's gaze for a moment before returning to the boy. They were light blue, made lighter by the contrast with her dress of dark blue taffeta.

She smiled when she recognized Dickie Howell. "Good morning, Dickie. And who have you brought us today?"

"I've brought you Captain Beck, Miss Gray," Dickie said.

"I am pleased to meet you, Captain Beck. I am Molly Gray."

As Jason bent over her hand, he noticed that she smelled faintly of lavender. "The pleasure is mine, Miss

Gray." He heard himself talking like a dandified landsman and found that he didn't mind in the least.

"Miss Gray, I must—" the uniformed man began.

"Oh! Forgive me," Molly Gray exclaimed. "Captain
Beck, may I present Captain Farren, of the San Francisco Blues."

"Captain Beck." Farren nodded curtly to Jason. He
was slender but not slight, with sandy hair and a full
mustache. Jason guessed he was not yet thirty. "Your
rank is maritime, I take it?" Farren said.

"It is."

"I won't stop just now, if you'll forgive me. I'm on militia business. Molly, I really think it best if I escort you
to the theater."

"For heaven's sake, David, I've made my way about
this city for years. Go along and see to your militia."

Farren was plainly injured by the rebuff. He tipped
his hat and marched off, his bearing rigid and military.

"It's this shooting," Molly Gray said to Jason. "It
has given them all an excuse to run about in their uni-
forms and they love it." She carried a silk parasol,
which she opened now and twirled above her head, although she stood in the shade of the veranda. She was
never still, moving about lithely, appraising Jason almost brazenly. Her skirts were buoyed out by petticoats and they swayed about her legs as she moved,
emphasizing her slender form. It seemed to Jason that
he had never seen any form quite so lovely in all the
ports he had visited, but he recognized the resurgence
of appetites held in check at sea and kept them from
showing in his face.

"Are you truly a sea captain?" she asked.

"Truly, Miss Gray. I command the ship *Sarah B.
Watson*, arrived in this port yesterday."

"I see. And will you be with us long?" The brogue of
an Irish colleen had slipped into her voice. She seemed
almost to be toying with him, or playing a role. Jason
felt off balance, unaccustomed as he was to a woman's
banter.

"I don't exactly know. There is some difficulty about
my cargo. When my business is done, we will up anchor
and be off with the tide."

"I hope your business will not be done too quickly, then. Mrs. Rockwell charges five dollars a day or thirty dollars a week, including board. Twenty dollars a week if you prefer to dine out. There are many fine restaurants in San Francisco, but I would caution you not to miss Sarah's cooking."

"The kitchen here comes well recommended," he said.

"I am pleased to hear you say so," said a new voice. Mrs. Rockwell stood in the doorway.

"This is Captain Beck, Sarah. He is master of a ship that bears your name. I'll leave you now, Captain." Molly Gray started off, then stopped and looked back at Jason. "Oh. I should tell you that Mrs. Rockwell keeps a temperance house. Can you walk softly when you have been tippling, Captain?"

She went off down Jackson Street, twirling her parasol on her shoulder. Jason was entranced by the swing of her hips as she walked.

He became aware that Sarah Rockwell was watching him. "I will pay for one week in advance, including board, if that suits you, Mrs. Rockwell." One week, and I hope it's no longer.

"It suits me very well, Captain." Sarah Rockwell smiled, but a change came over her expression and she looked at him strangely, almost fearfully. "You are— yesterday, in Montgomery Street, when—"

He knew her then. She wore no cape now, and no bonnet in the privacy of her home. Her hair was rich auburn, piled atop her head in a simple twist.

"Please, come in," she said. "I must thank you again. You may have saved my life."

She stepped aside as Jason and Dickie entered, and favored the uncomprehending boy with a smile. "Captain Beck stopped me from blundering into the middle of Mr. Casey's fight with Mr. King yesterday."

"You was there too?"

"I was. We witnessed the spark that has set the town on fire. And where have you been, young man? It has been some time since we've seen you here."

Dickie didn't meet Mrs. Rockwell's gaze. "I've been busy."

"Have you thought about my offer?"

Dickie shrugged.

"Well, come to supper tonight if you like. Mr. Norton would like to see you. Now run along to the kitchen and have a fresh muffin while I show Captain Beck to his room."

When the boy was gone, Sarah Rockwell led the way up the stairs. "I have told Dickie he may live here if he wishes," she said. "There is something about him. I think he's better than the rest."

"So do I."

"Do you? Good. Then maybe he really has a chance. But he must come to me of his free will."

The oil lamp on the wall at the head of the first landing was a ship's lamp, brass and gimballed, a mate to the one in the foyer. As they reached the landing, a door opened and a young man in a satin gown of emerald green peered out. His hair was uncombed, his eyes still heavy with sleep. Behind him, the curtains were drawn, his room dark. "What sort of day is it, Sarah?"

"A lovely day, Mr. Trelayne," she said briskly. "Time for you to be up and about. Molly has already gone to the theater."

Trelayne grunted something and withdrew into the darkness.

"They are theatrical people," Sarah Rockwell said as they started up to the third floor. "I hope you don't object."

"A seaman learns not to be particular about his bunk-mates. That is—" He broke off, embarrassed.

She surprised him by laughing.

"I'm sorry, I did not mean to—"

"Don't apologize, Captain. You will only make it worse." She brought her amusement under control. "Mr. Trelayne is a theatrical manager. Miss Gray is his leading actress. All the same, I assure you this is a respectable house."

"I'm sure it is."

The room she showed him was one of two that occupied the space beneath the gabled roof. It was sunny and clean and the dormer window offered a view of the bay. Jason set down his valise and stepped to the window.

"I hope you will be comfortable," she said. "I find that sailing men like to overlook the water."

"Aye." From where he stood he could pick out the *Sarah B. Watson* among the ships at anchor, her poles naked in the morning breeze when they should have been hung with canvas and straining against the stays, far from land. His chest tightened with longing for the sea. Sarah Rockwell came to stand beside him.

"Which ship is yours?"

He pointed. "That one there, between the barkentine and the merchantman."

"She is a fine vessel." Something in her voice told Jason it was more than an idle compliment. "Miss Gray said she bears my name."

"Her name is *Sarah B. Watson*."

She met his eyes for a moment, then moved away from the window. "I offer only breakfast and supper. As Miss Gray said, I allow no spirits in the house, and no drunkenness."

He paid her for the week and cast one more look at the *Sarah B.* before descending to reclaim Dickie Howell from the kitchen and set about the day's business.

Chapter 6

David Farren walked down Jackson Street to Kearny. He crossed to the northeast corner and waited in the shade of a doorway. He felt conspicuous in his uniform. He had worn it the afternoon before, when the Blues drilled with the Continentals and the Wallace Guards south of Market Street, but that was before James Casey shot King of William. Yesterday, the militia drills were mostly for show.

There were fewer pedestrians and horsemen than he would have expected at this hour of the morning. Men stood in the streets in small groups, talking among themselves, and there were scarcely any women in evidence. Many businesses that would normally have been open were closed.

Farren had spent the night on duty at the jail. The crowd had grown, but remained quiet. At eleven o'clock, Captain Frederick Macondray, commanding officer of the California Guards, had appeared at the jail. At the same time, two brass six-pound fieldpieces belonging to the Guards were brought into Broadway. They were not loaded, but gun crews stood beside the guns and their presence had a subduing effect on the crowd.

Macondray had knocked at the jail door and after a short delay he was admitted. In a matter of minutes he reappeared. He held up his hands for quiet and addressed the crowd from the steps of the jail. He had assured them that Casey was safely locked in a cell, and he promised that the patrolling militia would see to it that Casey would neither escape nor be taken elsewhere.

"Is that why we're here?" Farren had muttered to Ashe.

"If they think that's our purpose, it is all to the good."

To Farren's surprise, men at the fringes of the gathering began to drift away almost before Macondray had finished speaking. "Van Ness tells them to go home and the crowd doubles. Macondray says the same thing and they trot off like sheep."

"They know what side he is on," Ashe said.

By midnight, the last straggling onlookers had left the street before the jail and the militia were left alone. Their footsteps echoed softly between the blocks of buildings. The Lancers' dragoons took up positions at the street corners. They dismounted and dozed beside their horses, throwing an arm over their saddles to keep themselves upright. At half past one, two men came up Broadway and talked briefly with Captain Macondray. When they left, Macondray spoke with the gun crews, who withdrew with their fieldpieces soon after.

As the new day dawned, the block on Broadway between Kearny and Dupont remained inviolate, as if it were under a seal of sanctuary. Passersby stopped in the closest cross streets but they did not linger for long. At half past seven, Colonel J. R. West, commanding officer of the First Infantry Battalion, which included the companies on guard at the jail, had arrived on foot. He was a solidly built man with a rasping voice that gave gravity to his slow Southern cadences. Before coming to California in '49 he had been a United States senator from Louisiana.

"You may dismiss your men," he told Macondray and Ashe.

"But there is no relief, sir," Farren said.

"The city is quiet enough now," West said placidly. Without seeming to do so, he drew Ashe and Farren aside as Macondray dismissed his men. He brought a folded copy of the San Francisco *Chronicle* from beneath his coat and pointed to an announcement published on the front page amid the advertisements there. It in-

structed all members of the 1851 Committee of Vigilance
to report to 105½ Sacramento Street at nine o'clock that
morning and called for new volunteers to join the revived organization.

"The street outside that building is full of men already." West spoke quickly and Louisiana receded into
his past. There was more of California in his tone now,
all business and urgent for whatever the day might hold.
"Macondray knows this. He has taken his fieldpieces off
somewhere. I don't know just where. Now that the vigilants have decided to organize, they won't allow any
mobs to stir things up. What we must know by the end
of the day is, will your Blues hold fast? Muster your
men quietly, Captain Ashe. In small groups, if need be.
Send a few men you can trust to sound out the other
companies. Tell them not to argue with any who appear
to be going over. Captain Farren, I have a task for you."

West had instructed Farren to get some breakfast and
to meet him at Jackson and Kearny streets at a quarter to nine. Farren had returned to Mrs. Rockwell's to
freshen himself and bolt as much breakfast as the time
allowed.

Now, at the appointed meeting place, Farren took out
his watch. He was a few minutes early. On a normal
weekday morning he would have been at his law offices,
listening to his partner, Volney Howard, declaim about
trivial points of law as if he were Chief Justice Taney
giving his opinion from the bench. Howard was pompous, and sometimes an ass, but he was twenty years
Farren's senior and the fact that he had been a United
States congressman before coming to California had
helped him to build a substantial practice. Among his cli-
ents was Colonel West, who was an assistant city alder-
man as well as a commander of militia. Farren had
recently handled the redrafting of West's will and some
other small matters. Apparently as a consequence, West
had selected him for a special mission.

A group of men marched down the middle of Kearny
Street, stepping in unison although they wore no uni-
forms and carried no arms. Behind them, walking on the
sidewalk, Colonel West sauntered as if he hadn't a care
in the world. He was dressed in civilian clothes and he

smiled amiably as Farren stepped from his doorway to meet him.

"Much to-do, eh, Captain? Men marching about. They'll have no shortage of volunteers, I should say."

"No, sir."

"We have a new general of militia." West spoke conversationally as they walked. "An army man, but a banker now. Fellow named Sherman. Managing partner of Lucas, Turner and Company. Montgomery Street at Jackson. A sound man, from what I hear. Kept his head in the panic last year and brought his bank through with colors flying."

"But he has some military background?"

"He came to this coast with Colonel Mason. Spent the war at Monterey. Rose to be adjutant general of the Division of the Pacific. No experience in battle that I know of." West said this last as a footnote, without judgment. "He is to be sworn in this morning at the mayor's office. See what you make of him."

They had arrived at the Plaza. West stopped in front of the City Hall, which faced on the square from the east side of Kearny. It was an impressive building, as its former owner, the famed impresario Thomas Maguire, had intended. It had been Maguire's fourth and last Jenny Lind Theater, built on the ashes of earlier structures lost to fires in '51. Maguire had overreached himself in building the four-story brick edifice and sold it to the city soon after it was completed.

"An adjutant general should know something about organization," Farren ventured.

"So he should. The rest will depend on what he is made of. Meantime, I must see what forces he will have to command. Oh," West called back as they parted. "I have recommended you to be his adjutant."

Farren climbed the steps and held the door for a tall, loose-jointed man some years his senior who preceded him down the hallway to Mayor Van Ness's chambers.

"I will get this one." The tall man opened the door.

"Here he is now." Mayor Van Ness rose from behind a huge mahogany desk as Farren and the tall man entered the room. "We are very glad to see you, General."

"I haven't taken the oath yet," the tall man said

brusquely. His black suit was disheveled and a trifle worn. When he removed his hat he revealed unkempt reddish hair.

"You know Captain Farren, I see." Van Ness was forty-eight and stout, with graying hair and florid skin. Despite the pleasant breeze that came through the open windows facing on Kearny Street, he was perspiring.

"Captain Farren and I arrived together by chance."

"Oh, well then, Captain Farren of the Blues, General Sherman."

The grip Sherman offered Farren was strong, the hand surprisingly hard for a banker's.

"And may I present Judge Terry of the supreme court."

Terry, who had not risen when Sherman entered the chamber, got to his feet now. He was nearly as tall as Sherman and more solidly built. His chin whiskers were unruly beneath a clean-shaven upper lip and his eyes were heavy-lidded, which gave him a disdainful appearance.

"Judge Terry." Sherman offered his hand. "I know you by reputation, sir. I take it you are here to administer the oath?"

"I am here at the governor's request, sir, to take the mood of the city following King's shooting."

"Where is the sheriff?" Sherman asked of the mayor.

"Sheriff Scannell sent word to say he judges it not prudent to leave the jail just now, in view of the talk about forming a vigilance committee."

"Talk!" Sherman uttered the word as a harsh bark. "Is that what he calls it? There is a notice in today's papers calling for all red-blooded vigilants to report for duty at nine o'clock this morning. Sacramento Street is full of men falling over themselves to join the rebels, and he calls it talk? How many men did the Vigilance Committee put under arms in fifty-one?"

"Seven hundred," Van Ness said. "No more than eight."

Sherman had been away from California from 1850 until the spring of '53 and had missed the first outbreak of organized vigilantism. The Vigilance Committee had remained in existence for three months and hanged four men. It was still possible to provoke heated discussions about which, if any, of those dispatched by the organization had been guilty of hanging crimes.

"There are at least two thousand men in Sacramento Street just now," Sherman said. "We will have to act quickly and decisively if we are to put a stop to this thing."

"Hear, hear," Judge Terry murmured his approval.

"Judge, we will use you in your official capacity, seeing as you are here." Sherman's manner was that of a man taking command. "It won't hurt to have myself sworn in by a justice of the state supreme bench." Sherman turned to Van Ness. "Have you a Bible?"

The mayor produced a King James version from his desk drawer, and with Judge Terry presiding, Sherman took the oath as major general of California militia.

"How is King of William?" Sherman asked Van Ness when the swearing-in was completed.

"Hmm? Oh. They have moved him to a room in Montgomery Block. Dr. Cole holds out hope of recovery. Doctors Toland, Hammond and Bertody are consulting."

"The man's a scoundrel," Sherman said.

"Not that Casey is any better," Terry added. It seemed to Farren that Judge Terry offered the remark tentatively, to sound out Sherman's own opinion.

"He is a low sort," Sherman acknowledged. "All the same, when he was county treasurer his books balanced to the cent. And he's no coward. He proved that in the brawl with Bagley."

"And King of William is a failed banker," Terry said. "That does not sit well with you, I imagine."

Sherman's ruddy countenance darkened. "It does not, sir. He had a hand in the worst financial panic this city has known. What's more, he announced repeatedly in his paper that he would meet any challenge. When Casey called him out, he wouldn't fight. The man's a scoundrel."

Terry nodded. "His fate is in the physicians' hands now."

"We must keep Casey alive until the passions of the mob have quieted," Sherman said. "There's time enough then to hang him properly, if he warrants it. Is there anything you can do to keep things in hand?"

"The law is corrective, not preventive, General," Terry said. "It must be broken before it can act. The moment the vigilantes step across the line, I will urge the governor to use every means at his disposal to put them down."

It seemed to Farren that Judge Terry was eager for that moment to arrive. Terry was a Texan, one of many in San Francisco, one of a select few who had served in the Rangers with the legendary Jack Hays during the Mexican War. He had been elected an associate justice of the state supreme court the year before. Now, with Chief Justice Murray too ill to carry on his duties and the court's third judge, Heydenfelt, out of the state, Terry was acting chief justice. For the time being, the power of the supreme court of California was vested in a single man.

A burst of cheering came from outside, where a company of militia marched south along Kearny Street to the loud approval of a knot of onlookers.

Sherman watched the marching men pass by, then turned to Farren. "I understand the militia companies have been withdrawn from the jail. Why?"

"Colonel West's orders, sir. He believes the vigilants will not move against the jail until they have organized."

"I understand too that many in the militia are sympathetic with the Vigilance Committee. Where do you stand, Captain?"

Farren stiffened. "The Blues will remain loyal, sir, so long as Captain Ashe and I are in command."

The door to the mayor's chamber opened and a man stepped inside. He wore a city marshal's tin badge pinned to his coat.

"Them's the California Guards, sir, goin' over to the Vigilance Committee," he said to the mayor. "As cocky as a bunch of Irishmen on the way to a saloon."

"Are they armed?" Sherman demanded.

"Not so's you could see."

"Thank you, Marshal North," Van Ness said. North withdrew.

"How many of the other companies can we count on?" Sherman asked Farren.

"That's hard to say just yet, sir. As a rule, they will stay loyal or desert en masse. The City Guards will go over for certain. You can count on Captain Riggs and his Marion Rifles. The Continentals too. Most of them, anyway. I wouldn't put money on the rest."

"You served in the Mexican War, I am told."

"Yes, sir."

"In Mexico?"

"Yes, General."

"So far as I can determine, every veteran presently in California saw active service in Mexico, saving myself. Still, I am the general here now."

William Tecumseh Sherman was thirty-six years old. He had resigned from the Army three years before, certain he would never rise above the rank of captain. During the Mexican War, while his fellow officers had distinguished themselves at Matamoros and Chapultepec, he had languished in Monterey, California, where the Mexican dons, far from being hostile, had entertained the American officers royally at every opportunity and seemed blithely indifferent to the fact that the *yanquis* had seized California by force of arms. Now, against his better judgment, Sherman found himself the sham general of a militia that was evaporating from the city's streets even as he took an oath before God to uphold the laws and the constitutions of California and the United States of America. Was he so desperate for military honors? He thought it unlikely that he would get any here.

Sherman's hard eyes admitted nothing about his private doubts. He drew himself up to his full height and ran a hand through his tousled red hair. "Gentlemen, I accepted this commission at Governor Johnson's insistence. I was assured that my role would be largely ceremonial and would take very little of my time. It may be that it will turn out to be something quite different, but that is not in my hands. For now, the immediate task is to see what men and arms we can depend on."

"Any company that disbands as state's militia is obliged to leave their arms and ammunition at the armories," Farren said.

"Let's hope their sense of duty lasts long enough for them to fulfill that obligation." Judge Terry's caustic tone suggested he did not put much faith in the deserters' sense of duty.

"Captain Farren, you will continue in command of your company and you will also act as my adjutant," Sherman said. "I want you to learn what has become of the California Guards' arms and see to the state of the armories. The inventory doesn't have to be exact. While you're about it, discover as best you can the sentiments of the other militia companies."

"Colonel West and Captain Ashe are doing that now, sir."

"Good. Report to me at my bank this afternoon." Sherman clapped his hat on his head and started for the door.

"As to a uniform, General—" Van Ness began, but Sherman cut him off with a snort of derision.

"I will wear a uniform when I have some troops who will obey my orders, Mayor. Until then, I am general in mufti, and probably just as well."

Chapter 7

ason and Dickie found Stephen Kent speaking with Ned Rollick in the ground-floor rooms of Farnum & Kent. He broke off when he saw them enter. "There you are. You've seen the state of things? It's bad luck, this vigilance business. Couldn't have come at a worse time."

"What's it to do with us?"

"This is not just some rabble, Jason. The best men in the city are involved in it. Abel Calvert and I have been up half the night trying to reason with them. Many of the city's firms are closed up tight, but I have persuaded four men to meet with us about our rice."

The offices of the four merchants were within a few streets of one another in the business district. At each of the first three firms Jason and Kent were given the same evasive answers to their inquiries. Mr. Brown and Mr. Liebling and Captain Macondray all shared a reluctance to become involved with rice at this time.

The mood of the commercial district was very different from the previous day. Then, Jason had felt the optimism and youthful vitality of the gold port. Now most of the businesses were closed. The doors of some firms bore notices referring to "unsettled conditions" in the city. Here and there a storefront or warehouse was open, here and there an occasional drayman hauled his goods, but the men in the streets gathered in tight knots to talk softly, and there were no ladies in evidence at all.

"Have you a ship's boy on your ship?" Dickie Howell asked Jason. They were walking north on Montgomery.

"Every good vessel has a boy. The *Sarah B. Watson* is a China clipper, lad. Naturally she has a ship's boy. His name is Stritch."

Dickie was disappointed. "I was hoping you might be in need of a boy."

"You'd like to go to sea, eh, young Richard?"

"Don't get him started on that," Kent said. "The sea is his dream."

"When I'm grown enough," Dickie said defensively. "It's not fair that I'm small for my age, I say. But Mrs. Rockwell says God's plan for each of us is made plain in time." The boy didn't appear to take much comfort in Mrs. Rockwell's interpretation of the Creator's grand design.

"Do you know anything of ships?"

"Yes, Captain. I can name the sails and the spars, and some of the hauling ends. I don't know them all, but I go aboard the ships when I can and the sailors show me about."

"Do you know what time we must meet Finn Warren at the Noggin of Ale?"

"Four bells of the dog watches, you told him."

"Aye. And what time is that by landsmen's reckoning?"

"Six o'clock."

"You know your ship's bells, then."

"Every boy on the wharves knows ship's time, Captain. There are three watches in every twelve hours, beginning at midday and midnight. One bell every half hour, up to eight, then start again."

"And the dog watches, what are they?"

"The afternoon watch from four to eight is split into two, at four bells."

"Why?"

"So the port and starboard watch don't stand the same watches every day, Captain. But I don't know why that is."

"Good lad. Always admit when you don't know something. Never be afraid to ask. We change watches to keep the men on their toes. Stand the same watch every day and a man grows careless." He regarded Dickie soberly. "I tell you what I will do. If I hear of any ship that needs a boy, I will send them to you."

"Thank you, Captain!" A thought sobered Dickie. "But don't tell Mrs. Rockwell. She doesn't think much of ship's boys. She says God intends a better life for me."

"Does Mrs. Rockwell speak for God often, then?"

"Not very often. It's just her way of saying what she thinks."

In the next premises Kent entered, Jason was surprised to find himself welcomed by Jonathan Frye.

"Come in, Captain Beck, come in!" Frye greeted him heartily. "Please forgive me for not stopping last evening to make your acquaintance." The merchant was a changed man from the surly tippler of the night before. He was rock-steady on his feet and his eyes were clear.

"Mr. Kent has told me of your cargo," he said to Jason when the three men were alone in Frye's private office. "I don't deal in grains myself. Never have. Too uncertain for me. Real estate, now, that is something you can count on. You can stand on a piece of land."

"But you know the merchants in this town," Kent said. "We will sell at a very attractive price. For fifteen percent in advance, you can represent the cargo exclusively."

"I will do what I can. In my view, it will be a few weeks before flour is reasonable. Things will come into balance then."

Kent leaned forward in his chair. "Listen here, Frye. There has been some talk of late. I won't say where I heard it, but I have heard of an effort in rice now that flour is falling. A new monopoly."

Frye's face darkened. "If the talk is true, I hope those men break out in boils on their backsides." He rubbed his chin, which was clean shaven beneath a flowing mustache that joined his side-whiskers. "Anyone with rice on his hands is hurting now. But if they keep it off the market until the flour is exhausted, they could make up their losses."

"I can't wait that long," Jason said. "I've a profitable cargo awaiting me in China."

Frye brightened. "If there is a cartel in rice, it can

work to your advantage, Captain. Your cargo is offshore. Without warehouse costs, a man who owned your cargo would be in a position to sell low." He was speaking rapidly now. "With a hundred tons of rice—"

"A hundred and fifty," Kent said.

"With that much he can sell at the first good offer and break the cartel." Frye was delighted. "The price will plummet and they will lose their shirts! With that incentive, I may find you a buyer." He held up a cautioning hand. "I make no promises of course, but if I were to inspect the cargo myself I could vouch for its condition."

"I will take you aboard today. Right now, if you like." Jason felt hope spread through him like the warmth from the brandy punches at the Bank Exchange.

At the Pacific Wharf, Finn Warren offered to take them out to the *Sarah B. Watson* in his dory. "I ferry ships' officers now and again," he told Jason as they helped Frye into the high-sided boat. "It keeps me on the water."

They were four, Kent having remained ashore to attend to other business. With Jason in the bow and Dickie and Frye in the stern, Finn put up the dory's single sail and the boat flew over the water.

"Captain's alongside!" called out a voice when the dory was still thirty yards from the *Sarah B. Watson*. The bosun piped them aboard as if the clipper were a navy ship and Jonathan Frye a visiting admiral. Jason was pleased to see that the vessel was shipshape and all the men aloft or on deck were occupied with some task or another.

Dickie Howell kept close by Jason's side, looking about the ship with eager eyes.

"A fine-looking vessel, Captain Beck," Frye said. "Still, it's not much of a name for a clipper, *Sarah Watson*. Why have you not given it a name to fit the times? *Flying Cloud, Empress of the Seas, Gem of the Ocean*, something like that?"

"So a ship is christened, so she remains, Mr. Frye. 'Tis bad luck to rename her." Jason concealed his distaste for the very idea. Hearing that Farnum & Kent never renamed their vessels had drawn him to the house in the first place. Learning that they respected other maritime traditions as well, and did not press their captains to overload their vessels, had reinforced his growing loyalty to the firm.

Melchior hove in sight from the foredeck. "Didn't expect ee back so soon, Cap'n."

"I've brought Mr. Frye to see our rice, if you will see to my friend here. He would like to be a ship's boy someday. Richard Howell, this is Melchior, first mate of the *Sarah B.* He's a regular terror when given cause, but you are safe with him." He beckoned Jonathan Frye toward the forward hatchway, which stood open to air the hold.

"So, young Dick. Ee's a friend o' the skipper's?" Melchior extended a hand. Dickie screwed up his courage and stuck out his own. It was enveloped in a grip as callused and hard as a blacksmith's. "Want to be a ship's boy, do ee? Well, we'll have Stritch to show ee about. Ahoy, Rob Tinker!" Melchior called to the bosun. "Where's that Stritch got to?" Tinker was whipping a frayed footrope in the mainmast shrouds, working swiftly with a needle and a leather sailmaker's palm.

"Stepped into the galley to fetch me an orange, Melchior," was the reply. "He'll be back in a jiff."

"What a soft ship she is," Melchior said to Dickie. "Oranges, now we're in port. Come all the way from Spain or Tahiti, I'm bound." He loomed over Dickie Howell and gazed upon him, and Dickie drew back in spite of himself. He was used to men of the sea and their rough ways, but Melchior's imposing bulk daunted him and the bright eyes beneath the mate's thick black brows threatened to bore through him.

"You wanted me, Mr. Melchior?" A youth six inches taller than Dickie and a year or two older stepped to the mate's side. He tossed an orange to Rob Tinker.

"This here be Dick Howell, Stritch. Cap'n brought him to see the vessel. Has it in mind to be a ship's boy. What do ee think o' that?"

The boy looked at Dickie distastefully. "He's puny, ain't he?"

"You were scarce bigger'n him when you come aboard, Stritch, and look at ee. Go along now and show'n the ship."

"Beg pardon, sir, but I'm due to go ashore."

"Avast, boy," Melchior cautioned him. "Ee will set foot ashore at my pleasure or not at all. Now show this lad the *Sarah B.* from stem to stern, and *tomorrer* ee can go ashore with the starboard watch."

Stritch opened his mouth to protest further, knew it was futile, and tugged his forelock. "This way." He led Dickie to the fo'c'sle, which was empty now that the port watch was ashore. Dickie tripped going through the hatchway and nearly fell.

"You're all thumbs and two left feet, like every land-lubber," Stritch observed.

"That's as may be," Dickie said. "But I have worked the docks of San Francisco and I know a thing or two about ships." He looked about the fo'c'sle and wondered what it would be like to live in the cramped space for months at sea. There were two dozen or more narrow bunks stacked in tiers of three, and space to hang a dozen hammocks. The place smelled of salt and tar and old clothes.

"Where's the hawse hole?" Stritch tested him.

Dickie pointed to the hole where the anchor chain passed through the bow of the ship. The chain and its mechanism were in the center of the fo'c'sle, while the capstan was on the foredeck above. "That's it, there. I'm not claiming to know as much as you, mind. I might as well ask you to name the wharves of San Francisco from north to south."

"It's a lively port, I hear."

"The liveliest this side of Singapore. You might learn a thing or two, with me to show you about."

"Such as?" Stritch couldn't entirely disguise his interest.

Dickie's hand went to his back, beneath his short coat. "Such as this." His hand flashed through the air and a small dirk embedded itself into a bunk post.

Stritch laughed. "Not bad, for a puny lubber." His own hand went to the haft of a knife at his waist and in a twinkling it stood in the same spot, a handsbreadth from Dickie's.

Dickie grinned. "I should have known a ship's boy would know how to handle a shiv." They went together to retrieve the knives. Dickie struggled with his, which seemed to be stuck fast. Stritch pulled his own knife out with one hand, turning away as he sheathed it in the leather scabbard the sailmaker had fashioned for him. Before he knew what was happening, Dickie had his knife hand in a viselike grip and the dirk at his throat.

"I might show you how to do this, if you like," Dickie said in his ear. He released the larger boy and stepped back, tensed for a countermove.

"I can fight with knives right enough, but not with you," Stritch said. "Not here. You come aboard with the skipper. He'd have me flogged if I was to cut you."

Dickie's eyes widened. "Would he?"

Stritch shrugged. "There's never been a man flogged aboard the *Sarah B.* since I come aboard. None since Cap'n Beck took command, they say. I'm not sayin' he wouldn't flog me, mind, if I was to cut you, but I'm willin' to be friends if you'll show me the shore. I don't get no rum aboard ship. Maybe you'd know where a ship's boy can drink with the sailors ashore?"

"That's easy. But first you've got to show me the ship."

"I'd be ashore now, but for you," Stritch said. Then he smiled, abashed. "That, and I spilled the breakfast slops in the galley and had to stay aboard to clean up. So let's say I show you the ship, and you'll show me the sailor's life ashore."

"Done," said Dickie Howell.

Chapter 8

avid Farren presented himself at the Montgomery Street offices of Lucas, Turner & Company a little after two o'clock. The bank was an attractive three-story brick structure that Sherman had erected on the northeast corner of Montgomery and Jackson. Lucas, Turner occupied the entire ground floor, while the second and third stories were let out. Farren was ushered immediately into Sherman's private office, where he found Colonel West with Sherman.

"The California Guards' arms and ammunition were not turned in at the armory, sir," Farren reported after a brief greeting. "I was told they were 'sequestered.' A friend of mine is a lieutenant in the Guards. He has joined the vigilants himself but he doesn't want to see bloodshed."

"Fine way he has of showing it," Sherman said sourly. "Did he tell you what use the arms will be put to?"

"Not in so many words, sir. May I speak frankly?"

"Captain, you may speak frankly to me at all times. So far, we are three blind mice, waltzing in the dark with a cat of unknown disposition."

"Well, sir, I am pretty sure they hid the arms so they can be used by the vigilants later, but my friend said they won't take action unless we move against them."

"And we can't move against them unless we have arms ourselves," Colonel West said.

Sherman paced the confines of the small room. "What we have here is a novel form of the Mexican standoff. Instead of two adversaries armed to the teeth, each waiting for the other to commence hostilities, we have two parties bound to be adversaries, neither visibly armed, each awaiting some demonstration of the other's intentions." To West he said, "How are the other companies taking sides?"

"Much as I expected, General." Unlike Sherman, West thought better when he was at rest. He had not moved from where he sat beside Sherman's desk since Farren entered the office. "We will have the Blues and the Marion Rifles, and a good many of the Continentals will stick. Most of the other companies will join the vigilants. I don't know if you are aware, General, but the California Guards have two fieldpieces. The guns were at the jail last night but Captain Macondray sent them off before dawn."

Sherman paused in his rounds. "Missing as well?"

West nodded. "With powder and shot."

"Damnation and hellfire." Sherman spoke the words pensively, more like a blessing than an oath. He resumed his restless pacing. "We must do what we can to limit the damage. It might be a good idea to collect the arms of the militia companies until we know for certain how they stand."

"That may do more harm than good, sir," Farren said. "The men who are loyal will feel you don't trust them. It may sway them to the Vigilance Committee."

"It is a risk I think we must take. We must gather what we can. If we can deny the vigilants some of the arms, we may at least perpetuate the standoff."

Sherman sat at his desk, seized a piece of paper, and began to write quickly. "Captain, you will take this to the police office in City Hall. It is an order for them to collect the militia arms and put them in the guardrooms at the jail and the Court House. We don't want them all in one place."

"What about ours, sir? The arms of the Blues and the Marion Rifles?"

"If they are safe in the armories and guarded by men you know and trust, let them remain where they are. Or remove them to a safe place if you think best. I leave that up to you."

Sherman got to his feet and handed the note to Farren. "If King survives for a few more days, we may have time to raise reinforcements. If he lives, this whole business may peter out, but we must prepare for the worst. Take that order to the police now. Then go to the jail and give my respects to Sheriff Scannell. Tell him I suggest he issue a call to the leading citizens to form a posse comitatus to guard the jail. If the vigilants are going to muster their men, we had better put ours in a row so we can count heads."

Two men were with Molly Gray in the boardinghouse parlor when Jason Beck came down the stairs for dinner. The actress rose from the divan as he entered.

"You didn't tell me you had seen the shooting yesterday, Captain." She was resplendent in a lavender evening dress. In the relative privacy of the parlor, she wore no covering on her lustrous black hair. "You met Mr. Trelayne this morning, I understand."

Jason recognized the younger of the two men in the parlor as the bleary-eyed figure he had seen briefly when Mrs. Rockwell showed him to his room.

"We weren't properly introduced. I am Thomas Trelayne." The theatrical manager was younger than Jason's first impression had led him to believe. Jason judged he was in his middle twenties. When he smiled, he revealed sharp, rather prominent canine teeth that gave him a somewhat feral look. He was clean shaven and his attire was a rebuke to the somber colors worn by most gentlemen for evening wear. His silk cravat was royal blue, his trousers a fine tan worsted. A ruby ring shone on his right hand. He was shorter than Jason, of slight build, and he was quick on his feet when he stepped back to present the other man.

"You don't know Mr. Norton. He is a true forty-niner and a distinguished member of this city's merchant community."

Norton bowed slightly. "I am honored, Captain Beck. Mrs. Rockwell has told us something of you and your ship."

Jason detected an odd accent in Norton's voice but he couldn't place it. The merchant had bulging eyes and a receding hairline. The velvet collar of his chesterfield coat was worn and one of his cuffs was beginning to fray. Jason himself was wearing his one white shirt, a plain black cravat, and a coat that was musty from lying too long in his sea chest. He felt comfortable in Norton's company.

"One member of our cast is absent this evening." Trelayne clearly enjoyed playing the role of host. "Captain Farren is a lawyer, but he also commands a company of volunteer militia. They have been called out—"

The French doors to the dining room were opened from within, and Sarah Rockwell entered the parlor.

"Ah," Trelayne exclaimed. "The leading lady makes her entrance."

Her evening dress was gray silk, trimmed with black lace, tied with black ribbon bows at the shoulders. A black cap covered most of her auburn hair.

"Mrs. Rockwell tells us you saved her yesterday, when Mr. Casey shot King of William," Molly Gray said.

"I did nothing of the kind," Jason protested.

"He is modest too," Trelayne murmured.

"Not at all. I stopped Mrs. Rockwell without thinking," Jason said truthfully. "Like everyone else, I was watching the duelists."

Trelayne pounced on the word. "So it was a duel!"

"Casey asked King of William if he was armed and he gave him warning. He said something like, 'Prepare to defend yourself.'"

"And as it turned out, King of William was armed!" Trelayne was triumphant. "They found a five-shooter in his pocket."

"Dueling is an uncivilized practice that is forbidden by the constitution of this state," Sarah Rockwell said firmly.

Norton cleared his throat. "The code duello is an ancient institution, Mrs. Rockwell. It has provided a means for men to settle their differences."

"So long as men shoot each other over some imagined slight we are no better than barbarians."

Trelayne snorted. "Without dueling, we would lose some of the best scenes in the theater."

"If duels were fought only on a theatrical stage, I should be very happy," Sarah Rockwell replied. "From what I saw, King of William made no attempt to defend himself."

"That's true." Jason was reluctant to contradict her. "All the same, he had one hand inside his coat, and plenty of time."

"Is that important?" Molly had seated herself once more and she leaned slightly forward now. The posture emphasized the perfect symmetry of her breasts and presented them for Jason's inspection.

"In a street duel, a man is not required to wait until his opponent draws a weapon," Norton said.

"Honestly, there is no justice in the world." Trelayne sighed. "Captain Beck was ashore less than a day and he witnessed the most exciting event San Francisco has seen in years. *I* could make use of it. To see a real duel! What ideas it would give me for staging fights in my plays."

"Duel or not, it has brought commerce to a standstill," Jason said. "I've a cargo of rice to sell, but the merchants are all caught up in this vigilance business."

"Which only the *Herald* has courage to condemn," Sarah Rockwell said with some heat. "Mr. Nugent says that there is no need for any new organization now. We have police and courts, whatever some may think of them."

Trelayne got to his feet. "Well, the mealtime conversation promises to be lively."

Sarah gave him a stern look. "You know very well I allow no politics at the table. From this moment, I forbid any further talk of dueling and vigilantes." She led the way to the dining room. "You have made quite an impression on Dickie," she said to Jason.

She had sent Dickie Howell to the kitchen when he and Captain Beck returned to the boardinghouse that afternoon. While Ingrid, the Swedish scullery maid, helped Sarah prepare the dinner, Dickie had eaten his supper and talked at great length about Captain Beck and his splendid ship.

"He tells me you are teaching him to read and write," Jason said.

"If we don't want to have the streets full of broken lives, Captain, we must do our best to mend them." She seated him at her right hand and left the others to take their customary places.

"That's a fine Boston chowder, Mrs. Rockwell," Jason said when he had tasted the soup.

"We make chowder in Maine too, Captain Beck." Sarah noted a measure of defensive pride in her voice and she softened it with a smile.

"I know the coast of Maine," he said. "Where was your home?"

"At Kittery Point."

"Molly and I are Sarah's subjects for a continuous lesson in New England cookery." Trelayne was mournful.

"Behave yourself, Tommy, just this once." Molly Gray gave Trelayne a cautioning look and leaned toward Jason. "Tell us, Captain. Of all the things you must do without at sea, which do you miss the most?"

Sarah saw how they looked at him, the exotic stranger in their midst, the sea captain with the long hair and the golden earring, and she saw how the sea captain kept his gaze on Molly Gray. Sarah's dress was more chaste than Molly's, revealing only a modest expanse of lightly freckled skin and scarcely a glimpse of her bosom. She felt plain beside the diminutive actress.

"Company, Miss Gray."

"Company?"

"The company of equals. People I can talk to without being conscious that they are mine to command."

Norton nodded sagely. "Aboard ship, the captain is king. He knows the loneliness of the absolute ruler."

"Careful now," Trelayne warned. "You have got him started, Captain. Joshua—Mr. Norton—adores to imagine himself an absolute ruler of infinite wisdom. He would right all wrongs and we would live together in boring harmony."

"Would it be so bad as all that?" Norton was petulant. "If I were king I could decree an end to dueling. Whosoever defied the ban, I would hang them. That would put a stop to it."

"I'm sure you would never be so bloodthirsty," Sarah said.

"It is America he wants to rule, Captain Beck," Trelayne said. "He takes a passionate interest in this land, for a man born halfway 'round the world."

"My father took our family from England to the Cape of Good Hope," Norton said to Jason. "But he might as easily have sailed westward to America. For a time I became the Wandering Jew, although I do not practice the religion of my fathers. But here I found a home. And is this not the nation that invites the wanderer to claim it for his own? Is not this city peopled with men who have come halfway 'round the world? Women as well, like Mrs. Rockwell and our dear Molly?"

"Precisely," Sarah agreed. "Without the courageous men and women who come to our shores, neither California nor the eastern States could grow as rapidly as they must if we are to keep the Union whole and strong."

"That sounds dangerously like political talk, Sarah," Trelayne chided her.

"Concern for the well-being of the Union should concern us all in these times. But you're right. I apologize."

"It is unusual for a woman to take such an interest in men's affairs, Mrs. Rockwell," Jason said.

"Men's affairs govern women, Captain Beck." There was a hardness in Sarah's tone, but she saw the meaningful look Molly Gray gave her. "Don't worry, Molly. I will not lecture Captain Beck on his first evening with us." To Jason she said, "My late husband's family did not approve of my politics. Molly doesn't either."

She rang a small silver bell and the scullery maid appeared. She was a plain, timid creature who cleared the chowder plates and brought on the fish.

"I discourage politics at the table because opinions are so contentious here," Sarah said. "But the truth is, Captain, in San Francisco it is not really politics the men care about most. It is money. They argue politics day and night, but I have never seen a place where money was more on everyone's mind."

"That's what brought us, isn't it?" Trelayne said. "Molly and I saw the golden glow even from Illinois. And you yourself, Sarah. Tell the truth now."

Sarah's answer was subdued. "It is not why I came, although it is why I stayed. But not for avarice. Grant me that."

"I would grant you the sun and moon if they were mine to give, fair Sarah." Trelayne's tone was conciliatory.

"Mr. Trelayne only pretends to be as greedy as the rest," Sarah said to Jason. "His true reason for coming here was to try new ideas in a town where the theater was not already set in its ways. Most theatrical managers compete for the best-known actors and actresses who come to California and keep them only so long as they are new and fresh. Mr. Trelayne is the first to create a repertory company. His productions are brilliant, although I should never say so in his hearing. He has earned the admiration of the public by the quality and variety of his entertainments."

"You see how she is, Captain." Trelayne basked in the compliment. "She will not permit a man to keep his humility intact. Alas, the truth is she has never seen one of my shows."

"My mourning doesn't permit it," Sarah said. "But I have read all the notices in the newspapers and I hear people talk about your plays."

"Sarah!" Molly said. "You must come to the first night of our new play tomorrow!"

"You know I can't."

"Why not? Oh, Sarah, really! No one can say you haven't mourned. But it is almost three years!"

"Two years, nine months and a week."

Molly's voice softened. "And even the strictest mourning ends after two and a half years. I'm not asking you to forget, Sarah. Only to see that you belong with the living. You have your whole life ahead of you. Mr. Rockwell would want you to live it."

"Do come, Sarah," Trelayne said. "It will do you good."

"Captain Beck can escort you!" Molly was pleased with her plan. "He will enjoy a night at the theater. Say you will, Captain. It will all be very proper. We have a supper onstage after the performance, catered by Martin's restaurant."

"There you are. The company of San Francisco's most lovely widow and a free supper into the bargain." Trelayne took Molly's hand as they awaited Jason's answer.

Jason dreaded the thought of an evening spent watching bewigged men dressed in tights making fools of themselves, but he could see no way to refuse gracefully. "I would be honored," he said. At this rate, he would be a landsman from stem to stern inside of a week, daubing pomade on his hair and brushing specks of dust from his boots.

Trelayne beamed. "Well, then, that's settled." As the fish course gave way to beef, he contented himself with small jests that kept the two women smiling.

When the meal was done, Jason excused himself to smoke on the veranda. Norton followed him and they sat together. When the cigars were lighted and they had settled themselves, the gray cat emerged from a shadow and jumped up to Norton's lap. "Have you met Kittery?" he said.

"Not formally."

"She answers to Kit. She takes some time to get used to newcomers." Norton scratched the cat's neck absently. "Have you spent much time in California waters, Captain?"

"I first saw California twenty years ago. I was bunking before the mast in those days."

Norton seemed pleased. "Then you played a part in opening this coast to American trade."

"We came for hides, and a good profit," Jason said. "The grand designs of American trade we left to others." He flexed his shoulders without thinking, reviving a movement that had been habitual after carrying bullock hides through the surf to a waiting longboat.

"All the same, you played your part. The trappers came overland to find new markets, and good Yankee ships came by sea. Before long the American government found the right moment, and California became American by an almost bloodless conquest. Thus are empires made, Captain, by seizing the moment."

"I am only a Yankee trader, Mr. Norton."

"And as such, in the vanguard of empire with every voyage you undertake. Those hides you took back to

New England became shoes for American feet and belts for the revolution of industry that is reshaping the world."

They smoked for a time in silence. The parlor window glowed with lamplight. Within, Jason could see Sarah Rockwell instructing Dickie Howell in penmanship. Trelayne and Molly came out of the house together to stroll in the dusk.

When they were gone, Norton leaned forward as if to convey a confidence. "Mind me well, Captain," he said. "Rid yourself of that rice as soon as you can. It is evil stuff."

"Rice, Mr. Norton?"

"Beware the men who deal in rice. Don't trust them. Sell your cargo and begone, or you will spend more time ashore than befits a sailor."

"I want nothing more than to follow your advice, Mr. Norton. But flour has pulled rice down to unprofitable levels, so everyone reminds me. If you know where I can sell my cargo, the commission is yours."

Norton reacted as if Jason had insulted him. "Well, of course you have no way of knowing. And I mustn't blame you. How could you know?" He puffed his cigar. "Not so long ago I was a wealthy man, Captain. Emulating Caesar, I came to San Francisco, I saw the opportunities, and I conquered. I owned all four corner lots at Jackson and Sansome streets. I had a cigar factory and a rice mill. I had a storeship to warehouse my goods. I was infected by the spirit of the time and place. There was no limit to my ambitions. And, like Caesar, I too fell from grace."

Norton's protruding eyes were fixed on Jason. "Rice, Captain. Rice was the cause. When the first cartel formed in 'fifty-three, they drove flour up in the winter and it was still high in June. Rice was high too, and scarce. It went up to thirty cents or more after the Manchus banned the export of rice from China. As the master of a China clipper you know all about that."

Jason nodded. Four years earlier there had been a famine in China. To keep foodstuffs at home, the Manchu overlords banned the export of grain. Before the ban the *Sarah B. Watson* had carried rice to Boston. On her next voyage she carried silk and ladies' fans, folding screens, lacquered boxes and carved ivory, and made a handsome profit. In Boston, rice had gone over forty cents a pound until new sources made up the loss.

"The first new rice came from Peru aboard the ship *Glyde*." Norton spoke the name as if recalling a dead relation for whom he never held any affection. "Two hundred thousand pounds aboard, and I got it for twelve and a half cents! But within days, more ships arrived with Peruvian rice. Within two weeks there were a million pounds of rice on that bay, begging for buyers." Norton pointed an accusing arm down Jackson Street, toward the water.

"At the same time, the flour merchants released their stocks and the price fell. I had hoped to corner the market in rice. Instead, I was very nearly ruined. I lost a good many of my holdings and mortgaged the others. But I will recover. I believe that. And it is just possible you have shown me the way. Would it not be poetic justice if rice were my salvation?"

"You'll help, then?"

"I'll do what I can. This vigilance business may seem—"

David Farren emerged from the dusk, bounded up the steps, and stopped when he saw the two men on the veranda. "The Vigilance Committee has enrolled fifteen hundred men today. By tomorrow they'll have two thousand under arms."

Farren went into the house and Jason rose to follow him, but Norton put a hand on his arm. "Do not let this civil alarm concern you, Captain. I know it seems that commerce has come to a halt, but that is an illusion. The Vigilance Committee is a sleeping brotherhood, now awakened. I was a member of the Committee in 'fifty-one. Soon I will join the new organization. Behind its closed doors, the business of the city continues."

Chapter 9

t breakfast the next morning, Captain Farren reported that the city was quiet, although the Vigilance Committee was still enrolling volunteers. He had been out to take the mood of the town shortly after sunrise and was off again before the meal was done, on militia business, he said. He would give no details.

When Jason left the house, the weather vane pointed west by north and the air was fresh. He found Sarah Rockwell negotiating once again with the same Chinaman who had provided her vegetables the day before. In the sunlight, her hair glowed deep red.

"Has Mr. Norton gone to his office?" Jason asked her. He had meant to tell Norton at breakfast that Abel Calvert had offered to keep a weather eye out for anyone who might be interested in a cargo of rice. He hoped the two men might coordinate their efforts.

"Mr. Norton has no office, Captain."

"I don't understand."

"Mr. Norton spends his mornings going about the town looking for opportunities. He picks up a few small commissions buying and selling. In the afternoon he is in his room with his papers and books. He hopes one day to have an office again."

Mrs. Rockwell's tone conveyed such compassion for Norton's reduced circumstances that Jason wondered if she even charged the merchant for his room.

"I will be gone much of the day," he said, "but I will come back for supper. What time does Mr. Trelayne's play begin?"

"Half past seven." To his surprise, she presented him to the Chinaman. "Su-Yan, this is my new boarder, Captain Beck. This is Su-Yan Quan. Or is it Quan Su-Yan? I can never remember."

"Quan Su-Yan in China, Miss Rockwell." The Chinaman spoke with scarcely any accent. "Su-Yan Quan in the Christian fashion. Praise the Lord Jesus." He bowed in greeting. "I am honored to meet you, Captain. But perhaps you prefer 'China boy plenty glad know captain fella.'"

"Not at all," Jason said, although the pidgin greeting was what he would have expected before hearing the Chinaman speak. Unlike most of his Celestial brethren, Su-Yan Quan wore Western dress. His vest, pants and coat were of the best worsted and his feet were clad in proper shoes instead of the cloth slippers favored by his countrymen. His attire would have been acceptable at the Bank Exchange, although he, as a Chinaman, would be excluded. The single oddity was his hat, which was a wide-brimmed miner's felt hat that shaded his face from the sun as he peddled his vegetables about the town.

"You are fortunate in your lodging, Captain Beck. Miss Rockwell keeps the best boardinghouse in San Francisco."

"It is Mrs. Rockwell, as you know very well," Sarah scolded.

"You are too young to be missus, certainly!" Su-Yan exclaimed. "In China, when a bride loses her husband before one year, she is 'missee' all over."

"That is nonsense, and you know it." To Jason, Sarah added, "He makes up any outrageous custom you can imagine and says it is ancient Chinese tradition."

"It is a true custom! I swear it on the Bible," Su-Yan protested. "When a woman's husband is dead before one year, she is a virgin bride again! If you marry this Captain Beck, he will certainly delight in you as for the first time!"

Sarah flushed crimson with embarrassment. "You will grow accustomed to him, Captain," she said. "He hasn't acquired our notions of propriety along with his devout belief in our Savior."

"Praise the Lord Jesus!" Su-Yan exclaimed. "Is it not right to speak of marriage? The captain is already married?"

"Why, I don't know if he is or not." Sarah regarded Jason with frank curiosity. "You haven't mentioned a wife, Captain."

Jason was aware that the Chinaman was looking on with undisguised interest. "There is no wife, Mrs. Rockwell. Few women are willing to spend months alone while their husbands are at sea. Fewer still that I'd be wedded to."

"Oh? How so?"

"If a woman likes companionship, she will be unhappy when I am gone and blame me when I return. If she enjoys solitude, she will resent my presence when I am ashore, and so we would both be unhappy. And now, as I am ashore on business, I had better see to it."

He tipped his cap to Sarah, gave the Chinaman a nod, and went on his way, feeling that he had taken part in a very odd encounter. Later, in retrospect, he regarded that encounter as the most pleasant part of another day in which he felt the shackles of the gold port tighten about himself and his ship.

It was half past nine when Joshua Norton saw Jonathan Frye come out of his firm's offices and start off along Montgomery Street, approaching the doorway where Norton had kept watch on Frye & Company for more than an hour.

"Mr. Frye." He stepped into Frye's path.

Frye's gaze held no welcome. "Mr. Norton. I have pressing business."

Norton put a hand in his pocket and brought out a large pewter coin bearing the emblem of the 1851 Committee of Vigilance, with its watchful eye in the center and the organization's motto inscribed around the border: *Fiat Justitia Ruat Coelum* — Let justice be done, though the heavens fall.

"I will not keep you long. In confidence, Mr. Frye. Are you involved in this new organization?"

"In confidence, I am. So are most of the responsible men in the city."

"And it has been my intention to join you," Norton said. "But there is no sense my ploughing through that mob on Sacramento Street. I'll come along in a day or two, when things are quiet."

"Suit yourself." Frye was impatient to be off.

"I want to inform you of a promising opportunity. I am aware you do not customarily deal in grains. What would you say if I told you I can offer you, or someone of your acquaintance, a shipload of fine Carolina rice at a price that will enable you to sell it well before those whose storage costs are high?"

"I would say you have been approached by Mr. Kent and Captain Beck."

"Ah. So you know of their vessel and its cargo." Norton was disappointed to find Frye a step ahead of him. "Have you any interest in the rice?"

"None. I really must be going."

Norton blocked Frye's way. Frye was known to avoid speculative investments and Norton hadn't expected the merchant to buy the grain himself. He made the offer as a courtesy, and to prepare the way for his true request. "I am willing to take the risk myself. All I ask is your help in obtaining the capital."

Frye hesitated. "What collateral would you put up?"

"I still own two lots at Rincon Point, free and clear. In exchange, I will split my profit with you. Sixty percent and forty."

"Fifty and fifty."

"Very well." Norton had been prepared to offer this at the start. He was glad he had let Frye gain the point.

"I am not in the business of lending money, Norton. If I find someone who may be interested in rice, I will approach him on your behalf."

The big man walked off briskly, swinging his walking stick, going south on Montgomery. Norton felt sure Frye's "pressing business" was a meeting of the Vigilance Committee's leadership. The *Bulletin* and the other newspapers that supported the organization said the prominent men who were guiding it met continually. The papers agreed that whether King of William lived or died would determine if the vigilance troops took to the streets.

Unlike the eager applicants who besieged the recruitment offices on Sacramento Street, Joshua Norton was not impatient to sign his name. They were moved by mob passion, many of them, whereas he was motivated by self-interest and a sound grasp of business. In '51 he had seen as soon as the Vigilance Committee organized that he must join it and contribute to its support if he wished to continue doing business with the city's most successful merchants, for they composed the bulk of the Committee's leadership. The associations formed there had continued to benefit him long after the Committee of five years before had ceased to function. To some extent he had been ostracized by his fellow merchants as his fortunes fell, but with Captain Beck's rice as a bargaining chip, he saw a chance to renew those relations now. The present resurrection of the Committee came at an opportune moment, one he would not let pass him by.

Jonathan Frye skirted the crowd that choked Sacramento Street and made for the side entrance to the rooms where the Vigilance Committee was enrolling volunteers. The door opened into Leidesdorff Street, a narrow passage that was scarcely more than an alley. In Leidesdorff he found two boys loitering, watching the door.

"You, boy," he addressed the smaller of the two. "I know you, don't I? What is your name?"

"Dickie Howell, Mr. Frye. I've carried messages for your firm."

"Do you know the banking house of Calvert and Winston?"

"Yes, sir. Montgomery at Merchant Street."

"And do you know Captain Macondray's warehouses?"

"Yes, sir." Again, the boy gave the location correctly.

"Very well." Frye withdrew a leatherbound notebook and a lead pencil from his coat. He wrote rapidly, tore out two sheets, folded them separately, and wrote a name on each.

"Can you read these names?"

"Yes, sir." Dickie looked at the names, trying to make

out Frye's careless scrawl, and he was heartily grateful for Mrs. Rockwell's reading lessons. "I know Mr. Calvert and Mr. Macondray."

"Very well. Give the notes to those gentlemen personally and tell no one else who sent them. When you have done that, come back here and ask for me at this door. Say only 'number fifty-three.' Do you understand? I may have more work for you today." He pressed two coins into Dickie's hand.

"Yes, Mr. Frye!"

"Go along with you, then." Frye rapped on the door with the head of his cane. When the door opened a crack he said, "Number fifty-three," and was admitted.

The large commercial rooms had previously been occupied by a general store of a style that had been more common in San Francisco a few years earlier, where anything from a lady's bonnet to an anchor could be bought under one roof. Now they were choked with men. Frye saw at a glance that the premises were inadequate for the Vigilance Committee's needs. Tomorrow, the organization would move its operations to a large warehouse farther down Sacramento Street. It was clear the move came none too soon.

Frye approached a man named Watkins who was overseeing the admission of the volunteers. They were let in five at a time to sign their names in ledgers that were supervised by five clerks at a long table. He drew Watkins aside.

"You know who I am?"

"Yes sir, Mr. Frye."

"Then you know I am on the Executive Committee. I want you to add this name to the list of those not to be admitted to this organization." Frye wrote the name on a page from his notebook, tore it out, and handed it to Watkins.

Watkins glanced at the paper. "Joshua Norton. Not to be admitted. I'll see to it, Mr. Frye." He folded the paper and put it in a pocket of his coat.

In the alley, Dickie Howell thrust the note for Macondray into Stritch's hand. "You deliver this one and we'll be back here twice as soon. It's just down there on Front Street, to the right. Macondray and Company."

Stritch had come ashore with the starboard watch two hours before. The port watch was back aboard the *Sarah B. Watson*, three of the men unconscious and all of them reeking of rum and brandy, Stritch said.

"I don't read too good." The admission cost Stritch a measure of his pride.

"You know your numbers, don't you? Go two streets down and one to the right. It's a whitewashed warehouse, two stories. Number 124. The numbers are over the door."

"I thought you was going to show me the town." Dickie had met Stritch at the wharf and whisked him off through the streets, saying only that there was excitement in town and work to be had.

"How much do you make as ship's boy?"

"Ten dollars a month."

Dickie opened his hand to reveal two gold quarter-eagle coins, each worth two and a half dollars. He handed one to Stritch. "San Francisco costs money. You help me today and you can spend a month's wages tonight." He had planned this day with care to impress Stritch. With the gold they would earn in the next few hours, they could pay for more elaborate entertainments than Dickie had originally intended.

Jason Beck paced the streets of the commercial district like a sentinel walking the decks of a man-o'-war. Jonathan Frye was not in his office. Farnum & Kent was manned by an apprentice clerk. Not even Ned Rollick was there. Jason wrote out a note for Kent, asking him to Trelayne's opening that evening, and he moved on. At the banking house of Calvert & Winston he was received by Winston, a pale, dour man perfectly suited to the role of the silent partner. Winston knew nothing of Mr. Calvert's whereabouts, still less about any efforts he might be making on behalf of Jason's cargo. "I am not comfortable with perishable commodities," he told Jason as he showed him out. "Grain rots. Gold doesn't."

A few more businesses were open than the day before, but the mood in the streets remained tense. In Sacra-

mento Street the crowd of men waiting to sign up with
the vigilantes never seemed to dwindle, no matter how
many were let through the doors into the recruitment
rooms.

Watching the restless throng of volunteers, Jason
came to a sudden decision. He hired a hackney cab from
the line in the Plaza and arrived in less than ten minutes
at the Pacific Wharf. A quarter of an hour later, thanks
to Finn Warren and his dory, Jason was standing with
Melchior on the deck of the *Sarah B. Watson*.

"All hands accounted for?"

"Port watch all back aboard, Cap'n. Starboard watch
ashore now, followin' your orders. I've said a prayer for
luck."

"Rob Tinker has left his sea legs ashore."

The *Sarah B.*'s bosun, a compact Vermonter, carried a
new main royal halyard unsteadily aft from the forepeak,
where spare ropes and all manner of ship's supplies were
stored. Close to three hundred feet of rope were coiled
on Rob Tinker's shoulder. As he clambered up the
shrouds he showed none of the spryness of an experienced seaman.

"They've been long at sea, Cap'n," Melchior said.
" 'Tis only in the way of a sailor to taste the landsmen's
grog when he's first ashore."

"And what about you, old friend? No grog for you?"

"You know me and grog, Jason. A mug o' grog and
I'm half-saved. Best I stay aboard these first days, I'm
thinkin', what with ee bunkin' ashore and all. Keep the
lads on their toes. There be time enough for me to see
the land when we unload the rice." When he spoke
thoughtfully, the Cornishman seemed to chew each
vowel for a time before finally turning it loose upon the
world.

"Aye." Jason nodded his approval. *Half-saved* in the
Cornish talk meant weak in the head. Melchior had a
prodigious thirst for rum, once he tasted the first drop.

Jason looked across the sparkling water to the city at
the edge of the harbor, the houses so bright in the midday sun. From here, the town was deceptively peaceful.
"Once they're back aboard tomorrow there's to be no
more leave for a time."

"No more to go ashore?"

"No more. Tell them it's just for a day or two. That might be truth, but I can't swear to it. There's trouble brewing, I'm bound."

"So say the lads when they come aboard," Melchior mused. "A shooting, they say. Some talk of hanging. I put it down to landsmen's foolishness. None t'do with the likes of we."

"Aye. But those same landsmen have the power to keep us here until the *Sarah B.*'s bottom is thick with barnacles."

Melchior knit his black brows, opened his mouth to say something, and clamped it shut.

"Out with it, man," Jason said.

"I've a feeling we're afloat in the devil's calm, Jason. The ship's as sour as a crab. Do ee feel her?"

The *Sarah B.* was solid beneath Jason's boots, steady in the absence of ocean swells. The waves of the bay were playthings, tossed off her oaken sides without effort.

"She seems contented enough."

"You ain't been sleepin' aboard, Cap'n. At night she's restless, like. She wants to be gone."

s he dressed for the theater, it seemed to Jason that he was preparing to play the part of a man enjoying himself while the city around him divided into armed camps. He was pleasantly surprised to discover that the play served as the perfect instrument to banish his cares, at least for an evening. The melodrama, *The Houri and the Bedouin* by name, was nonsense, but Jason laughed frequently and became engrossed in the nonsense despite himself. The drop curtain behind the actors was painted with a colorful scene of an Arabian oasis and from time to time he found it possible to forget that he was halfway around the world from the deserts that spread to the shores of the Arabian Sea.

Trelayne had provided a private box to celebrate Sarah's return to society. She invited Joshua Norton to join them there, and graciously included Stephen Kent and his wife, Ethel, when they greeted Jason outside the theater. Ethel Kent was as solidly built as her husband and as florid of face, although retiring where he was gregarious. She had sharp eyes and a sensible bonnet.

As they filed into the theater together, Jason glimpsed Kent's clerk, Ned Rollick, across the vestibule, and he saw Jonathan Frye with a stern-faced woman his own age, undoubtedly his wife, by her proprietary air. They were making for the stairway to the boxes on the opposite side of the auditorium and there was no opportunity to greet the merchant.

Molly Gray was captivating as the *houri* of the play's title. At one point in the melodrama she disguised herself as a young man, in the course of a subterfuge to evade her stern father and rendezvous with her beloved, the Bedouin. So effective was her disguise that the audience did not recognize her until she threw off her turban and loosed her hair, revealing herself to the Bedouin, whereupon the entire audience burst into applause.

"How does she do that?" Jason whispered to Sarah. He made a gesture to indicate Molly's apparent lack of breasts in her man's costume.

Sarah leaned close to speak into his ear and he could smell the freshness of her hair. "A lady's—prominence is dictated by fashion, Captain. Without the support of a corset, and perhaps with a band of cloth to—flatten the chest, it is not so difficult."

Sarah was intoxicated by the simple fact of being in a theater after nearly three years of seclusion. She wore an evening dress of wine-colored silk taffeta that she had bought in Boston before sailing for California, but had never worn until now. The neckline was more revealing than her mourning had allowed, and her cap exposed more of her auburn hair than was dictated by conservative fashion. She had planned her ensemble as a departure from the restricted colors of mourning, but she did not want to be judged too daring, least of all at the Theater Trelayne, where Molly Gray was the undisputed leading lady.

At the climax of the action, Trelayne came onstage on horseback and carried Molly off to the cheers of his tribesmen and the audience. When the curtain closed, bouquets of flowers for Molly pelted the stage. Even the "sky critics" high in the gallery—the uppermost balcony—gave their unqualified approval.

"Splendid, Trelayne!" Jason congratulated the author, who was also leading man, when Sarah took him backstage after the final curtain. Around them, stagehands were setting up tables on the stage for the promised supper. "It was fair sailing from start to finish. Bringing that horse onstage took me by surprise, I'm bound."

"I am very pleased you liked it, Captain. It means a great deal to hear such praise from a man of the world."

"Oh, I'm a man of the world's ports, maybe, but these entertainments are strange waters to me. Still, I have not enjoyed myself so much in a long time. Truly."

"Did you see beneath the simple romance, Captain?" Trelayne regarded him intently. He was still costumed as a desert Arab, his eyes flashing from a dark visage that was partly concealed behind a black beard and mustache.

"Underneath the simple tale of an Arab beauty and the desert chieftain who wins her heart, there is a lesson for us, I suspect," Sarah ventured.

"The hero gives up his throne to follow his heart. What does that tell you?"

"It tells me that the heart cares nothing for power and position," Sarah said.

Trelayne beamed. "Precisely."

"I had not thought of it in those terms." Jason felt out of his depth.

"The theatrical art, like the others, addresses the heart, Captain, not the head," Trelayne said. "Whatever you may think of my play, I want to make you feel as well. Now if you'll excuse me, I'll fetch Molly to greet her admirers."

Sarah and Jason stood apart from the bustle on the stage. Those who remained for the supper, by invitation, were drawn from the better-dressed patrons who had watched the play from the boxes and the dress circle. Abel Calvert spied Jason and made his way to his side, followed by the Kents, as Molly and Trelayne appeared from backstage to a burst of applause.

"Who is that creature?" Calvert asked.

"That is Molly Gray," Jason said.

Molly had transformed herself from a Mohammedan princess into a Christian lady once more. She had washed away the dark skin coloring without a trace, and the diaphanous veils of the houri were replaced by an evening dress of a soft rose color.

"She was the Arab girl!" Calvert said. "I have heard she was beautiful, but the stories don't tell the half of it."

"You see!" Kent said. "For three years I have badgered him to come to the theater. Now at last he learns what he has been missing."

Molly disengaged herself from her admirers and made her way to the little group. "Captain Back, I am so glad you could come." She gave him her hand and held it while she greeted the others. "Mrs. Kent. How good to see you."

Calvert bowed when Jason presented him to the actress. "Miss Gray, you are more fair than sunrise in the mountains."

"Why thank you, Mr. Calvert. I think." Molly was amused.

"There is no finer compliment from an old mountain man, I assure you. I have seen the sun rise in the Winds and the Bitterroots, the Gros Ventres and the Sangre de Cristos. Fair mornings with beaver just slapping at the water, waiting to be caught. And you outshine them all."

"Mr. Calvert came west before any of us, Miss Gray," Kent said by way of explanation. "He was a fur trapper before he came to California to seek his fortune."

"Found it, too, but that's neither here nor there." Calvert's eyes were so steady on Molly's that she dropped her gaze.

"You must tell me of your adventures over supper, Mr. Calvert." She took his arm and seated him beside her at the nearest table, as the staff of Martin's restaurant began serving. The meal was informal, with the guests seating themselves where they liked and introducing themselves to their table companions. The actress who had played the sister to Molly's houri took the chair on Jason's free side. Her name was Helena Trout.

"Molly thinks the world of you, Mrs. Rockwell," she said to Sarah before giving Jason a brief flutter of her limpid eyes. "And she has told us all about you, Captain Beck."

Judging by the way the actress occupied Jason's attention as the meal progressed, Sarah guessed that Molly Gray had told her there was a handsome sea captain ashore on leave and that he might welcome the attentions of a willing woman. Helena Trout was just short of shameless in the way she flaunted herself, but scarcely less brazen than Molly, who leaned often toward Abel

Calvert, as if the better to hear him over the din of conversation, and pretended not to notice when he looked down her dress.

"She does it to make him jealous," Jason said to Sarah when he managed to divert Helena Trout to the Kents for the moment. He was looking at Trelayne, who had found no vacant seat at Molly's table and was eating nearby, frequently casting black looks in Molly's direction.

"Their — *liaison* has never been smooth sailing," Sarah said. "Molly wants Tommy to marry her and she flirts with every handsome man who comes near to make him jealous. Instead he grows angry. I have warned her to use different tactics with him, but she is headstrong and proud, I'm afraid." She caught herself, feeling that she had said more than was proper. It was enough that Jason Beck had guessed the true nature of the relationship between Trelayne and Molly and was not offended by it, after her assurances that she operated a respectable boardinghouse.

Sarah herself had learned quite by accident that Molly Gray often spent the night in Trelayne's bed. Two years before, a few months after she had bought the boardinghouse where Trelayne and Molly were already established as permanent guests, Sarah had risen in the small hours to use the privy in the garden. On returning to the house, she had noticed that the brass lamp on the foyer wall, which she left turned low during the night, had gone out. She was in the act of relighting it when Trelayne's door opened and Molly Gray come out onto the second-floor landing wearing nothing but a nightdress. She looked down, saw Sarah looking up at her, and came down the stairs. Sarah built up the fire in the kitchen stove while Molly begged her please not to evict her and Mr. Trelayne. She told Sarah how she had met Trelayne in Chicago, and how the theater owners there would never let him put on the shows he wrote himself. Here in San Francisco the theater was only just beginning to attract a following, and all of Tommy's money was invested it it. They couldn't afford the better hotels, she said, and the only other boardinghouses that would take theatrical people were sordid places where Molly and Trelayne could never be happy.

When Molly was done, and had dried a few tears that came to her eyes in the telling, Sarah told her she had no intention of putting them out. The simple fact was that Sarah saw Trelayne and Molly Gray as outcasts, and she sympathized with them, for she was an outcast herself.

When the after-theater supper was over, the guests excused themselves and took their leave. Abel Calvert was among the last to go. "Miss Gray, you have gained a devoted servant."

"I hope you will come again, Mr. Calvert," Molly said.

"You can depend on it, ma'am. By one week from tonight I will know the play front to back. If Mr. Trelayne falls off that horse, I will take over the part myself."

He bowed slightly to Trelayne, tipped his hat to Molly, and took his leave.

"He's nice," Molly said.

"He is rich as Croesus," Trelayne said dryly. "Maybe he would like to invest in the theater."

"I will ask him," said Molly.

"I am sure you will have an opportunity." Trelayne's tone was sharper.

"For heaven's sake, Tommy, don't be a child. Come along now, let's close up."

Sarah and Jason waited while Trelayne extinguished the last of the gaslights and locked the front doors. Outside, the street was bright with moonlight.

"It's a beautiful night!" Molly took Trelayne by the arm. "I want to walk, Tommy. Let's go to the top of a hill and look over the bay."

"I am yours to command, my dear, though I don't know why."

Four men strode past the theater, walking in the middle of the empty street. "That's Captain Farren," Sarah said. "And Mr. Sherman." She knew the banker and his wife, Ellen, from meetings of the Franchise League, an organization devoted to improving the rights of free Negroes under California law. "He is general of militia now, Captain Farren tells me."

"That's Governor Johnson with them, or I miss my

guess," said Trelayne. "Where can they be going at this hour?"

When the men reached the end of the block, Trelayne turned to Sarah and Jason. "Thank you for coming, both of you." He took Molly's hand and they walked off up California Street, making for the hill.

Sarah and Jason walked north on Kearny, her hand warm on his arm. "She repairs the damage she has done as soon as she notices it," Sarah said. "And Tommy puts up with her."

"But for how long?" Jason wondered.

Chapter 11

ayor Van Ness called on Sherman at his
bank after lunch on Friday to inform him
that Governor J. Neely Johnson would be
down from Sacramento by the evening
steamer.

"There's a chance for reconciliation here." Van Ness
wiped his brow with an embroidered handkerchief.
"Considering his friendship with Coleman, I mean."

"Coleman? The commission merchant?"

"I forget you weren't here in 'fifty-one. Coleman was
the guiding light of the old vigilance organization and
they've handed him the reins of this one, I hear. He's
young and brash, but the others look to him. The thing
is, he operated a lumber business in Sacramento in the
early days and he knew Johnson then. As I understand
it, they're friends."

Shortly after the mayor departed, a policeman presented Sherman with a writ from the county sheriff. It
was couched in legal language and said that inasmuch as
Sheriff Scannel had *"good reason to believe that a serious
breach of the peace and riot are to be apprehended, and that an
organized attempt will be made violently to wrest from my custody a prisoner committed to my charge for safe-keeping, now,
therefore, by virtue of the authority in me vested, and in the discharge of my duty as Sheriff of the County of San Francisco,
you are hereby commanded to be and appear at half past three*

o'clock P.M. this sixteenth day of May, 1856, at the Fourth District Court-room in the City Hall. . . ." Et cetera, et cetera.

Sherman was gratified to see that Scannell had acted on his suggestion to call a posse comitatus. He sent a note to Scannell saying he would come to the jail at the close of business, and allowed himself a cautious optimism that was rudely banished when David Farren arrived at three o'clock.

"Our attempt to collect the arms has confirmed most of the militia in their commitment to the vigilants, sir," Farren said. "They are already organizing in companies, mostly commanded by former militia officers. Many are veterans of the Mexican campaigns. For what it's worth, General," Farren added, "there may be some of the Union Rifles and Jackson Guards we can count on, but not enough to form a company between them."

"We will attach them to your Blues if it comes to that. How many arms did the police collect?"

"A few of the oldest muskets, half of them broken. I sent three of my men about the town to visit the gunsmiths, sir. The stocks of guns and powder have been stripped from the city's shops."

Sherman managed a thin smile. "I admire an officer who can report bad news in a straightforward manner, Farren."

"I wish it was better news, sir."

"It is my fault, not yours. You gave me good advice and I ignored it. In hindsight, we would have done better to approach the militia quietly and sway them to our side by reason. That's spilt milk now. We learn from our mistakes and go forward."

Sherman said these words with more resolve then he felt. His first order as commander of the militia had been a serious mistake. A few more like that one and he might as well personally present the Committee of Vigilance with the key to the city.

At the jail, he was shocked to learn that fewer than sixty men out of the several hundred who received the sheriff's summons were willing to serve in the posse. The jail itself was not intended to withstand an armed assault. There were houses on either side of the single-story stone building and the rear wall was dug into the slope of Telegraph Hill. It was possible to step directly onto the roof from the hillside. Sentinels posted on the roof— there were four there now—could be shot down from above, and a small force could break through the roof or burn the building, no matter how many armed men might be inside.

Sheriff Scannell was a large, gruff man who greeted Sherman with deference. Sherman suggested that men be posted in the houses overlooking the jail. Scannell sent members of the posse out at once, but they returned within minutes to say that armed vigilantes already occupied the upper floors of the houses.

"You cannot hope to defend this place against a con- certed attack," Sherman told the posse. "But your pres- ence here will exert a moral influence. Let us hope that is sufficient." Feeling no confidence that it would be, he walked home to Rincon Hill for supper.

At eight o'clock, in the gathering dusk, he met David Farren at the steamer wharf to await the Sacramento boat. At half past eight they were joined by Judge David Terry. From above the Contra Costa hills, the almost full moon spread a path of silver light on the waters of the bay.

The boat arrived late, at a quarter past nine. "What is the news of Mr. King?" Governor Johnson asked when they met him at the gangway.

"The doctors say the vomiting has stopped," Terry said. "The sponge is still in the wound and I gather there was some argument about that. Dr. Cole was against leaving it, and he is now put off the case. The others ex- press hope for a recovery."

Johnson turned to Sherman. "General, when I asked that you accept this commission, the state of things was very different. Do you wish to be relieved?"

Sherman hesitated only for a moment before saying "No, sir." What else could he say? That he looked for- ward to strutting about in a uniform and plumed hat on ceremonial occasions, but preferred to retire to the safety of his bank when armed rebels threatened the city? "I understand you know Coleman, Governor. If you can use your friendship to head off these vigilantes, I would say that friendship has never been put to better purpose."

"Where is he now?" the governor asked. His dark hair and beard were thick and wavy, his face not yet creased with care. He was thirty years old.

"They are meeting at the Turnverein gymnastic hall," Terry said. "Each day they remove to larger quarters."

"Let us see if Mr. Coleman will listen to reason."

Johnson's manner reflected his awareness that he was on the state's business and suggested a certain self-importance, but he lacked the layer of cynicism that Sherman had perceived in most politicians. He seemed uncorrupted, and Sherman thought better of him for it.

They stopped at the International Hotel on Jackson Street, where the governor took a room and refreshed himself briefly before setting out for the confrontation with Coleman. The moonlit streets were nearly deserted. In other circumstances, Sherman would have perceived the town as serene. Tonight it was tense with waiting. A few blocks from the Turnverein Hall the four men passed the Theater Trelayne, which was just closing. Two couples in front of the theater watched the quartet pass by.

"Damn fine-looking women," Terry said.

"The black-haired one is Molly Gray," Farren said. "She is Trelayne's leading lady."

"In his bed as well as on his stage, from what I hear," Terry added.

A few days before, Farren had expected to attend Trelayne's opening. Then, his militia post was little more than membership in a gentleman's marching society. Now it seemed only slightly unnatural that he was in the company of the state's governor and his general of militia, bent on a mission that could mean life or death for James Casey, and perhaps for others as well, while the citizenry went about their amusements as usual.

"What sort of man is Coleman?" Sherman asked Johnson.

"Forty-niner," Johnson said. "He's supposed to be some sort of distant relation of President Washington. You can't always tell what he's thinking."

The gymnastic hall was on Bush Street, between

Dupont and Stockton. Governor Johnson knocked loudly on the heavy oaken door with the wrought-iron knocker.

"Who's there?" came a voice from within.

"Governor Neely Johnson."

The door opened a crack. "Who's that with you?" demanded the voice.

"Judge Terry of the supreme court, Major General William Sherman of the California Militia, and Captain Farren of the San Francisco Blues."

Hearing his full title spoken with so much authority made Sherman want to look about to see who such an august personage might be. They were shown to a barroom off one end of the narrow vestibule and left alone.

"There is something I have wanted to ask you, Sherman," Johnson said. "How did you save your bank last year? It was a miracle, from where I sat."

"I kept my doors open, Governor."

"As simple as that? You had the courage not to show fear?"

"I knew my bank was sound, And I had the help of a few good friends." There was much more Sherman could have said, but that was the truth in a nutshell. On President Washington's birthday the previous year, the banking firm of Page, Bacon & Company had failed to open following a run of several days on their bank, which took place when news arrived in San Francisco that their New York branch had failed and there were fears for the home office in St. Louis. At the time, Page, Bacon was the most respected bank in San Francisco. The next day, the doors of Adams & Company, second only to Page, Bacon in the public trust, had remained bolted, along with those of Wells, Fargo. Public confidence in San Francisco's banks broke, and the run extended to every firm.

At Lucas, Turner & Company, Sherman's tellers paid out $400,000 in coin and bullion on February 23 and ended the day with less than $50,000 in the vaults. Yet even in the midst of the rush there were hopeful signs. Some of the bank's wealthiest depositors asked Sherman if their money was safe, and being assured that it was, they left the bank without making any withdrawal. During the night, Sherman called in what loans he could and received vital help from two old Army friends, Joseph Libby Folsom and Richard P. Hammond. Folsom provided $25,000 of his own money and Hammond, as collector of the port, gave Sherman $40,000 in government funds entrusted to him for construction of a new Custom House. The next day the run petered out in the face of word that many respected men had made loans and deposits to Lucas, Turner, demonstrating their faith in its soundness. At the end of business on the twenty-fourth, deposits narrowly outbalanced withdrawals. By the start of the following week, Lucas, Turner & Company had replaced Page, Bacon and Adams & Company at the pinnacle of public trust, and Sherman repaid the life-saving loans.

The memory cheered Sherman perversely and he felt something approaching delight in his new predicament. Given the choice, he would gladly face San Francisco's reborn Vigilance Committee single-handed rather than having to live through another day like February 23, 1855.

A door opened and William Tell Coleman entered the barroom, accompanied by four others. Coleman was smooth shaven and smooth-faced. A long forelock was plastered down with pomade, nearly reaching to his left ear. He appeared agitated as he shook hands quickly with each member of the governor's party and introduced his colleagues as Miers Truett, Thomas Smiley, Isaac Bluxome and Abel Calvert.

Smiley's close-set eyes met Sherman's but he did not offer his hand. As contractor for the new Custom House, Smiley had approved Hammond's loan to Sherman's bank during the crisis the year before. Later he had sued Sherman, charging mishandling of the funds. Less than a month ago, the judge in the case had decided wholly in Sherman's favor.

Sherman shook Abel Calvert's hand firmly. Calvert & Winston had survived the bank run too. Sherman judged Calvert to be solid and dependable and he was glad to see the banker among those with Coleman.

Truett towered above the others, while Bluxome, whom Coleman introduced as secretary to the Vigilance

Committee, stayed close to Coleman's side. He was dark-bearded and dark-eyed, and he held a ruled pad on which he made notes during the ensuing conversation.

"Coleman, what the devil is the matter here?" Johnson demanded when the pleasantries were barely done.

Coleman faced the governor squarely. "Governor, we are of the opinion that this shooting in our streets has got to stop."

"There are lawful means for that. What is the reason for reviving this organization, when you have courts and juries?"

"The courts and the police are full of men like Casey. Some of them are no better than thugs. They stuff the ballot boxes to get themselves elected and they pack the juries."

"You're exaggerating," Johnson said. "There are honest judges and juries, if honest men don't shirk their duty." His emphasis on the last words was a pointed reminder that evasion of jury duty amounted almost to a civic amusement among the better citizens of San Francisco.

"We won't see Casey turned loose," Coleman said.

"Nor will I, if he's guilty," Johnson replied calmly, "but the time is long past for mobs and vigilantes."

"We have the people behind us, Governor." Coleman drew himself up to his full height, which was sufficient to look Neely Johnson in the eye. "Their representatives are gathered in this hall to determine on a course of action."

"*Elected* representatives?" Judge Terry inquired. There was a hard edge beneath the soft tone.

Johnson took Terry's cue. "You have popular support, I acknowledge that. And I propose a way you can use it for the public good. If your organization will back the civil authorities, I will guarantee that Casey will not escape punishment. There is a grand jury now in session. I give you my word that if King dies the grand jury will produce a true bill, and Casey will be tried as speedily as the law allows."

Coleman weighed the governor's offer. "The people have no faith in Sheriff Scannell and his crowd."

"I will take personal responsibility for the safety of the

prisoner," Johnson said. "I give you my word as the chief executive officer of California that if you support the constituted authorities in this, I will do as I have promised in order to save this city and the state the disgrace of mob violence."

"We will require a condition of our own," Thomas Smiley said. The plump merchant reminded Sherman of a bulldog guarding something he regarded as his own. "Some of our men must be allowed into the jail to see that Casey doesn't escape."

"Impossible!" Sherman protested. "The sheriff and the members of his posse would never stand for it. You could be the guard from a Trojan horse."

"Without this condition, the Committee will never agree." Isaac Bluxome spoke it as a pronouncement of fact.

"If we are to take you at your word, you must accept ours," Coleman supported him.

Johnson looked at Sherman.

"I am against it, Governor."

Johnson glanced at Terry, who shook his head, then returned his gaze to Coleman. "Is there no other way you will be satisfied?"

"There is none."

"Very well," Johnson said. "But your men must be limited to no more than ten. They will be assistant guards and under the orders of the sheriff."

With the governor's consent given, Sherman sought a way to reduce the risk. "You must notify the governor and withdraw your guards from the jail before you take any public action. On your honor as gentlemen."

Coleman looked around his circle. Truett and Bluxome nodded. Smiley shrugged.

"Fair is fair," Abel Calvert said.

Coleman held out his hand and Governor Johnson took it. "You have bound yourselves to abide by the law," he said. "We will go ahead to the jail. Give us a little time to prepare the sheriff for your guards before you send them along."

Sarah Rockwell bent over her pen, intent on her writing. She sat at the mahogany secretary in her bedroom beneath the stairs, just across the back hallway from the kitchen. Not long before, the kitchen clock had struck one. Unable to sleep, Sarah had risen and put on a dressing gown. She had not written her brother Peter in several weeks and she had missed yesterday's steamer, but it didn't matter that some time would pass before she could dispatch the letter. Writing Peter always eased her worries. He was her confidant.

Today's Herald *is much reduced in size. Supporters of the Vigilance Committee have withdrawn their advertising and canceled their subscriptions in an attempt to silence Mr. Nugent, but he is stalwart in his refusal to yield. He continues to proclaim Mr. Casey's right to a fair trial and today he wrote, "If the sacred position of a public journalist is to be degraded by the compulsory subservience to a cabal, we confess we have not the stomach for the office."*

This business upsets me more than I can say. You know how I feel about this place. You saw how happy I was when you came to take me home and I would not go. Do you remember what you said? "If I had found you miserable, Sarey, I would have carried you off by force. But I have never seen you so well." And I am still well, but for the loss of my husband. Yet if I had Haven to depend on, I would not be as strong as I am today. It may be shameful to say so, but it is true. San Francisco has been my sanctuary. It received me kindly after Haven's death, and when I was transformed from a wealthy widow to a boardinghouse keeper by the spite of the Rockwells, no one thought the worse of me. This disregard for class is what I like best about the city. What could be more welcome to a seaman's daughter from Kittery Point! I have come into my own here, Peter. I have learned how to depend on myself.

Brave-sounding words, yet today I write you for reassurance and comfort, although all this uproar will be past by the time you receive this letter, certainly by the time I can have a reply. Perhaps the vigilants, knowing the majority are behind them, will content themselves with acting as watchdogs over the judicial process. Every hour brings new speculation but no action as yet. I will write more when the issue is resolved.

I have a new boarder. Captain Beck is the master of the China clipper Sarah B. Watson. *He is lodging here while he attempts to sell his cargo of Carolina rice. He chafes at being forced ashore by commercial matters and has no patience for landsmen's affairs. Does this sound familiar? How often our father spoke in just those words! Molly is flirting with the handsome captain outrageously, of course, just as she flirted with David Farren when he moved here last fall. (Poor David still carries a torch for her. I must find him someone suitable. Now that my mourning is to end, I can be more active in society.)*

Sarah sat back and read what she had written, restraining an impulse to tear it up. How could she make a match for David Farren if she sold her house and left San Francisco? Should she tell Peter what she planned to do when she returned to the east? Would he help her? Would he understand that she sought justice and not just vengeance? These same questions had kept her awake, and writing to Peter had provided no answers.

None of her boarders had noticed her advertisement in the *Herald*, putting the house up for sale. The doings of the Vigilance Committee occupied their attention and Sarah was grateful for the distraction the unrest provided. What would they say when they learned she was abandoning them?

She rose from the desk and went out to pace the hallway. Seeing light from the parlor, she imagined that someone had forgotten to put out the lamp, but when she entered the room she found Jason Beck with a book in his hands.

" 'Tis always the same for me," he said, looking up. "The first nights ashore, I can't sleep."

Sarah pulled her cotton dressing gown closer about her. "Can I get you something? Some tea or cocoa?"

"Don't be troubling yourself, Mrs. Rockwell. 'Tis not for lack of anything that I am awake. It is too quiet for me to sleep."

"I think this city is never quiet." From her parents' house in Kittery Point, Sarah could hear the waves on the shore while lying in her bed. Here, at night, when the wind was off the bay, she could hear the bell buoys clang, and sometimes she dreamed she was a little girl in her old bed again.

"I miss the sounds of my ship," Jason said. "I hear the water against the hull. I hear the canvas and the ropes and the creaks below deck. No matter how sound a vessel may be, she breathes and she sighs. She makes love to the sea." He came to himself as if waking from a dream. He got to his feet. "Forgive me. I had no leave to speak that way to a lady."

"Please don't apologize, Captain. Your words were . . . poetic, not rude. Besides, I was not raised a lady. I came from humble beginnings, like you."

"Not so humble as me."

"Shall we contest our humility?" There was mischief in her eyes. With her hair down, dressed for sleep, he saw the young girl she had been not so long ago.

"Nay. I will grant that we are as like as two peas in a pod, if you ask it. But as we have attended the theater to mark the end of your mourning, I should like to know its cause, if you are willing to tell me."

She hesitated for only a moment before answering. "My husband died when we were crossing the Isthmus. We had been married for less than a year."

"I am very sorry."

"Molly is right. It is time I left that behind me."

"We carry the past within us, but we can live in the present."

"You are a philosopher, Captain." She was teasing him soberly.

"My philosophy is borrowed from books." He held up the volume in his hand, a copy of *The Pickwick Papers*.

"Then I will leave you in good company. I hope you sleep well."

When she was gone, Jason resumed his seat, but for the first time in as long as he could recall, a Dickens nar-

rative failed to hold his attention. He blew out the lamp
and sat in the dark, his thoughts measured by the ticking
of the clock on the mantel. If Sarah Rockwell's husband
died while they were crossing the Isthmus, why had she
not returned to Maine? he wondered. That was the natural course for a young widow. Instead, she had come to
California. Now, with her widow's weeds put away, she
would have suitors. She was a woman worth courting,
but not for a sailor who would be gone on the first tide
when his ship was rid of its cargo.

After a quarter of an hour the front door opened and
Molly Gray entered, stifling laughter. Trelayne was close
behind her. The foyer lamp cast a pale arm into the parlor but Jason sat in the shadows beyond its reach. He
saw Trelayne take Molly in his arms. Their lips met and
Trelayne's hand moved to Molly's breast. She murmured
something in his ear and they went up the stairs without
entering the darkened parlor, where the scent of Sarah
Rockwell's hair lingered in Jason's memory.

Chapter 12

On Saturday morning, Abel Calvert found Su-Yan Quan loading his cart with fresh vegetables and fruits in preparation for his morning rounds. Su-Yan's house was on Dupont Street south of Broadway, in a district called Little China. It was a frame house in the California style, equal in size to Calvert's own.

"Mr. Calvert. Good morning to you, sir!" Su-Yan bowed.

"Good morning, Mr. Quan." Calvert was struck once again by how well the Chinaman managed the r's in the English language. Like many, he had believed that the Oriental palate was incapable of producing the sound, but Su-Yan overcame the physical handicap, if indeed there was one.

"May I offer you tea?"

"No, thank you, Mr. Quan. I have things to attend to. I wonder if I might speak with you on a matter of business, if you'll overlook my lack of manners this once."

Calvert had taken tea with the Quans on two occasions. Su-Yan's home was very different from any white man's household, but Calvert was comfortable there. He had eaten in the lodges of the Arikaree and the Sioux, the Snakes and Gros Ventres and even the Blackfoot. He had lain with their women and he had lived for four years with an Indian wife. He was not easily put off by people with different ways. He would have enjoyed a good cup of China tea with Su-Yan today, but things were moving quickly and he had no time to waste. Refusing Su-Yan's offer of hospitality and launching at once into business would be considered rude. Like the Indians, the immigrants from the Celestial Kingdom preferred to sit and eat and jaw about inconsequential matters before getting down to serious talk. But like the Indians, the Chinese could shorten the preliminaries if pressed.

Su-Yan bowed, acceding to Calvert's request. He gestured to the covered porch that extended along the north and east sides of his home. The porch furniture was Western, the chairs and lounges wicker. The cushions were upholstered in a pleasant flowered print.

"Your wife is well, I hope," Calvert said when they were seated.

"My wife and my family are in good health."

Calvert approached his business obliquely, by discussing a matter of general concern. "The city is calm today. Most businesses will open, I think."

"And your bank?"

"Winston is there now." Winston lived for banking and he was honest to a fault. It would not occur to him to steal. Nor would he have the first notion how to guide the bank's policy without Abel Calvert to make those decisions.

"Perhaps a period of calm will allow sensible men to prevail." Su-Yan was asking for reassurance.

"Perhaps bears will sprout wings and fly."

"You expect trouble, then?" Abel Calvert was the only white man who spoke with Su-Yan as one man to another. The banker's observations offered him a window into the world of the *guey low*—the white devils—from which he had gained much insight over the years.

"When Injuns get all dressed up to go on the warpath, they ain't satisfied 'til they lift some hair," Calvert said.

"I am told the governor is in the city. Can he not calm the hot tempers, certainly?"

"The Committee of Vigilance threatens the governor's power. He will fight them if they try to take Casey from jail."

"You yourself are a member of this Committee, I believe?"

Calvert concealed his surprise. How in the devil did the Chinaman know that? "It is necessary to know what they plan if I wish to keep doing business with them."

"Does Governor Johnson have the means to oppose them?"

"We have the arms of most of the militia companies. A few remain loyal to the state."

"Then there is the possibility of conflict." This was what Su-Yan feared above all, but he said it matter-of-factly, as if making an observation about the weather.

"I hope not. Some of us are working within the Committee to keep the peace. We can achieve what we want without violence, if the leaders keep their heads."

" 'The king approaches his temple.' "

"I beg your pardon?"

"It is a Chinese saying, Mr. Calvert. I apologize. I was thinking aloud, as you say." The saying had come to Su-Yan's mind unbidden, from the Book of Changes. It was from the hexagram *Huan*, and it addressed the rigid frame of mind that overcame a ruler filled with the righteousness of his cause. By acting from his spiritual side, the wise ruler could see himself once more as part of the greater spirit of all men. Su-Yan hoped Abel Calvert's moderation would sway the Vigilance Committee to a wise course. "Perhaps good sense will prevail."

"There is no reason for this unrest to touch your people."

"We are like the leaves blowing in the wind, Mr. Calvert. Sometimes we are disturbed by matters not of our world. In time the wind passes and we come to rest."

"Even so, we all have some things in common. Take your people, now. They have a fondness for rice. Won't live without it, so you tell me. Just now rice is low. That's bad for the seller, good for the buyer. I might know where you could get enough top-quality rice to see your people through the summer, no matter what happens to the price."

Su-Yan was relieved to learn the true reason for Calvert's visit. "Certainly, rice is a staple in my community. For this reason we keep a reserve against troubled times."

"So your stores are adequate?"

"For the time being."

"Let me be blunt. If you had the opportunity to acquire plenty of rice at a price that would enable you to sell at a profit before anyone else in town, would you be interested? My bank could help you finance the purchase."

"I will be blunt as well, Mr. Calvert. As a merchant, I act for my people. I act with the consent of my associates, for the good of the community. We are strangers here. We must be conservative in our actions. Your offer is attractive, but it involves more risk than I judge wise for a man in my position."

Su-Yan was pleased with himself. As business conditions in San Francisco worsened over the past year, he had foreseen that white merchants would revive their speculations in essential foodstuffs. As before, they had tried to inflate the price of flour first. Rice followed flour as summer followed springtime. It was the order of things here. Thanks to Su-Yan and his colleagues, Little China had a reserve of rice large enough to wait out the fluctuations in the white merchants' markets.

"I am grateful for the help you have offered in the past," Su-Yan said, bringing the conversation to an end. "Certainly I trust we will do business again."

"Certainly. No reason not to. Where it benefits us both." Calvert got to his feet. After mutual expressions of goodwill and wishes for health and prosperity, he took his leave and walked back downtown feeling that his time had been very well spent. The visit with Su-Yan Quan had produced two pieces of valuable information. He had learned that the Chinese merchants would not meddle in the current speculation in grains, and this in turn reassured him that his bank's investments in the Chinese community were safe.

No other American bank would lend money to the Chinese, but Calvert had responded positively the first time Su-Yan approached him, back when the Chinaman was starting his vegetable business. As Su-Yan's enterprises grew, he had become one of Calvert & Winston's most important customers. The association was a well-kept secret. Calvert charged Su-Yan interest one half percent higher than he charged his white customers, although it had quickly become clear to him that Chinese business practices were just as predictable and just as sound as any white man's, although conducted with more subtlety. Someday he would reduce the rate he charged Su-Yan, but he would do it when he could get something valuable in exchange. Don't give away something for nothing. That was a principle even more honored in Little China than on Montgomery Street.

Whatever actions the Committee of Vigilance might take in the coming days, Calvert would do his best to see that they left the Chinese out of it.

He walked with a spring in his step. For the third day in a row the air was balmy, giving the city a deceptive feeling of benevolence. The shops were open and the streets were crowded. The expressions of the people revealed no concern more worrisome than getting on with business. In just a few days the city had accepted the new state of affairs, although beneath the surface things were far from normal.

Calvert tipped his hat to a pretty whore who gave him a crooked smile. He felt a stirring in his loins that was occasioned not by the whore but by the memory of Molly Gray as he had seen her last night, dark-skinned, with fire in her eyes, costumed as the Arab houri in Trelayne's play. The smell of her French lavender perfume, which no respectable woman would dare to wear, was fixed indelibly in Calvert's memory, as were the contours of her shoulders and breasts, which he had ample occasion to inspect during supper after the play. He had longed to touch her skin, so fair and unblemished, and the thought of kissing her set him on fire.

It was not only the attractions of Molly's flesh that exerted such a powerful effect on him. There was another stirring as well, for she touched memories he thought he had put to rest for good. When the houri appeared on the stage of the Theater Trelayne, Calvert's breath had caught in his throat. It was as if his Arikaree wife, Gray Dawn, had climbed down from the burial scaffold where a grief-stricken Abel Calvert had lovingly arranged her earthly remains. The houri's dark skin, the flashing eyes, the flowing black hair, all were the image of Gray Dawn, dead now for sixteen years, during which time the longing and the pain had never entirely left him. When he was seated with Molly Gray, seeing her without the paint and costume, she aroused those memories again. She touched him where he thought he had turned to stone, and awakened feelings that had only risen once before, in the arms of an Arikaree girl of nineteen winters who called herself Gray Dawn. In Molly Gray he sensed a spirit that was mate to his own.

"Damn foolishness," he said under his breath. At the corner of Montgomery, he turned into a doorway and presented himself to a clerk who knew him well. "Tell Mr. Frye I am here to see him."

When Abel Calvert left him, Su-Yan pulled the loaded cart into the shade of the house. From a bucket he took a ladle of water and sprinkled it over the vegetables. He repeated this several times, then covered the cart with a bedsheet. Today he would make his rounds a little later than was his custom.

On wakening that morning, Su-Yan had felt a vague foreboding. When Abel Calvert appeared, he feared the white man had come with bad news. Learning he wanted only to sell Captain Beck's rice had eased Su-Yan's fears somewhat, but still the foreboding lingered.

"I thought you were gone," his wife said when he entered her kitchen. With the help of her mother, she was making *ho fun*, the large rice noodles he liked so well.

"I will be below for a time. Do not disturb me." He descended the steep stairs to the cellar, which was divided into two rooms, one large, the other very small. The large room was a root cellar that extended beyond the foundations of the house. Building it had been expensive, but worth the investment. The walls and floor were cement and it remained at the same temperature year-round. It was almost empty now, with the approach of summer. In the fall, Su-Yan bought root vegetables and apples and gourds to store. When those things were our of season, he sold them at a handsome profit. The damp, cool air of the cellar suggested life lying dormant, fortune held in reserve, protection against danger, and it comforted him.

Taking a key from his pocket, Su-Yan unlocked a narrow door that led to the small room built behind the stairs. The floor and walls were of teak planks exquisitely fitted together and pegged. There was not a single nail in the room. The rug on the floor had been his mother's, and hers before that. A low wooden stand contained an altar, a shelf and a single drawer.

The room was his place of meditation. No one but he had set foot in it since it was finished. He bowed to the crucifix on the wall, then to the small Buddha that sat, jolly and squat, on the altar. From the shelf below the altar, which held a Koran and a Torah and a Bible as well as volumes on Confucianism, Taoism and Buddhism, Su-Yan withdrew the Book of Changes.

Seating himself cross-legged on the rug, he lit a stick of joss. He removed ink, paper and brush from the drawer, and the linen sack that held the yarrow stalks. He had gathered the yarrow himself in this new land the Chinese called *gum sahn*—the golden mountain— convinced that the plants native to California would give the surest guidance about how to conduct himself here. The flowering tops had long since found their way into teas and tonics. Yarrow was of great value for the health of women's reproductive organs. Su-Yan's wife had availed herself of much of it for that purpose, turning a deaf ear to her husband's suggestions that her organs would remain in good health if she readmitted him to her bed and exercised them in the manner nature intended.

Su-Yan felt a momentary annoyance but he put it quickly aside. He took care of his physical needs elsewhere, in the houses of prostitution operated only for Chinese, and sometimes with Western women as well.

He returned to the task at hand, shutting out all other thoughts. The bunching of the yarrow stalks, the transfer from hand to hand, the counting of those that remained, were actions rendered automatic by years of repetition. Six times he cast the stalks, pausing each time to dip the brush in ink and draw a line on the paper. When the hexagram was complete he looked at the six lines and a shiver of fear passed through him. The hexagram was *Po*.

It signified a breaking or splitting apart, and it was the only one among the sixty-four hexagrams of the *I Ching* that seemed unavoidably to bode ill.

Su-Yan forced himself to remember that the oracle did not predict the future. It merely reflected the moment. And in doing so, it revealed the *Tao* of the moment. But the *Tao* was the underlying flow that affected all events both temporal and spiritual, and a flow had direction.

He took up the Book of Changes and skimmed quickly over the familiar commentaries, seeking any hopeful sign. *The dark forces are rising*, said one sage. *They overflow the light and dispel it. There is nothing to be gained by going ahead*, said another. *Treacherous men are rising to power. Honorable men cannot prevent this. The wise man will sit quietly and bide his time. There is no blame in this course.* A small ray of hope. *Splitting apart means ruin*, said a third commentary. But ruin for whom? *The natural ebb and flow of fortune resembles the tides of the sea. Fullness follows emptiness.*

An image formed in Su-Yan's mind of a dark tide rising against the rocks on the shore, covering them. But the rocks bided their time and did not struggle against the black waters. In time the tide receded and the rocks emerged again, cleansed and renewed.

He turned to the second hexagram produced by the changing lines in the first. *There is much to gain*, the sages counseled. *New enterprises find their reward.*

Su-Yan took a deep breath and let it out slowly, releasing the last of his fear. The oracle confirmed that danger was abroad in the affairs of men, but if he behaved with wisdom and circumspection he could come through the difficult times unscathed and perhaps even profit by the experience.

nce again Jason paced the city to no end. He found Kent at his office after lunch, but the shipowner gave him little cause for hope. "Don't let the look of the town fool you," Kent said. "The firms and shops may be open, but business is at low ebb. We are caught in irons, Jason."

In the afternoon, Jason visited the *Sarah B. Watson*. The starboard watch was short by two when it came back aboard. The missing men were Grimes and a Kanaka named Little Jack. Grimes was no great loss, but no one was more nimble in the rigging than Little Jack, whatever the weather. The crew was surly at the news there would be no shore leave for a time. Melchior mustered the ship's company aft on the weather deck and Jason addressed them from the poop, saying the landsmen's quarrels were none of their affair and there was work to be done aboard. Leave would resume soon, he promised, if they must remain in port for long. He did not tell them that the prospects for selling the cargo were gloomy just now, but he told Melchior everything he knew about conditions in the city.

It was nearing suppertime when Jason approached Sarah Rockwell's boardinghouse. Joshua Norton arose from a chair on the veranda as Jason climbed the steps. "Welcome back to harbor, Captain Beck."

"I am too long in harbor, Mr. Norton. This damned

business will keep my ship here until the sea gives up her dead."

Norton was beaming at him.

"You seem in fine spirits, Mr. Norton."

"I have found the capital, Captain! I will buy your rice."

Jason was speechless, but Norton could scarcely contain himself. "I received word at midday that Mr. Calvert, of Calvert and Winston, wished to see me. They are bankers, you know. It was our own Dickie Howell brought the message, bless him. When I presented myself at Calvert's bank, Mr. Calvert received me like royalty."

Norton was so puffed up with pride it seemed to Jason that he might burst. "Somehow Mr. Calvert got wind of my interest in your cargo. He offered to lend me the money to purchase the exclusive commission to sell it, and of course I accepted! He will transfer the funds to my account on Monday. I have spoken to Mr. Kent already and we have agreed on the terms."

"That is wonderful," Sarah Rockwell said when they went in the house and told her the news, but it seemed to Jason that her reaction was subdued. "Should you be taking such a risk?" she asked Norton when he paused for breath in relating his triumph.

"Risk is a part of any business endeavor, Mrs. Rockwell. What matters is, I control the cargo. I will pay Mr. Kent now for the right to buy it within the next month at a fixed price, and a very good one, I must say. When I find a buyer, I take delivery of the cargo and pass it on to the buyer at once."

"What if you don't find a buyer?" Sarah said.

He brushed away her concern. "I am certain we will see a correction in the market soon. In a few weeks, Captain, you will be on the high seas again!"

Molly and Trelayne had stopped to listen as they prepared to go to the theater. "Shame on you, Mr. Norton," Molly said now. "You have robbed us of Captain Beck's company."

"What?" Norton was stung by the rebuke. "I was only trying to help."

"And you have helped more than any other man in this city," Jason assured him.

"I hope to see your ship before you sail, Captain," said Trelayne. "But I warn you, I get seasick in any weather."

"When she is docked to unload, you will all take dinner in the captain's cabin," Jason said. "She's steady as a rock at the wharf."

In the middle of the night, Jason started awake for no reason he could discern. A breeze stirred the curtains at his window and a patch of moonlight overlay the hooked rug. Kit, the gray cat, was curled up at the foot of his bed like a hedgehog. And then a spectral figure of white rose from the chair. Only the head and arms had distinct form. The rest swayed as if blown by the wind, and the sight brought to Jason's mind the memory of a headsail torn loose from its lines on the recent passage around the Horn. Freed from its battle with the wind, the wisp of canvas had remained aloft for a time, drifting to leeward, until it sank at last into the leaping waves.

He blinked to clear the sleep from his vision, but the phantasm remained. It floated toward him, silhouetted now against the window, and he saw it was not a phantasm at all but something real and intelligible. The flowing white shape was a thin cotton nightdress given substance by the outline of a woman's body.

"You're to leave us, Captain." Molly Gray put a hand on his cheek and the fragrance of lavender enveloped him.

"Aye. So it seems." His voice was strained and husky in his ears.

"Then this will be good-bye." She lowered herself to the bed and his arms went around her of their own accord, his hands moving over her body to assure himself it was real.

"Why, Molly?" he asked, when the patch of moonlight had moved across the floor and begun to climb the wall.

"Because I wanted to know you in this way." She sat up to look down on him, and he saw the perfection of her breasts, which his hands already knew. "Because you need the company of someone who is not yours to command. Because soon you will be gone. And because I am going to do something foolish and then you will no longer want me, even if you stay."

At breakfast, Molly wore a simple day dress of pale blue gingham. She flirted with Trelayne and treated Jason like a favorite brother, and she shared in the congratulations for the previous day's newspaper reviews of *The Bedouin and the Houri*, which were highly favorable.

David Farren had attended the Saturday-night performance. "This play is just the thing to improve the civic mood," he said. "If the city stays calm today, I'll begin to breathe easier." As on the day before, Farren had taken a walk before breakfast. He reported the streets still quiet. The morning was gray and breezy under solid clouds that hung low over the city.

Sunday breakfast in the boardinghouse was an elaborate affair that began a half hour later than usual. There were buckwheat cakes and corn dodgers, bacon and pork chops and scrapple, eggs and potatoes and several kinds of fruit. The leisurely enjoyment of the meal was a ritual, interrupted today by the arrival of Dickie Howell, who carried a letter for Farren.

Farren read it quickly. "General Sherman has asked me to Sunday dinner, and I must see the governor at his hotel first. I think I'll get a horse from the livery. It's a pleasant day for a ride."

"A sail is pleasant in any weather." Sarah turned to Jason. "What would you say to an outing, Captain Beck?"

"Are we to forgo church, then?" Jason tried not to sound too hopeful. Before breakfast, Sarah had invited him to accompany her to the Unitarian church.

"God will be glad to see two New England sailors testing the waters," she said. "My sloop is not so grand a vessel as yours, but she'll hold two points closer to the wind or you can have your next week's lodgings free."

"Now there's a challenge to whet a seaman's appetite," Trelayne said.

" 'Tis no challenge, Mr. Trelayne. Any sloop can point better to the wind than a ship. Mrs. Rockwell is offering me a fool's wager."

"But I ask nothing from you if you lose, Captain."

Sarah's eyes sparked and Jason saw that she was teasing him.

He felt more optimistic than at any time since Ned Rollick had first told him the cargo could not be unloaded. Even if Norton's scheme involved further delay, it gave him heart. If the city remained quiet today he would send word to the *Sarah B.* tomorrow, resuming shore leave for the crew.

"You need some fresh air." Molly touched Trelayne's cheek. "You're pale. Let's get some horses from the livery and ride to the ocean beach. We haven't been there in weeks. No! I know! Let's go sailing with Sarah and Captain Beck."

"I'm counting on you," Sarah said quickly. "It wouldn't be proper for us to go alone."

Molly laughed. "I don't believe San Francisco's respectable ladies would approve of theatrical people as chaperons."

"I am green at the very thought of Sarah's boat," Trelayne said. "A ride would be better."

Molly took his hand. "We'll ride to the beach and later we'll have supper downtown. Helena Trout told me about a new restaurant on Washington Street." Since the reform administration of Mayor Garrison, who had preceded Van Ness, San Francisco's theaters were closed on Sunday. Trelayne and Molly had the evening free.

Sarah saw that Dickie Howell was surveying the remnants of breakfast. "Sit down, Dickie. I'll bring you a clean plate." When she returned, she said, "When you have filled yourself up, you can come sailing with Captain Beck and me."

"Thank you, Mrs. Rockwell, but I've messages to carry for the Executive Committee. I'm making more money every day than I used to make in a week."

"Money is the root of evil, Dickie," Joshua Norton advised him. "If you stay after breakfast, I'll tell you a story."

Dickie liked Mr. Norton's stories, but he liked the feel of the gold and silver coins in his pocket even more. "Thank you, Mr. Norton, but I'll have to be getting downtown." He reached for the corn dodgers and the pork chops.

"If you were to accept Mrs. Rockwell's invitation and live here with us, I would tell you a story each evening before your bedtime." Norton watched Dickie hopefully, but the boy's attention turned to the fried eggs and buckwheat cakes, which he heaped on his plate as if this were his last meal on earth.

Jason carried his own plate to the kitchen, where Sarah was pouring hot water from a kettle into the dishpan. "You can't go back on your offer now. Not when you've promised me a sail."

"You're right," she said. "It is too good a breeze to stand on propriety. I will pack a picnic lunch and be ready in half an hour."

Sarah's boat was a trim little gaff-rigged sloop that bobbed at a mooring off North Beach in the lee of Meiggs' Wharf. By means of a rope that extended from a post on shore to a piling in the water, where it passed through a pulley, Sarah hauled the boat to the beach. It was a clever arrangement, made originally for the use of a Sicilian fisherman, that allowed her to enter the boat with dry skirts at any tide.

The sloop was just eighteen feet long, but broad of beam and surprisingly at ease in the swift currents and changeable winds of San Francisco Bay. As soon as the sails were up and the centerboard down, she raced over the waves. Jason noted that Sarah looked constantly from the telltale atop the single mast to the patterns of the wind and the waves.

"You didn't tell me you were a sailor."

"A lady isn't supposed to tell a gentleman all about herself. She is supposed to be modest. You are supposed to discover my secrets on your own."

He regarded her steadily and she soon turned away, showing a sailor's concern for the set of the sail.

"We could visit my ship if you like." Three miles downwind, the *Sarah B. Watson* swung from her anchor amidst a fleet of vessels resting idle.

"From your anchorage we would spend half the day beating upwind to Saucelito, and I intend to be there before noontime."

"We have a destination then?"

"Oh yes, Captain. I have planned this day to make

you forget your cares. Thanks to Mr. Norton you may soon be rid of your cargo and gone. I want you to remember San Francisco kindly."

"You shouldn't call me Captain aboard your own boat. You're the skipper here."

"I've grown used to Captain."

The first time they came about, she gave him almost no warning. "Ready about!" she called, and she put the tiller hard over as she said "Helm's alee," leaving Jason scrambling to handle the jib sheets while she took care of the mainsail.

She kept close to the shore for a time, tacking westward toward the Golden Gate. The morning clouds were retreating to sea. Before long, sunshine flooded the waters, interrupted only occasionally by small clouds that broke free of the gray mass offshore and scudded swiftly across the bay before the fresh breeze that came westnor'west.

Off a rocky point west of the city, Sarah put the boat out from shore on a reach that would take them across the channel. The deeper waters were choppy, the waves capped with streaks of foam. The sloop's bow threw up spray that flew back in their faces until Jason shifted himself farther astern, close to Sarah, trimming the boat to ride higher in the bow. He leaned back against the cockpit coaming, the sun warm on his back, and his worries about rice and landsmen's politics were far behind.

"What's her name?" he asked.

"*Katahdin.*"

"For Maine's tallest mountain."

"Have you been there?"

"Nay. 'Tis too far inland for a seaman."

"My father took me. We climbed to the very top. You should see the view."

"I like the view from high places. Most often from a ship's rigging, as you can imagine."

"I will take you for a better view than that today."

In the middle of the channel the waves were larger and the spray from *Katahdin*'s bow threatened to soak her crew to the skin. Sarah produced oilskin caps and long sou'westers from a compartment beneath the stern thwart. Soon she was indistinguishable from Jason so long as she kept her skirts tucked beneath her.

"I rarely sail in a dress," she said. "I wear bloomers when I'm alone, but I didn't want to shock you."

Jason made a face. "Those awful things. That woman should be keel-hauled."

"I agree with you that they don't look well, Captain. That's why I don't wear them often. But they are practical, and Mrs. Bloomer has many other noteworthy accomplishments. I don't suppose you have read her newspaper?"

"I didn't know she had one," Jason admitted.

"She wrote for her husband's paper first, when he had just the one in Seneca County. Her own paper was called *The Lily* and it had considerable success. I think it is a wonderful accomplishment for a woman to do so well in a man's occupation."

"If this newspaper of Mrs. Bloomer's was such a success, why do you speak of it as something over and done?" Jason's tone was carefully neutral.

A gust of wind heeled *Katahdin* until the waves lapped at the gunwale, but Sarah held her course, leaning outboard shoulder to shoulder with Jason to counterbalance the force of the wind. She braced herself against the thwart with a stockinged leg that was extended for a time beyond the shelter of her skirts. She did not retract the exposed limb and settle herself back until the gust subsided.

"Her husband bought other papers in the middle west and she wanted to help him with those. They share their lives fully, both the domestic side and the work too. I think there would be more happy marriages if we all did that." When Jason remained silent, she said, "Mrs. Bloomer's real cause is temperance, of course. She continues to lecture about the evils of rum."

"My first night at your house, you promised not to lecture me."

"And I don't mean to now. I apologize, Captain." A moment later she said, "I go on about women's issues because I missed a chance to learn much more about them. My aunt Sally offered to take me to the Women's Rights Convention at Seneca Falls, eight years ago, but I didn't go. I was sixteen then, and empty-headed as a lark. I have felt ever since that I missed my chance to be a part of something meaningful. Women have a role to play in the world, you know."

"That they do."

"And you think it is only to keep the home and hearth and look after the children."

"I said nothing of the sort. You might be surprised to know that I heard Elizabeth Cady Stanton speak once."

Sarah could scarcely imagine Jason Beck sitting in a lecture hall listening to Elizabeth Cady Stanton, who was second only to Lucretia Mott in the forefront of women's rights.

"It was in Boston, after my last voyage but one. It was a temperance lecture. She made sense, too. The men of the sea are a hard-drinking lot. I have seen lives ruined by rum that might have been set to rights by a bit of temperance."

They had come under the lee of the Marin headlands. The water was calmer here but the winds more variable.

"Dickie told me you began your life on the wharves," Sarah said. "I found it hard to believe."

"Because I'm a ship's master now? We're all capable of changing ourselves, Mrs. Rockwell. You believe Dickie can be more than he is now. You hope to change him, don't you?"

"Did you have someone to help you rise above that life?"

"Nay. I climbed out of the bilge by myself. It was a slippery ladder. I've had some falls."

Sarah met his eyes, seeking to read everything that lay beneath that brief recounting of his journey to manhood.

"So you see, my beginnings were more humble than most," he said, and it was he who looked away.

Chapter 14

David Farren arrived at Sherman's pleasant frame home on Rincon Hill just at noon, an hour before he was expected.

"The vigilants have notified the governor that they are removing their men from the jail, sir," he said when the maid summoned Sherman to the parlor.

Sherman was in slippers and a brocade dressing gown. He was tired and irritable following a bad night during which he had sat up for hours, periodically inhaling the smoke from burning nitre paper to quell an attack of asthma. His asthma troubled him more in San Francisco than any other place he had lived.

"How long ago?" he demanded.

"Just over an hour."

"What else did they say?"

"Nothing, sir. Governor Johnson showed me the note. It said, 'We beg to advise you that we have withdrawn our guard from the County Jail. By order of the Committee. 33, Secretary.' That's all."

"Damn them!" Sherman said. "They haven't a thimbleful of honor among the lot of them. But we knew that yesterday, didn't we."

The evening before, less than twenty-four hours after the governor's visit to the Turnverein Hall on Friday night, a delegation from the Vigilance Committee had called on Johnson at his hotel. It included neither

Coleman nor any of the others who had negotiated on the Committee's behalf at the hall. The spokesman, a man named Dows, repudiated any and all terms agreed to by Coleman, saying he lacked authority to make such a treaty. The delegation had promised only to notify the governor if they intended to remove their observers from the jail, and this they had now done.

"They mean to take Casey," Sherman said. "Excuse me, Captain. I won't be long."

Ellen Sherman joined her husband while he dressed to go out. "What news?" she asked, knowing the reply by his mood.

"From bad to worse. I must go. I am sorry, my dear. Tell the children I'm sorry too." Lizzy was nearly four, Willy not yet two. He could hear them playing in the yard.

Sherman patted his wife's abdomen. "How is the little one?" She was four months along with a new child.

"Resting peacefully. Be careful, Cump."

"I will, sweet. Don't fret." Ellen had only to call him by his family nickname, given for his boyish mispronouncing of "Tecumseh," and he was hers to command.

The day was brilliant, the sunshine warm. Farren left his horse at Sherman's and together they walked downtown. As they crossed Sacramento Street, Farren pointed toward the bay. "Look, sir." Two blocks away, coming up Sacramento, were columns of marching men flanked by a crowd of onlookers that moved along the sidewalks.

Sherman and Farren stood back as the front ranks of the vigilance militia approached and passed them by. The troops marched in columns of four, with no talking in ranks, and every man was armed with a musket. "I wish they were ours," Sherman said. Down the street, more troops turned into Sacramento from the side streets and the end was not in sight. Sherman touched Farren's arm and they worked their way out of the crowd. "Double time, now," Sherman said. At a military trot, they reached the International Hotel in a few minutes. They found Governor Johnson on the roof, looking in the direction of the County Jail, which was in plain view across Broadway. All the housetops in the vicinity of the jail were covered with people, and more were running up the slopes of Telegraph Hill.

"The vigilants are marching, Governor," Sherman said. "We must do something."

"There is nothing we can do," Johnson said. He turned on Sherman and demanded angrily, "Or am I wrong, General? Have we an army to put against this one?"

"We have two companies at most, sir. One hundred fifty men, if we're lucky."

"And the Vigilance Committee has three thousand. Maybe four."

"We can't just watch, sir!"

"Our time will come, General, perhaps even soon enough to save Mr. Casey. Coleman sent word they will punish no man without a trial. Judge Terry is in Sacramento conferring with the prominent men there. We may raise a regiment of volunteers if we can arm them adequately. And the doctors say Mr. King is better today."

From the street below came the sound of many feet marching in cadence. Stepping to the edge of the roof, the men saw that the vigilance columns were marching north along Montgomery Street. At the corner of Pacific they turned left, moving uphill. Along the way, the onlookers fell silent as the troops came in sight. The only sounds that reached those watching from the roof of the hotel were the tramp of marching feet and the occasional shouts of the officers, whose commands echoed through the streets.

"You could go to the jail and stand in the door," Sherman said. "There is still time."

"If I thought there were a chance that some body of the town's citizens would support me, I would go gladly," Johnson said. "But those who oppose the vigilants will have nothing to do with me now, because I made that agreement with Coleman."

"That is an outrage!" Sherman said. "You were trying to keep Casey alive and guarantee him a fair trial."

"If King lives there can be no capital charge, General. That is where our best hope lies now."

Dickie Howell stayed in the forefront of the crowd along the line of march so he would not be kept to the rear when the vigilance troops massed before the County Jail. To his surprise they did not march up Broadway as he expected. Instead, the marching column turned left up Pacific Street and divided in two at Kearny, one approaching Broadway along Kearny, the other on Dupont, so they arrived at the jail from both sides. They turned onto the wide thoroughfare and pushed the onlookers out of the street, forming a large hollow square before the jail.

As soon as the square was formed and the troops at rest, the following crowd flowed around the cordon, seeking the best vantage points from which to watch whatever was to take place. Dickie jostled and pushed with the rest, and when he arrived at the triple line of armed vigilantes that held the people back he had four gentlemen's purses in his pockets, each heavy with coins. Without opening them he knew they contained enough money to keep him fed for two or three weeks, possibly longer. He wriggled between two men and stood behind the vigilance soldiers.

"Stay there, boy," one ordered him. "No farther."

"Yes, sir." Dickie was the picture of obedience. He had a clear view of the jail and a group of unarmed men who stood within the hollow square. He recognized Mr. Frye among them, and Mr. Coleman and Mr. Truett, and Mr. Calvert as well.

The street fell silent. Those in the back of the crowd pushed forward until every space was full and all motion ceased. Sunlight glinted off the bayonets of the vigilance muskets. The wind rippled the flag that flew over the jail and fluttered the edges of coats and capes.

There was a rustle of movement at the east side of the square. The troops there parted to admit a team of horses accompanied by a squad of vigilance militia. "They have a cannon," a man said. Once it was in the open space even those in the rear of the crowd could see that the horses pulled a brass fieldpiece on a wooden gun carriage. The driver guided the team so the cannon pointed at the jail, then unhitched the horses and held them to one side while three members of the gun's escort loaded the piece with a solid shot.

Dickie wished Stritch were with him to share in the

spectacle. Nothing like this had taken place in San Francisco in his lifetime and likely never would again, and poor Stritch was kept aboard the *Sarah B. Watson* with the rest of the crew.

On Friday, Dickie and Stritch had earned twelve dollars each carrying messages for the Vigilance Committee. At the Noggin of Ale, Stritch had drunk brandy and porter, and when night fell he had followed Dickie in an eager daze to the back door of Fanny Boyle's whorehouse on Pike Street, near Dupont. For a quarter eagle each, Fanny had allowed the two boys to use a small room with peepholes where customers who enjoyed such diversions could watch other customers with the whores. Stritch's eyes had bugged out when he looked through the holes. They had watched for a time, and then, when Stritch saw one of the girls was alone, he had walked boldly down the hall and entered her room without knocking. She had tried to throw him out at first, but when he showed her a double-eagle coin she laughed and threw off her robe. She pulled down Stritch's pants and exclaimed, "Oh, look at him standin' to attention! So smooth and fine and young. And all for me? Am I the first? Tell me the truth now. I knew it! And such a handsome sailor boy too."

When Stritch emerged from the whore's room he was sober as a preacher and he stood six feet tall in his stocking feet. He would have promised Dickie Howell the moon and stars, if Dickie had asked for them, but all that Dickie asked was to be shown over the *Sarah B. Watson* again, until he knew every timber and every rope and every sail, so when the day came that he had a chance to serve as a ship's boy he would get the job without fail, no matter how many other boys might be pleading for the chance. Now, with shore leave forbidden the crew, he might never have a chance to see the ship again.

The same side of the hollow square parted again, this time to admit a four-in-hand coach that came to a stop near the jail, out of the cannon's line of fire, and now three of the Committee's leaders approached the jail. They knocked at the door and after a short delay the door opened and they were admitted.

The troops and the onlookers in the square remained perfectly quiet. Dickie began to make his way out of the crowd. Whatever the vigilantes intended to do with James Casey, they wouldn't do it here. They would take him away in the carriage to some other place and hang him there. Dickie moved toward Dupont Street. West of Dupont, Broadway rose steadily toward Mason Street, where it ended. By walking partway up the slope, he would be able to see which direction the carriage took.

He had reached the edge of the crowd when a hand fell on his shoulder from behind. He pulled away, fearing it might be a gentleman who had missed his purse, then turned about to find Stritch looking at him oddly. "Ain't you glad to see me?"

"How'd you get ashore?"

"Cap'n Beck sent word to the ship. He's sold our rice and give the whole crew leave to celebrate. We got shore pay, too." Stritch displayed a handful of coins, most of them copper and silver. "What's all that about?" He jerked a thumb at the crowd.

"The Committee of Vigilance is going to hang Mr. Casey, I reckon."

"A hanging? I ain't never seen a hanging."

There was a commotion in the crowd and a voice cried, "Here they come!"

"It's Casey!" said another.

"Come on!" Dickie led Stritch up Broadway at a run. From halfway to Stockton they could see above the heads of the crowd. The vigilance leaders came down the steps of the jail leading a man who was manacled hand and foot. They put him in the coach with three men to guard him and the coach left the hollow square at once by way of Dupont Street, with an escort of vigilance militia trotting beside it.

"They going to hang him now?" Stritch said.

"I reckon. Come on." Dickie led off at a run into Stockton Street, parallel to the direction taken by the coach. "We'll go ahead and get right up front," Dickie said as they ran. "Later on we'll go to the ship. You ain't forgot your promise, have you?"

"I ain't forgot," Stritch said. "You'n me's mates now. I'll learn you the *Sarah B.* from her bowsprit to her taffrail, just like I promised. Only I'd hate to miss a hanging. Rob Tinker says the bugger's prick gets stiff and he shoots his wad after he's dead."

At Sacramento Street Dickie turned left. On Friday, the Vigilance Committee had moved its headquarters to a large warehouse on Sacramento between Front and Davis streets. He guessed that was where the coach would take James Casey and he was elated to see it now, stopped before the vigilance warehouse. Only a few onlookers milled about in the street but more were arriving every moment, and now a larger crowd poured into the street from Kearny behind a second carriage. Dickie caught a glimpse of a man inside the coach whose face was ghostly pale.

They ran alongside the militia escorting the second carriage. "Who's that in there, mister?" Dickie asked the nearest man, who was panting for breath.

"Charles ... Cora. We're going to ... hang them two by two."

Chapter 15

hat was as seamanlike a job of sailing as I've seen." Jason made *Katahdin*'s painter fast to a cleat on the dock.

They were in the fishing village of Saucelito, on Marin's eastern shore. The few fisher boats that were not out trolling the waters of the bay and the sea beyond the Gate were moored offshore or tied up at the docks that looked quaint and spindly compared with San Francisco's massive wharves where the clipper ships berthed.

Sarah glanced at the sun. "What time do you think it is?"

"Seven bells, going eight."

She saw the wrinkles of amusement at the corners of his eyes. He was testing her, but she didn't mind. He judged it to be between half past eleven and twelve o'clock. She made the conversion without effort. In her youth, her father had instructed her brother Peter in the meaning of ship's bells, and how to box the compass. He had insisted that Peter learn to read better than he was taught in school so he might be a ship's officer someday, and Sarah had demanded the same lessons, unwilling to have Peter know things that she did not. Peter worked now in a shoe factory in Lawrence, Massachusetts, where a compass offered no guidance in his labors, and a steam whistle instead of a ship's bell marked the hours.

With Jason carrying the wicker picnic hamper Sarah

had stowed beneath the sloop's foredeck, Sarah led the way through the dusty streets to a livery stable. As soon as they were mounted, Jason saw that her equestrian ability was much superior to his own, sidesaddle or no. At the edge of the village, Jason's horse took it into his head to return to the stable, but Jason reined the brute about and kicked him into a gallop, and after that the animal accepted his lot without further rebellion.

They rode along the shores of a bay that narrowed steadily and ended where a stream issued into the salt water across flats of black mud that shone like the flanks of a beached whale. From there, the road led them straight toward the mountain that dominated the peninsula.

"It's called Tamalpais," Sarah said, following Jason's gaze. "That's where we're going."

The sun was overhead when they passed the busy sawmill at the foot of the mountain. Beyond the mill they entered groves of vaulting redwood trees where there were no sounds but birdcalls and the fall of the horses' hooves. They climbed the slopes by wagon roads made for the lumbering operations that had already stripped great areas bare in order to build the city of San Francisco and fuel the steam vessels that called there.

Sarah appeared to know the rutted avenues well. In less than an hour she led Jason to a place high on the mountain's southern flank that commanded a sweeping view of the sea. Below them, the western slopes were natural meadow, the tall grasses already brown and golden, the shorter grass kept green by the damp winds off the ocean. Offshore, beyond a blue band of water a few miles wide along the coast, a blanket of fog as white as combed cotton stretched to the horizon.

"Well, Captain? How does this compare with your masthead?"

Jason turned about to take in the panorama. To the east, across the bay, a single sharp peak rose beyond the hills of Contra Costa. On the southern peninsula, San Francisco was a cluster of houses huddled by the harbor.

" 'Tis steadier than a masthead."

"You like it."

"Aye. More than that. 'Tis what I love best aboard

ship, being able to see far. I'm a speck on the surface of the world in all its vastness. The ship and I are nothing. 'Tis much the same here."

"You make it sound as if we are insignificant."

"We are. Feel the strength of the wind! It comes thousands of leagues, all the way from the Japans. If you understand the power of the wind and sea, you understand that we are nothing. What is a man, compared to that? Or a woman, for that matter?"

"I'm not sure I like thinking of myself as nothing."

"A sailor knows his true measure every moment. He has the vastness of the sea to remind him. One mistake and we're gone, with none the wiser, and the world goes on without a care. It keeps you on your toes."

He took her by the hands and led her in a sailor's hornpipe. She learned the steps quickly. They spun about, and he drew her into his arms to keep hold of her. He felt a sudden want for her, and the desire to hold her tighter still, and so he stopped and let her go.

"I would not have taken you for a dancing man, Captain."

"Aboard ship, we dance with the deck and we dance with the waves."

"When you talk like that you take my breath away. I shall never forget what you said that first night, about the way a ship breathes."

"And makes love to the sea."

"Yes." She met his eyes for a moment before turning away. "Come. I promised you a picnic."

She unpacked the picnic hamper and spread its bounty on a gingham tablecloth. There were cold chicken and beef, half a loaf of bread, Jack's cheese from Monterey, two Seville oranges, and a bottle of wine, which Sarah pronounced "rough, like California, but suitable for the surroundings." The jouncing of her steed had broken one of the two glasses in the hamper, so they shared the other.

"Very flavorful," Jason said when he tasted the wine, although he preferred brandy or rum.

"The missions made wine. It is almost the only thing we have adopted from the Spaniards, besides the land.

My husband taught me a little about wine before we left New England."

"You came to California by steamer?"

"To Chagres, and overland to Panama." Her brow furrowed and Jason regretted his idle question.

"I'm sorry. I didn't mean to remind you of your loss."

"It is behind me now. Honestly. Our night at the theater was a turning point for me."

He cut a slice of cheese for her with his seaman's knife and another for himself. "Fine wines and steamer cabins to California don't sound like humble beginnings to me." He meant to tease her, but she was serious when she replied.

"I gained those things by marrying well, although that was not my purpose. My mother was widowed when I was sixteen. Father was a sailor. He rose to be second mate on an Atlantic packet, but the long voyages kept him away from home and my mother missed him, so he took a berth as first mate on a coastal lumber schooner." She broke off a small piece of cheese and put it in her mouth. "He was sailing from Maine to Boston in an early autumn storm. 'Beating upwind with green water in the scuppers at the best of times' is how he described those passages along the coast. During the storm the lumber on deck shifted and he went with two men to lash it down. Before they made fast the new lashings it shifted again and crushed him."

She held her morsel of cheese clenched in her hand. "With what Father had saved, Mother bought a boardinghouse in Kittery town, on the Post Road." After the move from Kittery Point, Sarah could no longer hear the waves from her bed.

"We managed well enough. I was the innkeeper's daughter, you see. I married a wealthy gentleman who stayed the night and came back from Pennsylvania to court me. His family thought I only wanted his money." She grew bitter at the memory. "They are stubborn, conceited fools. Anyone could see we were happy."

"And then he died."

"Yes. Haven left everything to me, but his parents went to court and overturned his will. It was their way of punishing the innkeeper's daughter who had lured their only son into marrying beneath his station."

"They left you with nothing?" Jason wrapped a piece of bread around a slice of beef and ate it.

"Haven had brought enough to set himself up in business here in California. The rest of his wealth was invested in the family enterprises. Railroads and Panama steamers, mostly. We traveled from New York to the Isthmus on a Rockwell vessel."

Sarah took Jason's knife and sliced an orange into six pieces with sure, quick strokes. "We took a river steamer as far as we could and then we crossed to Panama City on mules." She felt the anger building within her. "Haven wouldn't ride a mule. He insisted on having a horse. He was an excellent horseman. He rode alongside our little caravan, keeping up everyone's spirits. There was cholera along the way, but our party escaped, thank God. There were snakes and bats, and someone saw a jaguar, but Haven pooh-poohed the dangers. And then he fell from his horse and broke his neck."

She offered a wedge of orange to Jason and ate one herself. "It was months before I learned that Haven's parents wouldn't send me any more money. I had enough left to buy my house, and running a boardinghouse was something I knew. It became my refuge." She saw Haven in her mind's eye, one minute smiling the same merry smile that had won her, the next lying crumpled on the ground like some useless refuse cast off by the westering argonauts. It had happened within sight of Panama City.

Watching her husband interred with what ceremony the Spanish priest and the officials of the Pacific steamship company could muster, she was a helpless castaway on a foreign shore. And then within a matter of hours she had found a new resolve she never dreamed lay dormant within her. Faced with her fellow travelers' assumptions that she would turn back and return to the States, she had announced to the astonishment of one and all that she would continue on to California and the unknown. And in that moment she was transformed. Months later, in San Francisco, when she was certain that the Rockwells intended to deny her everything, she

bought her boardinghouse and planned her revenge.
Now, in a small iron chest in the armoire in her bedroom, there was enough gold to pay for her return to the
eastern States and to hire an attorney. The sale of the
boardinghouse would provide a reserve, and enough to
live on while she challenged the Rockwells for what was
rightfully hers.

"I have loved two men and they betrayed me," she
said to Jason. "At least my father was trying to save his
vessel. But he went off to sea like all you brave sailors
and he came back to us in a box made from the same
lumber that killed him. And Haven has no excuse at all.
Damn them for dying and leaving me!"

"In your husband's case you would do better to damn
the horse," Jason suggested.

"It was not the animal's fault! It was Haven's. He was
showing off to amuse the ladies. To amuse me, I suppose.
He made that poor dumb Spanish horse do tricks to entertain us. It grew frightened and it threw him. He died
because he was showing off, and I will never forgive
him."

The fog advanced as the afternoon grew long. It
flowed up the western slopes of the mountain and enveloped them as they made ready to leave their picnic
ground. By the time they set sail from Saucelito, it blew
thick through the Golden Gate, but it stayed above the
water and they could make out the southern peninsula.
Sarah offered the tiller to Jason and he made *Katahdin*
scud across the waves on a broad reach for the North
Point. They buttoned their sou'westers and pulled the
oilskin hats low over their eyes and they reached the
shore while the light still held.

As dusk darkened the waters of the bay, a sailing dory
passed close to leeward of the anchored clipper *Sarah B.
Watson*. Second Mate Rooney, a sandy-haired Irishman
who was the officer of the watch, returned the tillerman's
wave. He recognized the old Finn as the same man who
had ferried the skipper to the city and carried some of
the men when the crew went ashore on leave.

Once the dory was beneath the ship's bows, out of
sight of the watch on deck, Finn Warren hove to and

grabbed the anchor chain. "Up now, boys, and be quick," he said. "I'll be alongside at six bells to take you back."

Stritch threw off the tarpaulin that covered him and Dickie Howell in the dory's bow. He climbed the anchor chain first and poked his head through the hawse hole. There was the sound of snoring in the fo'c'sle. When his eyes adjusted to the gloom, Stritch made out the form of Brad Keith asleep and the other bunks empty. He squirmed through the hole with difficulty, skinning his knee on the anchor chain, then helped Dickie through.

They had waited at the Vigilance Committee's warehouse for hours in the midst of a restless crowd of men. Finally a guard announced to the crowd that the Executive Committee had begun the trial of Charles Cora but had adjourned for the night. It was then that Stritch and Dickie had decided to board the *Sarah B. Watson* like pirates and see how long they could avoid detection by the watch. "A gold doubloon to the man who gets to Cap'n Beck's cabin without being seen and leaves his knife on the cap'n's bunk," Stritch had proposed. When Dickie said he had no doubloons, Stritch said any gold coin would do. Once the contest was settled they would reveal themselves to the watch and Stritch would show Dickie around the ship before they returned to shore.

Now, crouched in the fo'c'sle, peering through the open hatchway of the fo'c'sle, they could see most of the weather deck. "That's Mr. Rooney," Stritch whispered, pointing to a figure seated on a keg by the deckhouse, smoking a pipe. "He'll have a seaman making rounds."

Before long a second figure came in sight, strolling the deck. "That's Grimes!" Stritch exclaimed. He clapped a hand over his own mouth when the sentry glanced toward the fo'c'sle. Brad Keith murmured in his sleep and rolled over, but he did not waken. Stritch waited until Grimes turned and started aft before whispering in Dickie's ear, "Grimes jumped ship two days ago. If there's to be a flogging under Cap'n Beck, he's the one to get it. Off you go, now."

Dickie could see that the forward cargo hatch was open, the cover resting ajar. Keeping low, he ran to the hatch. A ladder hung by hooks from the coaming. He

climbed over the lip and down the ladder and found
himself in the tween decks. The sides of the cargo space
were lined with sacks of rice, leaving a clear passageway
down the center. Over his head, he heard footsteps as
Grimes came forward again.

Dickie scampered aft. When Stritch showed him
around the ship three days before, they had not ventured
into the tween decks but he remembered a companionway rising from below into the captain's saloon in the
stern of the ship.

A sound like something hitting the side of the hull
made Dickie pause. He looked toward the bow and saw
Stritch drop down through the forward hatch. Dickie
continued aft and was relieved to find the companionway
where he hoped it would be. He climbed the steps silently and emerged cautiously into the captain's saloon.
On the port side, off the narrow passageway to the steward's galley, three doors led to the mates' cabins. The
captain's quarters lay to starboard. Dickie entered Captain Beck's cabin and closed the door behind him. He
put his knife on the bunk, which was twice as wide as
those in the fo'c'sle, and concealed himself in the captain's private head. By the faint light from the porthole
he could make out the copper tub and washbasin, and
the towels hanging from a brass rail. He would wait for
Stritch here and give him a fright when he came into the
cabin.

But Stritch didn't come. After a time, Dickie heard
voices on deck. Thinking perhaps the older boy had been
discovered by the watch, he crept from the captain's
quarters and through the steward's pantry where a porthole looked out on the weather deck. At first Dickie
could see no one, but then a movement caught his eye.
He made out two men near the main hatch. One pointed
forward, and when the other turned to look the first man
raised his hand and brought a belaying pin down on the
other's head with all his might.

ason and Sarah approached the house through the garden and entered by way of the kitchen. At the sound of their footsteps in the hallway, Trelayne came out of the parlor.

"You haven't heard."

Something wild in his expression caused Sarah to move closer to Jason, as if for protection. "Heard what?"

"The Committee of Vigilance took Casey and the gambler Charles Cora from the jail this afternoon. They haven't hanged them yet but it's only a matter of time."

Joshua Norton and Molly Gray appeared in the parlor doorway. "You missed some grand theater," Trelayne said. "They had thousands of men, but they didn't make a sound! It was all done in pantomime! Whoever staged it had a flair for drama."

"We were just on our way to the livery when we saw the crowd," Molly said.

Norton was downcast. "I shared the burden in fifty-one, but they turned me away. 'Joshua Norton not to be admitted.' Well, they can hang who they like. I've got your cargo, Captain, and they'll pay a pretty penny for it, I can promise you that. Oh, I'm to tell you your man Melchior stopped here this afternoon. It was after the business at the jail."

"Melchior, here?" Jason had given Melchior the location of the boardinghouse so he could send word if there were trouble aboard ship or anything else that required the master's attention.

"I'm to give you this." Norton handed Jason a piece of paper sealed with wax and stamped with the ship's seal.

Jason broke the seal and read the note. " 'All the lads ashore. Harbor watch aboard. Come to the Noggin of Ale.' " He looked at Norton. "What does he mean, 'All the lads ashore'?"

"He said he had brought the crew ashore on your orders."

"My orders? I gave no such orders." For a moment, Jason was held in the grip of unreasoning fear. Then he turned and ran from the house, the note still clutched in his hand. Outside, the last light was fading. The layer of fog over the town had thickened. Five minutes' running downhill brought him to the Noggin of Ale. It was full of men, mostly drunk, but he recognized no one from his crew and found Finn Warren's customary chair occupied by a stranger.

"You, miss!" He seized the barmaid by the arm and she drew back in fear when she saw his face. "Sorry, miss. No harm to you. Just tell me, has there been a big Cornishman named Melchior here today, from the ship *Sarah B. Watson*?"

"Him you want? Bless him, he's free with his coin, that one. Bought drinks all 'round. They've gone off to Fanny Boyle's an hour ago. If you're the skipper, I'm to send you along."

"Where is Fanny Boyle's?"

"On Pike Street, the far side of Dupont, between Sacramento and Clay. Up the stairway and knock twice. If you knock three times, you're the law."

Pike Street was narrow and dark. Midway between Sacramento and Clay a rickety flight of stairs clung to a dilapidated house, one of those thrown up in haste in the early days of the gold rush and never meant to last this many years. Jason took the stairs two at a time and knocked twice. The door was opened by a half-naked Negro girl whose breasts were hung with strings of false pearls. She was no more than seventeen years old and she was smoking a cigar. Her face, which might have been pretty, was ravaged by smallpox, but the skin of her breasts was as smooth as polished mahogany. She smiled at Jason, revealing yellow teeth.

"Come in, Jack Tar. Jine de party." Behind her, in a large common room that reeked of spirits and smoke and unwashed bodies, Jason spied Jolly Jim and half a dozen others from his crew. He shouldered past the girl.

"What are you doing ashore, Jim?" he demanded.

The Sandwich Islander smiled blandly. He was reeling drunk. "Evening, Cap'n!"

"Jim, where is Melchior?"

"Fucking, Cap'n. That room there." He pointed at one of the doors that opened onto the common room, then another. "Mebbe that one. I don't remember so good. I was fucking too."

Behind the first door, Jason found Rob Tinker on the bed with his pants about his knees, in the act of mounting a young whore from behind. The bosun spun around, his phallus waving like the mast of a ship in rough seas. Jason nearly gagged at the stench of rum and sweat and other more private juices.

"Hoy! Fuck off, now, this one's mine!" Tinker lost his balance on the bed and fell to the floor. "Oh, it's you, Skipper. Well, she's your'n if you want her." He tried to get up, got tangled in his pants, and fell again.

Jason jerked the bosun to his feet. "I'll have you flogged and taken to Boston in irons, Rob Tinker, if you're ashore without leave."

A portion of the bosun's sodden brain recognized that the threat was deadly serious. His manhood wilted obscenely. On the bed, the young whore covered herself with a filthy sheet and cringed against the wall. "You give us leave, Cap'n! It was Grimes brought it. From your hand, he told Melchior, and he had the money too! Shore pay, he said."

"Grimes deserted! Melchior would have put him in irons if he found him."

"So he would, Cap'n! But Grimes come back all on his own, see? Melchior left him aboard with Mr. Rooney to stand watch. Young Brad Keith too. Harbor watch right and proper, Cap'n!"

Jason flung Rob Tinker on the bed and turned to find

Melchior advancing on him. The first mate was naked from the waist up, his chest matted with graying hair, and his red-rimmed eyes were bright with anger.

"Leave off that man! That be a member of my crew and no landlubber have leave to touch a member of my crew!" He placed one hand against Jason's chest and shoved him back nearly to the bed where Rob Tinker was now cowering beneath the covers with his whore.

"He ain't himself, Cap'n!" Tinker warned, but Jason recognized the lack of comprehension in Melchior's eyes. He made a fist and slammed it into Melchior's midriff, knocking the wind out of him. As Melchior doubled over, Jason seized his ears and held his face an inch away from his own.

"It's me, old friend. It's Jason."

Melchior's anger left him and he smiled. "I be drunk as a lord, Cap'n, but 'tis all for the good. Sold the rice, ee have. Tomorrer we'll up anchor, eh? One good night ashore with the lads, after all this time."

Jason let go of Melchior's ears. "I sent no message and no money to the ship." He spoke the words slowly, keeping his eyes fixed on Melchior's, forcing the mate to listen and comprehend.

" 'Twas in your hand, Jason. Sold the rice, ee said. Shore leave for all the lads. Discharge cargo tomorrer."

"I don't know what's happened, Melchior, but something's amiss. We'll go to the ship now, all of us. We'll sort it out there. I want every man from the crew outside in the street in three minutes. We'll carry those who can't manage."

There were fourteen men from the ship in the whorehouse. Of those, ten could walk and some of those were able to help their besotted shipmates. "Quick, now," Jason ordered when they were all in the street. He led the way toward the wharves. The distance was not great, less than ten minutes for a sober man at a brisk pace, but tonight it took almost twenty.

Jason and Melchior strode ahead of the others, Melchior full of purpose now but weaving a little from side to side.

"I was set to clap Grimes in irons for desertion," Melchior said. "But he swore he squared it with ee, about being gone those two days. He swore it, Jason! And him havin' the money made me believe 'twas so. Ee sent no one to the vessel? No word?"

"No one and no word."

"Grimes had the letter, see? 'Twas scrawled on a bit of wrappin' paper, but you ain't much o' one for formality, Jason. No signature, not even a name, now I think of it. Gor damme, Jason, I never thought 'twere anything but the truth—"

Jason took Melchior's arm and came to a stop. They had arrived at Drumm and Pacific streets and the foot of the Pacific Wharf. Far across the black water, near Goat Island, somewhere among the ships at anchor, a brilliant orange light flared and swayed, illuminating the low-hanging fog with an eerie glow.

"There's a vessel afire." Jason broke into a run, racing between the shuttered stalls. In the distance, at the wharf's end, he could see moving figures. He leaped a gaping hole in the planks and kept going, narrowly missing a fall. As he neared the figures, he saw that they were men, three of them, and a boy. One of the men was Finn Warren. He and another were lifting something from a ship's boat to the wharf. It was an oblong burden, wrapped in a tarpaulin. By the way the men handled it, it could only be a body. Now the boy turned and Jason saw it was Dickie Howell.

"Captain! Captain Beck!" He ran towards Jason and he was crying. Jason caught the boy in his arms. Dickie's sodden clothing smelled of smoke.

Jason didn't dare ask what ship was burning. "Who's that there, Dickie? Who is it they've got there?"

Dickie seemed not to hear him. "Stritch and me, we were in the tween decks, and Stritch, he—"

"You were aboard the *Sarah B.*? Where is Stritch, Dickie? Is he still on board the ship?"

Dickie buried his face against Jason's neck, and Jason could barely make out the muffled words that escaped between the sobs. "He's dead, Captain. The *Sarah B.* is burned and Stritch is dead."

Book Two

Chapter 17

Jason reeled as he gained the porch. He stank of brandy and smoke. It was two hours past midnight, but lights showed in the windows. He steadied himself and knocked on the door.

For what seemed like a very long time there was no sound from within. Around him, the streets were deserted. He considered leaving. It was only a short way to Sarah Rockwell's house. If he could reach his room without being heard . . .

No chance of that. Melchior and Dickie would be there by now. He had sent them to the boardinghouse to carry the news and find themselves rooms for the night. There would be sympathy and questions and the story of the fire told over and over, and Jason was prepared for none of it.

The door opened to reveal a well-dressed diminutive woman with sharp eyes and graying hair that was fashionably put up. Her expression, pleasant at first, hardened into distaste as she looked Jason up and down.

"Who might you be at this ungodly hour?" It was the harsh voice of a harridan.

"Captain Jason Beck of the Farnum and Kent clipper ship *Sarah B. Watson*," he replied, presenting his full credentials and leaving aside the fact that the ship was a foundered hulk.

"Says you. You look like a common swab."

"I was sent by a boy named Richard—Dickie Howell."

A smile transformed the harridan into a gentlewoman who had fallen from better circumstances. "Bless his soul. Welcome, Captain. I am Mrs. Wickliff." Her voice was smoothly modulated. "Do come in."

The small hallway was tastefully furnished. Small oil paintings and watercolors hung in gilt frames. A flight of stairs led to the upper story. "You have not been here before," Mrs. Wickliff said.

"I haven't made port in San Francisco since fortynine, ma'am."

She smiled. "I had only a tent and three girls then."

"I am sorry to come to you so late."

"In our business we don't keep regular hours. We are here to suit your needs, Captain."

"I need a bath."

Mrs. Wickliff was much relieved by the request. "You shall have it. And a companion to bathe you. Have you any special preference? Nationality? Color of hair?"

"I like red hair well enough, but I leave the selection to you." Jason had found that nothing served more surely to win the good graces of a parlor-house madam than letting her choose the girl for the first visit. If he returned, he could make his own choice among the others.

"I will do my best to earn that confidence." Mrs. Wickliff ushered Jason into an opulent parlor. The oil paintings were larger here. The curtains were lace, the drapes of rich silk damask, the furniture plush, the carpets Persian. A piano stood against one wall.

"Brandy, or wine?"

"Brandy."

She selected a crystal decanter that was one of many on a mahogany sideboard. "Have you eaten, Captain? I can have the cook fix something."

"I'm not hungry." It was true, although he had last eaten on the ridge of Mt. Tamalpais. That pleasant interlude was a memory from a previous life, and the nourishment he took there long spent.

"Another time you must come to supper," Mrs. Wickliff said. "We serve every evening at half past eight.

Please sit down." She motioned to a chair. "I will only be a moment." She left him by way of a curtained doorway.

Jason brushed at the seat of his pants and found them gritty from the thwart of Finn Warren's dory. He remained standing, pacing the parlor and drinking the brandy, looking at the paintings and wondering how much he would have to drink to forget the night's happenings.

He and Melchior and the crew members who were sober enough to help had spent more than an hour rowing about the anchorage, searching for Keith and Grimes and Second Mate Rooney, in the hope they might have escaped the inferno. Other seamen and curiosity seekers from the waterfront were out in small boats, but none found anyone in the water. The body on the wharf, wrapped in a tarpaulin, was Stritch. He had been picked up by Finn Warren, who saw the fire and set out to save Dickie and Stritch and the harbor watch, and arrived at the anchorage too late to do more than pluck Dickie from the water alive and Stritch dead. In all probability Stritch had jumped from the ship to save himself, but he could not swim.

After ordering Melchior and Dickie to Sarah Rockwell's, Jason had entered the first waterfront grogshop he found, intending to drink himself insensible, but the brandy had made him lonely and sent him to find the comfort of a woman's arms.

Footsteps descended the stairway in the front hall. Jason caught a glimpse of a stocky figure in a cloak and top hat. As the man opened the front door and stepped out into the night, Jason recognized Jonathan Frye by his size and bearing, and by the gold-headed cane in his hand. He was glad Frye had not seen him. He wanted to be anonymous tonight, but he took it as a good sign that a man of Jonathan Frye's position patronized Mrs. Wickliff's house.

A blond girl entered the parlor through a curtained doorway that led to the back of the house. "Oh," she exclaimed softly when she saw Jason. She pulled her gown about her. Beneath it she wore only a negligee of dusky blue. "I am sorry. I thought there was no one here." She spoke with a Sandinavian accent. She was slim and tall and very fair.

"Don't be sorry. It's your parlor."

"We are supposed to be properly dressed here."

" 'Tis very late to be properly dressed." Jason surprised himself by attempting a joke. The girl rewarded him with a smile.

"I came for a brandy. A nightcap, you call it?"

"Aye. And the brandy is good. Let me pour for you." In all the houses of prostitution Jason had frequented, the girl was among the most lovely women he had seen. If her beauty was representative of the standards Mrs. Wickliff kept, this house was a rare find.

Mrs. Wickliff returned with a red-haired girl in tow. She frowned when she saw the blonde. "I see you have met Lucy. This is Yvette."

"I am charmed, *capitaine*." Yvette was unmistakably French. She was impeccably dressed, her manner correct, even a little reserved. Her beauty almost equalled Lucy's, although it was more flamboyant. There was a hint of hardness in the set of her lips, and something in her eyes as she looked at Jason promised lascivious abandon once they were alone. Her face was powdered and rouged, but not excessively. The blond girl, by contrast, was devoid of powder or artificial color. Her clear skin was pale, her whole demeanor fresh and unspoiled.

"You should not be here like that," Mrs. Wickliff said to Lucy.

"I invited her to stay," Jason said. "And, well, as you say, I have met Lucy. Not that Yvette is any less appealing. You understand."

"Of course, Captain. As you wish." Mrs. Wickliff's tone carried no resentment.

"Maybe another time," Jason said to the French girl.

"I hope so, *capitaine*."

Privately, Jason knew that he would not choose Yvette another time. As soon as he saw her, he realized it had been a mistake to ask for a girl with red hair. He had been thinking of Sarah Rockwell when he voiced the preference, but a substitute for Sarah was the last thing he truly wanted.

With Yvette dismissed and Lucy sent upstairs by Mrs.

Wickliff to prepare herself, the madam addressed the matter of money tactfully. "As this is your first visit, Captain, and because it is late, I would think you will want to sleep after your bath."

Jason became aware that he was very tired. "Yes."

"I will make you a special rate. One hundred fifty dollars for the night. You may sleep as long as you like and we will give you breakfast fit for the captain of a China clipper. Just put your things outside Lucy's door tonight and I will have them cleaned for you."

Four days earlier Jason would have laughed at the notion that such a figure was a special rate, but in the interim he had become acquainted with the local costs for everything from brandy to boardinghouses. It was not surprising that the price of whores stood in proportion to the rest. In his present condition he would have paid the sum Mrs. Wickliff asked just for a bath and a good night's sleep. To get Lucy's company as well seemed a bargain.

The room Mrs. Wickliff led him to was as far removed from the squalid brothel where he had found Jolly Jim and Rob Tinker as if it were on another continent. It was a boudoir as elegant as any Jason had seen, not excluding those belonging to ladies of his acquaintance, and Lucy was a gracious hostess. She had brushed her hair and put on a satin robe the color of persimmon. She took his coat, seated him beside a low table, offered him champagne, and joined him instead in another glass of brandy when he chose to keep steady on his course. A large copper tub sat in one corner of the room. As they drank their brandy and talked, a Chinese girl came and went, pouring buckets of hot water into the tub until it was three quarters full.

When the Chinese girl had left for the last time, Lucy lowered her gaze and said, "Captain, I must ask you a favor."

"Ask away."

"I am flattered that you chose me. Yvette is very beautiful, and very accomplished."

"You are more beautiful. And I have no doubt you are every bit as accomplished." The brandy was going to his

head at last, making him giddy and bringing the compliments easily to his lips.

"You are kind. I hope you will be as kind when I tell
you the favor I ask. My last guest was—vigorous."

Jason was surprised to see that the girl was blushing.

"He made me sore. Here." She rested one hand between her thighs. The gesture was neither suggestive nor
crude. Jason found it touching.

"This man, was it Jonathan Frye?"

"No. Why do you ask?"

"I saw him leaving."

"He visits someone else in this house. Do you know
him?"

"Only by chance. Business to do with my ship." As
soon as he said the words, the image of the burning ship
returned. He had managed to put the memory aside for
a short time, and in that time he had begun to regather
his strength.

He tossed down the last of his brandy. In recent hours
he had drunk at least a quart. "What you need is a hot
bath."

"Yes. That will help. But if I cannot make love, I ask
you to stay with me tonight anyway. That is the favor.
When I came to the parlor I wanted the brandy to make
me sleep. I wanted to be alone. But now I want to be
with you. I can't explain it, but you comfort me. If you
will do this for me, I will pay you whatever amount you
gave to Mrs. Wickliff. It will cost you nothing."

Jason had heard flattery from whores around the
globe, compliments both crude and polished and every
shade between. This girl was in earnest.

"What is your full name, Lucy?"

"Lucy Greta Thorsen." She pronounced the surname
with a hard *T*.

"How old are you?"

"I will be twenty-three in August."

"Well, Lucy Greta Thorsen, if we get in that tub and
then in the bed, it would take a woman with more than
twenty-three years' experience to keep me awake longer
than five minutes. So we will sleep together, and I will
gladly pay for the privilege. And if you put your arms

around me, there is even a chance I will dream sweet dreams."

Just don't let me dream of the ship, dear God. Don't let me dream of Keith or Rooney. Don't let me see them pale and cold, resting on the muddy bottom of the bay. And don't let me think about tomorrow until it is here and half-gone.

Lucy preceded him to the copper tub, where she untied the robe and let it drop to the floor, followed by her nightdress. She stood naked before him, letting him see her. Jason felt short of breath. She was blond both topside and below decks, and her body was stunning, from the graceful curves of her belly and her bottom to the upturned breasts that splayed apart as if to receive him.

She got into the tub and watched him while he undressed.

"You're making me aware of my nakedness," he said as he tested the water. It was just right, almost too hot to bear.

"Men like to look at women with no clothes. I like to look at men with no clothes. Some men. I like to look at you. You are hard like a young man."

"Not where it counts."

"You will be hard there when the time comes."

The Chinese girl had left a sponge in the water and a cake of perfumed soap on a small silver tray beside the tub. Lucy washed him, making him stand so she could soap his legs and his privates, and he washed her in turn, lingering over her curves and enjoying the look of her standing before him with rivulets of water coursing down her flanks. He grew hard from the sight and the feel of her, but he remembered her bruised condition and he washed between her legs gently, with his hand.

When they were dry and in the canopied bed with the lamp turned low, she kissed him. Her lips were very soft.

"Careful," he said. "You'll wake me up."

"Shh. I will put you to sleep." She kissed his cheeks and eyes and his forehead and his nose, her unloosed blond hair trailing featherlike caresses across his face. She rested her head on his shoulder and lay still until his breathing deepened. Then she slipped out of bed and gathered his things to put them outside the door for cleaning before she snuffed the lamps and rejoined him, being careful not to disturb his rest. Remembering what he had said, she put her arms around him and held him while he dreamed.

Jason's first awareness was of the ship's deck beneath him, rolling on gentle, regular swells. He was lying on his back, bathed in warm sunshine that seemed to be particularly concentrated at his groin. Still asleep, he became aware that he was rigid with desire. He struggled to rise, but something held him down. Somewhere beyond his vision a woman was laughing softly.

He opened his eyes to find Lucy atop him, impaled on him. Sunshine filtered by the drapes bathed the room with soft light.

"Good morning, Captain." She leaned forward to kiss him.

"Good morning." He moved to meet her. "You are better."

"Much better." The words escaped her lips in a whisper. She sat up straight and bore down upon him, leaning back on her hands. Her breasts thrust toward the ceiling as she let her head fall backward. Her skin glowed bright pink and glistened with a faint sheen of sweat. The sight of her abandoned to his gaze, rising and falling on his flesh, threatened to bring on his climax, but the lingering dullness of sleep was his ally. He contained himself, waiting for her, letting her control the pace.

She rode atop him for a long time. At last her movements grew slower and longer. Her body trembled with the intensity of her concentration on the place where they were joined. She bent forward, doubling over, folding in on herself, her hair surrounding his head like a golden veil. Her forehead touched him. The moment was so intimate that he could contain himself no longer, but she was ready now, and they lost themselves in each other.

"Oh, Captain," she said after a time. They lay side by side, touching each other like lovers. "Will you come to see me again?"

"Yes." *Promise nothing to a whore.* That piece of advice

had been given him by the Marblehead seaman who bought him his first whore at the age of thirteen. He had followed it until now, but he made the promise willingly.

He breakfasted on beefsteak and four eggs, griddle cakes and honey, melon from Mexico and three cups of strong India tea. The Chinese girl who had brought the bathwater the night before ate with them. Jason learned that her name was Barbara and that she was one of Mrs. Wickliff's girls, not a servant as he had assumed. Lucy and Barbara occasionally laughed at private jokes but they never ignored him. They made him feel as if he were in the dining room of a respectable home, among friends.

When he stepped into the street, he could think of the ship and his missing crewmen without pain. His clothes were clean, and he himself was fortified and healed. The pain that had tormented him the night before like a physical wound had turned now to anger. It sent him downtown, propelled by a raw sea wind that promised to strengthen as the day grew longer.

At the Vigilance Committee's warehouse on Sacramento Street, a guard blocked Jason's way when he tried to approach the door. "Hold on now. What's your number?"

"No number yet. I've come to sign aboard."

single huge storeroom occupied the entire ground floor of the warehouse. Several companies of vigilance militia were drilling on a makeshift parade ground, their footsteps soft on the rammed-earth floor.

"Captain! Captain Beck!" Ned Rollick approached Jason from the tables near the door, where two dozen men were lined up to enlist.

"Once a clerk, always a clerk." Rollick gestured toward the tables. "They have me keeping the rolls. Are you here to see Mr. Kent?"

"He's one of you?"

"He is on the Executive Committee. They are conducting Mr. Cora's trial."

"I must see him right away." Jason wondered that he had not guessed sooner the reason for Kent's absences, and Rollick's, from the firm's offices in recent days.

Rollick led him to the upper floor of the warehouse, which was brighter, thanks to skylights in the flat roof, than the gloomy cavern below. Partitions had been hastily erected to create several rooms, small and large. The smell of fresh-sawn wood was strong.

"Wait here, Captain." Rollick knocked on a door and let himself into a room against the northern wall of the building. He returned a moment later, followed by Stephen Kent, who seized Jason's hand in both his own.

"Jason, I am sick at heart."

"Aye. She was a grand ship. How did you hear?"

"The news is all over town."

For Jason, the loss of the *Sarah B.* was personal, an intimate grief. Until now he had not considered that it was a matter of public interest, but the knowledge heartened him, for it suited his purpose in coming.

"I am glad to find you here, Stephen," Jason said. "I need an ally."

"And surprised to find me, too, I'm bound. I would have told you, but these men set great store by secrecy. It goes against my grain, I don't mind saying. If we are right in what we do, we must stand up for the world to see and face the consequences if we are wrong."

"I think better of them for having you among the leaders."

"Abel Calvert and I have decided that it is better for us to be part of the Committee than to be left on their lee side, if you take my meaning. Some of the others—well, they would run before the wind if we let them." Kent's expression turned mournful. "You know they found your mate?"

"Mr. Rooney? Is he dead?"

"Yes. I'm sorry. And Seaman Keith too. Found aboard the hulk this morning by divers. They were badly burned, I'm afraid."

Jason felt only an intensifying of his anger. He told Kent his plan then, and Kent nodded his approval before returning to the room where the Executive Committee was meeting. Within moments, a guard escorted a pale and worried-looking man from the room. The guard took him to a small wooden cubicle, one of several that stood along the north wall, opened the door, and pushed him in. A short time later the door to the Executive Committee's meeting room opened again and Stephen Kent beckoned Jason to enter.

He strode in and refused the offer of a chair. In his mind, he was on the poop deck of the *Sarah B. Watson*, addressing his own crew. This was how the vigilantes must see him. He was not here to beg. He had come to tell them what he planned to do.

There were two dozen men seated at six pine tables that were placed to form a square-cornered U. Jason stood at the open end, facing those at the tables. He knew Stephen Kent, Abel Calvert and Jonathan Frye, and he recognized two others among those who looked at him, some with curiosity, others with indifference.

He rested his gaze on the black-bearded visage of Isaac Bluxome. "Mr. Bluxome, do you know me?"

"I cannot say that I do, sir." Bluxome had a ruled writing tablet before him and a pencil in his hand.

"Well, I know you. You commanded one of the companies that put down the Hounds in forty-nine. My men and I assisted you."

Bluxome adjusted his spectacles and peered at Jason. "Yes, by Jove! Forgive me, Captain. I should have known you at once. You were a younger man then." Bluxome's voice revealed his New York origins.

"Is there any man here who wasn't younger in forty-nine?" Jason said. This brought laughter from those around the tables.

In July of 1849, when Jason was stranded in San Francisco by the loss of his crew, a band of rowdies had briefly menaced the town. They were layabouts and former soldiers who were too lazy to work in the mines, and they called themselves the Hounds. There was no police force then, and the rowdies grew bold. They robbed honest citizens in broad daylight, they took what they wanted from the stores, and they put a pistol to the head of anyone foolish enough to protest. One Sunday night on a drunken spree, they had terrorized the inhabitants of "Chilitown," below Telegraph Hill. They burned the Chileans' tents and shanties, violated several women, shot one boy, and sent the residents fleeing for their lives.

The next morning, while the Hounds were asleep, the citizens of San Francisco organized several companies of volunteers. Jason and a few of his men lent a hand. Before the day was over, the leaders of the gang were arrested and the others had fled the city. Within a week, the Hounds were tried and convicted and put aboard outbound vessels, banished from California forever, in the absence of any jail or penitentiary to hold them.

Jason turned to a patrician gentleman on his right. "Mr. Gillespie. You served with us too. You told me you built the first bungalow in Hong Kong and you came here aboard the *Eagle*. You said you brought the first Chinamen who came to California."

Gillespie smiled. "Your memory serves you well, Captain. Like your own ship's crew at that time, my Chinamen left me for the mines. How can we help you?"

Jason was pleased that the offer of help had come from a member of the Committee even before he made his proposal.

"Gentlemen, my crew and I will join you, but for one purpose only. We are seamen. Landsmen's affairs are not our concern, except in this one matter. We are going to find the man who burned my ship. With your help, we will find him all the sooner. You have the people on your side. If they know we are working with you, they will help us. If your men keep their ears open for anything that may lead us to the guilty man, that's three thousand pairs of ears helping us in our work."

"Four thousand now." The speaker was Charles Doane, the grand marshal of the Committee, commander of the vigilance police and militia. Alone among the members of the Executive Committee, he wore a military uniform.

"All the better," Jason said.

"Perhaps as a captain of militia—" Miers Truett began, but Jason cut him off.

"I'm no soldier, to go marching up and down."

"What are you asking is entirely outside our plans," Thomas Smiley said irritably.

"It fits our plans perfectly, if we intend to root out crime and corruption," Stephen Kent replied. "A noble ship has been burned in our harbor. That is a crime as serious as any arson done previously in this city. And I would say the same if the *Sarah B. Watson* belonged to another firm."

William Tell Coleman rapped gently on the table with a walnut gavel. For two days he had been mediating disputes, acting as the voice of conciliation and reason. He had blundered badly by dealing with Governor Johnson without first consulting the Committee leadership. They had overridden the agreement he had made and he had lost stature as a result. He would have to tread carefully if he hoped to consolidate his power. In Captain Beck's suggestion, he saw a way to bring the Executive Committee into unanimity, at least for a time.

"No one disputes your sincerity or the seriousness of the crime, Mr. Kent," Coleman said. "At issue here is the method for solving it."

"Captain Beck has given you the method," Kent said. "He and his men will find the bilge rat soon enough."

"We can't have undisciplined freebooters acting in the Committee's name," said Thomas Smiley.

"It's justice we're after, not booty!" Jason shot back.

Kent threw him a warning glance. "If you had served a day aboard Captain Beck's ship, Mr. Smiley, you would never doubt the discipline of his men."

"He would have to be under our orders." Smiley yielded ground grudgingly. His porcine eyes darted about the tables, judging who supported Captain Beck and who opposed him.

"I can't come running to you every time I want to turn around," Jason said. "We operate independently or we'll go it alone."

"That won't do, Captain," Coleman warned. There were murmurs of assent from around the table.

Kent saw that the Committee would brook no challenge to its power and he sought a way to mollify them. "Captain Beck can help us as well. He and his men will inform the Committee of any wrongdoing they uncover on the waterfront. For our part, we will inform Captain Beck of anything we learn that may lead to the men who burned his ship. What more could you ask for?"

Abel Calvert spoke for the first time. "Rangers," he said. The others looked at him, wondering what on earth he was talking about. "Captain Beck and his men will be the Committee's rangers."

"A company of rangers," Smiley mused, liking the idea.

"A company of marines," said Jason Beck.

The men of the Executive Committee looked at one another.

Kent smiled. "There you are." With a word, Abel Calvert had turned the tide in Jason's favor. Rangers or marines, it didn't matter. Both carried associations so favorable that no man could object. None wanted to, judging by the approving looks that now replaced the members' skepticism. From Rogers' Rangers in the French and Indian Wars to the Texas Rangers in the war with Mexico, the exploits of America's rangers were a proud part of her history, as were those of the United States Marines, who had distinguished themselves against the British, the French, the Tripoli pirates, and the Mexicans.

"A company of marines," Miers Truett said with finality.

"Detached for service on the San Francisco waterfront, under Captain Beck's command," Jonathan Frye said. "I will be glad to serve as liaison with Captain Beck's marines, if the Committee approves."

At two o'clock, the crew of the *Sarah B. Watson* mustered at the offices of Farnum & Kent. The night before, after the fruitless search for Rooney and Keith, Jason had told the men to find doss houses, although he knew half of them would bed with whores, and he had ordered them to gather at the firm's place of business today. Then, he had no plan in mind beyond rendering himself painless with brandy. Now he had obtained the Vigilance Committee's cooperation without putting himself or his men directly under the Committee's orders, and the success fortified him.

Kent was still at the vigilantes' warehouse, engaged in trying Charles Cora, so Jason took over his second-floor office.

"Well, Melchior, 'tis a new day," he greeted the mate with the best face he could manage.

"Aye, and us on a lee shore, Cap'n." After assembling the crew, Melchior had left them in the rooms below while he came to humble himself before his captain. He doffed his sea cap. " 'Twas my fault. I never should've come ashore."

He motioned Melchior to a chair and sat on the edge of Kent's desk. "There are to be no recriminations, Melchior."

"That note, 'twas so much like ee, I believed it and never doubted." He shook his head. The graying curls swayed and steadied like loosely coiled wire. "Poor Stritch drownded. Brad Keith and Mr. Rooney charred in hellfire. I will carry them to my grave, Jason."

"No more of that, old friend. You found a berth at Mrs. Rockwell's?"

"Aye. She asked for ee last night, and again this morning."

Jason flushed, remembering where he had been last night. There would be time later to make amends. It was time now to instill his own sense of purpose in his men.

"That boy run off," Melchior said. "Young Dickie. Soon's ee left us last night, he run off. Ain't seen the black of his shadow since then. Mrs. Rockwell, she be worried about him."

"He seems to take care of himself well enough." Hearing the boy was missing, Jason was worried too, but wharf rats had a way of surviving. "Have you eaten?"

"Aye. She sets a good table, that woman."

"You will need your strength. Now tell me again what happened when Grimes came aboard yesterday."

"It were just gone eight bells at midday," Melchior began. He repeated what he had told Jason the night before, about Grimes coming to the ship with the note he said he had received from Jason's hand, and shore pay for the crew. "If only I'd looked closer at that paper, I might o' seen it weren't your hand."

"What's done is done," Jason said. It was time for revenge, not guilt and blame. "Grimes brought the other boats with him?"

"Aye. Three boats in all."

"Think now, man. What did the oarsmen look like?"

Melchior twisted his cap in his enormous hands. "Now you ask it, I recall I first took one of the others to be Little Jack, come back to stand up for deserting, like Grimes. He were small, about the same as Little Jack, but I never got a good look at him. Jolly Jim rode in that boat, I think." The mate shook his head. "The truth be, Jason, I scarce paid attention to the boatmen, so glad I was to get ashore. If I'd stood aboard we'd still have a ship today."

"Stop blaming yourself, man!" Jason took hold of Melchior's shoulder. It felt like an oaken bulwark beneath his hand. "Let the sea claim her dead, old friend. If you had stayed aboard, we would be mourning you, instead of Keith and Rooney, God rest their souls. And God pardon me for saying so, but I am grateful you are here alive today. Now tell me what you would do if the world was in your power."

Melchior was momentarily puzzled, but then his eyes lit up with new interest. "I'd hang the scum that burnt the *Sarah B.*"

"Aye. And that's what we will do. But understand this. Whether you stay with me now is up to you. You can join me, or you will be released from the ship's company with pay until the day the ship burned, and no blame for going your own way."

"I signed articles with ee long ago, Jason."

"That was to serve aboard ship. This is something new. Every man who stays will have ship's wages and his lodging paid for until this business is done. When it's over, he will be discharged here in San Francisco or given passage to Boston at Farnum and Kent's expense, as he chooses. If with God's favor we find a new ship here, I will take any man aboard the new vessel in his old position, you before all the rest."

"Show me the papers, then, and I'll sign."

Jason pointed to a ruled sheet that lay on Stephen Kent's desk. He offered a pen, and Melchior signed his name.

"You bring the men up one at a time now, Jolly Jim first," Jason said. "No man to leave the premises until I say. And send up Ned Rollick."

Rollick had accompanied Jason to the firm's offices, released from his vigilance duties by Stephen Kent with the consent of the Executive Committee. While Jason and Melchior questioned the members of the crew, Rollick wrote down a summary of their recollections in a neat hand. The testimony from the interviews, along with all other evidence concerning the fire, would go to the insurers in Boston by the first steamer.

"This little England man, he don't say much, he just row the boat," Jolly Jim said when Jason asked him about the small boatman.

Jason sat at Stephen Kent's desk, flanked by Melchior

and Ned Rollick. Jolly Jim was uncomfortable before the three men, and gave no evidence of the good spirits that had earned him his name.

"What about the other boats?" Jason asked. "Who rowed them?"

"One fella named Tom. Ireland man, I think. And Grimes."

"Last night you said Melchior left Grimes to stand watch."

"Aye, Cap'n," Melchior spoke up. "Troia rowed Grimes's boat ashore. I told Grimes I would flog him if he set foot on land again afore ee'd passed judgment."

Jason returned his attention to Jolly Jim. "You're sure the small boatman was English?"

"Sure, Cap'n. Little England man."

Questioning the rest of the crew didn't take long. Kept aboard ship after sampling the gold port's fleshpots and grogshops, the men had been so eager to return ashore when Grimes brought the counterfeit message, they hadn't taken much note of the men who rowed them to land. They confirmed what Jolly Jim had said about the boatmen, but contributed little more.

When the last man left Kent's office, twenty-one had signed to serve in Jason's company of marine irregulars. Only five men drew their pay, which they planned to invest at once in mining supplies and passage inland to the gold country. These five would receive letters from Farnum & Kent releasing them from duty in San Francisco and protecting them from maritime law, which said a sailor could only leave his ship in her home port.

Jason addressed the remaining men in the firm's reception room on the ground floor. "I want Grimes," he told them. "He'll know who sent the boats out to the ship and he'll know who the other boatmen were." He paused to let the words sink in. "Don't try to take him alone. Follow him, see where he goes. Then fetch a shipmate and take him however you can. But I want him alive."

Chapter 19

hile the crew spread through the town, drifting into the grogshops and doss houses and pushing academies like an inquisitive tide, Jason and Melchior, with Jolly Jim and two others, sailed to the Goat Island anchorage in Finn Warren's dory to see what could be salvaged from the *Sarah B. Watson*. The clouds were solid overhead and the air was full of moisture, enough to dampen the clothes on Jason's back and the skin on his face. The wind promised rain. Out over the sea, visible between the heads of the Golden Gate, gray veils stretched from the low clouds to the darker gray of the water.

A yellow buoy marked the sunken hulk that had been a China clipper, although the masts and spars were plain enough to see, rising nearly two hundred feet above the waves. The poop was awash, the fo'c'sle and the bows mostly burned away. When the fire burned through the hull, the flooding seawater had soaked the rice in the ship's hold and she sank like a stone to the bottom that lay only a fathom beneath her keel at low water.

"She'll spew rice for a month." Jan deLoesseps, the sailmaker, a solid Dutchman, pointed to a bloom of swollen grains that rose from the forward hatch and drifted to leeward. Beside deLoesseps, Rob Tinker was a sober shadow of the man whose depraved coupling Jason had interrupted the night before.

"Steady and level, she is, Jason," Finn Warren said. "The bottom is soft here. She'll rest well enough until she's towed off or a winter storm breaks her apart."

"She went down fast, Cap'n." Melchior was appraising the condition of the spars. The mainmast and the mizzen were sound. Only the foremast had continued to burn after the ship sank. It was a charred pole, with remnants of the braces dangling from the blocks at the ends of the blackened yards. If a ship burned from the deck down, the masts and yards were consumed long before the fire breached the hull.

Jason peered through the greenish water. He could see the ship's weather deck plainly. Around the hatches and along the starboard bulwarks the decking was burned through but the ship had sunk before the whole deck burned off.

"She was fired below decks, just as Dickie said."

The night before, when he had calmed the boy enough to get the rudiments of his story, Dickie told him of seeing strangers aboard the ship, and then of smoke and fire. He had tried to say more, but Jason had turned all his efforts to searching for Seaman Keith and Second Mate Rooney. Later, he hadn't the stomach for starting after the cause of the fire. The fact of the ship's death was enough to bear. Now he wanted to know every detail of the boy's story, but that would have to wait until he could speak with Dickie again. Here, the remains of the *Sarah B.* confirmed that she had been sunk by design.

Jason looked aloft. "We'll save what we can. Yards and topmasts we'll float ashore. Whatever sails and ropes aren't burned, we'll take them too."

"Poor old Jim," Jan deLoesseps said. He was looking down at the remains of the deckhouse, where he and Second Mate Rooney had sat for many an hour during their watches together. They had shared a love of pipe smoking and they had argued about the merits of different tobaccos until the rest of the watch was driven to distraction. "To think that he is gone." DeLoesseps put his head in his hands.

They spent the afternoon in the rigging, clambering up the shrouds from the dory, walking out the yards where the footropes held fast, hauling lines through blocks, and inspecting the sails that had escaped the flames. Finn Warren left them there, perched in the spars, for long enough to sail to the docks and return with a longboat in tow. With all hands working hard they managed to bring down the mizzen topsail and topgallant, together with the braces and the other lines for those sails, all but the halyards and downhauls for the moving yards. Those ropes would be used to lower the yards themselves on the morrow.

At dusk, Jason and Melchior returned to the boardinghouse in a light rain, their wet clothing stained with tar. Atop the gable, the wrought-iron ship sailed sou'west into the squall with all sails set.

Jason was ready now to face the condolences that he felt sure would be heaped upon him, but instead of becoming the center of attention on his arrival he found most of the household's sympathy directed at the forlorn figure of Dickie Howell, who was seated in the kitchen, wrapped in a blanket. Sarah Rockwell and Ingrid moved from stove to table, urging food on the boy although he had already eaten his fill, while Joshua Norton looked on.

"The lad spent all the night and all of today trying to discover the fiend who burned your ship," Norton told Jason.

Jason put a hand on Dickie's shoulder. "How did you expect to find him, all by yourself?"

"I don't know, Captain. I just had to try. I went through the dram houses, looking for anyone who smelled of smoke." Dickie rose abruptly from the table and ran from the kitchen. Jason heard the thump of small feet running up the stairs, then along the landing and up to the top floor.

"He has taken the loss of the ship and your boy Stritch very hard," Sarah said. "He blames himself."

"Blames himself? What for?"

"You had better ask him."

Jason found Dickie face down on the bed in the vacant room on the third floor, next to his own. He sat on the bed and patted the boy's shoulder awkwardly. "Now, young Richard. What's this about?"

Dickie rolled on his side. Wet streaks glistened on his cheeks. "It's my fault Stritch is dead, Captain."

"Nonsense."

"It is. It was my idea to go aboard the ship. I didn't know he couldn't swim! Honest, I didn't."

Jason had learned to swim off the Boston docks, but fully a third of his crew had never mastered the skill. "Suppose you start at the beginning. Tell me how you came to be aboard the ship when the fire started."

Dickie wiped his face with a small fist. He told Jason about finding Stritch in the crowd at the jail, and how Stritch had wanted to see the hanging, and of Stritch's idea to play at pirates aboard the *Sarah B.*, once it was clear there would be no hanging then. He told how they got out to the ship, and of going into the tween decks to avoid the watch on deck. "I thought the tween decks would be full of rice, but it was almost empty," Dickie said, still puzzled by the discovery.

"Grain is a heavy cargo. A ship full to the main deck with rice is barely afloat. She'll founder if she takes on water in a storm."

Dickie stored away this knowledge with the rest of his nautical lore. He told how he had waited for Stritch in Jason's cabin, and of hearing voices on deck, and seeing one man hit another over the head.

"Did you recognize either man?" Jason's pulse quickened.

"It was too dark, Captain. I saw the man who was hit fall down and then I hid in your cabin again. I was frightened."

"There is no shame in that, Richard. Was that all you saw before the fire began?"

"No. I hid for a while and then I went out and looked again and I saw—" Dickie's eyes grew wide. "I remember something, Captain! I saw a man with a hook instead of a hand!"

"You're certain? He might have been holding a cargo hook."

"No! When I looked again, I saw two men. One short man and another man. They went to the main hatch and the short man dropped down inside. The other man passed something to him. A jug of some kind. He had a hook instead of a hand! I'm certain."

"All right. What did you do then?"

"The man with the hook went for'ard and I couldn't see him anymore. I wanted to find Stritch, so I went down the aft companionway. That's when I smelled the smoke. There was smoke in the tween decks, and I smelled turpentine too."

"Turpentine. Not pine tar? We had oakum and pitch aboard for caulking."

"I'm certain it was turpentine, Captain. I called down the companionway for Stritch, as loud as I dared, but there was no answer. The smoke was too thick to see in the tween decks, so I stayed where I was, calling to Stritch, but the smoke came up the companionway and finally I went out on deck. There was smoke from the hatches and flames for'ard, and no one about."

"Already in their boat and gone, then. What part of the ship was burning?"

"The deckhouse was burning. There was smoke from all the hatches and flames on the starboard side, and I think the fo'c'sle was burning too. I couldn't see for'ard because of the smoke, but I heard someone coughing and then Stritch's voice called Mr. Rooney's name. I called back to him and he said 'They've killed Brad Keith, Dickie.' Then he said 'I'm on fire,' and then I heard a splash."

"He went over the side, poor lad. If he'd got clear of the fire he might have lowered a boat amidships. Go on."

"The wind was blowing the flames aft. I jumped overboard and I swam 'round and 'round calling for Stritch but I never seen him." The boy's breath caught in his throat.

Jason gripped his shoulder. "It's all right, lad. You did what you could. You're lucky to be alive."

Fresh tears rolled down Dickie's cheeks. "If we hadn't been playing aboard ship this never would have happened! It was my fault."

"It was the fault of the men who set the fire." And the fault of the man who paid them. Jason had no doubt that someone paid to have his ship burned. "You've done no wrong, Richard. Remember that. You've told me much. You have done well."

The deed was done by Grimes and two others. A short man—possibly the Englishman who rowed Jolly Jim's boat—and a man with a hook for a hand had helped him. They set the fire below decks to burn through the hull and sink the ship quickly. Most likely the man Dickie Howell saw knocked on the head was Mr. Rooney. Kent said Rooney was found aboard, but he didn't say where. Probably they pitched him into the hold, hoping his body would be consumed by the fire. They must have found Brad Keith asleep in the fo'c'sle and killed him there.

Three men killed, and all for a cargo of rice. From the first, Jason was certain the reason for the fire was the rice, not the ship herself. Someone didn't want the rice on the market. But who, and why? Grimes held the answers. When he was found, he would give them up.

"I thought Dickie might like to hear a story." Joshua Norton ventured into the room holding a plate of cookies, followed by the gray cat. "You're to sleep here tonight, young man, by imperial orders. Mrs. Rockwell sent these for you." He set the plate on the bed. "I cannot say how sorry I am, Captain. For the ship and that accursed cargo."

"You did what you could to rid me of it," Jason said.

"So I did. Today, with Mr. Calvert's loan in hand and my bargain sealed with Farnum and Kent, the rice would have been mine. And instead of recovering some of what I lost by my earlier folly, I should have compounded it."

Jason hadn't considered how close his own loss had come to snaring Norton too. He left the merchant with the boy and went down to the kitchen, where Sarah Rockwell was ministering to Melchior's hunger. Afloat or ashore, in high spirits or low, the mate's appetite was prodigious.

"How is Dickie?" Sarah asked.

"He is mourning for his friend, but he will be all right. I've told him he is not to blame."

"Thank you for that."

" 'Tis only the truth. He is a good boy, Mrs. Rockwell,

and he did no wrong. See he gets his rest and feed him again when he wakes. He will be himself soon enough."

"What about you, Captain? What will you do?"

"I'll find the men responsible for burning my ship."

"And when you find them?"

"I will hang them from a yardarm for the world to see."

Sarah opened her mouth to speak but she closed it and said nothing. She set a plate of food before Jason, and when he would eat no more she sent him to bed.

Melchior remained, chewing methodically. "Thank ee, ma'am," he said when at last he pushed his plate away. " 'Tis only the food from your table has got me through this day."

"Captain Beck is blessed to have such a devoted officer at a time like this." Sarah was still somewhat in awe of the enormous mate.

"Nay. 'Tis friendship binds us, ma'am. And a debt I owe 'n."

"A debt?"

"Aye. A debt for my life."

"Captain Beck saved your life?"

" 'Twas not written I should be here now, ma'am. Eight years since, my ship was pooped by a rogue wave off the Cape of Good Hope. Broke in twain and went down with all hands in scarce more'n the time to tell of it. All hands save me. I held fast to a spar. The fore royal spar, it were, not that ee'd know or care. I knew it by the length and the girth of it, and by the footropes that I fashioned myself not three months afore. I reckoned 'twas vanity to keep hold of it. No more'n vanity and striving after a wind, as the preacher says. Soon enough I'd tire and let go, I reckoned, and then I'd be drownded like the rest. All my shipmates gone. But I held fast through the night just to see the sun put up its head once more. The clouds broke during the night and I seen the Southern Cross, so pretty off my stern. I reckoned I'd see the sunrise and then let go."

Sarah stood with a dishrag in her hand, checked on her way to wipe the stovetop clean, all her attention on the Cornishman.

"Come the sunrise, 'twere as pretty a sea as ever you

seen. Just a few clouds, for decoration, like. So I watch the sunrise and take a last look around and here be Cap'n Beck with all sails set, scarce more'n a half mile to suthard. That were afore the *Sarah B. Watson*, but I never set eyes on a prettier vessel than that one. Cap'n Beck spied a bit o' wreckage and turned to look for any poor souls left alive, and all he found was me."

"It was not your time to die."

"So 'twould seem. 'Tis a burden to owe 'n for my life, but Cap'n Beck does what he can to ease the weight of it."

"Surely he asks nothing in return."

"Nay. And there's the burden." He got to his feet and loomed over her. "See, missus, I shunned the life I were born to, and p'raps I went against God's will. We're mining folk, the Cornishmen, but I turned my back on the mines after one look at them cramped holes full of dust and dark. I went to sea instead, to live beneath the sky, with the sun and the moon and the stars and the wind, as God intended a man to live, I always thought. But what if the Lord sent that wave and sunk my vessel just to bring me home to His mercy, by way of teaching me a lesson? And Cap'n Beck, by saving me from the waters, confounded His will again? There's a debt I can never repay, not in a lifetime."

When Sarah was done in the kitchen she went to the third floor and found Joshua Norton seated in a chair by Dickie's bed, telling the boy a story. Kittery, the gray cat, was curled up on the bed beside Dickie, sleeping soundly.

"Let him finish the story, please," Dickie begged when Sarah said it was time for him to sleep.

"You tell her what it's about," Norton said to Dickie, "and then I will finish it. There's not much more."

"It's about a boy who lives all alone in a great forest," Dickie said. "He has a magic lantern and a magic axe."

"His father is a woodcutter," Norton added. "He was once the woodcutter to the king, but he offended the king by falling in love with the king's daughter and the king banished him to the very depths of the royal forest."

"Let me tell it!" Dickie insisted. "The only trail that

leads out of the forest goes over a bridge that is guarded by a terrible troll."

"Does the boy have a mother?" Sarah asked.

"He did, but she died," Dickie said. Norton gave Sarah a meaningful look, glancing from her to the boy, which Sarah took to mean that the tale was a disguised story about Dickie himself.

"The boy's name is Richard," Dickie said. "The woodcutter isn't really his father. He found the woodcutter's cabin while he was wandering in the forest after his mother died. She left him a magic lantern that keeps him safe from all the wild beasts, and he was almost out of lamp oil but he found the woodcutter's cabin and he was safe there. The woodcutter adopted him, and then one day he went off to cut wood and he never came back."

"That's where we are now," Norton said. "Winter is coming on. And we should tell you that this axe of Richard's—a hatchet, really—was a gift from the woodcutter, and it had special powers. It enabled the boy to cut all the firewood he needed, and the woodcutter had cautioned him always to take it with him when he left the cabin. But he had only enough food to last a month, and so, as the end of the month drew near, and the woodcutter had not returned, Richard went off to look for him. He took his mother's lamp and the hatchet the woodcutter gave him and he walked and he walked, following the trail that led out of the forest, until he came to the bridge where the terrible troll lived.

"Richard hoped he might tiptoe across the bridge without waking the troll, who slept all the day long, but it was evening, and the troll was waking up. When he heard Richard tiptoeing across the bridge, the terrible troll rushed up to the far end to block Richard's way. He was four feet tall and horribly ugly. He was very strong, and he had long teeth like a wolf, and most of all things in the world, he liked to eat little children."

"You will frighten the boy out of his skin," Sarah said.

"That's the way these tales are," Norton said. "Full of fearsome things, but it comes out all right in the end, as we shall soon see. The troll cried, 'Who is this, crossing my bridge?' And Richard said, 'I am Richard, the woodcutter's son, and everything in the forest belongs to the king, not to any old troll.' Well, that made the troll very angry and he rushed at Richard to eat him up, but Richard held up his mother's lamp and the light blinded the troll. And now Richard raised his magic hatchet and with a single swipe he chopped the troll's head right off, and to his amazement the troll vanished in a puff of smoke with a loud pop, just like this."

Norton put a finger in his mouth and popped it out with a *pop* that made Dickie laugh.

"Trolls are no laughing matter," Norton said seriously. "For as soon as that troll disappeared, another one rushed out from beneath the bridge. Once again, Richard held up his lantern and chopped the troll's head off, and he vanished with a *pop*. A third troll came out, but this time, before the troll could come up on the bridge, Richard chopped at the bridge with his magic hatchet and in no time at all he reduced it to a pile of kindling. And he said, 'There! Now you have no home. It is better that the travelers should get their feet wet wading across the stream,' which was not very deep at all, 'than to be frightened by a terrible old troll.' But when he looked to where the third troll had been Richard saw that it wasn't a troll at all, but his father, the woodcutter. And with him on the bank of the stream were hundreds of people, all cheering him. They were all the people the troll had captured over the years, you see, and they had all been turned into trolls, but when Richard chopped down the bridge he destroyed the troll's home and freed them all. And now, to Richard's wonder, the dark forest became much lighter, and the trees were full of singing birds and the stream was a beautiful place where the gentle creatures came to drink.

"The people he had saved lifted him up on their shoulders and carried him down the path, out of the forest and across the fields and meadows until they came to the castle of the king. When they told the king what Richard had done, he welcomed them, and especially the woodcutter, for the king's daughter had not smiled or spoken a word since the woodcutter was banished to the forest. The king begged the woodcutter to marry his daughter, for only then would she smile and speak again. Of course the woodcutter said yes, and the wedding was the grandest the kingdom had ever known. It made the king very happy to see his daughter smiling again, and to hear her voice, and he gave them a castle at the edge of the forest, which was no longer a fearsome place. And do you know who lived with the woodcutter and the king's daughter in that castle?"

"Richard did!" Dickie said.

"Shh," Norton cautioned him. "You'll wake Captain Beck, who had a terrible day, just as you did. Now tell me how you think the story ends."

"They lived happily ever after?"

"Just so. And with that, you must go to sleep, so you will have happy dreams."

"I'll dream about having a magic axe so I can kill all the trolls."

"And don't forget your lantern." Norton looked on while Sarah tucked Dickie in and kissed him good night. They left the door ajar so a little light from the lamp on the second-floor landing could enter Dickie's room, and they went downstairs together.

"If only our childhood dreams could come true," Sarah said.

"But they can," Norton said. "The symbols in the fairy tales show us the way. The hatchet is the strength of courage and the lamp shines with the light of truth and understanding. With courage and understanding, we can overcome our fears and make our dreams come true."

"When I was a little girl I wanted to be a fairy princess and live in a castle. You have always wanted to be an emperor. Those things can never be."

"Can't they? To those in your house, you are more than a princess, Mrs. Rockwell. You are the fairy queen who reigns in this castle, and you give us shelter."

Sarah smiled. "I always thought I was the one taking shelter here."

"You see?" Norton beamed. "Each of our dreams comes true in its own way, and they needn't be put off by the realities of the ordinary world. All we need is the courage to fight for what we believe in."

"You make it sound so simple."

"Oh, it isn't simple at all. It is hard work to be courageous, as you well know." Norton took Sarah's hand and kissed it quickly before giving her a shy smile and retreating to his room.

In her own room, Sarah combed out her hair and put on her nightdress. She sat at her secretary and began a letter to Peter by telling him of the dreadful fire and the deaths it caused.

With Melchior, the mate, in the second-floor room beside Mr. Norton's, and Dickie in the room next to Captain Beck's (at least for tonight), the house is full for the first time in many months, yet I cannot rejoice in this, she wrote. She turned the wick on the lamp a little higher.

> *Tragedy has brought Melchior and Dickie here, and kept Captain Beck ashore for what promises to be a longer stay. He regards San Francisco—the city that has been my safe harbor—as a purgatory, and now I find my sanctuary threatened by events I am powerless to affect. In this morning's Herald—a valiant clarion that cries out alone against this unauthorized army—Mr. Nugent gives the Vigilance Committee their due and admits that they conducted their march on the jail yesterday with discipline and order, yet he also says, "Justice is supine and her ministers are bound hand and foot."*
>
> *What are we to think of these men who have seized the city? Are they good or evil? I know only that normal business is at a standstill, the municipal authorities are impotent, and everything hangs on the life of one man—James King of William. If he lives, we still may draw back from the abyss. If he dies, there is no telling what actions that event may provoke. At the very least, it will doom James Casey to swift execution, but I fear it may unleash a mob spirit that will be difficult to restrain.*
>
> *Before Captain Beck and Melchior returned this evening, Mr. Norton and I were speaking about the vigilantes. Since the Vigilance Committee rejected him, he takes an increasingly dim view of them. I wondered whether they will ever willingly yield the*

power they have seized. Mr. Norton observed that all the elements of the French revolutionists' Committee of Safety are present here, and he spoke ominously of how the noble ideals of the revolution were tarnished by the Terror and the guillotine.

Chapter 20

Are you Captain Beck?"

"I am."

"I am Beverly Cole."

The impeccably dressed young man who presented himself to Jason in the Bank Exchange was tall and slender. His skin was very fair, all the more so in contrast to his curly hair and beard, which were glossy black. Bright eyes looked at Jason from beneath delicate brows and a high forehead where the hair was receding at the temples, although Cole was four years short of thirty. He supported himself on crutches, and showed evidence of being in some pain when he moved about.

It was Tuesday, the twentieth of May, the second day after the fire. Jason had risen that morning to find Dickie Howell already up and gone. The boy returned after breakfast with a note from Stephen Kent, asking Jason to meet Dr. Cole in the Bank Exchange saloon at one o'clock. Jason had invited Dickie to accompany him to Kent's office to see what the crew might have learned, but Dickie excused himself, saying the trial of Charles Cora by the Committee of Vigilance was a steady source of employment, as he took messages hither and yon to summon witnesses.

Kent's note to Jason did not say who Dr. Cole might be or why Kent wanted Jason to meet him, but Cole provided the reasons at once.

"I was asked to examine the remains of your crewmen, Captain. Post-mortem examinations are a specialty of mine." Cole's voice was softly modulated but his handshake was firm. He swung himself about and led Jason to a table.

Few of the saloon's patrons paid any special attention to Cole, nor did Jason's presence occasion anything like the interest it had provoked when Stephen Kent first brought him to the saloon five days before. In less than a week he had become known, his piratical hair and gold earring no longer curiosities.

Once seated, Cole set aside his crutches and hailed a waiter girl. Jason ordered brandy punch. Cole held up two fingers, then turned his attention to Jason. "You are a man of the sea, Captain, so I needn't mince words. You have seen death in most of its forms, I imagine."

"Too many times."

"The remains of your seaman and second mate were badly burned. Yet medical science can offer some evidence as to the cause of death in each case. A section of the sailor's lungs revealed that he had breathed a good deal of smoke before he died. Very likely he would have been asphyxiated by it, but someone helped him along. There were several stab wounds in both lungs, any of which might have caused death. He was stabbed in the back while he was lying down, probably while he slept. It is possible he never regained consciousness."

"Thank God for small blessings," Jason said.

"As for your second mate, that is an interesting case. He was found in the remains of the galley."

"Someone saw a man knocked over the head. They must have knocked him out and put him there."

"Unfortunately, Mr. Rooney's condition won't permit determining if he was struck a blow on the head. However, I found neither smoke nor water in his lungs. In other words, he was dead before the fire began. And I found the cause of death." Cole paused for effect, but Jason said nothing. Dr. Beverly Cole was a man much impressed by his own skills as a physician. He would tell soon enough what he had found.

The waiter girl returned with the brandy punches.

Cole made no protest when Jason paid, accepting the courtesy as his due.

"There is an incision in Mr. Rooney's heart," Cole said when the girl had left them. "The wound was instantly fatal. It came from below. It was made by a short blade, sharpened on both edges. Judging by the location of the incision, I should say the stroke was delivered underhand, like this."

He brought up his hand as if holding a knife, stopping it just below Jason's sternum, angling up toward the heart.

"Under the ribs, you see? The man who did this knew what he was doing, and he was a cold-blooded son of a bitch. He was standing face-to-face with your mate and he took him unawares. It's possible the murderer was short, although a taller man could have delivered the fatal blow if he were careful not to strike too high." Cole leaned back, evidently satisfied with himself. "I don't mind telling you, Captain, that wound was damnably hard to find."

Stephen Kent appeared in the midday crowd, spied them, and approached the table, out of breath. "I hoped I might join you, but I wasn't sure I would be able to come. As it happens, we are done with ... the matter that has taken up so much of our time. Rum business, I can tell you, but it's done. Now, Doctor, you've told him what you know?"

"I have."

"Good. We will need your report for the insurers."

"How soon after the report is done can we expect a draft for the settlement?" Jason said to Kent. Between persuading the Vigilance Committee to aid his search for the incendiaries and beginning salvage efforts on the ship, he had not found time to speak with Kent about the insurance until now.

"Just as soon as the steamers can carry our report to Boston and bring back authorization."

Jason was dumbfounded. If the settlement depended on authorization from Boston, there could be no draft for a new vessel in less than two months. "The company must have an adjuster here."

"So there is. I took him to see the ship yesterday, but

that's not the problem." Kent's discomfort was plain to see. "I have dreaded telling you this, Jason. Bean and Jameson's settlements have been drawn on the bank of Palmer, Cook and Company. That bank got in a great deal of trouble in the financial panic last year and never got out of it. There are lawsuits under way. To make matters worse, the firm mucks about in politics, mostly with the Democrats. As you can imagine, they have suffered since the Vigilance Committee came into power. The fact is, they haven't the capital to pay a settlement such as ours."

"What about another bank?"

"We'll get the money all right. I promise you that. But it will take time. Bean and Jameson is in the process of making arrangements with other banks. Sadly, until the new arrangements are complete, each draft must be authorized by the home office in Boston."

The insurance firm of Bean & Jameson was smaller than many, but solid as bedrock and conservatively run. Much like Farnum & Kent, they accepted only risks they had weighed carefully and judged to be prudent. In consequence, their rates were lower than most of their competitors. This benefit, coupled with the firm's soundness, had persuaded Farnum & Kent to insure their vessels with Bean & Jameson. Jason himself had approved the choice, but he had never dreamed a sensible business decision would keep him ashore in California for two months or more. If the ship were insured with Lloyd's, at a higher cost, they could have a draft within the week on any bank in San Francisco.

"What word is there of Mr. King today?" Kent asked Dr. Cole.

"I was put off the case on the second day, Mr. Kent."

"I am well aware. That is why I ask. We are—that is, I am interested to hear your opinion precisely because you disagreed with the other doctors."

"Very well," Cole said. "I will put it in a few words. King of William's wound was not mortal, but the treatment he has received will prove to be, in my opinion. Doctors Toland and the others left the sponge in the wound. I believe the wound would close if they removed it. With the wound healing, they could remove the tourniquet."

"Yesterday the reports were encouraging. They said he was resting well."

Cole shook his head. "If the sponge does not kill him, the tourniquet will surely do so."

Somewhere in the street outside, a bell sounded once, then again.

Kent pulled a fat watch from his pocket. "It isn't two o'clock yet." Before he could open the case the distant bell struck a third time and a fourth, and now the first bell was joined by a second, and then another. In the saloon, conversations stopped and heads were raised. The room fell silent. All across the city the bells were slowly tolling. The men nearest the door stepped into the street.

"What can it be?" Cole wondered. Kent and Jason rose. Jason offered a helping hand to Cole but the young doctor waved him away and hoisted himself on his crutches.

In Montgomery Street, the pedestrians were motionless, listening, all but three Chinamen who hastened along, making for Little China. A passing drayman reined in his horses. The day was brilliant, the air clean and cool. The rain the night before had cleaned the streets and still held down the dust.

Somewhere out of sight a cry was raised. A moment later, a man appeared at a run from Jackson Street, calling out as he went, "King of William is dead! King of William is dead!"

Cole's expression as he heard the words revealed satisfaction and a measure of pride, not only in his calling, Jason judged, but also in the dramatic way his prophecy about King of William's demise had been proven correct.

When the runner had passed by, those in Montgomery Street began to speak all at once, addressing their acquaintances, or complete strangers, whoever chanced to be nearest. First one group and then another started off along the street, walking south. Soon every person in sight was moving in the same direction.

"Where are they all going?" Beverly Cole wondered aloud.

"To see the hanging." A man who had come out of the

Bank Exchange removed the napkin tucked in his vest, wiped his mustache and chin whiskers carefully, and handed the napkin to a waiter girl before he started off after the crowd.

"I must leave you, I'm afraid," Kent said.

"I'll walk along with you," said Jason. "Dr. Cole?"

"My business is saving lives, not taking them."

When they were beyond the doctor's hearing, Jason said to Kent, "Cole seems fit enough. Why is he on crutches?"

"He shot himself." Kent saw Jason's surprise. "Not on purpose, of course. He was packing for a horseback journey. His pistol fell to the floor and discharged. The ball passed through his stomach. That was two years ago and the wound is still not fully healed, they say. Come." He took Jason's arm and turned left at Clay Street, taking them out of the stream of pedestrians that was moving along Montgomery. "How is the salvage going?"

"Melchior is out there now. We will save most of the sails from the mizzen and the main. The main course is lost. The mizzen might be patched." The courses were the lowermost sails on each mast.

"It isn't much of a silver lining to our misfortune."

"When we get a ship, Jan deLoesseps will fit the sails we save. It will reduce the cost of rigging her."

They were at Sansome Street. Kent stopped to face Jason. "I am more sorry than I can say about this delay, Jason. As soon as the authorization for the settlement arrives, you will have the best vessel money can buy. I promise you that. There are some decent hulls afloat on this waterfront. When we can spare Ned Rollick from his duties at our headquarters, I will have him make inquiries."

Three men came running along Sansome. "Don't miss the hanging!" one called out as he passed them by.

"These people will be disappointed," Kent said. "There will be no hanging today."

"You're certain?"

"We began Casey's trial only yesterday. It will take some time, even now that King is dead."

"It's a proper trial, then?"

"Yes and no. Under the rules, the accused can select

any member of the Executive Committee to defend him. We call witnesses and all that. But we require only a majority to convict, and that doesn't sit well with me. In a regular court it takes a unanimous verdict to hang a man, but with Cora we did no better than the jury at his trial last winter. A bare majority to convict. I had some hope we might save him still. Now that King is dead I fear he'll go to the gibbet with Casey."

"I don't see that this man Cora has anything to do with your Committee."

"Neither do I, Jason, if the truth be known. They said we must take Cora to show that we stand for justice, against the corrupt courts and police. If we took only Casey, it would appear we were out for revenge." Kent shook his head. "It's a rum business, I'll tell you. Mr. Calvert and I are doing our best to keep the others in check."

"With luck, I will bring you an incendiary or two to try before long," Jason said. "When I do, I will see them hang, unanimous verdict or no."

They shook hands and parted, Kent going toward Sacramento Street, which was already crowded with men and women gathering around the vigilantes' warehouse. Jason followed Sansome Street to Pacific. He turned right to the wharf and there he found Dickie Howell waiting for him.

"They've made me a special messenger to the Executive Committee," Dickie announced. "I'm to carry messages between Mr. Frye and your marines, as well as my other duties." The boy looked much improved from the despondent figure of the night before. He was obviously pleased to have a role in Jason's work.

"You know who we are looking for?"

"Yes, Captain. Seaman Grimes and a small Englishman and the man with a hook."

"All right. You keep a weather eye out for them as you move about. This afternoon I will be at the *Sarah B.*'s anchorage. You know where Finn Warren ties up his dory?"

"Halfway along the wharf, on the north side."

"Aye. We come and go from there. We'll finish the salvage tomorrow, if not today."

Ten minutes later, Dickie was on Front Street at Sacramento, where vigilance militiamen were pushing the people back from the front of the warehouse. A company of dragoons arrived in a clatter of hooves to assist the soldiers on foot.

Dickie turned into a store belonging to the firm of Attro & Jones, which concealed a private entrance to the Committee's warehouse. He asked for Abel Calvert and was shown to the back room. Calvert rose from a chair when he saw Dickie.

"You're a coon who keeps his word," Calvert said. "I like that in a man." He handed Dickie a gold coin and a piece of paper that was folded in three and sealed with wax. "This note is more important than all the others," the banker said.

"Are your soldiers marching again?"

"No soldiers. This is my own affair. You take that paper and you go like the wind to Mrs. Rockwell's. You give that paper to Molly Gray, but not when anyone's about, 'specially not Trelayne."

The sun was down when Jason returned to the Pacific Wharf from what remained of the *Sarah B. Watson*. He was grimy once more from an afternoon spent dismantling rigging.

Dickie Howell was waiting for him where Finn Warren tied up his dory. "You're to come with me, Captain," Dickie said. "Mr. Frye sent me to fetch you. He will meet us at Dr. Cole's surgery."

"I have seen Dr. Cole earlier today."

"He has something more to tell you. That's all they said. Just to bring you."

The darkening streets were quiet, the buildings hung with funeral wreaths and black bunting. Between the wharves and Cole's office, Jason counted five squads of vigilance militia marching on patrol. In Jackson Street a rider reined in beside one squad long enough to exchange a few words with the man in charge, then raced on.

Beverly Cole's office was on Montgomery Street, in the premises of Little's Drug Store. Jonathan Frye opened the door at Dickie's knock. "About time. Dr. Cole would tell me nothing until you arrived."

"I don't like to repeat myself," Cole said. "Now I will tell you all. You stay here," he ordered Dickie. "This is no business for a boy."

Cole led Frye and Jason through a short hallway to the room in the back that served as his surgery. As they entered the room, Jason smelled turpentine. Cole struck a match and lit a gaslight set in a brass sconce on the wall. Jason's eyes, accustomed to the dusk outside, squinted at the bright light.

A body draped with a sheet lay on the examination table. Jonathan Frye lifted the corner of the sheet with the tip of his cane and turned it back so the head and shoulders of the corpse were exposed. The man was naked, his skin gray and lifeless. A freshly sutured scar ran down the center of his chest.

"Do you recognize this man?" Dr. Cole asked Jason.

"It is one of my seamen. Hubert Grimes."

Dr. Cole seated himself at a small desk and wrote on a tablet of paper. "Grimes. Hubert. Do you know the place and date of his birth?"

"That was in the ship's papers. Gone now, with everything else. He was from Connecticut. Hartford, I think. He was about twenty-four. He drowned?"

"Lungs full of water," Cole said. "You could wring them out like a sponge. Two fishermen pulled him from the bay."

Jason knew how the body would feel to the touch. He had taken enough dead men from the sea to know that texture too well. "Grimes deserted on his first shore leave. He was one of the men who brought the boats to the ship to take my crew ashore on the night of the fire."

"You think he set the fire?" Frye said.

"He had a hand in it. He knew who sent those boats."

"Perhaps he had a grievance against you, Captain?" Frye suggested. "Something to make him want revenge when he was drunk?"

"Ten days before we made port my second mate had him standing double watches for shirking his duty. That's not enough cause to burn a ship." Was it enough to give Grimes a motive for stabbing Second Mate Rooney in the heart? Perhaps, if Mr. Rooney was to be killed in any event in the course of the arson.

"One never knows how the inferior mind works, eh, Doctor?" Frye said.

"Much the same as the superior mind, Mr. Frye, under the same circumstances." Cole finished writing and rejoined the two men. "You smell the turpentine, of course. His clothes, there." He indicated a heap of sodden clothing in the sink.

"Dickie Howell was on the ship that night," Jason said. "He smelled turpentine when the fire began." Jason's certainty that the fire was set to destroy the cargo of rice wavered. Could it have been only a seaman's grievance, nourished by rum until it grew beyond reason?

"The fire may have spread faster than Seaman Grimes planned." Frye gazed thoughtfully at the body. "I imagine he panicked. Jumped into the bay and drowned."

Beverly Cole shook his head. "He did not jump. You can put money on it." He turned Grimes's head to the side, manipulating the corpse as matter-of-factly as he might have handled a roast of beef. He took Frye's hand and placed it against the back of Grimes's head. "Here. Do you feel it?" Frye withdrew his hand as soon as Cole released him. He took a handkerchief from his coat and wiped his fingers carefully.

"Here, Captain." Cole guided Jason's hand. "I doubt another doctor in San Francisco would have noticed this."

"There's a lump."

"Just so. In my opinion, someone knocked out your Seaman Grimes and tossed him in the bay, where he drowned."

as Grimes one of 'em, that's what I want to know," Melchior said at breakfast the next morning. "Did he have a hand in the fire?"

"They may have used him to get aboard or he may have been in with them," Jason said. "It doesn't matter now."

Joshua Norton was intent on the conversation. "I see what you mean. Whether he helped them knowingly or not, they killed him so he could not identify them."

"Aye. That is one more death they must answer for." Each time Jason awoke during the night, he had cursed Providence for delivering Grimes to him dead and wondered how he would ever find the men who had burned his ship. When the roosters sang to greet the sun he had still not found the answer.

"Grimes was your only suspect?" David Farren said.

"We have two others."

"Aye." Melchior gave a grim chuckle. "Comes to it, we may hang every small Englishman in San Francisco, and every man with a hook for a hand."

"If you take an eye for an eye, you abandon the rule of law," Farren said.

"It seems to me this city has abandoned it already," Jason said.

"You would see no cannon in the streets and no pris-

oners taken from the lawful authorities if I were king."
Norton was only half in jest.

"I would be the first to enlist in your army, Mr.
Norton," Farren said. "I feel a complete fool, holding a
commission in the California militia and standing by
while the vigilants run freely in the streets." He was
dressed today in civilian clothes, his militia uniform put
away until he could wear it to some purpose.

"Is there nothing Governor Johnson and General
Sherman can do?" Sarah asked.

"The governor has gone back to Sacramento." Farren
offered nothing more, but when Jason and Melchior had
left for Farnum & Kent to meet with their crew, he came
to the kitchen, where Sarah was washing dishes.

"You mustn't ask me about General Sherman and the
governor when Captain Beck is with us, Sarah. You forget he is in with the Vigilance Committee."

"That is only so he can find the man who burned his
ship! And I don't believe for a minute that he would repeat anything he heard in this house." Sarah's anger
arose less from outrage than a fear that Farren was right
to be cautious. The lawyer and Jason Beck were in opposite camps. The division created in the city by the rise
of the Committee of Vigilance had entered her household, and she resented the intrusion as much as anything
the vigilantes had done.

"I'm sorry," she said. "I will keep to my own rule
about avoiding political discussions at mealtimes. In any
event, we are alone now, so you can talk freely. Are you
doing nothing at all to oppose the Vigilance Committee?"

"We can do nothing until they act."

"You're saying there must be bloodshed?"

"There must be a blatant violation of the law. If they
hang Casey and Cora, a great majority of the people will
support them, as they have supported them from the
start, but some will oppose them. If the Committee does
not disband soon, the governor will request the enlistment of new militia on behalf of the state. Then we will
find our recruits."

"Why doesn't the governor request new militia now?"

"Because we haven't three companies of men to their
forty. Because we haven't enough arms for the men who

are loyal. Until the vigilants act or disband, we can do nothing."

A gentle tapping sounded at the kitchen door. Sarah opened it to find Su-Yan Quan on the back steps. The gray cat slipped past his legs and trotted into the kitchen.

"I must get to my law office," Farren said, and took his leave.

"Very good day, Miss Rockwell," Su-Yan greeted Sarah when Farren was gone.

"Not so good, Su-Yan." The day was gray and cool. A raw wind blew off the sea and the air smelled like rain, but Sarah was not referring to the weather.

"Troubled times, certainly that is true," Su-Yan said.

"What will happen, do you think?"

"It is not given to me to foresee the future."

"It is not given to any of us, Su-Yan."

"Perhaps. In my world, sometimes one is permitted to see ahead."

"If you can see ahead I wish you would tell me what is to come, so I can prepare myself."

"In the old religion, we are taught to prepare for what is to come by making ourselves perfect now. Perfect for this moment that is now, and then gone. Jesus Christ teaches the same, certainly? To be good now, in the expectation of heaven?"

"You could put it that way." Sarah realized that she was discussing the philosophy of religion with an Oriental purveyor of vegetables. She felt slightly foolish, but as she picked over the contents of his cart she reflected that there were few Christians whose belief in divine providence was more devout than Su-Yan's, and it occurred to her that there was no less reason to listen to his opinions of religion than to those of any Occidental. There was more, perhaps, since Su-Yan knew the teachings of both Buddha and Jesus, while born Christians rarely subjected their beliefs to the scrutiny of comparison.

"Your house is for sale," he said.

"What? Oh. Yes. Yes, it is."

"You have had inquiries?"

"No. No inquiries."

"In the present conditions the price will seem high to some."

"Do you think it's too high?"

Su-Yan surveyed the house and grounds soberly before answering, as if he had spent his life dealing in real
estate. "It is a fair price, Miss Rockwell."

Sarah chose enough vegetables for two days and sent
Su-Yan on his way with her thanks. She pumped some
water in a pan and set the parsley and the carrots in the
water to keep them fresh before returning to her bedroom and sitting down to finish the letter she had begun
two nights before.

> *The only one who has noticed my advertisement
> for the house is my Chinese greengrocer. He says
> my price is fair, and I know you will think I am
> mad, but when he gives his opinion I accept it with-
> out a doubt. Something about him commands be-
> lief. To sell now I will have to take less than the
> house is worth, and that goes against my grain.
> Oh, Peter! What shall I do?*
>
> *I am more frightened today than ever before. Mr.
> King died yesterday and instead of riots and witch-
> hunts an absolute calm prevails over the city. I
> wish you were here to walk through the streets with
> me as I did yesterday afternoon with Molly, so you
> could feel what I feel.*

She wished Peter were here so she could talk to
him. She wished for someone she could trust absolutely.
Someone who could tell her that her fears were ground-
less and that the Committee of Vigilance was acting in
the best interests of San Francisco and its citizens.
Someone who could tell her what to do. But Jason Beck
was working hand in hand with the vigilantes and her
other boarders had their own concerns, and no one
seemed to feel, as she did, that the earth had slipped
from its orbit and was careening toward an uncharted
part of the heavens.

> *The town is draped in mourning, people talk in
> whispers, and everyone is waiting for the other shoe
> to fall. At times I think I would be less fearful if
> there were rampaging mobs in the streets. Somehow*

the silence is more terrible. In today's Herald, *Mr.
Nugent says that the trials of Casey and Cora
must still be in progress or the Vigilance Committee would make the verdicts public. Mr. Nugent im-
plores the Committee once more to return the
prisoners to Sheriff Scannell, but that is a vain
hope now. The* Alta *and all the other papers save
the* Herald *side completely with the vigilants, and
I find myself more and more outraged by their acceptance of the state of things. The* Alta *says that
the public's desire for justice in the matter of Mr.
King's death must surely produce decisive action on
the part of the Committee soon, as though we had
no police, no courts, no honest judges, no means
whatever for punishing a murderer without these
self-appointed men meeting in secret to determine
the fates of Casey and Cora and all the rest of us
as well. Mr. King's funeral is tomorrow, following
services at the Unitarian Church on Stockton.*

A light rain was falling when Su-Yan knocked at the
kitchen door of Mrs. Wickliff's parlor house. He was
greeted by Ferdinand, the burly cook, who disregarded
the rain and scrutinized the vegetables minutely before
inviting Su-Yan into the kitchen, which was warmed by
a large stove. At the table, three scantily clad prostitutes
were taking a late breakfast.

"Hello, Su-Yan," Lucy Thorsen greeted him. Lucy
was always courteous to him and she was more careful
in her dress than the others. The French woman, Yvette,
turned to favor him with a languid smile. Through the
arm hole of her sleeveless nightdress he could see her
breast. She put her arm over the back of the chair, which
made the breast rise up towards him, displaying its small
pink point.

Concealing his distaste, Su-Yan accepted a cup of coffee from Ferdinand and sipped it as they conducted their
business. He took care not let his impatience cause him
to give in too easily on the matter of price. Only Mrs.
Sarah Rockwell, of all his customers, did not haggle over
price. When he learned that this was her custom, he had

reduced what he charged her to only a little over the customary rate.

As the negotiating drew to a close, Lucy finished her breakfast and rose. "I will find Barbara."

"You 'ave no time for me this morning, Su-Yan?" Yvette stretched like a cat to display her svelte form to full advantage. She had fair skin and red hair. Through the thin fabric of her nightdress Su-Yan could see the dark cloud between her legs.

"For you, I am free," she said. "Just one time. So I can see what a yellow prick looks like."

"Leave him alone, Yvette." Ferdinand was abrupt with the French whore. The kitchen was his domain. "He's a Christian. And a married man."

Yvette pouted. "So are most of my customers."

Su-Yan excused himself and went out to wait on the kitchen porch. He seated himself in a bentwood rocking chair and slowed his breathing, allowing his mind to go blank to recover his composure. The French girl attracted him, but it was unthinkable to consort with a whore where he came to the back door as a vegetable peddler. He patronized the best brothels in Little China, where he was welcomed as an elder in the community and treated with respect.

A lifetime of practice allowed him to enter a meditative state in a matter of moments. As a boy, he had followed his teacher's advice that he imagine he was about to hear a beautiful piece of music for the first time, or the voice of the woman who was to become his wife, but he had abandoned such tricks long ago. He had no taste for music, and the voice of his wife was as familiar to him as his own. Now he simply put aside his thoughts and listened for whatever the world might tell him.

He was aware that time passed, but he did not measure it. There was a rustle of silk, and a hand placed lightly on his shoulder. He looked up and saw that his daughter had prepared herself to receive him. She wore a jacquard gown. Her hair was brushed, combed, and coiled at the back of her head. Small, elegant slippers peeped from beneath her gown. She bowed low to Su-Yan.

"What have you learned, Daughter? Will there be violence?"

"One man thinks so. Others say not."

They spoke Cantonese. His daughter's voice was very pleasant to the ear, as a Chinese woman's voice must be. Bo-Ji was her birth name. The Catholic missionary who christened her had named her Barbara without considering the difficulties it presented to those whose native tongue was Cantonese. It was almost as hard for Su-Yan to say his daughter's Christian name as that of Sarah Rockwell.

"The women say much the same," he told her. "The usurpers have the power to prevent violence. I overheard one man say the civil authorities have too few men and guns to oppose them." He had listened at Mrs. Rockwell's kitchen door this morning for as long as he dared. He was very glad to know that Governor Johnson did not plan to move against the Vigilance Committee for the present.

"Then our people are not in danger?"

Su-Yan admired his daughter's fine black hair, so like her mother's when she was young. "There is always danger in a barbaric land. But even if violence comes I think we are safe enough. Are you well?"

"Very well, Father."

"You have seen our doctor?"

"Every week, Father."

He stood. "Tell that vulgar French woman to cover herself when I am here. And give my best wishes to Lucy."

"Yes, Father." She bowed again as he left her.

Su-Yan continued his rounds, saddened, as always, by the necessity for placing his daughter in a house of prostitution, and worst of all in a house frequented by *guey low*. If she were in a house of Chinese, for Chinese—but then there would be no reason to place her in such a house at all. It was necessary that she be here. Together, he and Bo-Ji learned more about the doings of the *guey low* than the rest of the Chinese in San Francisco put together. On his daily rounds, Su-Yan exchanged meaningless chatter with the white women of the city. So it would appear to any casual listener and so it seemed to the white women themselves. But no woman's chatter was meaningless. What the men would not say to one another, they told their wives. The wives in turn told the Chinese greengrocer things they would not say to another white woman, thinking it meant nothing to him. What the white men would not tell their women, they told to the Chinese whore they bedded, for she was not part of their world.

The first Bo-Ji had lived more than two millennia ago, and she had sacrificed her life rather than risk the appearance of unvirtuous behavior. It pained Su-Yan that his daughter had abandoned her chastity at his command, but in following that command she displayed obedience, which was one of the cardinal virtues. And she followed the rest of the Four Virtues in an exemplary manner, demonstrating reticence, domestic skills, and a pleasing manner at all times when she visited the family at home, and while working for Mrs. Wickliff too, according to the reports Su-Yan received from Bo-Ji's employer.

Bo-Ji served her father and her people well. But the intelligence she gained did not come without a price. Since Su-Yan had instructed Bo-Ji to enter Mrs. Wickliff's house, his wife had denied him completely in the physical aspect of marriage. They slept apart. Their relationship was cordial and correct in every other respect, but she had taken her revenge.

onestly, you would think the President of the United States had died, or a senator at the very least." The jostling of the crowd pushed Sarah against Jason's side.

"Don't speak ill of the dead." Molly crossed herself.

Trelayne took her hand in his. "I wouldn't be too free with the Cross. After Democrats, Catholics were King of William's favorite targets."

It was midday Thursday. James King of William's funeral cortege was formed outside the Unitarian church on Stockton, but the greatest mass of the people were gathered along Montgomery Street, where the procession would pass when the memorial service was done. By working their way slowly forward, Jason and Sarah, accompanied by Trelayne and Molly and Farren and Norton, had reached Montgomery near the corner of Washington, across from the Bank Exchange saloon.

The flags hung at half-mast and black drapery adorned every building in the central district. Throughout the morning, the city's bells had tolled even more somberly than two days before, when the news that King of William had died was first carried around the town.

The morning's newspapers revealed that a post-mortem examination had been performed on the deceased by the doctors who failed to save his life. They had discovered tubercular masses the size of a man's thumb in King's lungs. The doctors expressed their view that this illness of the lungs had contributed to the victim's demise. Dr. Beverly Cole's opinion was solicited by a reporter from the *Alta California*, but it was not fit to print.

The day was hot under a clear sky. The westerly breezes were languid, scarcely bothering to stir the flags. Here and there along the funeral route, some of the men had removed their coats. Sarah had put on mourning dress, but Molly owned nothing so somber. Her dilemma had been solved by Trelayne, who went to the theater and brought her a silk dress of dark gray from the costume trunks. It had an elongated jacket bodice and three stiff flounces that widened the skirt, each ringed with stripes of lighter gray. Dressed properly for a funeral, Molly still managed to catch the eye of the gentlemen within her sight. In the unexpected heat of the day she was perspiring beneath her clothes.

"Men don't have to do anything different at all for a funeral," she complained to Trelayne. "They just wear what they wear every day. It isn't fair."

"Life isn't fair, my dear." He squeezed her hand.

"There's General Sherman." David Farren pointed out a tall red-haired man across the street. The woman at his side was holding his arm. "That's his wife with him."

"He isn't afraid to bring a lady into the streets," Sarah said pointedly. Supported by Trelayne and Norton, Jason had tried to persuade Sarah and Molly to remain at the boardinghouse on the grounds that anything was possible with feelings in the city at a high pitch, but the women had refused to stay behind. Sarah said the funeral was the most important public event to take place since her arrival in San Francisco, and she would see it no matter how much she might disapprove of the people's unreasoning adulation of a man who had taken the city's journalistic standards to a new low.

"Come over," Farren said. "I'll introduce you."

"I know the Shermans," Sarah said, and she led the way across the street.

"Good day, Mrs. Rockwell." Sherman tipped his hat. "I am sorry we missed the meeting of the Franchise League."

"The meeting was canceled," Sarah said. The Negro

rights organization held its monthly meeting on the third Tuesday of each month. The date for the May gathering had fallen on the eighteenth—the day King of William died. Sarah had arrived at the meeting place two nights before to find a notice posted on the door, canceling the meeting "out of respect for San Francisco's fallen martyr."

"You know my wife, of course," Sherman said. A round of introductions followed, in which Norton was presented last.

"Mr. Norton." Sherman's greeting was cool, but it was embarrassment, not dislike, that caused his reticence. After Norton's decline following his failed attempt to corner the rice market in '53, the notes for several of his properties had come into the hands of Sherman's bank.

"Always a pleasure, Mr. Sherman." Norton wrung Sherman's hand warmly, then turned to Jason. "My first place of business in this city was just there, Captain, at the corner of Montgomery and Jackson, where Mr. Sherman's bank now stands." He pointed to the brick bank, a block away. "Through the workings of fate, a good deal of my former property has passed through Mr. Sherman's hands. You may think it odd, but I take pleasure in this happenstance, for Mr. Sherman is the most honest man in San Francisco. It wouldn't do to have my holdings in the hands of a scoundrel."

Sherman changed the subject by addressing Jason. "Very bad business, losing your ship. You have my sincere condolences."

"If condolences were coin, I would have a new ship already. But I thank you, General."

"I am general of nothing, just now, Captain Beck, and I should think 'Mr. Sherman' would do very well in this gathering."

Piqued at being left out of the conversation, Molly Gray favored Sherman with her most fetching smile. "I imagine a banker must know a good deal about other bankers in the city."

"I have done business with most of them at one time or another, Miss Gray," Sherman said.

"Perhaps you know Abel Calvert."

"Only in passing. A real pioneer, I understand. From

what I know of him, he represents the best of the breed. He has raised himself to a responsible position in the city by sound business and a strong sense of honor."

"But of course one banker would be reluctant to speak ill of another," Trelayne said.

"Perhaps," said Sherman. "I can't speak for all bankers, only myself. When I have nothing good to say of a man, I keep my mouth shut."

Sarah gave Molly a warning glance, but Molly's delight in her victory was cut short by a murmur from the crowd as the funeral procession entered Montgomery Street from Jackson and turned south into the sunlit avenue.

A company of vigilance militia marched in the lead. Six drummers in their midst beat a grim tattoo on muffled drums. Next came the hearse, drawn by four black horses. Behind the hearse were the family, followed by members of the city's civic organizations, drawn up in rows. Along the sidewalks, men who had taken off their coats in the heat put them back on now, to show proper respect for the dead.

"It is a black day for California," Sherman muttered as the vigilantes marched by. "I would sooner be ruled by a dictator than the likes of these rebels."

"My sentiments exactly," Norton concurred. "Although I would prefer a benevolent despot, if that is to be the way of things."

The onlookers fell in behind the cortege when the last of the organized mourners passed by, lengthening the procession steadily as it moved along Montgomery, which was crowded along its length.

Farren took Sherman a little to one side as the throng around them thinned. "The sloop-of-war *John Adams* made port yesterday from the Sandwich Islands. She is anchored off North Point."

"Who is the captain?"

"Lieutenant Boutwell, they say."

"What sort of man is he?"

"Captain Ashe says he is steady. They are friends."

"Good. We may have need of the Navy before this is over."

"Look there," Trelayne said. "Where are they going?"

The funeral cortege continued southward on Montgomery toward Market Street. There it would turn right to Geary and follow that thoroughfare due west to the Lone Mountain Cemetery, which lay a mile beyond the city. At Sacramento, just two streets away, many of the followers were turning left, toward the bay, leaving the hearse and the official mourners to proceed attended by only a fragment of the disorganized multitude they had recently gathered in their wake.

"Something is happening there," Jason said.

"More parading at the rebel stronghold, I should think," Norton ventured with some bitterness. "They are great ones for strutting up and down."

"I want to see them marching." Molly started off alone and the others followed, Trelayne stepping quickly to overtake her. Jason took off his pea coat and slung it over his shoulder.

Once in Sacramento Street, they saw that the crowd, which was growing larger every moment, was held back at Battery, two streets east of Montgomery. Below Battery, the street was clear to Front and on to Davis, guarded by lines of vigilance militia. As on the day they seized James Casey and Charles Cora from the jail, the militiamen were armed with muskets fitted with stiletto-like bayonets. Atop the vigilance warehouse and on several of the nearby buildings, armed sentries patrolled the rooftops.

"What are they up to now?" Norton demanded irritably, but he followed along until they were stopped by the throng.

Sherman's wife clutched his arm. "Cump!"

The others followed her gaze. At the nearer end of the vigilantes' warehouse, narrow platforms extended from two of the second story windows, supported at their outer ends by ropes hung from heavy beams that projected from the roof. A man stood on each platform, his hands bound behind his back. The two men, like the platforms they stood on, were connected to the overhead beams by ropes.

"What are they—" Molly Gray's face grew pale.

"They are going to hang them," Jason said.

Ellen Sherman clung to her husband. "Can you do nothing?"

"Nothing," he said. "Let us be grateful that if anyone is to be hanged it will be two wretches like Casey and Cora."

"Even wretches deserve better than lynching."

Sherman softened. "Yes. And bless you for reminding me. Come, my dear." With a nod to the others, he guided his wife away.

Joshua Norton looked from Sarah to Molly. "I think we would do well to follow the Shermans' example."

"I cannot leave this place." Sarah's voice was strained, her eyes fixed on the platforms and the figures there. One of the men was speaking to the crowd, but his words were carried away by the freshening breeze.

"My God, look at it!" Trelayne whispered. "Who is in charge of these arrangements? Can he know how perfectly theatrical this is?"

"For God's sake, Tommy!" Molly said. "They are about to kill two men."

Yes, and Abel Calvert is one of the murderers, Trelayne thought, but he did not speak the words. He took Molly's hand in his own. "This is no place for you," he said. To his surprise, she did not resist, but allowed him to guide her away, with Joshua Norton walking on her other side.

Sarah scarcely noticed that the trio had left. Jason touched her arm. "Let us go too, Sarah."

She shook her head. Coming on the scene unexpectedly and knowing what was about to happen, she could not voluntarily leave. She feared that the memory of the event would haunt her, but she knew that she must bear witness to what took place here.

"They haven't the right!" she said. "Only the law can take a life, and even that is wrong in the sight of God." A man turned to look at her. She met his eyes and he looked away.

There was movement above the figures on the platforms. Two men stepped to the edge of the roof. They wielded axes, chopping at the ropes that held up the platforms, and now a plaintive cry came from one of the standing figures, the four words plainly audible up and down the street. "Mother! Oh, my mother!"

Twice the axemen struck in unison, three times, and at almost the same instant the ropes parted and the platforms dropped away from beneath the feet of the doomed men.

arah reeled and clutched Jason, pressing her face against his chest. His shirt smelled of pine tar and sweat and salt air, and the smells comforted her. In her mind's eye the men were still falling. She had looked away before they reached the ends of the ropes. She wanted them to fall forever, all the way to hell, if that was where they belonged. She would not look up. But then a sound reached her ears, a collective murmur of satisfaction from the crowd that sent a chill along her spine, followed by a few cheers.

"Come along now," Jason said gently. Half supporting her with an arm around her waist, he took her away, pushing through the onlookers that had gathered behind them, until they broke free of the crowd.

"Murderers!" a man in the rearmost rank of the throng cried out. "Murderers!"

"You could be next," another man said. A scuffle broke out and the onlookers fell back, giving way to the combatants.

"Look out!" Even as someone cried out a warning, a blade flashed in the sunlight. Two men wielding knives careened toward Jason and Sarah, one pursuing the other. Before Sarah knew what was happening, Jason thrust her aside. He blocked the first man with his arm and hissed as the knife cut through the sleeve of his coat. He seized the man's arm and twisted it abruptly, causing the hand holding the knife to open and bringing a cry of pain from the man's lips. Jason flung the man aside and turned to meet the pursuer, knocking his blade aside and putting the point of his own seaman's knife at the second man's throat.

Jason smelled the brandy on the man's breath and he felt himself tremble. He wanted to thrust the knife home and feel the blood warm on his hand. Only a sensation that strong could wipe away the sight of the two hanged men shuddering in the throes of death.

"Jason."

He saw the fear in Sarah's eyes, and the look stayed his hand. "There's been enough killing for one day," he said to the man. His voice was harsh and unnatural. "Unless you're bound to die."

The man dropped his knife and backed away. Jason lowered his blade and picked up the knives the two men had abandoned at his feet. He held out his hand to Sarah. She took it and allowed him to draw her close.

"Mrs. Rockwell! Captain Beck!" a piping voice called from nearby.

"Jason, it's Dickie."

The boy was in the grip of a man who held a musket in one hand and Dickie's arm in the other as he pushed his way through the crowd, which was beginning to break up now that the hanging was done. Dickie reached out to Jason and Sarah with his free hand. "Mrs. Rockwell! Captain! Help me!"

Jason blocked the man's way. "What are you doing with this boy?"

"That's my business, friend, not yours." The man tried to force his way past Jason, presenting his musket with one hand and keeping a firm hold on Dickie with the other, but Jason brushed the musket aside and stopped the man at arm's length. He felt the rush of anger in him, unquelled.

"I am Captain Jason Beck, Vigilance Marines."

The man saw the danger in Jason's eyes and became suddenly humble. "Sorry, sir. Francis Baker, Vigilance Committee police. This boy was picking pockets." Baker dug in his coat. He produced a pigskin pinch-purse and a gentleman's wallet. "The boy had these. I caught him taking another, but I give it back."

Jason fixed Dickie with his gaze. "Is this true, young Richard?"

Dickie considered a lie and knew it would fail. "Yes, Captain."

"Why, Dickie?" Sarah demanded. "Why did you steal?"

"That's how I make my living, Mrs. Rockwell." He was contrite, but he would not beg for forgiveness.

"What will you do with him?" Jason asked Baker.

"Put him in the Committee's cells." Baker looked at the boy. "Might give him Casey's cell, now that it's vacant."

Dickie had stopped resisting the vigilante's grip. While the two men talked he slumped as if defeated, relaxing his body so it seemed small and weak. He felt Baker's hand grow lax and he made his move suddenly, twisting free and flinging himself toward Sarah.

"Please don't let him take me! They'll hang me up like they done them two!" The tears that came to Dickie's eyes were real enough, as was his fear. He had seen the two men jerked up short by the ropes. While they twitched about, he had taken advantage of the moment by reaching for an onlooker's purse. The vigilante's hand had descended on his neck at the same moment.

Baker moved to recover Dickie from Sarah's arms but the look she gave him made him draw back. "We'll put him in a cell overnight, sir," he said to Jason. "In the morning we'll send him to the home for delinquent boys."

Jason glowered at Dickie. "He deserves whatever punishment you think fit."

"Are you forgetting that you were an orphan too, Captain?" Sarah's eyes were cold. "Did you never steal to assure your own survival?"

"Aye. But I was never caught. When you are caught, you have to pay the price. That is the way of things."

"So you would give him to the vigilantes? You would let them terrorize a poor boy who has just seen them hang two men?"

"Would you turn him loose to steal again, ma'am?" Baker asked.

"No! He needn't steal at all. I have offered him a place in my own home. I will see to his needs and I will answer for his behavior." She clung to Dickie fiercely, as if by keeping him from the vigilantes' justice she could bring back the two dead men.

A small crowd had gathered around them. At Sarah's words, a few approving murmurs came from the women, but one man laughed aloud. "I know that one. He's a wharf rat. You'll never change his ways."

"Which will it be, young Richard?" Jason regarded Dickie sternly. "Mrs. Rockwell's house or the cells of the Committee?"

"Mrs. Rockwell's, I guess."

"You must be sure, lad. If you put yourself in Mrs. Rockwell's care, you must do as she says. There will be no more stealing. No running off to join your wharf-rat friends whenever you please. Do you understand?"

Dickie nodded solemnly.

"I can vouch for Mrs. Rockwell," Jason said to Baker. "If she says she will look after the boy, she will do it."

How much of Baker's reluctance was genuine and how much was put on for Dickie's benefit, Jason couldn't tell. "If you say so, sir," the man said. "But if we catch him again, it's the Committee cells for certain." Baker turned on Dickie for a last time. "They are small and dark, lad. Don't you forget."

Sarah kept a grip on Dickie as she turned and marched him quickly away with Jason bringing up the rear. "It is time someone taught you the difference between right and wrong, young man."

"Me mum taught me that!" Dickie protested. "She told me God would punish me if I was bad, and He's done it straight along."

At the boardinghouse they found Joshua Norton smoking on the veranda. He greeted Dickie warmly when he learned that the boy would be living in the house, and he offered to tell him a story before supper, but Sarah said there would be no rewards for a common pickpocket, not until he showed that he was as good as his word and meant to abide by her rules in his new home. She took Dickie to the parlor and sat beside him on the divan.

"When people live together they agree on rules of behavior," she told him. "In the grown-up world these rules are called laws. You saw today what happens when the laws are disregarded."

"Yes, ma'am. I guess Casey and Cora had it coming."

"That's not what I meant." How could she explain? He saw the vigilantes marching through the streets unopposed and the people cheering while two men died, and like most of the grown-ups he was deceived into believing they were in the right. "Dickie, the Vigilance Committee is ignoring the laws we have all agreed on and what they are doing is desperately wrong. I don't expect you to understand, but I do expect you to abide by the rules I make in this house. The room on the top floor, the one beside Captain Beck's, that will be yours. If you have any belongings you are to bring them here. I will go with you to fetch them."

"I ain't got but a few things. You can trust me to go and fetch them on me own. I already give you my word I'd live here."

Dickie was so humbled that Sarah felt pity well up within her, but she kept it in check. There would be time later to show him forgiveness.

" 'I *have only* a few things.' 'You can trust me to fetch them on *my* own.' 'I already *gave* you my word.' " She regarded him silently for a moment to emphasize the lessons. "We speak properly in this house at all times. Do you understand?"

"Yes, ma'am."

"Very well. I will trust you to go on your own. But not today. Tomorrow you can go if the town has settled down. Until then, you will stay here. Have you eaten today?"

"I et some breakfast."

" 'I *ate* some breakfast.' From now on you will have three meals a day. Supper is at half past six. I expect you to stay in the house until then. You may borrow any book you want from the shelves in the parlor without asking. And I imagine if you ask Mr. Norton, he will lend you books from his room. Would you like some bread and cheese now?"

"Yes, please."

"All right, but first ask Captain Beck to come to the kitchen."

"We're bunkmates now, Richard," Jason said when Sarah had seated him at the kitchen table so she could inspect his wounded arm.

"Yes, Captain." Dickie was pleased to realize this was so.

Sarah rolled up Jason's blood-soaked sleeve. The gash was long, but not deep. Along half its length the blood had already congealed, stanching the flow, and there was no pulsing in the bleeding that remained. "How does it feel?"

"I've scratched myself worse on a barnacle." The arm throbbed but it would heal cleanly.

"Men are all the same, playing at heroes." Sarah wet a cloth and washed the cut with lye soap. "Where will it end, Captain?"

"The vigilance business? 'Tis not for me to predict an end to landsmen's madness. And it was Jason earlier today."

"I apologize if I was informal."

"Nay, I did not mean that. It pleased me that you should use my Christian name."

"I'm not sure it is proper."

"Proper be damned. Your household is much like a ship's company. There is formality and respect when needs be, but that doesn't lessen the friendship among you. 'Tis less restrained than a ship's company, where some men must give orders to others. You have made me welcome. And we are friends, are we not?"

"Yes. We are friends. And I thank you. I am not certain I should have come safely through this day but for you."

Dickie sensed that something more than the words alone conveyed had passed between the grown-ups, but he couldn't guess what it was. Ingrid, the scullery maid, arrived just then. Mrs. Rockwell and Captain Beck were silent while Mrs. Rockwell bandaged his wound with a strip of clean linen and Ingrid pottered about the kitchen making a racket and a mess as she began preparations for supper.

For the rest of the afternoon the boardinghouse was quiet, everyone keeping mostly to themselves. It seemed to Dickie that when they did speak, much of what the grown-ups said had a meaning that was beyond his understanding. When Melchior came, in Dickie was in the parlor, searching for a book simple enough that he could read it, and he overheard Melchior and Captain Beck speaking in the foyer. "You know of the hanging?" Captain Beck said.

"Aye, Cap'n. I were there, and some of the others. I sent 'em through the crowd like sharks on the hunt, but we seen no fish."

The next to enter the foyer were Trelayne and Molly Gray. They took no notice of Dickie, who had settled on Mr. Dana's *Two Years Before the Mast*, and was curled up on the divan.

"Why must we change, Molly?" Trelayne was saying as they came through the door. They lowered their voices then, but Dickie could hear them plainly.

"Because I will not go on like this," Molly said. "We must go forward, or not go at all."

The grown-ups came to the parlor before supper and they talked of politics and the law, and the right and wrong of the Vigilance Committee's actions. "This new organization is too big," Mr. Norton said darkly. "They won't be able to control it." That, at least, Dickie understood, and he wondered what would happen if the Vigilance Committee could not control their men.

He expected Mrs. Rockwell to send him to the kitchen to eat with Ingrid, who chewed with her mouth open and said hardly a word to him when he stayed to supper, but when it came time to go in to the dining room Mrs. Rockwell announced that because Dickie was to be a regular member of the household he would henceforth eat with the grown-ups. This pleased Dickie very much, although he was so tired from running about the city all day long that he could barely keep his eyes open during the meal. After supper Mrs. Rockwell put him straight to bed in clean sheets that smelled of sunshine.

He dreamed of Stritch and being aboard the *Sarah B.*

Watson. They were sailing through the Golden Gate, bound for Macao, but then it was suddenly night and the ship was on fire again. Dickie tossed in his sleep and cried out, but he did not awake. In his next dream he was in the Vigilance Committee's cells, so small and dark he could not stand upright or see where he was. There were rats in the cell, running about the floor and over his feet, and then the door opened and men were coming to hang him. He cried out again and was glad when he woke up to find Molly Gray sitting on his bed with a lamp in her hand. Outside, it was dark. The window by his bed was open and the night air had turned cool.

"Miss Gray? It's really you. I was dreaming."

"It must have been a terrible dream. You should have seen your face. I didn't want to wake you, but when I saw you were dreaming I shook your shoulder." She stroked his hair. "I wondered if Mr. Calvert might have sent me another note today."

"Oh! Yes! I forgot. There was no note, but he did give me a message." Calvert had told him the message before the funeral procession left the church, but the excitement of the hanging and the terrifying grip of the vigilance policeman had driven everything else from Dickie's mind. "He said to tell you that he would be at the same place tonight at eleven o'clock. He said he would wait for half an hour."

Molly kissed him on the cheek and he smelled her lavender scent. "Thank you, Dickie."

"I'm sorry I forgot."

"It doesn't matter. It's only a quarter after ten." She helped him get settled, tucking the blankets around him before she picked up her lamp. "Have you said your prayers?"

"No. I forgot that too."

He made to get up so he could kneel at the bedside, but she motioned him to stay where he was. "God will hear you if you're lying down, just as well as when you're kneeling."

"He will?" The idea was new to Dickie.

"He will hear you if you are sincere."

She left him to make his prayers in his own way, but she left his door ajar, as she had found it, admitting a slight glow from the ship's lamp on the landing below.

Dickie clasped his hands beneath the covers and prayed earnestly to God to forgive him. "Dear God," he said, "I am only a poor orphan boy. If you will forgive me, I will try to learn what is right, like Mrs. Rockwell says, and I'll live by the grown-up rules. Amen."

God's punishment for his wrongs had seemed more than he could bear in recent days. Stritch's death and the loss of the *Sarah B. Watson*, for which he held himself in part to blame, were calamities so far beyond his ability to redress that he had lost his will for a time. He had become careless, and that carelessness had resulted in being caught stealing by the vigilance policeman today. But if being taken in by Sarah Rockwell were the result of his wickedness, perhaps the lesson God intended for him was one of hope rather than punishment.

It was this chance that had led him to accept Mrs. Rockwell's offer. At that moment, any alternative to placing himself in the custody of the vigilance hangmen seemed the better choice. Now he dared to hope that it was something more, for he was worn-out with caring for himself. At times the burden crushed him. Now, for good or ill—but he fervently hoped it was for the good—he had placed himself in another's care. He had promised to live in Sarah Rockwell's house and do as she told him, and he meant every word he said.

As he drifted back toward sleep, Dickie allowed his thoughts to wander. The message he had carried from Abel Calvert to Molly Gray interested him. He liked secrets and it pleased him to know that grown-ups had them too. He wondered why Calvert met Miss Gray in secret and he wondered if she would go to meet him tonight. He raised himself up on an elbow to peer out the window. His room overlooked the garden and the drying grounds. If Molly Gray left the house by that route he would see her. The garden was illuminated by faint light of the moon, which had only just risen, and within it nothing moved.

I'll look again in a moment, Dickie thought, but the warmth of the bed and the clean smell of the sheets soothed him to sleep almost as soon as he lay back down. And so, without misgiving, he left his former life behind him.

Chapter 24

Friday, May 30, 1856
Dear Peter,

Eight days have passed since the hangings. I am writing before breakfast, which is the only quiet time of day now that my house is full. This letter will go out on the steamer Sunday, so you will have it soon after those relating the beginning of our public crisis.

The Committee of Vigilance has not massed their forces again, but neither have they announced any intention of disbanding. Their militia drill daily in the streets near the warehouse on Sacramento Street. They call it Fort Vigilance now and they have put up a flagpole on the roof. How long they intend to rule the roost, we do not know. I had hoped there would be some protest from the responsible citizens—instead the city has been utterly docile under the heel of this chillingly disciplined mob. There are stories, whispered in private, of homes being searched in the night and men carried off to the Committee's warehouse to be tried in secret. They say that Sheriff Scannell's jail-keeper, a man named Billy Mulligan, was arrested on his way to work yesterday, and that 'Yankee' Sullivan, the former boxing champion, whom the vigilantes denounce as a ballot-box stuffer for the Democrats, has been held for several days. Both Mulligan and

Sullivan are Irish, as you might guess, and I think it is no coincidence. The Irish and the Sydney ducks seem to be the vigilantes' special targets. The newspapers—except the Herald, *of course (the* Bulletin *is edited now by King of William's brother Tom and is as scurrilous as ever)—say the Vigilance Committee has no politics and that they are only arresting "known scoundrels" and other bad persons. So far as I can learn, the men they seize are working men given to voting Democratic, and I doubt you would find an old Whig or a young Republican among them. Some who fear the Committee's attentions are leaving town. Usually it is the rats who leave the sinking ship—here the rats are at the helm while decent citizens jump overboard to save themselves.*

Their motto is Fiat justitia, ruat coelum: *Let justice be done, though the heavens fall. I wonder if it occurs to them that if they bring down the heavens, that puts them in league with the devil? Arguing politics, which was the lifeblood of the city until two weeks ago, has ceased almost entirely. If you support the Committee, you can safely voice those views in public. To express criticism carries a risk. There are tales of citizens denouncing each other to the vigilantes. People are afraid to speak to their neighbors, and*

A gentle knocking sounded at Sarah's bedroom door, which she had left open. She turned to find David Farren peering in. He was dressed in his militia uniform. Sarah was glad she had put on a housedress after starting the fire in the stove.

"I'm sorry," Farren apologized. "I can't wait for breakfast. Is there anything to eat?"

"What time is it?"

"A quarter to seven."

"There is some of the roast beef. I can make you a sandwich. If you can wait a few minutes, I'll put on water for coffee."

"Just the sandwich will do. And I do apologize. I'm going away overnight."

"Away? Where?"

Farren let his excitement show. "We're making our move, Mrs. Rockwell. I can't say more. Not yet. But when I come back tomorrow I will have good news. We are going to show these rebels they can't have things their own way forever.".

Sarah fetched the roast from the pantry. "Do you have enough support in the city?"

"My partner, Mr. Howard, is a general of the state's militia. In Mr. Howard's case the position is mostly honorary, but it gives him a certain standing. Three days ago Howard met with Mayor Van Ness and several other prominent men. They wrote to Governor Johnson, formally setting forth the abuses of the Vigilance Committee and asking him to do whatever is needed to put them down. General Howard carried the letter to the governor." Farren glanced about as if the walls had ears. "Yesterday, Governor Johnson telegraphed General Sherman to meet him today at the Army headquarters in Benicia. We will take the afternoon steamer and spend the night."

"But you have no troops. You have said so yourself." Sarah kept her eyes on the carving knife as she sliced the beef.

"We will have them soon. I have come up with a legal strategem that will allow the governor to call up new militia. The vigilants have the men, they have the arms, they have the power. But they left us the *law* because they care nothing for it. It's our best weapon against this rabble. Now I really must go."

The kitchen clock struck seven. Farren took the sandwich from Sarah's hands. "Thank you. And please, say nothing of this to anyone."

Farren's optimism gave Sarah cautious hope. She put on the kettle and a pot of porridge to simmer and was about to return to her bedroom to continue her letter when Molly Gray came into the kitchen. Her hair was still down and bare feet peeped from beneath the hem of her dressing gown. "You haven't seen Tommy yet, Sarah?"

"Tommy never wakes before nine or ten o'clock. You know that better than anyone. What are you doing up at this hour?"

"I'm going out for breakfast."

The cat meowed at the back door and Sarah let it in. "It seems everyone in this household has a rendezvous this morning."

"Who else is up?" Molly's curiosity was aroused.

"Never you mind." Sarah poured milk into the cat's saucer. "Honestly, Molly, this has got to stop. You can't go on like this."

"Like what?"

"Do you think I am deaf, dumb and blind? I hear you coming and going at all hours of the night. You are meeting someone."

"I can't wait for Tommy forever, Sarah."

"Who is it?"

"Abel Calvert, if you must know."

"He is one of the ringleaders of the vigilantes!"

"Abel is a voice of moderation on the Committee!"

"Is it 'Abel' so soon?"

"Do you know what they wanted to do? Just a few days ago they were talking about removing the city officeholders, Mayor Van Ness and all the rest. But Abel and Mr. Kent talked them out of it. They agreed not to meddle in local politics."

"Not meddle! What do you call taking prisoners from the jail and hanging them?"

"Abel voted to acquit Mr. Cora." Molly waited for a reaction, but Sarah said nothing. "You should have been a man, Sarah. You get all excited about right and wrong, and politics, and rights for women. You would make a perfect politician. If you were a man you could be a senator or a governor, and you could give us all those rights."

"We aren't *given* rights, Molly! We *have* them under natural law. The Constitution recognizes the rights that we are born with, men and women alike."

"You see? You have such passion for things I don't understand. It's why I admire you. But I'm different. I just want to live a comfortable life. I want to be a lady."

"That is not so easy, even here."

"You can be anything in San Francisco, Sarah! All you have to do is watch for the chance and take it. Look at Abel. He came here with nothing."

For more than a week Molly had met Abel Calvert at least once each day, usually late at night or in the morning before Trelayne was awake. Two days earlier, the Theater Trelayne had opened *The School for Scandal*, a comedy that was a perennial favorite with San Francisco audiences. Calvert had attended the first night. After Trelayne and Molly had walked home to the boarding-house, and once Trelayne was in bed asleep, Molly had met Abel Calvert and they had ridden to the ocean beach. They walked on the sand, leading the horses, and he had told her about his life as a trapper. His stories of traveling through the Rocky Mountains while Molly herself was still a child had enthralled her.

Sarah stirred the porridge. "Is it really to be Abel Calvert, then?"

"He is a good man, Sarah. You heard General Sherman say he is the best of his kind."

"If it's any comfort to you, Captain Beck told me that Mr. Kent trusts Mr. Calvert. He says together they are doing what they can to keep the rest in check. But it's another thing for a man to trust a man. I hope you don't trust him too far."

"We have been very proper. On my honor, such as it is. Abel is courting me on the promise of things to come, nothing more."

"Not even a kiss?"

"Well." Molly managed to look both demure and mischievous at the same time. "You have to whet their interest. But he is a gentleman all the same. He holds my hand. He says I remind him of his Indian wife. It's very romantic, really. She died years ago and he has pined for her ever since, until he met me."

Sarah was spooning coffee beans into the grinder. "Is this what you want? To be a banker's wife?"

"Is it so bad to want money and comfort? You want your husband's money."

"Because Haven wanted me to have it! And because what the Rockwells did was wrong." Sarah put more of her strength into grinding the coffee than the job required. "You will break Tommy's heart."

"It's no more than he deserves." Molly glanced at the

clock. "I have to go. Just tell him I'm out for a walk, if he asks."

"You know I'm not a good liar."

Molly squeezed Sarah's arm. "I know. Just don't blurt out the whole truth. Do that for me."

With Farren and Molly absent, there were five for breakfast—Jason and Melchior, Dickie, Norton and Sarah herself. She sliced the rest of the beef and served it with potatoes and eggs, porridge and oranges.

"I will take Dickie with me again today, Mrs. Rockwell," Jason said as she spooned out the porridge.

On the morning after the hanging, when Jason suggested that Dickie might carry messages between Kent's office and the ship's crewmen if the need arose, Sarah had resisted the boy's further involvement in the search for the incendiary. She feared the reminders of the fire and Stritch's death would unsettle Dickie and might even lead him to abandon the house and run off to his wharf rat's existence. But she had realized that to keep him shut up would only make him want to break free, and so she let him go. He had made the honest portion of his livelihood by serving as a messenger before. She prayed that allowing him to continue that part of his previous life would encourage him in honest ways.

Thus far, her trust seemed justified. Dickie had promised to mind Jason's orders and return each evening at suppertime, and he had kept his word. He made no objection to Sarah's lessons in reading and writing each evening after supper, and Norton lightened the burden of his studies by telling the boy a bedtime story almost every night. In large ways and small, the others in the household had taken an interest in Dickie's welfare and made him feel welcome.

When the men were gone, Jason and Melchior and Dickie to pursue the elusive incendiary and Norton on his daily rounds to revive his commission trade, Sarah sat at her secretary to continue her letter.

There is still no progress at finding the men who burned Captain Beck's ship. With Seaman Grimes dead, there seems little hope of finding his confeder-

*ates. Four members of the crew have left Captain
Beck in the past week. There are times when I believe he is glad that the Committee of Vigilance
rules the city, so he can hang the incendiaries himself, if he finds them. I pray that in time his mur-
derous impulse will cool.*

Sarah was startled by the intensity of her anger at Jason Beck. He is a man, damn him! she thought, and
these are man things — politics and greed and alarm bells
in the night. Why can't he see that the corruption of the
Committee's power has him in its grip? Why can't he see
the right and wrong of it as clearly as I do!

She picked up the pen, dipped the nib, and wrote
quickly.

*It infuriates me that I see so much wrong
around me and all I can do is pour out my feelings
in these letters to you. You have told me I do this
well, putting words together to make pictures of my
life. But I am only a woman and a writer of letters.
If I were a man (breathes there a woman who
hasn't said this at one time or another) — If I were
a man I would write the truth as I see it about the
evil being done here in the name of*

She stopped with the pen poised above the paper, then
lowered her arm to the desk and sat very still. The house
was quiet. She did not know how long she sat without
moving. She was aware that the kitchen clock struck a
quarter to ten. Soon after, from the parlor, came the gentler chime of the clock on the mantelpiece. The kitchen
clock ran a few minutes fast each day and no amount of
adjusting would cure it of its impatience.

She sat a while longer. Then, as if freed from invisible
restraints, she wrote a quick end to the letter, folded it,
and set it aside. From a drawer she took the bundle of
letters she had received from Peter. Selecting one at random, she spread it before her. On another sheet of paper
she began to write experimentally, broadening her
strokes, glancing often at Peter's writing, trying to imitate her brother's undisciplined scrawl. When she was

satisfied that she could maintain something like his style, she took up a clean sheet and began to write rapidly, careless of the occasional scratched-out word or inky smudge made in her haste.

She wrote in bursts, then sat immobile, her soft brow furrowed, until the next burst moved her. An hour passed. She heard Trelayne come downstairs and go to the kitchen to warm himself some coffee, which was all the nourishment he took before midday. Soon he passed again over her head as he went back up the stairs.

When she was done, she held the pages at arm's length, viewing each one critically to be sure her feminine hand had not betrayed itself while she concentrated on what she wrote. Satisfied, she gathered the sheets together and carried them upstairs. She knocked on Trelayne's door and opened it at the sound of his voice. He was in his dressing gown and slippers, sitting, as she had been until moments before, writing, the empty coffee cup beside him. The floor around him was littered with balls of crumpled paper.

"I'm sorry," she said. "I can come back later."

"That's all right." He stretched himself. "Any interruption is welcome."

"What is it you're writing?"

"We need a new play, something original. How do you suppose the great writers get their ideas? I sit here in need, and my mind is blank as a slate."

"You said *School for Scandal* was doing well."

"It will run for a week at the outside. The vigilantes have people afraid to go out at night. We must change attractions often or we will lose our public."

"They love Molly in boys' parts."

Trelayne looked at her. "Yes, by God, they do. Good for you, Sarah! Next week I'll give them Molly in *Oliver Twist*. It will afford me a little time, but after that I will have to come up with something spectacular or go bust, if the stranglers are still at it."

He noticed the papers she held in her hand. "What have you got there?" She handed him what she had written. "For me? Sarah, you have no idea how I have longed for a billet doux from your hand—"

"Oh, Tommy, shut up and read it."

He read the first page. His eyes widened and he looked inquiringly at her. "Who wrote this?"

Sarah sat on the bed, greatly relieved. "I have just passed my first test. Does it look like a man's hand?"

Trelayne's eyebrows vanished behind his unkempt forelock. "*You* wrote it." He scrutinized the writing. "I never would take it for a woman's hand. Did you really write this?"

"Do you like it?"

"Like it! It's brilliant!" He raced through the rest, then exclaimed, "I had half decided the vigilantes might be right, but you have brought me back to the fold! If the people could read something like this, it would set the town on its ear."

"For that, I need your help."

At a quarter to four that afternoon, a young man of slight build tried the door of the San Francisco *Herald*'s office on Montgomery Street and found it locked. Within the dingy office, the printer bent over the press, his shirtsleeves rolled up to the elbows, his hands and arms black with ink. His face was smudged from wiping the sweat from his brow and pushing the hair out of his eyes. At the sound of the door latch being tested, he turned with a start and his right hand found a two-foot length of pipe that rested against the press. He brought it with him when he opened the door.

The caller was dressed as a laborer. The cuffs of his coat were frayed, and it appeared that neither coat nor pants had been recently cleaned by any method more thorough than haphazard brushing. He doffed his cap as he entered, revealing tousled hair. "I would like to see Mr. Nugent, if you please."

"I'm Nugent. If you've come to make threats, I only accept threats in writing. You'll find pen and paper there on my desk."

"No threats, Mr. Nugent. I assure you, you won't need that pipe."

Nugent estimated his visitor to be a few years younger than himself and twenty pounds lighter. Everything in his manner said that physical violence was not in his nature. Nugent set the pipe aside.

"I wish I'd had this yesterday. A fellow came in and said he had something for me. The next thing I knew he gave me this." He pointed to a bruise on his face, which his visitor had taken to be a smudge of ink. "They'd like me to line up with the other papers and support the Vigilance Committee, but I'll see them in hell first. If that offends your politics, give me a moment to pick up my weapon."

"I take no offense." The caller withdrew three folded sheets of paper from his coat pocket and offered them to Nugent. "I have something for your paper. You may find it interesting."

Nugent looked the newcomer up and down, with more care this time. He saw a reserved young man who made a show of humble petition, cap in hand. His mustache covered most of his mouth but his chin was clean shaven. It was a good chin, revealing strength of character. And there was intelligence in the eyes. The hand that offered the papers was clean, the nails smooth and short.

Nugent wiped his own hands on a grimy cloth. "What's the nature of this offering?"

"It is in the nature of a letter. I would prefer you read it for yourself."

"Spread it out on the desk there."

The young man did as he was bid. Nugent bent over to read, still wiping his hands. The cloth had absorbed enough ink to transform his fingers from black to gray, but could do no more. Partway through the first page, Nugent tossed the cloth in the general direction of the press and took the sheets in his hands, marking them at once with gray smudges. He read them through quickly, glancing occasionally at the one who had brought them.

"You write this?"

"I did, sir."

" 'Hermes,' eh. That your name?"

"A nom de plume."

"Hermes. That's a good one. It's a pleasure to meet the herald of the gods." Nugent offered his inky hand.

The other shook it, revealing soft skin and a fervent grip. "Conductor of souls and bringer of dreams."

"Let us hope that a return to tranquillity in this city is more than just a dream. May I know your true name?"

"I think for both our sakes it would be best if I were just Hermes for now."

"I take your point." Nugent contained his curiosity. "Hermes" was much more than what he appeared to be. His innocuous disguise was well chosen. It would allow him to go about the city unnoticed. "If you will entertain a suggestion, why not Mercury? You get all the Greek meanings, and another as well. To the Romans, Mercury was the god of merchants. Who better to herald the truth about a mercantile cabal like the Committee of Vigilance?"

The young man smiled, revealing even, white teeth. The canines were prominent and sharp. "I hadn't thought of that. Let it be Mercury by all means."

"I can't pay you for this. My advertisers have left me and my printer is in the vigilance militia. Most of my subscribers have canceled."

"But you'll print it?"

"With pleasure. It will be in tomorrow's edition."

"That is payment enough." The visitor turned to go, but he stopped with his hand on the doorknob. "I'm curious, Mr. Nugent. You supported the vigilantes in fifty-one. Why do you oppose them now?"

"Maybe I was wrong in fifty-one. It was a rough town then and the organization seemed necessary. But this isn't fifty-one. As you say in this letter, we have courts and police. If the people don't like them, they're free to vote them out at the next election."

"Good luck to you, sir."

"And to you. I hope not too many people know you wrote this."

"Just you and I."

"If you write more, let me have it."

The young man closed the door behind him and hastened on his way. Montgomery Street was full of activity, horses and drays and pedestrians all vying for space on the crowded thoroughfare. Without seeming to do so, he looked about as he moved along, watching for followers. No one appeared to have taken special notice of his arrival at the *Herald*'s office, or his departure. All the same he would approach the newspaper by another street if he came again. That would depend on Sarah.

"Well?" she demanded when he returned to the house, shorn of his mustache and dressed once more as himself. She drew him into the parlor, scarcely able to contain herself.

"He'll print it."

"Oh, Tommy! Do you think he suspected?"

"He believed I wrote it, if that's what you mean."

"You didn't go like that?"

Trelayne slumped a little, becoming humble. "You would never notice the fellow who visited Mr. Nugent. He was a study in anonymity. I would have liked you to see him, but I left him at the theater. We don't want Mr. Hermes coming and going from this house."

"Coming and going?"

"Mr. Nugent said he will be pleased to print anything you might write. Incidentally, you're to be 'Mercury' in the paper. He's the god of merchants." Trelayne smiled. "Isn't it lovely? Quicksilver. Bright and elusive. It slips from the grasp. Our Mercury will be all that, and more."

"I hadn't thought of writing again."

"Why not? You've made a start. Once they read tomorrow's paper, the whole town will be waiting for more, no matter which side they're on."

"Thanks to you."

"You owe me nothing, dear Sarah, but the debt I owe you is more than I can repay. I've never played a part in real life before. It's like nothing else I've done. On a stage, they know you're playing a part. Out there"—he flung a hand toward the street—"they believe I am whatever character I'm playing. It's magnificent, Sarah! It's the theater of the world."

Chapter 25

Sherman and Farren arrived at the Benicia landing by steamer on Friday evening just at dusk. The pleasant town stood on the northern shore of Carquinez Strait, the narrow waterway through which the Sacramento River flowed into San Pablo Bay. A few years earlier it had been briefly the capital of California and it was now the headquarters for the United States Army's Department of the Pacific. Six miles west lay the town of Vallejo and the Navy headquarters at Mare Island.

Governor Johnson and another man were waiting on the wharf. Johnson greeted Sherman and Farren warmly and introduced them to David Douglass, California's secretary of state. Farren had known Douglass somewhat when the latter served as U.S. marshall for Northern California before accepting his present position in Governor Johnson's administration.

"Your Captain Farren is no slouch at the law," Douglass said to Sherman. "This scheme is our salvation."

Sherman was not given to praising his subordinates in their presence. He addressed himself to Johnson, "Has Judge Terry issued the writ for Mulligan?"

"He went down on this evening's steamer. Sheriff Scannell will have it by now. You're sure they won't give up Mulligan?"

Sherman snorted. "According to the noble Committee,

Billy Mulligan is the devil's right-hand man. Now they've got him, they won't let him go."

"Good."

"We must be sure of the arms, Governor. I can't do a thing with unarmed men."

"General Wool is at the hotel. He is expecting us." Johnson led the way up the street from the steamer landing. The evening was warm. Sherman's neck itched under his starched collar, but neither Johnson nor Douglass removed their coats, so he kept his on as well.

"I think you should propose the plan as your own, Governor," Farren said as they walked. "It will carry more weight, coming from the state's chief executive."

"It might be best," Johnson agreed. "But I will remember where it came from."

Five minutes' walk up the gentle slope from the steamer dock brought them to the American Hotel, a two-story brick affair that had seen its heyday when Benicia was the capital. General Wool's residence occupied a suite of rooms at the northern end of the second floor, where they were protected from the heat of the midday sun.

"A pleasure to see you again, General," Wool greeted Sherman.

Sherman noted an ironic inflection on the last word. Wool had served with distinction in the Mexican War. In Sherman's few previous encounters with the Army commander, he himself had been a San Francisco banker with no military position at all, a fact that Wool appeared to have foremost in his mind as he made the governor's delegation welcome in his sitting room and offered brandy and cigars.

Lieutenant General John E. Wool was autocratic in breeding and appearance. His white hair was cut short and brushed forward over a high, rounded forehead. This style, together with an aquiline nose, combined to give him the look of the Caesars, an impression Wool did nothing to discourage.

To Sherman's astonishment, Wool proffered a deck of playing cards and suggested they should talk over a game of whist. He dealt the cards around and the game commenced, but Wool made no objection when Governor Johnson turned the talk almost immediately to the Vigilance Committee and the steps he proposed taking against them. In Wool's manner toward the young governor, Sherman imagined that he detected some of the same condescension the general so obviously felt for Sherman's militia rank, but as Johnson talked, Sherman felt a quickening of hope. The lack of will Johnson had displayed when the Vigilance Committee took Casey and Cora from the jail appeared to be replaced now by a firm clarity of purpose as he told Wool the fundamentals of Farren's plan: Judge Terry was already in San Francisco with a writ of habeas corpus for Billy Mulligan, the jail keeper who was in the Committee's hands. If, as expected, the vigilantes refused service of the writ, the governor would issue a proclamation calling on the Vigilance Committee to disband. If that too was refused, the state would enlist new militia. The purpose of this visit was to obtain the necessary arms.

Johnson turned to Sherman. "Tell us what you need, General."

"I need arms for at least a thousand men."

"I understand the vigilants have five thousand," Wool said.

"It's very hard to say, General," Sherman replied evenly. "They don't line them up for us to count. In any event, we have no need to match them man for man."

"Oh? Why not?"

"It is my intention to take the marine battery at Rincon Point. There are six thirty-two-pound guns that command a view of the city. I will arrest the leaders and order them to disband their organization. It will be easy enough if it's timed properly. If they refuse to yield, I will blow the Committee's block of warehouses to atoms."

Wool appeared to be taken aback by the boldness of Sherman's strategy. He looked at the cards in his hand, considering what Sherman had said. "I suppose it might work. When would you enlist your troops?"

"As soon as Governor Johnson gives the order."

"I am drafting the proclamation now," Johnson said.

"Everything will be done legally," Secretary Douglass added.

"There must be a proclamation," Wool insisted somewhat petulantly. "You must order the vigilants to disperse. If they don't obey, then you must order out the militia."

Sherman controlled his impatience. "That's our intention, General. Once I have the men enrolled, we will bring down the arms at night and take the battery at once."

"How will you transport the arms?"

"We intend to ask Commodore Farragut for a ship."

Wool seemed doubtful. "I can't speak for the Navy."

"Of course not." Johnson too was growing impatient. "General Sherman and I will see Farragut tomorrow."

"You have never commanded in battle, I believe," Wool said to Sherman.

Sherman felt his face grow warm. "That's true, General. I did serve in Florida during the Seminole War."

"You're sure of your ground? The vigilants haven't invested the battery?"

"I live on the hill above the point. The rebels have shown no interest in it whatever." Sherman did not add that he himself had been the one to propose that Rincon Point be reserved by the national government for military use in order to protect it from the rampant speculation in land during the early days of the gold rush. That foresight afforded him a good deal of satisfaction today.

Wool dealt the cards and sorted his hand with apparent interest. "I put down a mutiny once, in the war with Britain. That was on the northern frontier, in fourteen. It's much the same kind of situation here, on a larger scale. You just have to be firm, and sure of your ground."

He threw down the cards abruptly, bored with the game. "Well, gentlemen, it is growing late." He got to his feet. "Tomorrow we will inspect the armory."

He ushered them out, all smiles and goodwill, as if the evening had been a pleasant social event.

"You can't get a grip on the man!" Sherman exploded when they were in Governor Johnson's rooms at the far end of the corridor. "What will it take to make him say yes or no?"

"We'll get an answer out of him tomorrow," Johnson said.

"He must be sixty-five, if he's a day," Secretary Douglass said. "Ripe for retirement."

"We won't leave here until we have a firm commitment for those arms." Johnson was calm and determined.

"He's more like a *politician* than a soldier." Sherman spat out the word. "Meaning no disrespect, Governor," he added quickly, cursing his thoughtlessness.

Johnson smiled fleetingly. "I take your meaning, General."

"At least he's going to show us the armory." Sherman brightened at the thought. "If I'm right—"

"Let us hope you are."

Sherman slept restlessly. His spirits fell the next morning when General Wool presented the headquarters guard for Governor Johnson's inspection. Around the parade ground, the post was somnolent in the warmth of the morning, which promised a stifling day. Most of Wool's troops were garrisoned in Oregon and Washington to protect the settlers there against Indians.

"How would these do?" General Wool indicated the guards' ancient musketoons fitted with sword bayonets. They dated from the Revolution, and would be worse than useless against the longer-barreled weapons in the hands of the vigilantes.

Sherman tugged at his collar and did his best to keep his scorn for the smoothbore blunderbusses out of his voice. "We don't want to disarm your guard, General. Perhaps in your storeroom we shall find something you can spare."

Wool summoned a carriage and drove them to the arsenal, which lay north of the post, behind a low hill. When he ushered them into a large earthen bunker, one glance was enough to change Sherman's mood from discouragement to elation. Against one wall were kegs of cartridges. Stacked in orderly rectangles in the middle of the bunker were crate upon crate of rifles and muskets that Sherman recognized almost as readily as he would have known his own children. His own regiment had brought the arms around the Horn in '47 aboard the troopship *Lexington*. He had believed they were transferred to Benicia when the departmental headquarters was moved in '54, but until this moment he was not certain they were still here. In all, there were nearly four thousand long arms.

Sherman kept his triumph to himself and did his best to sound sober and thoughtful as he addressed Wool. "These will do very well, General."

"We will need your commitment before we proceed," Johnson said mildly.

"Hmm?" Wool looked from the governor to Sherman, then at Farren and Secretary Douglass. "Yes. Well. It must all be done legally. The writ and the proclamation and all that. When General Sherman makes his requisition, approved by you, Governor, I will issue the arms and ammunition."

"Gentlemen!" William Tell Coleman pounded the table with his gavel. "Gentlemen, please!" He kept up the pounding until the Executive Committee room fell silent. He glared around the tables. The group had grown to include nearly forty men. Despite the fact that most were many years Coleman's senior, they were abashed by his disapproval. He had recovered from his blunder in dealing with Governor Johnson and was firmly in control again. Since the hangings, Johnson, and Sherman, his general of militia, had been notable by their absence from the public arena.

This morning, the Committee's leadership faced their first setback and thus far they were not coping with it well. During the night, the imprisoned pugilist Yankee Sullivan had committed suicide in his makeshift cell. The Executive Committee had been summoned to Fort Vigilance shortly after sunrise, brought from their homes by messengers, to hear Dr. Cole's post-mortem report. It seemed the prisoner had managed to open a vein with the table knife from his evening meal and bled to death in a short time. While they were considering Cole's testimony, a messenger had brought several copies of the morning's *Herald*, which contained an anonymous letter signed "Mercury" that set the members at each other's throats.

"One at a time, please, gentlemen," Coleman said

softly into the quiet. "Or must we raise our hands like boys in school?"

"This letter writer is saying our actions are politically motivated." Jonathan Frye kept his temper under control with an effort.

"He is saying we bribed the doctors!" Thomas Smiley said. "Listen to this: *There are questions that have not been spoken publicly, questions that need asking. Such as, who stood most to benefit from the death of James King of William? The Committee of Vigilance would have had no excuse to organize if King had lived. It is almost beyond belief that decent men might have wished one of their staunchest supporters dead, but it would not be the first time unscrupulous plotters have created a martyr to their own cause.*"

"He is saying we let King die!" little James Dows exclaimed. "I'll tie the noose myself, when we find him."

"To give this 'Mercury' his due," Stephen Kent said quickly, "he approves of Dr. Cole. Look here. *We understand Dr. Beverly Cole has been named Surgeon-General to the vigilantes. We believe the good doctor to be an honorable man as well as a skilled physician. Now, at least, the unknown persons confined in the Committee's cells will have the best medical care.*"

Frye snorted. "That is a backhanded compliment if ever there was one. This fellow is a threat to the Committee's authority."

"No more of a threat than what John Nugent was already printing," Smiley said. "For my money, he wrote the Mercury letter himself."

Abel Calvert shook his head. "This Mercury is a different voice."

"A noose will stop it quick enough!" someone said.

"Gentlemen!" The single word from Miers Truett silenced a growing rumble of agitation around the tables. From his imposing height, Truett gazed down on those around him. "We organized to uphold American principles, gentlemen. Not to trample them. If we are confident in the righteousness of our cause, the barbs of the opposition press cannot hurt us."

"There ain't no opposition press," James Dows said. "There's just John fucking Nugent. I say hang the bastard and shut down the *Herald*."

Coleman smacked his gavel on the table. "We won't have that kind of language in these proceedings!"

Dows sulked and became even smaller in his chair.

"If we make a fuss about this letter, it will get all the more notice," Stephen Kent said. "Why not just let it die?"

Abel Calvert nodded. "Today's paper wraps tomorrow's fish."

"And what if he writes again?" Jonathan Frye asked. "What if this is the beginning of a series of letters?"

"We'll face that when we come to it," Calvert said. Like Kent, he hoped the matter could be laid to rest.

"We can put someone to watch the *Herald*'s office," Tom Smiley suggested. "Nugent's got few advertisers and fewer subscribers. We should be able to pick the man out if he comes and goes often."

There was a silence as the members considered Smiley's proposal. Isaac Bluxome raised his dark eyes from the tablet he had filled with notes in the past few hours. He glanced around at the members, then at Coleman. "Mr. Chairman, I propose that we have arrived at a sense of the meeting. We will not interfere with Mr. Nugent's right to publish his views. But we will post a lookout to watch for this Mercury. If he writes again, we will consider further action."

Coleman tapped the gavel lightly. "In the absence of objection, the secretary will so record the sense of the meeting."

When the members left the warehouse, going by twos and threes through the premises of Attro & Jones and out onto Front Street, Stephen Kent accompanied Abel Calvert.

"We mustn't let them interfere with the press, Abel," Kent said once they were in the street. "If we suppress Nugent or his correspondents, we threaten sacred principles."

"I would rather put this Mercury in a cell for a few weeks, if need be, than see him strung up because he gets this crowd too mad," Calvert said. "If he writes again, we may have to support arresting him to keep him alive."

"Like Yankee Sullivan?"

"That was bad luck. They never should have given him a knife with his meals, but how could they know?"

"It will not reflect well on us," Kent said.

"Can't be helped." Calvert took out his watch. It was past ten o'clock and the sun was warming the streets. "I've got to go, Stephen. I'm having a late breakfast with a friend."

"Molly Gray again?"

"How in the devil did you know?"

"You have been seen breakfasting with her three times in the past week. If you don't want to be noticed, you should choose a smaller restaurant, or another companion."

Calvert had taken Molly to fashionable places because he wanted to impress her. Whose business was it anyway? And what harm was done? "I'm going to ask her to marry me, Stephen."

It was Kent's turn to be surprised. "What about Trelayne? I understood that . . ." he trailed off, embarrassed.

"There was something—I don't know what and I don't ask," Calvert said. "Something in the past. That's all over now."

"Will she have you?"

"By this time tomorrow, I'll know."

Calvert left Kent and hurried on his way. He had sent Dickie Howell with a message to Molly that he would be delayed, asking her to wait until half-past ten and to give him up if he hadn't arrived by then. This morning he would take her to some out of the way café to propose, in case she made a fuss.

How much had there been between Trelayne and Molly? That was a question that nagged him and wouldn't let go. Molly wouldn't give him a clear-cut answer, although she led him to believe it was all innocent enough. For three years? Traveling together from Illinois? And Molly in Trelayne's San Francisco troupe since then? They had made their reputations together in this town. Yet she wanted him to believe that they were as fond of each other as brother and sister, and nothing more.

She doesn't want to lie to me, Calvert thought. That is why she won't say more. I should be happy for that. It means she truly cares. "I was fond of Tommy once," she had said, "but that's over. Believe me, Abel. It is over." It was as close as she had come to saying outright that what Calvert feared was true.

As always, when he thought of Molly he thought of Gray Dawn. She had another husband before him, and that didn't bother him. Because she was an Indian? He thought no less of her for that. Indians had different customs, which he came to know and respect. They hadn't the prudery of white men and women about matters of sex, but many tribes respected the bonds of marriage as absolutely as a pious white man. If a woman's husband died, his brother took her as a second wife, or as his first, if he had none. Abel Calvert was blood brother to Gray Dawn's first husband, Bear Tracks. When Bear Tracks died fighting the Sioux, Calvert had taken in Gray Dawn. She was scarcely nineteen, and afraid of him. In time, the fear left her. In more time, the love between them bloomed. It was like nothing else Abel Calvert had ever known.

He felt the pain of her death again, sharp like a wound from an arrow. It was a twofold pain—the hurt of loss combined with the hurt of betrayal. If only she hadn't betrayed him!

He blundered along the midmorning street, feeling like a stranger amidst his own kind. Were they truly his kind, or had he found his true kindred long ago, in the hide lodges of the tribes along the upper Missouri? That life was lost to him now, and Gray Dawn with it. But here in San Francisco, in this new life he had built for himself with the blessings of fortune, he had a second chance. If Molly would have him, he would show her all the love he had felt just once before. He would give everything she asked for and more. He would make her dreams come true, and she would never betray him.

Chapter 26

ason. Welcome." Kent shook Jason's hand heartily. It was Saturday evening, the last day of May. Kent had invited Jason to supper at his home and he was very glad for the company of a friend.

The house was at Powell Street and Union, looking down the gentle slope toward North Beach. The midday heat had been blown away by westerlies that freshened during the afternoon, bringing back the sea air.

In Jason's honor Ethel Kent had made a New England boiled dinner, with Indian pudding for dessert. Jason gratified her by eating two helpings of everything and praising the cornmeal confection enthusiastically.

"You go along now," Ethel told the men when the meal was done. She was glad to be left to her cleaning up, comfortable in the knowledge that her husband was at peace in his own home. Every night when Stephen returned, and sometimes in the morning, when the deliberations of the Executive Committee had kept him out all night, Stephen told her what had been decided or argued or done by the Committee of Vigilance since last he saw her. And every time he left the house, Ethel prayed for his safety.

"We may not get out of this scot-free, Jason," Kent said when they were settled on the porch, drinking port and smoking. "There are men organizing against us."

"What men?"

"Sherman, the banker. He and Governor Johnson have been meeting with General Wool in Benicia." Kent shook his head. "It wasn't like this in fifty-one. No one opposed us then. Now we have the governor against us and he wants to bring the Army into it. I won't vote to send our men against the lawful government."

Kent's news disturbed Jason. If the landsmen's turmoil became civil war, he and his crew might be caught up in it. Even if they stayed uninvolved, his hopes of finding the incendiaries would be held in abeyance until the governor or the vigilantes emerged triumphant. Thirteen days had passed since the *Sarah B. Watson* was burned. Eleven since Jason learned that Grimes was dead. And since then not a glimmer of information that pointed to the men who committed the crimes. " 'Tis like tryin' to catch hold of St. Elmo's fire," Melchoir had said that morning.

"We must smoke them out," Jason said now.

"Hmm? Smoke who out?" Kent was at a loss.

"The small Englishman and the man with the hook." On the bay, a medium clipper was beating upwind off Fort Mason, making for the open sea. At her topgallant yards, the sailors were shaking out the sails. Jason felt a surge of envy and turned his chair toward Kent's, putting his back to the water.

"Look, Stephen. We don't know enough about these men to find them. How tall are they? What do they look like? What color hair does the Englishman have? It's bad enough looking for a mackerel in a shoal of tuna. If you don't know what a mackerel looks like, it's hopeless. We must smoke them out."

"How do you propose we do it?"

"By offering a reward."

Kent paused in the act of bringing his cigar to his lips. "My God, I'm an idiot."

Jason smiled. "So am I. Why haven't we thought of it before? I don't know. All I know is that this morning I climbed up that slope"—he pointed to the crest of Russian Hill—"and I was at my wits' end. It came to me like a revelation and I felt the perfect fool."

"I will put it to the Executive Committee tomorrow." Kent stubbed out his cigar in the china ashtray and tossed down the last of his port. "I shan't be a minute." He went into the house and returned with the decanter. It was a cut-glass ship's decanter, squat and wide, with a tall neck.

"I don't mind telling you," Kent said as he poured the port, "this makes me feel a great deal better about going back to that warehouse. I've a purpose now." He set down the decanter and resumed his seat. "I am having doubts about our course, Jason. Not yours and mine. The Committee's. After the hanging, I argued that we should adjourn. So did Abel Calvert. No, said Tom Smiley, we've started good work here. We have a chance to rid the city of the criminal class. Most of the others backed him. Recently we have talked of adjourning when the work is done, but the threat from Sherman changes all that. They will never disband the Committee with their backs to the wall."

Kent leaned forward. "In the beginning, we swore our work had nothing to do with politics. 'No creed, no sectional issues, no party,' we said. It's on the Committee's seal. But some of the men we are arresting have committed no crime, unless it is criminal to be a Democrat. This Mercury fellow is right, Jason. We are persecuting our political enemies."

"Mercury?"

"A letter in today's *Herald*. He says we're in league with the devil, and a lot more. Some of them wanted to shut down the *Herald*, but we put a stop to that. Still, I don't know how long we can hold them, Jason. They've got the wind in their sails."

"Keep them on course, Stephen. When I've got the incendiaries at the end of a rope, they can go back to their business."

"There will be a fuss over this Sullivan affair. You've heard about that?"

"Aye. On the waterfront. Some say he was killed by your Committee."

Kent shook his white head. "Calvert and I made sure of that. We knew there would be talk and we questioned Dr. Cole at length. He stakes his reputation that it was suicide. All the same, it makes us look bad." Kent's eyes widened. "By Neptune, that will help! They want to

make a good impression now. I will put up one thousand
dollars of the firm's money as a reward for the men who
burned the *Sarah B.* I will ask the Committee to match
it, or do better."

"Will they go along?"

"It's the worst crime committed since we organized.
They can't go against it." Kent sat back in his chair.
"When we have the reward, we will publish a notice in
the newspapers."

Jason said, "Let's hope one of the incendiaries is the
sort who will value money more than friendship."

Farren crept into the house like a thief in the night,
entering by way of the kitchen, but Sarah was listening
for him. She was writing again in her best imitation of a
man's careless hand. She covered the letter with a piece
of blotting paper before she came out of her bedroom to
meet Farren with a lamp in her hand. She had kept the
fire going in the stove and the kitchen was warm.

"Would you like some hot cocoa?"

"That would be just the thing." His eyes were bright
and his cheeks were pink from the steamer voyage. His
sandy mustache, which was usually brushed and waxed,
was rough like a miner's from the wind and salt air of the
bay.

Sarah broke squares of rich Ghirardelli chocolate into
a small saucepan. Farren paced back and forth, his
pent-up excitement plain to see. "Well, what news here?
Did the Committee resign while I was away?"

"Yankee Sullivan died in that fort of theirs. They say
he took his own life."

Farren nodded. "We heard the minute we stepped off
the boat. And who is this 'Mercury' everyone is talking
about? Did you see that letter to the *Herald*?"

"I glanced at it." She put on a saucepan of milk to
warm as the chocolate melted.

"Talk about stirring up a hornet's nest. My God, what
courage."

"Did you have a pleasant trip?" she prompted, and the
question loosed a torrent.

"Pleasant? Yes! It was more than pleasant. It was a
success! General Wool has promised us the arms we

need, Sarah! He is too cautious by half for my taste. He's an old man and he has lost his will, if you ask me. And Farragut! The Navy can't take a hand in civilian affairs without orders from Washington City, he says. All we wanted was a boat to bring the arms down. He's got a sloop-of-war right there, the *John Adams*, but he claims she is laid up for repairs. He says in any event there is a standing order not to send Navy ships in support of civil unrest! How General Sherman kept his temper, I don't know. He explained to Farragut that we were trying to *put down* civil unrest, but it made no difference. Finally the old man said he would write the Department of War and send the *John Adams* down to the city when her repairs are made."

"It will take two months to get a reply from Washington," Sarah said.

"That's it exactly! He can stall forever. But we found a way around him." Farren puffed up like a rooster. "The fact is, it was my idea. I suggested to Governor Johnson that he must have certain extraordinary powers in the event of a civil emergency. I suggested he might commandeer a Pacific Mail steamer. He's having Secretary Douglass look into it. One way or another we'll find a boat."

He sipped from the cup Sarah handed him. "Oh, that is good."

From the foyer came the sound of voices, and the front door closing. "That will be Tommy and Molly," Sarah said.

Footsteps climbed the stairs. Farren waited for the sound of doors closing before putting a finger to his lips to invoke Sarah's silence and going off to his room, cup in hand.

Sarah sat at the table, sipping her cocoa and listening to the sounds of the house. Molly came downstairs and passed through the hallway on her way to the privy. She gave Sarah a whispered "Good night" on her way back, but did not stop to talk. Sarah waited, hoping Trelayne would make the same journey. When her cocoa was gone and he had not come down, she went upstairs. Only Trelayne's door showed light at the transom. Afraid to knock, she lifted the latch and peeped in to find him reading in bed. He looked up and saw her.

"*'But soft, what light through yonder window breaks? It is the east, and Juliet is the sun!'*"

Sarah motioned him to be quiet, although he spoke the words in a whisper. She closed the door and sat on the bed beside him. "Tommy, I must ask a favor. Tomorrow morning would you get up early for me?"

"*'She speaks—O, speak again, bright angel! for thou art as glorious to this night as is a winged messenger of heaven—'*"

"Hush! and listen to me. Will you meet Dr. Cole tomorrow when he comes out of church? He takes his wife to the Unitarian church each Sunday. You can disguise yourself as that fellow who took my letter to Mr. Nugent."

Trelayne's eyes gleamed with feigned madness. "*'Once more, into the breach'*?"

"Will you please be serious!"

"How can I be serious, dear Sarah, when your siren call lures me toward the theater of the world? You have only to tell me my part and I will play it. What is it you want from the good Dr. Cole?"

"Everything there is to know about how Yankee Sullivan died."

"You shall know it all, for we will ask him together."

Dr. Beverly Cole and his wife, Eugenia, left the Unitarian church on Stockton Street after the rest of the congregation, as was their custom. Cole preferred not to be jostled by the crowd while he negotiated the steps of the church on his crutches. Eugenia took his arm as any wife might take the arm of a healthy husband, but she steadied him as he descended the steps one at a time. She was very pretty and she was his true companion. They had been married seven years before, when he was not yet twenty and she sixteen.

As they started along the street, a slender gentleman about Cole's age stepped up to the couple, accompanied by a beardless youth of less certain breeding. The youth wore nondescript clothing that concealed his form and a slouch hat that hid much of his face.

"Dr. Cole, I believe?" The gentleman tipped his hat to Mrs. Cole.

"You have the advantage of me, sir."

"Theodore Trelawney, Doctor, although I daresay you won't know the name." He did not present the youth, who remained a step or two behind Trelawney.

"If this is a medical matter, I am at my surgery until six o'clock every day but Sunday."

Trelawney laughed softly. "Oh, I am in perfect health, Doctor, as you can tell at a glance, I'm sure."

Cole disliked the man's foppish air. Trelawney's attire was stylish to the point of exaggeration. His hair and his chin beard were shiny with pomade, his mustache waxed and curled. He wore pince-nez spectacles and carried a blackthorn walking stick as a vanity. Having taken the measure of the man, Beverly Cole judged him a coxcomb, all affectation and no substance.

"I won't take a moment of your time," Trelawney said. "I write the occasional bit of news for the *Alta*, and our readers are eager for more details of poor Mr. Sullivan's death. Were you present when he died?" Trelawney's eyes were fixed on Cole's, and there was a new seriousness in his purpose.

"I was not, sir. I was called at daylight yesterday and examined the deceased shortly thereafter. The rigor mortis had already taken effect."

"Then how can you be certain his wound was self-inflicted?" Trelawney searched the pallid face of the doctor, looking for anything that might betray deception or concealment. The newspapers had revealed that Sullivan died from loss of blood, but little more.

"The instrument was a common dinner knife, such as he was given with his meals. It was clenched in his right hand. The gash was in the bend of the left arm."

"But the gash might have been made by anyone, and the knife put in his hand when he was dead."

"That is impossible." Cole's reply was emphatic. "There was blood on the mattress and on the floor below. There was none elsewhere. If he had struggled in any way, it would have been all over the cell. The only possible interpretation of the evidence is that he cut his arm intentionally and allowed himself to bleed to death."

"But why, Doctor? Why would he kill himself?"

Cole had expected the Executive Committee to ask this question, but they had not, although he had the answer ready. "I spoke with the prisoner soon after his incarceration, Mr. Trelawney. He was convinced that no matter what he had done or not done, he would be executed by the Vigilance Committee. 'There is no earthly hope for me,' he told me, although I assured him otherwise. I concluded that the throne of his intellect was disturbed. I took precautions, but they were insufficient, as you know. If there is blame to be apportioned, I bear the burden of it."

"What sort of precautions, Doctor?"

"He was to have no spirits. Drink often aggravates delusions."

Trelawney pounced like a ferret. "Yet he was a known drunkard. And the withdrawal of drink is known to cause delusions."

"It was a medical decision, Mr. Trelawney. I drew on all my learning. If I was wrong, God will be my judge." Cole's manner suggested that no earthly power was competent to anticipate the Creator's verdict.

Trelawney smiled thinly. "Your dedication to your art is evident, Doctor. Please don't think I was questioning your ethics. I have every confidence that the other prisoners in the Committee's custody will receive the best of care, should they need it." The reference to Mercury's warning was intentional, and Cole bristled.

"I am sworn to heal, sir, and to save life to the limits of my earthly powers."

"Then I pray God to lend you His heavenly power as well, Dr. Cole." Trelawney tipped his hat again, bowed slightly, and withdrew with the silent youth at his side.

"Scarcely the sort of questions I would expect from the *Alta California*." Cole did not expect Eugenia to comprehend the delicate game of cat and mouse that had just been played out before her. "A very odd fellow, I should say. Come along, my dear." He swung the crutches and set out at his best pace, wincing from the pain in the old wound as he got under way. "What would you call his style of dress? It was a bit much, wasn't it?"

'*Outré,*" Eugenia said. "Just a trifle *outré.*"

"That is just the word for that popinjay. Precisely. You have a way with words, my dear. He is *outré*." Cole remembered the pale youth and thought it possible Trelawney was a pederast as well, but he did not share this thought with his wife.

"The man's a pompous ass, but I believe him." Trelayne looked over his shoulder and saw the Coles pass out of sight down Jackson Street. He and Sarah were walking south on Stockton. "I don't think he has a political bone in his body. He took the position with the vigilantes because he feels he is the best man for the job."

"And because it is a feather in his cap," Sarah said. "I don't think he is unaware of that."

"No. Not at all unaware, I should say." Trelayne looked Sarah up and down, admiring his handiwork once more. "Tell me the truth, Sarah. You are enjoying yourself, aren't you?"

Her eyes were shining. "Yes. I was right next to Mrs. Cole and she scarcely looked at me. I wouldn't have believed it possible."

"People believe what they see. They don't question their eyes. Here's a good-looking young man, Mrs. Cole was thinking. She fancied you."

"Tommy! You are incorrigible. And you are a consummate actor. If anything, she fancied Theodore Trelawney."

"She may pine for his memory, but she will never see him again. Too bad. I rather like him."

"Why can't you use him again?"

"He is too memorable. But I felt whimsical today. Cole will remember the questions Trelawney asked. And if he should happen to see his answers in Mercury's letter to the *Herald*, Theodore Trelawney will be at risk." The costume he had adopted to visit the *Herald* had been a wiser choice. Dressed as a common man, he would be taken for one of the common workingmen who supported the Committee of Vigilance in the thousands, with all the fervor of their ignorance.

"I would never write anything to put you in danger," Sarah said.

Trelayne waved away her concern. "I have a hundred

disguises. You write the letters and a host of different messengers will deliver them."

Trelayne's costume, like Sarah's, had come from the Theater Trelayne's wardrobes. In his enthusiasm for the adventure, Trelayne had left the boardinghouse before breakfast to prepare their disguises. As soon as breakfast was done, Sarah had slipped out of the house and met him at the theater, and in less than half an hour he had transformed her into a man. In ill-fitting men's clothes, with her hair concealed beneath the crown of her slouch hat and her breasts bound, as Molly's had been when she played a man in *The Houri and the Bedouin*, with a band of silk damask, Sarah had scarcely known herself.

Before they left the theater on their mission, Trelayne had instructed her in walking like a man. "Take bigger steps than you think proper for a lady. Watch the way I walk. And swing your arms as you move along."

Her first efforts had been less than convincing. "Move more freely," Trelayne had ordered her. "Walk as if you own the world."

In the streets, Sarah found it exhilarating to walk un-hampered by skirts and unrestricted by notions of what was proper comportment for a lady. On their way to the church, she and Trelayne had been accosted by three sailors who were weaving drunkenly in the middle of Jackson Street after a night of carousing.

"Ahoy, mates," one had called out to them.

"Here is your first test," Trelayne had said softly. "Remember, you are better than they."

"Beggin' yer pardon, sir, but we're told there's a house hereabouts," the one who had hailed them said.

"A house where a sailor can drop his anchor in friendly waters, so to speak," another said with a giggle.

"There is one parlor house that I know of, but it is not for the likes of you," Trelayne said.

"Better go to Pike Street where you belong," Sarah added. She had kept her voice as low as possible and gave it what she hoped was an air of aloofness.

"Not for the likes of us?" The worst of the three was barely able to stand. He lurched toward Sarah. "Fuckin' dandy boys!"

His companions held him back. "Don't mind him, sir.

We'll go along, just as you say." The first sailor's tone was respectful. He tugged his cap as they turned away. "I told you we was in the wrong part of town!" he hissed to the others as they reeled off down the street.

"Well done!" Trelayne exclaimed when the sailors were gone, and Sarah had glimpsed the full extent of her new power. It went beyond the joy of her physical freedom. For the first time since her body had begun to change from a girl's into a woman's, she could walk among men unintimidated by their desire.

Whether they were refined or coarse, most men appraised each and every woman they met. They judged her pretty or plain, they considered her hair, her eyes, her carriage, her manner of speaking—if she spoke—and her body, what they could see of it. This appraisal was sometimes discreet, sometimes blatant, but it was ever-present, forcing a lady to drop her eyes lest she give encouragement.

Sarah Titus had not been raised a lady. As her body blossomed she had heard every sort of comment, some kind and some cruel, from seamen and draymen, from fishmongers and dockside crimps and farmers' sons and gentlemen, and old men whose blood warmed again at the sight of a young woman's ankle. She had sometimes wished she might be plain—even ugly—to avoid men's stares. But she knew if she were ugly there would still be the looks, the appraisal, and then—instead of desire—revulsion or disdain. And how would that make a woman feel, to be an object of scorn each time she was found wanting?

They were in Kearny Street, crossing Sacramento, a block from the Theater Trelayne, where they would remove their costumes and become Tommy Trelayne and Sarah Rockwell once more.

"Mind your way, gents," cautioned a drayman whose horse had deposited a fresh pile of dung on the planks.

"Big steps," Trelayne said under his breath. "Swing your arms. That's it."

Sarah felt that she could fly above the rooftops merely by lengthening her stride a little more. Dressed as a man, she was invulnerable.

•　•　•

They returned to the boardinghouse after eleven o'clock and found it deserted. While Sarah took off her cloak and bonnet, Trelayne went up the stairs, opened his door and Molly's, then came down again.

"No sign of Molly?" Sarah said.

"We scarcely see her anymore." Trelayne's tone was wistful, but he hadn't meant to reveal his concern, even to Sarah. He pretended indifference. "Well, she can do as she likes."

"She will do as she likes, Tommy. Unless you take her in hand."

"What am I to do, Sarah?"

"Tell her your feelings. Every woman needs to hear that."

"I have shown her my feelings."

"It's not the same. Words touch a woman where the flesh cannot." Her own frankness surprised her.

He sulked. "Men need to be courted too, you know."

"She's afraid, Tommy."

"Of what?"

"Of losing you."

"So she plays up to every man in town?"

"It's her way."

"I won't take part in that game. Ah. There's the player now. Not a word."

Through the parlor windows they could see Molly coming up Jackson Street. She walked with a bounce in her step and she swung her folded parasol as she walked.

"Hasn't a care in the world, has she?" Trelayne couldn't keep the bitterness out of his voice.

"Hush, now. Show her what a nice man you can be."

He fought an impulse to take Molly in his arms when she opened the door and stepped into the foyer.

"Tommy. Sarah." She curtsied. Her cheeks dimpled as she smiled.

"You look very well, Molly," Trelayne said. In her Sunday dress, her cheeks flushed from her outing, she had never been so lovely.

"I feel very well. In fact I feel on top of the world. I feel as if I were San Francisco's leading lady." She opened her parasol and twirled it over her head, turning in a pirouette at the same time. She dropped the parasol in front of her face. From behind the mauve silk there came a soft giggle.

"It's bad luck to open that thing in the house," Trelayne said pettishly. He didn't like the feeling that Molly was excluding him from a secret.

"What has gotten into you?" Sarah had never seen Molly behave so strangely.

Molly raised the parasol. "Yesterday Abel Calvert asked me to marry him." The parasol revolved slowly above her head.

"And?" Trelayne felt cold, although the day was pleasant.

"And this morning I said yes."

Chapter 27

he four men in Sheriff Scannell's office at the County Jail waited in silence. Scannell, Farren and Judge Terry were all sitting. Sherman moved about restlessly. Scannell's chair was half-turned behind his desk so he could look out the barred window at Broadway. He was a large man who had the build of an Irish hod carrier, but Sherman knew that he wrote concise, literate reports in a disciplined hand.

It was midafternoon. Deputy Sheriff Harrison had left the jail over an hour ago to serve the writ of habeas corpus for Billy Mulligan at the Vigilance Committee's warehouse on Sacramento Street. The office was warm and stuffy, and the waiting made Sherman more impatient with each passing moment.

"Here he is," Scannell said.

Deputy Harrison rode up Broadway at a lope and dismounted. He threw his reins around the hitching rail, bounded up the jail steps and entered Scannell's office. Harrison was younger than Scannell but just as solidly built. He was the star batter on the sheriff's baseball team, which took on all comers in the Plaza on the first Friday of each month.

"Did they refuse the writ?" Judge Terry demanded.

"They're not such fools as to turn me away cold, Judge," Harrison said. "They kept me waiting outside that shitheel fort of theirs for a quarter hour. Maybe longer. Had to find someone with authority to receive the writ, they says. Shouldn't be bringing legal business on the Lord's day, they says. 'The Good Lord rested on the seventh day,' says I, 'but the law never sleeps.' They had the door half-open and I could hear them shouting inside. 'Find Mr. Truett,' they says. After a bit, here comes himself, Mr. Miers Truett, his head scrapin' the clouds. Shows me all around the place. Shows me upstairs too. They got cells built along the north wall. Wouldn't open 'em up, but I knocked on the doors and shouted for anyone inside to answer me, and none did. Claimed they was storage rooms, sir. Storage rooms with ventilation holes, and iron bolts instead of latches."

Sherman looked at Terry, who was still seated. "Well, Judge?"

"You ask me," Harrison said, "they took whoever was in them cells and hid 'em. They had plenty of time."

"Did they acknowledge holding Billy Mulligan?" Terry asked.

"Denied it to my face, Judge," said Harrison. " 'Never heard of the feller,' one of the guards said, but Truett give him a look and he shut up."

"They as much as admitted they had Mulligan when they first took him, Judge," Farren said. "They said he would turn loose every criminal in the jail if he stayed in his position."

Terry rose from his chair. "We have credible evidence that Mulligan is in their custody. The service of the writ was denied. I will so inform Governor Johnson."

Trelayne did not come downstairs at suppertime. After Molly's announcement that morning he had gone to his room, and he did not emerge when Sarah rang the small silver hand bell to call the boarders to table.

Sunday was the one night of the week when Trelayne and Molly were not at the theater. Their participation at Sunday supper usually made it a lively end to the weekend. Tonight it seemed to Sarah that there was a pall over the household, although Jason and Norton and Melchior congratulated Molly with genuine warmth when they learned of her engagement to Abel Calvert.

Because it was Ingrid's night off, Molly and Dickie

helped Sarah serve. When the food was on the table and the others seated—all but David Farren, who was absent too—Sarah went to Trelayne's room and found him bent over his secretary, writing furiously.

"Won't you join us?" she said.

"Hmm? No, thank you, Sarah."

"Can I bring you something?"

He scarcely looked up from his writing. "A piece of bread. A bit of cheese. anything at all."

She brought him a full meal on a tray and set it on the small table by his window. He sat in the ladder-back chair and began to eat ravenously.

"Are you all right, Tommy?"

"All right? Oh, you mean about Molly. Yes, Sarah. I'm all right. I have an idea for a play, that's all. Tell them I'm writing a play, and make my excuses for me."

When Sarah returned to the dining room she found that David Farren had come in late for supper. He gave her a look of such triumph that she guessed his preparations to confront the Committee of Vigilance were going well, but he glanced meaningfully at Jason, shook his head almost imperceptibly, and kept his attention on the conversation at hand, which concerned the search for the men who burned the *Sarah B. Watson*.

"Two weeks today they sent her to her grave," Melchior said mournfully. "Where've they gone to, those men? Bilge rats they be, eh, Jason? Worse'n that, but I won't say it in this company." He gave Sarah a shy smile.

"Tomorrow the reward notice will be in the papers," Jason said. "Perhaps it will scare them out, perhaps not. Either way, we must make preparations to leave this port." He met Melchior's doleful gaze. "Tomorrow we will begin to look for a ship."

The mate was transformed in an instant. "Gor damme!" he exclaimed, forgetting entirely where he was. "I never thought to hear them words from ee, Jason. Sweet to my ears, they be. Nigh a week now I been looking for a way to say to ee that vengeance is the Lord's, and not for the likes of we. And now you seen the light."

Sarah silently blessed Melchior, but Jason shook his head. "Nay," he said, "I'm not giving up my vengeance, old friend. I'll have it if I can, but 'tis time to look ahead as well."

As soon as it came, Melchior's joy faded. "But the settlement, Jason. Are ee forgettin' it'll be weeks yet afore we have the insurance money?"

"Hang the settlement. I've spoken with Mr. Kent about that, last evening when I supped with him. I told him we must find the money now, and he agreed. We will approach the bankers and merchants here for an advance against the insurance. We will offer a discount on a cargo carried to China, or a percentage of our profit on the first cargo we bring back here from the eastern states. Some way we'll get it."

"Gor damme!" This time Melchior cast an abashed look in Sarah's direction. "I'm askin' your pardon, missus. Yours too, Miss Molly. But praise God, my cap'n has found the way for us to cast off from this port."

"We'll start looking for a vessel tomorrow," Jason said. "The sooner we start fitting out a new ship, the better. There is trouble here, and worse to come."

"Worse to come?" Farren said.

"Aye," Jason said. "Mr. Kent says the Army may take a hand. Your General Sherman has been to see them. I'll take what's left of my crew and make sail for Whampoa in a longboat before I'll have them caught up in that kind of trouble."

Farren did not entirely manage to conceal his alarm at hearing Jason speak of General Sherman and the Army. He opened his mouth to speak, thought better of it, cast a worried glance at Sarah, and was much relieved when Trelayne appeared in the doorway to the parlor, his eyes wild with barely contained excitement. "Molly! When is the wedding to be?"

Molly was startled by his sudden appearance, and a little frightened, but she put on a brave face. "On the fourteenth of June."

"That's less than two weeks!" Sarah was shocked. The engagement was scandalously short. It would prompt speculation that there might be an as yet unseen reason for the sudden nuptials.

"It's what I want." Molly was defiant. "Abel wanted

to wait until the Fourth of July, but I made him agree to do it now."

"Saturday. Two weeks from yesterday." Trelayne's mind was racing. Proprieties were the least of his concerns. "We can do it. We'll close *School for Scandal* Thursday night and we'll forget about *Oliver Twist* for now. We'll rehearse through the weekend and open the new play a week from tomorrow, on the ninth."

"No one opens a new play on Monday," Molly said.

Trelayne smiled. "Exactly. There will be no risk of another theater opening something new on the same night. We will have the whole town's attention."

"Tommy, I—" Molly looked to Sarah for support, then rushed on to get the words out while she dared to speak them. "After the wedding I'm leaving the Theater Trelayne. Abel insisted. It was the one thing he asked of me. Mr. Maguire has agreed to take me on."

Trelayne's spirits flagged. "Maguire! Why him, of all people?"

Thomas Maguire was the most renowned theatrical manager in California, and Trelayne's particular rival. A forty-niner, Maguire had begun as a saloon keeper. He had opened his first theater over a saloon on Kearny Street, around the corner from where his present playhouse—the San Francisco Hall—now stood on Washington. Like all of San Francisco's theatrical managers, Maguire's fortunes had waxed and waned, but defeat had never kept him down for long. He had helped Trelayne get started on his own and Trelayne knew him to be a kind and generous man. Maguire would have been shocked to learn that Trelayne considered him a rival, but the one achievement Trelayne sought more than any other was to mount a production that outstripped Maguire's triumphs. Now he had it half-written.

They were all looking at him, wondering how he would take Molly's news. He kept his eyes on Molly. "There is still time, if you will stay with me until your wedding day. Do this for me, Molly, and I'll send you to Tom Maguire in a coach and four. We will open on the ninth and run just five days. Monday to Friday, and Saturday I'll toast your wedding. You'll triumph as never before. I've saved the best part for you."

"What is the play?"

"It's a classical piece in modern dress. I won't say more now, but you'll play a man."

"I love men's parts!"

"The first night will be a benefit for you. It will be my wedding gift."

Theatrical performances were frequently dedicated to the benefit of a popular actress or actor so the public could shower them with bouquets and gifts. Gold coins and flowers, even expensive jewelry, were thrown onto the stage at the conclusion of the evening. A favorite player could earn as much from one benefit as from a year of treading the boards for a weekly salary. Sarah suspected that Trelayne intended to bait Abel Calvert somehow by the benefit, but there was nothing improper on the face of it, and Molly was plainly entranced by the offer.

"Oh, Tommy. Yes, of course I'll do it."

"Good. Good. That's settled, then. Well, I've much more to do." He went as abruptly as he had come.

Chapter 28

he Monday editions of San Francisco's newspapers carried a notice prominently displayed on the news pages:

REWARD OFFERED

Farnum & Kent, shipowners and merchants of this city, will pay a reward of $2,500. for the identity of the person or persons responsible for burning the clipper ship *Sarah B. Watson* at anchor off Goat Island on the 18th ultimo. Persons with knowledge of this crime may make application at the firm's place of business on Sansome Street between Washington and Jackson.

The *Herald* printed the notice next to a column that contained a letter signed "Mercury."

When a boy brought the paper to the offices of Farnum & Kent, Stephen Kent verified that the reward notice was printed properly and felt renewed satisfaction over the amount offered. When he put the proposition to the Executive Committee on Sunday, Abel Calvert had been the first to respond, with two hundred fifty dollars of his own. To Kent's surprise, Jonathan Frye, who was notorious for his parsimony, had matched Calvert's contribution. The Executive Committee, place in the position of putting its money where its principles were, had voted a thousand dollars from the Committee's reserves to match Farnum & Kent's share.

Kent did not notice the letter adjoining the reward notice until Abel Calvert stormed into his office just before noon, waving a copy of the *Herald*.

"Have you seen this?"

"Our notice? Of course I have seen it."

"Not your notice! Mercury's letter!"

"Is there another?"

Calvert closed the door to the outer office, where Ned Rollick was gaping. "Listen to this." He lowered his voice and read with an intensity Kent had not seen in him before. *"Are the vigilantes so heartless that they will let a man cut his own veins in his madness, while many of their Executive Committee are tippling at the city's finest saloons? The effects caused by the sudden denial of a drunkard's alcoholic spirits are well known. Could they not give Yankee Sullivan a dram to ease his suffering? One dram of kindness might have prevented a needless death. And how many more deaths must we see before this mercantile junta retires into the obscurity from which it came?"*

"Well he might ask," Kent grumbled.

Calvert gave him a black look. "It gets worse: *Dr. Cole has admitted his mistake in the care of Yankee Sullivan. Let the Committee of Vigilance admit their mistake in organizing. Let them retire now, while they still have the good opinion of the public, however mistaken that opinion may be. Let them retire now, before the forces organizing against them take the field, where the triumph of law and order is certain. Through their spies, the Committee knows of the preparations being made to oppose them by force of arms. Let them retire now, before they commit greater crimes and earn greater retribution."* Calvert looked at Kent, awaiting a response.

Kent cleared his throat. "We have always been straightforward between us, Abel. Here in this office, I will tell you that Mercury is right. It's time for us to go back to our business. We've thrown a scare into the rough element. They will mind their p's and q's for a long time."

"That may be," Calvert admitted. "The Committee can't go on forever and I'm not saying it should. But don't you see? *He* knows *we* know about the governor's preparations! We've got a nigger in the woodpile, Stephen. I find that coon, by God I'll skin him alive."

It occurred to Kent that Abel Calvert was the one man on the Executive Committee who had the skills to perform that grisly operation.

Calvert paced the office. "This Mercury knows our business and that is intolerable! We have got to do something about it."

"Today's paper wraps tomorrow's fish."

"This isn't some redskin taking one shot at us and then keeping to cover. We've got an enemy here, Stephen. I'll side with you the next time we talk about adjourning, but I won't run for cover with my tail between my legs. Meantime, someone in the Executive Committee is spilling the beans."

Kent shrugged. "I've spoken to no one outside the organization. Have you?"

"'Course not."

"I was thinking of—well, forgive me. I understand congratulations are in order."

Calvert became almost boyish in his embarrassment. "How did you hear? The announcement won't be in the papers until tomorrow."

"I see Captain Beck every day. Mrs. Rockwell's house has been buzzing like a beehive since Miss Gray told them, as you can imagine. You're an old rascal, Abel."

"I'm a lucky man."

"Aye, you are that. We'll drink to your good fortune."

"That would be fine."

"You didn't—that is, you've made no mention of our business to Miss Gray?" Kent held up a hand to stave off the indignation he expected. "I know you are not an imprudent man, Abel. But in the flush of romantic feelings even the most prudent man sometimes forgets himself."

Calvert took no offense. "Molly doesn't care a whit for politics. She hates the whole vigilance thing because it takes so much of my time."

"When is the wedding to be?"

"The fourteenth. Saturday. You're to come, of course, you and Ethel."

"That's a short engagement."

"We're neither of us babes in the woods. We know

what we want and we're going about it right quick. Convention be hanged, we say. Let the blue bloods turn up their noses."

Kent saw that Abel Calvert was besotted with love. In Boston, a banker who married an actress would be ostracized. In San Francisco, Calvert would keep the place he had earned in the city's financial community, and he would be envied.

On Tuesday, Sherman spent the morning stalking about his office. Occasionally he sat at his desk and shuffled through the papers awaiting his attention. He signed a few and gave them to Benjamin Nisbet, his assistant. For the time being, most of the running of the bank was in Nisbet's hands. The younger man was capable, but short as pie crust with customers, a fault that no amount of hinting seemed able to correct.

It was after midday when David Farren entered the bank. He came straight to Sherman's office and tendered a sheet of foolscap bearing the telegraph company's letterhead. "It has already gone to the printers. By two o'clock it will be posted all over town. The governor has gone us one better, I'd say."

Sherman read Governor Johnson's proclamation rapidly. *Whereas satisfactory information has been received by me ... an unlawful organization styling themselves the Vigilance Committee, have resisted by force the execution of Criminal process.... Now therefore, I, J. NEELY JOHNSON, Governor of the State of California, by virtue of the powers vested in me ... do hereby declare said County of San Francisco in a state of insurrection—*

"Good God!" Sherman exclaimed softly.

Farren grinned, immensely pleased. "He has reworked it considerably from what I suggested. I would guess that Judge Terry helped him." Farren had drafted the outline for the proclamation himself, after a day spent poring over law books in his firm's offices. He had given Johnson the outline at Benicia, but the phrase *a state of insurrection* had not appeared in his draft.

Sherman read on. *I do hereby order and direct all of the Volunteer Militia Companies of the County of San Francisco ... to report themselves for duty immediately to Major General*

William T. Sherman commanding Second Division California Militia.... I furthermore order and direct that all associations, combinations, or organizations whatsoever, existing in said County of San Francisco or elsewhere in this State, in opposition to, or in violation of, the laws thereof more particularly the association known as the Vigilance Committee of San Francisco, do disband, and ... yield obedience to the Constitution and Laws of this State....

"It will be in the evening papers today and all the papers tomorrow," Farren said. "This came for you, as well." He handed Sherman a second sheet, which Sherman glanced at briefly. It was Governor Johnson's formal order to Sherman to call up the militia.

"Place a call for volunteers to run in tomorrow's papers," Sherman said. "Be sure to cite the authority of the Governor's proclamation. The state's quartermaster general will arrive by this afternoon's boat from Sacramento. A man named Kibbe. Do you know him?"

"I have met him, sir. He is sound. Very good at organization."

There was a knock at the door.

"Meet him at the boat. Take him to the City Hall and arrange some rooms for our recruitment."

The knock came again, more insistent.

"Come!"

Benjamin Nisbet put his head in the door and asked if Sherman would see his old friend Henry Halleck.

"I am always in to Mr. Halleck. You go along, Captain. Give Quartermaster Kibbe any assistance he needs."

Farren stepped aside on his way out to admit two men, one tall and tending to portliness, the other leaner and older.

"You know Joe Crockett, Will." Henry Halleck pumped Sherman's hand in greeting. They had been classmates at West Point and had come around the Horn together in '47 aboard the *Lexington*. Early in the gold rush, Halleck had left the Army and invested wisely in real estate. In a few years he had become a rich man. His most notable achievement was building the Montgomery Block, where James King of William had recently died.

Halleck came right to the point. "We hear that you are about to take a stand against the Vigilance Committee."

"There are no secrets in this city, it seems. You had better read this." Sherman took Johnson's proclamation from his pocket and handed it to Halleck, who read it with Crockett looking over his shoulder.

"Good God," Halleck exclaimed, echoing Sherman's own reaction. "The fat is in the fire now." He handed the paper back to Sherman.

"Look here, Sherman," Crockett said. "You know I stood guard in the jail when the sheriff called the posse. No one deplores the current state of things more than I, but let us admit that it *is* the state of things."

Joseph Crockett had been speaker of the Kentucky House of Representatives before coming to California to practice law. He had little of the politician's manner, a fact that had earned Sherman's respect from their first meeting.

"If you arm your troops, that may lead to fighting," Halleck said.

"All that is necessary to prevent it is for the vigilantes to stand down," Sherman said. "If they resist the execution of the laws, they must expect consequences."

"They don't want to go down in defeat," Crockett said. "It is a matter of appearances."

"Do you prefer the appearance of the city and the state powerless before this mob?" Sherman glared at Crockett, then returned his attention to Halleck. "Have you thought what the results may be for California and the rest of the nation if no efforts are made to resist this Committee while they overthrow the laws? My God, Henry, what would your wife's grandfather think of this business?" Halleck's wife, Elizabeth, was the granddaughter of Alexander Hamilton. Sherman pictured the principal author of *The Federalist Papers* spinning like a dervish in his grave.

Halleck's habitual expression was grave and it did not vary now. "We've been speaking with some solid men in this town, Will. We want to work for conciliation before this leads to more bloodshed. Three men are dead. Four if you count Sullivan. Let it stop there. Give us a chance.

We'll find a way for the Committee to disband with honor."

"Honor!" Sherman barked. "What about the honor of the state? What about the *law*!"

"Armed conflict among our own people would be a terrible blot on the history of this state and a tragedy for its citizens," Crocket said.

Sherman felt the righteous outrage leave him. "You're right, of course. We must avoid armed conflict if possible. I cannot publicly recognize your effort. But if you can work out a compromise that does not dishonor the state, I will urge the governor to accept it."

"Crockett and I have been to see Coleman," Halleck said. "He told us in confidence that many of their Executive Committee are tired of the whole thing. Casey and Cora are gone, and that's taken the steam out of it. They will disband within a week. Ten days at the outside, if the state doesn't move against them."

"I won't hinder them in any way. But I must go ahead with my preparations. If you want to bring about conciliation, tell your friends on the Vigilance Committee to get on with their packing."

Chapter 29

or three days, Jason and Melchior looked at rotting hulks and bluff-bowed, wallowing merchantmen. On Wednesday afternoon, June 4, when Dickie Howell brought word from Farnum & Kent that a storeship anchored off Rincon Point was for sale, Jason said, "At least we know it will float."

His spirits lifted a little when Finn Warren's dory approached the moored storeship off the point's eastern shore. Although dismasted, the vessel had the concave bow and trim lines of a true clipper. *"Pride of the Seas,"* Jason read the ship's name in peeling paint on her stern.

"She's built by Donald McKay," Dickie said. Donald McKay of Boston stood head and shoulders above the rest of America's shipbuilders. Even a San Francisco wharf rat felt his pulse beat a little faster when he saw a McKay ship.

Jason looked at the note Dickie had brought from Stephen Kent. "Christened February fifty-two. She came to San Francisco on her maiden voyage that same year, and never left."

"She'd be a fair vessel, that one," Melchior mused.

Finn Warren dropped sail as they neared the ship. He fitted the oars in the locks and rowed the dory around her so they could look at her from all sides. Jason peered through the murky water at the growth of seaweed and barnacles on the ship's hull below the water-line. "She'll need a good scraping and new plates."

" 'Tis easy enough to heave her down," Melchior said. " 'Twill give the lads something to do. They'll work alongside the riggers with a good will, I'm bound."

"What do you think of the name?"

"Pride of the Seas?" Melchior's massive shoulders rose and fell. " 'Tis the modern way. I'm fond of a woman's name, like the *Sarah B.*"

Jason preferred a woman's name as well. *Sarah B. Watson.* Or Sarah T. Rockwell. She was too much on his mind of late. It was time to be turning his attention to fitting out a new vessel and leaving the Golden Gate in his wake, before he lost his bearings altogether and yielded to the longing for a woman who was his match. Each time in the past when he had let his feelings for a woman run free he had come to a choice between the woman and his ship. And each time, choosing the ship had caused the woman such grief and himself such remorse that he had finally vowed to hold his feelings in check until he might find some way to embrace both a woman and a ship in his life. Or until he was willing to give up the sea. But by then he would be in his grave.

He looked again at Kent's note. "They want too much money for her. We'll beat them down or make them pay to refit her. How would you rig her? Skysails or no?"

They talked of skysails and split topsails and improvements to the *Sarah B.*'s style of rigging while they sailed back to the Pacific Wharf. "You two go to Farnum and Kent," Jason instructed Melchior and Dickie when they reached the foot of Pacific Street. "If there is anyone to claim that reward, keep him there and send young Richard to find me. I'm going to the Vigilance Committee's warehouse to tell Mr. Kent we've found our ship."

He set out along Davis Street. In his note, Kent had said he would be at the vigilantes' warehouse for much of the afternoon. If there were a way to buy *Pride of the Seas,* together they would find it, and there would be time enough still for revenge. Even if the stars smiled on the enterprise and the ship were bought tomorrow, it would take at least two weeks to scrape her and fit new copper plates to her bottom and rig her and fit her out.

Two weeks, and that would be a miracle. Three weeks or even four was more likely. Time enough for revenge.

Time enough to approach the problem from upwind, and maybe take the man behind it all by surprise. Since the fire, Jason had made no headway. Once Grimes was dead, instead of trying to find the men who went aboard the *Sarah B.* to burn her, he should have been working to discover the man who paid them. Who would have the motive to destroy the cargo? Someone with an interest in rice or flour. One of those in the flour monopoly, or perhaps in the conspiracy in rice that followed on the first cartel's heels. The men who took part in those schemes might include some of the very same merchants Jason would approach now to invest in the new ship. He would ask questions and listen carefully to the answers. In the meantime, if the promise of a reward flushed out a bilge rat who had a tale to tell, all the better.

Thus far, the reward notice had produced only a pair of bungling conspirators who hoped to gain the money by fraud. Yesterday, two seamen had entered Farnum & Kent an hour apart, one stinking of rum, the other of brandy. Each swore that the other had burned the *Sarah B. Watson*. Their stories of how the fire had been set were ludicrous. When the second man made his appearance, Jason had threatened him with dire punishment at the Vigilance Committee's hands if he did not confess his deception. Terrified, the man admitted that he and his shipmate had fallen out after conniving to claim the reward. He was mortified to learn his friend had come to Farnum & Kent first.

No other informants had applied at the firm. Today the talk of the town, on the waterfront as well as in the commercial district, was the governor's proclamation, which raised the prospect of armed conflict in the city streets within a matter of days. Jason felt he was racing against a gathering storm.

"Good day, Captain."

Jason recognized Ned Rollick approaching him with outstretched hand and Adam's apple bobbing. He had arrived at Sacramento Street, near the Vigilance Committee's warehouse. "Good day to you, Mr. Rollick. Has anyone come for our reward?"

"I have not been at the offices since this morning, Captain. I am on other business." Rollick nodded toward the warehouse, where armed sentries paced the roof.

"Is Mr. Kent there?"

"He is." Rollick kept his voice low. His habit of swallowing before he spoke vanished when he was on familiar ground. "I'm afraid the Executive Committee is in closed session just now. No one to be admitted. There is some concern about the governor's proclamation, as you may imagine. They are preparing to take measures."

"What sort of measures?"

"You will know before I, Captain. In your position as commander of our marines, you may well be part of them. Walk with me, if you will. I must get to Portsmouth Square and back to Fort Vigilance within the half hour."

They set out at a brisk pace. "Listen here," Jason said. "You know a good deal about the business of Farnum and Kent."

"I do."

"I may have found a vessel. Has Mr. Kent told you of our intention to borrow against the insurance settlement?"

"He has."

"We will need the money soon."

Rollick's Adam's apple bobbed. "It may be that I can make some inquiries within the Vigilance Committee. I often deal with bankers and merchants for Mr. Kent. The fact is, I know some of them better than he does. Many of those men are in the organization."

Rollick was thinking aloud, marshaling his thoughts as he spoke. If he could find a way to facilitate the purchase of a ship for Farnum & Kent's top skipper, the firm would be in his debt. Advancement and a rise in salary could follow. Lately he had been discouraged by the slow pace of his progress. In Captain Beck's new venture he saw an opportunity that could benefit Ned Rollick as well as the firm.

"I will do what I can, Captain," he said. "For the present, leave this in my hands. Once I have reported back to the Executive Committee this afternoon, I may have some time free. Leave it to me for now."

They turned the corner from Clay into Kearny, and Portsmouth Square lay before them. In the sloping rectangle of the Plaza, which was bounded by an iron fence, at least two hundred men were gathered. They were separated in three groups of roughly equal size. In the center of each group, a man was addressing those around him. Across the Plaza, by the fence along Washington Street, a few youths were throwing a baseball, but their attention was on the groups of men.

"Timid as rabbits." Rollick's tone was scornful. He was looking at the City Hall, which dominated the block between Washington and Clay. Jason saw that men were passing through the arched portals in twos and threes to enter the public building. Above the cupola, the American flag stood out to the east, flapping in the wind.

"Look at them," Rollick said. "They advance like rabbits, scared of their own shadows. Then they see their fellows in the Plaza and they take courage. Scoundrels and layabouts, every one of them. There are two more. And three over there." He noticed Jason's incomprehension. "They are volunteers, Captain. That is where Mr. Sherman is enrolling his new militia."

At six o'clock, when Captain Farren closed the doors to the makeshift recruiting office, nearly eight hundred men had signed the rolls. Among the officers put in charge of the newly formed companies were some who had served with Sherman in the Army. Several others had commanded companies of the state's militia before the rise of the Committee of Vigilance. Captain Richard Ashe had insisted on retaining his position as commander of the Blues' Company A, despite his federal position as naval agent.

With Sherman and Farren in the recruiting room were Quartermaster General William Kibbe, who was gathering up the enlistment sheets, and Colonel J. R. West. In the state's reorganized militia, West was Sherman's second in command.

The room was at the southern corner of the City Hall. Like the mayor's chambers, at the far end of the corridor, it commanded a view of Kearny Street and the Plaza. Outside, the last of the volunteers were leaving the Plaza, hurrying home for a bite to eat before coming back at seven o'clock to be drilled. Sherman wanted the populace—and the vigilants' watchdogs—to see the state's forces in training.

"They're mostly laborers," Farren said. "A few gentlemen among them. Rather more Sydney ducks than gentlemen, I'm afraid."

"A majority have seen military service," said Quartermaster Kibbe. Like Colonel West, he was a solid figure of a man, and intensely loyal to the state, but of an altogether different temperament. While West was a leader, Kibbe's natural bent was to organize things, which he did very well. Just now he was arranging the recruitment forms in neat stacks by company.

"Under good discipline, these men will be a force to be reckoned with." West's Louisiana inflections imparted a relaxed confidence to the statement.

"Motivation is a necessary quality in a soldier," Sherman said. "He must believe in what he's fighting for." He allowed himself a small smile. "Many of these are the very sort of men the vigilants have persecuted. I think we will find they are well motivated."

Privately, Sherman had feared that few would dare to enlist in broad daylight to oppose the Committee, no matter what the governor's proclamation said. The success of the first day's recruitment heartened him immensely. He turned to West. "Following this evening's drill, you will arm those men who have previous military experience."

"With your permission, General, I will instruct the men to take their arms to their homes. By dispersing the guns, we will make it impossible for the vigilants to take us by surprise and disarm us."

Sherman gave his assent to West's suggestion at once. He felt no doubt, no need for hesitation. He was following his instincts. Trust the officers, make the decisions, be confident in command. Act! After all the waiting it was finally time to act. Still, if Halleck and Crockett were right—

Mayor Van Ness entered the room and motioned to Sherman. "Two gentlemen to see you sir. They are in my office." The mayor was visibly nervous as he conducted

Sherman down the hallway. "I had no idea they would come here. I didn't know whether to receive them or not. I hope I'm doing the right thing."

On entering the mayor's chamber, Sherman recognized Abel Calvert at once. The second man's face was familiar, but Sherman could not place him until Calvert introduced him as Stephen Kent, of the shipping firm Farnum & Kent.

"We have come on behalf of the Committee of Vigilance," Calvert said without preliminaries.

"I can have nothing to do with members of an unlawful committee." Sherman chose his words with care. He wanted to know why the men had come. "I am surprised to find you involved in this business, Calvert. I should have thought to see you with Halleck and Crockett and their conciliation group."

"You might say that Mr. Kent and I are the conciliators within the Committee." Calvert's manner was straightforward, neither belligerent nor defensive.

"Perhaps we might have a few words with you as concerned citizens," Kent proposed.

"Very well. But you must understand that what we say here cannot in any way be construed as a communication between myself and the Vigilance Committee."

Calvert nodded. "We understand. As concerned citizens then, we beg you not to go ahead with forming this militia. The Committee has nearly completed its work, and will soon quietly disband. We—they—have no wish to see a collision of arms in the streets of this city."

"I am very glad to hear you say so, Mr. Calvert."

Kent looked hopeful. "You will delay arming your companies?"

"I said nothing of the kind. When I have an adequate force assembled, I will act in accordance with the governor's orders. If the rebels truly wish to avoid a clash, they can do so by disbanding now."

"You chased the Seminoles in Florida, I'm told," Calvert said. "I've lived with Injuns. Came to know a thing or two about them. Some things they understand better'n a white man. They know there's a time to fight and a time to walk away."

"The state has walked away from the first day, Mr.

Calvert, because we hadn't the means to oppose you. You have murdered two men and imprisoned more. God knows what else you will do before this is over."

"One day, General," Kent pleaded. "Halt this effort for one day, and we will try to persuade the Executive Committee to announce a date for our adjournment."

"I am sorry, gentlemen. I can make no such agreement."

Sherman turned on his heel and left the room, sure that Calvert and Kent would discern his doubts if he stayed, fearful they would guess his plans. He was not as sure of his ability to confront the vigilants as he made out to be, but being approached twice in two days, first by Halleck and Crockett and now by Calvert and Kent, bolstered his confidence. He had only the bare beginnings of a military force, inadequately armed and not yet capable of marching together in line, and already he had received offers of help from concerned mediators and overtures from the enemy.

Overtures, but no promises, he reminded himself. And a formidable obstacle to compromise remained: the Committee would adjourn only if the state did nothing. They would retire in triumph—if indeed they meant to retire at all—with the state of California lying prostrate before them, vanquished and docile.

Sherman was convinced that such an adjournment would do more lasting harm than an armed victory by the rebels over the state's militia. The obstacle was insurmountable. And so he would act. Today Governor Johnson had sent his order to General Wool to requisition arms and ammunition for the militia Sherman would continue to enroll tomorrow and the day after that. The Committee of Vigilance would look on, expecting to see the new companies in training. They would calculate how soon Sherman might act, and they would make preparations to meet his threat—too late.

The state's militia would train by day while the enrollment continued. On Saturday, three days hence, while the ragged new companies drilled in the Plaza, a Pacific Mail steamer would take the arms and ammunition aboard at Benicia. After dark she would bring them down to Rincon Point, where Sherman would arm his men. In the small hours of Sunday morning he would invest the marine battery and load the thirty-two-pound guns while the rest of his companies surrounded the Vigilance Committee's warehouse and commanded the sentries to throw down their arms.

He would strike before even a madman would think his forces ready, and he would achieve complete surprise.

Chapter 30

fter supper on Wednesday, Jason and Joshua Norton stepped out to smoke together on the veranda, as had become their custom. Jason had a special reason for wanting a moment alone with the merchant this evening. Norton anticipated his topic by saying, "Nothing new since you baited your trap, Captain?"

"Nothing. I am taking a new tack and I need your help."

"I will give it gladly." The tip of Norton's cigar glowed brightly.

"If my ship was burned to keep our rice off the market, who would benefit most?"

"Those who already had rice on hand."

"A cartel, you mean. Men conspiring to drive up the price. I've thought of all this, Mr. Norton, but it hasn't brought me any closer to the man who ordered the fire set."

Norton nodded sympathetically. "This city is unlike any other, Captain Beck. It has as yet no established order. Unlike most of the world's ports, the supply of basic commodities has not settled into regular channels here. That is what makes a successful cartel possible—men who control the supply of an essential foodstuff keep it back. Where the merchant community is stable, a few men may control flour, a few others rice, and so on. Here, every man orders what he wants when he thinks the time is right. A dozen men may organize a cartel to withhold flour, but any day may bring ships loaded with flour ordered by someone else. There is great risk in such an effort. As a consequence, desperate men try to find certainty where there is none. Bills of lading are bought and sold and stolen in order to learn what others have ordered. There is every sort of chicanery."

"My first night in this house, you said that flour rose first in fifty-three, just as it did this year."

"The patterns are too similar for coincidence, in my view. In January of fifty-three, flour was at fifty dollars a barrel and there was talk of bread riots. It rose later this year, and never got so high, but I will stake what's left of my reputation that some of the same men were involved in the recent effort. It had their mark. But this is not fifty-three, and that was their undoing."

Norton leaned forward, his bulging eyes shining. "Business has been bad for two years now. This past winter was the driest since the American occupation. Miners need water for their flumes. Without it, there is not enough gold coming from the mines and everyone suffers. With their capital reserves gone, the weakest members of this year's cartel could not stay the course. Facing bankruptcy, they sold, and flour fell. It happened that rice shipments were high. The arrival of these shipments helped to break the flour monopoly. The price of both commodities fell until rice was unprofitable, which provides the incentive for a new monopoly to bring it up."

Jason was deep in thought. If cartels were unusually perilous here, they would be attractive only to men who were both daring and greedy. But greed was a driving force in San Francisco, and uncommon daring was common coin among those who had borne arduous journeys to arrive on this distant shore, so recently unknown. "How can I learn who besides Farnum and Kent ordered rice?"

"Ask the bankers. Bankers finance merchants. If you can discover who ordered rice, learning which of those men conspired to withhold it will be far easier."

"I have met two bankers here. Mr. Calvert and Mr. Sherman. I will start with them."

"If I may make a suggestion, use Mr. Calvert to make inquiries within the Vigilance Committee."

"You think they are involved?"

"That organization embraces the most important merchants in the city. And the most desperate."

"They are helping me search—" Jason let the thought go unfinished. In more than two weeks, the Vigilance Committee's cooperation had produced no information and no suspects. If someone within the vigilance organization was involved in burning the *Sarah B.*, that person was in a position to shield his henchmen from discovery.

"Although I am excluded from the Committee, I have friends in the merchant community," Norton said. "It may be that I can learn a thing or two on my own." He puffed hugely at his cigar. Jason could see the dark eyes fixed on him through the smoke. "I too lost something when your cargo burned, Captain. I lost an opportunity to recover my earlier loss in the same accursed commodity. Do you know, I have not eaten a grain of rice since eighteen fifty-three."

When Norton went up to bed, Jason found Sarah in the kitchen, kneading bread dough.

"If there were good news, you would have told me," she said.

"Two thousand five hundred dollars we are holding out, and the city turns up its nose. Somewhere there is a man who wants that money and knows enough to earn it."

"He is afraid." Sarah voiced the thought without thinking.

"Aye. But of what?"

"Of the killer." It seemed to Sarah that someone else was speaking for her. "His henchmen must fear him very much. And they fear to incriminate themselves."

"A man may be forgiven a lesser crime if he gives information that points to a murder."

"Yes. In a court of law. But it's the Vigilance Committee who will try these men." She left the dough and turned to him, her hands white with flour. "If you were the incendiary, and if you stood in that crowd and watched Casey and Cora hang, would you trust the forgiveness of the Vigilance Committee? Would you come forward, Captain?"

"There is talk they may disband," Jason said. "Mr. Kent told me they will deport the men they hold in their cells. Tonight, he says. Maybe that will satisfy them."

That afternoon he had returned to the vigilance warehouse with Ned Rollick and waited until the Executive Committee ended its wrangling. The full measure of what Kent had relayed to him gave him some reason to believe his cautious hope might be warranted. When Kent came out of the meeting room, he had told Jason that some on the Executive Committee, Kent and Calvert in the vanguard, had argued for adjournment of the full Committee once the prisoners were deported, but that a majority had voted not to adjourn so long as the state's new militia was organizing.

"We're doing our best to head off a clash," Kent had said. "I can't say more. Not even to you. But if our efforts succeed, there will be no war in these streets."

Kent had received Jason's news about *Pride of the Seas* enthusiastically, and promised to do all he could to find someone to advance the money to purchase her. Calvert had called to him then and the two of them had gone off together while Jason returned to the boardinghouse.

"Will you sit with me in the parlor when you are finished here?" he said to Sarah now. "It eases me to talk with you."

"Not tonight, Captain. If you don't mind. I will finish up here and go to bed."

When Jason had gone upstairs to his room and the bread was set to rise overnight, Sarah retired to her bedroom. I must watch this business of telling small lies, she thought. She had wanted to say, Yes, I will sit with you, but she had much to do before Trelayne returned from the theater.

While Jason and Norton smoked on the veranda, she had entered the darkened parlor to light the lamps. As she reached for the matches she had heard their voices from the porch through the open window. She had not listened for long, but she left the parlor without lighting the lamps, and with Mercury's next letter already taking form in her mind.

The masculine style of writing came easily to her now. She filled a page and a half, blotted the last lines, and set the letter aside. She would finish it later, when she and Trelayne returned from the waterfront. She removed her dress and petticoats and corset, keeping only her chemise, then wrapped herself in a dressing gown and went to Trelayne's room, creeping like a thief in her own house.

She lit the lamp and opened the wardrobe. A foulard neck scarf hanging from a hook inside the door would do to bind her breasts. She rummaged through the suits and found the least flamboyant. When they had gone together to interview Dr. Cole, it had struck Sarah that she and Trelayne were much the same size. In her own dress and petticoats her shape was so different from a man's that she had never noticed the similarity before.

The suit of clothes fit her well enough but Trelayne's shoes were too large for her feet. She stuffed a little tissue paper in the toe of each one and laced them tightly, and found she could walk comfortably. In men's clothes again, without a corset to hamper her movements, she felt supple and loose-jointed.

She kept watch from the parlor windows, prepared to duck into her own room if Molly and Trelayne come home together, but when he come he was alone. His eyes widened when he saw her and a look of puckish excitement came over him. He tucked a stray wisp of hair back under her hat, which was a derby he rarely wore. "A little soot from the stove, I think, to darken your chin. Come."

In the kitchen, he rubbed soot on his fingers, then on her chin, smoothing it until it was just a shadow that would pass in dim light as a day's growth of beard. "Molly isn't home yet, I take it? Damn the man! Courting her under my nose."

"You must let her go, Tommy. It is too late."

"I know. I do know, Sarah." He stood back to appraise his handiwork and gave a satisfied nod. "Thanks to you, I have something to distract me from a morbid contemplation of my failings. Where are we going tonight?"

•　　•　　•

It was after midnight when the doors of Fort Vigilance opened and a small delegation marched forth, escorted by a company of armed militia. They proceeded at a swift pace along Front Street to the Broadway Wharf, where the steam tug *Hercules* was moored. Smoke rose from the tug's stack and drifted low across the water, borne on the dank air.

"Stand back there," the commander of militia ordered two late-night idlers who were loitering on the wharf. "Vigilance Committee business."

"Go to it, boys," said one of the pair. He wore a gentleman's cloak and a top hat. A beard hid much of his face.

"Who've you got there?" the second loiterer asked. He was clean shaven beneath a derby hat, and his voice was soft.

"Mulligan and some others. We're sending 'em off on a sea voyage." Several members of the militia laughed at this witticism and the two loiterers joined in good-naturedly.

"Good riddance," the bearded one said. The pair watched solemnly as the former jail keeper and five other men were led aboard the tug. When the vigilance delegation was back on the wharf, crewmen cast off the lines and the tug swung away from the wharf with much churning of the big side wheels.

The loiterers walked along with the militia as they left the wharf, chatting amiably and congratulating them on a job well done, before bidding the delegation good night. As soon as the militia were out of sight, the loiterers acquired a new sense of purpose. They turned up Broadway and walked briskly, their long strides falling naturally in step with each other.

"They will remember us when they read my letter tomorrow," Sarah smiled.

Trelayne smiled. They were crossing Montgomery and his eyes glinted in the gaslight. "Yes, but who will they remember? A bearded gentleman and a younger man with a derby hat whom no one will ever see again. We're will-o'-the-wisps, Sarah. If we keep this up, we'll give them the shivering fits."

•   •   •

On Thursday morning, Jason and Stephen Kent walked the two blocks from Farnum & Kent to the offices of Frye & Company, where they had an appointment to meet with Abel Calvert and Jonathan Frye.

The day was bright and brisk, with a promise of warmth to come. Calvert was waiting for them at the corner of Montgomery Street. "Let me do the talking once we're inside," he said. "First we'll build a fire under the griz, then we'll pacify him with sweet honey."

"You don't think Mr. Frye is involved?" Kent asked.

"I do not. Frye doesn't traffic in grains. But let him think we suspect him, he'll work that much harder to steer us to the men involved."

On entering Frye & Company, the three men were shown at once into Frye's private office. When the clerk withdrew, Calvert turned on Frye and poked a forefinger at him in accusation. "You said last month you heard talk of a rice cartel."

The portly merchant was taken aback by Calvert's accusing tone. "You heard the same talk, Mr. Calvert. We all did."

"I heard it from you, Mr. Frye. Who did you hear it from?"

"I don't recall. I would have to think about it."

"Think about it, then."

"What has brought this on?"

"Whoever burned my ship wanted to keep my rice off the market," Jason said.

"You and I, Mr. Frye, are in a position to find out who had an interest in rice," Calvert went on. "I'll look into the banks. You speak with our friends on the Executive Committee and see what you can learn about their dealings. Start with that fellow Smiley. He was in flour up to his neck. I don't trust the man. Jim Dows had the smell of a baker there too, for a while."

Frye didn't like the tenor of the conversation. "Starting that kind of talk within the Executive Committee will stir up trouble."

"No need to kick up a fuss. We'll do it quietly." Calvert's tone was soothing. "We will speak man to man, in private. And if someone on the Committee had a hand in this, who better than the Committee to deal with him as he deserves?"

"You're right." Frye's resolve grew firmer. "I must say you took me unaware with all this." He picked up the single flimsy sheet of that morning's *Herald*. "I don't imagine you have seen what our friend Mercury is up to today? It's uncanny, your coming here to talk about cartels."

He folded the paper and passed it to Calvert, who read the letter aloud.

"'Ask yourselves, honest citizens, who are these men that you follow so blindly. Is not the Vigilance Committee's executive rank composed mainly of merchants? Did they not in the winter of 1853 create a monopoly of flour and put it up to famine prices? Is it a greater crime to cheat at elections and stuff ballot boxes, crimes that have yet to be proven, than to cheat honest people by selling bad provisions, as some of these same men who rule us now have done? While the vigilantes make a great show of condemning riffraff and layabouts, their own greater sins go unpunished. Can this Committee find the villains who burned Captain Beck's ship and cruelly murdered his crewmen? They cannot, because to do so would unearth the villainy in their own membership.'"

"If he thinks he can get away with calling us murderers, he'll soon learn different," Frye said grimly.

"'Who else stood to benefit by the loss of tons of rice than the commission merchants of San Francisco, who for years have played with the fortunes and the very lives of our citizens while manipulating precious commodities to line their own pockets with gold.'" Calvert threw the paper on Frye's desk. "There's more, about Billy Mulligan and that bunch we deported. You'd think he could admit that deporting is a damned sight better than hanging."

"What if he's right?" Jason said. "What if it was someone on your Committee who burned my ship?"

Frye glared at him. "We'll know soon enough if he's right. All right, Calvert. You and I will make inquiries. But quietly. With discretion."

Jason rose from his chair. "I must get to the waterfront."

"Nothing yet on the incendiaries?" Frye said.

"Nothing," said Kent. "Good day, Mr. Frye."

Calvert took his leave in the street, pleading bank business that needed attending. He walked one block south along Montgomery, turned about, and returned to Pacific, where he looked around the corner toward the waterfront. Kent and Captain Beck were gone from sight. Calvert reentered Frye & Company and went straight to Jonathan Frye's office.

"You fool!" Frye hissed as soon as Calvert closed the door. "Are you mad, coming here with your talk of cartels?"

Calvert was scornful. "Simmer down, Jonathan. We're lucky they didn't think sooner to look into who has an interest in rice and flour."

"We must do something before this gets out of hand!"

"Get a grip on yourself!"

Frye sat heavily behind his desk. "You took me by surprise."

"I had to make it look good in front of them."

"What do we do now?"

"The way to make this whole business disappear is to get Captain Jason Beck on his way to China and out of our hair."

The door to Sherman's office was open. From his desk he could see the front doors of the bank. He glanced up often, watching for the boy from the telegraph office, who would bring word from Governor Johnson that General Wool was ready to deliver the arms the next day.

It was nearing four o'clock, the bank's closing time. To occupy himself, Sherman picked up the *Herald* and read Mercury's letter once more with relish. After virtually accusing the Vigilance Committee of conspiring to burn Captain Beck's ship, the letter reviled them for deporting Billy Mulligan and his cronies in the small hours of the morning. From the boasting of the vigilants, Mercury had been able to learn that the tug was to carry Mulligan and two others to an outbound Pacific Mail steamer before it reached the heads of the Golden Gate, and that the remaining deportees were to be put aboard the bark

Yankee, which would put them off in the Sandwich Islands.

This is the very same Billy Mulligan whom the Committee of Vigilance denied it held captive when Sheriff Scannell's deputy presented a legal writ for his release, Mercury wrote, adding that each and every one of those deported was Irish, and a Democrat. *It seems the Committee finds crime and corruption only among their political enemies. Hypocrites! They say they shun political motives and proclaim that they stand only for justice. Now are their lies revealed!*

Beware, ye merchants of tyranny! The forces of law are gathering around you. Courageous men are planning your downfall. Even now the state's loyal militia is drilling in the public streets and squares. Save yourselves while you may! Disband while the popular will is still blind to your perfidy, or prepare to reap your just rewards.

Under "Topics of the Day," the paper reported that more than 1500 men had been enrolled in the state's militia the day before. *It is expected that by tonight three thousand men will be enrolled in this city,* the account went on. *The Third, Fourth and Fifth Divisions of the State Militia, from adjacent regions of the state, have been ordered to hold themselves in readiness. If necessary, an effective force of ten thousand men can be brought to bear on the rebels.*

Sherman smiled when he read the inflated figures. If the opinions of the people were molded by the distortions of the pro-vigilance press, their confidence might be shaken by some distortions on the part of the opposition. Taken together with Mercury's warning, Nugent's editorial should give the rebels pause. The two pieces were so perfectly coordinated, they might have been written in concert.

The bank's clocks struck four and still no boy had arrived. A man entered the front door just as Nisbet rose from his desk to lock it. He tried to put the man out, but the man spoke briefly in his ear and Nisbet pointed him to Sherman's office.

"General Sherman, I am Colonel E. A. Rowe, Governor Johnson's military aide," the man announced as he entered. He was about Sherman's age, ramrod straight and powerfully built. Rowe's expression was serious as he closed the office door and took Sherman's hand. "I am afraid I have some very bad news," he said, "Yesterday I carried Governor Johnson's requisition to General Wool. General Wool has refused it."

"Refused it?" Sherman's voice was reedy. The blood pounded in his ears and he felt a familiar tightness in his chest.

"General Wool has declined the governor's request for arms. He says he has examined the laws, and he finds that no one other than the president has the authority to issue federal arms to state officials."

Chapter 31

olly Gray was at the kitchen table in her dressing gown, reading a scene from Trelayne's play, when Sarah came to the kitchen on Sunday morning. Kittery was purring in Molly's lap.

"I couldn't sleep," Molly said. "I've made the fire, but you better see that I did it properly." Her fine black hair was in disarray.

The kitchen smelled of smoke. Sarah saw that the stove was still damped down as she had left it the night before. She threw the drafts wide and opened the back door to ventilate the kitchen. The morning was clear, the air fresh and comfortable. She would let the fire go out after the midday meal. It was to be a special dinner for Molly and Abel Calvert, to celebrate their engagement. The Kents were invited and the full household would be there, all but David Farren, whom no one had seen since Friday breakfast.

"He gave us four days to learn our lines, Sarah!" Molly said. "We've never put on a new work with so little rehearsal. Tommy is like a madman. We have to work the whole afternoon today and the morning tomorrow." The first performance was tomorrow night.

"Remember," Sarah cautioned her, "Mr. Calvert isn't to come backstage tomorrow. After dinner today, you're not to see him until the wedding."

Molly pouted. "I'm sorry I ever agreed to your silly custom."

"It is so the wedding day will be magical," Sarah said.

"I know. And I do agree, Sarah."

Sarah's mother had taught her that a bride must not see her groom for a week before the wedding. The custom had been passed down by her mother's mother, and hers before that. Sarah's mother had not seen her own bridegroom for seven months before the ceremony. His ship docked and he had a night's sleep ashore before presenting himself to be married the next morning. From their union on the wedding night, Sarah's brother Peter was born. Sarah herself arrived in the world fourteen months after Peter.

"Tommy has been so strange," Molly said. "He's not himself."

"I should say he has been a perfect gentleman."

"That's what I mean. It's not like him. Usually he's poking fun at people. He used to make me laugh."

"Did you expect him to be the same as always with you engaged to another man?"

"I expected him to be angry. I expected him to throw me out of the theater the minute I announced my engagement to Abel. Instead he has me playing Mark Antony. For the first time in years, I am nervous about the part."

"The play is *Julius Caesar*?" Sarah knew very well what the play was to be. Trelayne had confided in her, but she wanted to know how much he had told Molly.

"It is an adaptation, Tommy says. He won't let us see anything but our own scenes. It is a comedy, in part, I think. It's hard, Sarah. This is our last production together." Molly's tone was wistful.

"You're not doing this just to make Tommy jealous?" Sarah said. "It's gone too far for that."

"No. This is what I want, Sarah. Abel is what I need." The pensive air left Molly's voice and she became her other self, worldly and self-assured. "Men like Tommy are dashing and handsome and romantic, but they're not steady. When you choose another man to marry, pick one who is steady."

Sarah wondered if Molly had any idea how much suffering she caused her dashing, romantic men. David Farren still looked at her with longing.

"You can help me with breakfast," Sarah said. "That will take your mind off things. You can make the pancakes while I clean the chicken for dinner. Then I'll help you with the eggs and scrapple." Sarah had arranged to have Ingrid come to help make the dinner and clean up afterward. Ingrid had pleaded that her church service would keep her until eleven o'clock.

"It's so quiet," Molly said. "Is it always like this?"

Sarah smiled. "Yes. That's what I like best about the mornings. The quiet before the whole town is a-bustle."

They worked together for a time, Sarah saying only what was necessary to instruct Molly in her tasks. As Molly spooned batter into a hot skillet, she said, "I will miss this house. And you, Sarah. But I will come back to see you."

Sarah had considered telling Molly about her planned departure, but if Molly knew, everyone would know, and Sarah wasn't yet ready for that. Other than Su-Yan Quan, only Joshua Norton had noticed the advertisement for the boardinghouse in the *Herald* and she had sworn him to silence on the subject.

"I may not be here forever," she said now.

"It wouldn't hurt you to see more of the world. There is *life* out there, Sarah."

"I have seen the world," Sarah said defensively. "I buried my husband in a squalid foreign land and I came on my own to California."

"Where you have lived like the virgin queen Elizabeth. Dear Sarah, you are my best friend in the world, and I only want the best for you. Don't hide from life."

It pleased Sarah that she might be Molly's best friend in the world. "I'm not as conventional as you think. I am a seaman's daughter."

"Who married well and is now a respectable boardinghouse keeper. But there are respectable men who can show you the kind of life I mean, Sarah. You may think Tommy and Abel are very different, and they are in some ways, but they are both alive."

"A moment ago, you told me to find a man who was steady."

"Not too steady. He must be alive too. Like your Captain Beck."

"He is not my Captain Beck."

"I have seen how he looks at you. He is a man, Sarah!"

"Captain Beck will go back to sea. That's the way with sailors. They go back to sea."

She remembered her father, and her mother's longing when he was away. But her mother had children and a home, and she treasured the times when her husband spent a few weeks ashore.

Molly brightened. "Abel is taking me to the gold country for our honeymoon. We will find a small inn, or camp out like trappers. I've told Mr. Maguire he will just have to do without me until I'm back." She giggled. "I'll surprise Abel by making pancakes."

"It sounds very rustic and peaceful." Sarah wondered if Calvert had planned his honeymoon as an escape from the running of the Vigilance Committee, or in expectation of its adjournment. There had been nothing in the papers since Thursday about the state's militia and its plans. Even the *Herald* had been quiet on the subject after a good deal of belligerent bluster when the enrollment first began.

Abel Calvert walked with a bounce in his step when he came to fetch Molly to church. He removed his beaver hat and bowed low when Sarah opened the door.

"The top of the morning, Mrs. Rockwell. You are the epitome of refinement and beauty, as always."

Sarah blushed at this gallantry. Calvert had done his best to win her over since his betrothal to Molly, and he had succeeded in some measure. He was considerate and polite, and Sarah had come to see that he genuinely cared for Molly.

"Is that Abel?" Molly called down from the second-floor landing. "I will be right there."

As Molly came down the stairs, Calvert felt his heart swell in his chest. She wore a yellow dress as bright as the sunshine. If Gray Dawn had put on a white woman's dress, this is how she would have looked—once she had adjusted to the strange feel of the corset and the rest of the undergarments—young and beautiful and as proud as the Queen of England.

"Molly, my love. Never was a man so lucky. No one will hear a word of the sermon with you sitting in church looking like that." He kissed her hand. "When you are mine, my old trapper friends will turn in their lonely graves out of pure jealousy." And my, wouldn't their withered peckers rise at the sight of Old Abe sporting with his new bride on his wedding night. Shinin' times.

"You are in high spirits today, Mr. Calvert," Sarah observed.

"There are days when all the gods are smiling, Mrs. Rockwell. This is surely one of them." He kept the other reason for his high spirits to himself. The city would know it soon enough, and those who supported the Committee would celebrate.

"Will you come to church with us, Mrs. Rockwell?"

Sarah smiled. "Who should make your dinner if I did?"

Calvert inhaled deeply, testing the smells that came from the kitchen. "Roast chicken on a Sunday! It takes me back to my boyhood on the Monongahela. We'll do your dinner justice today, Mrs. Rockwell." He gave Molly his arm and together they set off.

It seemed to Sarah that she had never seen a man of middle age so bewitched by love. "One o'clock sharp," she called after them.

She was basting the chicken when David Farren came in the kitchen door with a black look on his face. His boots were dusty, his clothing rumpled, his hair askew when he doffed his hat. His walk was unsteady and she smelled brandy on his breath.

"David? Where on earth have you been?"

"Forgive me. I shouldn't appear in your house in this condition. I only came for a change of clothes. But I saw them—Molly and that man. Did he say anything?"

"Mr. Calvert? He is as addlebrained as a schoolboy today."

"I didn't trust myself to speak to him. I waited in the garden until he left. They are all laughing at us."

"Laughing, why?"

"You haven't heard? No, of course not. It won't be in

the newspapers until tomorrow." Farren drew himself up as if to make a formal speech. "General Sherman has resigned as general of militia."

Sarah's breath faltered. "Resigned?"

"General Wool went back on his solemn promise to furnish us with arms. General Sherman and I have been in Benicia with Governor Johnson, but we couldn't change Wool's mind. The effect is that we have no militia except in name. The vigilants have won the day. I fear they may have won the war."

Sarah was speechless. The spoon in her hand dripped pan juices on the floor. "Oh!" she exclaimed, when she saw what she was doing. She shut the oven and fetched a rag to wipe the floor. "Sit down, David. You need a cup of coffee."

Farren did as he was bidden, becoming abjectly apologetic. "You shouldn't see me like this. Really, I will change my clothes and go." He started to rise again.

"Sit still, for heaven's sake." She filled an enamelled mug with black coffee and set it before him. "Drink this and tell me what happened."

"We were on the verge of moving against them. All we needed were the arms. Damn Wool anyhow!"

"How could he go back on his promise?" Sarah sat across the table from Farren, her dinner preparations forgotten for the moment.

"They got to him, that's why! They bribed him or threatened him or God knows what. Wool and Farragut were against us from the start, anyway. Damn them all!" Farren reddened. "I'm sorry. I'm not myself. I haven't slept much."

"I have heard much worse. Now start at the beginning, and try to make sense this time."

"The waste of it, Sarah! In three days we put together a battalion of militia that was equal to the task." He sighed. "We were to have the arms last night. There's no harm in telling you now. I could tell the city, for all the harm it would do."

"You said they got to General Wool."

"The blackguard! A general in the United States Army is — I suppose he is as weak as other men. General Sherman learned three days ago that Wool had gone back on his word, but he kept it secret. He hoped to shame him into keeping his promise. There was a group of men in Benicia. Crockett and some others. A party of conciliation, they call themselves. They came on the same steamer as we did and they gave Wool the perfect excuse not to deliver us the arms, all in the name of a peaceful resolution. Just avoid a clash, they said. General Sherman thinks they favor the vigilants. Judge Terry says the same thing, in harsher terms. He says they lined Wool's pocket." Farren tossed back the last of the coffee as if it were brandy.

"They bribed him?" Sarah was shocked.

"We can't prove it. But each of the 'conciliators' has friends and business associates who sit on the Executive Committee. It doesn't take a great stretch of the imagination to see how an offer could be made to Granny Wool through them."

"Does General Sherman believe this?"

"All he said was 'How can one tell if a dishonorable man has been bribed?'" Farren slumped in his chair. "We're finished, Sarah."

"Mr. Nugent said your companies were armed with the latest weapons. He says you have plenty of ammunition."

"Mr. Nugent is doing his best to confuse the enemy, but it's not enough to win the war. My law partner, Mr. Howard—General Howard—he's to replace General Sherman, for all the good it will do."

"Oh!" Sarah got suddenly to her feet. "I've forgotten the Indian pudding. I bought the cornmeal especially so I could make Indian pudding." Jason Beck had spoken of the Indian pudding Ethel Kent made for him, and Sarah would not be outdone. She brought cornmeal and a crock of molasses from the pantry. "Mr. Calvert is coming to dinner. It's to celebrate his engagement to Molly. Can you set politics aside?"

"I wouldn't trust myself." Farren got to his feet. "I always thought that Molly and Trelayne—when I realized Calvert was courting her, I felt like a fool for not being there first."

"I know, and I am sorry. I would prefer it was you."

"Well, I shall be off." He waved away her concerned

expression. "Don't worry about me. I will eat downtown and spend some time at my office. I will help General Howard to do what he can, but it will be too little, too late." He was embarrassed once more. "I'm sorry you saw me like this. It won't happen again."

"This is your home, David. You have shelter here, no matter your condition."

He gave her a grateful smile and left, still unsteady but no longer ashamed.

Jason and Melchior and Dickie were the last to arrive for the midday meal, coming in the door when the food was already on the table and Sarah was about to invite the others into the dining room.

"You are a man of your word, Captain," she said.

"I promised I would have Dickie here all shipshape at two bells of the afternoon watch, Mrs. Rockwell. Here he stands, ready for inspection."

The boy's Sunday clothes were still presentable although he had been to the wharves with Jason and Melchior and gone from Sarah's care for more than three hours.

"We've been to see Captain Beck's new ship," Dickie said.

"She's not mine yet, young Richard."

Dickie was undaunted. "We went aboard her today."

"And what sort of vessel is she, Dickie?" Sarah said.

"She has fair lines." Dickie was fair to bursting with pride and he could not contain his secret for a moment longer. "I'm to be her ship's boy."

"You were not to say that, Richard!" Jason said. "Not until I spoke to Mrs. Rockwell." To Sarah he said, "I would not take him without your permission. He broke a promise by speaking of this to you now."

"It's all right, Captain. I know he dreams of going to sea. We can talk about it later. Now our dinner is ready." Whatever else might happen on this day, Sarah was determined that the dinner should take place as planned, with nothing amiss to mar the celebration.

Stephen Kent rose from the divan where he was seated beside his wife. "I've been to see her, Jason. A good hull, it seems to me."

"And so it should be, for what they are asking."

Kent glanced at Calvert and said, "Well, we are here to celebrate Abel's good fortune. We must put off talk of business."

Molly Gray was pouring champagne as the guests entered the dining room. Even Dickie Howell was given a small glass. When everyone was seated, Calvert raised his glass to Sarah. The wine glowed in the warm midday light of the sunny dining room.

"To our gracious hostess. Molly and I thank you with all our hearts for this celebration. And I thank you most humbly for making me welcome in your home." The glass trembled slightly in his hand. He drank, then said, "I know you do not approve of my participation, and Mr. Kent's, in the Vigilance Committee, but you have—"

"Sarah doesn't allow politics at the table," Molly said. She put her hand on Calvert's to soften the rebuke.

"A very wise policy, Mrs. Rockwell. Forgive me."

Sarah began serving the soup. "You are forgiven. And we will have no more toasts until we have eaten, or I will be too giddy to serve." She had not drunk champagne since her own wedding day, but she had taken a glass in the kitchen before dinner to quell a fear that Abel Calvert's high spirits were caused by the knowledge of General Sherman's resignation. Today it was she, more than her guests, who needed to banish the thought of politics from the dinner table.

"I must thank you again," Calvert said, "for allowing my champagne to be served in your house."

"My mother taught me moderation in all things, Mr. Calvert. I am moderate in my abstinence." This brought laughter from the others, and the rest of the dinner went better than Sarah had expected. Trelayne was unfailingly polite, but subdued, except when Calvert inquired about his new play.

"Molly tells me you have something special planned." Calvert's initial nervousness had subsided and he was enjoying himself.

"Indeed, Abel. May call I you Abel?" As the gentleman guest of longest residence in the house, Trelayne was carving the chicken. He paused with the silverhandled knife in the air, awaiting Calvert's reply.

"I don't stand much on formality. Still got too many habits from the mountain life. By all means let's be Abel and Tom, and let's have a preview of this new play."

"It derives from the classics, but we will perform it in modern dress." The thought of Calvert's reaction to the play filled Trelayne with anticipation. He attacked the chicken with renewed zeal, severing a thigh joint with a single stoke. "It is a morality play, of sorts. I don't want to say too much about it. It would spoil the surprise."

"Nothing immoral, I hope," Calvert said.

Trelayne repressed an urge to laugh. "No. Nothing like that. There is one surprise I can reveal to you all. Our own Joshua Norton will play a part in the production."

"Mr. Norton!" Sarah chided him. "You didn't tell us."

"I have taken a vow of secrecy." Norton's prominent eyes were gleeful. "But inasmuch as my manager has broken it, I will say that I play the part of an emperor."

"For Joshua, it is a dream come true," Trelayne said, and this provoked renewed laughter.

"Mr. and Mrs. Kent will accompany me to the theater," Calvert said. "It will be like the opening we attended together, the evening I met Molly."

"Your courtship ran longer than the play," Kent said, "but only just."

Trelayne seated himself and raised his glass. "I give you Miss Molly Gray and Mr. Abel Calvert. May they always be as happy as they are on this day."

Molly blushed and Calvert beamed at the gracious gesture. "Of course we want you to come to the wedding." He had wondered about inviting Trelayne but he was confident now that it was the right thing to do. To all appearances Trelayne had accepted the fact of Molly's marriage, and what lay in the past was truly past. "Mrs. Rockwell. Mr. Norton. Mr. Melchior. You too, Dickie. You're all invited. There will be proper invitations sent 'round tomorrow. You'll have one too, Captain Beck. I hope you'll be here."

"I see no way that I can leave this city for the present," Jason said. His concerns had been pushed aside by the wine and the gaiety, but they returned to him now.

"Since the day I set foot ashore, I have not known when I might leave this port. It is no different now."

Calvert looked to Stephen Kent and Kent nodded. "I think the moment has come, Abel."

"Well, Captain," Calvert said. "As you know, I was prepared to advance Mr. Norton the capital to buy your rice. Not out of charity, you understand. It was a sound investment. Your fire put an end to that, and I saw no other way to help you until Stephen's—Mr. Kent's—young clerk approached me about advancing the money to buy a new ship. As I told him at the time, my bank could not advance such a sum. But in the interim I have assembled a group of business associates. A small consortium, if you will. Together we have raised the capital. You can have a draft on my bank tomorrow, if you like."

"Do ee mean we're to have the ship?" Melchior asked. He had been reserved in the company of folk he considered his betters, but the talk of ships emboldened him.

"That is exactly what he means." Stephen Kent was smiling broadly. "Abel told me before the meal, Jason. I'm sorry we kept it from you until now, but he wanted to announce it to everyone at once."

"This is most generous." Jason's surprise was evident.

"It is good business for us all, Captain." Calvert was expansive in his magnanimity. "In return for our loan, my little group of investors will receive a small discount from Farnum and Kent for cargoes shipped on their vessels. Everyone involved will benefit."

"Even I will forgo moderation to celebrate this news," Ethel Kent said. "I give you Mr. Abel Calvert, benefactor and friend to Farnum and Kent." She raised her glass, which she had only sipped until now, and emptied it at a gulp.

Calvert could scarcely contain his satisfaction. He had already discussed with Su-Yan Quan what items of trade might find a ready market in Canton just now, and the discount rate would apply to cargoes arriving from the eastern States as well. Best of all, fitting out the new ship would occupy Captain Beck's attention until he had left the Golden Gate behind.

Chapter 32

t half-past five that afternoon, Sarah left the house with Mercury's latest letter concealed in the inner pocket of her dress. She had composed it in her mind while helping Ingrid wash up after dinner and wrote it in half an hour when the washing was done.

Ten minutes' walk brought her to Kearny and California streets, where she found the front doors of the Theater Trelayne locked. In the alley at the back, the stage door opened at her touch. The theater was silent. A single lamp lit the narrow hallway that led past the dressing rooms to the stage. She took a breath to call Trelayne's name, but she let it out softly. When she carried Mercury's letters she felt like a thief and she took on some of a thief's caution. Trelayne had said that he would dismiss the cast at five. She preferred not to be seen if anyone else were still in the theater.

A short stairway led to the wings. The backstage was dark. Somewhere onstage a faint light shone. Sarah passed through the wings and emerged behind a curtain of black gauze that hung as a backdrop. The curtain was made from yard-wide strips of cheesecloth that Trelayne had bought at a bargain. An importer had ordered bolts of the flimsy cotton weave at a time when there were still few cows in San Francisco, and little demand for cheesecloth. Sarah and Molly had dyed the fabric in a huge kettle in Sarah's garden. The skin of their hands held the dye for days and they had joked about finding work in a minstrel show.

A sound came from the stage, which was divided in two by a partition. The side of the partition facing Sarah was painted to resemble a marble-columned public building. The nearer half of the stage was set as a street. Beyond the partition, out of sight, a lamp burned. Sarah advanced cautiously. Behind the building's facade, the interior was represented by a single large chamber furnished in the modern style with an enormous desk and several chairs. Through the gauze, Sarah made out movement near the desk. At first the dark form made no sense, and then she saw that Trelayne was sitting in a chair and Molly was seated on his lap, straddling him. The bodice of her dress was unbuttoned, revealing her breasts. Her skirts were pulled up about her thighs and her head was turned toward Sarah, catching the lamplight. Her eyes were closed, and she was smiling.

Sarah realized with a start what she was seeing. She drew back, afraid to make a sound. Behind her, the stairs were thirty feet away through the wings. Had the floor creaked when she walked to the stage? She couldn't remember. She tried to look anywhere but at the couple on the chair, but there was something compelling about the intensity of their involvement. Molly's motions were rhythmic and strong. She leaned back, her hands gripping Trelayne's shoulders, grinding herself against him. By her movements, and the sounds that reached Sarah's ears, Molly imparted a depth of desire that Sarah felt as a physical force.

Sarah closed her eyes but the image remained. There could be no question that Molly was the aggressor, or that it was her need which propelled the act, and Sarah felt that a mystery had been revealed. In her brief marriage to Haven Rockwell she had experienced nothing that could arouse such a passion in her, and yet she knew beyond a doubt that this power was a part of her as well.

Sarah opened her eyes. Molly's mouth was open in a silent scream. Sarah trembled, as if taken by a sudden chill, and turned to go on silent feet, across the stage and down the stairs and through the narrow hallway and out into the alley again, where the cool wind and the glare of the afternoon sky seemed unreal to her, as if they were part of an enormous stage setting, and only what she had left behind her in the dark of the theater was genuine.

Trelayne fastened the small buttons at the front of Molly's dress one by one, every movement of his hands conveying tenderness and affection.

"I have missed you," she said.

"Why are you marrying that man?"

"Because he can give me what I want."

"Didn't I always give you what you wanted?"

"You can't give me respectability, Tommy. You can't give me a place in society. Do you know how it hurt me in Chicago, to have men assume I was a whore because I worked in a theater? They expected me to fuck them in the boxes between the acts!"

"Using that word in anger is not ladylike."

"I'm not a lady! Don't you know how many ways they had to remind me of that?"

"The way to be accepted as a lady is to play the part."

"That's what you always said. And you're right, I know. Oh, Tommy!" She beat her small fists against his shoulders in frustration.

"Able Calvert is an uncouth fur trapper who plays the part of a gentleman," Trelayne said. "He's good at it. So good he can tell tales of his buckskin past and use the mannerisms of a trapper to make himself stand out from the crowd. He is a superb actor."

Molly hadn't thought of Abel as an actor. "He is not uncouth."

"He comes from uncouth origins. He is a self-made man. I taught you to be a self-made woman. A lady, if that's what you want. In San Francisco you need only play the part for a time and you will be accepted as a lady. You will become a lady. This is a city where people can change themselves. Caterpillars become butterflies."

"I expected you to try to change my mind. Instead, you're telling me I'm right."

Trelayne buttoned the last button and looked into her eyes, saying nothing.

"I miss the way you make me laugh," Molly said. "All

this vigilance business has made Abel so serious. I don't think I have laughed since the day I became engaged." Tears welled up in her eyes. "Oh, Tommy, I'm a fool."

"You want things I can't give you. You want a life that is not mine. You want position and reputation, and now you've got them. With Calvert and Maguire you will have it all."

"I don't care about Maguire! *You* taught me. You made me what I am." She wiped away her tears with her fingers, delicately, as if she were applying makeup. "I will stay, if you'll have me."

Trelayne felt a rebirth of hope. "Would Calvert permit it?"

A hardness came into Molly's voice. "Abel Calvert does not tell me what to do. If I tell him I have decided to stay in your company, he will agree."

"You are so sure of him?"

"He doesn't know me the way you do, Tommy. He never will. I can control him."

He took her face in his hands, tilting it toward the lamp. "Your eyes are captivating in the light of the stage, but it was your lips I noticed first. When you speak your lines, a man hears everything you say because he watches your mouth. He wants to kiss those lips. And the women envy you, but not so much that they resent you. They want their gentlemen friends to look at them the way they look at you."

Molly gazed at him, utterly vulnerable. It was the way she had looked at him on the night he first met her. He had gone to a third-rate melodrama in which Molly played the ingénue. After the play he had taken her to a restaurant and bought her supper. She had never tasted wine before. When he began to undress her in his room, she had stared at him in just this way. Not shy or afraid, but wide-eyed with wonder. She had been sixteen years old.

"You go on now." He helped her to her feet. "Go home to Sarah and be as sweet as you can be. Don't let her suspect. Tell no one you're even thinking of staying in this theater until you have told Calvert. Pick the right moment. And remember you are playing a role." Sarah would not be there when Molly got home, but he could not let Molly know that he knew.

At the stage door, Molly kissed him. She clung to him for a moment, then opened the door and was gone.

He could scarcely believe what she had offered him. She would be married to Abel Calvert but he would have her still. And in time, anything was possible. The new play might destroy Molly's affection for him entirely, but it might have another effect. If it sowed dissension between Molly and her betrothed, it could drive them apart before the wedding. It might prevent the wedding altogether.

A knock sounded at the door and he let Sarah in. "It's good you're a bit late," he said. "I kept a few of the actors to go over their lines."

She reached through the placket at the side seam of her skirt and withdrew the letter from the pocket. He read it quickly and gave a soft whistle when he was done. "You are fearless, Sarah. If a few others wrote so bravely, the vigilantes would be put aboard the next steamer."

"I hide behind a Roman god. And a dear friend who takes all the risk."

"You have given my craft new meaning. If every actor played roles in real life, we would all outshine the Booths. Oh! I haven't told you! Edwin Booth will be in the play! I saw him yesterday and he agreed. It will cost me twice what I'm paying Molly, but it will be worth it. His Cassius will make the merchants squirm!"

He looked at the letter again. "You write as well as any man, Sarah. You could make your way doing this."

"Do you think Mr. Nugent would print these letters if he knew they were written by a woman?"

"He would now. At the start? I can't say."

"Be careful, Tommy."

Trelayne smiled wolfishly. "If I were careful, I should book passage on a fast vessel and board her as soon as the curtain falls tomorrow."

"Will you be home for supper? I'll serve the leftovers from our dinner."

Trelayne shook his head. "No, thank you, dear Sarah.

Tonight I'm on the town. I can never sleep well before a first night, so I'll have a bit of fun."

When she was gone he rummaged in the costume trunks for the things he would need. The first item he selected was a wig of longish hair, tied at the back like a sailor's. The second was a sailor's cap and the third an eye patch on a thin band of cloth. Once in place, the patch and the cap would help to secure the wig. The smallest piece of his costume was a gold earring. Portraying Jean Lafitte and Blackbeard, he had worn rings in both ears. Molly had pierced his ears and he hers, but that was long ago, in Chicago.

The fifth item was a gunnysack. With these five things on hand, Trelayne donned a gray beard and mustache. He dusted white powder into his own hair to turn it gray. He put on a worn but once elegant suit of clothes and he selected a formal walking stick. He practiced walking in the bent over but still dignified manner of an elderly gentleman. He concealed the five items in the pockets of his coat and cloak and he took his supper at Delmonico's on Montgomery Street, an establishment only slightly less grand than its namesake in New York. With the better part of a good bottle of wine in him, he walked the few blocks to the office of the *Herald*.

"Good evening, sir." Nugent scrutinized him closely after admitting him. "Ah. We know each other, I believe."

"Quite so. I think you'll find this of interest." Trelayne placed a folded edition of the morning's *Herald* on the counter. He had delivered the last two letters in the same manner, folded in the *Herald*, so prying eyes would see nothing passed between himself and Nugent.

"You rouse my curiosity, sir," Nugent said. "Coming as you do in new guise every day."

"Curiosity killed the cat," Trelayne said. "My intention is to survive. To that end, I have the help of a good friend who is knowledgeable in the art of disguise."

"Until tomorrow, then," Nugent said.

"I will come late tomorrow. I am going to the theater."

"So am I. Perhaps we will see each other there."

"I doubt it." Trelayne gave Nugent a sly wink and took his leave. He walked down Commercial Street and turned right into Leidesdorff. Once in the narrow street

he ran to the back door of the American Exchange, a saloon that faced on Sansome Street. Twice in recent days
he thought he might have been followed from the *Herald*,
but each time he had given the man the slip. Tonight he
had planned his moves carefully. The rear entrance of
the saloon was in deep shadow, partially protected by a
fence that enclosed the garbage and ash bins. As soon as
he was in the doorway Trelayne removed the folded gunnysack from his coat pocket. He shook it out, removed
his cloak and hat, beard and mustache, and bundled
them into the sack. He rolled up the cuffs of his trousers
and turned up the collar of his coat. He took a handful
of ash from the saloon's ash bin and dusted the suit with
ashes, heavier here, lighter there, to make the coat and
pants disreputable. He donned the wig and eye patch
and cap, and slipped the gold earring into his ear.

With his transformation complete, he peered from the
darkness and saw a man approaching cautiously along
Leidesdorff. As the man drew abreast of the American
Exchange, Trelayne lurched from the doorway, startling
the man so that he drew back.

"Steady on, there, mate." Trelayne clutched the man's
sleeve and spoke with a Cornish roll in his vowels.
"Haven't got a coin for a poor beached Jack-Tar, have
ee?"

"I'll give you a quarter eagle if you've seen an old gentleman come down this street in the last five minutes."

"Aye, mate! He come along 'ere, just as ee said. Gone
out that end o' the street. Kept lookin' back as if the
devil was after him."

The man slapped a coin in Trelayne's hand and ran off
toward California Street. The coin was a half-dollar.
"Hoy! This ain't a quarter eagle!" Trelayne called after
him indignantly, but he was laughing under his breath as
he slung the gunnysack over his shoulder and left the
street from the other end. He turned down Sacramento
toward the bay. Passing in front of Fort Vigilance, he
was startled by a shaft of light that reached across the
street as one of the large doors opened, then closed
again.

"Ahoy! Be that a saloon?"

"No saloon here, Jack-Tar," came a voice from the

shadows. "Vigilance Committee headquarters. Move along, now." Trelayne made out guards on either side of the doorway, armed with muskets. Low breastworks, made of sandbags, had been added in recent days to protect the guards' positions.

"I'll sign up, then," Trelayne announced. "Bit of fun, hanging the toffs. When's the next hanging to be?"

"We'll string you up, if you don't move along," came a voice from the roof.

Trelayne looked up and saw the silhouette of a man peering down at him. He waved and reeled off toward the waterfront, where the grogshops kept late hours.

A burst of laughter drew him to a corner tavern where the tobacco smoke was thick and the ceiling low, supported by hand-hewn timbers. He bought two brandies from a barmaid and drank the first down in a gulp, which seemed to please her. He gave her back the empty glass and pinched her bottom, which pleased her more.

"There's more where that came from," he said with a sailor's leer. "When we're alone."

"Cost you gold." Her look was brazen. She had hair the color of straw, and plump curves, and she in no way reminded him of Molly Gray.

"You there!" A hand plucked Trelayne's arm, pulling him around. It belonged to a man who stared at him with bleary eyes that were wide with surprise.

"Lord strike me if you ain't the spittin' image of Michael Dunn! Let's have a look at ye." By his speech, the man was unmistakably Irish. He was a little taller than Trelayne and a little older. "One eye, just like you, Michael had, but no patch. Had spectacles made special, one side clear glass, t'other black as night. Poor Michael. Dead these five years." The Irishman crossed himself. "You like to give me a start. Wouldn't have the price of a gin, now would ye? For me heart, it is."

Trelayne caught the barmaid by the arm when she passed near him again. He slid his hand to her buttock when she stopped beside him. "One gins, love, and a brandy. The best you've got."

"The best costs the same as the worst, love. It comes from the same bottle." She laughed and wiggled her bottom against his hand.

"Tom's the name," said the Irishman, when the barmaid moved off. "Tom's in yer debt, mate." He peered hard at Trelayne and prodded him tentatively with one finger. "You seem real enough, but who's to say a ghost can't make himself solid flesh if he takes a mind to? Swear you ain't Michael's ghost."

"I swear it, friend."

"Swear on yer mother's grave."

Trelayne put his hand over his heart and swore. His mother was sleeping soundly in Chicago by his father's side, so far as he knew, but he swore with a will. Irish Tom was a character worthy of Mr. Dickens at his best and Trelayne took in everything about him, from the manner of his speech to the unsteady nods of his head when he forgot to hold it up.

"Poor Michael. Dead five years and a fortnight, and you're his spittin' image."

The barmaid returned, pressing her breasts against Trelayne's arm as she gave out the drinks. He paid her with a gold coin and waved away her attempts to give him silver coins in return. This munificence caught Irish Tom's eye, as Trelayne had intended. He plucked Trelayne's sleeve and gestured toward the back.

"Let's find a table, you and me." He beckoned stiffly with his left hand, and Trelayne saw that he wore a leather glove on it, although the right was bare. He walked with a limp that threatened to topple him at every step until Trelayne took his arm to steady him.

"Sure, that's better now. I bent me pin on a rock, and it were a slimy rock covered with shit. Gettin' out of a boat, I was. Three weeks since. Three weeks today. Slipped on a shitten rock and bent me pin, and it's cursed slow to mend, I can tell you that."

Irish Tom slopped his gin on the table as he took his seat, and without a moment's hesitation he bent over and licked it up with his tongue as neatly as a cat.

Chapter 33

y God, what a bottom the barmaid had! Firm as a pork roast." Trelayne spread his fingers to demonstrate the shape.

It was Monday morning and they were in Stephen Kent's office. Trelayne had returned to the boardinghouse after one o'clock and he had slept like a dead man until almost nine. When he awoke, Jason and Melchior were gone from the house, but he had found them here with Kent and Dickie Howell, awaiting Abel Calvert, who was to bring them a bank draft for the purchase of *Pride of the Seas*. Trelayne was wide-awake now as he relived the encounter with Irish Tom.

"Ee's certain he were an Irishman," Melchior said.

"As Irish as Saint Patrick. And such a character! I can tell you every detail of his face and his dress. He moved like this." Trelayne stood and walked around the room, limping slightly and leaning a little to one side. "He injured the left leg not long ago, getting out of a boat. 'Slimy rocks, covered with shit,' he says. 'Slipped on a shitten rock and bent me pin,' he says."

Trelayne abandoned the imitation of the limping Irishman and spun toward Jason. "Three weeks ago yesterday he sprained it, Captain! At midnight. Getting out of a boat under the old battery on Telegraph Hill. The tide was out, he said, and he slipped on the rocks. What do you think of that?"

Jason felt the hairs on his neck rise. "Where was he—"

"Where was he going in a boat that night? Well you might ask." Trelayne was taking as much pleasure in telling the tale to his audience of three as from any role he had played in his life, except perhaps his role of the night before. "There were a dozen or more small boats out to see your ship burn, you said. And no crime in rowing out to see a fire, to be sure. But there's more, Captain." Trelayne's eyes fell half-closed. He swayed and adopted the speech of an Irishman. The transformation was sudden and uncanny. " 'Poor Michael. Would ye say a man that burned could have a ghost?' "

Trelayne became himself again. " 'Burned in hell?' I ask him. It was unreal, Captain. I felt like a character in a scene penned by the Bard. My lines were written for me. 'Burned in hell?' I ask. 'That may be,' says Tom, 'but he burned in the here and now afore that.' Now he leans right up to my face and I will tell you his breath was strong enough to asphyxiate a horse. 'Michael was burned in this city by a mob,' he says. 'Caught him setting a fire. June of fifty-one, it was. Found him with lucifers in his pocket and the smell of turpentine on his hands and they pitched him in the flames.' "

"Yes, by Neptune!" Kent exclaimed. "I heard the story at the time, Jason. It was the last of the great conflagrations that year. The arsonist was thrown alive into his own fire when the people caught him. Grim business."

Jason's scalp was tight with anticipation. "Go on," he said to Trelayne.

"You're right, Captain. We're not at the end of the tale just yet." Trelayne leaned close and became the drunken Irishman once more, his tongue licking often at his lips as he spoke. " 'Poor Michael had bad luck,' he says. 'Billy and me, our luck held. Luck o' the Irish, you might say, even though Billy's a pom. Got away clean, we did. Tom Leary, says I, you're a lucky man.' "

Trelayne resumed his seat, the customary alertness returning to his expression. "Odd, isn't it? I didn't remember his full name until just now. He was far gone by then. Drowning in his cups. I'd stake a pouch of gold dust that Tom Leary doesn't remember me today, or anything he said. It would give him the shivering fits. He was putting his head in a noose if I told the stranglers."

"But he had no hook?"

"No, Captain. He didn't use his left arm much. He kept it at his side, as if it might be crippled. He wore a glove on the hand."

Jason turned to Melchior. "You said one of the men who rowed out to the ship with Grimes was an Englishman. What did Jolly Jim say about the other?"

"He said t'other were an Irishman named Tom."

"Yes. An Irishman named Tom. But neither Tom nor the Englishman had a hook. Where is the man with the hook?"

"Perhaps young Dickie was mistaken." Kent looked at the boy.

"I'm not! I know what I seen!" Dickie had listened to Trelayne's story with his mouth agape.

" 'I know what I saw,' or Mrs. Rockwell will skin us both," Jason said. "All right, lad. You seem certain enough."

"P'raps this Tom Leary can tell us of a man with a hook," Melchior suggested.

"Don't forget his friend Billy, Captain." Trelayne dropped into character in an instant. " 'Billy and me, our luck held. Luck o' the Irish, you might say, even though Billy's a pom. Got away clean, we did.' "

"Aye," Jason said. "Got away clean. But now we know their names. Tom's the Irishman and Billy's the Englishman. And the man with a hook makes three. We'll gather the lads. Jolly Jim to lead one group, you the other, Trelayne, if you'll help us. You're the only two who know these men by sight. I'll join you later. Just now, Mr. Kent and I have an appointment with Mr. Calvert and Mr. Frye."

"Only too glad to be of assistance, Captain. I'll have to go to the theater a few hours before curtain time this evening. Until then I'm yours to command."

"I'm grateful." Jason rose to go. "What was the tavern where you found Tom Leary?"

"The Noggin of Ale."

•   •   •   •

Jonathan Frye left his office at half-past ten. A meeting of the Executive Committee was called for two o'clock. With Sherman out of the way, the mood would be optimistic. Still, the business with Wool had been a near thing. If Governor Johnson and Sherman had managed to arm their troops the whole affair could have taken a very bad turn. Even with Wool's refusal to issue the muskets, there were repercussions. That morning, the city's newspapers had printed a notice from General Sherman, explaining his resignation from command of the state's militia. In it, he had not directly accused General Wool of breaking his solemn word, but he made it clear that the Army's failure to supply arms had rendered him impotent and was the motive for his withdrawal.

The *Herald*'s acid-tongued Mercury, already a vexing thorn in the side of the Committee, was probing deeper in the wound. *Has the corrupting influence of the Vigilance Committee reached beyond the bounds of the city?* his letter asked this morning. *Is General Wool's dishonorable refusal to provide assistance to General Sherman in putting down these self-appointed satraps another signal, if more were needed, of their pernicious influence? Has the Committee suborned the highest ranking federal officer on these shores? None but the guilty parties themselves can provide the answers, and they are keeping their own counsel, cowering in the safety of their so-called fort, now piled about with gunnybags, hiding their deliberations and their unbridled ambitions from the world.*

Frye scowled as he strode along. Something would have to be done soon to silence Mercury's speculations. Today he himself would propose to the Executive Committee that an arrest warrant be issued, but over the next few hours he had personal business to transact. It was business that would benefit him long after the Vigilance Committee adjourned, long after Captain Beck and his cargo of rice were forgotten, and looking forward to it now raised his spirits in anticipation.

He walked at a good pace along Dupont, swinging his cane, until he came to the foot of Telegraph Hill. At Green Street he turned uphill. At the third house from the corner he knocked at the door of a two-story frame building. The woman who opened the door welcomed him effusively. She showed him up a flight of stairs built on the uphill side of the building. They led to the third story, where she ushered him into a newly furnished apartment. Frye inspected it with care, opening the cabinets in the kitchen and the drawers of the bedroom dresser to see that everything was arranged as he had ordered. The dresser drawers were full of gloves and scarves and women's undergarments, and the armoire contained six dresses, both day and evening, as well as hats and shoes, all new. Before leaving, Frye received two keys to the apartment and counted six fifty-dollar gold coins into the landlady's hand, which caused her to blush with pleasure as if he had propositioned her.

From Dupont and Green it was less than ten minutes' walk to Powell and Clay and the house of Mrs. Wickliff. Half an hour after entering that establishment, Jonathan Frye was panting in the arms of Barbara Quan, his body covered with sweat.

"You are very strong today, Jonathan."

He rolled off her. "With you, I am insatiable. Just give me a moment to catch my wind. Fetch me a gin and water."

Bo-Ji was glad he had reached his climax quickly. In the first flush of his lust he cared nothing for her pleasure, or for the discomfort his energetic coupling might cause her. She was tense and unsatisfied, but her satisfaction would come later.

Frye lit a cigar. When she returned with his gin, and a brandy for herself, he blew a warm stream of smoke at her breasts and stroked her black hair.

"Shall we have a bath? I could send for hot water."

"No. I want you all sweaty and smelling of sin." He sipped the gin as if it were wine. "You are good for me, Barbara. You make me believe in myself." Mrs. Frye had just the opposite effect on him, with her constant fretting about the Vigilance Committee and the governor's proclamation and the slow state of business at present.

He had almost torn Barbara's clothes from her today, he was so eager to have her. She had been dressed to go out and the layers of her clothing seemed endless. But he had remembered in time that they were expensive clothes he himself had bought for her and he had limited the damage to a few popped buttons and a tear in her chemise.

He set the gin aside and caressed the Chinese girl with fingers that were gentle now.

Bo-Ji felt her arousal return. Frye's virility excited her and he could be a skillful lover when he wanted to. She stroked him, trying to ignore the smell of a man who drank and smoked too much and did not bathe daily. Many American men smelled worse, even among the wealthy merchants and bankers who patronized Mrs. Wickliff's. Bo-Ji was constantly offended by the lack of cleanliness among Occidentals. Often she could coax Jonathan into a bath with the promise of washing him in special ways that he liked. On the days when that ruse failed she closed her mind to the odor and drank a little more brandy to dull her senses. She was very careful never to offend her customers, Jonathan Frye most of all, for if she handled Jonathan Frye with care, he could give her what she wanted more than anything.

"I am a fool, Barbara."

"Fools don't become rich."

"Even so, in pursuit of riches I have ventured into dangerous waters." He chuckled and drank the gin. "That's a good one. I'm not a sailor, and I don't go on the water myself, but I venture into dangerous waters all the same." He held her against him and stroked her buttocks lightly with his fingertips. "Do you like rice, Barbara?" His hand slid down farther and found her weakness.

"Rice is the staple food of my people."

Frye laughed. "I was speaking of commerce, not cuisine."

"I know very little about commerce, Jonathan. As I have told you, I hope to learn more. From you, if you will teach me."

"I should say you have good business instincts. You have situated yourself with a respectable firm of the better class. You are a successful businesswoman, in your own way."

"You make it sound so serious."

"Business is serious. Look at mine. I deal in many commodities. All the essentials of life. Building materials.

Clothing. Wine. Foodstuffs. Spirits. What are they for, but to satisfy men's appetites? Men need food just as they need women. We are much alike, you and I. We merely satisfy different appetites." Inwardly, he rejected the notion that he and a Chinese whore were in any way connected by class or commercial acumen, but women like compliments. It had never occurred to him before to praise a woman's ability in business. The effectiveness of his tactic impressed him. Barbara was more at ease now and she was responding enthusiastically to his caresses.

"You remember our talk about your having a place of your own? Where I would have you to myself."

Bo-Ji opened her almond eyes and tried to concentrate on what he was saying. "I remember, Jonathan."

"It would be in a good part of town. Better than this."

"I could not live on the money I make only from you."

"You would have a generous allowance, of course."

She was watching him closely, gauging his sincerity. His hand lay unmoving between her legs, which made it easier to keep her mind on the negotiation at hand. "Every conversation is a negotiation, daughter," her father counseled her. It was his most frequent admonition.

"What would I do all day?"

"Do? Take the air in your carriage. What do women do all day?"

"Would I have a carriage?"

"That might be possible."

"I should like to learn more about commerce, Jonathan."

"Commerce is a man's world."

"In Little China as on Montgomery Street," she agreed. "But I am American, Jonathan. American women have opportunity. Mrs. Wickliff has her own business. Someday I will too." She would let him think she only wanted a house of prostitution. He would understand that. Many whores dreamed of having their own houses someday.

Already she had learned far more from Jonathan Frye than he suspected. From the first time Frye chose her in Mrs. Wickliff's parlor, Bo-Ji had asked him politely about his business affairs and she had listened carefully to the answers. She had persuaded her father that Frye could be an important source of information, and he had told her all he knew of Frye's business affairs so Bo-Ji could better understand whatever Frye might reveal to her. She judged Jonathan Frye to be crafty, astute, and unscrupulous. All were qualities much valued by the merchants among her people. Now, at last, she had asked him directly for his help, holding out the promise of something he wanted very badly in exchange.

"Very well," Frye said. "I will teach you about commerce. I will teach you about my business. In your new apartment. When you have agreed to see only me. So long as you receive other men, I will teach you nothing."

Frye spoke as if making a calculated business proposition. And so it was. But it was much more as well. His feelings for the eighteen-year-old Chinese prostitute constituted an obsession. He recognized it for what it was but saw no reason not to indulge it. She was beautiful, and wise beyond her years in the ways of physical love. Given time, she could learn to respond to the feelings of his heart as well. But she must be his alone. The thought of other men touching her made him tremble with rage. Now, as always, he hid his jealousy from her view, and he did it very well.

"You are saying yes? You really will teach me?" She pressed herself against him, her hand finding him.

"First things first. When you are situated away from this house, our lessons can begin. Tomorrow evening I will show you a place I have in mind."

"You have found a place already?" For a moment her composure faltered, and he saw her girlish delight.

"Tomorrow you will see it. As I say, I have been thinking that I would like to have you to myself."

Bo-Ji had nourished this thought tenderly, letting him think it was his own from the start. She nuzzled his neck. "Must I wait until tomorrow? Can we not go today? This evening? We could dine afterward."

"Not tonight. Tomorrow I will come for you." This evening, Frye was to take his wife to the theater. It was not something he looked forward to. He did not care for popular entertainments, as his wife was well aware. But she insisted they keep up appearances, and attending the theater occasionally was a concession Frye made for the sake of domestic harmony. On Saturday, Abel Calvert would be married to the actress Molly Gray. Tonight's opening was to be in her benefit. At Calvert's invitation, many of the Executive Committee would attend. Frye would endure the evening to please his wife, and he would carry with him pleasant memories of the day.

Beneath Bo-Ji's touch Frye had grown hard again and his hand had resumed its explorations in her sensitive places. She pulled him atop her and guided him into her, at the same time wrapping her arms about him and thrusting against him slowly. She was astonished at how easily she had gained her objective. He had given her everything she wanted, and so soon! Tomorrow she would see her new home, where she would receive only Jonathan Frye and where her father would never set foot. It was the first step in taking her revenge. From Jonathan Frye she would learn the principles of commerce. With his help she would invest the money she had saved. When it was possible, she would open her own trading business. It would be small at first but over time it would grow and her influence in Little China would grow with it.

Bo-Ji estimated that it would take ten years to bankrupt her father in repayment for his forcing her into a life of shame.

"From this moment, I do not want you to be with any other man," Frye said. "Will you promise me that?"

"I promise, Jonathan."

He clasped her to him and rolled onto his back. "Now do the things you know how to do. Show me your whorish tricks."

Chapter 34

Uncertain titters sounded in the audience as the curtain parted to reveal the stage of the Theater Trelayne. A score of actors in modern dress were positioned onstage. The faces and hands of the actors were blacked and they wore woolly black wigs, as in a minstrel show. It was this discovery that prompted the laughter in the audience. Behind the actors, a cloth backdrop represented a scene that was familiar to every person in the theater. It showed a view of Kearny Street along the east side of Portsmouth Square, with City Hall squarely in the middle.

"Hence! home, you idle creatures, get you home," commanded one of two actors wearing the glazed-brim caps and single-breasted blue coats of the San Francisco police. The speaker and his companion confronted a rabble of poorly dressed citizens. *"Is this a holiday?"* demanded the same policeman. *"What! I know you not. Speak, what trade art thou?"*

"Why, sir, a coal man," answered one of the rabble.

"So thy dusky visage would announce," said the second policeman, *"were it not for the negritude that so abounds in thy company. Are they coal men all?"*

"Nay, sir. Good men all, come to honor Caesar."

"Wherefore honor Caesar?"

"Why, therefore, sir, for he passes here *within the hour."*

Sarah observed that the hidden meaning in the substitution of a "coal man" for the original play's cobbler escaped the audience, as Trelayne had guessed it might, although laughter punctuated the comic exchange. Already, knowledgeable playgoers in the audience saw that Trelayne was departing from Shakespeare's text, and a breeze of whispering flowed beneath the gaiety. In the newspapers and on the bills posted about town the play was heralded as *Caesar in California, OR, The World Turned Upside Down*. The whisperers were speculating about what direction Trelayne's satire might take, and how Shakespeare's world would be upended.

As the scene progressed, the mood of the audience remained both expectant and unsettled. The style of Trelayne's invention was not what they had anticipated. Minstrel lampoons of Shakespeare's classics were a staple fare of the California stage, but they were customarily presented as afterpieces, the humorous playlets that followed the main drama of the evening. Here, despite the burnt-cork faces and the wigs, there was none of the usual minstrel japery, no broad Negro dialect. The humor was in Shakespeare's style, stemming from plays on words and veiled meanings.

When the second policeman recalled noble Pompey, whom Caesar had slain, he added a new rebuke to Caesar, for having tarried with Cleopatra in Egypt. *"Would that fatal asp had lain against her bosom long ere Caesar's lips!"* he cried. *"Oh, Caesar! You plucked the flower of Egypt and now she too is turned to dust. Your kiss is like the adder's, boding ill to friend and foe alike!"*

A banjo in the pit struck up a slow rhythm and the rabble onstage broke into reverential song:

> *"Go down Moses, way down in Egypt's land*
> *Tell ol' Caesar to let Cleopatra go!"*

This brought a swell of laughter from the audience, and the laughter lingered as Caesar and his retinue entered from the opposite wings. Here too every face and hand, every exposed patch of skin, was blacked.

"My God, it's Norton," Jason said as he recognized the bulbous nose and prominent eyes of Caesar's dark visage. He identified Helena Trout, the company's second lady, as Portia, the wife of Brutus. Another actress of the company played Caesar's wife, Calphurnia. "Where is Miss Gray?" he whispered to Sarah.

"Look closely at Mark Antony."

Jason peered at the slight figure by Norton's side. "By God, so it is." Molly Gray was dressed in the top hat and Sunday suit of a San Francisco merchant and she sported a large diamond ring. When she spoke her first lines, which were not intended to call much attention to Antony here, her voice was somehow not a woman's. It was the voice of a soft-spoken man.

A actor clad like a field hand on a Southern plantation stepped from the rabble, feeling his way with a stick. *"Caesar! Beware the ides of May."*

"What man is that?" Joshua Norton demanded imperiously.

Trelayne, as Brutus, answered from among Caesar's retinue. *"A blind soothsayer bids you beware the ides of May."*

"He is a dreamer. Let us leave him."

"It was the ides of March," Sarah said as Caesar led his procession into the wings.

"Aye, but not tonight, it seems," Jason replied.

They were seated in the center of the dress circle, with Abel Calvert and the Kents. Trelayne had offered them a box if they preferred, but urged them to sit "in the thick of it" this evening. "You will feel the temper of the audience better there," he had advised them, "and you will see better in the third act, when the stage is partitioned." Lacking this advice, several prominent men from the Committee of Vigilance sat in the first tier of boxes. Jason recognized William Tell Coleman and Thomas Smiley with their wives, seated in a box over the edge of the stage. Next to them the tall figure of Miers Truett and the shorter one of James Dows were unmistakable. Across the way, Jonathan Frye sat with the same stern-faced woman who had accompanied him to see *The Houri and the Bedouin*.

The house was rapt while Edwin Booth, as Cassius, kept Brutus behind when Caesar departed and, in roundabout fashion, first tested Brutus's loyalty to Caesar and then invited him to join the conspirators who were already plotting Caesar's assassination. The eloquent words were Shakespeare's own, yet they seemed fresh and alive to Jason's ear. He had read the play many times on long voyages but had seen it performed only once before, and that time poorly, in Hong Kong, by British Navy officers and ratings. Here the drama was vivid, and he could not imagine two actors better suited to the parts of Brutus and Cassius than Trelayne and Booth. They were young, passionate conspirators, and they spoke their lines as if the thoughts were born at the instant they voiced them.

Beside Jason, Sarah gripped the arms of her chair with fingers that flexed unconsciously from time to time, whitening at the tips. She feared Trelayne's satire would become so pointed that he would enrage the vigilantes too soon, but he kept his barbs sheathed as Brutus committed himself to the conspirators' cause and Caesar turned aside well-intentioned warnings meant to keep him from danger. Together, Cassius and Brutus propelled the assassination plot toward its goal. Little more was made of the blackened faces of the actors, and the audience grew accustomed to the oddity of masquerade Negroes speaking cultured English.

The story, for the most part, was Shakespeare's. The conspirators feared that Caesar's ambitious nature would lead him to accept an emperor's crown, sealing the fate of the dying republic. Sarah recognized a greater stress than Shakespeare had placed on Brutus's love of Caesar, and on some warnings that what followed Caesar might be worse still, and she perceived that a new theme was emerging—even the conspirators acknowledged that Caesar, however ambitious, stood for justice. If anything, they said, he was too forgiving of his enemies.

When the curtain closed at the end of the second act, signalling the intermission, Sarah said, "I would like some champagne, Captain, if you don't mind escorting me."

"I am pleased to escort you. In truth, I am interested to see how the ladies and gentlemen of San Francisco are enjoying Mr. Trelayne's version of the play." In the vestibule, Jason bought two glasses of champagne and led Sarah to a corner from which they could observe the crowd.

Sarah's evening dress was of teal silk, the flounces edged with gold thread. Haven had given it to her in New York before they sailed for California and she had never worn it in public until now.

"There's Captain Farren," she said, spying him with the Shermans and the Volney Howards. At Farren's suggestion, Sherman and Howard had agreed to appear together at the theater as a signal to the public that Sherman bore no shame for his resignation and that he supported General Howard in his new office.

Coleman and Frye and the others from the Vigilance Committee were gathered in a group, Abel Calvert among them, standing a little apart from their wives, who had formed a circle of their own. Some of the Committee members nodded politely when Sherman looked their way, the greetings formal and correct, if distant.

"There is as much drama here as on the stage," Jason observed.

Sarah surveyed the throng and pointed out a few of the notables to Jason. Thomas Maguire had come to see Molly Gray in her last production before she became his leading lady. Mayor Van Ness was in attendance, as were Judge and Mrs. David Terry, and Colonel and Mrs. West. The gathering was representative of the divided city, but here the Committee of Vigilance mustered only its most prominent leaders, not its troops, and the sides were more even.

"Look there." Sarah directed Jason's attention to a rather slight man who moved through the crowded vestibule with a tall, stately woman on his arm. "It is Colonel Hays."

"Jack Hays? The Texas Ranger?"

Sarah was pleased by Jason's astonishment. No hero of the Mexican War shone more brightly in the popular imagination than Colonel John Coffee Hays, leader of the Texas Ranger regiment. His reputation extended from the Atlantic to the Pacific, and in San Francisco it shone especially brightly. He had arrived in the gold port in January 1850, and was elected sheriff three months later. In the rough days of the city's boom, he was an indomitable force for law and order. Reelected by increasingly large majorities, he gave up the office in 1853 when he was appointed United States surveyor general for California by President-elect Franklin Pierce. Hays's presence at Pierce's inaugural ball in the nation's capital had occasioned so much attention that he had retired into an out-of-the-way corner to avoid embarrassing the president.

Those who knew of Hays only by reputation were always surprised to find that the figure behind the legend was a slender, unassuming man of no more than middling height.

"Which side is he on?" Jason said.

"He shuns politics. But I believe he had some kind of brush with the vigilantes in fifty-one. Look! He's going to speak with General Sherman."

Hays led his wife through the crowded vestibule. When he reached the Shermans and the Howards he greeted them warmly, drawing black looks from the vigilance leaders.

If the early acts of *Caesar in California* had allayed Sarah's fears, the opening scenes of Act III soon revived them. The stage was divided now by the partition representing the facade of City Hall, complete with mock marble columns. Kearny Street was on the left, outside the hall, and a single chamber, representing the hall's interior, was on the right, behind the facade. As the third act began, the chamber was occupied by a gathering of gentlemen awaiting the arrival of Caesar, who entered the street set from the wings with a small retinue, moving through a crowd of onlookers.

"The ides of May are come," Joshua Norton proclaimed when he spied the blind Soothsayer in the throng.

"Ay, Caesar, but not gone," replied the Soothsayer, and then, in a departure from Shakespeare's text, he added, *"Regard the final portent of your doom."* He pointed with his stick as a man stepped from the crowd close to the footlights to challenge another man upstage, near the backdrop.

"Come on! Come on, now!" the challenger called. *"Arm and defend thyself! Your published lies endanger the republic!"*

The challenged man folded his arms, one hand within his coat. *"That cannot be, for I am Republican."* Nervous laughter from the audience broke the hush, as the listeners grasped the play on *republic* and *Republican.*

"Usurper!" the challenger cried. He drew a pistol from beneath his cape and fired.

"Oh, Lord!" The other staggered. *"Oh, my arm!"*

There was a stirring in the audience and Sarah felt a chill. For a moment she was back in Montgomery Street with Jason by her side, seeing the street duel for the first time.

Men from the crowd helped the wounded man offstage. *"The council awaits. Come, Caesar,"* Cassius urged, but Caesar held back as two policemen approached the challenger and escorted him away. *"Is he ta'en?"* Caesar asked.

"He is, Caesar," Mark Antony assured him. *"He will meet thy justice soon. Shall you be merciful?"*

"Nay, for his act is an affront to justice, and I am Justice itself, though but a man of flesh and blood. Yet there may be more here than meets the eye."

Sarah marveled at how effectively Joshua Norton conducted himself as Caesar, delivering his lines as if he had played the part many times before. When Cassius drew Caesar to the door of City Hall and ushered him into the chamber where the gentlemen awaited him, Sarah gripped the arms of her chair, knowing what was to come. A petitioner would approach Caesar, be refused, and then the conspirators would strike. Here, Trelayne had warned her, the innovations in the play would become more pointed.

In the chamber, an ally of Cassius drew Mark Antony aside and led off him into the wings, while a dignified man bowed low before Caesar, a petition in his hand.

"Most powerful Caesar, I bow before you with humble heart to plead my case. Too fervently thy supporter acts in striking down thine enemy! You, Caesar, saw the act just now, yet you saw not the honest heart within the man who will soon face thy too cold justice. Be not blind, Caesar! Acknowledge the difference between friend and foe and treat them not alike, for thy foes, though they call themselves Republicans, would tear down thy temples and give the city to the mob."

Norton, who had seated himself behind the huge desk that dominated the chamber, rose now to his feet.

"Stand straight before me and leave off thy low, crooked curt-sies and base spaniel fawning. I hear thy plea. Stand before me as a man when you seek justice! Look me in mine eye so thou wilt see that I am Justice, and know that true justice must e'er be tempered by mercy. My temples are the palaces of justice and so I will be merciful to him that defends them, e'en as I will be just to those who would tear them to rubble. Though they call themselves Republican, they are enemies of my republic! They shall find harsh judgment at my hands, for I am Justice incar-nate, though but a man of flesh and blood!"

Unnoticed, Cassius and the other conspirators had drawn near to Caesar as he spoke. Now Cassius drew a huge bowie knife from his coat and cried out, *"Then pierce flesh and let flow blood! Speak, hands, for me!"*

He stabbed Caesar in the neck. A gout of blood ap-peared, provoking gasps from the audience even as the other conspirators clustered around Caesar, stabbing him repeatedly. At the last, Brutus thrust his dagger into Caesar's side. With a gasp, and a murmured *"Et tu, Brute? Then fall, Caesar!"* Joshua Norton collapsed to the stage.

"Liberty! Freedom! Justice is dead! Run hence, proclaim, cry it about the streets!" Cassius cried, holding high his bloody dagger.

There was not a sound in the auditorium. Sarah's breath caught in her throat. She looked to the boxes where the vigilance leaders sat. Jonathan Frye's mouth hung open. Across the way, William Tell Coleman's ex-pression was grim and Miers Truett whispered in Jim Dows' ear. Sarah half expected them to storm the stage, calling for Trelayne's head, but they sat as if bound to their chairs, staring. Had none of them marked Tre-layne's substitution of *Justice is dead* for *Tyranny is dead* in Shakespeare's words? Did they not see that the world of the original play was truly turned upside down? Where the Bard of Avon depicted Caesar as a budding tyrant, Trelayne had transformed him into the incarnation of Justice, defender of the republic, a dispenser of mercy who would have spared James Casey's life. Where Shakespeare's conspirators acted to save the Roman re-public, here Brutus and Cassius and the rest were the as-sassins of Justice and of the California republic too.

If the vigilance leaders had seen themselves in Caesar's murderers, they did not know how to respond. And now, as he had done in the early acts, Trelayne soothed them by returning to the play as written. While half the councillors fled the chamber, carrying the news to the crowd in the street, Trelayne, as Brutus, bent over Caesar and arose with his hand wet with blood.

"Stoop, citizens, stoop, and let us bathe our hands in Caesar's blood, and besmear our swords: then we walk forth e'en to Portsmouth Square, and waving our red weapons o'er our heads, let's all cry, Peace! freedom! and liberty!"

The conspirators congratulated themselves on bringing liberty to the city, and when Antony came to them humbly, asking leave that he might address the citizens at Caesar's funeral, the conspirators agreed. Then, leaving Antony alone to prepare Caesar's body for burial, Brutus and Cassius and the other conspirators passed through the partition and into Kearny Street, where Brutus would address the crowd before Antony, to sway them to the conspirators' cause.

Molly Gray, a small and dapper Antony in her gentleman's Sunday suit, was alone now with the crumpled form of Joshua Norton. By an ingenious manipulation of the lighting, the street scene grew dim as the citizens gathered silently around Brutus, who held forth his arms and addressed them silently, in pantomime. A single orange beam shone down on the City Hall chamber from above, focussing attention on the forlorn figure of Antony, who held out a hand toward Caesar's body as if beseeching him.

"O, pardon me, thou bleeding piece of earth, that I am meek and gentle with these butchers!" The words were spoken so softly that the audience had to strain to catch them, all but the last, when Molly raised her head toward the door and spat out "butchers!" like a curse. As soon as it rose the anger died, to be replaced by a sorrow so palpable, as expressed in Molly's bearing, and in her voice—which suggested a man made hoarse with grief—that Sarah's vision blurred with tears. From the parquet floor to the gallery—the highest balcony—the theater hung on Antony's words.

"Thou art the ruins of the noblest man that ever lived in the

tide of times. Woe to the hand that shed this costly blood! Over thy wounds now do I prophesy, a curse shall light upon the limbs of men; domestic fury and fierce civil strife shall cumber all the parts of California!"

As Molly spoke, her voice gathered strength. A tension grew in her body. She seemed to increase in size as she raised her head and turned to face the audience.

"Blood and destruction shall be so in use, and dreadful objects so familiar, that mothers shall but smile when they behold their infants quarter'd with the hands of war. All pity chok'd, with Justice fallen dead, and Caesar's spirit, ranging for revenge, shall in these streets with a monarch's voice cry HAVOC, and let slip the dogs of war; that this foul deed shall smell above the earth with carrion men, groaning for burial!"

The last words rang out in the stillness.

A pair of hands clapped somewhere in the gallery. On the parquet, another pair joined the first, then another, and the applause rose like the sound of a wave breaking on the ocean shore. Sarah got to her feet. Nearby, a few others followed her example. Jason found himself standing beside her, and soon those who remained seated were the minority, stared at from every side. Embarrassed by this attention, even a few of the vigilance leaders rose, although they kept their hands at their sides.

The tribute ended and the audience resumed their seats as the scene was transformed once more by a shifting of the light, leaving Antony in dimness while the street beyond the partition brightened. Men from the crowd around Brutus entered the chamber. They lifted Caesar's body and bore it into the street set while the assembly there chanted the popular song "Carry Me Back to Old Virginny" in the manner of a funeral dirge.

As the song ended, Trelayne—who had left off Brutus's pantomimed speech when Caesar's body was brought forth—began speaking aloud now, assuring the citizens of his love for Caesar, whom he slew only for the good of the city: *"Not that I loved Justice less, but that I loved San Francisco more! Had you rather that Caesar were living, and live like slaves under his justice, than that Caesar were dead, to live like free Republicans?"*

"No, Massa, no!" cried the crowd onstage, taking on,

for the first time, the servile attitudes and thick dialect of Negro slaves.

Now Brutus looked beyond the stage to the audience. *"Who is here so base that would be a bondman? Who is here so rude that would not be a free man?"*

"None, Massa, none!" cried the citizens onstage. *"We wants to be free, Massa! Show us de way!"* They milled about, gesturing grotesquely in a broad parody of uncultured slaves, but almost at once their movements took on a common rhythm, becoming a kind of shuffling dance. The band in the pit struck up the familiar melody of Stephen Foster's "O! Susanna," and the black-faced citizens burst into song:

"To live a slave for all my life is wearing mighty thin,
I'se gwine to California, where stealin' ain't a sin.
I'll take along a barr'l o' flour and sell it with a smile,
One ounce o' gold for every pound, that's how I'll make my pile.
O! Jerusha, Who's it gwine to be?
I'se gwine to California to get rich and be free!
O! Jerusha, Who's it gwine to be?
I'se gwine to California to get rich and be free!"

"Oh! Jerusha" variants of the song were well-known to the audience, who had heard innumerable parodies in minstrel shows given on San Francisco stages. They smiled and nodded, welcoming the moment's levity, and so were unprepared for the sudden stop to the singing and dancing as one old man in the crowd called out to Brutus:

"Show us de way, Massa!"

"No!" Brutus's stern refusal rang out harshly in the sudden quiet.

"Did I slay Caesar to advance myself? No! I slew him for the good of all, and I have the same dagger for myself when it should please the city to need my death. Do not ask me to serve. From among you the leaders shall be chosen! Who would'st lead in Caesar's stead? Surely there is one known to all whom you would place above you?"

"Fetch de coal man!" came a voice.

"Yes! Fetch de coal man!"

"Hyah he is! Bring him for'ard!"

A man was pushed from the crowd. It was the same black-faced coal man, wearing the same soot-smudged clothes, who had appeared in the first scene of the play. He looked about now, bewildered. *"What would you with me, great Brutus?"* he inquired timorously.

"Nay, not great Brutus, Coal Man. Come thou hither. Stand up here with me and I'll step down. Thou shalt preside over us. A free man to lead us! All hail, Coal Man!"

"All hail, Coal Man!" echoed the crowd, and from the audience there came a buzz of whispers as they recognized now the satire in the Coal Man's name. The poor fellow was thrust toward the podium where Brutus stood, which was made of three flour barrels placed together. Lifted by the crowd, he was raised up beside Brutus, who stepped nimbly down, leaving the Coal Man alone.

In the foremost box, a chair scraped the floor. William Tell Coleman got to his feet, glaring down at those on the stage, who paid him no mind. He cast a meaningful glance at the vigilance leaders nearest him, offered his arm to his wife, and escorted her from the box. Before he was gone from sight, Thomas Smiley got up, and James Dows. Miers Truett rose to his full height, then stooped to leave the box. They made much of their leaving, careless of the disturbance they caused. There was movement in the dress circle as several gentlemen departed with their wives, and now the scattered protests became an exodus. In the second and third circles, in the orchestra, on the parquet, they rose by fits and starts, with shuffling feet and muttering as they went.

But now Antony left the darkened chamber of City Hall and stepped into the brightly lighted street set, from where he addressed not the crowd of actors but the audience: *"Friends! Forty-niners! Countrymen! Lend me your ears!"*

"They will all go," Sarah feared.

"Nay," Jason reassured her. "They will stay to hear him, I'm bound." Even as he spoke the exodus slowed to a trickle, then stopped. Some of those who had left their seats found others and sat again. The theater was still half-full. Jonathan Frye looked to where Abel Calvert sat, but Calvert motioned him to keep his seat. Onstage, the Coal Man was forgotten by the citizens, who turned toward Antony.

"I come to bury Caesar, not to praise him." Molly kept her eyes on the audience, and here again the theme of justice slain was added to Shakespeare's words.

"The evil that men do lives after them; the good is oft interred with their bones. Let it not be thus with Caesar! The noble Brutus has told you that Caesar was ambitious: if it were so, it were a grievous fault, and grievously hath Caesar answer'd it. Yet Caesar stood for justice; justice in him dwelt; and so dies Caesar, dies justice too. Here, under leave of Brutus and the rest—for Brutus is an honorable man—come I to speak in Caesar's funeral. He was my friend, faithful and just to me: but Brutus says he was ambitious; and Brutus is an honorable man."

Molly had scarcely noticed the departures from the auditorium. She was aware of a commotion in the house and saw some moving toward the doors, but her attention, her being, was given to Antony's oration.

Trelayne had sworn her to keep the new thrust of the address secret. She had rehearsed alone in her room and she had practiced the speech aloud just three times, walking in the evening near Sarah's house. She had spoken only Shakespeare's words in dress rehearsal, yet she knew Tommy's altered lines as well as any she had ever played. They belonged to her and she spoke them as her own, her passion growing as Antony praised Caesar's merits one by one, conveying the love he held for Caesar—and for Justice, slain by the same hands—yet always reminding his listeners that Brutus said Caesar was ambitious, and Brutus was an honorable man.

"You must embody the tragedy, Molly," Tommy had instructed her. "Brutus *is* an honorable man. He has acted out of honor. Look at me. I am Brutus. I have acted for the good of San Francisco. I have killed the one man who stands for justice, and I am wrong. Yet with all my soul I believed I was doing right. That is the tragedy. You know in your heart I was wrong, but there is no hint of sarcasm when you say 'Brutus is an honorable man.' You *love* Brutus."

He was watching her now, from the fringes of the crowd onstage, his eyes bright in his blackened face, and she knew without breaking her rhythm that she was perfect. The lines and the meaning of the lines came from her heart, and she spoke with true conviction.

She was become Mark Antony.

"O masters, if I were disposed to stir your hearts and minds to mutiny and rage, I should do Brutus wrong, and Cassius wrong, who, you all know, are honorable men. I will not do them wrong; I rather choose to wrong the dead, to wrong myself and you, to see Justice cast down, courts closed and judges scorned, than I will wrong such honorable men!"

The crowd was with her now, their love of Brutus waning, his soothing reasonings forgot, pushed aside by Antony's passion for Caesar and for Justice. Unnoticed, Brutus, Cassius, and their fellow conspirators slipped singly into the wings.

Antony bent over Caesar's body. *"If you have tears, prepare to shed them now,"* he commanded his listeners, and he showed them Caesar's cloak where the conspirators' daggers had rent it. The onlookers' anger turned toward the assassins, guided by Antony's skillful words, as he described the plotters' betrayal and Caesar's death—

"Then burst his mighty heart, great Caesar fell, and so was Justice fallen! O, what a fall was there, my countrymen! Then I, and you, and all of us fell down, whilst bloody treason flourished over us!"

Trelayne had counseled Molly to count to ten after delivering this line. She counted instead to twenty, turning her head slowly to sweep the auditorium with her gaze. She saw Abel Calvert in the dress circle, but she could not tell if his expression conveyed pride in her or awe at the spectacle.

In Molly's hand, Caesar's torn cloak dripped calf's blood that had been concealed in small balloons of India rubber, which burst as the conspirators struck Norton with their false knives. Around her, some of the actors made a show of weeping over Caesar's bloody garment.

"O, now you weep. And I perceive you feel the dint of pity; these are gracious drops. Kind souls, what, weep you when you but behold Caesar's vesture wounded? Look you here, here is himself, marr'd, as you see, with traitors!"

Now the fury of the mob rose and the tear-streaked faces shouted, *"O traitors! Villains!"* *"We will be revenged! Let not a traitor live."*

But Antony held them back. *"Stay, countrymen! Good friends, sweet friends! Let me not stir you up to such sudden mutiny! You go to do you know not what!"* Molly's voice became softer. *"Yet stay awhile, for I will read to you Caesar's last will and testament."*

"The will! Let's stay and hear the will!"

Molly drew a paper from her coat and unfolded it. *"To every citizen of San Francisco he gives five hundred dollars in gold."*

"Most noble Caesar! We'll revenge his death!"

"Stay! There is more. He hath left you his planked streets and his wharves and his public buildings, great and small, yet these are the least of his bequests to you, good citizens."

"What more, Antony? What more?"

Where Shakespeare's Caesar has bequeathed only tangible things, Trelayne's now promised more enduring gifts:

"To each and every one, he bequeaths the fruits of liberty: freedom in your homes and when you walk abroad, freedom to enter a business or not, as you choose; freedom from tyranny— domestic and foreign—and more. But you must secure these freedoms to yourselves, if you will it, for Caesar is slain, and Justice cast down by the hands that slew him!"

"Caesar was ambitious!" The voice came not from the stage, but from the dress circle. Men and women in the audience looked about to see who had spoken.

Molly Gray turned toward the voice. *"Yes, Caesar was ambitious! for Caesar was Justice, and justice is ambitious to bring peace and liberty where tyranny would reign!"* She paused to let those words be heard, and then, *"Now ask you this: would you have justice served by imperfect men, or Justice slain and imperfect men let loose upon the world? For so long as justice is administered by men, it will be weakened by ambition, frailty and greed. Yet no ambitious justice can do greater harm than unfettered men, once the guiding reins of law be cut asunder."*

She flung out a hand toward Caesar's body. *"Here was a Caesar with justice in his heart. When comes such another?"*

"Never! Never!" cried the citizens around her. They were in a frenzy now. *"Come away! We'll burn his body in the holy place, and with the brands we'll fire the traitors' houses! Go, fetch fire!"*

Hoisting Caesar's body on their shoulders, the mob surged from the stage and was gone. Turning to the audience once more, Molly stepped forward to address the house. *"Now let it work. Mischief, thou art afoot! Take thou what course thou wilt!"*

The curtain drew closed behind her, leaving her alone before the footlights, and the applause broke like thunder.

avid Farren dropped into a seat behind Jason and Sarah. "Look at them!" He had to shout to make himself heard over the tumult. From the parquet, flowers flew toward the stage and bouquets fell at Molly's feet. The sound of coins striking the stage was like a metallic rain.

Sarah leaned close to Farren's ear. "That was your voice just now."

"Trelayne put me up to it." Farren was gleeful.

"I would not have thought you could find so many people in San Francisco to cheer in opposition to the Vigilance Committee," Jason said.

"You see here the state's militia in mufti, Captain," Farren said. "The officers are here"—he gestured to the parquet and dress circle, then pointed up to the gallery— "and the soldiers are above. We have packed the house. And by God, we have shown them our numbers tonight! I am glad you take no offense."

"Captain Beck leaves landsmen's matters to landsmen," Sarah said.

"A wise policy. You'll be glad to leave all this behind, I imagine. But for those of us who remain, this evening is a triumph."

"The triumph is Molly's," Sarah said.

"And we owe much to Trelayne as well," Farren reminded her. "What an inspiration to cast himself as Brutus. The vigilants thought he was on their side until he turned the play upside down!"

Onstage the curtain opened and the full cast came from the wings to join Molly. Members of the audience surged up the steps at either side of the stage. A gentleman admirer presented Molly with a necklace of pearls in a velvet-lined box. Others pressed to the edge of the pit with offerings of their own, amidst cries of "Author! Author!"

"Let's go down," Sarah said. Flanked by Jason and Farren, she made her way from the dress circle and through the crowd to the stage.

Trelayne stepped forward from the assembled cast, but the din only ceased when Molly stood beside him and raised his hand with her own.

"Good citizens, I thank you," Trelayne said. "Here stands Brutus humbly before you, vanquished by a worthy adversary." He bowed to Molly, which provoked a cheer from her fervent fans. When it died away, Trelayne said, "The Bard hath writ full two acts more. Yet our play upon the play must end here, incomplete, for on the greater stage in which we dwell the battle is yet to come. So doff we now our slavish guise—" Here he removed his wooly wig, then Molly's. The cast followed suit, revealing white foreheads above burnt-cork faces. Molly removed the pins holding her own black hair and it fell about her shoulders, prompting a new burst of applause.

"Let none of us be slaves!" Trelayne said when quiet was restored. "Though justice is cast down, we are still free men! Tonight in your homes and tomorrow in our troubled streets, ask you this: Where next will this benighted city find a Caesar with justice in his heart?" This brought renewed cheers, but Trelayne raised his hands to quell it. "And now I remind you that this performance is dedicated to the benefit of our own Miss Molly Gray. Be generous, gentlemen, for our gifts make up her dowry!"

The men around Molly pressed offerings into her hands until she called to Helena Trout and other members of the cast for help. Dickie Howell, who had been privileged to watch the play from the wings, struggled through the crush around Molly and held up a handful of gold coins. "There's lots more, Miss Gray!"

"You gather them for me, Dickie, and I will give you one in ten."

"Truly? I'll get them all!" As he broke clear of her admirers he careened into Abel Calvert, who thrust him violently aside. Dickie fell, scattering his booty. His cry of surprise and the clatter of the coins on the planks of the stage caused a sudden hush.

"Come here, Molly." Calvert reached out a hand. The gathering around Molly Gray parted. She came forward tentatively, searching Calvert's face. When she took his hand, he drew her close to him. "Leave these things."

"But Abel, they are my—"

"I said leave them!" He knocked the gifts from her hand. "When you want gold and jewels, I will give them to you. You will keep nothing from these people."

"Mr. Calvert, the gifts are only a tribute to Molly's acting," Sarah Rockwell said. "They are wedding gifts." Jason stood at her side, watching Calvert for a sign that he meant harm to Molly or Sarah or anyone else.

Those on the stage moved closer around the banker, their dark faces menacing. Calvert kept his eyes on Sarah. "Molly will accept no tribute from this company, Mrs. Rockwell. I am taking her out of here now."

"You agreed you would not see her until the wedding."

"Nevertheless, I am taking her. I will obtain a room for her at the International Hotel. I will not see her again until Saturday. But I tell you this. She is not to set foot in this theater again. Nor is she to set foot in your house, or any other place where that man is present!" He pointed an accusing finger at Trelayne, as if aiming a musket.

"Molly—" Sara began.

"I'll be all right, Sarah." Molly allowed Calvert to guide her from the stage and across the parquet. Jonathan Frye was waiting near the doors. He raised his gold-headed cane and pointed it at Trelayne.

"You have gone too far, Trelayne! Mark my words! You have gone too far!" He fell in behind Calvert and

Molly as rear guard, and together they passed from sight.

It was after midnight when Trelayne left the theater. Before stepping into the alley and locking the stage door behind him, he looked both ways, alert for any lurking forms. He had infuriated the most dangerous men in the city tonight, and he did not put past them a quick and brutal reprisal.

He was dressed as himself, after considering a disguise and rejecting it. His first destination was the boarding-house, where he would receive Mercury's commentary on the play. The sight of a stranger coming and going from Sarah's house, whether an overdressed dandy or a pigtailed Jack-Tar, might arouse further suspicion. In time it might lead someone to make a connection between the boardinghouse and the *Herald*, and that would never do.

He entered the house boldly, drew the drapes in the parlor, lighted a lamp, and left it burning when he crept from the back door ten minutes later, dressed in his laborer's costume, with Sarah's letter in his pocket. He kept to the shadows in the garden and passed through the yards of several other houses before emerging on Pacific Street, but he did not go straight to the *Herald*. He made instead for Montgomery Street, where the saloons were doing lively trade. As he moved along the street he gazed through the windows of the drinking houses, as if in awe of the glittering chandeliers and fine-clothed gentlemen within. In the Bank Exchange he saw Jonathan Frye and several other leaders of the Vigilance Committee conferring grimly. Abel Calvert was not among them.

Straying off Montgomery toward the waterfront, Trelayne took a mug of porter in a workingman's tavern. The sentiments expressed by the drinkers, vigilantes to a man, favored hanging Thomas Trelayne and his entire company on the morrow, without bothering to try them. Unremarked and unhindered, Trelayne left the tavern and returned to the gaslit streets, wondering where he would find an audience to cheer *Caesar in California* at the next evening's performance.

He himself would play Mark Antony. Booth would

make a worthy Brutus, if he were willing to finish out the week. If the Committee of Vigilance did not bribe or threaten him. If the theater were allowed to open at all.

But without Molly it would never be the same.

" '*O, she doth teach the torches to burn bright!*' " he said to a pair of saddle horses hitched outside the Metropolitan Exchange. " '*It seems she hangs upon the cheek of night like a rich jewel in an Ethiop's ear! Beauty too rich for use, for earth too dear! So shows a snowy dove trooping with crows, as yonder lady o'er her fellows shows.*' " The lines from *Romeo and Juliet* came as easily to him as breathing. He and Molly had played the parts many times. In their first year together he had trained her by assigning her to memorize many of Shakespeare's famous roles, and her aptitude had astonished him. She remembered not only her own part but the others as well, and she could still recite complete scenes from memory.

Nearby, a public clock sounded a single stroke. It was followed by others, bells near and far sounding when each judged the time was right. Trelayne hastened on his way, once more the innocuous laborer, but conspicuous in empty streets all the same. He had more to do this night than merely deliver a letter. Already Captain Beck and Jolly Jim were prowling the waterfront taverns. Trelayne was to visit the Noggin of Ale alone so as not to arouse Tom Leary's suspicions if the Irishman were there.

At the *Herald*, John Nugent was waiting. "I have just come from the Theater Trelayne. Did we attend the same play, by chance?"

"We did." Tonight Trelayne spoke in his humble laborer's voice.

"My own commentary will run beside your letter." Nugent met Trelayne's eyes. "I hope no one else discerns the same hand that wrote the play in these letters."

Trelayne was pleased to be found out.

Nugent smiled broadly. "Bravo, Brutus." He seized Trelayne's hand and shook it. "It was wonderful to see those pompous asses squirm in their seats once they got the gist of it. I'm surprised they stayed as long as they did."

"Will they let me run out the week?"

Nugent shrugged. "The worst they've done to me is burn some of my papers in the street. They haven't smashed my presses. They haven't thrown me in one of their little cells demanding to know who writes these." He held up the letter. "Perhaps a modicum of human decency holds them back. If not, God help us when they drop their righteous pose. You and I will swing from the same gibbet then, Mr. Trelayne."

"Or be marched aboard the same steamer."

"There's something to pray for, if you're a praying man. If we're lucky, we'll be put off in the Sandwich Isles. I have often wondered what the *wahines* wear beneath their skirts."

Sherman was having a bad night, although it had begun in bliss. On their return from the theater, Ellen had looked in on the children, sent the maid to bed, and then seduced him gently. He had lain almost insensible when the lovemaking was over, clinging to the pleasant oblivion it engendered.

Ellen had been the first to speak. "Promise me that you'll be only a banker from now on."

"Oh, I'll keep the bank afloat," he said. "The truth is, Ellie, banking doesn't suit me."

"Then whatever you do, promise me that you will always come home to me so we can be together like this."

"I promise you that with all my heart."

Satisfied, she had turned on her side to go to sleep, but she moved against him, needing his touch. She placed her back against his shoulder, the softness of her bottom against his hip, and the soles of her feet against the warmth of his calf.

Sherman had lain awake after her breathing became deep and regular, unwilling to sleep and lose the profound sense of comfort that pervaded him. He prayed silently, thanking God for Ellen and the kind fortune that had placed him in her father's house when he was just a boy.

Sherman's own father, a judge on the Ohio supreme court, had died when he was nine, leaving his mother a widow with eleven children to care for. To lighten her burden, Tecumseh, the eldest boy, was taken in by

Thomas Ewing, one of his father's closest friends and later a United States senator from Ohio. Cump was raised in Ewing's household with Ewing's children from the age of nine until he went off to West Point at sixteen. On his visits home from the military academy, Sherman saw Ellen Ewing blossom from his childhood playmate into a fetching young woman. After three long years in California with the Army, he returned home on leave in 1850 and married her, unwilling to be parted from her again for so long. He still felt like a bashful groom each time he saw Ellen when they had been apart, even for a few hours.

She was his life's companion. He wanted nothing more than to remain in her embrace while the world around them went to hell in a basket, but the play at the Theater Trelayne had revived his anger at the Vigilance Committee and his need for vindication. These thoughts kept him awake and brought on the asthma, which forced him to prop himself up with several pillows and sit gasping for breath. Eventually he slipped out of bed without waking Ellen, donned a robe, and went to his study, where he burned scraps of nitre paper in an ashtray and sat inhaling the fumes.

Why was it so damnably important that he find some way to bring the Committee of Vigilance down?

Because they were in the wrong, and their very existence was a threat to the American notions of liberty. He had seen that from the beginning. He had tried to take a stand against them and he had been frustrated at every turn. Now, with no public position at all, he was powerless and alone. All that was left to him was the bank, and the blessing of his family and friends, who had never failed him.

Sherman got suddenly to his feet, feeling a surge of hope. He paced the study, wheezing slightly, but feeling the tightness in his chest begin to loosen. In the bank crisis of '55 he stood alone for a time and he feared he might go down, but he had survived it with the help of his friends. Richard Hammond, whom he had known since West Point, had loaned him public funds that he had no right to lend, on the strength of Sherman's word and their friendship. Hammond's wife was Sarah Hays, the sister of John Coffee Hays. The Hammonds lived on Rincon Hill, only a few streets away from the Shermans. The two couples often dined together, and on several occasions Jack Hays and his wife, Susan, had been present when Sherman and Ellen visited the Hammonds' home.

Tonight, at the Theater Trelayne, Hays had made a gesture of support for Sherman and Volney Howard and the forces that were opposed to the Committee of Vigilance. Sherman wondered what Coleman and the rest would say if they knew that he and Hays had spoken only of their children. A month ago, Susan Hays had given birth to a daughter, Kitty. Sherman's own son Willy had turned two the day before, and Hays had greeted the news that Ellen was expecting again with warmhearted congratulations. None of which detracted from the importance of the Texan's conspicuous gesture. On the basis of that gesture, and his acquaintance with Sherman, would Jack Hays be prepared to risk offending the president of the United States? Sherman allowed himself a cautious hope that the answer might be yes.

When he returned to bed, Ellen murmured, "Are you all right, Cump?" She turned over and put an arm across him when he lay back against the pillows. He could feel the swell of her pregnant belly against his side. Outside, the first light of dawn was turning the sky gray.

"Yes, dear," he assured her. "I am all right."

⚔ Chapter 36 ⚔

It was his fiancée up there last night!" Jim Dows bobbed in his chair, trying to make himself taller as he accused Calvert. "She told all the world that justice is dead in San Francisco!"

"She's a woman!" Calvert snapped. He was standing so that every man in room could see him clearly. He glared at Dows. "Do you think she understood what that play was about? To her it was a job of acting. We had a talk last night. Molly wept when I told her what she'd done. It nearly broke her heart."

It was half-past eight on Tuesday morning. Few of the Executive Committee had slept well, but all were present. The number of members was stable now at forty-two.

Calvert felt the sweat beading on his forehead but he did not want to reveal his nervousness by wiping it away. "There were nine hundred people in that theater. A damn sight less when we cleared out. Are you afraid of a few hundred men?" He thrust an arm at the ceiling over their heads, one finger outstretched. "If we ring that bell up there we'll have four thousand of our militia here in half an hour!"

Five days before, on the fifth of June, the bell from the Monumental firehouse on the Plaza had been brought to the warehouse and mounted on the roof. In 1851, the Monumental bell had been used to assemble the first Committee of Vigilance. On May 22 of this year it had sounded to call the members when King of William died. Henceforth, if needed, it would sound from atop Fort Vigilance, which was defended now by sandbag embrasures and a six-pound cannon.

Calvert looked around the table. "There's two ways to handle Trelayne. We can arrest him and let the whole city know we're afraid of him and his play. We could even trump up a crime to charge him with, but everyone from the governor to the chimney sweep would see through it. Or we can just act like we don't give a damn."

"And let the city laugh at us until we're powerless." Dows' tone was scornful.

"We can't go around arresting twenty or thirty people just because they poke fun at us! Not if you want to finish what we started out to do." Calvert sat down.

Coleman tapped his gavel lightly. "All in favor of arresting Thomas Trelayne?"

Even Dows kept his hand down. Stephen Kent leaned close to whisper in Calvert's ear, "Well done, Abel."

"Motion denied," Isaac Bluxome said. He made a notation on his writing tablet.

Grand Marshal Charles Doane brandished the flimsy sheet of the morning's *Herald*. "If you want to arrest someone, it's this Mercury we should go after! He says we're no better than Ethiopians!" He read from the paper. *"It would seem the Coal Men and the Flour Men and the Salt Pork Men of this city took umbrage at Mr. Trelayne's satire. They departed in a huff, while the blackamoors on the stage of the Theater Trelayne conducted themselves with more honor."*

Doane threw the paper on the table. "I won't be called a nigger by anyone!"

Able Calvert sat back in his chair, content to leave Mercury to the others. Trelayne was safe for the time being and that was what mattered to him. He wanted to risk nothing that might upset Molly again before the wedding. Her tears of remorse had been genuine enough, but when Calvert had turned his ire in Trelayne's direction, Molly's mood had changed suddenly. "You are not to hurt him, Abel!" she said. Calvert feared her anger, although he would never admit it to her or anyone else. She stood up to him, which was one reason he loved her. The only sure way he knew to turn aside her wrath was to give her what she wanted. He had promised to protect Trelayne and he had kept his promise. Given time, others might do for him what he longed to do with his own hands.

"If our friend Mercury simply stopped writing, who would know what happened to him until this is all over?" Jimmy Dows was saying. "No one knows who he is. He came out of nowhere."

Jonathan Frye smiled. "You're suggesting we could send him back where he came from and no one would be the wiser."

"I move we arrest the *Herald*'s correspondent known as Mercury," Tom Smiley said. Since the establishment of the Committee he had grown steadily more rotund and more truculent.

"Second the motion," said Frye.

"On what charge?" someone wondered aloud.

"Wanted for questioning," Smiley said. "Believed to be involved in election fraud. Having carnal knowledge of a Great Dane on Sunday. Whatever you like." This brought a few chuckles, but the mood around the tables remained sober.

"And when we find Mr. Mercury, we put him aboard the first vessel to the Sandwich Islands," Dows said.

"No." Miers Truett shook his head slowly. "At liberty, he might continue to taunt us. We imprison him until this is over."

Smiley nodded. "There's no need for a trial. We just lock him up. Deport him when it's over."

Stephen Kent had been briefly encouraged by the vote against arresting Trelayne, but he saw now that the members' anger had only been diverted to a different enemy. Since General Sherman's resignation, the mood of the Executive Committee had hardened perceptibly. "We agreed to arrest and try only men guilty of crimes against the people of this city," he said.

"Whoever this Mercury is, he skulks about like a thief and hides behind a nom de plume," Smiley said.

"As do most of those who write for the newspapers,"

Kent reminded him. "It's traditional." Kent looked to Abel Calvert for support, but Calvert was lost in his thoughts.

Isaac Bluxome cleared his throat. "I think a case can be made against this Mercury. His letters amount to sedition."

"Sedition involves undermining lawful authority," Kent objected. "We would have to have a legal opinion, wouldn't we?" He wished there were a good lawyer on the Committee, but the Committee had trampled the law and evaded a writ of the state's supreme court, and San Francisco's lawyers resented the vigilantes' intrusion in the realm of their learned expertise.

"How can we uphold the laws if Mercury undermines us?" Frye said.

"We agreed to respect freedom of the press," Kent said.

"Mr. Nugent is free to print what he likes," Coleman said. "But if it should happen that Mercury no longer offered him letters, how could he print them?"

Kent was at a loss. Every objection he raised was countered with a logic that was no logic at all. The Executive Committee had become its own authority. It made its own rules, changing them to suit the needs of the moment.

"Can we catch him, that's the question," Dows said. "The way I hear it, our watchdogs can't get his scent." He looked at Frye, who was the Executive Committee's liaison with the vigilance police.

"They have seen several men come late at night," Frye said. "Some of these men have taken pains not to be followed. It may be that our Mercury is using confederates to deliver the letters. The next time anyone behaves suspiciously when leaving the *Herald*, we'll bring him here for questioning. We'll arrest all of Mr. Nugent's correspondents if we have to. Once we have them in custody we can separate the wheat from the chaff."

"Move the question," Isaac Bluxome said from within his black beard.

Charles Gillespie and three other men joined Stephen Kent in opposing the motion. Coleman and Bluxome and Truett voted with the majority. Abel Calvert abstained.

"Motion passed." Bluxome made another notation. "Mr. Chairman, a member has requested an opinion on our liability to federal prosecution."

The statement caused a moment's silence. Tom Smiley shrugged. "What can the government in Washington do against us? Nothing, that's what. Even if Farragut and Wool turned against us, what could they do against six thousand men?"

Miers Truett glowered at Smiley. "You are advocating secession."

"We've talked of it in private," Jim Dows said coolly. Nothing in his tone conceded the great disparity between his physical stature and Truett's. "It's time we spoke of it here. Not armed insurrection, if it can be avoided. But separation, that's something to think about."

"He's right." Coleman surprised every man in the room by agreeing that the topic was timely.

Charles Gillespie cleared his throat. Since supporting Jason Beck's request for assistance from the Committee, he had hardly spoken in the meeting room. As one of the elder members and as one of the long-standing Committee of Thirteen, he commanded respect. "In fifty-one, neither the governor nor the local authorities opposed us," he said.

"Except for Jack Hays," Jim Dows reminded him.

"Nevertheless, we were never in defiance of the state," Gillespie said. "Now we are. The governor's proclamation accuses us of insurrection. There may come a time when we will have to answer that charge."

"There can be no federal prosecution if California is no longer in the federal Union," Jonathan Frye said.

Truett slapped the table with his enormous palm. "I did not join this Committee to take California out of the Union!"

"Nor did I," said Stephen Kent.

"It is pointless to discuss the issue unless we believe we have enough support in the state to do it," said Bluxome.

"The people are for us," Dows said.

"In this city, yes," Coleman said. "But we are fooling ourselves if we think that support is as lopsided in Sacramento and Stockton as it is here." He turned to Truett, who sat at his right hand. "Tell the members what you told me."

Truett swept his eyes around the tables as he spoke. "At the request of the chairman, I have made inquiries through our supporters in Sacramento. These include men on the governor's staff. Governor Johnson receives letters of support more than equal in number to those advocating our course. His correspondents cite the federal Constitution incessantly. They say we are trampling it. They say we are the enemies of liberty. A letter from Marysville says all the leading men of that town are ready to answer the governor's call to arms."

"They're exaggerating," Dows protested.

Truett turned his great head like a gun turret, bringing his gaze to bear on Dows. "If this state were evenly divided, will you take the responsibility for starting a civil war?"

Dows was silent and Stephen Kent spoke into the quiet. "Is this what we've come to? For fear of standing before a federal judge will we set the state on fire?"

The members looked at one another and looked away. Less than four weeks earlier, in the hot blood of righteousness, they had organized to avenge James King of William. Now a street brawl threatened to become the goad that could push California to the brink of secession.

"I won't be a party to this." Stephen Kent got suddenly to his feet. "Not to arresting a man for writing letters and not to this kind of talk. I resign from this body and from the Committee as a whole."

"There can be no resignations, Mr. Kent," Coleman said. "We agreed on that at the outset."

Kent strode to the door and turned back to face the members. "I joined this organization in good faith, to uphold the laws. You have broken that faith. I do not consider myself bound by the conditions imposed at the founding of this Committee. If any man feels I have questioned his honor, you know where to find me."

He went out the door and closed it behind him, leaving a rising current of conversation among the members.

Coleman struck the table forcefully with his gavel to restore quiet. "If we discipline Mr. Kent, the quarrel will become public and it will act to undermine this organization. Without objection, I recommend we let him go." He looked around the tables. No objection was offered. "If there are others who feel they can serve no longer . . ."

Again, no one spoke. Coleman tapped the table. "I think we have done enough for today. The meeting is adjourned."

Smiley took Jonathan Frye's arm and kept him behind as the members left the room. "Between the two of us, will you be satisfied with Mercury in a cell?"

Frye snorted derisively. "Nothing of the sort. Once we have this fellow in our hands it takes only a simple majority of the Executive Committee to hang him. I think we can manage that."

On the floor of the warehouse Stephen Kent spied Ned Rollick and beckoned to him. "Come along, Ned," he said when the clerk joined him. "It isn't the love of justice that moves these men. It is the love of power. I have resigned, and we're well quit of them."

Rollick swallowed hard. "Wouldn't it be best if I remain where I am, Mr. Kent?"

"Remain? I just told you I have resigned from the Committee."

"I'm only thinking of what's best for the firm, sir. Mr. Calvert has promised us a loan. Isn't it possible your resignation may endanger that understanding?"

"I suppose so." Kent hadn't begun to consider the consequences that might follow his resignation. "Damn them all! If only they would listen to reason!"

"If I stay, I may persuade Mr. Calvert to keep the agreement." Rollick spoke his thoughts as soon as they were formed. If Kent would let him stay he saw a way to assure his own future, no matter if the vigilantes disbanded voluntarily or were overthrown by their adversaries. "Another thing, sir. They may regard you as their enemy now. If I were to refuse to resign with you I would gain their confidence. I would be in a position to keep you informed of their doings, as they may affect our business."

Kent looked at Rollick with new respect. "You've a head on your shoulders, Ned."

Calvert and some other members of the Executive

Committee appeared at the head of the open stairway. "I must be seen to defy you," Rollick said quickly. "They must believe that I have chosen the Committee over my loyalty to you. I must defy you and you must discharge me. Of course I will remain in your service, but only we two will know it."

"Very well. Do what you must."

Rollick raised his voice in anger. "In these circumstances, I cannot remain in your employ, Mr. Kent!"

"The devil take you then, you damned whelp!" Kent turned on his heel and stalked from the warehouse without a glance at anyone.

The vehemence of Kent's attack took Rollick by surprise. He recoiled and stumbled into Abel Calvert. "Excuse me, sir," he said.

"What was that about, Rollick?"

Rollick drew himself up. "Mr. Kent wanted me to resign from this Committee. I told him I could not."

"Good for you," Calvert said. "We need every man. What is your position with us now?"

"I have assisted with the enrollment from the start, sir. I am in Captain Webb's company of our militia and have the honor to be elected a delegate from my company." The delegates from each company formed a Board of Delegates that reviewed the verdicts rendered in trials before the Executive Committee and ratified them before the sentences could be carried out.

"Mr. Calvert." Rollick adopted a humble tone. "May I hazard a guess that you agreed to assist Mr. Kent's purchase of *Pride of the Seas* because you judged it to be a good investment?"

"You may. And you'd be right." Calvert, as always, was direct.

"Well, sir, there is no reason Mr. Kent's resignation need endanger that investment. He has a sound mind for business, but he is proud, as you know. If I were to act as go-between, perhaps I could smooth things over."

"Perhaps you could," Calvert said. "And I would be in your debt. You see Kent this afternoon. Tell him I've put you on at my bank and you've come on my behalf. Say I hope our friendship won't be affected by this business today. And you tell him my offer stands. *Pride of the Seas* is in both our interests. He'll see that. You do that and I'll make you chief clerk, responsible to my partner, Winston."

"Thank you, sir. I will do my best."

As Calvert went to rejoin Coleman and the others, Ned Rollick could scarcely contain himself. He prided himself that he had an eye for opportunity, and in the Vigilance Committee he had found opportunity beyond his dreams. Early on, he had learned that being connected to a member of the Executive Committee had its advantages. Merely by hinting at the trust his employer placed in him, he had got himself elected to the Board of Delegates from his militia company. In time he had become an influential voice on the board, and he found that the responsibilities of his new position suited him well. After Cora and Casey were hanged and rumors had circulated that the Committee would soon disband, he had found himself reluctant to think of returning to Farnum & Kent as an ordinary clerk, even as personal clerk to Mr. Kent.

Thus far the Committee had not disbanded and Ned Rollick had kept an eye out for further opportunity. Now, thanks to Mr. Kent's resignation, he had come to the attention of Abel Calvert, who was one of the most influential bankers in the city. In time there was no telling where that connection might lead. In the blink of an eye, he was chief clerk to Calvert & Winston, and so long as he continued to serve Farnum & Kent as well, he would collect two salaries.

Ned Rollick was very pleased with himself.

Chapter 37

n Friday morning, at Sarah Rockwell's request, Trelayne invited Jason Beck and Melchior to attend the closing performance of *Caesar in California* that evening. Melchior had not yet seen the play and Jason found that he was interested to see it again, with Trelayne now playing Mark Antony and Edwin Booth as Brutus instead of Cassius. It was arranged that after the performance they would eat a late supper with Trelayne and then the three of them would make the rounds of the waterfront taverns, where four nights of searching had failed to turn up any trace of Tom Leary or his friend Billy. Jason and Melchior spent the days working on *Pride of the Seas*, which had been towed around to the Vallejo Wharf, and the nights in the taverns, and they got very little sleep.

When Jason and Melchior left the house after breakfast, Sarah gave Dickie a note for David Farren, who had already gone to his law office. When Dickie delivered the note, Farren hired him for the day, promising him five gold dollars to carry several messages, including one back to Mrs. Rockwell and one to the telegraph office, and that afternoon to perform a very important and highly confidential errand that required of him the utmost discretion.

The fog did not leave the city during the day. When Farren walked home late in the afternoon, small beads of mist gathered on his woolen cloak. He found Sarah in the kitchen, preparing dinner. She told him that Ingrid was dismissed for the evening and that Joshua Norton had accepted without question her explanation that there was to be a small private supper for a few old friends of Farren's. Norton had gratefully accepted her offer to bring him his meal on a tray.

With the arrangements confirmed, Farren waited in the parlor for the special guests who had been invited by means of messages carried by Dickie Howell. The first to arrive was Captain Richard Ashe, commander of Company A of the Blues. Ashe was the only one in whom Farren had confided the purpose of the dinner.

Soon after, Judge David Terry and John Nugent chanced to arrive at the same time, Nugent by foot and Terry on horseback. "Dick, you damned horse thief!" Terry burst out when he found Ashe in the parlor. The two men pounded each other on the back like the old comrades-in-arms they were, having served together in the Mexican War. "Is this a reunion, Farren?" Terry said. "Is that why you've brought us here?"

"In a way, Judge. But it is something more as well."

"Damned mysterious business instructions in your note. Take precautions not to be followed and all that."

"If you don't mind, I will wait until our other guests are here to reveal the purpose. Mr. Nugent, I'm David Farren, Volney Howard's law partner. I'm afraid you are invited as a private citizen, not as a representative of the fourth estate. I must ask you not to write about the conclave, but I promise that what you hear tonight will give you a unique understanding of what we hope will come about as a result."

"That is good enough for me, Mr. Farren," Nugent said. "Ah, now my interest is truly aroused," he added when Sherman appeared from the back hallway, having come in by way of the kitchen.

"Judge. Captain Ashe. Mr. Nugent." Sherman had approached the boardinghouse on foot from the west after taking a circuitous route through town, making certain that no one was following him. "What time is the Oakland boat?" he said to Farren.

Farren looked at the clock on the mantel. "It was due forty minutes ago. It may have been late."

Five minutes more passed before voices from the kitchen announced the backdoor arrival of the final guest. Sarah came first, showing the way along the hall, followed by Dickie Howell and John Coffee Hays.

"John! And Dick, and David too. This is a grand surprise." Hays strode forward to greet Nugent and Ashe and Terry. His thick hair was reddish brown. He had a light mustache and chin beard, but his large hazel eyes were his most arresting feature. They moved like a hawk's beneath prominent, arched brows, and they shone with an inner light.

Hay's animated reaction to the unannounced presence of three old friends was everything Sherman had hoped for. Hays had known Terry since they were boys together in Texas. Terry had served under Hays in the Texas Rangers, in the same company with Richard Ashe. John Nugent had chanced to pass through Texas in 1849 when Hays was preparing to leave for California. Nugent signed on with Hay's group for the difficult passage along the Gila River route and on to San Diego. On the way, Hays and Nugent became fast friends. In California, Hays and Dick Ashe had met again as colleagues when Hays was sheriff of San Francisco and Ashe sheriff of San Joaquin County.

Sherman had learned these facts in a quiet talk with Richard Hammond on Tuesday—the day after Trelayne's new play opened—in which Sherman had asked to know who Hays's special friends might be. Learning that the select group included Terry and Nugent was providential. Sherman was counting on that friendship now. The present company included a lawyer, a supreme court judge, and two former peace officers, both now serving in federal positions. Bound together by friendship and united in their respect for the law, these men were the natural enemies of the Committee of Vigilance.

"To what do I owe this pleasure?" Hays was pumping Nugent's hand. Even the usually reserved Terry was smiling. Disdainful in most company, he was modest before Jack Hays.

"This lad brought an invitation to my office," Nugent said, indicating Dickie Howell. "I have no idea why."

"We have General Sherman to thank, I believe," Terry said. "But why here?"

"The choice of a rendezvous was mine, Colonel," Farren said. Like Sherman, he was heartened by the warmth among the old friends. "General Sherman is known to the vigilants. As are you gentlemen. This house is not a place any of you frequent. Dickie, did you bring Colonel Hays the way I told you?" He had summoned Hays by telegram from his home in Oakland, across the bay, and instructed Dickie to meet him at the ferry.

"Yes, Captain. And I made certain no one was following."

"I thought I was being led through a labyrinth," Hays said. "If we were in Texas, I would recommend Master Howell to scout for the Rangers."

This pronouncement from the legendary Jack Hays made Dickie forget, for the moment, any thought of ever going to sea.

"I gather this is something more than a reunion of old comrades?" Hays looked from Farren to Sherman.

"So we have been advised," Terry said.

Sarah Rockwell delayed the need for explanations by opening the dining-room doors. "Gentlemen. Please come in. I will leave you alone when I have served so you can conduct your business."

Dickie helped Sarah serve the soup and he accompanied her when she retired to the kitchen after setting a silver bell by Farren, which she instructed him to ring when they were ready for the next course.

"I envy you, Captain," Hays said to Farren when he had tasted the soup. "When I first came to California, I did not eat this well."

"Mrs. Rockwell sets a fine table." Tonight there was wine on the table. Sarah had agreed at once when Farren suggested that relaxing her prohibition might improve the chance for a successful outcome to the clandestine gathering.

"I hope you will regard what promises to be an excellent dinner as some compensation for the manner in which you were brought here, Colonel," Sherman said to

Hays. "May I ask how much you know about the present state of affairs in this city?"

"The vigilance business began before I went off on my last survey," Hays said. "I read the newspapers, yours most carefully, of course, John." This earned him a grin from Nugent. "From the rest of the San Francisco papers, you would think our Savior and His Apostles were running the Committee of Vigilance, but you have balanced my view."

"I feel like a voice in the wilderness," Nugent said.

"What does the mining country think of the vigilance business, sir?" Farren asked Hays.

"They are not so caught up in it as the people here. The papers in the interior tell both sides of it."

"Could the rebels win over the rest of the state?" Sherman asked.

"Not by a long shot. Some of the miners have had occasion to practice vigilante justice themselves. They might side with this bunch if they're brought into it, but you could raise a regiment in Sacramento and Stockton to stand against them."

"We have taken steps in that direction," Farren said. "Governor Johnson has alerted General McCorkle's division in Butte County, as well as companies in Tulare and Coloma, to make themselves ready for service."

"We have raised the better part of a regiment here in San Francisco," Sherman said. "If we can arm them, it's our best hope of achieving surprise."

"Are your men ready?" Hays said.

"I can speak for the Blues," Ashe said. "Captain Farren's company and my own have stood firm since the first day. Give them a chance and they will show the vigilance rabble that we're more than Sunday soldiers."

Farren grinned. "Judge Terry hasn't given General Howard a moment's rest, sir. He is at our law offices every day with demands for more drilling and ideas on how to move against the Vigilance Committee when we have the arms."

"General Howard is not with us this evening," Hays observed.

"Considering your federal position, we thought it best that you not confer directly with him." Farren was re-

lieved when Hays nodded his acceptance of this explanation. The truth was that Volney Howard was out of his
depth in his new position. He had little military experience, and as a consequence the officers had little confidence in him. Morale in the state's militia was declining.
At Farren's urging, Howard had adopted Sherman's plan
to take the battery at Rincon Point. Unlike Sherman,
Howard would act only if he had a virtual certainty of
success.

"Governor Johnson has obtained a hundred and fifty
muskets in Sacramento," Terry said. "If necessary, we
can bring the arms of the other militia divisions here."

Sherman shook his head. "Too hard to do that without
arousing notice. They may not be in the majority outside
the city, but there are many who sympathize with the
vigilants. The word will get out and we will lose surprise.
Without it, there will be fighting."

"Why arm yourselves, if not to fight the vigilants?"
Hays's hawklike eyes probed Sherman.

"Fighting in this city will involve everyone, not just
the soldiers," Sherman said. "It will create wounds that
will last for a generation. Whatever else they are, the
vigilants are American citizens, not British redcoats or
Mexican dragoons."

"They oppose everything we stand for, sir," said
Farren.

"So they do," Sherman said. "But they are blind to
their failings. May God preserve this Union from righteous men of inadequate understanding."

"Must we avoid fighting even at the risk of seeing
these men take California out of the Union?" Farren had
two trump cards to play this evening. This was the first.

Hays was shocked. "There is no risk of that, surely."

"The idea has been spoken in their councils, sir. One
of the Executive Committee who has no liking for that
kind of talk approached Mr. Halleck. Mr. Halleck came
to see General Howard on behalf of the conciliation
group. The vigilants are taking discreet soundings
around the state to see if they have enough support to
create a Pacific republic."

"Good God," Sherman exclaimed softly. "You see
why, don't you? By that means, they would remove

themselves from the reach of American justice when this is all over."

"Make no mistake, Jack, they are rebels," Terry said to Hays. "They have established an armed force in opposition to the state. The government cannot enforce the laws."

"They have conducted themselves with discipline."

"Yes, while they broke the laws! I have never seen Judge Lynch dressed up so elaborately or attended by such a retinue, but I recognize his evil countenance, despite the fancy costume!"

"If they try to secede from the Union, there will be civil war," Hays said. "If they do not, if they disband quietly, wouldn't that be the best outcome?"

"The worst possible evil would be in allowing them to go unchallenged," Terry said. "We must make them back down publicly!"

"I have believed from the start that these flour merchants will give in if they're faced by a determined force," Sherman said. "I still believe it."

"But your force must be armed," Hays said.

"We will have the arms, sir," Richard Ashe said. "Enough for a few companies. We have Captain Farren to thank."

Farren took his cue. "The state's militia is owed over one hundred of the Army's muskets. They belong to us! General Wool is obliged by law to hand them over."

"Each year the state receives a quota of arms from the federal arsenal at Benicia," Ashe explained. "We haven't had all of this year's issue. The shortfall is in General Howard's division. The exact number due is one hundred thirteen. If the governor requests the arms, General Wool can't refuse."

"A hundred and thirteen from the Army, and a hundred and fifty in Sacramento," Sherman said. "Two hundred sixty-odd muskets and rifles, and we have that many more among the loyal companies in the city. Call it five hundred."

"We can arm six companies," Ashe said.

"You can arm eight if you give muskets or rifles to three fourths of the men in each company and be certain the rest have revolvers," Hays said. For seven years before the Mexican War, Hays and a few undermanned companies had protected the region between San Antonio and the Rio Grande from incursions by Mexican irregulars and the ever-present danger from Comanches. Without Samuel Colt's revolvers, the job would have required several hundred more men.

"You have brought me here for a purpose," Hays said now. "What would you have me do?"

Sherman had been waiting for Hays to pose the question. "If we can avoid involving you, we will. In extremity, the governor will request your aid, unofficially, to appeal to the Texans in the vigilance ranks."

Terry understood Sherman's plan now. "There are hundreds of our boys in the Committee, Jack. Maybe a thousand. A word from you could be decisive."

The young men of Texas had been called on disproportionately to fight the Mexican War, which took place on their doorstep. At the war's end many of the veterans, fresh from one adventure, set off on another when they heard of the discovery of gold in California. Texans represented a significant presence in San Francisco and in the ranks of the vigilance militia.

Hays looked from Terry to Sherman. "By asking the Texans to change sides, you think I might swing the balance?"

This was the decisive moment. Sherman had prepared his appeal with the utmost care. "Above all, we want to avoid fighting. Our aim is to force the rebels to capitulate publicly in the face of the state's militia. We believe an appeal from you to the Texans, and to the citizens generally, might weaken support for the vigilants at the decisive moment."

"You have thought this out," Hays said.

"As best I am able."

"You have the instincts of a politician."

"God forbid! You will see me in hell before you see me in politics, Colonel."

Hays laughed. "You're a man after my own heart, Sherman. I was offered the governorship of Texas and I ran for my life. But I believe your brother does not share your views."

Sherman scowled. "I did my best to encourage John

in a respectable line of work, but I failed." Hays laughed again, and Sherman smiled in spite of himself. Two years earlier, John Sherman had been elected to Congress from Ohio. Since then, Tecumseh Sherman had held his tongue in his correspondence with his brother, but his general impression of politics and politicians had not changed.

Hays ran a hand through his thick hair. He glanced at Terry and Ashe, who, like Sherman, were awaiting his reply. "I serve in my present position at the pleasure of the president. But I will speak out to prevent civil warfare if the governor calls on me. When will you arm your men?"

It was Farren who answered. "It will take some days to get the arms from General Wool, sir. I have telegraphed Secretary of State Douglass. He is preparing the request. We should be ready to move by the end of next week."

A soft knock sounded at the door to the kitchen.

"Who can that be?" Sherman wondered.

Sarah Rockwell put her head into the dining room. "Are you ready for the fish?"

The men looked at their soup plates, which had been empty for some time now. When the fish was served, accompanied by champagne, Judge Terry raised his glass.

"Gentlemen, I give you the committee of vigilance." To the surprised looks this proposal aroused, he replied with a sly smile. "Oh, I don't mean the mercantile cabal we seek to overthrow. *We* are the true committee of vigilance, my friends. We here and two others: Mercury, our will-o'-the-wisp gadfly, who stings like a wasp, and Mr. Trelayne, whose play states the issue so eloquently. We are the vigilant few who understand the threat posed by these men. We stand for the Constitution and those it protects: the individual against the tyranny of the majority; the established authorities, however imperfect, against the usurpers. To us, gentlemen, the vigilant minority. May we bring the despots down."

he day of Abel Calvert's wedding to Molly Gray dawned without a dawn. The thick fog that seemed almost to touch the church steeples brightened only grudgingly. At mid-morning there were raindrops on the windowpanes and Molly was in despair.

"Oh, Sarah, my wedding day is ruined!"

They were in the bedroom of Abel Calvert's house. The grandfather clock in the parlor below had recently struck ten. The bedroom windows overlooked North Beach. Across the water, Alcatraz Island was barely visible through the mists.

Sarah had brought Ingrid to help with the wedding dinner, which was her gift to Molly. Calvert was neat for a bachelor, but he knew nothing about hosting a social event in his home. With his grateful consent, Sarah had engaged two women to cook and Ingrid to serve while she herself oversaw all the arrangements for the meal.

"It will be a lovely day, even if we never see the sun." Sarah did her best to sound encouraging, but her mood matched the weather. "Come here and stop fretting."

She began to unbutton the tiny, satin-covered buttons at the back of Molly's wedding dress. Four days earlier, it had fit Molly perfectly. Today, the waist was loose on her and it wrinkled as she walked.

Abel Calvert had charged Madame duRoi, the foremost dressmaker in the city, to make the most beautiful dress ever seen in San Francisco, and Madame duRoi had fulfilled her commission. It was cream silk taffeta with flounces of gold brocade and a lace-trimmed bodice that matched the lace of the veil, which fell to Molly's knees in back. Although the wedding was to take place in the afternoon, the dress was in the evening style, with a low neck and short sleeves, to show off Molly's graceful neckline as well as her bosom.

"I am being punished," Molly said.

"Whatever for?"

"For taking the part in Tommy's play. I knew perfectly well what it was about. I knew it would anger Abel, but I took the part anyway. I wanted to show him that I have a mind of my own. Of course when he hauled me off to that hotel I told him I had no idea that Tommy was poking fun at the vigilantes."

"Did he believe you?"

"I am a good actress, Sarah. But I should be better to him." She stood silent for a time as Sarah worked at the dress, trying to fashion two small tucks in the waist.

"Abel kept his word, you know," Molly said. "He didn't see me all week. I wrote him a note saying I wouldn't marry him if he excluded my friends. I sent him to you to be sure you all would come. All but Tommy. Abel was adamant about Tommy."

"He was very gracious."

Abel Calvert had called on Sarah Wednesday afternoon to apologize for his behavior at the theater and to renew the invitations to the wedding ceremony for Sarah's guests. He had made special mention of Captain Beck, but none at all of Trelayne. Sarah had risked a cautious question about the intentions of the Vigilance Committee, which Calvert had answered frankly, saying that their business was almost done, but he added that some of the members were enjoying themselves and would put off disbanding as long as they could.

Sarah had dared nothing more, although there was much more she wanted to know. She could not give up the habit of pursuing information about the enemy's plans, although she had not written as Mercury since Monday night, after the opening of *Caesar in California*. On Tuesday, in the course of venting his wrath at the vigilance organization, Stephen Kent had told Jason that the Executive Committee had issued an arrest warrant for Mercury. Jason had mentioned the warrant, and Kent's resignation from the Committee, to Sarah, as evidence that the vigilantes were more concerned with arresting a letter writer than an incendiary who had burned a clipper ship on San Francisco Bay.

Sarah had seen at once that it was Trelayne, her courier, who was in the greatest danger.

"You can't stop now!" Trelayne had said. "You've set this town on its ear."

"They have hanged two men. There is no telling what they might do if they think you're Mercury."

"But I'm not. Not really." Then he had realized the implication of what he said. "I'm sorry, Sarah. I'm a selfish lout. I would never let them suspect it was you."

"And I can't put you in danger to protect me."

"But don't you see? We have nothing to fear! They're looking for one man who visits John Nugent and hands him the letters. I have been half a dozen men already! I could be a woman if it comes to that. You write your letters. I'll lead these miserable stranglers a merry chase."

Despite his repeated urging she had refused, unwilling to endanger his life. Readers of the *Herald* had found no letters from Mercury for four days now. In the *Bulletin*, Tom King had commented on Mercury's silence and offered it as proof of cowardice.

"It is so easy to control Abel, really," Molly said now. "He hasn't had me yet, Sarah. And he wants me terribly. I don't know how he can stand the waiting."

"You are shameless."

"How else can I make him do what I want? Oh, I'll never make it through the day in this corset!"

"Hold still, Molly, for heaven's sake! You'll have to be careful of these pins. Wait, I know. Where's that girl? Ingrid!"

When Ingrid's dull face appeared in the doorway a moment later, Sarah sent her to fetch a wine cork.

"It is a pretty dress, isn't it" Molly said.

"It is beautiful and you know it. I would die to be seen in a dress like this. Now do keep still."

"What was your wedding like, Sarah?"

"It was lovely." Sarah's tone belied her words.

"I'm sorry. I didn't mean to remind you of Haven."

"It's not that. I had a beautiful dress that cost a fortune, and I had a miserable time. Haven paid for the dress and his mother found out. 'If that girl can't afford a decent dress, why doesn't her mother make her one,' she said."

"He told you that?"

"Yes."

"Men are simpletons. Why would he tell you something to make you feel bad?"

"Haven was not wise in the ways people have of hurting one another. He was a little naive, for a man of his background." Sarah smiled. "My mother would think I was putting on airs if she heard me talk like that. 'French words is it now, Sally?' she'd say. 'Plain, honest American words ain't good enough for you?' Poor Mother. They treated her like a servant at the wedding, and me too, some of them."

"They sound like a rotten bunch. You're better off without them. Oh, I don't mean—I know you loved Haven."

"They bullied him too. We came to California to get away from them. He wasn't practical and grasping and interested in making money more than anything in the world. He liked to paint watercolors. Did I ever tell you that? I think he would have liked to be an artist."

Ingrid returned with a wine-stained cork.

"Thank you, Ingrid. Remind Mrs. Halloran to baste the roast every quarter hour."

"Yes, ma'am."

Sarah broke small pieces of cork and fitted them on the points of the pins, which were inside the waist, hidden in the tucks. When she was done she rebuttoned the dress and stood back. "There. Walk around." Molly moved tentatively about the room, watching Sarah anxiously.

"It's perfect. Really, Molly. You have never looked so beautiful."

"Lord, Molly, if that isn't the truth." Calvert stood in the doorway.

"Abel! Get out!" Molly stamped her foot.

"I ain't in, sweet thing. Just came to see how you were feeling." Calvert wore a smart black tailcoat and trousers, and an embroidered waistcoat of burgundy silk over his boiled and starched shirtfront. From his hair—which was slicked back with rosewater pomade—to his varnished boots, he looked every inch the prosperous banker and the proud groom.

"You mustn't see me in the wedding dress before the ceremony! Go, Abel, please!"

"I'll see you in it and out'n it soon enough. What's the difference?"

Sarah moved to the door and closed it partway to hide Molly from his view. "It's bad luck, Mr. Calvert."

"The fact is, Mrs. Rockwell, I don't know what to do with myself."

"Then go out of doors and smoke a cigar, or walk about," Sarah urged him. "Reflect on the loss of your bachelorhood and what you're about to gain. But do go, or Molly will be a nervous wreck."

"Sorry, Molly my love," Calvert called past Sarah. "You're prettier than a summer morning in the mountains, and I'm the luckiest man on earth. Don't let an old superstition fret you."

Molly sank onto the bed as Sarah closed the door. "My aunt Maude's husband saw her in her wedding dress before the wedding. He died six months later."

"Get up from there or you'll wrinkle the dress," Sarah ordered her. "How did he die?"

Molly stood. "It was a bullet. At Chapultepec, I think."

"You can't blame a bullet in the Mexican War on his seeing your aunt Maude in her wedding dress. Now cheer up, or I will pinch your cheeks to make them red."

"I just want some sign that I'm doing the right thing. Is that too much to ask?"

"The only sign you need is in your heart, Molly. What does it say?"

"It says I've gone too far to turn back."

The sun appeared as the first guests arrived, just before noon. In a short time the fog and clouds receded beyond the crest of Russian Hill and a circle of blue sky wreathed the city. When Sarah stepped out of doors, it seemed to her that the clear sky was centered on Calvert's house, and that all the bad omens were confounded.

A Negro groom stood at the gate to hold the carriage horses steady while the passengers stepped down. The guests gathered in the garden while waiting for the ceremony to begin. They drank champagne and exclaimed at the good turn in the weather, and they admired the house. It was built of bricks brought around the Horn from Philadelphia, a solid, respectable two-story house for a solid, respectable banker. On the south side, a rose garden was enclosed by young boxwood hedges that had taken hold quickly in the mild climate. On the west, a brick terrace was situated to catch the afternoon sun. It gave a view of Russian Hill and the headlands of Marin.

When the members of Trelayne's theatrical company arrived, the guests formed into two distinct groups, the actors taking over the rose garden and the groom's friends moving around to the terrace. Among the later arrivals, Thomas Maguire joined the actors, as did Joshua Norton and Dickie Howell, who walked over with Jason from Sarah's boardinghouse. When Stephen and Ethel Kent entered the garden, Calvert emerged from the house to greet them.

"Mrs. Kent, Stephen. Captain Beck. Glad you could come, all of you. How is the ship progressing?"

"We've the masts all stepped," Jason said. "We'll begin hoisting the yards tomorrow."

"She's a fair vessel," Kent said. "And she'll be fitted out better than any other ship on the seas, thanks to you."

Calvert was plainly nervous. He put his hands in his pockets, then took them out and straightened his coat. When Sarah approached carrying a silver tray laden with brimming champagne glasses, he said, "I hope the sunshine has put a stop to Molly's talk of bad luck, Mrs. Rockwell."

"Molly is feeling much better. And I think the bridegroom could be allowed a glass of champagne before the service."

Calvert reached eagerly for a glass, drained it, and took another.

Jason accepted a glass and walked with Sarah as she moved to the next cluster of guests. "No luck?" she said.

"No luck." On Monday morning, Trelayne's tale of meeting Tom Leary was so vivid, Jason had felt certain that finding the Irishman would be a matter of hours. Since then it had proved no easier to catch incendiaries with names than without them. The only Irishman called Tom to be found at the Noggin of Ale was the bartender, who came near to weighing as much as Melchior. The searchers had grown bolder as the week progressed, asking for Irish Tom and English Billy in all the grogshops and doss houses, Jason with Jolly Jim and Melchior with Trelayne, but so far as the waterfront was concerned, Tom and Billy were phantasms.

"Fit out your ship," Sarah said. "Those men will meet their judgment in good time, whether you find them or not. Oh, thank heaven. Here is the minister at last, and Su-Yan as well. Excuse me."

She set her tray on a rattan lawn table and went to greet the minister. Su-Yan Quan was trotting down the road between the shafts of his vegetable cart as the Reverend Mayhew LaFarge descended from his buggy and passed the reins to the groom. LaFarge was a prematurely balding young man of modest stature. Since coming to San Francisco, Sarah had attended three weddings at which he presided. He had an aptitude for ritual and managed to make the traditional service seem fresh and joyful each time.

LaFarge tipped his hat. "Everything is in good time, I trust, Mrs. Rockwell?"

"The guests are here, Reverend. We will begin as soon as the bride is ready."

LaFarge surveyed the house and grounds. "A grand day for a wedding. And I think the garden will serve very well. Mr. Calvert explained his theology to me, and I am comfortable with it."

"He has never explained it to me."

"This is Mr. Calvert's church." LaFarge spread his arms wide to encompass the land and the bay and the sky. "He told me of his years in the great mountains, living among the savages and hunting the wily beaver. The Indians' reverence for nature impressed him. They consider it unnatural that the white man closes himself away from nature to worship God. I must say, I see some wisdom in that. And here we are, under God's sky, enjoying His heavenly light."

"We're very lucky to have the sun," Sarah agreed. "Have some champagne, Reverend. I'll bring Molly as soon as I can."

"I don't mind if I do, thank you. Such a lovely day. God smiles on the sacrament of marriage." LaFarge trotted into the garden with an eagerness that Sarah suspected was prompted as much by the promise of champagne as his enthusiasm to perform the sacrament. She scolded herself for the uncharitable thought and stepped into the road where Su-Yan was waiting near the guests' carriages.

"I am sorry to be late, Miss Rockwell," the Chinaman said. "I must certainly provide the best vegetables for a wedding."

"I never doubted you for a moment. Just take them around back and give Mrs. Halloran what she wants."

Su-Yan's smooth forehead knit up with concern. "An Irish lady is cooking for the wedding? Not a wise choice, Miss Rockwell. Irish ladies cook vegetables too long."

"Is that an old Chinese saying?"

"A new Chinese saying. Made in San Francisco by Quan Su-Yan." Su-Yan smiled. "But it is true, certainly. It will pass into the wisdom of the Celestial Kingdom."

"I will tell Mrs. Halloran not to overcook the vegetables."

"You are very wise."

"If you will stop by my house this week, I will pay you then. I didn't bring any money, and I don't want to bother Mr. Calvert now."

"The bridegroom is not wise in money matters on the wedding day. He thinks only of the secret passage where he will soon find great joy."

"You are incorrigible. Go and give those things to Mrs. Halloran, or our guests will go hungry. Oh, my God." Sarah was looking past Su-Yan, up the road that led to the city. Trelayne was coming down the hill dressed in his finest suit. His hat was tipped back and he strolled with a jaunty gait, as if he hadn't a care in the world. Sarah started forward, but Abel Calvert passed her at a brisk walk, and then even if she had run she could not have prevented the meeting.

"What are you doing here?" Calvert demanded while there was still twenty feet between himself and Trelayne.

"I have your invitation." Trelayne innocently produced the folded paper that the messenger boy had delivered on Monday, along with the rest of the invitations for Sarah's house.

"That was sent before—You know damn well what I mean."

Trelayne's jaunty air vanished and he seemed to diminish in size. "I don't apologize for the play, Calvert. I abhor what you and your vigilante friends are doing. But Sarah—Mrs. Rockwell—said this was to be an event free of politics. A day of truce. I hoped I might accept this invitation in that spirit, to celebrate the marriage of a dear friend. And to wish you both well."

Calvert was taken aback by Trelayne's appeal, which was made in an attitude of genuine humility. From the terrace and the garden, the guests were watching the confrontation.

"Very well," he said. "For Molly's sake." He offered his hand and Trelayne took it, plainly grateful. A few moments later, when the guests gathered in the rose garden for the ceremony, Calvert saw that the two groups were mingling freely now. The truce imposed by the wedding day had been transformed by his magnanimity into a mood of true conciliation, and he felt a measure of satisfaction fitting to the occasion.

The Reverend LaFarge conducted the service with an almost reckless enthusiasm, and his zeal was contagious. He stood at the center of the garden facing the sun and the assembled guests, his surplice flapping in the breeze that had come up when the fog cleared. Jason remarked to Sarah that the good reverend looked like a small ship under sail.

Abel Calvert took his place before the minister, Molly appeared small and exquisite on Joshua Norton's arm, and the enthusiasm with which she received her husband's kiss at the close of the ceremony drew murmurs of appreciation from the gathering. Trelayne joined in the conversation at the wedding dinner and genially deflected a few barbs concerning his play that were thrown his way by members of the Committee of Vigilance. They made jovial remarks about Mercury's sudden silence, but William Tell Coleman scowled at those who raised dangerous topics at a time of celebration, and the moment passed.

The guests were served at three tables set up in the dining and sitting rooms, and a fourth outside on the brick terrace. The ladies looked with awe and some fear at an Indian lance over the fireplace in the sitting room when they learned that Abel Calvert had won it by killing its former owner.

Sarah oversaw the service in the kitchen, approving each dish before it was passed. When she emerged to join the guests, the meal was nearly over. She found Jason eating alone on the terrace, watching the sails on the water.

"It's a good breeze." She sat beside him.

"Aye." He returned to himself from far away. " 'Tis a good breeze. We might have another sail in your *Katahdin* on a day like this."

"I would like that."

From where they sat they could see the little sloop tossing at her mooring, as if eager to test the wind.

"The dinner is excellent," Jason said. "You'll make some man a fine wife." He paused with his fork halfway to his mouth. "I suppose that was a stupid thing to say."

Sarah smiled. "No more stupid and thoughtless than most things men say to women. For some reason I find it difficult to be angry with you."

"You didn't throw me out of your house when I joined the vigilantes. I'm grateful for that. Once I find a good anchorage I don't like to move about."

"I thought that moving about was all a sailor wanted. Going from place to place."

"At sea the ship is my home wherever the winds take me. Here I'm a castaway." He started to say something more but returned to his food instead, wiping the plate with a crust of bread and popping it into his mouth.

"I always think you're keeping something from me."

"I am." He regarded her steadily. "Will you walk with me when this is over? May I walk you home?"

"Sarah! There you are!" Molly had removed her veil. Her black hair was pinned up in an elegant coil. A few loose ends blew in the wind as she stepped onto the terrace. "Come see! You too, Captain. We have a musical band from the Monumental fire company! It's Mr. Coleman's wedding gift. We're going to have dancing!"

The Monumental Engine Company's brass band proved most adept at martial airs suitable for a company of volunteer firemen marching on parade, but they managed some lilting tunes, and the wedding guests danced willingly to the music, martial or otherwise, with high spirits. Abel Calvert demonstrated a mountain trapper's jig, which encouraged several of the Theater Trelayne's company to attempt a mazurka they had learned from a troupe of Polish dancers who had performed at the Music Hall some months before. These displays did much to persuade the more staid guests that dancing on the brick terrace or the lawn of the garden was acceptable and tame.

At the close of an energetic polka, Jason and Sarah found themselves near Molly, who had danced with David Farren. She was flushed and happy. "Miss Gray?" Jason bowed to the bride. "I'm sorry. Mrs. Calvert? May I have the honor?"

Molly moved into Jason's arms and he took her gracefully across the brick terrace as the band began another tune. "You dance beautifully, Captain Beck," Molly said.

"You are beautiful even when you're standing still, Molly."

"If you had paid me such gallant compliments when we first met, I might have married you."

"Instead, you warned me that I would want you no longer. You said you were about to do something foolish. I'm glad you changed your mind."

"Oh, but I didn't, Captain. And now your eye is set on another."

"Am I that transparent?"

"Only to me. Does she know?"

"We understand each other, I think."

"I'm not sure she understands you."

"I will be going to sea before long."

"And so you won't tell her of your feelings?"

"It wouldn't be fair."

Molly frowned. "Why do men think women cannot make up their own minds? Tell us how you feel, and we will know if it is right to match your feelings with our own."

Jason felt a hand on his shoulder and he found Trelayne by his side. Trelayne bowed to Molly. "Would the most lovely bride in all of California favor a poor wretch with a dance?"

Molly regarded him with caution. "Have you been drinking, Tommy?" His eyes were bright, and she recognized the flowery eloquence that wine brought out in him.

"Only enough to cushion my fall from grace, dear Molly. I am on the rocks of despair, but I will make repairs to the leaking hull and sail on alone. One dance with the bride and I will make my departure."

Molly moved into his arms. "One dance." She saw that Abel was watching them and she smiled pleasantly as Trelayne guided her away. "How did the rest of the week go?"

"Good houses, and the play went well enough. I could never match your Antony."

"I loved it, Tommy. And I enjoyed tweaking the noses of the mighty."

"It is more than a game, Molly. These men are a threat to liberty."

Molly made a face. "Don't exaggerate. They're just like boys, playing at king of the castle. Oh, Tommy, how will I ever stand all those merchants and bankers? They'll come to dinner and I will be expected to play hostess while they talk of money."

"It's what you wanted, my love." There was a hint of malice in Trelayne's voice.

"Don't be mean. I want us to be friends."

"You'll be going to Maguire now."

"It's best, for a while. Abel is jealous and angry. When some time has passed, you can offer me a role as a guest star. Just for a week. Like Mr. Booth in our play. We can start like that, and in time I will rejoin the company."

Trelayne was shocked by the calmness with which she planned to deceive her husband. "There is still hope for us, then?"

"You are part of my life, Tommy."

"Part, but not all."

"You couldn't give me what I want. You said so yourself." She stood back in his arms to look at him, puzzled by his manner.

"You haven't a particle of morality," he said.

"Tommy!"

The change in Trelayne was sudden and frightening. He held her close and hissed in her ear. "Do you think I want to be your paramour? A harem slave for the grand respectable lady?"

"We could still see each other. I thought you wanted that." She kept her voice low and guided him farther from the other couples on the terrace.

"I wanted to change your mind! I wanted you to see what you mean to me! Do you really think I could share you with him?" For a moment Trelayne's expression displayed his true feelings and Molly was stunned by the pain she saw there.

"Do you think I will be kept on a string while you open your legs for Abel Calvert, and him laughing behind my back because he stole you from me?" Trelayne pushed Molly away from him violently. She reeled into Jason and Sarah, nearly falling. Nearby, Calvert was dancing with Ethel Kent. He excused himself curtly and started toward Molly, but Trelayne reached her first.

"So sorry, Mrs. Calvert. I tripped on the bricks," he said for all to hear. Then he spoke for her alone. "Now watch and see what kind of a man your trapper really is."

"I think you had better go," Calvert said.

"Just what I had in mind. My muse is calling." Trelayne's tone was mocking. "I am working on an droll piece about a newlywed couple. You must come to the opening."

"We'll be in the mountains on our honeymoon," Calvert's voice was taut.

Trelayne stepped close to Calvert and said softly. "I'm

sure you'll enjoy the honey. Your wife is a skillful whore."

Before Trelayne could move or draw a breath he was flat on his back on the brick terrace with Abel Calvert atop him and a large skinning knife at his throat.

"Abel, no!" Molly screamed.

"Calvert!" Jason's cry was a warning. His hand found his own knife at the small of his back, beneath his coat. The sound of alarm in his voice brought Melchior from the garden at a run. When he saw Jason was in no danger, he came to a stop.

"I am not armed," Trelayne said with extraordinary calm, considering his position and Calvert's rage.

"Mr. Calvert!" Miers Truett reached Calvert's side in three huge steps and took him by the shoulders. "This is not how gentlemen settle their differences."

"Gentlemen be damned!" Calvert exclaimed. "He said my—" He saw now that everyone was watching him, the ladies keeping well back while the men gathered around. He released Trelayne and got up. In the course of his rising, his knife returned to a sheath somewhere at his left side, hidden by his tailcoat.

"All right then, we'll settle it like gentlemen." Calvert was in control of himself now, but there was no disguising the malice in his eyes as he watched Trelayne dust himself off. "Mr. Trelayne has insulted my honor."

"What did he say?" Tom Smiley demanded.

"I will not repeat his words."

"There is no need," Coleman said. "Mr. Trelayne, I remind you that this is Mr. Calvert's wedding day. In deference to the occasion, I beg you to retract whatever you may have said."

Trelayne smirked. "When hell freezes over, Mr. Coleman, or when your band of usurpers returns power in this city to the elected officials. Whichever happens first."

Coleman reddened and turned to Abel Calvert. "Can you forgive what Mr. Trelayne said, as a benevolent gesture on your wedding day?"

Calvert's eyes flicked to Molly. "I cannot. I demand the recourse that a gentleman has the right to expect."

"I can't be involved," Coleman said. "Not in the present state of things. But there is nothing to prevent you calling on others to act in your behalf."

"They're talking about a duel," Sarah said, as much to herself as to Molly.

"No," Molly said. "No! Abel, you mustn't!"

Calvert turned on her, and his face was very hard. "You are my wife now, ma'am. This is men's business and I will thank you to keep out of it."

"One more thing, gentlemen," Coleman added. "Dueling is against the law. Your meeting must not take place in San Francisco or the Committee will be forced to take note of it. Mrs. Coleman?" He held out his arm to his wife and conducted her to their carriage.

"Captain Beck?" Trelayne addressed Jason. "Would you be so good as to act for me? And you, Mr. Norton?"

Jason hesitated. He had never been involved in a formal duel and had only a vague notion of what was expected. Men of the sea generally settled their quarrels quickly and brutally, without formalities.

Norton sensed Jason's doubts. "Honor calls," he said.

"All right."

"Stephen?" Calvert looked to Stephen Kent.

"Me?" Kent was taken off guard. "I had rather—yes. Of course." He shook off Ethel's hand as she tried to hold him back.

"And Jonathan?" Calvert turned to Frye.

"With pleasure." Frye looked at Trelayne as if he would like to fight the duel himself.

"Ladies," Abel Calvert addressed the women. "I am sorry this occasion has been shamed by such an event, but my honor will not allow me to let a gross insult pass. Mrs. Calvert and I beg you to enjoy yourselves awhile longer." To Molly he said, "You will of course remain with our guests." He left the terrace and went into the house. When he was gone, Trelayne took Jason and Norton to one side, spoke with them briefly, and left the grounds without another word to anyone.

hen the seconds were done conferring, the wedding party dispersed quickly, the mood of celebration irrevocably broken. Sarah helped the hired women clean up and put the dishes away, and when that was done she sent them home and dismissed Ingrid and made one last effort to see Molly. Molly had locked herself in the bedroom, refusing to see Calvert unless he called off the duel, and Calvert had taken himself off to the shore at North Beach. Sarah talked to Molly through the bedroom door but Molly would not open it, so Sarah left the house to its misery and started for the boardinghouse. She found Jason seated on a rock by the roadside, watching the boats on the bay. "Dueling is a barbaric relic," she said.

"It is the way of things. Would you rather Calvert had cut Trelayne's throat then and there?"

Sarah pulled her cloak about her, falling into step beside him as he started up the street. The afternoon was growing long, and thick clouds were rolling over the top of Russian Hill. Already they covered the city and extended out over the bay. It was as if the brief interlude of blue skies and sunshine had been a mistake, now corrected.

"In the morning Tommy will be sober. He'll come to his senses." She tried to put more confidence in her words than she felt. "Anyway, Abel and Molly will be gone on their honeymoon."

"Affairs of honor must be settled within twenty-four hours, Mr. Norton says. Kent and Frye agree."

"You men and your honor! That custom is designed to promote duels. It allows no time for common sense to prevail."

"Honor isn't concerned with common sense."

"It will be tomorrow, then?"

"Aye. In the morning."

"Abel Calvert fought Indians! Tommy is no match for him."

"Trelayne will be all right."

Sarah sought further encouragement. "Are you sure?"

"Trelayne will be all right. There will be no one killed." Trelayne had told Jason and Norton what weapons he chose before leaving Calvert's house. Norton was on his way now to the theater, where he would meet with Trelayne and select them.

"Can you promise me there will be no bloodshed?"

"As nearly as I can promise anything, Sarah, I promise you no one will be killed."

They had reached the crest of the low rise that separated North Beach from the city. The breeze ruffled Sarah's skirts. She wrapped her arms about herself as they walked in silence the rest of the way to the boarding-house. She led Jason through an alley and into the fenced garden, where the last of Thursday's wash was still hanging in the drying ground because she hadn't had the time to take it in. The huge iron pots where the sheets and whites were boiled stood cold now, like the abandoned drums of some long-gone native tribe. They were silent reminders between wash days, nagging Sarah by their presence every time she walked to the privy. Her back was still sore from the washing.

"Will you help me for a moment? Just put out your arms." She pulled the wash from the line and hung the linens over Jason's outstretched arms. "I hope no one notices a ship's captain helping a poor woman take in her wash."

"I won't mind if they do."

"You were going to tell me what it is that you have kept from me," Sarah said.

"So I was."

In the kitchen, she laid the linens in a large basket where they would keep clean until she folded them and put them away. Tomorrow afternoon, she and Ingrid would do the ironing. She stirred the coals in the stove and put in a few pieces of kindling. At last she turned to him. "Well?" she said.

"First I was here for only so long as it took to unload my ship and put her in ballast for Canton. Then we seemed to be on opposite sides in this vigilance business."

"You're not a part of the vigilance business, Jason. You are after the man who burned your ship. I don't want you to hang him if you catch him, but I understand your need to find him." She added more wood to the fire. On the back of the stove, the kettle began to mutter.

"You still haven't told me your secret. You have told my why you kept it, but not what it is."

He waited until she replaced the lid on the stove and adjusted the drafts, and turned to face him. "I have feelings for you, Sarah."

"And I have feelings for you." The kitchen clock ticked off some part of a minute. "Am I too bold?"

"A sailor is accustomed to women who speak frankly."

"But not ladies who do."

"No."

She moved the kettle to the side of the stove, where it would keep warm. "I have told you before that I was raised a sailor's daughter. Now I want to tell you something else. I have been with only one man in my life. There was no one before my husband and no one since." She moved to his side and took his hand. "Come."

She took him to her bedroom, wishing it were more feminine somehow, more like a lady's boudoir. She drew the curtains, and the light in the room became intimate.

There was a moment, when he helped her unfasten her corset, when she felt awkward and embarrassed and feared she had been too rash. To her wonder, all the uncertainty left her as she stepped out of her chemise and stood naked before him. He had removed only his coat, but although he was clothed and she was not she felt perfectly at ease. She helped him now, first with his cravat and then his trouser buttons.

"I had a husband once," she reminded him. "I know how men's clothing is fastened. It's all such a mystery at first. So different from women's things."

"Women's things are impossible."

"We seem to have dispensed with mine easily enough." She removed the pins that held her hair and it fell to her shoulders.

"Aye. And it's a shame you ever cover this body with clothing." He touched her breasts. She closed her eyes and swayed against his hands.

They were together then, first standing on the woven rag carpet beside the bed, his skin warm to her touch, then in the bed. She was not sure how they moved from one place to the other and she had only a limited memory of what took place on the bed where she had slept alone since coming to San Francisco. She lost herself in him, relearning the pleasure and the comfort that were to be found in a man's arms and finding more of both than she had known with Haven. At the end, she heard someone crying out. It came from far away, but the voice was hers.

When she was herself again, Jason was holding her. His chest was shaking and he was laughing silently.

"Am I so comical?"

"Oh, Sarah. You have restored my faith."

"In what?"

"In God and man. And woman."

She raised her head to look at him.

"At sea," he said, "some resort to unnatural practices in the absence of women. Many, I suppose. Some keep to those practices on land. I have always shunned them, even when I was an ordinary seaman. As captain, it is unthinkable to consort with a common sailor in that way, although some do. Others prefer the cabin boys. At least poor Stritch escaped that abomination on my vessel, God rest his soul."

He was quiet for a moment. "In moments of weakness, I have prayed to God to preserve me for a natural union. Now you see how much He loves me. Look at the glory He has given me in you."

"That's blasphemy," she scolded him gently. "This is not a union blessed by God."

"Ah, Sarah. Give the Old Boy credit for more wisdom than we poor mortals reveal. Did you not cry out to him in your joy? Was it not something like a prayer?"

Her face grew warm. "Yes, I suppose." She looked away, unable to meet his eyes. "I don't know what made me do that."

He regarded her steadily. "How long were you married to your husband?"

"Six months and five days."

"Did you never . . . cry out like that with him?"

"With Haven I felt close, and tender. But I never lost myself like that. It's frightening."

"Aye. It is a little. But 'tis glorious as well." He looked to her for confirmation. "Is it not a prayer of thanks, for being able to give yourself to me so completely? And I to you?"

"Yes."

"Then why are you embarrassed?"

"Because I am not ashamed to be here with you like this, talking like this. If that makes any sense at all. I should be ashamed, but I'm not. Haven and I never talked about our—physical union."

"Never talked during the act, I'll warrant."

"No. Haven was shy."

"Are you happy now, here with me?"

"Yes."

"Then you have no reason to be embarrassed." He pushed the covers off her and roamed her with his eyes, which seemed almost black in the soft light of the room. She saw that he was ready for her again, and she touched him. He pulled her atop him, parting her legs, and entered her.

"No reason to be ashamed," he said. "Not when you give another such joy. I will tell you something most women don't know, and fewer ladies. Nothing is more pleasurable to a man than a woman who is unashamed to reveal her desires."

"You have had many—much experience."

He held her close. "Moments such as this don't come from experience, Sarah. They are rare. 'Tis a kind of magic that sometimes happens between two people. That is why I say these moments are blessed by God."

She raised herself up, moving atop him, wanting him with all her being. Jason let himself go now, no longer needing to guide her. He lost himself so completely that for a time he thought the rhythmic creaking of the bed came from a ship's timbers, and he was at sea once again.

"Tell me about your boyhood," she said while he was still drifting on the waters. Haltingly at first, he told her.

Sarah had seen the Boston waterfront with her father, but the picture Jason painted of his life there was very different from her girlish view of stalwart seamen and jovial stevedores. Those men had been kind to her because she was a mate's daughter and because some of them were kind men. In Jason's experience, a wharf rat's life was a struggle for survival in a world where everyone looked first to his own needs before offering kindness to another. Even so, some had been kind to him, whores and seamen and landsmen, and Sarah saw that he had taken his example from those men and women. He had seized every opportunity to better himself, and at the first chance he had escaped the Boston wharves and become a ship's boy. From then his life was less worrisome. He had seen London when he was eleven and rounded Cape Horn for the first time at sixteen, bound for China.

"Have you told Dickie any of this?" she asked.

"A little."

"He's lost, then. I have no chance against you."

"I am not your enemy, Sarah."

"I know that," she said, and they were silent again.

The room was almost dark when he spoke. "I have told you why I kept my feelings for you to myself. Now you must tell me why you concealed yours."

"Because I sensed what kind of man you are. You already have a mistress."

"On my honor, Sarah!"

"Peace, Jason, I'm not impugning your honor. But what I say is true. The sea is your mistress. You will never give her up for a woman on shore."

"Then why . . ."

"Why give myself now? For the same reasons. Because I know what kind of man you are." She moved closer to him. "I know it doesn't make sense. I was feeling lonely. Molly is gone from this house, and she was my friend. She is still my friend but it won't be the same now. And so I gave myself to you and you have restored my faith. In God and man, and myself."

"You kept back your feelings because you know I will go back to sea, and now you reveal them for the same reason?"

It was the first time she had seen him confused. "I can't explain it, Jason. But I ask nothing of you, no more than you can freely give. And I promise you this: I will never ask you to give up the sea."

After that they spoke of matters less consequential, and they lost themselves in each other once more. They slept intertwined, and Sarah wondered how she had ever slept alone for so long. She woke at first light, but he was already gone, and the cat, Kittery, was asleep where Jason had lain beside her.

Chapter 40

he driver of the first hackney carriage pulled to a stop where the woods opened onto a broad meadow. "There's no one will bother you gents here," he said.

"Others use this place?" Jason asked.

"Not so much as a few years ago. The law don't look kindly on it, but the law don't come lookin' for trouble, neither."

"Wait within the woods," Jason instructed him.

They had come across the bay on the first ferry. The meadow was well beyond the town limits of Oakland, although the drive from the ferry wharf had taken no more than a quarter of an hour. The pasture was surrounded on three sides by woods, mostly the live oaks that gave Oakland its name, mixed with manzanita and bay laurel. No human habitations stood in sight of the meadow, which stretched down toward the water.

"Mrs. Rockwell is worried about you," Jason said to Trelayne. "She hopes there will be no bloodshed."

"Oh, blood and gore isn't my plan at all, Captain. I have something more elegant in mind."

As Calvert emerged from the second hack he eyed the long leather case in Joshua Norton's arms, but said nothing.

"It's a pity your bride won't see your moment of glory, Calvert," Trelayne said. "She's still sleeping, I suppose. I imagine you exhausted her after all that waiting."

Calvert turned purple in the face and lunged at Trelayne, but Jonathan Frye and Stephen Kent seized him and held him until he brought his temper under control.

Trelayne's remark cut Calvert to the quick, for Molly had spurned him on their wedding night. "My wedding day is ruined!" she cried when he had finally persuaded her to admit him to the bedroom. "And all because you couldn't keep your temper."

"What about Trelayne!" Calvert's pent-up frustration gave his reply a hard edge he hadn't intended.

"Tommy's a fool!" Molly's eyes had flashed with anger. "But you should know better."

She didn't allow him to see her undress. When they were in bed at last, Molly in a flannel nightgown that covered her to the ankles, she had warded off his attempts to caress her. "I can't consummate our marriage with that duel hanging over us, Abel. Promise me you'll forget about Tommy. We'll ride out to the beach tomorrow to take the air. When we come home I'll make it up to you."

Calvert had refused to forgo the duel and she had turned away from him. "If you kill him, I will never forgive you," she said.

The sweet smell of her had kept Calvert awake all night, aching with desire that was mingled with rage. He had considered forcing himself upon her, as was his right, but he knew that if he took her against her will he would lose her forever. Thoughts of what she might have kept from him about her years with Trelayne obsessed him through the long night, his jealousy painting lurid pictures of Molly in Trelayne's arms. Whether or not his imaginings were justified, Calvert wanted to hurt Trelayne badly. But for Molly's sake he would try not to kill him.

An arm of fog extended across the bay and washed over the Contra Costa hills a few miles north of the dueling field but here the sun shone brightly. The men removed their coats, all but Dr. Cole, who was present to treat the duelists and judge the severity of their wounds. When the seconds came together to discuss the rules, he kept apart, looking pale in the sunshine, resting on his crutches.

"Gentlemen," Stephen Kent called after some minutes had passed. He beckoned the duelists to approach. "As your seconds, our first obligation is to beg you both to reconsider. It is not too late to make amends here. There is honor in magnanimity, and there is virtue in Christian forgiveness." He turned to Calvert. "As your friend, Abel, I ask you to pardon whatever offense Trelayne may have offered."

"His remark was unforgivable," Calvert said curtly.

Trelayne smirked. "So long as Mr. Calvert wants a lesson in humility, I am willing to provide instruction."

"Let's get on with it," Jonathan Frye grumbled.

Joshua Norton opened the long leather case. "Mr. Trelayne offers Mr. Calvert a choice of weapons. Foils or swords."

"It was up to me, I'd pick Green River knives," Calvert said.

Trelayne was calm, almost languid. "If you leave it to me, I will take the foils. They require more finesse."

Calvert's grip on his temper loosened for a moment. "I ain't no French dandy, to be playing with knitting needles! Pistols or muskets will do the job well enough. Let's have fowling pieces if that's your style!"

Trelayne said nothing. Calvert grudgingly selected a saber. "One knife's as good as another, I reckon." He tested the heft of the blade and swung it through the air.

Trelayne took the other, and Norton set the box aside. He nodded to Jason, who left the group and walked a short distance away, where he began to scrape a broad circle with his bootheel in an expanse of bare earth.

"My colleagues have selected me to set forth the rules," Norton said. "As you see, Captain Beck is marking a circle on the earth."

Alone among those present, Calvert recognized the bare ground for what it was. There had been a salt lick here not long ago, before Americans took over the land where Mexican cattle had grazed for fifty years. Gathering to lick the salt, the cattle had destroyed the grass, which was beginning to recover at the edges.

"Mr. Trelayne and Mr. Calvert must remain with the

circle, once the signal is given to begin," Norton continued. "The only weapons permitted are the sabers Mr.
Trelayne has provided. If a man falls, the other will allow
him to regain his feet. If a man is wounded, there will be
no further action until Dr. Cole has inspected the wound
and judged whether the injured party is able to continue.
The contest will continue until one man yields, or until
Mr. Calvert declares that his honor is satisfied."

The duelists and their seconds joined Jason on the
bare ground, where he had marked a circle twenty feet
in diameter.

"Gentlemen," Norton addressed the seconds. "Are you
armed?"

"We are," Stephen Kent replied on behalf of himself
and Frye.

"Captain Beck?"

Jason drew aside his coat to reveal a Navy revolver.
Norton turned to the duelists. "It is the duty of the seconds to uphold the roles. If either man breaks these rules
and threatens the life of his opponent in the course of
such a breach, he may be immediately dispatched by the
seconds of the other. Is that understood?" He fixed each
combatant in turn with his bulging eyes. First Calvert
and then Trelayne nodded.

"Very well. Gentlemen, take your positions. Mr. Kent
will give the signal to begin."

Calvert took a posture with his feet braced, the saber
upraised before him. Trelayne stood casually, his blade
loose in his hand, the point toward the ground. The fog
was cool on his face. He thought of Molly Gray, and the
surprising coolness of her skin the first time he had
touched her.

"On your guard," Kent said. "Begin."

The saber in Trelayne's hand came alive. It touched
Calvert's blade on one side, then the other. The steel
rang. Calvert lunged and swung his saber through the
air where Trelayne had been. It made a sound like a
bedsheet tearing.

"Over here." Trelayne knocked Calvert's beaver hat
into the dust with the tip of his blade.

"Stand still and fight!" Calvert took another broad

swipe. Trelayne's saber darted in and cut the sleeve of Calvert's shirt.

"Watch your guard," Trelayne advised him. Calvert felt a tug at his hand and he gaped as he saw his saber sail through the air and land at Jason Beck's feet, outside the circle.

Trelayne stood idly while Jason passed the saber to Kent, who returned it to Calvert. "Begin," said Kent, and the blades clashed again.

Calvert was sweating. Trelayne seemed to be everywhere at once. But a knife fight was still a knife fight. Look for an opening. Make one by disguising your moves. Guard your belly and your neck. Take a cut on the arm if you have to, but protect your gut. Calvert had seen a man gutted by a Blackfoot lance. Poor Georgie Tobin, in the mountains less than a year, bleeding to death with his guts falling out of his belly, and nothing Calvert or the other trappers could do for a wound like that. Calvert had the Blackfoot's scalp in a trunk in his attic at North Beach and the lance over his mantel.

The memory of killing the Indian gave Calvert heart. He feinted, tossed the saber to his other hand, and slashed at Trelayne's arm. Something struck the side of his head and sent his vision spinning.

"Hold!" Joshua Norton cried. "Dr. Cole."

Beverly Cole swung himself into the circle. There was a livid mark on Calvert's cheek. Minuscule drops of blood lined one edge of the welt.

"It is only a bruise," Cole said. "The stroke was delivered with the flat of the blade." If Trelayne had used the edge, he would have split Calvert's cheekbone and killed him outright.

"Stop it now, Abel," Stephen Kent said. "You're no match for him."

"Give the signal!"

"On your guard," Kent said reluctantly. "Begin."

Calvert gripped the saber in both hands. He advanced on Trelayne, hacking at the air in front of him with quick strokes.

"Lightly, Abel, like this." Trelayne knocked Calvert's blade aside and pricked him in the chest, not hard enough to draw blood, but hard enough to make a small tear in Calvert's shirtfront.

"Damn you!" Calvert charged. Trelayne stepped backward and tripped on a root that protruded from the dust. He stumbled and fell. Calvert raised his saber, feeling an immense satisfaction.

"Calvert!" Jason Beck's voice contained a warning that penetrated Calvert's anger. Beck had his Navy pistol in his hand.

Calvert stepped back. Trelayne rose, hatless now.

"That's enough, Abel!" Kent begged him. "Say you're satisfied."

Calvert spoke with difficulty. "I'll be satisfied when I find out if he bleeds red like the rest of us."

This time, at the command to begin, Trelayne took the offensive. As Richard III, as Henry V, as a host of other sword-bearing heroes in plays ranging from Shakespeare to low melodrama, he had spent a lifetime beneath the proscenium arch preparing himself for this moment, and he saw now that all his training as an actor had served one purpose—to prepare him for the theater of the world.

Trelayne was in his glory. For the first time he fought without knowing the outcome of the contest. No playwright had ordained the ending. He toyed with Calvert. He nicked his clothing in a dozen places. He cut Calvert's left suspender. He gave him a welt on the left cheek to match the one on the right, being careful this time to raise not even a single drop of blood.

Calvert was panting. Trelayne watched him closely, gauging the intensity of his rage, watching for the breaking point.

"Come on!" Calvert exhorted him. "Finish it, if you've got the stomach for it."

He lunged and Trelayne stepped aside, cutting Calvert's remaining suspender as Calvert passed him. Calvert's pants dropped around his knees. Trelayne stepped close to him just long enough to say in his ear, "You know what I like best, Abel? It's when she wraps her legs around me. Did she do that for you?"

Calvert let out an incoherent cry as Trelayne danced out of reach. He raised the saber high and charged at the actor, but he tripped on his trousers and fell. He arose awkwardly, bending over to pull up his pants. Trelayne delivered a stinging blow to Calvert's buttocks with the flat of his blade and sent him sprawling in the sun-warm earth.

Trelayne turned his back and strolled to the far side of the circle. Calvert struggled to his feet, holding his pants up with one hand, swinging the saber wildly with the other.

"I'll gut you, you bastard!" he roared.

Trelayne stepped out of the circle. "I yield," he said, but Calvert was beyond hearing. He crossed the line with his saber held high and dropped to the ground like a sack of flower when Jason Beck brought the barrel of his Navy revolver down on Calvert's skull.

Joshua Norton considered the fallen man dispassionately. "Under the rules you might have killed him," he said to Jason.

Trelayne felt light enough to rise into the sky with the birds. Overhead, the bright orb of the sun was a light that shone just for him.

arah Rockwell drew the pruning knife gently
through a small azalea stalk and put the cut sprig
in a jar of water. If it put out roots, she would
begin a new bed of azaleas in front of the house.
The sunshine was warm on her back. She
looked up and saw that there was a ghostly ring around
the sun.

It was Wednesday afternoon, the fourth day since
Molly's ill-fated wedding, the third since the duel. Sarah
had come to the garden hoping the task of pruning
would calm her, but she was still unsettled. Since the
duel the mood in the boardinghouse had been subdued,
almost melancholy. On Monday morning, Trelayne had
posted a notice on the doors of the theater saying it was
closed while a new work was in preparation. He gave
the company a week's leave with pay, and every night he
accompanied Jason and Melchior and Jolly Jim to the
waterfront to search for Tom Leary. During that time,
Jason had not returned to Sarah's bed.

"Miss Rockwell?"

Sarah had not noticed Su-Yan's approach, although
some part of her had been aware of the sound made by
his cartwheels. She chose enough vegetables for two
days and invited Su-Yan into the kitchen while she
fetched her coin purse from the bedroom.

Dishes were stacked by the tinned sink and the kettle
rumbled on the stove, full of water for the washing. Su-

Yan remained near the open door for the soothing effect
of the cool breeze. That morning he had awakened to a
sense of foreboding, as though a new element had entered the flow of events. He had taken his tea to the
small room in the cellar to consult the oracle before his
wife awoke. The casting of the stalks had calmed him,
but the sense of premonition returned when he recognized the hexagram *Ming I*, which indicated misfortune
in the affairs of men and harm descending from those in
authority. The oracle confirmed the impression of power
only temporarily restrained that Su-Yan had gathered
from his daughter's reports and from his own soundings
in the *guey low* community.

The Committee of Vigilance had been very quiet of
late. The dragon was sleeping, but *Ming I* signalled a
change. The dragon would soon awaken, and the dark
power was still firmly in control

Sarah Rockwell returned with her purse. As she
counted out the coins, she said, "Su-Yan, do you take an
interest in our politics?"

He replied cautiously, "Politics affect every man, Miss
Rockwell."

"Yes, of course. But that is not the same as taking an
interest." She looked at him directly. Su-Yan reminded
himself for the ten thousandth time since coming to the
Golden Mountain that what was rude in China was no
more than simple curiosity here.

"My people regard politics as part of life. Like you, I
take an interest in life."

"Will you have some tea with me?" Once more, she
took him off guard.

"Thank you. I cannot." He concealed his distaste. She
wanted to talk with him as an equal, and that was unthinkable. She was a woman and a barbarian and he was
a respectable man.

His refusal deterred her for only a moment. "Su-Yan,
what do your people think of the vigilantes?"

"In China, powerful men have always ruled. It is the
way of the world."

"Do you understand that under our Constitution and
our laws, these men are criminals?"

"Men in power can choose what laws to obey."

"But that isn't right! The laws must be the same for everyone."

"This is a dream, Miss Rockwell. It is a beautiful dream, but life is not the same as a dream."

She managed a smile. "Is that an old saying in China?"

"It is a fact, as an American would say." He bowed and turned to go, but paused in the doorway. "I will give you an old China saying, as a gift today, Miss Rockwell. In China, we say, 'Where the contest is averted, there is no victory, no defeat.' This is what is best for the spirit, but most Christians do not think of the spirit when their enemies confront them."

Sarah tried to hide her disappointment. "Why must you always talk in riddles?"

Su-Yan spoke as if instructing a child. "If I imagine I can tell you what will happen in your home or in this city, I may be wrong. But if I tell you the eternal way of the world, I will certainly be right."

Jason stood atop Russian Hill and looked toward the lowering sun. The ephemeral ring that had circled it earlier in the afternoon was gone, but Jason had seen the omen. A ring around the sun was a weather sign. A change would come soon.

Some seamen believed that solar rings foretold more than the weather. "When there's a ring around the sun, don't trust your luck for three days and nights," Finn Warren had warned a younger Jason Beck more than twenty years ago. Finn had counseled him to fashion a Turk's-head bracelet from a bit of old rope and wear it on his left wrist for three days and nights when he saw a solar ring.

In the Golden Gate, a trim hermaphrodite brig was working out to sea, beating against a steady breeze from the west. Jason read what the sky and the wind and the water told him, and he considered how he would prepare his own ship for what the weather might bring. In the North Atlantic, seeing a ring around the sun, he would make ready for a storm. Here the change would be less threatening. Dangerous storms were unknown on the coast of California in June. But a change would come.

In the boardinghouse parlor the mercury barometer was down this morning from the night before.

Jason swayed and nearly lost his balance. He was perched atop a small boulder that was the highest point on the hill. For a moment, watching the brig, he had imagined himself aboard her, leaning to windward to accommodate the shifting deck.

He stepped off the rock, turning away from the water, and discovered a tall woman coming toward him. She wore a calico dress and a short cloak and she carried a parasol. A rakish hat shaded her face. Her feet moved nimbly as she approached him through the low brush. She looked up, saw him watching her, and she smiled. "Ahoy, Captain." It was Lucy Thorsen.

"Ahoy yourself. What are you doing here?"

"I climb the hills often. Even whores like to take the air."

"Why do you speak of yourself that way?"

She laughed lightly. "I am a whore, Captain Beck."

"I only meant—" He wasn't certain what he meant. She was so young and so pretty—

"You meant that unpleasant truths should not be spoken? Why must it be unpleasant to say what I am? We are friends, are we not?" She was enjoying his discomfort.

"We are friends, Lucy Greta Thorsen."

Her voice softened. "If I had known of your loss on the night you spent with me, I would never have let you pay. I was very sorry to hear about your ship."

Jason realized that it was a month to the day since the *Sarah B. Watson* burned. He had not kept his promise to visit Lucy again.

"Now you have a new ship."

"How did you know?"

"You would be surprised what men tell a whore, Captain." She came close to him and looked into his face. Her eyes were level with his own. "I have seen you here before."

He smelled the scent of her skin and remembered that scent enveloping him. "I didn't see you."

"No. But I have watched you. You stand on that rock and you look out to sea."

"Aye. Why do you come here?"

"It's a place where a whore can walk without attracting unwelcome attention."

"In this city a . . . whore can go where she pleases, it seems to me."

"It is not the way it used to be. When I first came here we walked the streets day or night, and the gentlemen bowed when we passed. We set the fashions. If the truth be told, we still do." She pirouetted to display her finery. "No respectable woman would admit it, but they don't want us to outshine them, so they imitate us."

"You were young when you came here."

"I was eighteen. Many girls were younger."

"Have supper with me."

"All right."

They started down the hill toward the town. "When you saw me here before, why didn't you show yourself?" Jason said.

"Oh, Captain. I shouldn't tell you." Her light air faltered and a small sadness showed in her eyes. She came to a stop and he stopped beside her.

"Tell me all the same."

"You have touched me."

"Touched you?"

"A whore does not allow men to touch her, even while they are naked with her. Even when they are inside her." She looked into his eyes when she said this, and there was no trace of embarrassment in her manner. "But you have touched me. Here." She put a hand over her heart. "And you have not returned to me again. I hoped you would come and you didn't."

"I have been looking for the man who burned my ship."

"I know."

"I have thought of you."

Lucy smiled, her good spirits returning. "Today when I saw you I said to myself, I will go to him and I will see if he is glad to see me. And you are. Come, now. I will show you a place to take supper where no one will notice us together."

Together they walked down the slope and along Vallejo Street toward Telegraph Hill. Here the westerly winds were gentler, the evening warm. At Stockton, Lucy entered a wooden building that displayed no sign. Inside, men and women sat at small tables and talked jovially, as if they were members of the same family. The restaurant smelled of garlic and herbs and good cooking. A plump woman greeted Lucy warmly in Italian. She gave them a table in the back room. Among the other diners not a word of English was spoken.

"Do you like Italian food, Captain?" Lucy asked him.

"There are Italians in Massachusetts, but I have not often eaten their food." He had sailed six of the seven seas, but never the Mediterranean.

Lucy was pleased. "I am glad I can show something new to the sea captain who has sailed around the world."

"How did you find this place?"

"The woman who seated us? Domenica is her name. I met her at church."

"You're Catholic?"

"Yes. Not so many are Catholic in Denmark. Here there are more. Mexicans and Italians, and some of the French. Domenica thinks I need to be fat. She brought me here after church to feed me."

There was no written menu. Domenica herself waited on them, bringing first a clear soup with tiny beads of dough in it, then a plate of noodles and small peas in a cream sauce that was flavored with herbs. After the noodles she presented a small roasted chicken, which she divided between them, served with potatoes and green squash. They drank rough red wine from water glasses and poured more from a china pitcher. When they stepped into the street again, the western slope of Telegraph Hill was golden from the light of the setting sun.

Lucy stood so close to Jason that he could feel the warmth of her breath. "I would like to spend the night with you, Jason." It was the first time she had called him by his Christian name.

He hesitated. "I am stopping at a boardinghouse."

She nodded. "You are at Mrs. Rockwell's. But I know of a private place. Come."

They climbed Green Street, behind the County Jail, where she led him up a flight of rickety stairs. She opened the door with a key that she took from a potted plant and showed him into a refined sitting room. The furniture was elegant and there were etchings on the wall. Through one door was the kitchen, through another the bedroom. An alcove off the sitting room had been furnished with a small dining table and two chairs.

Lucy watched Jason look about. "It belongs to a friend. You remember Barbara? She had breakfast with us."

"The Chinese girl."

"Soon she will leave Mrs. Wickliff's and live here. A gentleman wants to have her for his own. You know him. It is Jonathan Frye."

"Should you be telling me all this?"

"I have no secrets from the man who has touched my heart. I tell you these things in confidence and I know you will not repeat them."

She led him to the bedroom. The etchings here showed men and women disporting themselves at love. Lucy sat on the satin cover of the canopied bed and began to unbutton her shoes. Jason took his purse from his pocket and searched for gold coins among the silver. When Lucy saw what he was doing she threw her shoe on the floor and stamped her foot.

"I did not bring you here for money? No money!" Tears sprang to her eyes and Jason felt unspeakably clumsy as he sat beside her and took her in his arms.

"I'm sorry."

She clung to him, her voice muffled against the rough wool of his pea coat. "There will never be money between us again." She pulled back and wiped her eyes, suddenly very brave. "I ask nothing of you. I don't ask you to rescue me from a life of shame, or to take me away with you when you go. I want to be with you because you have touched me, here." She took his hand and placed it over her heart. Through the layers of calico and silk he could feel the soft warmth of her breast and the beating of the heart within.

Her lovemaking was passionate and unrestrained. Her knowledge of his body and her own equalled that of any woman Jason had ever known, yet nothing in her manner resembled the practiced actions of a woman who was accustomed to being with many men. She was impetuous and spontaneous, as if discovering true abandon for the first time. When she arrived at the peak of her pleasure, she trembled in his arms until he feared she would lose consciousness. When at last they lay exhausted she traced the gold ring in his ear with one finger.

"Oh, Captain."

"You called me Jason before."

"Yes, but you are my captain now. I am your little boat." She giggled softly, the sound something between the laughter of a woman and a girl. "You move your tiller this way and that way, and I turn at your command."

Jason laughed. She rolled atop him and placed the tip of her nose against his. "Again?"

"Not yet, I'm afraid." He clasped her to him and held her tightly, to contain the affection that welled up within him.

She kissed his ear and said, "If I bring you food and water, will you stay in this bed forever?"

"Food and water and brandy."

"And brandy."

In the middle of the night he dreamt a dream that was lit by fire. He knew his ship was burning, but he could not see her for the thick mists that hung over the water. He was alone in a ship's gig and he rowed frantically hither and yon but got no nearer to the fire. And then, in the dream, he knew he was dreaming.

He opened his eyes. The room was pitch-dark. He did not know where he was until he sensed the warm body next to his and smelled the faint scent of Lucy's hair. He stretched himself, and the movement wakened her. She raised her head and drew away from him, suddenly alarmed.

"Who—Oh, Jason!" She clung to him, burying her head in the crook of his neck. "Oh, Jason. I am so glad it is you."

Her hands moved over his body, reassuring herself, and his passion stirred. Their joining was different this time, everything done with great care and tenderness. When they were spent, the room was turning blue with the first light from the east.

"I don't want to sleep," she murmured when he closed

his eyes, still holding her. "When we slept before, I forgot where I was. I forgot you were with me."

"I forgot too," he said. He remembered the dream.

"Remember your promise. You must never leave here."

"I have to meet Barbara's friend Jonathan Frye at ten o'clock. He is to give me information about the merchants who conspired in rice. One of them may have burned my ship."

He held her, content to remain awake until the city was alive around them. Once again she had comforted him and restored his will to face the world and its cruelty.

He thought of Sarah Rockwell and he pushed his guilt aside. Better to renew himself with Lucy, who expected nothing of him, than with Sarah. *I will never ask you to give up the sea,* she had promised him. But what else would she ask, and what then would he give in return?

In spite of himself he dozed, and when he woke again it was to the touch of Lucy's hands caressing him. Sunlight was shining in the window. She saw his eyes were open and she said, "You are my captain and I am your little boat. See? Your tiller is ready to steer me."

She moved to sit astride him, but there came a gentle knocking at the front door. "Wait," she said. She took a robe that was too short for her from the armoire and she closed the bedroom door behind her. Jason got out of bed and reached for his pants, unwilling to risk confronting Jonathan Frye unclothed in the bedroom Frye had prepared for his Chinese mistress, but before he could put them on, Lucy peeped in to say, "It's only Barbara. Come out when you are dressed." She cast a sad look at his flagging tiller and left him.

When he emerged from the bedroom Barbara greeted him with a smile. "I am so glad to find you here, Captain Beck." Lucy was making coffee. Barbara had brought fruit and fresh sweet rolls, and they breakfasted together in the kitchen after Lucy dressed.

"I must go now," Lucy said while Jason was still eating. "I didn't tell Mrs. Wickliff I would be out last night. She will be angry with me."

"You're her favorite," Barbara said. "Be nice to her

and put her in a good mood so when I tell her I'm leaving, she won't kill me."

"You will tell her today?" Lucy said.

"This afternoon. Tomorrow will be my first night in my new home. But you and Captain Beck must come again. I will visit my mother overnight and you will have the apartment to yourselves."

"We couldn't do that," Jason said.

"I have dreamed of having a place of my own so I can do what I like, Captain Beck. I like having you here. I like seeing Lucy so happy."

Lucy gave Barbara a dazzling smile. She picked up her parasol and Jason rose to go with her but she motioned him to stay. "Finish your coffee," she told him. "Barbara doesn't mind."

When Lucy was gone, Barbara put on an apron and splashed water in a pan to wash the few dishes they had used, clearly enjoying herself. They chatted, and at a pause in the talk Jason said, "May I ask how much you know about Mr. Frye's business?"

"Lucy told you?"

"Yes. I will not repeat anything she said. On my honor. And I will understand if you prefer not to speak of Mr. Frye."

Barbara dried her hands on a small towel. "There is no reason not to speak of him, Captain. He is helping you look for the men who burned your ship."

Jason wondered how much effort Frye had put into the search, and what he would have to say this morning about members of the Vigilance Committee who might be monopolists in rice. Thus far, Frye's promises of help had produced nothing at all.

"I know very little of his business, really," Barbara said. "He trades a good deal in land. He has imported almost every sort of merchandise over the years. But he doesn't speak much of business with me. It is not a woman's affair." She was trying to imagine why Captain Beck had asked about Jonathan's business. Because she could not guess the answer she decided to say nothing. She had learned from her father that information was precious. It might be revealed for a purpose, but lacking a purpose, it should be guarded until its true value was known.

A small clock on a sideboard in the sitting room struck nine times.

"Well, I must be off," Jason said. "I thank you for your kindness. You and Lucy must be very good friends."

"Yes, Captain, we are." She followed him to the door and she smiled when he looked back from the bottom of the steps.

After an unpleasant breakfast with his wife, it occurred to Jonathan Frye that even half an hour with Barbara before his meeting with Captain Beck would improve his spirits and allow him to lie with more conviction. He planned to tell Beck that he had made confidential inquiries among the members of the Executive Committee who traded in grains, but had discovered no evidence of a rice cartel. In reality he had spoken to no one. If any members of the Executive Committee had conspired in rice, Frye wanted to know nothing about it. What Calvert might have done by way of fulfilling his promise to Kent and Captain Beck, he did not know. Calvert had not mentioned the matter again, and Frye was more than content to let sleeping dogs slumber undisturbed.

Calvert had been foul-tempered since the duel with Trelayne and he had kept to himself, appearing for meetings of the Executive Committee and spending the rest of the time at his bank. Frye had spoken privately to him only once since Sunday, in an effort to cheer him. He had pointed out that whether or not by design, the Theater Trelayne was closed and Mercury was silent. Denied arms by General Wool, the state's militia was impotent and the Committee's enemies were in disarray. Calvert had looked at Frye as if he were a fool, and went on his way.

The day was bright, with a cool westerly wind and a few high clouds that were gathered in ripples like the surface of the bay under a light breeze. As Frye neared Green Street he felt a stirring in his loins at the thought of Barbara. They had planned to spend tomorrow night

together in the apartment for the first time, but she had
told him she would be here today to finish arranging everything to her taste. He would surprise her, and they
would inaugurate their life in the apartment now, spon-
taneously.

When Frye saw the sailor swinging down the stairway
at the side of the house, he thought the man must have
come to the wrong place and been sent away. But the
door was ajar and he caught a glimpse of Barbara's face.
She was smiling, watching the man go down the stairs.
The man wore a gold ring in his ear and his hair was
tied at the back, and then he turned and Frye recognized
Captain Beck. He walked away like a man on top of the
world.

When Barbara opened the door at Frye's knock, her
surprise was evident. "Jonathan. Why didn't you use
your key?"

"I wouldn't want to startle you, my dear. You might
be entertaining."

"What a thing to say. No one comes here." She carried it off so well, Frye would have believed her if he had
not seen Beck leaving and Barbara's smile. She was lying, and why would she lie unless she had something to
hide?

"Of course," he said. "Well then. I thought I would
come by and surprise you, but I haven't much time." The
bedroom door was open. From where he stood he
couldn't see the bed.

"Would you like tea? I can make breakfast for you."

He marveled at her composure. If she knew that he
was supposed to meet with Captain Beck at ten o'clock,
she gave no sign at all. "If I wanted tea, I would go to
a hotel or a tea shop."

"I wanted our first time here to be perfect. Not
rushed. I had planned—" She stopped as he walked into
the bedroom.

The four-poster bed of cherry wood was rumpled and
unmade. A vivid image came to Frye, of Barbara with
Captain Beck in this bed, as abandoned and lascivious as
she was with him. He felt the rage building in him but
he held it in. He tossed his cane on the bed and called

to Barbara to come into the bedroom. When she joined him she said, "I came in the night and slept here. I—"

"No! No more lies. Get undressed."

Her fingers trembled as they moved to the buttons of her dress. Frye watched in silence as she removed the dress, her petticoats, stockings and shoes, corset and chemise. Her breasts and thighs were unmarked. "Turn around," he said.

There were no marks on her back either, which merely meant that Captain Beck was not the kind of man who marked his women. Perhaps he liked them to mark him, scratching his back with their fingernails in the heat of passion.

"All right," Frye said.

Barbara turned back to face him and as she turned he hit her. She fell back onto the bed and he leaned over her.

"Was he good?"

"Who?" She cowered beneath him.

"Captain Beck, you stupid whore! Do you think I am blind? I saw him leaving you and I saw the pretty smile you gave him."

He struck her face with his fist. "Did he tell you what a pretty Chink bitch you are? Is that why you brought him here?"

She wiped her mouth with the back of her hand. It came away bloody. She looked at it, and then at Frye. The fear was gone from her eyes now, replaced by a coldness he had not seen before. "He was the best man I have ever had."

He hit her again, first with his right hand and then with the left. It was some time before he paused to reach for his cane.

hey were five at supper—Jason and Sarah, Melchior, Dickie and Norton. "Captain Farren told me he would not be here this evening, but Mr. Trelayne did not," Sarah said with some irritation.

"Mr. Trelayne spends all his time in the grogshops now," Melchior said. "He takes it personal, like this Tom Leary is playing hide-and-go-seek with him."

Jason knew that part of Sarah's irritation was directed at him, for missing supper without notice the previous evening and for staying out all night. He had apologized, but had offered no explanation when he returned to the house today, and she had asked for none.

Conversation during the meal was fitful, lacking the will to sustain itself. The soup went and a leg of mutton arrived. Dickie broke a silence that had lasted for several minutes by saying, out of the blue, "Are we ever going to talk about whether I'm to be the ship's boy on *Pride of the Seas*?" Three times since Miss Gray and Mr. Calvert's engagement dinner he had tried to speak to Sarah about it, but each time she had put him off.

Jason glanced at Sarah. She hesitated only a moment before saying, "That will be your decision," as if his right to choose were beyond question.

"Mine?" Dickie was at a loss.

"When Captain Beck is ready to set sail, you will have

to decide whether you are going to go with him or stay here with me."

This silenced Dickie for the rest of the meal. The notion that he would have to make the choice for himself had never entered his mind. Was it possible that neither Sarah nor Captain Beck knew what was best for him, and so they had avoided deciding his future, each hoping the other would state the case for his shipping out or staying ashore so forcefully that there could be no argument?

"May I have a story after my reading lessons?" he asked when they were finished with the dessert.

"After you help Ingrid with the dishes, you may have a story if Mr. Norton is willing," Sarah said.

"Willing, as always." Norton favored Dickie with a smile. "In the meantime, a word with you, Captain Beck, if I may. Will you come to my chambers?"

Norton's "chambers" consisted of a single room that resembled a library more than a bedroom. The walls were covered with shelves from floor to ceiling, leaving bare only the windows and the door and the wall where the bed stood, and the shelves were full of books. More books were stacked on the dresser and beneath the bed and atop the writing table, where they shared the space with piles of paper covered with writing in a cramped hand. Jason's eyes picked out *The Adventures of Baron Münchausen* and *Gulliver's Travels* side by side on one of the shelves.

Norton beamed with pride. "As you see, I have converted my remaining assets to something that will never lose value." He swept a hand about the room. "Knowledge, Captain. Answers to all the questions of man. Knowledge that will raise your spirits, too, if you know where to look. I keep my spirits here." He pulled out a thick volume, reached through the gap, and withdrew a bottle of brandy.

"In this house?" Jason said.

Norton put a finger to his lips and looked for all the world like a naughty boy. He retrieved two glasses from a drawer in his dresser and poured the brandy.

"To your health, Mr. Norton," Jason said.

"To the confusion of our enemies." Norton's large eyes

were wide, and Jason realized the merchant was keeping back a secret.

"You have something to tell me."

"Have you wondered where I have been keeping myself every day since Sunday?" Norton said.

"We both have our business to attend to."

"Quite so. But my business this week has led me into dark pathways. Tell me, what did you think of Mr. Calvert's house?"

Jason couldn't imagine what Calvert's house had to do with the dark pathways of Norton's life. "He has a good view of the water."

"As it happens, I once owned that lot. I chose it for the view. I had hoped to build my own home there in time. That was before the devil ship *Glyde* arrived with her cargo of rice. I lost that lot, among several other properties, following my ill-advised speculation. Imagine my surprise when I arrived for the wedding to find that Mr. Calvert has realized my dream without knowing a thing about it."

Norton watched Jason to see what effect his revelation was having. "You see, Captain, until now I have believed that my fall from grace was the work of fate. But our little chats about the doings of San Francisco's merchants, and seeing Mr. Calvert's house, have made me face a dark possibility. I faced it three years ago, and looked away. I preferred to attribute my failure to my own bad judgment. To think that someone set out deliberately to ruin me—that was too much."

"And now?"

"I have spent the past four days in the office of the county clerk. The records of property transfers are kept there, you see. It takes some time to go through them, but in just four days I managed to trace the titles to every piece of property I lost in fifty-three. Would you believe that every single lot has passed through the hands of one man, or is still owned by him?"

"What man?"

"Jonathan Frye."

Jason's pulse quickened. "Including Calvert's lot?"

"Bought by Jonathan Frye from Page, Bacon and Company. They held many of my notes for a time, after my misfortune. Frye sold the lot to Calvert for a small profit. He still owns my property at the corners of Jackson and Sansome streets. Three more lots in North Beach as well. He has sold two others to Calvert."

"It is hard to believe that one man would end up controlling your properties unless he planned it that way," Jason said.

"Just so. What is your impression of Mr. Frye?"

"He weighs each act for the benefit it will bring him." Norton's huge eyes flared. "Precisely."

"Frye doesn't deal in grains," Jason said. "How would he plan your downfall if he had no hand in grains?"

Norton refilled Jason's glass. "I hoped if we put our heads together, we might work it out."

"Do you have anything to connect Frye to what happened?"

"Only his interest in my property."

"Who offered you the *Glyde*'s cargo?"

"Goddefroy and Selim, importers. They approached me themselves. Nothing to do with Frye that I know of."

"Still, he might have been behind the offer." Jason drank off his brandy in a gulp. He felt a growing excitement. That morning, Frye had not kept his appointment with Jason, nor had he returned to his office all day. If Frye were involved with Norton's failure in '53, he might know a good deal more than he was telling, not only about conspirators in rice and flour, but about the fire that destroyed the *Sarah B. Watson* as well. And if Frye suspected that Jason was on the verge of discovering his involvement—

There were voices from below, and the sound of footsteps pounding up the stairs. A knock sounded at Norton's door and Sarah Rockwell threw the door open before Norton could move.

"Sarah?" Jason saw the alarm on her face.

"You had better come down."

In the foyer, Lucy Thorsen stood with Melchior and Dickie Howell. Ingrid gawked from the parlor door.

"Captain Beck!" Lucy's face was streaked with tears. "You must come quickly!"

"She has a friend outside in a hackney," Sarah said. "She says she is hurt."

Jason followed Lucy from the house. When they were outside, Lucy began to talk very quickly in a soft voice. "I forgot my hat and I went by this afternoon to get it. I don't know how long she was lying there. I know I should have taken her to Mrs. Wickliff's, but I was so frightened, Jason, and I thought of you. Oh, please, you must help her!"

When the hack driver saw them, he said, "If she's bled all over the seat, you'll pay for the cleaning, missy."

"I'll pay," Jason said. The hackney was a brougham, the passenger space fully enclosed. Lucy climbed into the carriage and struggled to lift something on the seat. Jason leaned in to help her, and when he saw what it was his breath stopped. Lucy held the Chinese girl Barbara in her arms. Her tears, which she had kept back for a time inside the strange house where she had come in desperation, were flowing now. "It was so hard to get her dressed," she managed to say. "Every time I moved her, I hurt her. I am so sorry to bring her like this."

Barbara was clad only in her robe and a pair of satin slippers that Lucy had put on her feet. Her hands and forearms were bruised and bloody. Her face was almost unrecognizable. Her eyes, which opened now to look first at Lucy and then at Jason, were like two dark jewels, horribly out of place in the violated flesh that supported them.

"Who did this?" he said.

"Jonathan came . . . he thought that I . . ." Barbara's voice was a strangled whisper and each word caused her pain.

"Frye!" Jason's face grew livid with rage.

Lucy's hand seized his with surprising strength. "Not now, Jason! First we must help her."

"Yes, of course." Jason lifted Barbara in his arms and he carried her to the house.

"Oh, my God!" Sarah's hand flew to her mouth when she saw the girl's face. Dickie was staring dumbstruck.

"Do you know where Dr. Cole lives, Richard?" Jason said.

"Yes, Captain. It's the third house on Clay Street, up the hill from—"

"Never mind. Tell the hackman. You go with him,

Melchior. Bring Dr. Cole to this house if you have to carry him."

"Aye, Cap'n. Come along, lad."

Jason moved for the stairs. "I will put her in my room," he said, but Sarah took hold of his arm.

"No. Bring her to mine. We can care for her properly there."

It was a quarter to eleven when Beverly Cole lowered himself into a chair at the kitchen table and set his crutches aside. He accepted the coffee Sarah offered him, wrapping his hands about the cup. Lucy had not left Barbara's side since arriving in the house, except to fetch clean water from the kettle at the doctor's request, and more linen for bandages. Now, with Barbara sleeping, she followed Dr. Cole to the kitchen to hear what he had to say.

"She is a strong girl." Cole's soft voice was made softer by fatigue.

"Will she live?" Jason asked.

"Oh, yes." He sipped the coffee. "Lacerations on the scalp bleed a great deal. It has to do with the supply of blood to the brain. Wounds to the head are alarming, but often not so serious as they first appear."

"Did she say anything?" Jason was aware of Sarah's eyes on him.

"Very little. That's to be expected. Once someone badly injured is in the care of a physician they let go and leave the doing to him. Miss Quan has let go now. You must leave her to sleep until she wakes. Then give her whatever fluids she will drink. Broth, if you have it." He directed these instructions to Sarah.

"Miss Quan?" she said.

"Miss Thorsen gives me to understand that is her name."

Sarah looked at Lucy. "Is she related to Su-Yan Quan?"

"He is her father," Lucy said.

"We will have to tell him, but I don't know where he lives. Do you, Miss—Thorsen, is it?" There had been no introductions. Sarah knew only that the tall blond woman was well enough acquainted with Jason to seek him out when she was in dire need.

"Lucy Thorsen, Mrs. Rockwell. Yes, I know his house."

"We'll send Dickie in the morning," Sarah said. "If Su-Yan learns of this now he will only come and make a fuss and disturb Barbara." With all the excitement in the house Dickie had refused to go to bed. Now he was drowsing in his chair.

"You are very kind to help her," Lucy said. She turned to Dr. Cole. "Will she be scarred?"

Cole shrugged. "It is hard to say. Her nose is broken, of course. I reset it as best I could, but it may not be just the same as before. I've sewn the worst of the lacerations. As for the rest, we will see."

Sarah said, "We are very grateful to you, Doctor."

"There is also a fracture of the right wrist. She used her arms to protect her head, and it is just as well. I will come by tomorrow morning on my way to the office. And now I must get home. My wife worries about me when I am called away in the night." Cole heaved himself upright and slipped his crutches under his arms. Somewhere in the distance a fire bell rang.

The hackman was asleep in the back of his carriage beneath a woolen lap robe, the horse dozing in the harness. When the hackney had returned with Melchior and Dickie from fetching Dr. Cole, Jason had told the driver to wait. A double eagle had silenced the man's complaints. Jason held the door while Cole clambered in. "The bastard who did this thing is a brutal man, Captain," Cole said. "He beat her with a stick."

From downtown, a second fire bell joined the first.

"He is on the Executive Committee, Doctor. And that girl is a prostitute. How will the Vigilance Committee judge one of their own when everyone knows what she is?"

"They are honorable men, most of them. I will testify to what I know about this crime. I will make the charge, if it comes to that. What is his name?"

"First I will find him, and then the world will know it."

Cole made as if to speak again, but he saw the set purpose in Jason's expression and he said nothing more.

Jason watched the hackney pull away. A third bell sounded, much nearer. Brought out by the alarms, Melchior and Norton and Sarah and Dickie were on the veranda. The moon, low over the hills of Contra Costa, made long shadows in the streets and a cool light that would brighten as it rose higher.

There was shouting from down Jackson Street. A group of men came in sight pulling a fire engine through the Stockton crossing, all heaving with a will on the long rope. Off to the southeast, a glow lit the sky. Dickie said to Sarah, "Can we go see?"

" 'Tis a fair fire, by the sound," Melchior ventured. There were several bells ringing now, near and far, to summon more volunteer companies to duty.

"Aye," Jason said. "We'll see what it is. Richard, you're to stay by me and not go running off."

"Dickie, no—" Sarah began, but the boy was already off the veranda and racing to Jason's side.

" 'Tis not a night for sleep, it would seem," Jason said to her. "He'll be safe with us. Tell Lucy we've gone. We will come home soon. Mr. Norton, you'll stay with the ladies?"

They walked down Jackson, looking south on each of the cross streets. The fire was on Kearny, several blocks away. When they drew nearer they could see that the burning building was at California, on the southwest corner. They crossed Sacramento and passed by a red-and-gold fire engine, its suction hose dropped into a cistern in the street. Firemen lined the long wooden pump handles at both sides of the engine, bobbing up and down like jack-in-the-boxes.

Already several dozen onlookers had gathered to see the fire. More were arriving every moment, some in their nightclothes. Firemen with hooks were pulling down the flaming structure's north wall. The power of the fire was mesmerizing. Jason stared in wonder as the wall crashed into the street, revealing the building's interior, and then he recognized the familiar auditorium, the ascending balconies and the broad stage all in flame, shimmering, as hosemen directed their arcs of water into the flaming interior of the Theater Trelayne.

"And so in its destruction, the grand old hall achieves a spectacle that far surpasses any poor efforts we mounted on that stage," said a voice. Trelayne had come out of nowhere and was standing beside them. "I was on my way home," he said. "Another night of cheap brandy and no thirsty Irishman." He stared at the fire. "It's grand, isn't it? You can feel the hunger. It devours every scrap of fuel as fast as it can, and then it dies. It's the drama of life acted out in a few minutes."

Closer to the conflagration, a fire captain directed his men through a speaking trumpet. It occurred to Jason that he looked like Gabriel preparing to sound his horn for the Judgment Day.

Nearby, a fireman pulling a hose from a pump engine passed through a cluster of men, thrusting them out of his way. "Stand aside, you bastards." The men wore hard leather fire hats like his own, but they made no move to help him.

"Show us how it's done, Paddy!" one encouraged the hoseman, drawing laughter from his friends.

"Why aren't those men fighting the fire?" Jason said.

"Ah, yes, there is drama in the street as well." Trelayne took a new interest in what was going on around them. "Those men are Monumentals, Captain. The very same company that played such lively airs for Molly's wedding. They are vigilance to a man. Half of them are on the Executive Committee, people say."

Jason recognized Thomas Smiley and James Dows among the group of idlers. "They won't fight the fire because your play offended them?"

"Offended them? Yes. Took them to task. Named them for the tyrants they are!" Trelayne shouted this last, but the noise of the fire drowned out his words. In the auditorium, the gallery lost its hold on the supporting wall and fell to the parquet. The sound of its falling was smothered by the rush of the flames and the shouting in the street.

"They will let the theater burn for spite?" Melchior was outraged.

"The first engine was the Crescent Number Ten, by a

twist of fate," Trelayne said. "They were James Casey's company, until the stranglers hanged him. The Empires were next. They worked like Turks, but the fire had taken hold. They are mostly Irish, the Empires and the Crescents, mostly Democrats. Not one man is in the ranks of the vigilants, I'll lay money. My hat's off to them. The Monumentals came in a great rush and stopped dead in their tracks when they saw what building was on fire."

The charred stench that pervaded the street reminded Jason of the night his ship burned. It was the smell of hellfire and brimstone. The works of man rendered into ashes and smoke. He looked about in the crowd, searching for the portly figure of Jonathan Frye and not finding him.

The clouds that rose from the fire now were more steam than smoke. Only the eastern wall of the theater, on Kearny Street, still burned. A hook-and-ladder crew ventured near enough to grapple the wall. "Lend a hand," they cried, heaving at ropes attached to their irons. Even a few of the Monumentals took hold of the ropes. The wall swayed and fell.

"Jake!" A fireman came running for the fire captain with the speaking trumpet. "We've got a body 'round the back!"

"Hold up there." A policeman blocked the way when Trelayne and Jason tried to enter the alley off California Street where the fireman and his captain had gone. The policeman was the warden of the alley, thirty yards of mud and stink. It was more authority than he had been permitted to wield since the Committee of Vigilance came to power.

"This is my property," Trelayne said. "I am Thomas Trelayne."

The policeman looked Trelayne and then Jason up and down, and gave a shrug. "You best leave the boy here."

"I'll mind the lad," Melchior offered.

In the alley the ground underfoot had turned to mud, black from soot and ashes, and the heat from the smoldering ruins was like tropical sunshine. Jason and Trelayne found four men midway along the passage. All the firemen's efforts had been concentrated on the alleys at the start of the fire, to prevent it from jumping to the nearby buildings. Here, the theater wall was still standing, like a piece of scenery from some too-real production about a great conflagration. The firemen were clustered around a dark shape on the ground outside the stage door.

"I am Thomas Trelayne," Trelayne announced.

"Jake Gallagher, captain of the Crescents," said the man with the speaking trumpet. "No way to tell who he is." He touched the blackened corpse with the toe of his boot. It was charred from head to foot, retaining the shape of a human being only in the general form. There were no features, no details. The body had been washed down by the hoses, which did much to suppress the smell of charred flesh.

There was something pitiful about the posture of the corpse, it seemed to Trelayne. It lay curled at the feet of the men as if huddled against a bitter cold. How a living person could be reduced to a burnt husk in a matter of minutes was harder to comprehend than the destruction of the theater.

"Where was he?" Trelayne asked.

"In the hallway." A fireman gestured toward the stage door.

"Let's get him into the street," Gallagher said. "We can wrap him in a bit of canvas."

The firemen took hold of the corpse. They wore thick leather gloves that allowed them to handle hot tools and burning timbers. They lifted the body and something small fell to the ground.

"He's lost a hand there," Gallagher said, as if the object were a coin purse or a hat.

"Mother of God." One of the firemen dropped the leg he was holding and crossed himself.

"Set him down," Jason said. "On his back. That's it. Look there." When the men first inspected the corpse it had been lying on its side, the arm hidden. They could see now that the victim's left arm ended not in a hand, but in a steel hook.

"What's this, then?" Gallagher demanded, pointing to the charred hand that lay beside the body.

Jason picked it up and examined it. "It's a false hand."

Trelayne peered at the object. "All made of leather. It's ingenious." His eyes met Jason's. "Mr. Tom Leary. I thought it was only a glove."

"You gents know this feller?" As captain of the first company on the fire, Gallagher had certain responsibilities. The city authorities, cowed by the vigilantes, clung to those functions that remained to them. They would want a written report.

"His name was Tom Leary," Trelayne said. "Clever fellow. He knew that people remember a man with a hook. The leather hand made him anonymous."

"What was he, this Tom Leary?" Gallagher asked.

"An incendiary," said Jason. He set the burnt leather hand on the body and he saw that something projected between the fingers of the other hand, the real one that had been flesh and blood and bone. He pried open the fingers, surprised at how easy it was. Clutched in the palm, protected there from the fire, was a cylindrical object with curving sides. Jason lifted it to catch the moonlight.

"It's the bowl of a pipe." The protruding object that he had seen between the dead man's fingers was the stub of the pipe stem.

"Leary didn't smoke," Trelayne said. "I was with him for three hours." He took the bowl and inspected it closely. "It isn't much of a clue."

"It's more than we've had until now," Jason said.

At the mouth of the alley, John Nugent was waiting with Melchior and Dickie, barred from entering by the policeman.

"Mr. Trelayne!" Nugent said when he saw them. "What can I possibly say? How horrible. My God, who is that?" He watched as the firemen carried the body away.

"That is the man with a hook." Jason was looking at Dickie. "The one young Richard saw aboard the *Sarah B. Watson* on the night she burned."

"Ee was right all along then, lad." Melchior put a hand on Dickie's shoulder.

"Say nothing of this, Mr. Nugent," Trelayne said. "I beg of you." He took Nugent by the arm and walked off with him a short distance, talking urgently for only the newspaperman to hear, telling him of Tom Leary and his connection to both fires. "If his confederate reads of this in the newspapers, we will never find him or the man who put them up to it."

"I won't say a word, but I need an account from Mercury to do this night's events justice," Nugent said. "Why have you been silent? It has been more than a week."

"There were . . . considerations." Trelayne thought of Sarah's fears for his safety and he sought a way to overcome them. "I think we should meet somewhere other than your office. I was followed leaving there."

Nugent's concern was immediate. "Have they—"

"I have given them the slip. Even so, there is no need to tempt fate too much. Meet me outside the Unitarian church at half-past three and be sure you are not followed." The summer solstice was two days away and the nights were short. By four o'clock the eastern sky was turning light. It was best to conduct Mercury's business in the dark, if Sarah would agree to write a letter.

Nugent regarded the wreckage that had been the Theater Trelayne. "Are you insured?"

Trelayne shook his head. Fire insurance was prohibitively expensive in San Francisco. The underwriters had long memories.

"It is not hard to imagine who might have paid that poor devil to burn your theater," Nugent said. "But what do a theater and a ship have in common? Bring me that story, Mr. Trelayne, and I will make your Tom Leary the talk of the town."

When they returned to the boardinghouse, Lucy was sitting with Barbara, who still slept, and Sarah was boiling chicken bones and vegetables to make a broth, as Dr. Cole had prescribed. Norton was in the parlor, nodding over a book, but he came wide-awake at the news of the fire and the discovery of Tom Leary. The story had to be told and retold until everyone knew it, and then Sarah ordered Dickie to bed. She tried to persuade Lucy to sleep as well, saying she would make up the divan in the parlor with sheets and blankets, but Lucy would not be

moved from Barbara's side and so Sarah made the divan
for herself.

When Jason started upstairs she stopped him. "Who
is Lucy Thorsen, Jason?"

He saw how much the question cost her and for a mo-
ment he was ashamed. "She is a friend, Sarah. Someone
I met soon after I arrived here. Barbara is her friend.
Don't ask me more."

Chapter 43

I n the morning Sarah decided to serve breakfast in the kitchen to each of her guests in turn, as they awoke. She made corn porridge and biscuits. She cooked sausage patties and moved the skillet to the edge of the stove where they would keep warm while she made coffee. She set another frypan to heat for eggs.

The first to come downstairs was Dickie, still excited about the night's happenings. He ate porridge and eggs and sausage and he told Sarah all about the fire again, and how Tom Leary's false hand was on top of his body when the firemen carried him out of the alley. "I told you I saw a man with a hook aboard the *Sarah B.*," he said.

"I never doubted you, Dickie."

Dr. Cole arrived while Dickie was eating. He examined Barbara, said the worst was past, and pronounced himself satisfied with her condition. He urged Sarah once more to give the patient whatever fluids she would drink. He cautioned her against moving Barbara for at least another forty-eight hours and he took his leave, promising to return again that evening.

When Dickie was done eating, Sarah got directions to Su-Yan Quan's from Lucy and sent Dickie with a note, asking Su-Yan to come to the boardinghouse at once without telling him why.

"There's porridge there," Sarah said when Lucy ventured somewhat hesitantly into the kitchen after Dickie was gone.

"Barbara is sleeping," Lucy said.

"I will make you some eggs." Seeing the blond woman in daylight touched a memory that Sarah could not place until Lucy stood beside the stove, watching her cook the eggs, and she noticed once again that they were much the same age and that Lucy was taller than she.

"On the day Mr. King of William was shot," Sarah said, "you were walking on California Street Hill in the afternoon. We watched a ship arrive together."

"Oh! It is you! You were wearing a cloak."

"And you were wearing a hat. I thought you were very daring. And you said—" Sarah remembered the rest of what Lucy had said that day and she felt her face grow hot.

"I told you I was not a lady."

Sarah busied herself with the eggs, taking them from the pan to a plate. When her eyes met Lucy's again she wasn't ready for the direct, open manner of Lucy's gaze. For a moment Sarah let her own discomfort show, and with it her anger.

Lucy dropped her eyes and said, "I apologize for coming here. I should not be in this house." She turned to go out of the kitchen and Sarah knew that if she said nothing, the blond girl would go out the door into the street and she would disappear into the city.

"Wait," Sarah said. "Please."

"Mrs. Rockwell, I don't want to—"

"Here now, sit down and eat." She brought the plate to the table and pulled out the chair. "How old are you?"

"Almost twenty-three, Mrs. Rockwell."

"I am twenty-four, and much too young to be called Mrs. Rockwell by anyone my own age. Now sit down. Do you take coffee?"

"Tea, please, but—"

"We will have tea together. Here. You sit here and I'll just pour the water." Lucy did as she was told and began to eat. She used her knife and fork as gracefully as a respectable dowager aunt. She took small bites and chewed with her mouth closed, all the time casting short glances in Sarah's direction like a child wondering if the risk of punishment was truly past.

Sarah found her own behavior incomprehensible. Her anger and resentment were real, but Lucy disarmed them without even knowing that she did it. How was it possible that anyone who lived a prostitute's life could be so innocent and so vulnerable? She brought the teapot to the table with two cups. "How long have you been in California?"

"Not quite three years. I came in August of fifty-three."

"So did I." They looked at each other, not quite believing the coincidence. "How did you meet Captain Beck?" Sarah asked, unthinking, but at once she said, "No, don't tell me. I don't want to know."

The back door opened and Dickie came into the kitchen, followed by Su-Yan Quan. "Su-Yan." Sarah rose to greet him. "I am sorry to bring you here without explanation, but I didn't want to give you bad news in a note. Your daughter is here."

Su-Yan looked at Lucy, uncomprehending. "Bo-Ji is here?"

"She is hurt, Mr. Quan," Lucy said. "The doctor has seen her and she is all right."

Sarah led the way across the back hallway to her bedroom. Su-Yan stopped in the doorway as if turned to stone. Barbara was awake. Her head was wrapped in bandaging that covered one ear entirely and most of her forehead and chin. More bandages covered her nose. During the night, the coloring of her bruises had deepened. The swelling distorted her features and one eye was almost swollen shut. Black silk ligatures showed in two of the exposed wounds.

"She was beaten," Lucy said. "Her nose is broken, and a bone in her wrist. Doctor Cole set them."

Su-Yan moved to the foot of the bed without taking his eyes from Barbara's face. Barbara made a feeble gesture. "What is it, Bo?" Lucy leaned over Barbara. "Tell me what it is."

Barbara managed to whisper a single word. "Water."

Sarah brought a glass from the kitchen and offered it to Barbara's lips as Lucy raised her up. Water ran down her chin as she drank because her cheeks and lips were swollen, but each time Sarah held back the glass so Barbara could catch her breath, she motioned for more. When the glass was empty Lucy lowered her back against the pillows.

"Thank you," Barbara managed to say, in a voice that was a little stronger now. Her eyes came to rest on her father. She spoke in Cantonese, haltingly at first, then with more assurance, explaining to him what had happened, acknowledging that she was at fault, for being blind to the *Tao* and putting herself in danger. She kept nothing back. She told him she had hated him for prostituting her and how she had planned her revenge. Having abandoned virtue, she forsook obedience, seeking to confront her father and defeat him in business and thereby to humiliate him in the eyes of the Chinese community. She told him too that her interest in commerce was genuine, and that she still wanted to dedicate her life to working for her family and her people. Her mistake, she saw now, had been in linking her genuine passion to learn with the negative feelings of revenge and hatred. She had strayed from the way of the *Tao* and her punishment was the result. She said that the decision about her future was up to him now. If she learned, it would be from him. If she entered business, it would be with his help, working at his side.

Su-Yan listened impassively, letting Bo-Ji say what cost her so much effort to say, and all the while knowing that the fault was his as surely as if he had beaten his daughter himself. He had placed her in a respectable brothel where he believed she would be safe, but he saw now that by debasing his daughter he had created bad fortune for her, and through her for his family as well, and the weight of his shame threatened to crush him. He spoke to her soothingly, accepting her apologies and her protestations of respect and obedience, and being careful not to contest or reject her view of the tragedy. It was not a wrong that he could correct in a moment. The mending would take much time and effort. The girl showed great courage in taking the whole burden on herself and it must be lightened gradually, so she would believe she had removed it herself.

In every word Bo-Ji said, Su-Yan saw her intelligence and her fortitude, and he cursed himself for not appreciating sooner the measure in which she possessed these qualities. Now, by extraordinary fortune, through the impenetrable wisdom of the *Tao*, he had the opportunity to redress his bad judgment in wasting such an exceptional daughter in the life of a prostitute. He would teach her all he knew and train her in his shadow, and in time they would work not in opposition but in harmony.

"We know who did this," Sarah said. "His name is Jonathan Frye."

"He is only the instrument that shows us the error of our ways," Su-Yan said. He bowed deeply to Sarah. "Of course I will pay you for assisting my daughter, and I will move her as soon as I can summon a carriage."

Sarah bit back a sharp reply. She composed herself and said, "In America it is not our custom to accept payment for acts of Christian charity."

"Nevertheless, my honor requires it. Please. I insist."

"If you insist, you will offend me deeply."

Su-Yan reddened but gave no other sign of his embarrassment. "Naturally, I have no wish to give offense, but—"

Barbara interrupted, speaking forcefully to her father in her whispery voice. When she fell silent Su-Yan bowed deeply to Sarah again. "My daughter says that I must follow the customs of this land. She tells me that I may be allowed to express my gratitude, which is beyond measure."

"I accept your gratitude," Sarah said. "As for moving your daughter, that is quite impossible. Dr. Cole expressly forbade us to move her for at least two days."

Su-Yan hesitated only for a moment. "With your permission, I will summon a physician to see to Bo-Ji's well-being."

"Dr. Cole was here half the night and he has seen her again this morning," Sarah said. "He is among the most respected physicians in San Francisco."

"I believe I may offer to pay for his services without giving offense," Su-Yan said. "And I mean no offense to Dr. Cole if I bring one of our own physicians here to suggest further remedies." He bowed again and left them.

"Their doctors know some things ours do not," Lucy said. She herself had been treated by Su-Yan Quan's physician to abort a pregnancy. The doctor had given her an herbal infusion that caused a miscarriage. It had left Lucy so weakened that she spent five days in bed, but she had avoided an operation that might easily have killed her. The Chinese doctor had instructed her in Oriental methods of preventing conception and since then she had not become pregnant again.

"Let's see if she will drink some broth," Sarah said. When she returned with the broth Lucy was sitting beside Barbara on the bed. They were talking in whispers. When Sarah came in, Lucy said, "Barbara wants to see Captain Beck. She has something important to tell him."

"You can see him when he comes downstairs," Sarah said to Barbara. "First you must drink some of this broth. It will make you stronger."

Together, Lucy and Sarah raised Barbara up and fed her the broth a spoonful at a time. Overhead there were sounds of movement, and footsteps coming down the stairs. A moment later Jason appeared in the bedroom doorway. "How is she today?"

Barbara motioned him to approach her. He bent over the bed and she spoke too softly for the others to hear, and then he said, "She wants to speak to me in private."

Sarah and Lucy withdrew, closing the door. Barbara moved one bandaged arm to indicate that Jason should sit on the bed beside her. "I lied to you yesterday, Captain," she said. "I ask you to forgive me."

"There is no need, lass."

"Yes, there is. Because what I am about to tell you will put you in danger."

Twenty minutes passed before Jason emerged from Sarah's bedroom. During that time Joshua Norton and Trelayne came downstairs. Norton ate a bowl of porridge and two fresh peaches. Trelayne confined himself to biscuits and coffee.

When Jason came to the kitchen Sarah said, "Will

you eat something?" He met her gaze and she was taken aback by the depth of the anger she saw in his eyes.

"I will eat. There is much to be done today. I don't know when I may eat again." He sat at the table and he cast his black gaze at Norton. "Jonathan Frye has dealt in rice and flower since the day he came to San Francisco. He has kept in the background by trading through middlemen."

"Are you certain?"

"Aye. Barbara Quan knows much about his business and she has told me all she knows. Frye made his fortune in fifty-three, in rice and flour."

"Then I was right," Norton said. "He planned my downfall to secure my property."

"Aye, and we are fools not to have seen it sooner. Until now we never considered that a man could speculate in both grains and play one against the other, but that is what he has done." Sarah set a plate before Jason and he began to eat.

"How did he manage it?" Norton said.

"First tell me how a man could learn that rice was on its way from Peru."

"In the old days, some of the commission merchants maintained agents in the major ports who stole or copied bills of lading and forwarded them here by steamer. They arrived weeks ahead of a sailing vessel. Months, if the ship was coming 'round the Horn."

"Frye could have learned that ships were taking on rice in Lima and Callao."

"Yes. But how could he know I would buy the first shipload? And how could he profit from that knowledge?"

"Suppose Frye held flour in fifty-three and learned that rice was coming," Jason said. "Suppose he arranged for the first cargo to be offered to you. You bought it, and now Frye put his stocks of flour on the market, selling through his middlemen. He recovered his investment and started a panic in flour, which guaranteed that the flour on hand would be traded quickly. Bakers and hotels and restaurants all bought it, and flour was shipped to the interior as the price fell."

"The crack in the cartel came from the top, not the bottom!"

"Aye. Now more rice arrives, and Frye is ready. The price falls because flour is plentiful. He buys rice when it hits bottom, again through his agents. He influences his friends without their knowing he is involved himself. They buy rice too. By forming a new monopoly, they hold it until the flour is gone and the price of rice goes to the sky, which benefits Frye as well."

Norton's bulging eyes seemed about to pop out of his head. "That is just what happened! Two months after the collapse of flour, rice was as high as gold, but it was too late for me."

"And all the while Frye was invisible. No one suspected he was behind it. He could bide his time and buy up your mortgaged property as he pleased."

"The blackguard!"

"Aye. And he was involved in grains again this year."

"Did he burn your ship?" Sarah said.

"I am sure of it. And Trelayne's theater as well."

"He gave me warning," Trelayne said. "At the theater he said, 'You have gone too far.'"

"We must prove he carried out his threat." Jason turned to Norton. "Can you learn who was the first to sell flour this year?"

Norton nodded eagerly. "I will ask among the men I know. I will make it seem a matter of personal interest."

"Good. In the meantime, we will trace the arsonist."

"But why burn the ship?" Trelayne said. "Why not do as he did before and turn your rice to his advantage?"

"This time he didn't know the rice was coming." Jason got to his feet. "Perhaps he simply didn't trust his luck a second time. Perhaps when the *Sarah B. Watson* arrived, he panicked. Whatever the reason, when I can prove he's guilty I'll see him hang. Come, we've much to do."

The front door had scarcely closed behind the departing men when David Farren opened the door from the back porch and stepped into the kitchen, startling Sarah. He was unshaven and his clothes were rumpled, but his eyes shone with an excitement that was almost fanatical. "Who is going to hang?"

"Captain Beck believes Mr. Frye burned his ship."

"Even if it's true, the vigilants will never condemn him."

"Four men died!" Sarah protested. "And he may have burned Mr. Trelayne's theater as well."

"I heard about that," Farren said. "So did our old friend Mercury. Listen to this." He held a copy of the morning's *Herald* in his hand. He opened it now. *"Shall we fight to protect only our friends from the scourge of fire, which destroyed this city half a dozen times in its early years? Shall we laugh while men die? The unfortunate wretch who perished in the Theater Trelayne might have been saved by those same Monumentals who swelled the crowd and stood idly by while the theater burned to the ground. Today, this city owes homage to the brave men of the Empire and Crescent engines, who led the assault on the conflagration. Let us honor them, while the Monumentals and their insurrectionist brethren feel the shame of their cowardly deeds, which may go beyond failing to fight the fire. Let the Monumental bell hang in silent shame over Fort Gunnybags. Let us pray that it will ring nevermore, until the day when it rests once again atop the Monumental firehouse and sounds only to summon good men to their neighbors' aid, not to revolt against the just powers of the community."*

Sarah took the paper from Farren and read the letter as if seeing it for the first time. The decision to resume writing as Mercury had been as much hers as Trelayne's, although she had let Tommy think he had persuaded her. For ten days her wrath at the Committee of Vigilance had been penned up. Trelayne's plan to meet Nugent away from the *Herald*'s office was all that Sarah needed to set pen to paper, once she heard of the fire and Jonathan Frye's involvement. She had written the letter after the rest of the household was in bed at last, and she had slept for only a few hours after that. Now seeing her words in print made her feel that her efforts were worth the risk.

"Fort Gunnybags!" Farren said. "That's priceless!"

The vigilantes' sandbag fortifications had been dramatically strengthened three days after the opening of *Caesar in California*. Since then, Sarah had been longing to christen the warehouse Fort Gunnybags. Farren's reaction gave her hope that the term would become popular.

"I have better news still," Farren said. "This morning the sloop-of-war *John Adams* came down from Mare Island to patrol the waterfront. Commodore Farragut sent her 'for calming effect.' Today, General Wool will release one hundred thirteen muskets to the state's militia. Governor Johnson has shipped a hundred and fifty more from Sacramento. I've come for my uniform and then I'm off for Benicia to receive them. This time we're going to win, Sarah! The arms will come to the city tonight. By morning, we will have eight companies of the state's loyal militia ready to face the Committee of Vigilance."

Book Three

Chapter 44

Jan deLoesseps held the pipe bowl to catch the light from the window of Kent's office and he scrutinized it carefully with a Hollander's appreciation for good craftmanship.

"Missouri corncob," he said. "Fine quality. There is good flavor to these pipes." He knocked some of the dottle into his hand and rubbed it between his fingers, then smelled them. "Virginia tobacco. Nothing special, but good enough in its way."

Melchior had found the sailmaker at his doss house and had brought him here where Jason and Trelayne and Kent were waiting. Since resigning from the Committee of Vigilance, Kent had put all his energies into fitting out *Pride of the Seas*.

"Could I buy a pipe like that one in this city, Jan?" Jason asked.

"Aye, Captain. The best tobacconist in town is on Front Street near Vallejo, between the livery and a warehouse. A small shop, but the Jew fellow who owns it knows his pipes." Ashore for a month, Jan deLoesseps had come to know the city's tobacconists and he spoke with authority. "Corncob's not so much in fashion here. He's the only one who carries it. Now I think of it, he had this tobacco too. Or one much the same. I tried it once, but it ain't to my taste. I'm fond of Turkish, when I can get it. Mr. Rooney preferred Virginia tobacco, for all my work at persuading him to give it up."

• • •

Billy Bemis pulled his collar up against the afternoon wind. At midday, bright sunshine had bathed the bay for an hour and the air grew warm enough to make the gentlemen sweat beneath their black wool coats, but the patch of blue sky soon yielded its brief victory to the solid layer of gray-white fog that had lurked along the coast for two days now. By two o'clock the fog had piled into a looming mass twice as high as the heads of the Gate, sending long plumes inland to spread over the city and the bay.

Ever since he woke that morning, Billy had wanted a smoke. At first he thought to spend the whole day abed with the whore, but the woman had lost her ability to excite him and he had grown restless for want of his pipe. Now, as he turned into Front Street, he picked up his pace when he saw the tobacconist's sign.

He felt an itch at the back of his neck and he paused to scratch it. Across the street, a big Kanaka seaman was looking in Billy's direction. The man moved on when Billy turned into the shop.

A loud squawk from overhead startled Billy nearly out of his skin. "Avast, you son of a bitch! He's a buggerhole, this one!" In his impatience, Billy had forgotten about the parrot. It hung in a cage where it could look out on the street through the half-round window above the door. Billy cursed under his breath, but not so the parrot could hear. It was no use talking back to Schoyer's parrot. The bird knew more obscenities in more languages than a Malacca whore.

Billy breathed deeply, savoring the mingled scents from a score of tobaccos. Schoyer himself emerged from a curtained doorway. He was a thin Viennese Jew. "And what might I do for you, my friend?"

"You're a dicksucker," the parrot observed dispassionately.

"I've lost my pipe. One of your corncobs. The good ones."

Schoyer placed the little Englishman by his voice. It had an edge to it, daring the world to contradict him. He never wasted words or money. It had been five years or more since the little Englishman bought a new pipe, but he came in for tobacco from time to time.

"Some of the Virginia tobacco too, I imagine? The usual?"

Billy drew himself up, pleased to be recognized as a steady customer. "That's right. The small packet."

When the transaction was complete, Billy surveyed the street through the shop's grimy window. The big Kanaka was strolling along the far side of the street and now Billy remembered where he had seen the seaman before.

"Got a back door, have you?" Billy patted his coat, assuring himself that the dirk was in its place.

"Backdoor bugger!" the parrot shrieked. "Up the old dirt road!"

"Through here." Schoyer held aside the curtain. His living quarters were small and neat, the bed little more than a cot.

"I owe a fellow money," Billy said, certain that the Jew would understand his wish to avoid a debtor.

The back door gave onto a narrow alley. Schoyer looked up and down, then motioned Billy out.

"I'm obliged." Billy went so far as to tip his hat. He moved along the alley and cursed as he stepped in fresh dog shit. He scraped his boot hastily on the edge of a crate, impatient to distance himself from the tobacconist's. He came out of the alley on Broadway, turned up toward Battery and strode smartly along the street. At Battery he turned left, slipping among the pedestrians, moving faster now. Four blocks along, at Clay Street, he turned left again, back toward the wharves, pausing at every cross street to glance behind him.

"Time for a bit of a holiday," he said to himself. He should have kept to his rule and taken the Sacramento steamer that morning. Get out of town after a job. Take no chances. Now it would be the afternoon steamer. He would come back in the autumn when the weather along the coast turned warmer.

Billy fished the pipe and the packet of tobacco from his pockets and filled the pipe half-full. It didn't pay to get it too hot the first time. Best to work up to a full bowl. It wouldn't be the same as the old one, not for weeks to come, but he needed a smoke.

He had returned to his room and searched it high and

low this morning after he left the whore snoring in her sweat, knowing all the while that he had taken the old pipe with him last night. He remembered the comforting feel of it in the left outside pocket of his coat. Now that same pocket was half torn away. Billy had no idea when or where the damage had been done, but the pipe must have fallen out at the same time. When the job was over, it wasn't there.

He struck a lucifer and waited until all the phosphorus had burned before touching the flame to the pipe. It tasted as much of corncob as tobacco. He smelled the dog shit on his boot again, and he cursed all the dogs in San Francisco. There had been few dogs back in '51. Only cats, then. At least cats took the time to bury their shit.

A ship's chandlery had a boot scraper beside the door. Billy scraped the shit off methodically, puffing on his pipe, taking care not to miss the angle of the heel.

He exploded in a fit of coughing as a strong hand clamped his shoulder. Choking and gasping, he tried to wrench away and turn around, but the grip was like a vise.

"Let's have a look at you, now." The voice was not at all friendly. Billy was lifted up and flung against the wall of the chandlery. He fell to the planks of the street, knocking the wind out of him and making his head spin.

"Bugger hell!" he exclaimed. He rolled over and looked up at his attacker. The man loomed over him. He was a seaman with his hair tied at the back and a gold earring in one ear.

"Who in hell are you?"

"I am Captain Jason Beck of the ship *Sarah B. Watson.*"

Billy fought back the cold fear that coursed through him. He had never seen the man before in his life. Of that he was certain. How much did he know for sure, and how much was he guessing, that was the question. He might know nothing at all.

"Never heard of you or your ship, guv." Billy got to his feet, keeping his back to the wall and his hands in view. One knee was skinned and his head throbbed where it had bashed against the brick wall.

"Don't lie to me, Billy."

At the use of his name, Billy clenched his hands to keep from trembling. The breeze brought him the smell of smoke on the captain's clothing. It had the odor of Billy's midnight handiwork.

"Jim! Come have a look!" Jason called without taking his eyes off Billy.

Billy became aware of three men standing at a distance. They came forward now, the big Kanaka among them. The other two he didn't know. One was even bigger than the Kanaka, who was peering at him intently.

"Sure, I know you. You row the boat, little England man. What else you do? You burn my ship too?"

"I didn't burn nothing!"

Jason took two steps forward and he seized Billy by the throat. "You met·my seaman Grimes when he deserted. You used him to get aboard my ship and then you or your friend Tom Leary knocked Grimes on the head and threw him overboard. You burned my ship and you killed four of my men." Beck's voice was thick with menace. Billy had to clench his sphincter to keep from voiding in his trousers.

"Last night it was Tom Leary's turn to get knocked on the head, wasn't it, Billy?" The man who spoke was the smallest of the four and even so he was larger than Billy. "Is that how you do it? You kill your confederates one by one so there's no one left to point the finger?"

"I don't know you, mister!" How in God's name did they know about Tom! Billy had watched the theater burn clean to the ground, enjoying the show as much as the vigilance muckamucks in the crowd, and then he had gone off to find a whore.

"You should know your victims, Billy." The man's voice was hard. "I am Thomas Trelayne, manager of the Theater Trelayne. You and Tom Leary paid my theater a visit last night."

"I can't breathe!" Billy's voice came out thin and strained. At his throat, Jason's hand loosened a little. "I don't know any Tom Leary or any theater!" Billy did his best to believe that he was being wrongly accused against all reason, but it was hard with Captain Jason Beck holding his neck and looking murder at him. "I spent last night with my doxie, guv! You ask her if I didn't. Sally Shears is the name."

Captain Beck held his free hand in front of Billy's face. He opened it to reveal a blackened object that was somehow familiar. A stub projected from one end. "It's your pipe, Billy. Found in Tom Leary's hand."

He remembered Tom falling, grabbing at his coat as he went down. Didn't hit him hard enough the first time! Tom clutched the left outside pocket of his coat, the one where he kept his pipe. He heard the sound of cloth tearing, but he was intent on the second blow, the one that put Tom out the way the first should have done. Should have used the sodding dirk in the first place!

"It ain't mine."

"Look again, Billy. 'Tis just the same as this one." Jason let go of Billy and bent to pick up the new pipe that Billy had dropped when he threw him against the wall.

"Cap'n!" Melchior cried a warning.

Billy felt invulnerable and intensely alive. His hand went under his coat and came out with a thin dirk all in a blur of purposeful movement, striking for Captain Beck's body, the blade lancing toward his belly. During his lifetime Billy had used his dirk against a score of men and three women without so much as a scratch in return. The mate aboard the *Sarah B. Watson* had been the last one. That was too easy, the man taken unawares. He had turned to look at Billy, not believing the first stab, which would have been fatal on its own, so Billy stabbed him twice more.

Billy felt an almost sexual anticipation as he lunged toward Captain Beck's midsection. He could already feel the blade slip effortlessly into the man's flesh and see the surprise on his face as the life slipped away from him.

But Jason had exposed himself deliberately, inviting the attack. He had let Billy think he would have the new pipe in his hand, but the pipe lay on the planks of the street and Jason's hand held his own knife, coming up now while the other hand deflected Billy's arm. The dirk flashed harmlessly past Jason's left side and Billy gasped with astonishment as Jason's knife entered his chest below the sternum.

For a moment Billy looked up at Jason as if to ask a question and then the strength went out of him. Jason withdrew his knife with a jerk and allowed Billy to fall to the planks of the street.

"My God, Captain." Trelayne took a step backward.

Jolly Jim smiled with pride. "Ain't no little England man catch our cap'n sleeping."

Jason knelt beside Billy. "Who paid you to burn my ship?"

Billy tried to focus on the man above him. He wanted to spit in his face, but gave up the effort. What did it matter now?

"The big man. Sodding bastard." Blood spilled from his lips.

"What big man? What was his name?"

Billy shrugged. He meant it as his answer. Don't know the sodding bastard's surname, he meant to say. Know his Christian name, but if I speak it, the life will run out of me and I will die. They stared at him, waiting for more, Captain Beck and the big Kanaka, the other one—even bigger—and the theater manager. Captain Beck shook him and repeated his question.

"What was his name, damn you!"

"Called himself Jonathan." The words bubbled out with a good deal of blood, borne on the last breath of Billy's life.

"Number?" the door guard demanded. The sentries atop the fortified warehouse were hunched against the wind. It was a quarter to six. As the afternoon grew longer, the layer of cloud over the city had deepened and spread until it obscured every remnant of blue.

"No number. I'm Captain Beck. I must see Mr. Frye."

A large man in a uniform came along the street, making for the door. He glanced at Jason as he passed by, and he stopped.

"He's all right. I'm Grand Marshal Doane, Captain Beck." Doane ushered Jason into the warehouse. The great room was crowded with vigilance militiamen gathered in groups, talking in low voices among themselves. Stands of muskets were clustered along the back wall.

"I remember you from the first day you came to us," Doane said. "What luck with your incendiaries?"

"I have just found the last of them. I must see Mr. Frye."

"You can't see him now, I'm afraid," Doane said. "The Executive Committee's in session. It may be some time. You can write a note if you like. I'll give it to Mr. Frye myself."

"I must speak with him in person."

"I will tell him you're here. Now if you will excuse me." Doane had the air of a man on important business. He left Jason and climbed the stairs to the second floor.

Jason felt at his waist where the Navy revolver was tucked in his belt beneath his coat. His seaman's knife, wiped clean of Billy's blood, was in its place at the small of his back.

Killing Billy Bemis had begun his revenge. Here, in the vigilantes' fort, it would end. He would confront Frye before the Executive Committee and the assembled militia, he would tell them what Frye had done, and he would challenge him. There would be no seconds, no delay to prepare for a formal duel. It would happen now, as soon as Frye appeared. A street duel with street rules. Challenge him, be certain he is armed, and kill him.

Jason estimated that there were four hundred men in the warehouse, loosely grouped in companies. On his earlier visits there had never been more than a few dozen. At this time of day it was usually deserted, the members at home eating their supper. Today the men glanced often at the stairs leading to the second floor. They were waiting, but waiting for what?

Jason saw Ned Rollick in one of the groups. He caught the clerk's eye and beckoned him to his side. "What's going on here, Mr. Rollick?"

"A hundred rumors, Captain. They say that Governor Johnson and General Howard are about to attack the city. Some say the naval sloop *John Adams* will bombard these headquarters and land her Marines. Others say General Howard has armed his militia and we will have to fight a battle in the streets." Rollick did not appear to relish the prospect.

There was a murmur from the men in the warehouse. William Tell Coleman was coming down the stairs, followed by Truett and Smiley and Abel Calvert. Jonathan Frye was behind Calvert. Jason left Ned Rollick and moved toward the stairs. He lost sight of Frye for a moment as the men clustered about the vigilance leaders when they reached the floor.

"Captain Beck." Abel Calvert stepped from the throng. Jason had not seen Calvert since the duel.

"Mr. Calvert. I am glad to see you looking well. I hope your head ..." He was momentarily at a loss.

"My head is very hard, Captain, as you may have gathered. I want you to know I bear you no ill will. You were entirely within your rights as Trelayne's second." Technically, because Trelayne had yielded at the last moment, Calvert had won the duel, but that in no way lessened the humiliation he had suffered at Trelayne's hands.

"You are generous," Jason said.

"No. But I try to be fair. What brings you here today? Something about the ship? All going well? Your men have everything they need to put her right?"

"We have, thanks to you." For a time, Jason had feared that Calvert might withdraw from the arrangement with Farnum & Kent out of anger over his part in the duel, or because of Kent's resignation from the Vigilance Committee, but the rigging of *Pride of the Seas* was nearly done. She looked more like a ship each day and Calvert's bank paid the bills as promptly as ever.

"You will be on your way before long," Calvert said. "You want my advice, you'll forget about finding the scum who burned your boat and weigh anchor as soon as this one is seaworthy." He waved a hand at the men around them. "This outfit is going from bad to worse."

"We found the incendiary an hour ago," Jason said.

Calvert was suddenly very alert. "Where is he now?"

"He is dead."

"Who was it?"

"An Englishman named Billy. His accomplice died last night at the Theater Trelayne."

"It is over, then."

"No. They were paid to burn my ship. I believe they were paid to burn the theater as well. By someone on this Committee."

"Who is it?" Calvert asked.

"Until I say his name, there's no one knows it but me." It wasn't true, but no one in the Vigilance Committee would hear it from Jason's crew or Sarah's household.

"And once you speak that name here, it's loose on the wind." Calvert nodded. "All right. You keep shut for now, Captain. Tomorrow, if things go our way, I'll call the Executive Committee into session. We'll bring the man in and you can accuse him to his face."

"It's true then. You are expecting trouble."

"We're taking steps to prevent it. I can't say more. Nothing personal, Captain. Executive Committee only. That's the rule. Once it's settled, you come see me. If a man in this organization has done what you say, we'll put him on trial quick enough."

Jonathan Frye was talking with Marshal Doane and Tom Smiley. Calvert's back was to them.

"And if he is guilty?" Jason said.

"He will hang just as high as Casey and Cora."

In his mind's eye Jason saw Frye dangling from a window of the warehouse, just as Casey and Cora had met their fate. That would be justice indeed. But it was too risky leaving Frye to the Vigilance Committee or any other court where the judgment was uncertain. Jason gauged the distance between himself and Frye. A dozen steps through the crowd, his knife at Frye's throat while he told them all what Frye had done, and then the challenge.

Frye had been clever to support the search for the arsonists. More clever still to act as intermediary between Jason's marines and the Committee. He had probably known where to find Billy and Tom Leary all the while! If he hadn't thrown caution to the winds and burned the theater too—

Wait, now. Trelayne's play had offended not just Frye but the whole Committee of Vigilance. Was Frye acting alone when he hired Billy to burn the theater, or was he acting for all of them? They were gathered around him now, Coleman and the rest, talking something over and glancing often in Jason's direction. What if they were all in it? What if they were involved as well in burning the *Sarah B*? Then it was not just Frye he must bring down, but the entire Committee of Vigilance —

They came toward him in a group, Coleman in the lead and Grand Marshal Doane beside him, with Frye on his other side and Truett and Smiley and little Jim Dows coming behind. Jason saw now that one of Frye's hands was bandaged. The knuckles of the other were bruised and swollen from beating Barbara Quan.

It was Frye who spoke first. "This Committee has co-operated with you fully, Captain," he said. "We hope now that you are prepared to cooperate with us. When Marshal Doane told me you were here, I said, 'That is just the man for the job.' "

"Governor Johnson has obtained arms for this rabble militia of his," Coleman said impatiently. "If they get them there will be hell to pay."

"We cannot have warfare in the streets, Captain," Doane said. "Everyone agrees on that."

"We want you to intercept the boat carrying these arms," Frye said. "Our men will make up the boarding party, once you find the vessel."

"How are they coming?" Jason kept his eyes on Frye. The merchant stood less than an arm's length away. He could draw his knife and put it through Frye's heart before any of the others knew what was happening.

"They will be brought by schooner from Benicia to-night."

"How many men aboard the schooner?"

"Three or four, so far as we know. We will provide you with a vessel."

"There is a sloop making ready at the Commercial Wharf," Doane said. "She's called the *Malvina*."

"I want my own men for handling the vessel," Jason said. "I'll take no landsmen as crew. I want men I trust."

"Are they loyal?" Frye asked.

"They are loyal to me." To forestall debate, Jason turned on his heel and left the warehouse.

When he was gone, Jonathan Frye found the man who was to lead the boarding party and spoke with him privately. His name was John Durkee and he had been a San Francisco policeman, the only one of that fraternity to join the Committee of Vigilance. He was now a member of the organization's small and select force of paid police. He had a full beard but no mustache, and his eyes drooped at the outer corners, which made him appear sad, although he was not an emotional man.

"You can take your men to the wharf now," Frye told him. "You understand what you are to do?"

"Yes, sir," Durkee said. "If there's any shooting, I'm to kill Captain Beck and make it look like it was done by someone aboard the schooner."

Chapter 45

he clock on the parlor mantel said twenty-five minutes after six when Jason entered the boardinghouse. A fire burned in the hearth and the smells of cooking came from the kitchen. Dickie Howell was reading at the table in the parlor where he took his lessons from Sarah. He looked up as Jason peered into the room.

"Is Melchior in the house, Richard?"

"Yes, Captain. In his room. Supper is in five minutes."

"Bring Melchior down, lad."

Jason went along the back hallway. Through the kitchen door, he saw Ingrid at the sideboard and a strange Chinaman bending over a pot on the stove. There were voices from Sarah's bedroom. Jason knocked on the door and opened it. Sarah and Lucy were on the small divan by the window. Su-Yan Quan was sitting beside Barbara, who was propped up on several pillows.

"I am glad to see you better," Jason said to her.

"Mrs. Rockwell has taken good care of me, Captain. My father brought a Chinese physician to take over my care."

"Dr. Cole was put out, I'm afraid," Sarah said.

"Is Jonathan—" Barbara began, remembering now what she had told Jason that morning. "Did you—"

"There is more to this than Frye now. Sarah, I must

speak with you." He led her to the parlor, where
Melchior and Dickie were waiting.

"General Howard's law offices are shut up tight. I
must find Captain Farren."

"Captain Farren is not here," Sarah said.

"Has he gone to Benicia?"

Sarah hesitated, unsure how to respond.

"The Vigilance Committee knows General Howard is
expecting arms from the governor," Jason said. "They
have a plan to intercept them."

Sarah turned pale. "Are you sure?"

"The arms are to come from Benicia by schooner tonight. Is that right?"

"Yes, but how—"

"They have sent me to intercept them."

"But if you are working for them—"

"I wouldn't be telling you this if I intended to do it! I
let them think I am rounding up my crew to man their
sloop. It will delay them awhile. But when I don't come
back they will send someone else. What schooner is coming from Benicia?"

"The *Julia*," Sarah said. "Captain Farren is bringing
the arms to General Howard. He will be aboard."

"Melchior and I will go in your little boat. She's fast
enough and we won't attract notice. We'll find the *Julia*
and warn Farren."

"You will not," Sarah said. "You will blunder about all
night on the bay, if you are not swept out to sea on the
tide."

"Now look here—" Jason began, but she cut him off.

"Tell me what the tide is doing now, at this moment."

"The tide? I couldn't say, but—"

"It is on the turn. In three hours it will be at full flood.
Do you know where the current is strongest? Do you
know where the shoals are? If you find the schooner before the turn, can you make your way back against the
tide by following the backwaters along the shore?"

"There will be danger, Sarah. There is no need for
you—"

"The need is *mine*! This is *my* bay and *Katahdin* is *my*
boat. I will change my clothes and be ready in ten minutes." She left them gaping after her.

"She be fit for a sailor's wife, that one," Melchior said.

Jason turned to Dickie, whom no one had paid a moment's notice since the three grown-ups entered the parlor. "Richard, I want you to find Finn Warren. Tell him to take his dory to Angel Island and lay off the shore where he can watch for a schooner coming down from San Pablo Bay. If we miss the *Julia*, he can warn her. He is to tell her the Committee of Vigilance knows about the arms."

"Yes, Captain!"

"Tell him to watch for a sloop named *Malvina* too. That is the Vigilance Committee's boat. When you have found Mr. Warren, you are to come home and you're to stay here. Do you understand?"

"Yes, Captain," Dickie said with less enthusiasm.

"All right, you have your orders," Jason said, and Dickie was off and gone. "How many men have we now?" Jason asked Melchior.

"Seventeen, Cap'n. Fourteen from the *Sarah B*."

Since news went out on the waterfront that Farnum & Kent had bought *Pride of the Seas* and were fitting her out for the China trade, the size of Jason's crew had recovered from a low of seven. A number of the old crew had returned, and three new men were hired already. By the time the ship was ready to make sail, she would have a full complement.

"You and Jolly Jim round them up," Jason said. "But only the men from the *Sarah B*. If you find any more of the old crew, offer them a week's sea wages and bring them along. See they are armed. Have them at Mr. Kent's offices by midnight. Fetch Mr. Kent from his house to let you in." He considered what else he might do to prepare for the eventualities of the following day and decided there was nothing. "If this night's work goes well, tomorrow we will know who burned our ship and Trelayne's theater. God willing, our ship's company will have a hand in bringing them to account."

Along the shore of North Beach the air was chill off the water. No idlers lingered on Meiggs' Wharf as they might have done on a warmer day. Jason and Sarah reeled in *Katahdin* from her mooring in the lee of the wharf and made ready to sail. Once they were aboard the little sloop and pushed off, Sarah took the tiller while Jason hoisted the sails. They trimmed the sheets together and the sloop stood away from the shore.

They sat on the windward side of the cockpit, clad in oilskins. Sarah's hair was tucked beneath a dark wool watch cap. Under her sou'wester, she wore a pea coat and a sailor's woolen pants. The sloop's passage was swift on a reach that took her to leeward of Alcatraz Island. In the deepest channel, where the tides moved fast, the water was black beneath a thick layer of fog that seemed nearly to touch the sloop's mast. From the Golden Gate, the baying of the steam foghorn at Fort Point sent a baleful warning across the water.

Katahdin topped a wave and rode the crest for a short time before sliding into the trough. Jason put one arm behind Sarah to steady her.

"Even if we warn Captain Farren, how will he get the arms ashore?" she said.

Jason had weighed the problem since Frye told him of the Committee's plans, but he had found no solution. A schooner might outsail a sloop if she knew the vigilance pirates were after her, but the vigilantes would be guarding the city's waterfront in case the *Malvina* failed to overtake her prey. "Where are they to come ashore?"

"At Rincon Point. General Howard will take the marine battery and point the guns at Fort Gunnybags. It was General Sherman's plan."

"It's a good one," Jason said. "The vigilantes outnumber the state's militia ten to one. Those guns will make the difference." The answer came to him suddenly. "We'll send the arms to Oakland!"

"Oakland?" Sarah couldn't imagine what good the muskets could do across the bay in Oakland.

"Captain Farren can commandeer a ferryboat or a tug in the governor's name," Jason said. "We can take it at the point of a pistol if we must." The plan was forming in Jason's mind as he spoke. "*Pride of the Seas* was moored off Rincon Point when we bought her. There is plenty of water for a ferry or a tug at the wharves there."

"They won't be expecting a steamer."

"Nay. They'll be looking for the *Julia*. We'll bring our

boat to the point while they're still searching the bay for a schooner." And if the wind should drop before dawn, as it often did, a steam vessel could still make the crossing while the *Malvina* sat becalmed.

Jason reached for the picnic basket Sarah had packed in haste before they left the boardinghouse. "Now I've an appetite. What was it you brought for our supper?"

They ate slices of pork Sarah had cut from the dinner roast before leaving the house. There were chunks of cheese and bread as well, and a jug of water that Jason wished were brandy.

There was no sunset. Far to the west, obscured by the mass of fog that clung to the coast and overflowed the bay, the sun dropped into the sea and the light dimmed as if a curtain had been slowly drawn across a vast window.

Angel Island loomed large before them. Sarah came about to gain the channel between the island and Marin. The water was deeper there than east of the island, she said, and the tide preferred that route to San Pablo Bay. The current pulled them along and *Katahdin* skipped over the waves, throwing spray from her bows. As they cleared the channel they fell off the wind, turning northward.

"Look there." Jason pointed overhead. A patch of dark blue sky showed through the thinning clouds.

"We will be in the clear soon." Sarah was pleased that what she took for granted surprised a man who had circumnavigated the world. In summer the fog poured through the Golden Gate, but north of Angel Island the air was warmed by its passage across the broad peninsula of Marin, which had baked in the midday sun, and the northern reach of the bay was often clear while San Francisco was dank and gray.

Katahdin soon left the fog and clouds behind. Overhead, the stars winked on one by one. The air turned warm, and Jason and Sarah put aside their sou'westers.

"We are losing the wind," Jason said.

"It's often calmer here."

" 'Tis a good school for a sailor, this bay," Jason said.

"I learned to sail on the coast of Maine," Sarah said. "My father and my brother Peter and I used to go out in the wintertime. We wore woolen underwear and woolen trousers and woolen seaman's sweaters from Norway that he brought home from Oslo, and woolen socks in our rubber boots, and sou'westers on top of it all. And we were still cold."

"Yankee sailors are the best in the world because they sail on the North Atlantic."

"The most dangerous of the seven seas."

"Aye," Jason said. "Did you dress like a boy then too?" He remembered the first time they had sailed together, and how she had tolerated the encumbrance of her skirts, but not without complaint.

"Yes. I was a tomboy. My mother called me a hoyden when I was too much for her."

"But your husband made you a lady."

They had not spoken of her husband since the afternoon of Molly's wedding. A picture of Haven Rockwell came to Sarah's mind, and she was surprised that he appeared young in her memory. When I am old he will still be young, she thought. I have left him behind.

"Haven knew that appearances matter to some people, and he believed it is a courtesy to behave well. But he understood my nature. He didn't try to change it."

"He was a good husband, then."

"Most men wouldn't agree with you. They believe a woman should remake herself in the image of her man, as if that were possible."

"I have never wanted that," he said. "A seaman's wife must be her own woman, with her husband gone for months at a time."

"Some wives go to sea with their husbands. Captains' wives."

"Aye." The long voyages of the merchantmen had overcome the sailors' prejudice against women on board ship. Some captains' wives fared well, others less so. "Would you go to sea with me?"

Sarah was silent for so long he thought she had not heard him, or perhaps that he had only imagined he spoke the question aloud. At last she said, "I won't compete with your mistress, Jason. She is stronger than I."

Half an hour later, Sarah could make out Point San Pablo on the Contra Costa shore and Point San Pedro jutting from the coastline of Marin. The narrows between the two points marked the southern limit of San Pablo Bay. The wind had continued to weaken as *Katahdin* sailed northward with the tide. In the channel, the water was rippled by the breeze but there were no waves. With the tide pushing into San Pablo Bay, no southbound sailing vessel would be able to make headway through the narrows unless the wind increased.

"If *Julia* can't make way against the current she will anchor and await the turn," Sarah said.

"When will it turn in the narrows?"

"An hour after it begins to ebb in the Golden Gate."

"After one o'clock, then."

"Yes."

"We'll heave to here, or anchor if you've got one."

"I have a kedge. We'll anchor there, so we'll have the wind behind us." Sarah pointed toward the western shore.

She trimmed the mainsail and put the tiller over, pointing the sloop toward a small bay between Point San Pablo and the next promontory to the south. With the wind on her port beam, *Katahdin* slipped quietly through the water. As they entered the sheltered waters of the little bay they left behind the rushing tide, which was nearing full flood, and entered a backwater that carried them toward the southern promontory. In its lee they dropped the sails and put out the kedge anchor.

The sloop drifted about her anchor line uncertainly, pushed by the shifting breezes and the currents of the backwater. Sarah found herself nodding, and she moved so she could rest her head on Jason's shoulder.

"I can't stay awake," she said. "Let me sleep for just a little while."

"I'll stand the first watch."

The water lapped at *Katahdin*'s hull and Jason's warmth was comforting. Almost as soon as Sarah closed her eyes she slept a dreamless sleep. When Jason shook her to wake her it seemed that only a few moments had passed, but the stars had turned in the heavens and the little sloop had swung about on her anchor. She was holding steady now, and Sarah judged that the incoming tide was slowing. The moon, waning but still fat, had risen, and it stood now a handbreadth above the Contra Costa hills.

"If you can stay awake for a bit, I had better get some rest," Jason said.

"Yes. I'm all right now. You can stretch out here." She moved across the cockpit, where she could keep a watch on the narrows. Jason lay on his back on the seat along the side of the cockpit with his feet on the stern thwart. In a short time his breathing grew slow and regular.

To keep herself awake, Sarah thought about the events of the past two days and she wondered what more she might have said in Mercury's letter that would appear in this morning's *Herald*, to make the vigilantes think twice about opposing the state's militia. She had left the letter on Trelayne's bed, with instructions that he was to send Dickie to the *Herald* to arrange a meeting between Trelayne and Nugent beyond the view of the Committee's spies.

Where the contest is avoided, there is no victory, no defeat. Su-Yan's words came to Sarah unbidden. His advice had not been on her mind when she wrote the letter, but averting a violent contest was her heartfelt aim and she had used every bit of information at her command toward that end.

While David Farren prepared for his trip to Benicia that morning, he had told Sarah the full extent of Governor Johnson's preparations to assure the Committee's downfall. Even if the rebels won the contest with the state's militia, the governor, in consultation with Judge Terry, had taken measures to assure that the ringleaders would soon find themselves in federal court, facing charges of insurrection and sedition. At midday on Friday, unknown to any but Johnson and Terry and David Farren, two men had sailed for Panama aboard the Pacific Mail steamer, bearing a letter from Governor Johnson to President Franklin Pierce in Washington. The emissaries were Judge Augustus Thompson, recently the United States land commissioner for California, and San Francisco's postmaster, Ferris Foreman. Governor Johnson's letter requested that President Pierce order General Wool and Commodore Farragut to give the state every assistance in putting down the Committee of Vigilance.

With Thompson and Foreman safely on their way and beyond the Committee's influence, Sarah had revealed their mission in her letter to the *Herald*. The news would be an unwelcome surprise for the Committee. Sarah hoped it would make the leaders see that a battle with the state, even if they were victorious, would gain them a harsh judgment when they stood before a federal court.

Yet the fact that Governor Johnson had sent the emissaries meant that he was not confident the military plan to bring down the Committee would succeed. If it failed, and if a violent clash were the result, no judgment of any court could repair the wounds, both real and symbolic, that would be inflicted on San Francisco and her citizens. At the very best, with no undue delay en route and with a swift and positive decision by President Pierce, the governor's delegation would not return for two months. How much blood could be shed in that time? And if the Vigilance Committee put down an armed attempt to overthrow them, how would they deal with those who had attacked them?

Sarah looked at Jason's sleeping form. She had brought him here to help prevent the Vigilance Committee from seizing the state's arms. By so doing, she was acting to preserve the chance that the state's militia might overthrow the Committee before the day was out, but as soon as the militia was armed the chances for armed conflict would rise a hundredfold.

A movement caught Sarah's eye. The vessel was a sloop of about forty or fifty feet overall. It came from the south, carried toward San Pablo Bay by the tide and the freshening southwesterly breeze. Sarah bent low so her silhouette would not be visible above *Katahdin*'s boom and the furled sail. On the deck of the larger sloop she could make out figures moving about. As the boat crossed the shining path of moonlight on the channel, Sarah saw that the men on deck were armed with muskets.

Chapter 46

ickie Howell found Finn Warren at the Noggin of Ale. The old salt was more than willing to undertake the task of spending the night on the dark bay, watching for the schooner *Julia*. He invited Dickie to come along as crew, but Dickie explained that he was ordered to return to Mrs. Rockwell's and stay there. The truth was, Dickie would very much have liked to go on with Finn Warren but there was something else he had to do. It wasn't much out of the way and now seemed his best chance to do it undetected.

Ten minutes after parting from the old seaman outside the grogshop, Dickie was in Merchant Street above Montgomery, testing the back window at the premises of Calvert & Winston, bankers. He had been in Mr. Calvert's offices often since the banker had agreed to lend Farnum & Kent the money to buy *Pride of the Seas*. From the start of refitting the ship, Dickie had spent as much time at the Vallejo Wharf as possible, to learn all there was to know, and Melchior took Dickie with him when he went to see about sailcloth and ropes and ballast and oakum and water barrels and all the other things required to make a neglected vessel seaworthy once more. "It'll do ee good to learn these things, young Dick," Melchior had told him. "Cap'n Beck's of a mind to make a mate or a master of ee, if I know'n."

Several times they had stopped at Calvert & Winston

to present bills for the bankers to pay. Twice on these occasions, Melchior and Dickie were shown into Mr. Calvert's private office and Mr. Calvert had asked Melchior questions about the ship and how long it would take to make her ready. On their most recent visit, Dickie had noticed that one screw securing the latch of the office window was loose. He had meant to say something to Mr. Calvert about it, but Sarah had warned him not to interrupt grown-ups' talk. When Melchior and Calvert were done with the day's business, Dickie's attention had wandered to some papers on Calvert's desk. Something there caught his interest and the loose screw had slipped his mind. If Calvert hadn't repaired the latch in the meantime, the window should yield to a good strong push.

Dickie heaved on the window and was startled when it shot up with a thump. The other screw must have been loose too. He looked up and down the street. The glow of gaslights spilled into Merchant from Montgomery, but there was no one within Dickie's sight. He climbed through the window headfirst, tumbled to the floor, got to his feet and closed the window behind him.

He sat on the floor behind the desk, out of sight of the window, to collect himself. His heart was pounding and he was breathing as if he had just run the length of Montgomery Street. Never in his wharf-rat days had he broken into private premises to steal. All his stealing was done in the street, where he could run in any direction to get away. Here he felt closed in, and he wondered if a piece of paper were worth the risk, but the only way to find out was to do what he had come to do.

He was here because a miracle had happened to him that evening before supper. Before Captain Beck came into the house he had been reading Mr. Dickens' *Oliver Twist* in the parlor, struggling over a passage in which Oliver was given a five-pound note by Mr. Brownlow, a kindly gentleman who had cared for Oliver when he was ill, and was sent with it to pay a debt Mr. Brownlow owed to a bookseller, when suddenly poor Oliver was set upon by a young woman who dragged him off into the presence of the evil Fagin and the frightening bully Bill Sikes.

From the moment the girl Nancy took hold of Oliver in the street, Dickie's finger had ceased to move beneath the words as a guide to his eyes. He had skipped over a few of the longer words but he followed the story without effort for several pages, growing outraged and alarmed to see Oliver abused by the heartless bystanders, who believed Nancy and would not heed his appeals for help. Dickie had been nearly in tears at the injustice of Oliver's plight when he realized that he had been *reading*, just as Sarah said he would.

"Something quite wonderful will happen to you very soon, Dickie," she had told him not three days before. "When you read alone, it will seem like hard work at first, but then something magical will happen. You will find that you are reading without working at it, as if the words were speaking to you from the page. I was just your age when that happened to me. The magical part is that once you have begun to read, you will never forget how."

Dickie had been about to go to Sarah's room to tell her of his astonishing feat when Captain Beck arrived and sent him upstairs to fetch Melchior, which put Mr. Dickens and poor Oliver completely out of Dickie's mind for a time. When Captain Beck had told him to find Finn Warren he had realized that this was his chance to test his newfound reading ability and to learn if the paper he had seen the other day on Abel Calvert's desk might be truly important. The name *Sarah B. Watson* had caught his eye, and Dickie had peered at the sheet to see what it might say about the ship, but Mr. Calvert had distracted him by pointing to the trapper's rifle that hung on the wall. Mr. Calvert had made a great fuss about the rifle on Dickie's previous visit, and Dickie couldn't understand why he was telling him all about it again, swearing on his honor that it had saved his life a hundred times or more. When Dickie looked again at the desk, the paper with the *Sarah B. Watson*'s name was no longer in sight and then Dickie knew as sure as he was born that the rifle had been only a way to distract him, like two boys pretending to fight while a third lifted a gentleman's purse from his pocket. While Dickie was distracted, Mr. Calvert had hidden the paper. But why? That was what he had come to find out.

The desk was as Dickie remembered it, cluttered with papers. He picked up a sheet at random and held it toward the dim light from the window, peering at the writing. It contained columns of figures and very few words to test his reading ability. A quick inspection showed that the rest of the sheets in the same pile were also covered with columns of numbers.

Where had he been standing? Mr. Calvert had sat in his chair behind the desk and Melchior sat there, in the chair provided for visitors. Dickie had stood near the front corner of the desk, here.

He examined the stack of papers nearest to him. The top sheet was a letter. It was written in a neat hand and was not hard to read. Sarah sometimes showed him the letters she wrote her brother Peter. Dickie liked her letters, with their stories about the city and its happenings, but this one was boring. It was all about money and business and something called "interest." There were a lot of words he didn't understand, but Sarah had prepared him for that. "Don't worry about the words you don't know," she had told him. "You will learn them in time. Read the words you do know. Often you'll find that you can make sense of something even though you don't know all the words."

Her advice had worked for *Oliver Twist*, but here, even when he understood most of the words, Dickie still didn't understand what the letters were about.

He leafed through the papers quickly. They were all letters until he got halfway down. There he found a number of printed forms with spaces left to be filled in. The word VESSEL was printed by the first space, followed by a line where the name of the vessel was written in by hand. On the first form, the name was *Stag Hound*. The rest of the sheet was filled with a written listing of articles that seemed to have nothing in common—kegs of nails and barrels of linseed oil and hogsheads of wine and bolts of silk and packing crates with pianos and furniture and books and pickaxes. After each item there was a number in a space at the right-hand edge of the page.

Dickie thumbed quickly through the pile, wishing he had stayed at home to learn whether Oliver Twist ever got free of Fagin and Bill Sikes. There were only a few dozen sheets in the middle that had to do with ships. The rest were letters, like those on top. He pulled out the middle section and took the pages over to the window to see them better. The names of the vessels shone like beacons from the pages, calling him to the sea: *Ringleader* and *Sea Serpent*, *Flying Cloud* and *Neptune's Car. Sarah B. Watson.*

This was the paper he had seen! Below the ship's name, on the line marked FIRM, *Farnum & Kent* was entered in a bold, flowing hand, just as Dickie remembered it. Why Mr. Calvert had bothered to hide it from him, he couldn't imagine. But Calvert had hidden it from his view without any reason to believe that an eleven-year-old boy would be interested in it, so Dickie folded the sheet and pushed it down into the front of his pants. He took several of the other forms for good measure and put them in the inside pocket of his coat, before shoving the rest back into the middle of the pile.

In his haste, he disturbed the balance of the pile. It toppled and fell, all the sheets above the middle slithering to the floor in a mess. As Dickie bent to pick them up, a shadow passed across the window. He froze, for fear that his movement might draw the eye of the passerby, but the shadow moved on.

Dickie pushed the papers together hastily, squaring them up as best he could before replacing them carefully atop the corner pile on the desk. He ducked again, this time behind the shelter of the desk, when three men paused outside the window for a few words before one parted from the others and all three went on their ways. Dickie counted to twenty-five before venturing near the window to peer up and down the street. He assured himself that there was no one in sight, then eased the window up, being careful to make no sound. Just as carefully he climbed through the opening, landing on his feet this time, and turned to close the window behind him.

A hand took hold of his coat collar and lifted him off

the ground. It was like a bad dream. His legs flailed in the air but he stayed in the same place.

Abel Calvert turned the struggling boy around. "Well, well. What have we here?" He patted Dickie's coat with his free hand and felt the wad of papers. When he took them out and looked at them, his expression grew very stern.

As afternoon turned to evening, Trelayne explored the better saloons on Montgomery Street. He took a perverse pleasure in playing the part of Thomas Trelayne, the brilliant theatrical manager who had bearded the lions of the Vigilance Committee and now quaffed brandy punches in their favored taverns. He hoped he would see Jonathan Frye so he could goad him into challenging him. He had no intention of toying with Frye as he had toyed with Calvert. A few minutes of sword-play, just enough to let Frye see he was outmatched and to see the fear in his eyes, and then kill him with a neat stroke that wouldn't bleed too much. Trelayne wondered what it would feel like to kill a man. Watching Captain Beck kill English Billy that afternoon had been an extraordinary experience. Now Trelayne stalked his own prey with the smell of blood still in his nostrils.

But he did not find Frye on Montgomery Street, nor did he see any of the other merchants who were known to sit on the vigilance organization's Executive Committee, so he dined in Delmonico's and returned to the boardinghouse, where he found the letter Sarah had left on his bed. Dickie was not in the house and Joshua Norton was setting out to look for the boy. Trelayne dressed himself as an elderly gentleman and took the letter to the *Herald*'s office. He regretted the loss of the costumes and accoutrements at the theater, which limited his choice of disguises to those things he kept at the boardinghouse for developing new characters. The beard and mustache he wore tonight were somewhat moth-eaten.

He was disappointed to note that no one took the slightest interest in his disguise or his evasions, even when he strolled out of the *Herald* office as bold as brass and paraded the length of Montgomery Street. When he returned to the boardinghouse, he hoped he might at least fool Norton and Dickie for a time, if they were home. His form shriveled and he put more weight on the cane he had swung jauntily on Montgomery Street. He climbed the steps to the veranda one at a time, as an old man might, pausing to catch his breath before he advanced to the door.

A shadow rose from a chair on the veranda. "Excuse me, sir," said a woman's voice. "Are you looking for Mrs. Rockwell?"

"Eh?" Trelayne cupped his ear. "Who's that?" He spoke in the fragile voice of an old man.

Molly stepped into the light from the parlor window. "I'm a friend of Mrs. Rockwell's. I'm afraid she isn't at home."

"Friend? Says you, missy. Creeping around folks' house in the dead of night? You call that a friend? Shameless wench! A trollop if ever a trollop was born!" He brandished his cane.

"No, really," Molly stammered, taken aback by the attack. "My name is Molly—"

"Molly Malone!" The old man leered. "Selling cockles and mussels, are we? Come, show me your mussels. If you are a very nice girl I might show you my cockles."

Molly's mouth fell open and her timidity vanished. She raised her parasol and struck Trelayne about the head and shoulders. "You are hateful! You frightened me half to death."

"Peace, Molly." Trelayne warded off the blows with his arms. Finally he took hold of the parasol. "That's enough. Come inside now. There are ears in the night." He took her by the arm and ushered her into the foyer. By the parlor clock, it was twenty minutes before ten.

"Come up while I change." Molly's presence had brought Trelayne to his senses and he was impatient to shed the disguise. The elderly gentleman did not belong in the boardinghouse. Always before he had slipped into the theater to remove his disguise before coming home, but the theater was gone and he was acting now on a larger stage where the duels and the hangings were in earnest.

Molly's eyes glinted in the lamplight of his room. "It's not a very original costume," she sniffed.

"It's not meant to attract attention." He stepped behind the Chinese screen to change.

"I have been waiting forever." By the chimes of the parlor clock, she had waited for less than an hour. She had seen Ingrid leave and since then had heard no sound from inside the boardinghouse. "I am so sorry about the theater, Tommy. I only heard this afternoon when Su-Yan came by with the vegetables."

"In time I will miss it," Trelayne said. "For now, the fire has given me wonderful roles." He peered around the screen. "I have been manning the battlements of liberty."

"Don't tease me."

"I am serious, Molly. Things are coming to a head. You had better keep to your house tomorrow. It won't be safe in the streets." He disappeared once more and emerged a few moments later wearing clean pants and a seaman's thick wool pullover. His feet were bare.

"What will you do, Tommy?"

"What is there to do? Perhaps Mr. Maguire will take me on."

He meant it in jest, but Molly was in earnest when she said, "I will find a way to help you. I promise."

"Maybe you can ask your husband to extend me credit."

Molly flushed. "I might have, before that awful duel. He was so angry."

"Would you rather I killed him?"

"I didn't come here to talk about Abel."

"Why did you come, Molly?"

"When I heard about the fire I thought of you all alone and it broke my heart. Who would do such a thing, Tommy?"

"The men who set the fire are dead."

"How do you know?" Her eyes were wide and her body was tense, like a cat prepared to flee from danger.

"One died in the fire. Captain Beck and I found the other this afternoon. He attacked Captain Beck with a knife and Captain Beck killed him. The same man burned his ship. Now we're after the man who paid him."

"You know who it is?"

"We know."

"And you won't tell."

"You're married to one of the vigilante leaders, Molly."

"Is it one of them? Is Abel involved?"

"They're all involved! Can't you see that? They are a pack of thieves who cloak themselves in righteousness to hide their sins. What do you think my play was about?"

"It wasn't Abel! He would never do a thing like that."

"It is not Abel." He touched Molly's hair, repeating a comforting gesture he had used more times than he could remember. "Won't he miss you? It's late, Molly."

Molly turned petulant. "He hasn't been home all day and he sent a messenger boy to say he won't be home to-night." She looked at him with the same soft eyes that had captivated him in Chicago, when she was just six-teen.

Trelayne moved his hand to the cool skin of her cheek, then brushed the tips of his fingers across her lips. They were softer than the petals of a flower. She took his hand in her own and placed it on her breast before drawing him into her arms.

ason started awake suddenly. He had no idea where he was. High above, the gibbous moon shone down on the little boat. In the east the black horizon was silhouetted now by the first hint of new light from the east. A steady breeze ruffled the water.

He remembered then. When he could keep his eyes open no longer he had wakened Sarah and she took over the watch. How long had he dozed? It seemed like a moment, but the moon was high in the sky.

Sarah was asleep with her head on his shoulder. In the narrows between the two bays a schooner was sailing close-hauled against the southwest breeze.

Jason shook Sarah awake. "What is it?" She was dull with sleep. "Oh! I fell asleep! Oh, Jason, I'm sorry."

"No matter. If that's the *Julia*, we've come to our senses in time."

It was the work of a moment to raise *Katahdin's* anchor and hoist the sails. The ebb tide pushing southward through the narrows bore the schooner swiftly along, even though she had the wind against her. She was carrying only her mainsail and one jib. Jason could make out a lone figure at the schooner's helm, hauling on the main sheet with both hands while bracing a knee against the wheel. Where were his men?

With the wind behind her, *Katahdin* slid almost silently through the water on a course to intercept the larger vessel. Jason stood, steadying himself against the center-board housing, and cupped his hands to his mouth. "Ahoy the schooner! What vessel are you?"

"Who wants to know?" the helmsman demanded.

Sarah put over the tiller and brought *Katahdin* on a course parallel to the schooner's and upwind.

"I am Captain Beck of the ship *Sarah B. Watson*."

"Captain Mannix of the *Julia*. What can I do for you?"

"We have important news for Captain Farren concerning your cargo."

"You're too late, Captain Beck. A gang of vigilance pirates boarded me two hours ago. Ten of 'em, there was, with pistols and muskets. My passengers and cargo are likely in that fort of theirs by now, or soon will be."

The sun was an hour in the sky and the bay was flat, the surface of the water only rippled by the light breezes, when the *Malvina* was sighted by a vigilance sentinel on the Commercial Wharf. The longest day of the year promised to be calm and hot. *Malvina* drifted languidly through the ships anchored off the wharves, sometimes losing headway altogether as the breezes waxed and waned. By the time the sloop dropped her sails at wharfside, an hour more had passed. Abel Calvert, Jonathan Frye and Miers Truett were on hand to greet her, accompanied by a score of the Committee's militia and a freight wagon drawn by two draft horses.

When the sloop was made fast, the three members of the Executive Committee stepped aboard. They were greeted by the policeman John Durkee. The evening before, when Captain Beck had failed to appear at the wharf, the Committee's leaders had hastily gathered men with sailing experience to crew the *Malvina* and placed Durkee in charge of the vessel. Their confidence was rewarded now by the presence of fifteen long crates on the sloop's deck.

"Mr. Durkee, well done," Calvert said.

"Thank you, sir." Durkee motioned to one of his men. "Bring 'em up on deck." A moment later, three men were brought up from the sloop's cramped cabin. They blinked in the sunlight.

"Why on earth did you bring them?" Truett said.

Durkee was taken aback. "I thought it best to keep 'em out of any further mischief, sir."

"Taking the arms to prevent civil strife is one thing," Truett said. "Kidnapping is another."

"Don't put ideas in their heads," Calvert warned Truett under his breath.

"You have no right to those arms and no authority to hold us," one of the prisoners said.

"Says who?" Frye demanded.

"I am Captain David Farren of the San Francisco Blues. These men are Lieutenant McNabb and Private Maloney."

Frye laughed. "And a fat lot of good it does you, eh?" He poked Farren in the chest lightly with the tip of his cane.

Farren knocked the cane away. "We are transporting this cargo by the express order of the governor. Seizing it is an act of piracy."

"You are relieved of your cargo by order of the Committee of Vigilance," Calvert said impatiently. There would be no debate here about the Committee's actions. "You'll come along with us while we decide what to do with you. Mr. Durkee, we'll take four of your men as escort. You see to it that the crates are transferred to that wagon and put where they will be safe. Mr. Frye will tell you where."

Calvert led the way off the sloop with Truett following. Durkee motioned to four men, who prodded the prisoners up the gangway. Frye stepped close to Durkee and spoke with him briefly in tones no one else on the deck could overhear. He gestured once over his shoulder toward the wharf and the streets beyond and then hastened after his friends.

Once they were back at Fort Vigilance and safely inside with the prisoners, Calvert spoke quietly to Truett and Frye. "We've got the arms and there's nothing these three can do about it. I say we turn them over to Mr. Bluxome, let him get their names for the record, then turn 'em loose."

Truett gave his assent and Frye could think of no

sound reason to object. Calvert issued brief orders to the four guards and dismissed the prisoners from his mind.

He took his watch from his pocket. It was half-past seven. At eight, the Executive Committee would meet to hear his report on the capture of the state's arms. After that, the militia companies that had been kept in readiness since the previous day could be dismissed. Many of the Executive Committee had been awake all night and would no doubt go home to get some rest. In a few days, there was no reason they couldn't talk about adjourning the Committee.

Calvert looked forward to a good breakfast at home. Most of all he looked forward to seeing Molly. She had submitted to him two days after the duel, and although there was still a certain awkwardness to their lovemaking he felt confident that in time, when the troubles of the moment were forgotten, theirs would be a joyous union.

Before going home he would have to take some food to Dickie Howell. What in hell was he going to do with the boy! He had locked him in his office closet and he had put a notice on the door of the bank saying it would not open until Monday due to Vigilance Committee business. By Monday he would have to find a solution. Turn him loose, and Dickie would say what he had found on Calvert's desk. Even if the telltale papers were destroyed before anyone came looking for them, the boy's story would raise doubts and questions. Some smart aleck would put two and two together, and the bank and all Calvert's achievements would come crashing down around his head.

No, by God. He had worked too hard to lose it all now.

"Mr. Calvert, sir, if I may have a moment."

Calvert found Kent's clerk, Ned Rollick, at his side. The fellow moves like a Blackfoot, Calvert thought. You never see him coming. "Well, what is it?"

Rollick swallowed nervously. "Sir, I took it on myself to keep watch on Mr. Thomas Trelayne since yesterday. It occurred to me he might take action against you, sir, or another member of the Executive Committee, on account of his theater being burned."

"Why should he come after us?"

"Well, sir, I chanced to overhear Mr. Kent speaking with Captain Beck's mate yesterday in the firm's offices. They believe the man found dead in the theater after the fire was one of the incendiaries. Yesterday afternoon Captain Beck caught the other one. He killed him."

"I know all this. Captain Beck told me himself."

"Did he tell you that the man he killed named someone on the Executive Committee as the one who hired him?"

"He did, but he's keeping the name to himself."

"He gave it to Mr. Kent, sir. It is Mr. Frye."

"The devil you say!"

"Yes, sir. And there is something more. In the course of keeping watch on Mr. Trelayne, I have learned that he is the one who has been writing letters to the *Herald* as Mercury."

Calvert was momentarily speechless. Knowing that Kent and Captain Beck suspected Frye of hiring Billy Bemis opened possibilities that Calvert had barely begun to consider. Learning that Trelayne was Mercury swept those thoughts aside in a rush of exultation. He no longer had to protect Trelayne for Molly's sake! As Mercury, Trelayne was fair game.

But if Trelayne was Mercury, how did he get his information? From within Mrs. Rockwell's house? Captain Beck wasn't privy to the doings of the Executive Committee—but Stephen Kent was, and Mercury stopped writing at the same time Kent resigned! In the new letters, yesterday and today, the *Herald*'s mysterious correspondent revealed no new intelligence from within the Committee of Vigilance, although much knowledge of the state's efforts. Had Kent been working against the Committee all along?

"Tell me what you saw," Calvert said.

Rollick was perspiring lightly in the cool warehouse. "Knowing Mr. Trelayne boards at Mrs. Rockwell's house on Mason Street, I arrived at the house yesterday about dusk. Soon after, a woman left by the back door. A scullion by the look of her. Mr. Trelayne came up Jackson Street a short time later. He was in the house only ten minutes before he came out again. The light showed in his room, then it went out, and then he came out."

"Get on with it, man!"

"That is important, sir, because the man who came out of the house after Mr. Trelayne's light was put out was apparently an older man and he wore a beard, but he was Mr. Trelayne's height and size and I was sure it was he, so I followed him."

"He wore a disguise!" Calvert exclaimed. As an actor, Trelayne was a master of disguise. In disguise, he could have gone anywhere to gather information for his letters to the *Herald*! He could have come inside Fort Vigilance. He might even be enrolled in the Committee's militia under a false name.

"The bearded man went to the offices of the *Herald* on Montgomery Street, sir."

"By God, we've got him now! Well done, Rollick."

"That is not quite all, sir. Believe me, Mr. Calvert, what I am about to tell you I will never breathe to another living soul. On my honor, sir." Rollick's Adam's apple bobbed twice.

"Well, what is it?"

"When Mr. Trelayne returned to Mrs. Rockwell's house, sir, there was someone waiting for him. It was . . . It was the actress Molly Gray. That is to say, sir, it was your wife, Mrs. Calvert."

Calvert felt a cold calm settle over him. He fixed Ned Rollick with his gaze and the clerk blanched, but he screwed up his courage and said, "She went inside with Mr. Trelayne, sir. So far as I could tell there was no one else in the house. I saw that I could reach the roof of the veranda by way of a trellis. Mr. Trelayne's window overlooks that roof, sir. I climbed the trellis and . . . Sir, I will never speak of this to—"

Calvert seized Ned Rollick by the front of his coat. "Spit it out, boy. Now."

"I saw Mr. Trelayne remove his false beard, sir. He and Mrs. Calvert talked for a time, sir, and then . . . and then they were intimate. Of course I left at once."

Calvert pulled Rollick closer and for a moment the clerk feared that Calvert was in the grip of some sort of seizure. He was trembling and his breathing was very rapid. When he spoke, his voice was barely his own. "You know Watkins, the police captain?" Rollick man-

aged to nod. "Tell him I believe Trelayne is Mercury.
Tell him I want Trelayne found and followed, but not arrested. Tell him I expressly forbid anyone to go to Mrs.
Rockwell's boardinghouse. Say the police are to follow
Trelayne and report to me if he is found in the streets
but no one is to go to the house. You take one man and
you tell him nothing, only that you're to watch for
Trelayne. You go to Mrs. Rockwell's house and you follow Trelayne anywhere he goes. Every hour on the hour,
you send word to me here. I want to arrest Trelayne myself, if possible. Do you understand? If you find him, tell
no one except me. If the police find him first—well, I
will find a way to do what must be done."

Calvert loosened his hold on Rollick and seemed about
to free him, but suddenly he jerked the young man up
close against his face again and he spoke in a ghastly
whisper. "If you tell anyone what you have told me,
about . . . what you saw, I will slit you open and feed
your guts to the fish."

He pushed Rollick violently away and Rollick fled.
For a moment he had feared that Calvert might kill him
on the spot. He would surely kill him if he knew that
Ned Rollick had watched Trelayne and Molly Gray until
their passion was spent and they lay insensible in each
other's arms. The variety and intensity of their coupling
had astonished him and the image of Molly Gray's unclothed body burned brightly in his memory, but more
brightly still shone his own future now, when Calvert
forgave him for being the messenger who bore such bad
tidings. By the sheerest chance, he had learned the iden-
tity of the mysterious Mercury, who had aroused the
Committee's ire. At the same time he had given Abel
Calvert a reason to kill Thomas Trelayne, and by so
doing he had put the banker in his debt for reasons that
could not be revealed to the world at large. In time, he
fervently prayed, this act would redound greatly to the
benefit of Ned Rollick.

Chapter 48

t was almost noon when Sarah returned to the boardinghouse. After she and Jason had intercepted the *Julia*, the schooner took *Katahdin* in tow. With Jason and Sarah acting as crew, Captain Mannix made use of every breath of wind and still it had taken all morning to travel the ten-odd miles back to the city. Captain Mannix swore that in his seven years on the bay he had never before seen anything approaching so perfect a calm.

Sarah found the house quiet and no one about. There was a fire in the stove. A kettle simmered at the back. In her bedroom, Lucy was reading to Barbara. Barbara's swellings were as bad as ever, but her attempted smile was genuine and her eyes showed new hope.

"I slept in the parlor, on the divan," Lucy said. "I hope that was all right."

"Yes, of course." If Lucy had chosen Jason's room that would have grieved Sarah, but from the start Lucy had shown great consideration for her feelings. It was by her consideration that Sarah saw how much Lucy herself cared for Jason.

"Where is Mr. Trelayne?"

"He was gone before I woke up," Lucy said. "There has been no one here all day since the Chinese doctor came."

"Not even Dickie?"

"No one has seen him since last night. Mr. Norton

went looking for him in the night and again this morning."

Sarah took the stairs two at a time, grateful for the absence of skirts to trip her. Dickie's room was neat, his bed made. There was an air of absence, perhaps even abandonment. She wondered if the promise of warfare in the streets had lured him back to his waif's life for a time.

"We are expecting Barbara's father," Lucy said when Sarah returned. "When he comes I will go to Mrs. Wickliff's for a change of clothing, unless you need me."

"Can you do something for me first? Can you go now? I'll stay with Barbara."

"I will do anything at all for you, Sarah," Lucy said, and once more Sarah was disarmed.

"Captain Beck has gone to Mr. Kent's offices. Farnum and Kent, on Sansome between Washington and Jackson streets. Tell him Dickie is missing and see if he can spare some of his crew to look for him. I will stay here in case Dickie comes home." She wanted to be in the house if Trelayne returned. All night she had worried that he might be careless in passing her letter to John Nugent, and might be found out. She needed to see for herself that he was all right.

She watched from the parlor as Lucy set off down Jackson Street. The blond girl walked with long strides, as Sarah walked when she was dressed in men's clothing. And then a movement caught Sarah's eye. A man peered from behind the house across the way after Lucy had passed by. He watched her go down the street, then stepped back out of sight.

Sarah kept watch a while longer. Twice the man's head appeared from behind the same corner of the house across the way. Each time he was looking in the direction of Sarah's house. Certain now that he was keeping watch on the boardinghouse, Sarah left the parlor and went up to Trelayne's room. On several occasions she had watched Trelayne disguise himself for his visits to the *Herald*. She knew where he kept his false whiskers and the gum mucilage he used to apply them. She hadn't thought until now that she might use them herself, but if she were to be accepted as a man in broad daylight she would need a thorough disguise.

Half an hour later she came downstairs dressed in Trelayne's laborer's clothes, which she concealed under a full-length cloak of her own. She would leave the house as herself. In her pockets she had a close-cropped beard and mustache, a wool tweed cap, and a pair of plain glass spectacles that made her look serious. She would go to Molly's to change herself into a man, beyond the view of the vigilance watchers. Abel Calvert would be at his bank or occupied with the Vigilance Committee's business and Molly would be alone. She could help apply the false whiskers and she would enjoy seeing Sarah playing the part of a man.

When she went to her bedroom to tell Barbara she was leaving, Sarah was much relieved to find Su-Yan sitting with his daughter.

"If Mr. Trelayne comes home, tell him I believe the house is being watched by men from the Vigilance Committee," Sarah said. "They're behind the house across the street and they may come for him if they see him. He'll know best what to do. If Dickie comes home, please keep him here."

"At last!" Stephen Kent exclaimed when Jason entered the offices of Farnum & Kent at midday. Seventeen of the *Sarah B. Watson*'s ship's company were gathered in the firm's rooms, as they had been since midnight. Finn Warren was with them.

"We have failed," Jason said. In the end, the night's work came down to that.

"We feared something happened to ee and Miss Sarah," Melchior said.

"Nay, nothing. We missed *Malvina* in the night and we failed. What's become of Captain Farren? Does anyone know?"

"Aye, Jason," Finn Warren said. "They turned 'em loose, and I was there to see it. I seen the *Malvina* come down the bay this morning, right past where I was hove to off Angel Island. Last night I never caught a glimpse of her. Then this morning she come right past me, so I followed along. I seen them take those men off her at the wharf and I went along to that fort of theirs. No one told me about arms aboard the schooner, or I might of followed them instead."

"It's all right, old friend," Jason said. "You did what you thought best."

"Aye, and p'raps it were best after all. I didn't reckon to wait long, but I'd scarce been outside the fort for half an hour when out they come again, Cap'n Farren and the other two, set free. I told Cap'n Farren you was off on the bay to warn him and he sent me here to wait for you, reckonin' you'd come here when you got ashore. He went to swear out a complaint against the Vigilance Committee for piracy. In federal court, he said. He's waiting for you now at Cap'n Ashe's office. Told me to send you there."

"Ashe is the U.S. naval agent," Stephen Kent said. "He opposed the Committee from the start. Commands a company of militia. He keeps rooms at Kearny and Washington, the northwest corner, over Palmer, Cook's bank. It's at the corner of the Plaza."

"He says if'n you seen any of it, you're a witness to piracy," Finn Warren said.

"I saw nothing, but Captain Mannix of the *Julia* saw it all. He'll testify, I'm certain." Jason felt the beginnings of new hope. Under United States law, piracy was a hanging crime. Once convicted in a federal court, the sentence was mandatory and there could be no appeal. Under that threat the Vigilance Committee might back down, but where was there a federal court that would give them an honest trial?

He noticed among the seamen a face he hadn't seen since two days after the *Sarah B. Watson* dropped anchor off Goat Island. It was Little Jack, the nimble Kanaka, who had deserted on his first shore leave. "You've come back to us, Jack."

"Aye, Cap'n. Ready to stand up for punishment."

"I find Little Jack, Cap'n," Jolly Jim said. "I tell him he come back with me, I will speak for him. He got drunk on leave, Cap'n. Fuck too much, drink too much. 'Fraid to come back after one day. More 'fraid after two days. He don't have nothin' to do wid the fire. I talk to him long time, he say he got nothing to do wid it. I b'lieve him."

"And you're ready to sail with us again, Jack?"

"If you'll have me, Cap'n. First port we make, I don't take no shore leave, stand harbor watch 'round the clock. First ten ports if you say."

"You will stand double watches the first week at sea," Jason said. "After that, we put the old business behind us. We are a new ship with a new crew."

The street door opened and Ned Rollick stepped inside. He was surprised to find the rooms crowded with seamen. "Mr. Kent, a word, if you please."

They went up the stairs to Kent's private office. After a moment, Kent called down the stairs, "Jason! You had better hear this."

When Jason entered Kent's private chamber, Kent closed the door and said, "Rollick has been acting on my behalf since I resigned from the Committee. He has pretended to support them in order to keep me apprised of their intentions. Tell him, Ned."

Rollick bobbed his head and swallowed. "The arms that the *Malvina* seized have been taken to a storehouse on Front Street, between Pacific and Jackson. It is an older building with new oaken doors."

"They're not at the vigilantes' fort?" Jason felt as alert as if he had just awakened from a long night's rest.

"Tell him who the storehouse belongs to," Kent said.

Ned Rollick said, "It belongs to Mr. Frye."

"How many guards?" Jason asked the clerk.

"Only two," Rollick said. "So as not to arouse suspicion."

"Our best chance will be after dark." Jason thought for a moment longer. "I must go to Captain Ashe and tell him."

Downstairs, he found the crew gathered around Lucy Thorsen. In the midst of the rough seamen, her beauty was startling. "Mrs. Rockwell sent me," she said to Jason, and she told him of Sarah's plea for help in finding Dickie. Jason ordered the starboard watch to look for the boy until four o'clock, when the port watch would take over the search. He instructed the men to eat and get some rest while they were off duty and to return to Farnum & Kent at nine o'clock that evening.

Lucy left the firm's offices with him, and when they were alone in the street, she took his arm and they walked together, Lucy's long strides matching themselves to his haste. "Mrs. Rockwell is worried about the boy," she said.

"He will be somewhere in the streets, watching the goings-on. When it's over he'll come back."

When they stopped at Washington and Kearny streets she put a hand over his heart and she said, "Tell me the truth, Jason. Mrs. Rockwell has touched you here. Is it not so?"

"Aye," he said, for it was the truth. It was true that Lucy Thorsen had touched his heart as well, but his other mistress, the sea, had the strongest claim on him of all and so he said nothing more as Lucy walked away.

In the rooms above Palmer, Cook & Company, David Farren introduced Jason to Captain Ashe, Judge Terry, and General Howard. The other two men present had accompanied Farren to Benicia to receive the state's arms. They were Lieutenant McNabb, of Ashe's company of the Blues, and Reuben Maloney, a private in the same company. Like Farren, they had been taken prisoner by the vigilance pirates and released.

"We were building our case against the vigilants when you arrived, Captain," Farren said. "The leader of the boarding party was a vigilance policeman named Durkee. He's the one we'll go after. Through him we hope to condemn the Executive Committee. Did you see anything of the piracy?"

"Nothing. But Captain Mannix will testify. He'll swear out a complaint if you like."

"An affidavit from the master of the schooner will help," David Terry said. He was sitting behind the only desk in the room, organizing the legal maneuvers. "If Durkee says he was ordered to seize the muskets, the whole vigilance leadership will stand before a federal judge."

"I have other charges to bring against Jonathan

Frye," Jason said. He was gauging the mood in the room.

"Captain Farren has told me about the arson," Terry said. "If what he says is true, it's enough to hang Mr. Frye even without the piracy."

Reuben Maloney rubbed his red nose with a dirty hand. "I'd like to see them stranglers get a dose of their own medicine."

"So would we all," said Ashe. He sat on the corner of the desk.

"With proper arms, we could put five hundred men against the rebels by midafternoon," General Howard said. "But our last hope of arms is gone."

Howard was a few years older than Jason. His hair was graying and he had a furrow of worry between his brows, beneath the rim of his Kossuth hat. The hat was the only thing military about his dress. Otherwise he looked like what he was, a San Francisco lawyer.

"Where are your militia troops now, General?" Jason said.

"They are mustered in their armories awaiting orders."

"Our Blues and the Marion Rifles are just up at Dupont and Jackson, over the firehouse," Farren said. "The Continentals are on the corner there." He pointed out the window, down Kearny past the City Hall, to the corner of Clay Street. "We have some arms, but not enough to make a show against the Vigilance Committee."

"Can you muster your new companies if you had arms for them?" Jason said.

"We could send runners from the Blues and Continentals."

"Would you act to recapture the governor's arms if you could?"

"What do you mean?" Ashe got up from the desk.

"The muskets are in a storehouse on Front Street between Pacific and Jackson."

Judge Terry sat bolt upright. "How do you know this?"

"My shipowner has a man in the vigilance militia."

"Why didn't they take the arms to Fort Gunnybags?" Ashe wondered. "That's where we thought they were."

"Because they're afraid I might issue a writ for them!" Terry got to his feet and came around the desk. "If we found the arms on their premises, we'd have them dead to rights. By God, this is a piece of luck!"

"We still have a chance to get the muskets and arm our men," Farren said, almost disbelieving it.

Terry's blood was up. He turned to Ashe and said, "Now you've got a reason to call your sloop-of-war."

"Yes!" Ashe exclaimed. "If Boutwell will bring the *John Adams* down off Sacramento Street, he can back us up from the water."

"Lieutenant Boutwell is ordered not to put his men ashore," Farren told Jason. "But his orders say nothing about using the guns aboard the sloop."

"Of course he'll have to send a boat to Mare Island to let old Farragut know what he's doing," Ashe said. "Without a wind it could take over a day or more for him to get a reply." He sat in the chair Terry had vacated and reached for pen and paper. "I will write out a letter telling Lieutenant Boutwell of the piracy and formally requesting his help. I'll take it to him myself."

"Will he do his part?" General Howard said. "I must be sure of him before committing my men."

Ashe paused in his writing. "Once Ned Boutwell takes a stand, you couldn't ask for a better man."

It seemed to Jason that Howard was looking for obstacles, while Ashe and Terry were searching for ways around them. They looked at Howard now, awaiting his reply.

Howard nodded. "Very well. It's worth a try. If we have a gunboat at the vigilantes' rear, we may still bluff them into submission with four or five companies of good men."

"Thank you, General," Terry said. Jason saw that it cost the jurist an effort to be polite to Howard. "What you must do first is order Quartermaster Kibbe to issue a formal request to the vigilantes, demanding the return of the state's arms. That is the only legal effort we need make. If they refuse, they confirm an act of piracy." Terry grinned at Jason. "Thanks to you, Captain, the legal moves are just our pawns. They will give our enemies something to think about. While they hesitate, we can bring our knights and rooks into play."

"My men and I know the waterfront," Jason said. "We will reconnoiter the storehouse."

Terry laughed a short bark of glee. "That will serve the sons of bitches right! Take their storehouse, arm our men, and arrive at the doors of Fort Gunnybags before they can ring their damned bell!!"

The door shook suddenly under the impact of an insistent knocking from the other side. At a nod from Ashe, Farren opened it. A stocky man stood in the doorway. Three more men were behind him on the landing.

"Captain Ashe?"

The naval agent stepped forward. "I'm Ashe. Who are you?"

"Name's Hopkins. Sterling Hopkins." Hopkins' tone was like his knock, demanding and loud. He was clean shaven but for a small goatee and he had large, rather limpid eyes beneath heavy brows. "I have a warrant for the arrest of one Reuben Maloney, said person bein' known to me and bein' now within these premises."

Chapter 49

erry moved to Ashe's side. "I am Judge David Terry of the state supreme court. You may come in and present your warrant, but you will come in alone."

Hopkins stepped uncertainly into the room. Ashe motioned Farren to close the door. He twisted his hand to mimic turning a key in a lock. At the sound of the bolt sliding into place, Hopkins looked about nervously.

"Where is your warrant?" Terry demanded. He stood a head taller than Hopkins.

Alone among strangers, Hopkins' manner was less assured. He cleared his throat. "I have no paper. My warrant is given by spoken order of my superiors."

"And who might they be?" Terry inquired acidly.

"I am empowered to arrest Reuben Maloney in the name of the Committee of Vigilance."

Ashe took a step toward Hopkins. "Maloney is a private in the San Francisco Blues and I am his commanding officer. Tell your Committee they can't arrest anyone in my office!"

Hopkins seemed to find strength in Ashe's defiance. "I can have this buildin' surrounded by a thousand armed men inside of half an hour."

"I serve the president of the United States," Ashe said sternly. "You tell your masters they had better think twice about assaulting a federal officer."

length. "You can't call for help if we cut out your tongue, can you now, Mr. Hopkins?"

Hopkins backed toward the door. The skin of his face glistened damply where the light from the window struck it. "I've come here on orders of the Committee of Vigilance. Seein' as you're gentlemen, you'll let me go, havin' stated my business."

Ashe turned the key and let Hopkins out. He brushed by his three companions and started quickly down the stairs. Ashe closed the door and relocked it. "Do you know who that was?"

"He said his name is Hopkins," Farren said.

"It took me a moment to remember where I heard it before. He's the man who put the nooses around Casey and Cora's necks! They called for a volunteer and he stepped up. Bragged about it later, by what I heard."

"They know about Captain Farren's complaint and it's got them worried," Terry said. "They're trying to rearrest the witnesses who can harm them."

"Why did he only ask for Maloney, then?" It was the first time Lieutenant McNabb had spoken since Jason entered the office. "Here am I, big as life. I'm an officer and he only wants Maloney? It doesn't make sense."

"As my lieutenant, you represent the authority of the state," Ashe said.

"That's right," Terry agreed. "He said nothing about Captain Farren either. If they are reluctant to tamper with the state's commissioned officers, that means they fear the government in Washington will support Governor Johnson."

"Maloney holds no commission," Jason said. "He's fair game."

"Fair game for the hangman, you mean!" Maloney was very pale.

"We all went to Benicia at General Howard's orders," Farren said. "They can't touch you for what you've done."

"Just the same, I'd feel better with a few dozen of the Blues backin' me up," Maloney said. "That Hopkins was put out proper by the way Cap'n Ashe tossed him out. He'll be back."

Ashe looked to Terry. "Our armory is two streets away."

"All right." Terry nodded. "The Blues' armory it is." He turned to General Howard. "Go now, General. Have one of your men carry Quartermaster Kibbe's demand for the arms to the vigilantes' fort and await a reply."

Ashe thrust a paper in Howard's hand. "Get this to the *John Adams*, sir. Have someone take it out. I'll do what I can as a federal officer to protect Maloney."

"Good luck to us all," Howard said as he left them.

When Howard was gone, Ashe brought a rifle and a shotgun from a closet. He passed the rifle to Terry. The jurist inspected the cap with the quick assurance of someone long accustomed to firearms. "Are you armed, Captain?" he asked Jason.

"A knife and a pistol, Judge."

The holster at David Farren's belt was empty. Terry looked at McNabb and Maloney. "You men?"

"The vigilantes took our weapons," McNabb said.

"We'll make do with our fists, if it comes to that," Maloney said. The efforts being made on his behalf were doing much to restore his confidence.

In the street, the party moved north along Kearny toward Jackson. As they reached the corner, a shout came from down Jackson. "There they are!" Five horsemen with Hopkins in the lead came galloping from the direction of the waterfront.

"The armory is there, third floor of the Crescent firehouse!" Ashe pointed up Jackson to the near corner of Dupont, just one street away. The six men broke into a run.

The horses' hooves thundered on the planks of Jackson Street. Hopkins, in the lead, raced past the runners. He reined in sharply and jumped from his mount in midblock, in front of another engine house, the Pennsylvania No. 12. With enemies before and behind, the men on foot came to a halt.

"Reuben Maloney, I arrest you in the name of the Vigilance Committee!" Hopkins charged the men who shielded Maloney in their midst.

Jason blocked Hopkins' rush and he careened into Ashe and Terry. The rest of the vigilantes were off their horses now, rushing to Hopkins' support. Untended, three of the animals ran off down the street. Another reared and pawed the air as its rider tried to control it.

Ashe lurched into Jason. "We must protect our witnesses," he said in Jason's ear. "Get McNabb to the armory."

"Come on!" Jason grabbed McNabb by the arm and started up the street. When they were halfway to the corner he slowed his pace, looking back. No one was following. One vigilante was running down the street after the fleeing horses. Another still struggled with his panicked animal. The three who were engaging Terry and Ashe and Farren had them backed against the brick wall of the Pennsylvania engine house with Maloney cowering in their midst. A vigilante held Ashe's shotgun in one hand and a pistol in the other. Hopkins had Terry's rifle by the barrel.

"Get to the armory!" Jason said to McNabb. He turned and started back down the street, drawing his revolver.

"I am a supreme court judge!" Terry shouted. "I order you to leave this man alone!" He tussled with Hopkins, trying to wrest loose his rifle. Hopkins kept hold of the barrel and pushed Terry, knocking him into the vigilante with Ashe's shotgun. The man's pistol discharged inches from Terry's face.

"By God!" Terry cried. Letting go of the rifle, he drew his bowie knife and plunged it into Hopkins' neck. Hopkins let out a mangled cry of pain.

The combatants' struggles ceased at the same moment. Terry's knife was raised, ready to strike again. Dark blood covered the end of the enormous blade. Ashe and the two vigilantes gaped at Hopkins, who held his neck with one hand. Blood gushed between the fingers. With his other hand, he reached out toward nothing in particular, his mouth open in silent astonishment. He backed away from the others and staggered into the street, half falling, half running, crying weakly for help.

Momentarily forgotten, Farren pushed Rube Maloney up the street. They sprinted past Jason, making for the corner, where McNabb was waiting by an open door.

"Come on, then!" Jason shouted to Ashe and Terry.

The cry released the two men from their trance. They ran, leaving the dismayed vigilantes behind. From the Pennsylvania firehouse, men came out to help Hopkins.

Jason was the last through the doorway to the Blues' armory. A steep stairway led to the third floor of the Crescent firehouse and an iron door at the top. Ashe pounded on the door and shouted his name. A bar clanged and the door opened. Inside, the armory was a bastion prepared for a siege. Thin shafts of light came through rifle slits in the iron shutters that protected every window.

The enclosed space was sweltering. The seventy-odd men in the rooms had removed their jackets and their shirts were soaked with sweat. They gathered around Ashe and Farren, glad to see their officers and eager for their news, which Ashe and Farren related in a few words.

"Do you think I killed him?" Terry said.

"Either way, they'll be coming for you, sir," Ashe said. "They'll be coming for us all."

"Lookouts to the windows," Farren instructed the militiamen.

Jason heard a sound like a bell buoy in the distance, but they were too far from the water and there was no wind to rock a buoy. He held up a hand. "Listen."

From across the rooftops of the city came the tolling of a bell. *Tap, tap,* and a pause. *Tap, tap.*

For two weeks since the Monumental Engine Company's bell had been removed to the roof of Fort Vigilance, it had hung silent on a sturdy frame erected by the vigilantes. Now, in the streets, pedestrians and horsemen stopped at the sound. *Tap, tap*—the ominous interval— *tap, tap.*

Draymen unhitched the horses from their wagons and gentlemen freed Thoroughbreds from the shafts of their buggies. Gaudily dressed miners and soberly attired merchants became a motley cavalry, racing to Sacramento Street in answer to the bell. For every horseman there were ten men afoot pelting toward Fort Vigilance, taking heart as their numbers swelled until Front Street and Davis and Sacramento itself were choked to the walls of the buildings.

They soon learned there was to be no orderly mus-

tering of the militia companies in the warehouse today.
No drawing up in lines and marching quietly through
the city with grim expressions to scare the living day-
lights out of every Democrat and Sydney duck within
sight or hearing. As fast as the men poured through the
doors of Fort Vigilance they were armed and rushed
back outside so others could come to grab a musket. Today it was muster in the streets and the devil take the
hindmost, and overhead the bell kept up its tolling—

Tap, tap—enough time to take a deep breath in the
pause—*tap, tap*.

At the first sound of the bell, some cautious merchants
and shopkeepers locked their doors. Along the streets
that felt the rush of vigilante feet, others followed suit.
The shutters on the banks clanged shut. The halt of business spread across town as the word was carried from
mouth to mouth. When the bell fell silent at last, the citizens stopped where they were and listened. From the
center of town came the sound of a large body of men
moving through the streets.

In the Blues' armory, Terry said, "We must give them
what they want."

"They want Maloney," Ashe said. "Now they will
want you and me as well."

"Precisely."

"You mean surrender?" Ashe was shocked.

"How many muskets have you here?"

Ashe turned to Farren and Farren looked to a younger
man. "Lieutenant Reese?"

"Sixty, sir."

"And how many balls per man?"

"Twenty-five, but some of the men are short on caps,
sir, and there is not enough powder."

"The vigilants will have a few thousand men in that
street in a quarter of an hour," Terry said. He addressed
Jason. "You must get away, Captain. You too, Captain
Farren. Take McNabb with you. We must protect the
witnesses to the piracy."

"My place is here," Farren protested.

"Your place is to carry on the fight so long as there's
hope, David," Ashe said. "We'll delay them as long as we

can. You find General Howard. No, never mind Howard. Get the men and arms out of the Continental armory if you can and tell them to scatter. The vigilants may use this as an excuse to seize all the state's arms left in the city." When Volney Howard took over command of the newly organized militia he had countermanded Sherman's policy of allowing the men to take their arms home with them. Ashe had approved the change at the time. Now he wished he had not.

"Vigilantes comin'!" a lookout cried. "Comin' up Jackson!"

"Coming up Dupont too!"

"They've got a cannon!"

"Quickly now." Ashe led Farren, Jason and McNabb to the rear of the armory. He pushed open the shutters of a window there, revealing a flat roof six feet below. "Go as far as you can over the roofs. Come down in an alley and you should get away all right."

Jason threw a leg over the sill. "Tell your men to come to Farnum and Kent, shipowners, Sansome Street north of Washington, after you and Judge Terry have surrendered," he said to Ashe. "Tell them to come by twos and threes. Someone there will tell them where we are mustering." He dropped from the window and landed lightly on the roof below, then turned to help the others down.

Getting away over the roofs was easily done. They came down a fire escape in an alley and emerged on Pacific Street. At Kearny they saw that the street was packed with men down by the Plaza, where the Continentals' armory was located.

"They have surrounded the Continentals too," Farren said.

"Holding them all hostage until they have Judge Terry and the others," Jason said.

"Maybe they're going to take them all," McNabb ventured.

"If they take our men, we are lost," said Farren.

"Nay," Jason said. "So long as those muskets are in Mr. Frye's storehouse, we will find a way to use them."

relayne arrived at Fort Vigilance a few hours past dawn and he spent the morning in Sacramento Street with the idlers there. He was dressed as a miner today, with bushy eyebrows and a flowing mustache. There was a certain flair to the bright calico shirt and the broadbrimmed hat, and the boots gave him a feeling of authority. He strutted along the street with the rest of the layabouts, exchanging gossip. The town was rife with rumors that no one could confirm and all were reluctant to deny. There had been a gun battle on the bay during the night, some said, although if pressed, they could not swear they heard the cannon. Others said the Vigilance Committee had put General Howard aboard a bark bound for Tahiti. Trelayne himself contributed a fanciful tale that Jonathan Frye had been found *in flagrante* with a Chinese whore by vigilance militia who were searching house by house for the dastardly Mercury. He hoped if the story reached Frye's ears it might inflame him enough to bring him out of the fort to learn who was spreading it, but noontime came and went and he saw no sign of Frye or any of the other vigilance leaders.

The sun had risen at a quarter to five to celebrate the solstice. Trelayne himself had risen at half-past six feeling rested after only a few hours' sleep. The evening before, Sarah's note had told him that she and Captain Beck were off to prevent piracy on the bay and that

General Howard's militia would confront the Vigilance Committee today. She meant it as a warning, but the news only heightened Trelayne's expectations. After he had delivered Mercury's letter to the *Herald*, and still later, near midnight, after he walked Molly to the top of the rise overlooking North Beach and watched until she reached Abel Calvert's house, he had wondered where he might go to watch the drama unfold. But he had no idea where the state's militia would muster or where the arms were to be put ashore and so he had returned to the boardinghouse and forced himself to sleep while he could, preparing himself for whatever part fate might offer him today if the city erupted in war.

The morning *Herald* had called the citizens to rally to the governor's call. *San Franciscans!* Mercury cried. *Are we to submit like sheep to the tyrannous yoke of the vigilantes for full two months more while Judge Thompson and Mr. Foreman are carried to our nation's capital and back by steamer? Or shall we stand proudly at the wharf when they return, to tell them that we have put down the evil cabal in their absence? For San Francisco, for California, for honor, let us do the work ourselves! Let us suffer no longer! Let us proclaim that the hour of retribution is at hand! Today the forces of Law will enter our city to lift the yoke of the oppressors. Stand behind them and by your presence give notice to the vigilantes that their rule is now at an end!*

But the forces of law had been defanged during the night by vigilance brigands on the bay. That story was on every lip and it was uncontested.

The drama Trelayne still hoped to play out for an appreciative audience would be more modest, but he would do his best to act it well. As in his duel with Calvert, the outcome was not written in advance, which heightened the drama for both participants and spectators. In his coat pocket he had a revolver. He had fired it often in modern melodramas, charged only with a little powder and wadding. Now it was loaded with lead balls and a full measure of powder in each cylinder. The weapon was a tool of his trade and he had rehearsed with it as diligently as he had practiced with swords and rapiers. For all of Calvert's bravado, Trelayne felt certain he could have killed the mountaineer in a duel with pistols.

Of Jonathan Frye he was still more sure. Before the day was done Frye would come out of the warehouse and Trelayne would be waiting.

Tap, tap. Atop Fort Gunnybags a sentinel struck the Monumental bell with a hammer. *Tap, tap.*

Trelayne allowed himself to be swept along in the rush that followed. Men came to Fort Gunnybags from every side. They poured through the doors, calling numbers to the guards. "Five hundred seventy-eight," Trelayne shouted. No one questioned him or gave him a second glance. He took a musket and went back into the street. By moving from one company to another as if searching for his own, he kept watch on the doors of the fort. Still no one from the Executive Committee came forth. When the militia marched off up Sacramento Street, two companies stayed behind to form a line around the block of buildings that included Fort Gunnybags. Trelayne joined the line and settled himself to wait. It seemed there was to be a spectacle after all. He would bide his time and allow it to play itself out. When Jonathan Frye made an entrance he would await a moment when he could command the full attention of the other players, and then he would take center stage.

"You in the armory! I order you to surrender yourselves in the name of the Vigilance Committee!"

The streets around the Crescent firehouse were packed with men. The speaker stood beside a brass fieldpiece that was aimed at the building.

In the Blues' armory, David Terry peered through a rifle slit. "Who is that?"

"Colonel Curtis," Ashe said. "He commanded the gun at the jail when they took Cora and Casey."

"Load!" Curtis's command could be heard by every man in the armory. In the street below, the gun crew moved through the practiced routine of loading the fieldpiece. Behind the gun, the thronged militia were silent.

"Light the match," Curtis ordered.

A man carrying a linstock lowered the forked end of the long pole. Another struck a match and held the flame to the larger match wedged in the linstock's fork. It was tar-soaked to keep it burning in the wind and it smoked black as it caught light.

"Let us reason with them," Terry said dryly.

Ashe opened a full-length shutter in the south wall and stepped onto a narrow iron balcony.

"Hang him!" cried a voice from the crowd.

"Put a ball through his heart!" urged another.

Colonel Curtis raised a hand for silence.

"We are prepared to discuss terms for the surrender of this armory." Ashe's words carried over the heads of the mob and the vigilantes raised a cheer.

"What are your terms?" Curtis asked when he could make himself heard.

"Judge Terry and I will meet you at the bottom of the stairs under your guarantee of safe conduct."

"You have it."

"Hang him!" the same voice insisted again, but the tone was less strident, as if the speaker sensed that there would be no impetuous murder today, and was disappointed.

When Ashe opened the door to the street, Curtis stood alone outside. Ashe and Terry remained within the shadow. Curtis stepped into the doorway to speak with them. Ashe was in his shirtsleeves. Terry still wore his coat. After the confined heat of the armory, the cool stairway was refreshing.

"Colonel." Ashe knew Curtis socially. They had not seen each other since the Committee of Vigilance organized.

"Captain Ashe. Is Reuben Maloney with you?"

"He is."

"We must have him, and the two of you as well."

"All in good time," Terry said. "First we must agree on certain terms."

"You are in no position to dictate terms."

"There are seventy-five men upstairs," Ashe said. "We have arms and ammunition."

"You can blow down the walls with your cannon and have the citizens of this city watch as you pull our bodies from the rubble," Terry said. "Or you can hear our conditions."

"Colonel!" A man came running up Jackson from the direction of Kearny calling out to Curtis as he drew near.

"Dr. Cole . . . is with Hopkins," the runner reported. He was a stout man, a baker before the vigilance business began and now on any day when the militia was not needed. He was unaccustomed to running and he panted between bursts of words.

"Hopkins . . . is alive. Dr. Cole . . . instructed me to tell you that . . . his condition is grave. . . . The blade opened the larynx and the esoph . . ." The runner paused as much for want of memory as air.

"The esophagus," Terry supplied.

"Thank you, sir. The blade opened the larynx and the esophagus . . . and cut a branch of the carotoid artery."

"Carotid," Terry corrected him, as if they were discussing an operation he had performed to save Hopkins' life.

"Dr. Cole says if Hopkins survives the next few hours he may live." At a nod from Curtis, the messenger withdrew.

Colonel James Curtis was thirty years old. His father had served aboard the *Chesapeake* and the *Constitution* in the War of 1812. When he stood before the County Jail on the eighteenth of May, he had been fully prepared to blow the door open if that were necessary to extract Casey and Cora. If the likes of Sheriff Scannell and Billy Mulligan chose to stand by a murderer and a whoremonger, they deserved to die with them, he had reasoned. On the day King of William was buried, he had held his company and his cannon in readiness in case anyone tried to prevent the hangings. Here, faced with the United States naval agent for San Francisco and the acting chief justice of the state supreme court, Curtis was experiencing doubts about the rightness of his course for the first time in his service to the Committee of Vigilance.

"State your conditions," he said.

"I will surrender myself on a guarantee that I will not be harmed by your mob," Terry said. "This guarantee to be given in writing by no fewer than two members of your ruling body. Maloney and Captain Ashe will surrender under the same guarantee. We will submit to trial before your Committee, but not to the passions of this rabble."

"I will convey your terms to the Executive Committee." Curtis turned to go.

"A word of advice, Colonel," Terry said.

"I need no advice from you, Judge."

"All the same, I offer it." The languor of the hot Texas plains rose most thickly in Terry's voice when he was containing his volatile temper. "Your so-called Committee of Vigilance is at the brink of an abyss. Until today you have merely assassinated the Constitution of the United States and risked throwing this state into anarchy. But you have kept to your own rules, however far beyond the pale of the law. Your leaders believe in the rightness of your cause and have attempted to conduct themselves with honor, as they are given to see it. The people, inflamed by a slavish press, support you." Terry spoke as if he were on the bench, reviewing the merits of a case before pronouncing judgment.

"By seizing the state's arms you are guilty of rebellion. By taking them on the bay, you are guilty of piracy. If you persist in your course, you will all end up on the gallows."

"History will judge us." Curtis had not contemplated its judgment until now. He stepped out of the doorway into the hot sunlight. "I will let you know when the members of the Executive Committee have arrived to conclude the surrender."

An hour passed, and then another. The air remained calm, the sun hot. In the ranks of the vigilance militia there were French *chasseurs* who had fought the establishment of Louis-Philippe's Second Empire, and Prussian hussars who had fled the collapse of Germany's own revolution. Easily persuaded that governments were corrupt and oppressive, they had been among the first to heed the Vigilance Committee's call. They stood stoically now, long accustomed to being rushed from place to place and made to wait for hours while the officers decided where to rush them next. Around them, the American troops were less patient. There was grumbling in the ranks that became more insistent and subsided only when a dozen members of the Executive Committee made their appearance at last, coming up Jackson Street in a group, surrounded by militia, as they had marched to the County Jail to relieve Sheriff Scannell of James Casey and Charles Cora. Here too, a carriage followed behind to carry away the prisoners.

When the delegation came to a stop, Abel Calvert moved to the front, beside Jonathan Frye, where he could see everything that happened. Colonel Curtis shouted to the armory, then accompanied Miers Truett and Thomas Smiley to the door by the firehouse to confer with Ashe and Terry.

Calvert shifted from foot to foot in the hot sun and he tugged occasionally at his starched collar, which scratched his neck. It was almost five o'clock. Ned Rollick would come looking for him at Fort Vigilance and would not find him. All day Rollick and a man named Sandlin had watched Mrs. Rockwell's boardinghouse without catching a glimpse of Trelayne. The only oddity they had reported was the sight of Mrs. Rockwell arriving at the house at midday dressed as a sailor. She had left again soon after, in a cloak and bonnet, and had not returned.

In other circumstances Calvert might have been amused by all the fuss and bother. Ring the alarm! Muster a few thousand men in the streets, frightening women and children. Then stand and wait half the afternoon while less than two hundred state's militia barricaded in their crackerbox armories tried to figure out if you had them whipped. In his present mood, Calvert was more than ready to see a little powder burned. The fieldpiece might be only a six-pounder, but it would knock down a brick wall quick enough.

When a runner from Colonel Curtis brought word of Terry's demands to Fort Vigilance, the Executive Committee had been planning a defense against the federal warrant that was issued for John Durkee on the basis of complaints by Farren and Captain Mannix. Durkee was ordered into hiding and the matter set aside, so the members could wrangle over how to respond to Terry's terms. They had chosen Truett and Smiley to sign the paper promising that no harm would come to Terry if he gave himself over to the besiegers. Truett because he was known to be moderate and dependable. Smiley because he would take no guff from the Committee's enemies. Show the membership that the factions in the Executive Committee stood united in this matter. Same promise of safe conduct made for Maloney and Ashe.

And then, almost as an afterthought, the vigilance leaders had decided to end the threat from the state's militia for good. The vote had been unanimous. Terry and Ashe and Maloney must surrender first, then both armories and all the men. It was the demand for the surrender of the Blues that was holding things up now. That would stick in their craw, but they had no choice. The militia would be held until all the remaining arms were rounded up and then they would be let go, and to hell with whoever didn't like it.

The troops in the street raised a cheer. "There they come," Frye said.

Judge Terry emerged first into the slanting sunlight, tall and apparently calm. Behind him, Rube Maloney looked this way and that, plainly in mortal fear. Terry stepped into the waiting carriage as if he were going to the theater.

Calvert remembered the last time he had been to the theater and his bloodlust returned full force. Once he had Trelayne in his sights, he would blow the little dandy's lights out without a second thought. For all he knew, Trelayne was in the crowd now, laughing at him behind that shitheel grin of his.

With all eyes on the carriage as it pulled away, flanked by musket-toting militia, Calvert's gaze searched among the civilian onlookers. It would be just like Trelayne to enjoy the spectacle, laughing behind his hand all the while. *Damn his fornicating eyes!*

No! That wasn't what he would do. He knew Calvert would be here while the Committee's legions were mobilized. And he knew how best to stab Calvert in the back. He would go to Molly!

"Where is Ashe?" Jonathan Frye said to Truett when the negotiators rejoined the delegation.

"Captain Ashe refused to leave his men," said Truett. "He said our demand for the surrender of the state's militia changed the whole picture. Mr. Coleman has ordered Colonel Curtis to wait them out. If the armory does not surrender by sunset, Curtis will fire one round. We are going now to deal with the Continentals."

"Are you coming, Abel?" Frye said to Calvert.

"Hmm? No. You don't need me." He stepped close to Frye and spoke softly. "I have a hunch where I can find our friend Mr. Trelayne."

"Do you, by God? You will save us all a deal of trouble if you shoot him where he stands. The damned trials are a waste of time."

"If I find him, he'll be no bother to anyone." Calvert set off along Dupont as the delegation turned in the other direction. Earlier in the day he had informed the Executive Committee that Trelayne was Mercury and of the steps he had taken to assure Trelayne's arrest. He had not mentioned his order to the police to tell him of Trelayne's whereabouts. With any luck, by the time the day's business was concluded and the Executive Committee thought to ask about Trelayne, Calvert would have found and removed the source of their concern.

If he found Trelayne with Molly, he would shoot Trelayne first, but not to kill him. Then he would shoot Molly, just as he had shot Gray Dawn, while Trelayne watched.

Calvert let out a groan that sounded loud in the empty street. Why had Gray Dawn betrayed him? He never knew. He never gave her time to speak. When he saw her in the Gros Ventre's arms he had plugged the buck, killing him dead atop her, the blood running over her breasts. That was what Calvert remembered most vividly, her breasts red with blood.

He had reloaded the Hawken calmly—powder, patch and ball. He had shut out the words she was saying, about how she loved him still, and how he had driven her away with his moods and his jealousy. He had reloaded calm and sure, and the moment the powder was in the pan he threw down on her and let fly, shutting her off in mid-cry and killing her deader than any animal he had ever killed before. Deader than the beaver he had trapped for their hides, deader than the elk and moose and bison and deer and rabbits he had killed to eat, deader than the men, red and white, he had killed because they wanted to kill him. Nothing had ever looked or felt so dead to him as Gray Dawn. He held her in his arms until she was cold, her blood and the Gros Ventre's drying on her and on him, gluing his buckskin to her skin, so he had to pry himself loose at the last. But even while she was still warm and supple he knew she was terribly, irreversibly dead, because he had known her alive. No one had ever been more alive.

Some part of his spirit had died that day. Now it was time to kill what remained. At least Gray Dawn had given herself to him heart and soul for a time. Molly had never loved him. He could see that now. She had used him, loving Trelayne all the while. They had laughed about him behind his back. Molly had played him for a fool, but now the play was over.

What if he was wrong, and Trelayne wasn't with her now?

Kill her just the same. Then find Trelayne. Tell him before killing him. That would be almost as good. Tell him Molly was dead, give him just time enough to understand, then kill him.

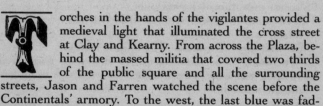orches in the hands of the vigilantes provided a medieval light that illuminated the cross street at Clay and Kearny. From across the Plaza, behind the massed militia that covered two thirds of the public square and all the surrounding streets, Jason and Farren watched the scene before the Continentals' armory. To the west, the last blue was fading from the sky. It seemed to Jason that the sun had remained in the heavens for twice its normal span.

The troops were quiet. It had been a day of waiting, but the waiting was nearly done. Captain Ashe and the Blues had surrendered an hour before.

Two men stood near Jason and Farren. The one wearing spectacles sidled closer. A voice that seemed oddly soft for the bearded face said, "It is a sad day for the friends of liberty."

"Aye." Jason looked more closely at the man as he stepped still nearer. The second man, who was smaller, stayed in the background.

"It is me, Jason," Sarah said in her normal voice.

"Sarah? My God, you—"

"Shh. Just listen. Men are watching the house. They are after Tommy. They think he is Mercury."

"Trelayne is Mercury?" Farren was dumbfounded.

"Be quiet!" Sarah cautioned. "Watch for him, please! If the vigilantes find him, he is in terrible danger. We have been looking for him everywhere."

"You should not be out tonight," Jason said. " 'Tis not safe for you."

"They have the arms. Now they have the militia as well."

"We're going to recapture the governor's arms," Farren said. "Stay clear of Front Street, Sarah."

"What will you—" Sarah began, but another familiar voice called to Jason from nearby.

"Captain!" Joshua Norton hastened toward Jason and Farren, out of breath and plainly delighted to see them. "At last I have found you."

Sarah moved off without a backward glance, and Norton scarcely noticed the bearded figure. He took Jason by the arm and he spoke in a confidential tone. "Success, Captain. I have done as you charged me, and I have come to report what I have learned."

Jason was at a loss. Sarah and her small companion were walking off toward Washington Street.

"The men who sold flour early this year, Captain. I have their names," Norton said.

Jason remembered the conversation of yesterday morning, after Barbara had told him of Frye's involvement with grain. It seemed like something that had taken place long ago, although he had barely slept or eaten in the meantime.

"The first sales were made by James Dows and Clancy Dempster," Norton said. "The auctioneer who handled the sale was Tom Smiley."

"What about Frye?"

Norton beamed. "After the sale Jim Dows made a large deposit to his account at Lucas, Turner and Company. The very same day he drew a large draft. Mr. Sherman authorized it himself, in view of the amount. Fifteen thousand dollars, Captain. Paid to the banking house of Calvert and Winston for the account of Jonathan Frye."

"Dows was acting for Frye," Jason said.

"I was able to discover that Mr. Smiley and Mr. Dempster bank with Mr. Calvert as well." Dempster, like Smiley and Dows and Frye, was a member of the Executive Committee.

"How did you learn all this?"

"I learned of the sale from my merchant friends. We owe the banking intelligence to Mr. Sherman. I have just spoken with him. He is there, with Colonel Hays." Norton pointed to two men who were standing a little apart from the vigilance troops, on the steps of the City Hall.

"Lucas, Turner has handled Jim Dows' business since they opened their doors," Norton said. "Mind you, Mr. Sherman does not tell tales about his customers. I took him somewhat into my confidence. I may have played on his sympathy. If men set out to ruin me, I said, did I not have a right to know who they were? I told him my property has passed through Frye's hands and I told him of our suspicions."

"You have a good circumstantial case," Farren said, "but you will need proof."

"Calvert's bank has the proof," Jason said. "If Frye's accounts show deposits from those other men, the figures will condemn him."

"They are Calvert's friends," Norton said.

"Yesterday he offered to hang the man who burned my ship. Now he'll get the chance."

"I must be getting along after Dickie," Norton said.

"Dickie is here?" Jason said.

"We haven't seen him since last night. He will be somewhere in all this excitement, I am sure." With a wave, Norton left them.

There was a murmur from the assembled troops as the first of the Continentals came out into the torchlight. The vigilance militia formed a corridor so the prisoners could pass in a line of twos down Clay Street. Here, as at the Blues' armory, the prisoners were handcuffed in pairs. Leading the Continentals, his head held high, Colonel J. R. West walked alone.

"Come," Jason said to Farren. He led the way to where Hays and Sherman stood watching the surrender with somber faces.

"It is a dark night, Captain," Sherman said to Farren.

"By God, they have no right to treat those men like that!" Hays kept his voice low, but the passion in his words was evident. Beneath the arched brows his sharp eyes reflected the torchlight, giving him the aspect of a predator on the hunt.

"General Howard should be with his men." Sherman's tone was bitter. During the negotiations at the Continental armory, Volney Howard had moved among the vigilantes unmolested. He had inspected the troops inside the armory, left the premises, and then sent a letter ordering Colonel West to surrender in the face of the superior force arrayed against him. Since then, General Howard had been conspicuous by his absence.

"I respect an officer who sees to the welfare of his men," Hays said.

"I respect an officer who shows some trace of courage before the enemy." As soon as the words were out, Sherman regretted them. "I'm a fine one to talk. We came ashore in forty-seven ready for blood and thunder. All the Mexicans wanted to do was race their horses against ours. They generally won, too."

"Not a bad way to fight a war," Hays said. "I don't suppose we could challenge Billy Coleman to a horse race."

When the last of the state's militia emerged from the armory, the vigilantes closed in behind and followed them down Clay Street, every man so quiet that the onlookers spoke in whispers. After the pandemonium let loose by the sounding of the bell in midafternoon, the Committee had restored order to its legions. Now, as on the occasions of their earlier victories, they impressed the citizenry not by tumult and rage but by the eerie calm of their passage, marked by no drums or fifes, only the cadence of their shoes on planked streets, as if they were marching in some vast ballroom.

"They have it all now, those peacocks!" Sherman said.

"That is to our advantage," Jason said. "They are so confident, they won't be expecting a move against them."

Hays and Sherman looked at him as if he were mad. "What possible hope can there be of that?" Sherman said.

"The arms the vigilants took from me this morning are in a warehouse on Front Street," Farren said. While waiting for the Continentals to surrender, he and Jason had calculated the last, desperate gamble that remained to them.

"They have taken the armories and they fancy themselves cocks of the walk," Hays said thoughtfully. "They will be crowing tomorrow, but tonight they will sleep. How many men have you?"

"A score of Jack-Tars," Jason said.

"It is a small force."

"If I can't take that storehouse with twenty men, I can't take it with a hundred, Colonel. Once we have the governor's muskets, we can arm our reserves."

"If we have any reserves left, they are well hidden," Sherman remarked sourly.

"On the contrary, General. They were just marched down to Fort Vigilance."

"Our militia?"

"How will you do it?" Hays said.

"My men and I will take the storehouse," Jason said. "When we have the governor's muskets, six of my men will take the rest of us to the vigilantes' fort as prisoners. The muskets will come along in a wagon. We will be armed with pistols and knives under our coats. Once inside, we will overpower the guards and arm the prisoners."

"A Trojan horse, by God," Hays exclaimed.

"It might work." Sherman's dark mood was replaced by cautious hope.

"Let's get away from this place," Hays said. The last of the vigilance militia was gone from the square and the onlookers were dispersing.

They set off down Washington Street, falling into step without being aware of it, their feet giving a faint answer to the cadence of the departed vigilantes. "My crew is waiting at my shipowners'," Jason said.

"Why are you and your men being brought in as prisoners?" Hays asked Jason, probing for weakness in the plan.

"The Executive Committee gave me the job of intercepting the governor's arms last night. When I didn't come back, they'll have guessed I changed sides."

"No matter how small a guard they keep in that fort,

they can bring the rest back with that damned bell,"
Sherman said.

"We intend to silence the bell the moment we take the
warehouse," Farren said. "We will disarm the guards,
capture the bell, and arm our men. If the *John Adams* will
help, we'll have naval guns in reserve."

"General Howard never got a message to her, but we
did," Jason said. "I sent two of my men in a dory this
afternoon. They carried word that Judge Terry and Captain Ashe were taken by the vigilants. As I understood it,
Captain Ashe and Lieutenant Boutwell are friends."

"That should bring him down if anything will,"
Sherman said.

They had passed through the warm wash of gaslight
where Washington crossed Montgomery and were concealed once more by the gloom of the night. The heat of
the day lingered in the streets and buildings and the air
was warm.

"Halt!" came a voice from the darkness. Six armed
men stepped into the cross street at Sansome, fanning
out to block the way. "Identify yourselves," demanded
one of the six. Stiletto bayonets pointed at each of the
four men.

"Who the hell are you?" Sherman growled.

"Vigilance Committee." The leader's voice was rich
with confidence. "We are under orders to detain any
persons who may be bearing arms against the Committee."

"I am John Coffee Hays," the Texan said calmly.

"Colonel Hays!" One of the vigilantes stepped nearer.
He raised his musket so it was no longer aiming at Hays.
"Jack Beauregard, Colonel. I served with you at Matamoros. Colonel Walker's battalion." Beauregard had a
full beard and a mustache that concealed his mouth.

"It's good to see you, Jack." Hays's pleasure was genuine. "You were wounded, I think. How's the leg?"

Beauregard grew an inch in height. "Good as new,
Colonel. Just as a formality, sir, I have to ask if you're
carrying arms against the Vigilance Committee. We're
patrolling the streets tonight to keep the peace."

Hays held open his coat. "As you see, I am not carrying arms against anyone, Jack. I'll vouch for my friends."

"Thank you, sir."

Hays started off and Jason fell into step beside him. Sherman and Farren came along behind. All walked easier when they heard the boots of the vigilantes go off down Sansome.

"Keeping the peace!" Sherman grumbled.

"I hate to lie to a Texan," Hays said. "I assume the rest of you are armed to the teeth."

"They have cast off all restraint," Sherman said. "If there is a chance to bring them down, we must act now, or they will rule this city until Gabriel blows his horn."

"You and I can't take part," Hays cautioned him. "We can only advise."

"Advise and witness," Sherman amended.

"Yes. Whatever happens this night will be witnessed by both of us for the world to know."

"If they're rounding up the last of their enemies, it may mean the Executive Committee will be in the fort," Jason said.

"The vigilantes' caution is in your favor," Hays said. "The guards will be so proud to show a new batch of prisoners to their bosses, they won't think to ask who brought you or why."

Chapter 52

relayne lost sight of Jonathan Frye on the dark march back to Fort Gunnybags. To his surprise, the vigilance leaders went ahead on their own as soon as the first of the surrendering Continentals emerged from the armory. Trelayne's company, which had guarded the fort after the summoning of the vigilance troops and then became the escort for the delegation from the Executive Committee, fell in line near the middle of the column. When they arrived at the fort the prisoners were passing through a double column of vigilance troops at each of the wagon doors and Trelayne's company was dismissed in the street, the word given from man to man.

From the moment Frye had come out of Fort Gunnybags at midafternoon, Trelayne had remained within a few paces of him throughout the siege of the armories. Far from boring him, the long periods of waiting had intrigued him. After the alarums and the gathering of the vigilance army, the minuets of negotiation were interludes in which the tension simmered instead of boiling over. Trelayne was content to play a pawn as others directed the scene, never knowing when a miscalculation or a rash act on either side might shatter the setpiece movements of the troops and let slip the dogs of war. All the while he had watched for his moment. Now, with the main acts of the spectacle played out, it was at hand. But when the last of the prisoners went through the doors and Trelayne made his way inside, Frye was nowhere to be seen.

The large interior of the warehouse was lighted with a few dozen lanterns hung on pegs on the walls. They produced a dim illumination, but adequate, Trelayne judged. It was an eerie sort of twilight effect, suitable to the mood of the scene as the newly arrived prisoners were led in groups to the long north wall and directed to sit on the earthen floor.

By the foot of an open stairway to the second floor, Abel Calvert was talking with a plump man with piglike eyes. The banker had been at the Blues' armory when Judge Terry surrendered, but after that he had disappeared. It occurred to Trelayne that it would be almost as entertaining to stalk Calvert as Frye. They were a pair of thieves. Brothers in crime, in a manner of speaking. Of the two, Calvert deserved far worse punishment. By burning the theater, Frye had robbed Trelayne of his livelihood. Calvert had stolen his one true love, which was a crime beyond measure, beyond adequate retribution, but to kill Calvert was to hurt Molly, and that Trelayne would not do. She had given herself anew to him and she had restored him to a state of grace. For her, he would divert his wrath to Jonathan Frye . . . and yet . . .

But for Jonathan Frye he would not have been catapulted into the theater of the world, where he had found his true calling. The realization stunned Trelayne. Instead of shooting Frye, he should get down on his knees to him and swear undying fealty, for it was here, where the performance was not even noticed if done properly, that he had found a greater challenge and greater satisfaction than he had dreamed possible. There was no applause, no glow from the footlights, but there was a reward beyond any he had known on the boards of a stage. Here he took part in a drama that was always fresh, always changing, never repeated, and he alone in the cast had the peerless awareness of enacting a role.

But Jonathan Frye had no such boon in mind when he paid Billy and Tom to burn the theater, and so he would gain no forgiveness for his incomparable gift.

Trelayne drifted closer to the stairway, using the comings and goings of militiamen and prisoners to mask his approach. Perhaps Calvert would lead him to Frye. He circled behind the banker and the fat man and sat beneath the stairs on a keg, where he could make out some of what they were saying.

". . . good night's work, by God . . . soon take the rest of them. If they resist, they'll be shot down like . . ." That was the fat man. Now Calvert was speaking. ". . . take a hand in the ambush myself," but the fat one objected, it seemed. He spoke vehemently, leaning close to Calvert, so Trelayne could only catch a few words. ". . . give it all away . . . here and wait it out like the rest of us!"

"Excuse me. Do you have a cigar?" The request came from a tall young man who swallowed nervously as Trelayne looked him up and down.

"I don't indulge," Trelayne said in his miner's voice, which was a little rougher and deeper than his own.

"Nor do I," said the beanpole youth. "I thought I might begin today, by way of celebration. Our enemies vanquished and all." He took out a cheap watch and popped open the lid. "Ten minutes past. I am late. Thank God Mr. Calvert is occupied." He put the watch away.

Trelayne rose and stretched himself with a yawn. "You didn't see where Mr. Frye went? I've some business with him."

"Mr. Frye? No, I'm sorry," the beanpole said.

"Well, he's somewhere hereabouts." Trelayne tugged the brim of his miner's hat, pulling it lower over his face. He shouldered his musket and left the skinny youth. Calvert and the fat man had moved away from the stairs. He would go up and look for Frye on the second floor, just to see if he was there. He would challenge him down here, with both the vigilance and the state's militia to witness the duel, but first he would make sure of his victim's whereabouts.

The militiamen were lining up at the doors to turn in their muskets and go out of the warehouse. Before long there would be only a guard left to watch the prisoners. Better still. A majority of the witnesses would be friendly—

Trelayne became aware that two men with muskets in their hands had come up on either side of him. The bearded one on his left took him by the arm. "We've come to get you out of here, Tommy."

The voice was Sarah's. On his right, the figure was shorter. The youthful face was shadowed by a slouch hat and wore a mustache cropped close in the French manner.

"'I would I were thy bird,'" Trelayne said softly.

"'Sweet, so would I, yet I should kill thee with much cherishing,'" Molly took her cue.

"I hadn't thought to find my Juliet abroad in the night." Trelayne guided them toward the east end of the warehouse, where there was an open space. "How in God's name did you get in here?"

"The troops in the Plaza left their muskets against the fence," Sarah said. "When the Continentals came out everyone was watching them. We took two muskets and marched along with the rest. We've been looking for you half the day."

"I knew you would be in the midst of it all," Molly said. "You couldn't resist."

"Tommy, listen to me," Sarah said. "There have been men watching the boardinghouse since this morning. I'm sure it's for you and I'm sure they suspect you are Mercury. Last night, did you go to the *Herald*?"

"Dickie was not at home, Sarah. I had no other way."

"You really are Mercury?" Molly was in awe.

"I am but a mortal courier for the herald of the gods," Trelayne said.

"And in just as much danger," Sarah said. "We must all get out of here."

"Mr. Frye is somewhere about and I've unfinished business with him. Besides, where could we be safer?"

"The alarm may sound at any minute and we'll be called out there to fight our friends!" Sarah said. "Jason and Captain Farren are going to recapture the governor's arms."

"They have no men."

"They have Jason's crew, and they know where the arms were taken."

They had reached the end of the warehouse. They were alone, well away from the closest vigilantes, but Trelayne spoke almost in a whisper. "Then they are in great danger. I heard Abel Calvert and another man talking about an ambush, and rounding up 'the rest of them.'"

"We must warn them!" Sarah said. "Captain Farren said where it was ... on Front Street! Somewhere on Front Street."

"Abel knows about this?" Molly said.

"Yes. I'm sorry," Trelayne said, surprised that he really was. "He wanted to be in on it, but the other man told him the trap was already laid and he should stay here to wait it out."

Molly shook her head, as if to free herself of a troublesome memory. "He said he was the one voice of reason! He said he and Mr. Kent kept them in check, and I believed him. I think it was so, at first." She took Trelayne's hand. "*'If they do see thee, they will murder thee.'*"

He felt his heart falter in its work. "*'Alack, there lies more peril in thine eye than in twenty of their swords: look but thou sweet and I am proof against their enmity.'*"

"*'I would not for the world they saw thee here.'*"

"I'm glad we're all agreed on something," Sarah said. "Come. Now." They walked past the lines at the doors. Sarah said "Executive Committee business" to the guards, she and Molly handed over their muskets, and the trio walked without hindrance into the dark of the night.

"Mr. Calvert."

Calvert was speaking with Isaac Bluxome when Ned Rollick called to him and beckoned him urgently. Calvert excused himself and joined the clerk.

"Trelayne is here, sir."

"Where!"

"Just there." Rollick looked toward the east end of the warehouse where Trelayne and the two others had gone, but they were no longer in sight. His eyes searched and caught a glimpse of calico beneath a miner's hat passing through a door to Sacramento Street. "There!" Rollick pointed. "He's the one dressed like a miner, sir.

I spoke with him. He doesn't know me from Adam, but I have seen him at the theater. I'm certain it was he."

In the street, Trelayne and Sarah and Molly moved among the discharged militiamen who lingered in small groups. A scattering of onlookers stood about, hoping for a hanging or two.

"Mr. Kent's offices are on Sansome Street across Washington," Sarah said. "They may still be there."

In Front Street they saw no sign of life or movement along its entire length. In Washington the yellowish glow from the gaslights grew brighter as they neared Montgomery. They heard booted feet marching in Battery Street and hid in a doorway as a vigilance patrol tramped through the cross street and went on toward Market.

In Sansome Street no light showed in the offices of Farnum & Kent. Trelayne knocked on the door, softly at first, then louder. A lone figure at the corner of Jackson Street looked toward the sound and came closer.

"I would know that nose in a coal bin," Trelayne whispered to Molly and Sarah. He raised his voice. " 'Ho, fellow! What business dost thou in the night?' "

"No business, sir," Joshua Norton said. "I am searching for a lost boy."

"You haven't found him?" Sarah ran to Norton's side.

"Mrs. Rockwell? Is it you? And these others?"

"Players, Joshua, in the game of life," Trelayne said. "Sarah, you and Molly go with Joshua. I'm sure Dickie will go home now that the excitement is over. I will warn our friends if I can."

"Be careful, Tommy." Molly put a hand to his cheek.

"This once to play the herald, carrying word to save bold heroes from harm, I would risk life itself, dear Molly. But if you care for me, my care for myself shall know no bounds."

They parted, Norton and the two women going up Washington and Trelayne following it toward the waterfront. As he entered the cross street at Battery, a figure stepped from the shadows.

"Are you armed, Trelayne?" said Abel Calvert.

Trelayne brought out his pocket revolver and turned

sideways to Calvert as he took aim. "For Molly's sake, don't make me fight you again, Calvert. This time you'll die."

After a day of frustrations, Ned Rollick's hopes were about to come true. Calvert had told him to stay in the warehouse, but to remain idly behind, perhaps not to know until morning if all his efforts were worth it, was intolerable. When Calvert left Fort Vigilance, Ned Rollick followed. Outside, he could make out the banker easily by the distinctive shape of his beaver hat. Calvert looked up and down the block, spied the three men, the miner in the middle, and followed as they turned into Front Street. In Washington, where the light from Montgomery made concealment more difficult, Calvert hung back, but once the trio entered Sansome, he ran to the corner and watched from there. When Calvert trotted back toward Battery, Rollick moved quickly into the dark street and hid himself in the shadows. Trelayne appeared in the cross street and Calvert stepped into his path.

"Are you armed, Trelayne?"

Rollick heard Calvert's challenge clearly. He saw Trelayne's pistol in his hand, and the actor said something that ended with ". . . this time you'll die," but Rollick didn't understand the rest because he was already fumbling for the revolver he had carried all day, praying he would never have to use it. It couldn't end like this! He had worked too hard. If Trelayne killed Calvert he would lose his most valuable patron!

Calvert's hands were empty, his arms at his sides. Ned Rollick aimed the pistol with both hands, pointing it at Trelayne. He cocked the hammer and pulled the trigger.

There was a flash of light and a sharp sound, and something struck Trelayne in the chest like the kick of a mule. He staggered backward and fell to the planks of the street.

"God damn it!" Abel Calvert shouted. He pulled his pistol and pointed it toward the place where he had seen the flash. "God damn you! Come out of there!"

The echoes of his words bounced away down the

street and there was silence. Calvert ran forward and
bent over Trelayne. Trelayne's hands were clasped over
his chest. Calvert pulled them away and saw the bub-
bling hole. He took Trelayne's head between his hands
and shook it like a melon.

"Look at me, damn you!"

Trelayne's eyelids fluttered, then opened wide. Calvert
leaned close so Trelayne would hear. "I wanted to kill
you myself. Understand? The need to kill you was like a
pain inside me."

Trelayne coughed, spattering Calvert's wrists with
blood. His eyes closed.

"Damn you!" Calvert took hold of Trelayne's shoulders and lifted him a little. The eyes opened. Deep
within, the light of the spirit still shone. "I burned your
theater," Calvert said. "You hear me? I did it. I hired
Bemis and that other one, the one you found dead. I
hired them and I watched it burn. It was a pretty fire."

Trelayne coughed again.

"It wasn't supposed to be like this. It was supposed to
be a fair fight, dammit!"

Trelayne raised one hand and took hold of Calvert's
revolver by the barrel. With the other, he seized Calvert's
coat and drew him down until Calvert could smell the
blood.

"Molly is mine." The words were like a sigh.

Trelayne let go. Calvert fell back and scrambled to his
feet. There were voices in the streets and footsteps drawing near. Three figures came running from the direction
of Montgomery, silhouetted by the gaslight.

"Abel? Tommy! No, God!"

The smallest figure cried out with Molly's voice. She
ran to Trelayne's side and knelt on the planks and took
Trelayne's bloody hands in her own. The face that looked
up at Calvert bore a mustache but the eyes were Molly's
and they were full of hatred.

"It wasn't me, Molly! I swear it on my soul! It wasn't
me! Oh, God damn you all!" Calvert fled down Battery
Street, away from Molly's eyes and away from Trelayne,
away from the shadows where an invisible assassin had
robbed Abel Calvert of his last great desire.

• • •

Trelayne felt himself slipping away. The embrace of Molly's arms was feather-light. The image of her face glowed at the center of his vision. Her hat was askew and a curl of her black hair partially covered one eye. He wanted to brush back the hair, but he had no strength. He closed his eyes for a moment, or perhaps it was for much longer. He couldn't be sure. When he opened them, Sarah and Joshua Norton stood beside Molly. Sarah wore spectacles and a beard and a soft hat. She knelt and she touched his face as if she were comforting a child.

"Your mustache, Molly," he managed to say. "Take it off. The hat too. Let me see you." Molly removed her hat and her hair fell about her face. She plucked the mustache away and Trelayne smiled.

Heavy footsteps approached on the run. Vigilance patrols came from Broadway along Battery and from Front Street up Washington. They slowed when they reached the cross street where one man stood and two more knelt beside the body of a fourth, and then they saw that one of the two figures kneeling was not a man, but the actress Molly Gray.

From the corner of his eye, Trelayne saw his audience drawing near. "Hamlet, Molly. Act Five, Scene Two. Horatio."

"Tommy—"

"Act Five, Scene Two. For me, Molly. You are my only love." His lungs were filling with blood and the quality of his voice was ghastly.

Molly did not have to summon the tears or the requisite emotion. " 'Good night, sweet prince. And flights of angels sing thee to thy rest.' "

Trelayne moved his head a fraction of an inch to nod his approval. "Calvert told me he burned the theater. He . . ." There was more he wanted to say. Most of all he wanted a better exit line, but it was the best he could manage in the circumstances.

The militiamen were gathered in a small circle. They saw Trelayne's eyes close and they saw his breathing stop, but none moved or ventured to speak because their hearts were rent by the figure of Molly Gray. The sobs that racked her body originated from so far within her that no trace of sound escaped into the night air. Joshua Norton stood over her protectively, one hand on her shoulder and the other on Sarah's, mumbling strange words that no one present recognized as Hebrew prayers.

Chapter 53

hey were gathered in an alley on Front Street, Jason and Melchior and the crew. A few held revolvers but most were armed with belaying pins and knives. Every face but Jason's was blacked with soot. An old clapboard warehouse stood between the alley and Jonathan Frey's storehouse, a brick building painted gray, with new oaken doors. Around the corner on Pacific, Jan deLoesseps waited with a dray horse and wagon to carry the muskets to Fort Vigilance.

The night was warm and dark. The waterfront air carried the smells of tar and salt, sewage and rot and wet hemp. A single shot sounded a street or two away, and a man shouted something in rage. The men in the alley stirred. Jason looked up and down Front Street but nothing moved.

A black-bearded sailor named Troia made his way to Jason's side. "I can't find Little Jack, Cap'n." Since midday, a member of the crew had kept watch on the storehouse to be certain the governor's arms were not moved elsewhere. Little Jack had relieved Troia at dusk.

"He desert us again, I flog him myself," Jolly Jim said.

Melchior touched Jason's arm and pointed. Across the street, within the alley there, a match glowed briefly, shielded by a hand. The signal meant that Hays and Sherman and Farren and Kent were in position. They were to take no part, but they would observe what occurred. Farren had begged to have a hand in the attack, but in the end he was persuaded that as a witness to the Committee's piracy he should keep out of it, lest some eager vigilant seize the chance to silence his testimony.

"Off you go," Jason said to Melchior. The mate and six men moved out the back end of the alley to approach the storehouse from the other side. Jason stepped into the street, humming a shantey. As he neared the storehouse, he sang the words.

> "Heave up the anchor and get it aweigh,
> It's got a good grip, so heave steady I say,
> And we're bound for the Rio Grande.
> Ooohh, Rio,
> I'll sing you a song of the fish of the sea,
> And we're bound for the Rio Grande."

Two guards stood within the wide wagon doorway. The nearby gunshot had broken the monotony of their watch and made them alert. Long muskets rested in the dark corners where a casual passerby would not notice them.

"Ahoy, mates." Jason lurched just a little, like a man who had taken aboard a cargo of rum but was still in control of himself.

"Ahoy yourself, Jack."

" 'Tis a fair night." Jason waved a hand at the sky.

"Fair enough." The speaker raised a jug, offering it. Jason changed course toward the guards. Silent shadows crept from the alleyways on either side of the storehouse. Jason took the jug from the guard's hand and drank deeply. The cheap brandy burned his throat.

"Here's to your health, mate." He returned the jug with an unsteady bow. "May the wind be always on your beam."

The shadows rushed into the doorway, presenting knives at the guards' throats. Jason waved his own blade in front of their eyes. "Not a sound."

Jolly Jim passed his hands over the guards and relieved them of pistols and knives. "Quick now. Which door is open?" Jason said. To the left of the wagon entrance there was an ordinary man-sized doorway.

The first guard shook his head. "None." Jason pricked the other's throat with the point of his blade.

"What's the signal, then, mate?"

"Th . . . Thr . . ." Jason withdrew the knife until it was no longer touching the man's skin and gave him a friendly nod.

"Three knocks given twice." The guard raised a hand toward the man-sized door.

"How many men inside?"

"Just the one."

"Look sharp now, boys." Jason rapped three times on the smaller door, paused, and rapped again. The door was opened by a watchman holding a lantern and Jason was inside, his knife at the watchman's throat. Behind him, sailors pushed the two guards into the cavernous space.

Jason glanced quickly about. The light of the watchman's lantern lost much of its power within a few yards of the source. He could see that there was no floor between the ground and the roof, two stories above. Laden gunnysacks were piled against the nearest wall and crates of goods were stacked in rows higher than a man across the storehouse floor. He released the watchman but held him at knife point. "Where are the muskets?"

"They are not here!" The words boomed from the dark. A dozen matches flared into life among the rows of crates. There was a clatter of lantern shades lifted and dropped. The pinpoints of light grew into a dozen glowing orbs held in the hands of men who came forward to form a wide half circle about Jason and his crew. More men appeared at the edge of the light with muskets levelled at the intruders. The doorway guards and the watchman moved away from the sailors.

William Tell Coleman stepped into the illuminated space, flanked by Miers Truett and Jonathan Frye. Behind them, other members of the Executive Committee came forward. "Lay down your arms," Coleman ordered.

Jason dropped his knife. Around him, he heard the sounds of knives and pistols and belaying pins striking the earth floor of the storehouse. A militiaman thrust Little Jack forward into the light and he joined his ship-mates.

"Sorry, Cap'n," the seaman said. "I never hear 'em comin'. Guess I stand a lot more double watches now."

"Marshal Doane will read the order," Coleman said.

Grand Marshal Doane held up a sheet of paper so it caught the light from the nearest lamp. " 'By order of the Executive Committee, all persons found bearing arms against the Committee of Vigilance will henceforth be taken into custody and conducted to the Committee's headquarters, there to be confined until they no longer pose a threat to this community.' "

"What will you do when you run out of space in your fort?" Jason said. "Drop your enemies in the bay?"

"You were among the faithful, Captain Beck," Coleman said. "I am sorry to find you fallen into apostasy."

"I joined your mob to find the man who burned my ship." Jason brought out the pistol he had hidden in his belt at the small of his back. He pointed it at Jonathan Frye. "There he stands."

"There are a score of muskets aimed at you," Coleman said.

"He has hidden behind your muskets from the start. He hired men to burn my ship and he paid the same men to burn the Theater Trelayne. He murdered my crewmen as sure as if he did the deeds himself."

"He's lying." Frye puffed out his barrel chest to loosen the grip of fear that constricted his breathing.

"What reason could Mr. Frye have to burn your ship?" Truett asked.

"To prevent my cargo of rice from breaking his cartel."

"Mr. Frye does not deal in grains."

"He has traded in grains for years by acting through others," Jason said. "He caused the ruin of Joshua Norton in fifty-three. He was involved in both flour and rice this year, with the help of Smiley and Dows and a man named Dempster."

Jason strode past the vigilance musketeers. He aimed his revolver at the stacked gunnysacks along the south wall of the storehouse and he fired. A stream of rice poured out of a punctured bag. Jason cupped his hand in the stream and threw a handful of grains at Coleman's feet. "Frye wanted to keep it off the market until the flour was all gone so he and his friends could drive up the price. My cargo stood in his way."

"I'm storing it for Jim Dows!" Frye protested.

Coleman turned toward the short figure of Dows. Dows hesitated for only a moment. "Smiley and I bought and sold grains for Frye. Dempster may have been in it too. I don't know about his part."

"Shut up, you fool!" Frye was livid.

"Dealing in commodities through intermediaries is no crime, Mr. Frye," Truett reminded him. "Have a care, lest you condemn yourself by your own words."

"I had no part in burning any ship," Dows said.

"Who are the incendiaries, Captain?" Coleman asked Jason.

"One died in the fire at the Theater Trelayne. The other came at me with a knife and I killed him. Three men besides myself heard him say his employer's name was Jonathan."

"This is not the time or place to conduct an inquiry." Miers Truett's gaze was fixed on Frye and his deep voice was an ominous rumble.

"We will take the prisoners to the fort," Coleman said. "We will convene the Executive Committee and Captain Beck can call his witnesses."

Jason took aim at Frye again. "I want your word that he will hang if you find him guilty, or before God I will shoot him where he stands."

"No more threats, no more talk," came a new voice. Abel Calvert pushed Dickie Howell ahead of him through the smaller doorway to the street, which had remained open all the while. Calvert held the collar of Dickie's coat in one hand and a Colt's Navy revolver in the other. "Captain Beck, you will march your bullyboys under escort to Fort Vigilance. Now."

Jason lowered his revolver but he kept it in his hand. "If you harm that lad you will answer to me." His eyes moved to Dickie. "Are you all right, Richard?"

"Right enough, Captain."

"The boy's a thief." Calvert addressed Coleman and

Truett. "I caught him stealing from my bank. I want him held with the rest of the prisoners until Winston and I can go over the books to see if there is any loss."

Calvert was glad that the weight of the pistol and his grip on the boy kept his hands from trembling. Seeing Trelayne shot from the shadows had confounded him, and he had not yet recovered his equilibrium. He had fetched the boy from his bank first as a hostage, to protect himself against a certain charge of murder, but he saw now a hairsbreadth chance to save himself altogether. He would throw Dickie in a dark cell and scare the pee water out of him until the boy wouldn't dare tell about the papers he had found. He hadn't yet worked out what to do with him then, but there would be time enough later to decide.

"I'm not a thief!" Dickie insisted. He reached in his pants and brought out a rumpled paper. He held it out to Jason. "I found this in Mr. Calvert's office. I seen it—I saw it," he corrected himself, "I saw it when I was there before with Mr. Melchior."

"The lad's been to the bank many a time with me," Melchior said. Of all the men in the storehouse he was standing nearest to Calvert, but too far to risk a move.

"You see? He stole private papers." Calvert let go of Dickie's coat and snatched for the sheet, but Dickie dodged out of Calvert's reach and rushed to Jason's side, thrusting the paper into his hand. Jason unfolded it and saw what it was. He passed it to Coleman, who stared at it without comprehension.

"That is a bill of lading for my ship," Jason said.

"What of it?"

"Calvert knew our cargo before we ever arrived in this bay. He must have told Frye the rice was coming. It means they're in it together."

Frye brandished his cane. "I had nothing to do with the theater!" He realized what he had said and he rushed on, hoping to cover his error with bluster. "I had nothing to do with any of it. Don't you see what they're doing? They're trying to turn us against one another!"

"I offered a loan to Mr. Norton to buy your cargo," Calvert said. "Why would I do that if I intended to burn the rice?"

"To divert attention from yourself." Jason was growing more sure of Calvert's guilt with every moment. "Maybe you hoped to steal the last of Norton's land, but you changed your mind."

"It is no crime to have a bill of lading," Truett said.

"He had more of them," Dickie said. "There were lots of papers, with the names of other ships."

"Of course he had them," Frye burst out. "He was behind it from the beginning!" If he could just speak fast enough it would all be out in the open and there would be no danger from Calvert because everyone would know. "He has been in grains with me since fifty-one. The capital for our ventures came from him. Having Dows and the others do our dealings for us was his idea. So was burning the ship!"

"Damn you!" Calvert raised his revolver and fired. The explosion was deafening in the enclosed space.

Jonathan Frye dropped to one knee. Melchior lunged for Calvert and tackled him to the ground. Frye steadied himself with his cane, reached out a hand toward Jason Beck, and toppled forward on his face.

The smell of burned powder was harsh in the air. Melchior hauled Calvert to his feet and jerked the pistol from his hand. Miers Truett knelt beside Frye. He put his ear to Frye's mouth, then to his chest. He looked up at Calvert. "You have condemned yourself, sir."

"Marshal Doane." Coleman gestured at Calvert. "Bring him along with Captain Beck and his men."

Doane searched the banker for other weapons and found none. "I can't walk," Calvert said. His left ankle had buckled under him when Melchior knocked him down. To put weight on it now caused pain that was severe but not unbearable. "Give me his walking stick." He pointed to Frye's gold-headed cane, which lay beside the merchant's body. Doane retrieved the stick and escorted Calvert toward the door. Coleman held out a hand for Jason's revolver. He gave it over and followed his men into the street.

Outside the storehouse more vigilance troops were waiting, a dozen men held in reserve to protect the ambush from without. Hays, Sherman, Kent and Farren stood in their midst. "We found these four lurkin' across the way, sir," the leader reported to Coleman.

"You have no business here, Colonel Hays." Coleman was less assured than he had been in the storehouse.

"This is a public street, Mr. Coleman. Your men have no business detaining law-abiding citizens."

"There is nothing here to concern the surveyor general."

"We will see that Captain Beck and his men are treated fairly."

"What do you intend doing with them?" Sherman spoke brusquely to Coleman, as he had spoken when he was still general of the state's militia and had a reasonable hope of arming his men.

"We will take them to Fort Vigilance overnight, until tempers cool. Tomorrow they will be free to go. You can take the boy with you now if you like."

"What about Judge Terry?" Hays said.

"Judge Terry must stand trial. If Mr. Hopkins dies, it will go hard with him."

Hays held his temper in check. "And Captain Ashe? And the scores of men you imprisoned today whose only crime was remaining loyal to the governor?"

"I have every expectation that we will be lenient now that the threat of resistance is over." Coleman was almost benign as his confidence returned.

Footsteps sounded in the empty street. A dozen vigilance militiamen appeared out of Washington Street. They came to a halt, then turned into Front Street and approached the gathering. They marched in parallel rows of six. Between them walked three figures. One carried something in his arms. In the east, the moon was rising at last, casting a white light that gave the approaching militia and their charges a spectral air.

"Who goes there?" said Grand Marshal Doane.

"Sergeant Lemuel Teague, sir. Major Parks' company. A man's been killed. We was taking these people to the fort for questioning. We offered to send for a cart, sir, but this gentleman insisted on carrying his friend."

Those before the storehouse could see now that the object in Joshua Norton's arms was the body of a man. Molly Gray stood beside Norton, one hand on his arm, her face as expressionless as a stone. *"'What is it you would see?'"* she asked of no one in particular. *"'If aught of woe or wonder, cease your search.'"*

Jason stepped forward. "Sarah? Is that you?"

Sarah Rockwell took off her hat and unhooked from her ears the curls of thin wire that held her false beard in place. She peeled it from her face, bringing a murmur of surprise from the seamen and their vigilance guards. "Tommy is dead, Jason." She put her fingers against Trelayne's cheek. It was cool to the touch and oddly inflexible.

Molly gazed at her vacantly. *"'He is dead and gone, lady. At his head a green grass turf, at his heels a stone.'"*

Norton was staggering beneath his burden. Jason took Trelayne from his arms. "Who did this, Molly?" he said.

Molly gathered herself. She looked at Jason and Sarah and then at the men who were moving closer for a look at the body. As she spoke, her voice grew strong. *"'Let me speak to the yet unknowing world how these things came about. So shall you hear of carnal, bloody and unnatural acts!'"* Without Horatio's lines, which Tommy had given her, she could not have said a word. *"'Of accidental judgments, casual slaughters; of deaths put on by cunning and forc'd cause; and, in this upshot, purposes mistook fall'n on the inventors' heads! All this I can truly deliver.'"*

Supporting himself on Frye's cane, Abel Calvert reached out toward Molly, his palm turned upward in supplication. "Molly—"

The sight of him gave her strength. "You did this!"

"No, Molly! I swear before heaven. I swear by the love I have for you."

Molly gazed wistfully at Trelayne. "He knew how to love, but I betrayed him." She pointed an accusing finger at Calvert. "This man stood over his body with a pistol in his hand!"

"Molly, no!" Calvert protested.

"You burned his theater! Wasn't that enough? Did you have to kill him?"

"It's true I challenged him but someone else shot him!"

"Who was it?" Coleman demanded.

"I don't know! I never saw him!" Calvert felt his luck leave him, all the fortune he had gained by accepting the loss of the trapper's life and coming to contend with his silk-hatted enemies on their own ground. He had beat them fair and square and still they held his life in their soft city hands! "I swear before God I am telling the truth. Yes, I burned the theater! Because none of you had the craw for it! Trelayne made us a laughingstock, and all you did was sit and talk. That's what you're good for, the whole tribe of you. Talk and more talk. I did something! And now you've got to make up your minds to stand by your pardner when the fat's in the fire, or throw him to the wolves. This Committee will fall if I go down! You mark my words. You try a member of the Executive Committee for arson and murder and you're through. All of you. Disgraced and forgotten inside of a year. Is that what you want written on your tombstone, Billy Coleman?"

Jason saw Coleman waver. "You try him before your court or I will hold him for another. I'll hang him myself if I have to."

"Not you, by God, nor any man!" Calvert raised Frye's cane in Jason's direction. He fumbled with the gold head, swinging it aside on a small hinge whose purpose Jonathan Frye had demonstrated to him a half-dozen times over the years.

Jack Hays saw what Calvert was doing and understood what it meant. "The cane!" he cried. "It's a gun!"

Encumbered by Trelayne's body, Jason was defenseless. He stepped in front of Sarah and Molly. Hays and Coleman were moving toward Calvert, but another figure, larger than all the rest, was faster. Melchior closed on Calvert with his sailor's knife in his hand, moving between the banker and Jason as he charged.

Calvert's finger touched the trigger hidden in the head of the cane. The stick of ebony bucked in his hand. Melchior staggered and then was upon him, the knife parting the fabric of Calvert's waistcoat and neatly slicing off one gold button as it stole his life away.

Chapter 54

e have no wish to hang a judge of the supreme bench." Truett's voice, like his presence, filled Kent's office, although he sat still and spoke softly. He looked at them in turn—Coleman, Hays, and Sherman, Kent, Farren, and Jason Beck. Truett and Coleman had come alone to represent the Committee of Vigilance after sending the troops who had taken part in the storehouse ambush to Fort Vigilance with orders to stay there until the two leaders returned.

Farren represented the state's militia, and, by extension, the governor. Volney Howard had completed his abdication of authority by taking the morning steamer to Sacramento.

"Because Judge Terry is arrested we must try him," Truett said. "I will defend him myself if he will have me. In any case it will be a long trial. Tempers will cool."

No one knew of the night's events save those who had witnessed them. That condition had been agreed to by both sides at the start. Outside, a fresh wind was stirring the bay. Church bells sounded far and near, and each of the men remembered other Sunday mornings less fraught with strife and sorrow.

Stephen Kent sat behind his desk. The others were arrayed in front of him in chairs Ned Rollick had brought up from the ground-floor rooms. Kent was the eldest by far, the only man in the room with white hair, but he had no illusion that he was presiding over the negotiations. If one man determined the course of the bargaining, it was Jason Beck. He had not spoken since they settled themselves in the office, but each of the others accorded him a respectful awareness. More often than not the conversation followed his gaze, as if it conferred leave to speak. He was looking at Coleman now.

"We will be hard-pressed to set Judge Terry free if Hopkins dies." Coleman voiced the danger no one had dared mention until now. "Dr. Cole says his condition is very grave."

Truett nodded reluctantly. "The membership will want a life for a life."

Beverly Cole had not dared move Hopkins from the Pennsylvania engine house. Soon after the incident of the previous afternoon, he had ligated a branch of Hopkins' carotid artery to repair the damage done by Judge Terry's knife.

"You must find a way to change their minds." Hays was unyielding. "If you harm David Terry, I will move heaven and hell to bring you down in disgrace."

This was the sticking point. How could the Executive Committee promise to save Judge Terry in the face of six thousand armed men howling for his blood? Such a promise was precisely what Hays and the others demanded, and the threat they held over the Committee's head was terrible for Coleman and Truett to contemplate. If word of the night's events were let out—plot and counterplot, murders witnessed and unseen, charges of arson and more murder against members of the Executive Committee—the Committee of Vigilance would lose its authority at a stroke and its climactic victory of the preceding day would become a bitter defeat. Only the presence of Terry and Ashe and the other prisoners in Fort Vigilance compelled the Committee's enemies to keep silent for a time.

"We have accomplished what we set out to do." Coleman wished there were some way to end the whole thing now, but the events of the day before had raised the vigilance troops to a new pitch of excitement. They felt invincible, and they did not yet understand that by arresting David Terry they had sown the seeds of their own fall from grace. Coleman saw that now, as he had not seen it yesterday when he stood before the Blues' armory with the Committee's legions at his back. Already there had been fistfights in Fort Vigilance, and the Texans had declared they would take up arms against the Committee if a hair of Judge Terry's head were harmed.

The dissension in the ranks was sown by Mercury's letter in yesterday's *Herald*, which had called on the Texans to consider where their true allegiance lay. *In the vigilance militia there are many Texans, men who acquitted themselves with honor in the recent war with Mexico*, Mercury said. *Surely they will not now prostitute that honor by opposing the government of this state by force of arms and trampling the sacred freedoms they once fought to preserve?* The entreaty had struck a chord. Even in death, it seemed, Trelayne continued to threaten the Committee.

A knock sounded at the door. "Come," said Kent.

Ned Rollick looked in. "A message for Mr. Coleman, sir." He ushered the messenger into the room. The boy was perhaps fourteen, dirty and ragged, an older Dickie Howell who had not found a Sarah Rockwell to save him.

"Mr. Coleman, sir. I'm to give this to you." The boy handed Coleman a folded paper sealed with wax.

To prevent any chance of the negotiations being overheard, Ned Rollick had been instructed not to let anyone coming to the second floor out of his sight. He remained at the messenger's side while Coleman read the letter, but he kept his eye on the barometer on the wall and wished he were invisible. By a miracle he had accomplished his design of removing the last armed threat to the Vigilance Committee. He had lured Captain Beck to attack the storehouse and he had warned the Executive Committee that the attack was imminent. By another miracle, he was not suspected in Trelayne's death, but his position was precarious still. If either side learned the full extent of what he had done, all he might yet gain would be forfeit. For the present, he intended to conduct himself so inconspicuously that few would recall any part he had played in the night's events. In time he would find a way to remind those whose gratitude could serve him best.

"No reply." Coleman waved the messenger out and Rollick retired with the boy.

As soon as he saw what the note said, Coleman knew that he would tell the others. Give them a point in their favor, maybe gain one in return. "Lieutenant Boutwell has moved the sloop-of-war *John Adams* to the foot of Sacramento Street. He has sent the Executive Committee a letter warning us to free Dr. Ashe and not to harm Judge Terry."

Stephen Kent brightened. "He's got you under his guns."

"The matter remains," Truett said. "How are we to free Judge Terry if Hopkins dies."

Jason looked at David Farren and Farren felt the beginnings of an idea. "Colonel Hays, do you remember what we once discussed? That you might act to influence the Committee's troops and the public at large? What if you were to publish a card in the paper? Something to the effect that you have known Judge Terry since boyhood, and testifying to his character. At most, you might express your concern for his welfare. There would be no need to mention the Vigilance Committee directly at all."

Coleman was wary. "You must not take a stand against us," he said to Hays.

"Your concern for Judge Terry will make the members of the Committee think twice," Farren went on. "The Texans will give great weight to your opinion, and most of the men remember when you were sheriff here."

Hays nodded his assent. "I will publish a notice in tomorrow's papers." He turned his piercing eyes on Coleman. "I must have your promise that you won't harm Judge Terry."

"You have it," Coleman assured him. "Terry can make a solid case for self-defense. Given time for reason to prevail, I am sure we can acquit him in the Executive Committee. But there must be no public opposition to the Committee in the meanwhile. No discussion of the crimes committed by Mr. Calvert or Mr. Frye. Most particularly no statements by you, Colonel, beyond the notice, or you, General Sherman."

"I will agree to that," Sherman said, "if you will release your prisoners today, including Captain Ashe."

"We will release them before noon," Coleman said. Then he added, "All but Reuben Maloney. We've made him the villain in the—incident concerning the governor's arms. We must keep him if we're to free the others. A sacrificial lamb, if you will. But he'll come to no harm, I give my word. We'll hold him for a time and then banish him."

Sherman nodded grudgingly. There were more important fish to fry here than Reuben Maloney. "You will disband your Committee when Judge Terry is freed." He wanted this condition burned in the memory of everyone present. In exchange for Judge Terry's life and the immediate freedom of the imprisoned militia, the Committee of Vigilance would keep its authority for a time, but only for a time. More important to the leaders, the agreement would allow them to keep the goodwill of the populace and perhaps thereby to secure posterity's blessing.

Coleman nodded. "Agreed."

"You must be done when the governor's emissaries return from Washington," Sherman added. "If the president orders General Wool and Commodore Farragut to assist the state, they will move against you."

"Judge Thompson and Mr. Foreman can't be back until the middle of August," Truett said. "There is more than enough time."

"We're settled then?" Coleman felt easier. "Colonel Hays will put a card in the paper testifying to Judge Terry's good character, nothing more. Nothing to incite our men against us."

"Thirty of your men saw what happened last night." Farren, the lawyer, was looking for loopholes. "Can you keep them quiet?"

"They are ordered to remain at the fort until we return," Coleman said. "Mr. Truett and I will speak to them." He would assure the ambushers that any man who breathed a word of what had transpired at Jonathan Frye's storehouse would find himself deported on the first available vessel and put ashore at Tierra del Fuego.

"You are to say nothing to disparage Mr. Trelayne's memory," Farren added. Coleman nodded his assent.

Kent felt the weight of Jason's dark eyes on him.

"Other men died as well," he said. "You must say something of them."

"An early-morning brawl on the waterfront," Coleman offered. "Four men dead. No witnesses. Dr. Cole will be the soul of discretion and the burials will be done with a minimum of fuss. We can keep it quiet in our papers."

"I will speak with Mr. Nugent," Hays said. "The *Herald* will go along."

"I'm taking Melchior with me," Jason said. Having broken his silence, he looked away, unable to bear the eyes of the others upon him. Even seen through the panes of Kent's second-story window, the sky comforted him. The day promised to be cooler than the one before, the wind steady and westerly. He was glad there was a wind. "We're afloat in the devil's calm," Melchior had been fond of saying when the air was still and the heartbeat of the sea was locked away beneath glassy waters.

The wagon that Jason had intended to carry the governor's arms to Fort Gunnybags had been used instead to take Melchior to Dr. Cole's surgery. Jason had instructed Dr. Cole to preserve the body as best he could until he could take Melchior to sea and bury him there. A few days, a week at most, and *Pride of the Seas* would sail. Then Melchior would rest in the deep.

"There is the matter of Captain Beck's ship to settle," Stephen Kent said. "I'll lay odds Calvert helped us just to get Captain Beck on his way before he could learn who burned the *Sarah B.*"

"There is a certain justice in Mr. Calvert providing a replacement," Truett suggested.

"He was paying the bills as they came," Kent said. "There are riggers and stevedores to be paid, provisions yet to go aboard."

"My bank will advance you the funds to complete your preparations and get Captain Beck to sea," Sherman said, taking them all by surprise. "Mrs. Calvert believes there is a will but knows nothing of the terms. It may take weeks to settle the estate. Jonathan Frye was Mr. Calvert's executor. In his absence, Mr. Truett has asked me to serve with him as coexecutor and I have agreed. I have every reason to believe Calvert's estate can meet his obligations." To Kent he said, "Tell me what you need, and you shall have it."

Jason paid little attention as Sherman and Kent settled the details. It was landsmen's business. Soon he would be on a new deck, feeling the power of the sea and wind as they bore him along. There he would find his peace, alone with the winds and God. The scars inflicted by landsmen's madness would heal in time and he would be whole once more.

The others were standing now. Jason rose and joined them as they left the office and descended the stairs in a body. Once in the street, they shook hands until every man had felt the grip of all the others, putting the seal on the bargain they had struck together before they went their several ways. For the landsmen, the agreement presaged the end of the Committee of Vigilance and the return of San Francisco to her elected officials, however noble or corrupt they were in fact when the name-calling was done. It would mean a return to lesser positions for some whose stature had increased with that of the Committee. For others, the sound of marching feet would no longer bring fear.

These concerns were as remote from Jason's thinking as the deserts of Araby. He tasted the sea on the west wind and he knew only that he had spent the morning in a small room with a handful of men whose lives he could not imagine, and at last they had set him free.

Chapter 55

f I were emperor of this land, I would forbid you to go," Joshua Norton said. He met Sarah's eyes and looked away. Around them the passengers and visitors swirled on the deck of the steamer *Golden Age.*

It was Monday, the fifteenth of September. In the early years of the gold rush the mail steamers had left San Francisco on the first and fifteenth of each month, and steamer days came near to assuming the nature of holidays. Now, with more steamers plying between the Isthmus and the Golden Gate, the mails went more often, but departures on the first or fifteenth still seemed to carry a special significance for those who were sailing and those who came to see them off.

"Have you found new quarters?" Sarah asked Norton.

"Oh. Yes. A small hotel. It won't be the same, of course. We were . . ." Norton seemed to have lost his train of thought, and then Sarah saw that he was silenced by his emotions. He breathed deeply and sighed. "We were a family, Sarah. The first I have had since my own relations died. It won't be the same without you to look after me. And I do miss Tommy."

"We all do, Joshua."

"Yes." He looked across the bay. "There will be no justice, you know. Not until governments are administered by kindly men."

"At least we have our own government back."

"Yes. Somewhat the worse for wear. And who is to say when those men will organize again?"

The bargain made in Stephen Kent's office on June 22 had held, even when the Committee of Vigilance broke the agreement by hanging two more men late in July for murders unrelated to the vigilantes or their activities. The Executive Committee let it be known among their opponents that the hangings were necessary to quell the bloodlust of the more rabid elements in the Committee, in order that David Terry could be freed and the Committee disbanded without causing an uprising in the ranks. Hays and Sherman and the others kept their word and made no public protest, despite their outrage, for the sake of Judge Terry.

On August 7, after a lengthy and contentious trial, the Committee set David Terry free. Sterling Hopkins, the man Terry stabbed, had stubbornly refused to succumb to his wound so Terry could be charged with murder. Rumor had it that friends of Judge Terry offered Dr. Cole several thousands of dollars to assure Hopkins' survival. According to the story, Cole contemptuously refused the money, assuring the man who offered it that his professional pride would allow him to do no less than his utmost toward that very end, and that no amount of money could influence him additionally in that direction.

The Executive Committee's verdict acquitting Terry was confirmed by the Board of Delegates after several ballots and much arm-twisting by the leaders. Terry was released from Fort Gunnybags at two o'clock in the morning, spirited out the back door so a mob of several hundred irate vigilants in Sacramento Street would not prevent his going. With Miers Truett's help, he was put aboard the sloop-of-war *John Adams* until morning, when a Navy longboat carried him to the Sacramento steamer.

Eleven days later, on the eighteenth of August, the Committee of Vigilance paraded its troops through the streets and publicly adjourned. Since then, the *Herald* had reported that the Executive Committee continued to meet, and charged they had recently put another of their political enemies aboard an outbound steamer, enjoining him never to return, on pain of death.

Through David Farren, Sarah knew a good deal more

than was known by the public. She had written about each event in the caustic language of Mercury, summoning her most scathing criticism for the hangings. But the letters were never delivered, nor had she intended they should be. In the last one, which was packed in her steamer trunk with the rest, she had fulminated over the return of Judge Thompson and Postmaster Foreman from Washington City on August 12, carrying President Pierce's refusal to intervene in the affairs of California. With Judge Terry free and the Committee about to disband, Governor Johnson had understandably hoped to keep the news secret for a time, but the Committee's tireless spies unearthed it and on the fourteenth it was published in the San Francisco newspapers.

For Sarah, writing the letters had been a way of expressing her feelings and still keeping them to herself. The men of the Executive Committee believed that her brave courier had been Mercury and that their most galling critic was dead, and Sarah was glad to let Trelayne carry to the grave the grudging respect of the men he had taunted so eloquently himself from the stage.

Lucy Thorsen swept across the crowded deck to join Sarah and Norton, resplendent in a dress she had bought for the voyage. She was as excited as a young girl. "The purser has arranged for me to share your cabin, Sarah. He is a very nice man and I gave him a quarter eagle for his trouble."

"You'll spoil him before we've even cast off," Sarah cautioned her. She often found herself feeling maternal toward the younger woman. Lucy was irrepressible. Where Sarah felt sadness at leaving San Francisco behind, Lucy thought only of the adventure that lay ahead.

"Of course I will spoil him," Lucy said. "And then he will spoil us. He has already promised us that we may sit at the captain's table."

"There is Molly at last," Norton said.

Molly was waving to Sarah from the wharf. She and David Farren had just arrived in Molly's carriage, a new phaeton drawn by a matched pair of grays.

"Do you think she will have the good sense to keep him this time?" Norton said to Sarah while Molly and Farren negotiated the crowded gangway.

"I hope so," Sarah said.

"My friends are abandoning me." The farewell was making Norton melancholy. Until three days ago, they had all lived in the boardinghouse together. Now Molly was settled at the International Hotel and Farren had bought a small house. When Sarah and Lucy were gone, Norton would be alone.

Sarah sought to comfort him. "You are a man who will always have friends, Joshua."

A steward passed along the deck calling, "All ashore that's going ashore!" The steamer's whistle let loose a warning toot.

"Oh, Sarah! If I had missed you I would never have forgiven myself." Molly threw herself into Sarah's arms. "You will write?"

"Of course I will, but will you?"

"I'm not much good at it. I know! I'll have David write. He can write letters for both of us."

Sarah gave Farren a smile. "I will look forward to them."

"We were rehearsing," Molly said. "Mr. Maguire is a tyrant, Sarah. I told him my dearest friend on earth was going away and I must say good-bye. I just left in the middle of rehearsal. If he doesn't like it, he can find another actress. After all, it's not as if I need the money."

Molly was rich. Sherman's inquiries into Abel Calvert's estate had turned up a new will, made a week before his wedding, in which he named Molly as his sole heir. After the outstanding debts were settled the balance would be enough to keep Molly comfortable for the rest of her life, if she managed it wisely. By virtue of the inheritance and her widowhood, Molly had acquired sudden respectability and a good deal of renown.

"Last call! All ashore that's going ashore!" The steward's voice and the steamer's whistle were more insistent now. Already the crewmen were lifting the mooring lines from the pilings while others made ready to haul the gangway inboard.

"Take good care of her, David," Sarah said. She embraced Farren.

"I will."

Molly hugged Sarah again and gave Joshua Norton a

kiss on the cheek. "I'm not leaving, you know," he said. He was very red and very pleased.

"I know," Molly said, "but I've wanted to do that for ever so long."

As soon as Farren and Norton and Molly were on the wharf, the crewmen heaved on the lines and the gangway slid onto the steamer's deck. The starboard wheel began to turn, sending eddies of water churning among the pilings. Slowly at first, then more rapidly, the *Golden Age* gained way.

On the wharf, Su-Yan and Bo-Ji Quan stood apart from the clamoring throng of well-wishers as the steamer swung out into the bay. They were dressed in stylish Western clothes, which occasioned some stares and some rude comments from the *guey low*, made just loud enough to be overheard. Su-Yan and Bo-Ji acknowledged neither the stares nor the words.

"Mrs. Rockwell is an unusual woman," Su-Yan said.

"Yes, Father," Bo-Ji agreed. She raised her hand and waved. At the railing of the steamer, Sarah and Lucy waved back.

The Quans had been the first to make their good-byes, the first to leave the steamer. Su-Yan was embarrassed by Sarah Rockwell's repeated expressions of gratitude, further embarrassed that he himself was incapable of adequately expressing his thanks and his continuing sense of obligation to Sarah for taking Bo-Ji into her home and caring for her.

Su-Yan had bought Sarah's boardinghouse. He had paid her advertised price, and when she had asked once more if he considered it unreasonable he had simply said no. By paying what she asked, with no negotiating, he had done as much as was possible in the earthly realm to repay his debt to her.

He had told her that he foresaw a not-too-distant day when the Chinese community would extend beyond the bustling streets of Little China. He said he was situating himself at the limits of that growth in his lifetime. "As a Christian," he had said, "I must keep one hand in each world." All of this was true, and yet not true. He might make the house his home in time, or it might become Bo-

Ji's home when she married. He had not decided yet. For now, the boardinghouse would become a parlor house of the first rank, where Occidental men of business could indulge their taste for mysterious women of the Orient. Bo-Ji would manage the house, and in so doing she would learn the principles of business first-hand.

Through what Bo-Ji had learned—in her rage at her father—from one white merchant, she had turned Jason Beck against the Committee of Vigilance and in the end they were brought down without conflict. The leaders had returned to their merchant trades neither humiliated nor destroyed. If one girl could acquire such power to affect the white world, what could ten girls do! Bo-Ji would help to select them from within the web of blood and commercial relationships that Su-Yan had established throughout Little China, and the benefits they brought to their people would affect the Chinese community in the Golden Mountain for a generation to come.

Already these plans had stimulated changes in Su-Yan's own business. He had hired a young man, the son of his second cousin, to pull the vegetable cart. Soon he would have three carts and three young men, each fluent in English and adept at making amusing conversation with *guey low* women. Henceforth he and Bo-Ji would manage his enterprises from a distance and they would be much less visible in the white world.

One question troubled him. If all this had come about because he had placed Bo-Ji in Mrs. Wickliff's, was his judgment wise rather than misguided from the start?

The *Golden Age* was beyond the ships at anchor off the waterfront. On the wharf, the well-wishers were gone, leaving Su-Yan and Bo-Ji alone. "Would you like to go to your new house?" he said.

"No, Father. Tomorrow we will go there. You will talk with the workmen and I will listen. Now I would like to go home."

"We will go home then," Su-Yan said. "Your mother will make us some tea."

The purser approached the two ladies at the rail of the *Golden Age* with some diffidence. They were young and exceptionally handsome, and Miss Thorsen had told him that Mrs. Rockwell was a widow. "It is warm and comfortable in the saloon, ladies," he said. "The steward's bell will sound for supper."

"Thank you. We will go in presently," Sarah said. The purser touched the brim of his cap and left them.

They were alone on deck, standing just forward of the starboard paddle wheel. The sun had set half an hour before. The western sky was banded with reds and yellows near the horizon. Sarah turned her back to the wind and leaned against the railing. Off the port beam, the California coast was a dark silhouette low on the horizon, nearly invisible against the dark of the sky. Already a few stars were visible over the distant shore.

"When we wake in the morning, will the land still be California?" Lucy wondered.

"I don't know. Someone will be able to tell us."

"Look. There is another ship."

Lucy pointed to a small speck of sail and Sarah turned back to the crimson glory in the west. The ship was hull down over the horizon. Clouds beyond the vessel were mounding up like castles, as if to capture the last light of the westering sun.

"It is too far to tell," Lucy said.

"It's not him. He will be in the Indian Ocean by now."

They had seen three ships during the day and a dozen lesser vessels—barks and brigs and a Danish brigantine named *Søren Larsen* that had passed near enough for Lucy to read the name on her bows and shout a few words in Danish to the delight of the sailors on deck. Sarah had identified each vessel in turn, pointing out to Lucy the number of masts and whether the sails were square-rigged or fore-and-aft, and how each combination determined the type of vessel. And although Sarah knew that Jason was halfway around the world, she had explained why each of the three ships they saw could not be *Pride of the Seas*, because it had split topgallants or did not have split topsails, or the headsails were wrong.

Pride of the Seas had cast off from the Vallejo Wharf on the twenty-eighth day of June, just a week after the climactic events of June 21. Finn Warren had sailed with

Jason as first mate. One last voyage, he said, with the best master afloat.

" 'Tis a great gift to have your affection," Jason told Sarah when they parted. "I thank you for it." She had remembered then what he said to her on the fateful night when they were alone in *Katahdin*, asking, in the reticent way of men, if she would go to sea with him as his wife.

Now, as she gazed at the great ocean, she knew she had been right to refuse. How could she contend with a mistress so powerful and restless? The waters were never still. Ever-changing, always on the run before the wind, they were the planet's breath, rising and falling to a stately rhythm that God had determined on the morning of creation. Once a man had found consolation on the bosom of the deep, how could he ever find contentment with a mere woman of the land?

They had talked of Melchoir for a time. "He said he owed his life to you," Sarah said. " 'Tis no consolation that he paid it back to save mine," Jason had replied.

Lucy too had come to see Jason off. Sarah had sent her a note, telling her when the ship would sail. Lucy had made her good-byes and left Sarah and Jason alone, not even waiting on the wharf until the ship cast off.

While a steam tug towed *Pride of the Seas* away from the wharf, Sarah had run to a livery and rented a horse. She had ridden to Fort Point and watched the ship pass between the headlands of the Gate. Oddly, she had felt no lack, no loss, when the sails dwindled to specs and vanished. In a short while she and Jason Beck had come to know each other as few people ever knew another in a lifetime. They had formed a bond between them that would sustain her in times of difficulty even if she never saw him again.

The day after *Pride of the Seas* sailed, Lucy had appeared at Sarah's door to say, "I am looking for a room." She had left Mrs. Wickliff's and the life in that house. She asked for Jason's room and Sarah gave it to her, and by that act of charity, Sarah banished the last of her jealousy.

The clear tone of the steward's bell sounded from its place at the entrance to the passengers' saloon.

"Shall we eat, Sarah?" Lucy said.

"I need to wait awhile. I'm feeling a little unsteady." Sarah put a hand to her stomach. The steamer was rolling gently in long swells that gathered beneath the waves and swept majestically toward the distant shore.

"You are a sailor's daughter," Lucy scolded. "You cannot be seasick."

Sarah laughed. "I have never been seasick a day in my life."

"All right, then. For the other, you are forgiven."

Sarah faced into the wind and breathed deeply, willing the queasiness in her stomach to go away. Mostly the upset feeling came over her in the morning, less often at other times of the day. Now that the worry about selling the house was over and they were on their way, she hoped that her high spirits would overcome the morning sickness altogether.

Lucy was the only one who knew she was expecting. She knew the symptoms well from observing Mrs. Wickliff's girls who became pregnant despite the precautions they took, and she had heard Sarah retching in a chamber pot on too many mornings not to suspect the truth. Once she knew, and when Sarah had told her what she intended to do after the child was born, Lucy had made her own decision, which she had presented to Sarah as something already done, not subject to discussion. She would come with Sarah to Maine and she would look after her during her confinement. Later she would help her care for the child while Sarah fought the Rockwells for her inheritance.

"You go in," Sarah said now. "I'll stay here a moment. Make my apologies to the captain and say I'll come along soon."

Lucy put her gloved hand on Sarah's for a moment where it rested on the rail, and left her.

Sarah had accepted Lucy's offer of companionship and aid with one condition—that they speak openly about Jason Beck. "We both care for him," Sarah told her, "but neither of us has claimed him."

"I did not make up to him, Sarah," Lucy had said. "He came into my life and he touched me here—" She put her hand on her heart. "No one ever touched me like that before. It was wonderful, but it was painful too. It is so hard, Sarah."

Sarah saw that Lucy's eyes were brimming with tears. "Another man will touch you there," she said. When Haven died, she too had believed her one love was gone forever, but it seemed that the heart knew its needs and would act to fulfil them, however little sense the yearnings made to the mind.

Where the contest is averted, there is no victory, no defeat. Sarah smiled inwardly. Was it possible that a fragment of Oriental wisdom could apply equally well to the contest of two women who cared for one man and a conflict as menacing as that between the Committee of Vigilance and the state of California?

She had heeded Su-Yan's warning and she had acted to prevent a confrontation in which Jason Beck and an unknown number of other good men might have died. While Jason slept beside her in *Katahdin*, she had watched the vigilance schooner glide up the channel into San Pablo Bay. An hour later, with the turn of the tide, she had seen it return. When it was gone, and the governor's muskets with it, Sarah had allowed herself to sleep, believing that all risk of conflict was past. Neither Jason Beck nor Governor Johnson's allies were to be so easily denied, and yet, despite their best efforts to arm themselves for bloody warfare, all their efforts had failed and neither side had suffered a grievous defeat.

Sarah dared not imagine she had been the sole agent of the final outcome. The responsibility was too great. Four men had died, slain by greed and deception, jealousy and revenge—forces too unpredictable for anyone to foresee or avert. But if the two sides had faced each other with guns in their hands, the carnage they unloosed might have filled a cemetery.

"Sarah!" A cry from astern caused her to turn away from the last glow in the west. A small figure came running her way.

"I have seen the whole vessel, Sarah! The second mate showed me the engine room. They have enough wood to go to Callao, the engineer said. He's a queer Englishman named Webster."

"I'm glad we have plenty of wood, but I hope they don't take us all the way to Callao."

She smiled, but Dickie had heard the catch in her voice and he noticed the wet streaks on her cheeks. "Why are you crying?"

"It's only the wind. No." She took his hand in her own. "I promised I would never lie to you. I was thinking of Mr. Trelayne."

"And Captain Beck?"

"Captain Beck too."

"The bell has rung for supper. Aren't you hungry?"

"Stand here with me for a moment. Give me just a moment. I don't want everyone to see me with red eyes."

She held Dickie with his back to her and her hands crossed on his chest, facing once more out to sea. "Do you miss him, Dickie?"

"Yes."

"Do you wish you had gone with him?"

"Sometimes." They had promised never to lie. It wasn't always easy for Dickie to tell the complete truth, but he found it easier as time went by.

On the day before *Pride of the Seas* was to sail, he had told Captain Beck that he would not go. To Dickie's surprise, Captain Beck appeared not to mind. "We're shipmates all the same, Richard," he said. "Haven't we sailed together on troubled seas?" Dickie didn't understand just what he meant, but it made him swell with pride to be called shipmate by such a man.

"You do understand, Jason," Sarah had said.

"Aye. He's a smarter lad than I was. With you as his teacher, he'll be the best of us all."

"He'll have other chances to go to sea."

"There will always be a berth for him on any ship I command. Send him to me when he's ready and I'll teach him whatever you cannot."

Pride of the Seas had sailed without a ship's boy. In a poor exchange, Sarah had provided Kittery, her cat from the boardinghouse, to keep the vessel free of mice and rats, although Jason swore by Neptune's trident he would never carry grain again.

Dickie was her child now. The certificate of adoption renamed him Richard Howell Rockwell. David Farren had seen to the legal matters. Sarah and Dickie had only to stand before a judge and swear that they each understood the gravity of the responsibilities they were undertaking. When they returned home from the courthouse, Molly had presented to Dickie the one coin in ten she had promised him from the first night of *Caesar in California.* The actors had gathered Molly's tribute from the boards after Calvert took Molly away, and Sarah had saved the money in her armoire with her own reserve of gold. They had divided it when Molly returned to the boardinghouse after Abel Calvert's death. Dickie's share came to several hundred dollars. Later, when Sarah explained to him why they were leaving San Francisco to go to the eastern States, he had pledged it to her, if she needed it, to use against the Rockwells.

With allies such as Lucy and Dickie at her side, Sarah knew she would inevitably vanquish the Rockwells. The battle would be fought in courts of law, which were the realm of man, but Sarah had walked among men dressed as one of them, and she had learned the secrets of their world. She knew that their dreams and aspirations were no more substantial than those born in a woman's breast. Men were no wiser, no more certain of their designs. They had no capacity not available to those they called the weaker sex, save their brute strength, which was useful only in war and manual labor. But still they led the way, plunging into the unknown without a care, because there was no one to hold them back. No wonder they would fight and die to keep their power!

God help me to use the courage I have found. Sarah addressed the sea, where it seemed to her that the spirit of God was more visible than any other place on the surface of the earth.

Dickie moved restlessly against her. "We'll miss supper if we don't go soon," he said.

Sarah released him. "Run ahead and open the door. I will make my entrance." As she followed him across the deck she walked straight and steady, instinctively meeting the steamer's roll. Her stomach was calm now and she was even a little hungry.

The Historical Characters

THE COMMITTEE OF VIGILANCE — In September 1856, John Durkee and Charles Rand were tried in U.S. circuit court in San Francisco for piracy in the hijacking of the state's muskets from the schooner *Julia* on June 21. The mandatory sentence for a guilty verdict was hanging with no possibility of appeal. Not surprisingly, the jury of solid San Francisco citizens brought in a verdict of not guilty.

Fearing that election results from San Francisco would be invalidated if the city were still officially in a state of insurrection at the time of the federal election in November 1856, the Executive Committee undertook negotiations with Governor Johnson through intermediaries to have his proclamation revoked. On November 3, the day before the election, the Committee returned to Quartermaster General William Kibbe the muskets they had seized on the bay on June 21. Johnson withdrew his proclamation, and a slate of People's Party candidates approved by the Committee of Vigilance gained a substantial victory in San Francisco, although Democrats triumphed in the rest of the state.

During the winter of 1856-57, William Tell Coleman, Miers Truett and Thomas Smiley were arrested in New York City on complaints sworn by Billy Mulligan, Reuben Maloney and others who had been deported from San Francisco by the Committee of Vigilance. Truett, in a dictation given to historian Hubert Howe Bancroft in the 1870s, said Maloney died before the case was resolved and the charges were dropped. Another source says the case was dismissed for lack of jurisdiction. I could find no information about the cause of Maloney's death or why Mulligan and the other plaintiffs did not pursue the case.

The Executive Committee continued to meet for at least three years after the general committee adjourned. Through the People's Party, the vigilantes and their supporters controlled San Francisco politics for the next decade.

WILLIAM TECUMSEH SHERMAN (1820–1891) — In his memoirs, Sherman wrote that when he resigned his commission as general of California militia on June 7, 1856, he declared "that I would thenceforeward mind my own business and leave public affairs severely alone . . . and I never afterward had any thing to do with politics in California, perfectly satisfied with that short experience." In fact, Sherman became briefly involved in trying to recover the state's hijacked arms. In late October 1856, he wrote Governor Johnson, offering to act as an intermediary between Johnson and the Committee. In the event, Sherman's assistance wasn't needed.

The following spring, Sherman advised his senior partners in St. Louis to close their San Francisco branch bank. On May 1, 1857, the banking house of Lucas, Turner & Company ceased doing business in San Francisco. Under Sherman's management during four financially perilous years, no depositor lost any funds entrusted to the bank.

In 1861, with the federal Union imperiled by secession and rebellion, Sherman rejoined the Army, and the rest, as they say, is history. Less well known than his victories for the Union and his pronouncement that "War is hell" is his enduring dislike of politics and politicians. In 1884 Sherman responded to a movement to place his name in nomination for the presidency at the Republican convention in Chicago by steadfastly refusing to have anything to do with it. When James G. Blaine was nominated, Sherman was much relieved. He wrote his brother John, a U.S. senator, "I would not for a million of dollars subject myself and family to the ordeal of a political canvass and afterwards to a four years' service in the White House."

JOSHUA ABRAHAM NORTON (1819?–1880) — On August 25, 1856, a week after the Committee of Vigilance paraded and disbanded its troops, the San Francisco *Bulletin* carried an item noting that Joshua Norton had filed for bankruptcy.

In September 1859, Norton appeared in the offices of the *Bulletin* and offered an edict proclaiming himself Norton the First, Emperor of the United States. The *Bulletin* printed the announcement with tongue firmly planted in cheek, but the idea charmed San Franciscans, and for the next twenty-one years Joshua Norton was the most celebrated eccentric in a city that has been noted since its establishment for its tolerance of eccentricity. Seats were reserved for Emperor Norton in the city's prominent restaurants and theaters. He traveled free on public transportation. He issued imperial scrip with which he paid for his necessities. He presciently ordered that a bridge should be built across San Francisco Bay to Oakland (less presciently, he ordered another built from San Francisco to Hawaii). He despised the nickname "Frisco" for San Francisco and decreed that anyone heard using it should be fined twenty-five dollars.

Norton collapsed and died on January 8, 1880, at the corner of Dupont and California streets. Ten thousand San Franciscans viewed his remains and twenty thousand attended the funeral. He is buried in Woodlawn Cemetery in Colma, California. His monument reads:

NORTON I
EMPEROR
OF THE UNITED STATES
AND
PROTECTOR OF MEXICO

JOSHUA A. NORTON
1819–1880

JOHN NUGENT (1825?–1880) — Sarah Rockwell's authorship of the San Francisco *Herald*'s "Mercury" letters is fictitious, as are the letters themselves, but the questions and misgivings she raises about the 1856 Committee of Vigilance were all raised at the time, many by Nugent himself in eloquent and compelling editorials. The boycott against the *Herald* by members of the Committee of Vigilance apparently forced Nugent to sell the newspaper for a time, although it was published continuously until January 1862, when it merged with the *Mirror* to become the *Daily Herald and Mirror.*

After serving as the U.S. commissioner to British Columbia for a time, Nugent returned to California and ran unsuccessfully for the U.S. Senate before reacquiring the *Herald.* He died in San Leandro, California, on March 29, 1880.

JOHN COFFEE HAYS (1817–1883) — The letter Hays published in the San Francisco papers following David Terry's arrest by the Committee of Vigilance, defending the jurist's character, is considered to have contributed to Terry's eventual release.

President Franklin Pierce had a policy of "rotating" his appointees by not reappointing them to the same office. Many urged him to make an exception in Hays's case, but Pierce stuck to his guns. Instead of reappointing Hays as surveyor general for California, he named him to the same post in Utah. Hays didn't want to take his family to live there and he resigned from government service. In 1859–60, he commanded a regiment in the Paiute War in Nevada.

Hays had been instrumental in founding the city of Oakland in 1851. Over the years he continued to promote its development. He donated portions of his large ranch as sites for churches (without regard to denomination) and city parks. When General Sherman paid a formal visit to Oakland in 1880, Hays rode in the escort of honor. His funeral in 1883 was the largest public event to take place in Oakland up to that time.

DAVID SMITH TERRY (1822?–1889) — Terry's hot temper continued to get him in trouble during the remainder of his career and ultimately caused his death. On September 13, 1859, he fought a duel with California's U.S. Senator David Broderick and killed him. Following the duel, Terry resigned from the bench and resumed the practice of law. He was a Confederate officer in Texas during the Civil War. In 1889, Terry himself was shot and killed by a bodyguard for U.S. Supreme Court Justice Stephen J. Field, who had served with Terry on the California Supreme Court, and with whom Terry had disagreed often and vehemently.

JOHN NEELY JOHNSON (1825–1872) — Johnson's opposition to the 1856 Committee of Vigilance while he was governor ended his political career in California. In January 1858, he returned to private life and subsequently moved to Nevada, where he practiced law and invested in silver mines, becoming wealthy. During the Civil War he fervently supported the Union and served as chairman of the Nevada Union State Central Committee. He was later a justice of the Nevada Supreme Court.

RICHARD BEVERLY COLE (1829–1901) — Although Cole's position as surgeon general to the '56 Committee enhanced his reputation, he took a stand against the Committee when it sanctioned the People's Party candidates in the fall elections. In a dictation given to the eminent (if blind, where the faults of the Committees of

Vigilance were concerned) historian Hubert Howe Bancroft in the 1870s, Cole said, "I was strenuously opposed to any such movement, which not only compromised the dignity of the Committee, but tended to detract from the value and importance of the service they had performed, in the minds of the community at large, and to create a suspicion as to their real purpose and aims. . . ." He ran for mayor against the People's Party candidate, "without any earthly hope of success, but purely with a view of placing myself on record as being opposed to the prostitution of this Committee to political purposes. . . ." As he expected, Cole lost the election, but his reputation as a physician grew steadily. He narrowed his practice to gynecological surgery and served as president of the American Association of Obstetricians and Gynecologists. In 1896 he was president of the American Medical Association's annual convention.

WILLIAM TELL COLEMAN (1824–1893) — In 1877, Coleman was called on once more to organize what was called this time a Committee of Safety, to help protect San Francisco against labor agitators and anti-Chinese rioters. With the approval of the president, the secretary of war, and the governor of California, the organization was armed with ammunition provided by the federal government and supported by federal troops.

JAMES REUBEN MALONEY (18??–1857) — The Committee of Vigilance held Maloney prisoner from June 21 until July 5, when they put him aboard a Panama steamer and warned him never to return to San Francisco under pain of death. He was thus not present to testify in the September trial of John Durkee and Charles Rand for piracy.

DAVID SCANNELL (18??–1893) — In a city dominated politically by the Committee and its supporters, Scannell had no hope of holding public office when his term as sheriff expired. He devoted himself instead to the Empire Engine Company No. 1. In the 1860s he was chief engineer of the volunteer fire department and he headed the city's paid fire department in the 1870s.

JOSEPH B. CROCKETT (1808–1884) — Crockett successfully defended John Durkee and Charles Rand in their September 1856 trial for piracy. He was later a justice of the California Supreme Court.

DAVID FARRAGUT (1801–1870) — At the start of the Civil War, Farragut was given command of a naval squadron in the Gulf of Mexico and ordered to take New Orleans, which he did in April 1862. He gained immortality in Mobile Bay in August 1864 by crying "Damn the torpedoes!" (which were submarine mines) and leading his squadron across a line of mines to gain the victory. He was promoted to rear admiral in 1862, vice-admiral in 1864, and admiral in 1866.

JAMES F. CURTIS (1825–1914) — Curtis, who commanded the cannon when the '56 Committee took Casey and Cora from the County Jail on May 18, and again at the surrender of the loyal armories on June 21, was elected San Francisco's first chief of police when the city's police force was reorganized that fall. He later served under Jack Hays in the Paiute War of 1859–60.

CAPTAIN FARREN OF THE SAN FRANCISCO BLUES — Contemporary records show that a "Captain Farren" commanded Company B of the San Francisco Blues militia company, but provide no further information about him. My character David Farren is entirely fictional, apart from his borrowed surname and his position in the Blues.

Acknowledgments

o one has contributed more selflessly to *The Committee of Vigilance* than Kevin J. Mullen. Author of *Let Justice Be Done: Crime and Politics in Early San Francisco*, and a former deputy chief of the San Francisco Police, Mullen is the foremost historian on law enforcement (or the lack of it) in San Francisco. He welcomed me into his home, gave me source books and the benefit of his expertise, and shared the information in his extensive files. He read an early draft of the novel and offered valuable comments. He has researched and provided answers to my bothersome questions in the midst of his own work. He responded to my inquires far beyond the call of duty, and he has made a devoted friend.

Robert M. Senkewicz, S.J., author of *Vigilantes in Gold Rush San Francisco*, referred me to important source material and shared his thoughts freely about the motives and actions of the 1856 Committee. For more than a century, most historians blandly accepted the San Francisco vigilantes' self-serving justifications for their actions. To date, Senkewicz's book is the most thorough and even-handed attempt to set the record straight. It provided me with important background and motivation for the novel.

I owe boundless thanks to the helpful staffs at the Bancroft Library at the University of California, Berkeley, and the Huntington Library, San Marino, California, which together house the surviving papers of the 1856

Committee of Vigilance as well as many other source materials bearing on the events in the novel. At the Huntington, Peter Blodgett, Virginia Renner and Elsa Sink were particularly helpful.

Irene A. Strachura, Reference Librarian at the San Francisco Maritime National Historical Park's J. Porter Shaw Library, provided valuable information on nineteenth-century merchant vessels and the San Francisco waterfront; Lisbet Bailey, the library's photo curator, sent me an essential chart of the bay. As always, the Teton County Library was a primary resource, thanks to Nancy Effinger and her staff.

Many others helped me and I am grateful to them all. Sam Andrew loaned and gave me valuable reference works from his personal library. Brent Blue, M.D., and his twin Cessna 340, 128 Charlie Kilo, enabled me to make many more research trips to San Francisco than I would have been able to afford by flying commercial. Bill Briggs made his laser printer available to me. Robert Woods Brown, M.D., gave me advice about the treatment of gunshot wounds, then and now, and referred me to valuable sources of period medical information.

My father, Alistair Cooke, gave me encouragement, valuable advice, and source books. Skipper Tony Davies and the crew of the brigantine *Søren Larsen* helped me to glimpse what sailing a nineteenth-century square-rigged ship must have been like. Charles duPont provided helpful information on period firearms.

Dave and Vera-Mae Fredrickson offered limitless hospitality and support during some of my long stays in Berkeley while doing research. Charlie Frizzell, who is my brother, though not by blood or law, took the jacket photo (which was not used, alas) and provided other photographic help; Charlie and Polly also hosted me during my Bay Area research trips, and their home is always a comforting place for me.

Newton Cope, Sr., Newton Cope, Jr., and Micarl Hill, of the Huntington Hotel in San Francisco, provided access to the hotel's collection of historical maps of San Francisco and gave me permission to photograph them. James E. Kern, curator at the Vallejo Naval and Historical Museum, was very helpful when I visited the museum and he suggested several valuable references.

Laurie Gudim offered insightful views on the I Ching and on human behavior. James Kimmins Greer, author of *Colonel Jack Hays*, facilitated my request for information on Hays's friend John Nugent. John W. Hays gave me information on his famous ancestor and pointed me in the right direction for further sources on Jack Hays and John Nugent.

Sydney Murray gave me some useful books before disappearing into the next phase of her life. Nancy Olmsted provided information on the San Francisco waterfront in 1856 and referred me to important maps of the period.

Fritz Richmond gave and loaned me valuable sourcebooks. Mark Rulli took me for a brief but exciting sail, and shared his knowledge of San Francisco Bay's weather and its tides; most important, he ended my two-year quest for a square-rigged vessel to sail on by referring me to Ocean Voyages in Sausalito, California, who sent me on my glorious voyage aboard the *Søren Larsen*.

David Rumsey generously provided copies of vital maps and helped me determine the configuration of the San Francisco waterfront in 1856. Nadya Tichman deserves special thanks for referring me to David.

Since 1950, when Richard Wilhelm's German translation of *The I Ching or Book of Changes* was rendered into English by Cary F. Baynes and published by Princeton University Press, this edition has been a primary reference for those interested in the I Ching. I have owned a copy for almost twenty years and I referred to it when writing about the I Ching in this novel. To the best of my knowledge I never quoted Wilhelm's text directly, but I may have paraphrased his translations of the ancient commentaries.

Finally, there are four people without whose help I might never have written this book. Candace Lake, in addition to representing my work for almost twenty years, has read drafts of each novel-in-progress and has always given helpful and discerning advice. Herman Gollob, without whose skillful guidance my first novel, *The Snowblind Moon*, might never have seen the light of day, encouraged *The Committee of Vigilance* when it was no more than an idea; he read an early draft of the novel and offered many helpful comments; my character Abel Calvert resulted from Herman's critique of that draft. Greg Tobin brought me to Bantam, ably and gently edited *South of the Border*, my second novel, and guided *The Committee of Vigilance* through three years of development before handing over the reins to Tom Dupree, who courageously waded through the semifinal draft not once but twice, and guided me expertly through the last crucial rewrite.

No writer has had better helpers and advisers than these. Any errors or shortcomings in the novel are my fault alone.

To anyone I have carelessly left out of this listing, I offer my heartfelt apologies and thanks.

John Byrne Cooke
Jackson, Wyoming
March 1994

About the Author

JOHN BYRNE COOKE's previous novels include *South of the Border* and the Spur Award-winning *The Snowblind Moon*. Cooke has worked as a bluegrass musician, filmmaker, screenwriter, and was Janis Joplin's road manager. He lives, writes and skis in Jackson Hole, Wyoming. He is the writer and creator of the documentary television series *Outlaws and Lawmen*, scheduled to air on the Discovery Channel in early 1996.

EYEWITNESS TO THE CIVIL WAR

The Civil War comes vividly to life. Here are eyewitness accounts—many available for the first time in decades—by generals, journalists, and ordinary foot soldiers, both blue and gray, who relive the conflict in all its terrible glory. Each volume brings you a human perspective on the war—its most decisive battles, its most remarkable personalities. Bantam's Eyewitness to the Civil War is American history at its finest— and a reading experience you will never forget.

All prices $5.99/$6.99 in Canada